Praise for the Full Spectrum series:

Full Spectrum

"State-of-the-art fiction by state-of-the-art writers.
Marvelous stuff."
—*Analog*

Full Spectrum 2

"A generous compilation of original short fiction, as
long and various—one realizes with surprise—as
Dangerous Visions."
—*The Washington Post Book World*

"If the heart of science fiction and fantasy is the
short story, then a collection such as *Full Spectrum 2*
surely must be its soul."
—*The Ottawa Citizen*

Full Spectrum 3

"*Full Spectrum 3* may be the best original anthology
ever produced."
—*Locus*

"High stand   series
is as themati   ginative
as ever   )

"Kudos . . . to *Full Spectrum*'s editors . . . for resuscitating
the form and for putting together in this volume such
a well-balanced diversity of themes and approaches."
—*Science Fiction Age*

Other Full Spectrum Anthologies

FULL SPECTRUM
FULL SPECTRUM 2
FULL SPECTRUM 3

FULL SPECTRUM
SPECTRUM
SPECTRUM
4

Edited by

Lou Aronica
Amy Stout
Betsy Mitchell

Bantam Books
New York • Toronto • London • Sydney • Auckland

FULL SPECTRUM IV

A Bantam Spectra Book / April 1993
Bantam paperback edition / March 1994
All rights reserved

"Fragments of the Women's Writing" copyright © 1993 by Ursula K. Le Guin;
"Motherhood, Etc." copyright © 1993 by L. Timmel Duchamp; "The Saints"
copyright © 1993 by Bonita Kale; "The Best Lives of Our Years" copyright ©
1993 by A. R. Morlan; "Embodied in Its Opposite" copyright © 1993 by John
M. Landsberg; "Foreigners" copyright © 1993 by Mark Rich; "The Googleplex
Comes and Goes" copyright © 1993 by Del Stone Jr.; "The Beauty Addict"
copyright © 1993 by Ray Aldridge; "In Medicis Gardens" copyright © 1985
by Jean-Claude Dunyach; translation copyright © 1993 by Dominique Bennett;
"The Woman Who Loved Pigs" copyright © 1993 by Stephen R. Donaldson;
"The Story So Far" copyright © 1993 by Martha Soukup; "Suicidal Tendencies"
copyright © 1993 by Dave Smeds; "The Mind's Place" copyright © 1993 by
Gregory Feely; "Ah, Bright Wings" copyright © 1993 by Howard V. Hendrix;
"Vox Domini" copyright © 1993 by Bruce Holland Rogers; "The Erl-King"
copyright © 1993 by Elizabeth Hand; "The Death of John Patrick Yoder"
copyright © 1993 by Nancy Kress; "Human, Martian—One, Two, Three"
copyright © 1993 by Kevin J. Anderson; "What Continues, What Fails"
copyright © 1991 by David Brin; "The Roar At the Heart of the World"
copyright © 1993 by Danith McPherson

SPECTRA and the portrayal of a boxed "s" are trademarks of Bantam Books,
a division of Bantam Doubleday Dell Publishing Group, Inc.
Copyright © 1993 by Bantam Doubleday Dell Publishing Group, Inc.
Cover art copyright © 1993 by SIUDMAK
No part of this book may be reproduced or transmitted in any form or
by any means, electronic or mechanical, including photocopying, recording,
or by any information storage and retrieval system, without permission
in writing from the publisher.
For information address: Bantam Books.

Library of Congress Catalog Card Number: 92-32681

If you purchased this book without a cover, you should be aware that this
book is stolen property. It was reported as "unsold and destroyed" to the
publisher and neither the author nor the publisher has received any payment
for this "stripped book."

ISBN: 0-553-56549-4

Published simultaneously in the United States and Canada

Bantam Books are published by Bantam Books, a division of Bantam Doubleday
Dell Publishing Group, Inc. Its trademark, consisting of the words "Bantam Books"
and the portrayal of a rooster, is Registered in U.S. Patent and Trademark Office
and in other countries. Marca Registrada. Bantam Books, 1540 Broadway, New
York, New York 10036.

PRINTED IN THE UNITED STATES OF AMERICA

OPM 0 9 8 7 6 5 4 3 2 1

CONTENTS

Ursula K. Le Guin	Fragments from the Women's Writing	1
L. Timmel Duchamp	Motherhood, Etc.	7
Bonita Kale	The Saints	47
A. R. Morlan	The Best Lives of Our Years	63
John M. Landsberg	Embodied In Its Opposite	84
Mark Rich	Foreigners	99
Del Stone Jr.	The Googleplex Comes and Goes	123
Ray Aldridge	The Beauty Addict	140
Jean-Claude Dunyach	In Medicis Gardens	205
Stephen R. Donaldson	The Woman Who Loved Pigs	221
Martha Soukup	The Story So Far	282
Dave Smeds	Suicidal Tendencies	300
Gregory Feeley	The Mind's Place	328
Howard V. Hendrix	Ah! Bright Wings	361
Bruce Holland Rogers	Vox Domini	400
Elizabeth Hand	The Erl-King	439
Nancy Kress	The Death of John Patrick Yoder	484
Kevin J. Anderson	Human, Martian— One, Two, Three	508
David Brin	What Continues, What Fails	547
Danith McPherson	Roar at the Heart of the World	583
	About the Authors	609

FULL
SPECTRUM
4

Fragments from the Women's Writing

Ursula K. Le Guin

A CHINESE LINGUIST HAS DISCOVERED A GROUP OF EL-derly women in Hunan who use an ancient script, written and read exclusively by women, which uses an inverted system of grammar and syntax "very different from Chinese." The writing resembles oracle-bone carvings from the Shang Dynasty (sixteenth century B.C.) and writing of the Chin Dynasty (third century B.C.). Local women believe the script, which mothers taught their daughters at home, was invented by a Song Dynasty concubine to relieve her loneliness, but Prof. Gong Zhibing thinks the language, too complex to be the creation of one person, is a relic of writing systems lost when Chinshi Huangdi, the First Emperor, united China in 221 B.C. Chinshi Huangdi unified Chinese writing by forbidding the use of all scripts except his official "small seal" characters. Men learned the new official writing. Women, barred from institutions of learning, kept the old script alive in private.

Most of the writing is poetry, autobiography, letters, and songs. Girls "would form 'sworn sister' relationships, using the script to document their bonds and correspond with one another long after they were grown and married. Few of the writings have survived, because the women asked that all their writings be burned when they died, so that they could read their favorite works in the afterlife."

Professor Gong met two women in their eighties who were able to read and write the language. The two, the only surviving members of a seven-member sworn sister "family," burned all the copies of a third sister's writings when she died this year.

—Quotes taken from *The China Daily*, Beijing, 1986

Fragments from the Women's Writing

Daughter: These are the characters
forbidden by the Emperor.
These are the bone words,
the cracks on the under-shell.
This is the other grammar.

Sister: I document our bond
and correspond to you
finger to finger, eye to eye.

Unwrap the old silk very slowly.

Daughter: Write in milk,
as I did. Hold it to the fire
to make the words appear.

Sister: Still my sleeves are dry,
but I saw a dark moon this autumn
a long way down the river.

My Lord was angry till I told him
it was my laundry list.
He laughed then, "Hen scratchings!"
and I laughed.

Daughter: Learn the language upside down,
inverted in the turtle's eye.
Use the bones for soup.

An army of men
of heavy red pottery
under the hill by the river
where we do the laundry.

Sister: His thighs are jade
and his staff a stiff bamboo,
but there's nobody here to talk to.

Do not burn all your songs, mother,
much as you may love them.
How can I sing smoke?
Leave me the one about autumn.

Sister: This form is my own.
I live inside these words
as the turtle in its shell,
as the marrow in the bone.

Sisters: This is a colder mountain
than the tiger's, and the bones
say only snow is falling.

Daughters: Keep my embroideries,
send my life after me.
My autobiography was the turtle's under-shell,
the small cracks in bones,
a silken thread, a drop of milk.
A life too vast
for the little writing of the Emperor.

I crack each word of your letter
and suck its sweetness.
How it will sing in the fire!

Sisters: Burn me, burn me,
let the snow fall in the river!

Mother: I entered college as a man
but they exposed my body
and wrote their small words on it
till it shrank to shadow.
I put on the turtle's shell
and crawled into the fire.
In the cracked oracle
you can read that the Empire
will fall.

Our characters
have always been forbidden.

Will the last daughters
unroll the silk kept secret
through all the dynasties,
or turn our words to fire?

Sister: I am lonely. Write.

Motherhood, Etc.

L. Timmel Duchamp

THE ROOM HAS A LONG, GLASS-TOPPED CONFERENCE table. The room's windows look out on the ocean, but the chair to which they direct her puts her back to the view. The man wearing a black-and-white polka-dotted tie identifies himself as Wagner. He introduces the bald man facing her across the table as Dr. Johns. Wagner asks most of the questions. The other man stares moodily over her shoulder, at the ocean.

"He called himself Joshua," she answers the first question. And: "I liked him because he was different," she answers the second.

The man across from her jerks his eyes off the ocean to stare at her. She blushes. Already she has made a mistake.

"Different, I mean, from all the other guys I'd ever gone out with," she amends. "He liked to talk about real things. And he listened, too. A lot. He had a cute laugh." She looks down at her hands, folded tightly and whitely together. "And the most wonderful brown eyes."

She gets stuck there, does not want to go on. Her eyes skim the walls, looking for the video camera. They are clever about these things, but she thinks she has found it, embedded in a metal sculpture. The bead of red light gives it away.

An "interview," is how they'd billed this ordeal. No one used the word *interrogation*. And no, they said, she was not under arrest. Though she cannot of course go home. If she were reasonable, she would understand why.

They kept telling her to be reasonable. To consider "the implications." They said that the interview . . . would help. Would help them, the "authorities." Who would know best what to do, much better than she. Who was only an inexperienced, nineteen-year-old . . . female. Who was in no position to judge the danger, to understand the stakes. She must trust them.

Right.

Wagner prompts her. He has moved to her side of the table. He perches on it, uncomfortably close to her. One of his feet rests on the chair to her right. The cuff of his somber black pant leg is rucked up. The black sock underneath looks as though it could be silk. Probably, she guesses, it goes all the way up to his knee. Certainly it covers his calf. She's sure that the skin of his leg is dead white. And crawling with coarse red hair. The hair on the backs of his hands and knuckles, certainly, is coarse red. And plentiful. Probably it covers his body.

"We saw one another just about every other night for a month before I first stayed over with him," she replies to the next question. She swallows, and looks away from Wagner's looming bulk, and wishes she could get away from him. He wants all the details, "Everything," he says. Like the prurient evangelist con artist who corners the timid into confessing all sin, all filth, all wickedness in their hearts. So she elaborates, "Yes, we slept together when I stayed over. In pajamas. Both of us. And wearing underpants."

God, Ulrike, he's so weird. *I mean, he said I couldn't sleep with him unless I'd keep my underpants on and wear at least the bottoms of the pajamas. He says he doesn't want to spoil our emotional relationship, which is what he says will happen if we rush ahead with the sexual side of things. He says he knows from past experience. And that I have to trust him.*

Telling it to Ulrike had (at the beginning, at least) made it seem all quite wonderful, an exemplar for what "normal" *should* be. But it hadn't *felt* "normal." It would be middle-of-the-night dark when Joshua's lips and fingers woke her. She'd hear his breathing, and her own, and other noises she knew involved her (or his?) genitals—*sexual* noises she couldn't identify. And little sounds coming from her own throat, that she couldn't mute, because of the explosive sensations rippling in wild, lingering streams of movement through her body. All the while a small observing part of her tried to visualize—as though to watch—what was happening, tried to fit it all into the fictional and theoretical ragbag that constituted her "knowledge" of Sex. His hands are now *there*, doing *this*, the detached observer would note. His right thigh is *there*. And his genitals are . . .

But little of it fit. And his genitals . . .

"Are you saying," the bald man grates, impatiently tapping the closed manila folder on the table before him, "that you never saw his genitals? Even once? That you never felt them with your hands? And that you didn't think it abnormal that after five months' sleeping together you still had not had intercourse with him?"

He sounds incredulous.

There is no way she's going to tell these men that only now and then had she managed to cop a feel, a vague fleeting touch to his genitals before Joshua had maneuvered them out of her reach. Joshua had claimed that her touching him there would turn him on too much. Timidly, she had suggested that since he used his fingers (et cetera) to bring her to orgasm, that she should do the same for him. How can she explain? In the night, she did think it weird. But she couldn't know for sure, because she'd never slept with a man before. And besides, Joshua always made her feel, well, *weird* for wanting more. Isn't it enough? he'd ask her. How can you miss what you've never known? Don't you enjoy what we do?

Sometimes they spent half the night coming. She recalls that one night he got up three times to change his underpants. (It is unreal remembering, with Wagner looming over her and Dr. Johns looking cold and dissatisfied and writing in a small thin script on the yellow pad to one side of the manila folder. They keep saying they want her to tell them everything. Imagine having them write *that* down. *Three pairs of underpants.* They'd probably ask her what his come smelled like. And whether it left stains.)

He had made her feel that wanting to touch his genitals was . . . immodest. Or at the least premature. Which was totally weird, considering all their discussions about Freedom and Being and the need to find Meaning in the face of an utterly random Universe. . . .

These men, she thinks, would feel comfortable with the archaic terminology she and Ulrike had used to discuss it. "Virginity," "hymen," and an "unnaturally prolonged state of innocence." And "clitoral versus vaginal orgasm . . ." They giggled when they used such language. But it was the only way she had known how to talk about it with Ulrike.

Now Wagner presses Dr. Johns's incredulity. She knows he must have figured out he's found one of her most vulnerable spots.

"Look," she says, "I'm nineteen. I'd never been with a man before. Sure, maybe I thought something might be a little strange. But hey, when you're new at it, *all* sex is weird."

Wagner lays his freckled hairy paw on her neatly (but tensely) folded hands. The touch of it, even the *sight* of it, makes her want to throw up. Talking about sex in general and about her and Joshua in particular with these creeps is obscene. "You're making me feel like an old goat, young lady," he says with one of those man-style chuckles (utterly unlike Joshua's frank crackups).

"But intercourse, you must have known that vaginal intercourse is the normal point of sexual relations," Dr. Johns lectures her. He raps his knuckles on the manila folder. "It says on your transcript that you've had three psychology courses. You can't expect us to believe you didn't know something was wrong!"

She is blushing again. And not only can she not stand a second longer of Wagner's touch, but her hands have started trembling. Chagrined, she snatches them away and buries them in her lap. Then she scoots her chair back from the table and glares up at him, though he's definitely too close for comfortable eye contact. (But what distance would be comfortable? A thousand yards?)

"What are you accusing me of?" she demands. "I've never heard that people have a legal obligation to report men who don't take every available opportunity to fuck a willing woman! I have a right to know what you think I've done wrong," she adds, though without faith that they're going to be willing to grant her any "rights" whatsoever, however de rigueur they were supposed to be.

"Now, Patty," Wagner remonstrates. "You know we're not accusing you of anything. We're talking public health, public safety here. We're talking *viruses*, Patty, *communicable* viruses. We're talking a virus that this guy whose name you won't tell us passed to you." He leans forward, so that his thickly freckled face is right up in hers. "Now I thought your doctor explained all that to you. Am I right?"

Patty. On top of everything else, their calling her that just about made her want to scream. But no way was she going to tell *them.* They'd probably just go on calling her that to bug her. And besides, as she'd long ago figured out, if adults you didn't know called you something you didn't ordinarily answer to, a name that was basically alien to you, it meant you were just that much more private from them, and that every time they used the hated name it reminded you of what jerks they were to call you something without first finding out what it is you wanted to be called.

Now the bald man in the navy silk suit opens the manila folder he's been persistently fingering. *Dr. Johns*, she sneers to herself. *Wagner*. Prurient jerks extraordinaire. Much, much worse than the doctor at the hospital. Whether they are as bad as the federal official who'd coerced her into submitting to the exam and photography remains to be seen. The vibes she is getting off Wagner, though, make her feel, in her gut, that they might be worse.

"I told you," she insists. "He said to call him Joshua. If he mentioned his last name to me, I don't remember."

Wagner shakes his head and sighs. "I can't believe a bright young lady like you could be so careless. You know you can't tell these days what you might be getting into, don't you? There's some pretty nasty STDs out there, raging out of control. Besides AIDS. You do know that, Patty, don't you?"

The doctor, now standing, leans over the table and arranges half a dozen or so photos—all 8 1/2 by 11 inches— down the center of the table. Pat stares at the little tuft of gray, like feathers, gracing the top of his shiny pink dome. He sits down and glares at her. "You've got a problem with denial," he announces. "But you can't deny *these*." He takes a stapled sheaf of pages from the folder and waves them at her. "Your DNA has mutated. Your blood doesn't match any known type, even though your medical records say you are type O. And your sex chromosomes now have three Xs and one Y. Which is to say, strictly speaking you're not a woman." He points at the photo nearest her. "And take a look at the eruptions of tissue, there." His words are coming through his teeth, as though he's almost too furious to talk.

Face aflame, she jumps out of her chair and grabs wildly at the photos. "How *dare* you," she seethes as she gets a look at her own pubic hair in larger-than-lifesize glossy black and white. "How dare you *slimeballs* turn my body into sleaze!" She wants to rip the photos to shreds and burn them. *Her* genitals, on public display. For creeps like these!

The doctor goes for the photos, to protect them, and Wagner for her—to slam her back into her chair and keep her pinned there by the shoulders. "Now Patty, I want you to calm yourself," he says.

"Take your filthy hands off me!" she spits, struggling to twist out of his hold.

"You're not going to get hysterical on us, are you?" he says.

The cold spot of fear inside her—that first appeared yesterday—spreads. When she refused to let them examine her, the federal guy also warned her against "getting hysterical," saying that if she did they'd have to give her something to calm her down. Totally cowed, she went along with everything, the crowd of masked witnesses, the cameras, *everything*.

"These photographs are the property of the federal government, young lady," the doctor scolds. "Perhaps you weren't aware of it, but intentional destruction of government property is a very, very serious offense. One you could go to prison for."

She folds her arms across her chest. "Government property," she sneers. "Of sleaze. I can just imagine."

"Important scientific evidence," the doctor snaps.

"Sleaze," she repeats. "Made and distributed without my permission, and definitely against my will."

The doctor looks over her head at Wagner. "People used to say that about Sigmund Freud, you know. But then there have always been people with minds too small and narrow to accept Science."

"And maybe Freud really was just a dirty old man," Pat mutters. She glares at the doctor, who looks as though he'd like to slap her—and ignores (as best she can) the increase of pressure on her shoulders. "Consider, after all, whose side he took in rape and incest cases."

The doctor's eyes lift, presumably to exchange knowing looks with Wagner. "This is intolerable," he says. "We
have about two dozen important questions it is essential
she answer. And she hasn't answered even one of them
yet."

The room is suddenly so quiet that Pat can hear the
surf of the ocean through the double panes of glass behind
her. The doctor's eyes are still focused over her head, so
she guesses the men are involved in some sort of silent
communication.

"It's really, you know, that Patty here doesn't yet
understand just how serious this situation is," Wagner
finally says. His hands lift from her shoulders. For a few
seconds she hears him moving around behind her. "And,
you know, girls her age are sometimes painfully embarrassed about anything to do with sex." His manly chuckle
rumbles briefly. "Especially with men our age." His face
is suddenly right next to Pat's. "Am I right, Patty?"

Embarrassed, right. You stupid boob.

But fear is gaining on anger. She feels too exhausted
to shove his face away, or scratch it, or do any of the
other things popping into her head every second he's bent
over her. "Yeah," she says, "that must be it." She coughs
delicately and scoots her chair to the right. "No offense,
but I think I must be allergic to your cologne." And she
puts her hand to her mouth and hacks loudly, to disguise
the giggles suddenly shaking her.

Wagner's breathing gets considerably heavier, but he
moves out of her face. She wonders how he's going to get
back at her. (There's no doubt in her mind that he will: he's
just that kind of guy.) A scenario involving drugs starts
playing through her mind. Is there, she wonders, really
something called *truth serum*? Can they shoot her up with
a drug that will make her babble indiscriminately?

She just can't stand the idea of reviewing her sexual relations with Joshua for creeps like these. And she
doesn't believe they have valid reasons for prying inside
her head. What she does with another person is none of

their business. It's her body. Which is sacred ground. Off limits. And no one's concern but her own.

The walls and window resonate with a fast rapping on the door.

"The CDC has arrived," Wagner mutters, presumably to Dr. Johns.

The door swings open and a blond giant fills the threshold. The thought flicks through Pat's head that the blond has been imbibing a Wonderland cocktail labeled DRINK ME. "Elliott Hardwick, CDC," he booms. "Apologies. My plane was late."

Though blonds are not Pat's type, she has to admit the man is a knockout. "A pretty boy," Ulrike would call him. He exudes energy and good health. You can see it rippling beneath his soft loose Pima cotton shirt, shining out of his purest of thick-lashed blue eyes, bursting out from his smile. She watches him shake hands, first with Baldie, then—leaning across the table—Wagner. She loves his salmon pink suspenders, she thinks they're perfect for the black jeans and pearl gray shirt. She only wishes he wore at least one gold ring in his ears.

"And *this*," the knockout says, crinkling his eyes in a major heat storm of a smile, "must be Patricia Morrow." He thrusts his hand at her. "How do you do. I'm Elliott Hardwick. Everyone calls me Sam, I hope you will, too."

He's overwhelming her. On purpose, she thinks. But she gives him her hand to shake.

"And what do you go by?" he wonders. "Patricia, Pat, Patty, or something entirely different?"

The blue eyes are like something out of a book, of the trashy romance sort. *Amused, knowing, powerful . . .* Also, he's still holding her hand after shaking it. She blushes, and clears her throat. "Pat," she says. "I go by the name Pat."

He nods, squeezes her hand and lets it go. It's almost a relief when he takes his eyes off her to swing his attache case onto the table and open it.

Wagner walks to the end of the table, rounds it and

walks back up the other side to the center. "If I could have a word with you outside, Sam," he says, jerking his head towards the door.

Elliott "Sam" Hardwick flashes his smile all around. "Sure, Bill," he says in such an easy way that Pat wonders if he has a West Coast background. "But you know, before we settle down to the hard work of eking out the story, what say we take a little break. My working style is just a lit-tle bit different." He *winks* at Pat. "I'd like, for one thing, if it's okay by her, to stretch my legs for a bit on the beach." He beams at Pat. "I bet *you're* up for a walk, Pat, am I right?"

Baldie makes a nasty sound in his throat. Pat shoots a quick glance at him. He looks as though he's swallowed something disagreeable, but though he tamps together the sheaf of photos with undue violence, he says nothing.

Pat shoves back her chair, grabs her bag and stands up. "Damned straight I'm up for it," she tells Sam.

He nods at her bag. "You don't need *that*."

Pat looks at Wagner, then back at Sam. She slings the strap of the bag over her shoulder and quickly rounds the table. Somebody ransacked her house last week. Her doctor was indignant when she suggested he might know who had done it. They're all sleaze, even Gorgeous Sam. And she knows she'd be a fool to forget it.

While Sam "snatches a quick briefing" from the Dynamic Duo, Pat waits outside. Scanning the beach, she wonders if there's any point in trying to run. Her guess is that most of the homes (if that's what they are) overlooking this beach are encased in heavy-duty security fences. But supposing she did get up to the street. She doesn't know the terrain in this La Jolla neighborhood. Buses aren't frequent. And taxis simply don't cruise residential areas looking for fares at ten A.M.

A sudden gust of wind makes her full skirt balloon up. *Surely you must have noticed*, her doctor had chided her for not having come in "at once." And now she's afraid to wear pants or any close-fitting skirts, except with a long loose shirt or sweater that could be counted on to keep the line of her crotch well disguised. As for what is *there* . . . it makes her queasy every morning when she wakes and finds all of it there, between her legs, crowding and sweat-making, scary because if you move or touch yourself the wrong way it can hurt, and making it so damned involved to pee, every morning its presence inexorable, something to be gotten used to all over again, like a bad dream about losing a body part that on waking turns out to be true. . . .

It can all be removed, quite easily, they say. Only they want to wait, to see just how far "it" develops. . . .

Every morning she's nauseated with revulsion, yes . . . but sometimes, especially in the evening, after a day of having accepted it, a perverse excitement breaks out of her, and she knows that though she wants it removed so that she can at least *look* normal (even if her blood and DNA will never again be), there's something powerful about the experience, too. And sometimes a secret voice in her head says there's something neat about being a freak. (If only she hadn't gone to the doctor in the first place.) And sometimes that voice whispers to her that there's a reason, there's a *meaning* in it all, that it's not just an accident of nature but a special event, fated to her in particular. . . .

And of course Joshua hadn't thought the changes in her genitals in the least bit odd. (Though of course he'd only seen the early stages.) And so she had in turn thought that maybe so much stimulation and excitement just naturally caused certain (small) changes, which she thought of as swellings. (But that was before everything had gotten out of hand.) It had made a weird kind of sense to her when she thought of all that blood suffusing those tissues for hours and hours and hours.

Such matters had always been mysterious to her. And so she had told herself that just because people didn't talk about the enlargement of the urethra and swelling just below it didn't mean such things weren't commonplace. It's not as though she had ever read any sex manuals or descriptive pornography that could be counted on to reveal such mature-audience side effects. And ever since she had been a little girl, she had been discovering that where sex and reproduction are concerned, the weirdest most unthinkable things often turn out to be true.

There still lurks in the back of Pat's mind the weird superstitious thought that the cause of the virus is to be found in the hours and hours of "messing around." A book that Ulrike had shown her, warning about such perversity, claimed that sexually stimulated women suffer "congestion" when they fail to achieve "deep vaginal orgasm," which (it claimed) can come only from "proper heterosexual intercourse." Ulrike's concern had been so embarrassing. It had gotten so that Pat hated to come home mornings and face the question *Well, did you finally do it? Have you lost the Big Vee?* And so she had mostly let Ulrike think they didn't do much besides, well, cuddle and *sleep*.

After about fifteen minutes Sam opens the door above and comes out onto the top deck. He waves at her, then starts down the stairs, past the middle deck and the hot tub, to the deck set on stilts into the sand. There he stops to remove his Birkenstocks and the beautiful salmon socks that match his suspenders. When he straightens up he gestures her to join him. Pat sighs, but heaves the bag back onto her shoulder and trudges over the bit of beach between them and up the bottom flight of stairs to the deck.

"Gotta say that after twenty days of Atlanta's temperature inversion, this is purely fantastic," he says, tossing a tube of sun block at her.

She catches it, looks at the label, then up at the sky. "The sun isn't hitting the water yet," she points out. "I really think this is overkill."

"If you knew the stats that I know," he remarks, "you'd never be caught out in UV rays without it."

She nods at his golden-tanned face. "But you go in for *tanning salons*?"

His eyebrows shoot up, and then he laughs. "Oh, you're referring to my face. Believe me, it only goes

down as far as my neck. From the slopes. Got this great
package deal, for weekend skiing this winter."

Pat sighs and rubs some of the #12 cream into her
face. She will humor him. But she wishes she weren't so
attracted to him. On top of Joshua, it makes her feel like a
nymphomaniac. Sam may be a dish, but pretty boys aren't
ordinarily her type.

They walk for a while along the water line, then pause
to look out at the lusciously turquoise water. They may not
have as long a stretch to walk as they would at Torrey
Pines, but this beach is certainly a lot more private. "I gather," Sam begins, "you've gotten into a pretty adversarial
relation, shall we say, with my colleagues." When Pat
snorts, Sam grins at her. "Right. You don't have to say
anything. But what *I* want to say about that is that all
that's just a problem of communication. We're basically
on the same side, Pat. Now I'm not saying it's *all* their
fault, but my guess is that your, well, negative reactions are
probably due to their not leveling with you, not explaining
what we do and don't know, and what you know and can
tell us that we need to know—and, maybe most important,
why we need to know."

Pat's heart starts racing. "Look, I just don't think any
of this is anybody's business but my own!" she exclaims.
"Okay, my body's fucking up. I understand that. But I'm
not a danger to anyone. I haven't done anything wrong.
Whatever my relationship with Joshua is is my own damned
business!"

Sam puts his back to the surf. The sun that pours onto
his face makes his eyes sparkle the same lush blue of the
water. "Pat, can I ask you to do something for me?"

He gazes intensely down into her eyes, and Pat has
to swallow several times. Even in the throes of so much
magnetism, she's practically squirming at her own reaction. She's convinced she's so transparent he's deliberately
manipulating her. She wishes she could say *Fuck you!*
and stomp off down the beach. But she can't. She's too
interested in milking every second out of him she can.

Instead, she says, "Will I be allowed to go back to classes when the new quarter starts next week?"

It makes her mad to hear the childish pleading anxiety in her voice. How could her voice so betray her, when she was feeling snarlingly surly at the very second the words came out? And it doesn't help when Sam lightly touches her shoulder and says: "I wish I knew the answer to that, because if I did I would tell you. But for one thing, I've just been brought in on this, so I can't begin to guess how things are going to go. Certainly we'll do everything we can to keep from disrupting your life any more than necessary. But I also have to add, Pat, that the answer depends a great deal on you. On how quickly we can get the most important questions answered. . . ."

Blackmail, Pat thinks. Covert, but intended. The bastard.

Pat drops her bag to the sand and shoves her hands into her skirt pockets. She wonders if all this would have been avoided if she'd gone home over break. But she and Joshua had planned to have an entire week together, and she hadn't been able to bring herself to tell her parents he'd (apparently) canceled. . . .

Better yet if she hadn't gone to the doctor to get an IUD in the first place. Then it would be just her—and Joshua's—little secret.

"No, Pat, please," Sam says quickly, seemingly reading her face if not her mind. "It's not going to help if you get pissed at me for telling you the truth. As I said before, what we have here is a mystery. A very frustrating and serious mystery. And though some of the answers will be hard to find, others of them, of almost equal consequence, are there, inside your head, if only you would give them to us."

Pat's hands, still in her pockets, ball into fists. "You *say* they're important. But what I *know* is that everybody wants me to surrender my privacy, just like that." Her face burns as she remembers the photos and Wagner's questions and sly innuendo. "Because to you people, it's nothing.

Like I have no rights. Like I'm this pornographic *object* you're all screwing over!"

Her outburst both embarrasses her and further fuels her rage. She can't remember ever talking to an adult this way before, except of course her parents and their co-members in the collective. Close to tears, she picks up her bag and taking big rapid strides resumes her progress up the beach. If the water weren't so cold she'd walk straight out into the surf, to hide.

"Pat, wait, please!" The wind whips Sam's words at her. "Please, if you would just stop for a minute and let me tell you what we need to know and why." He's caught up with her, and has her by the arm. "I know it would put a whole different spin on what you've been perceiving as a reckless invasion of your privacy."

Pat stops. Her breath is coming fast. She stares down at the sand. The man talks like the baby-boomer he is. "Right," she gasps. "I've heard it all already, from those goons up there." She jerks her head back up the beach. "They're grossed out. And they *think* I might be contagious!"

"Listen, I've seen your transcript. There's not a doubt in my mind that you can understand the specifics."

She looks at him, and twists her mouth into a derisory smile. *He* probably thinks he's being flattering. All her A's, and Advanced Placement and a double major in biology and English. Adults are always pretending that sort of thing is "impressive." Right. But she's still just a nineteen-year-old *female*. Which is to say, she's somebody to be browbeaten and manipulated and sidetracked from everything important.

His eyes scan the beach fronts, and he lifts his hand to his brow to shield his eyes from the sun. Pat wonders whether he sacrificed wearing shades on the walk—protection from the wicked UV rays bombarding them—so as to seem more accessible. He points to a concrete bench at the foot of some stairs not far from them. "Shall we sit for a bit?" he proposes.

Pat is glad for the chance to get the bag off her shoulder, so she shrugs and follows him into dry, loose sand. When they are settled, well above the high-tide mark (toward which the dirty-foamed water line is inexorably creeping), Sam, staring out at the water, begins: "I'm not sure how much you've been told. So what I'm going to do is tell you the story as it unfolded in the file they faxed me last night." Pat thinks of the photos, and her throat closes painfully. The very existence of such a file, and its being faxed who knows how many times to who knows how many people. . . .

Sam draws a deep breath. "That there was a problem first became apparent during your office visit to your gynecologist, to be fitted with an IUD." He looks at her. "It occurs to me from the things you've been saying that you might feel more comfortable talking with a woman, Pat. But I have to say that I assumed you wouldn't mind my being a man for the simple reason that you chose a male gynecologist."

Pat snorts. "Do you have any idea how hard it is to get a woman? Everybody wants them. And there aren't that many of them. So if you're in a hurry you don't have much choice. You know?"

Sam nods. "I see. Well, the problem is, we're in something of a hurry here, too, and all the principal investigators in this case are men. And like women gynecologists, women epidemiologists are hard to come by in a hurry, too."

Pat crosses her arms over her chest. She has to bite her lip to keep from flinging at him her own intention to become a medical researcher.

"But to continue." Again Sam gazes out at the water; and Pat does the same. "It seems your doctor initially diagnosed you as having a case of what is known as androgen-dihydrostestosterone deficiency. Which, in plain English, is a genetic condition that often does not become apparent until adolescence, in which the male sex organs make a late appearance in an individual that had previously been mistaken for female."

"That's interesting," Pat remarks. Some of the waves are coming in crooked. It amuses her to see them crash into one another from odd angles. "And I have to say it's the first time I've heard it." She smiles bitterly. "You see, my doctor never bothered to *share* his diagnosis with me."

"Well there were tests he was having done," Sam says quickly. "I'm sure he was just waiting for confirmation. But then when both the chromosomal analysis and blood chemistry reports came in, everything got much more complicated. Because, you see, the first startling thing was the discovery that your sex chromosome was polyploid." Sam looks at her. "To be specific, instead of having an ordinary diploid chromosomal pair, you've somehow got a quadriploid, a double pair. Given all the biology you've had, I assume you understand what I mean by *that*."

Pat frowns. "Except that it sounds like gibberish. I mean, how could I possibly have four sex chromosomes?"

"That's one of our mystery questions," Sam says drily. "Of course polyploidism is not completely unknown—in nonhuman species. Mostly in plants. Often engineered. And in such cases the mechanisms of reproduction are asexual. But that's neither here nor there."

"So I can think of myself as becoming like a plant?" Pat retorts.

Sam clears his throat. "I'm going to assume you mean that as a joke." His folded hands tug isometrically against his right black jean-clad knee, which he's raised a little above his left. "To continue. Your doctor had good reason to doubt his diagnosis, even before seeing the first batch of lab reports. For one thing, he knew from his examination that your female sexual and reproductive organs were all fully developed and morphologically normal. For another, because you were being fitted with an IUD, you were menstruating at the time of the examination. So right from the start there were reasons to doubt the diagnosis." Sam glances at her. "But one can hardly blame him for the mistake. Intersexes are usually discovered at birth, and forced into one sex or the other. An ob/gyn would be understandably fuzzy about the possibilities. So. Your test results start trickling in. The tissue sampled is indeed discovered to be male genital cells. Which seems to confirm the diagnosis. But your blood chemistry shows something else. First, that your sex chromosomal pair is not a pair, but one pair of each sex. Second, that your blood is no longer type O, as it had been when you donated blood in a drive at UCSD last fall. So, given all these mysteries, your doctor takes more blood from you, orders more tests, and seeks consults from colleagues in three different fields of specialization. And the new tests show estrogen in your blood." Sam grins at her. "And you know what that means, don't you?"

Pat snatches a quick look at him, then concentrates again on the water. "Sure. It means that my ovaries are working. Because estrogen is produced primarily in the ovaries, just as testosterone is produced in the testes."

"Right. So your doctor sees there's a problem, but a rather intriguing one. He—and one of the three specialists he's consulting—decides that you have two separate problems, unrelated. His idea is that you're an odd, hitherto unobserved case of intersex, a *true* hermaphrodite, manifesting organs of both sexes that are not only morphologically correct, but—as we now think will be the case—*functionally* correct. Which would be quite an interesting phenomenon, since intersexes on the whole tend to be sterile."

"But there's the problem of other cellular changes," Pat says when he pauses.

"A coincidence, your doctor believes." Sam chuckles. He has a pleasant, not unduly "manly" chuckle, Pat decides, though it doesn't compare with any of Joshua's so-infectious giggles, chortles and belly laughs. "But, needless to say, not what the hematologist thinks."

Pat crosses her legs, and catches herself mentally bracing for the squashing of her balls. She has half a dozen times in the last two weeks, on moving incautiously, been afflicted with horrible abdominal cramps. This time, though, the shift goes off safely, and the sensation of that extra bit of flesh pressing against sexually sensitive places is strictly pleasurable.

"The endocrinologist is also not so certain. And the oncologist is positive it's not."

"Oncologist!" Pat exclaims. "Are you saying this growth is cancerous?" The thought has not before occurred to her, for no one has said anything about changes other than in her blood type, her chromosomes and her genitals. But she sees now that she should have been worried about such a possibility all along.

Sam lays his hand over hers. "The indications are good that this is a controlled, directed growth, Pat. We can't be sure, of course. But the theory everyone's going with now is that the new genetic material is directing the growth." He sighs. "But that leaves open the question as to whether there have been other chromosomal changes. And, most important, what caused the change in your DNA to start with."

Pat snatches her hand away. "Well, it just burns me up that that damned bastard never mentioned any specialists, any doubts, any problems. Until yesterday I thought it was some kind of freak endocrine problem. That's what he led me to believe! And that once the so-called 'new tissue' had 'fully developed' it would be removed, and everything would be hunky-dory!" Her hands clench into fists. She'd like to pummel him. He's one of *them*, even if he is finally telling her *some* of the truth. (To manipulate her!) And it only makes matters worse that she's feeling *excessively* attracted to him—and in spite of the resentment. (And so what that he knows how to dress? That proves nothing. Her parents' generation's mania about judging people by hair and dress attest to that!)

Sam raises his legs, and staring at his bare toes, wriggles them. Even his feet are strong and shapely (though white white). "He's older, isn't he," Sam says. "Well, his generation was taught that women especially want doctors to be God. That you don't tell patients more than you have to, especially when you're not a hundred percent certain of what you think you know." He sighs, and lowers his legs. "You want to get your blood pressure up sometime, you should read through the ob/gyn journals of the nineteen fifties and sixties." He sweeps the air with his hand. "But to continue. Ongoing, intensive work is being done on your blood. The leading theory currently is that there's a virus at work." He shrugs. "The big breakthrough, though, came last week. When it was confirmed that your blood is infectious." Frowning, he looks her in the eye. "Did they tell you this part? That every blood sample put into contact with yours showed the same signs of alteration? Namely, the blood type altered, and an extra chromosomal pair was added. An XY pair for female blood, and an XX pair for male blood."

Pat gasps. "That's *incredible*!"

Sam snorts. "You could say that."

Which explains why they hauled her off to the hospital yesterday and wouldn't let her out of their sight.

"But of course the next mystery—beyond etiology and the like," Sam resumes, "is how the thing was transmitted to you. According to your file, when questioned yesterday you swore up and down that the only needles ever stuck into your body were of legitimate medical provenance. And we know from visual examinations that your hymen is still intact, that you have no vaginal or anal tearing. . . ." Sam clears his throat. "Don't you see, Pat. We need to know if this thing was transmitted sexually. Or if not, just how it *was* transmitted." He presses his lips together. "Your roommate's blood test has come up negative, so we know it can't be entirely casual, say through aerobic or dermal contact."

Pat thinks of how he put his hand on hers a few minutes ago—he's obviously confident he couldn't catch "it" from her in that way. "I don't understand what you're asking me." Her voice comes out small. And her cheeks, damn them, are burning again.

Sam executes a long elaborate ritual of cracking all

the joints on his knuckles one at a time. "You were being fitted for an IUD, presumably because you intended to have sexual intercourse." He frowns fiercely as he finishes the knuckles on the right hand and starts on the left. "You know, Pat, I feel compelled to interject here that if you're going to be having sexual intercourse you should be using a condom. Since there's more than simply contraception at stake."

"I told them all already," Pat snaps (wanting to ask him whether *he* uses condoms every time he has sex). "I was only seeing one man. Joshua. And I decided to get fitted just in case we did decide to . . . have sex. It wasn't that we were necessarily going to. But that I wanted to be prepared in case we did."

"Your roommate says you were out most nights over the last five months."

Pat swallows. It drives her nuts that Ulrike has been dragged in. Testing her. Asking her questions. And telling her what? That she, Pat, is carrying some new plague virus no one has ever seen before? The thought enrages her. "Yes," she seethes, "yes I slept with him. As I already told the others, with pajama bottoms." She glares at him. "Pretty damned funny, isn't it. That a man and woman who aren't married would sleep with one another without screwing. A real pair of freaks, right?"

Sam rises and plants his bare foot on the concrete bench, just at the edge of her skirt. "Why do you say that?" he wonders. Pat stares out at the ocean. The waves, it seems to her, are getting smaller. "What I'm really asking is, was there anything sexual? Did you, for instance, *kiss*?"

Pat's eyes fill with tears. "Yes," she answers. "Yes, we kissed. A lot."

"And petted?"

Her throat chokes with emotion. "Yes, if that's what you want to call it." Even though she's so furious she wants to destroy something, tears overflow her eyes.

"Genital petting?"

She stands up and crosses her arms over her chest. "I don't want to talk about it anymore," she announces.

"Pat. You know how sexually transmitted diseases are passed. You have to know what I'm asking and why. Don't you?"

She turns her back on him and the ocean. For a few seconds she listens to the surf beating on the sand and distant rocks. When she closes her eyes she can almost imagine she is on Torrey Pines Beach. She can almost imagine Joshua is nearby, his fingers ready to touch hers, his arms ready to enfold her when she presses herself close.

But Joshua is gone. And she is here, on this private beach, with an "investigator" wanting to know the details of her sex life with him. She hates them, all of them, for picking at her, for prying into her private self, for frightening Joshua away. A month ago everything was beautiful and life was a constant high.

She opens her eyes to the glare and turns and faces him. "His semen never touched my lips," she spits out. "I never even *saw* his penis. Okay? But he . . . we had . . . cunnilingus." Her tongue trips over the word, so technical, so nothing to do with the real thing. She stares out at the water. "And I had no cuts or sores in the pubic area at any time. Is that what you wanted to know?"

The world is silent, except for the surf and the cry of a gull circling overhead. Then, "Yes, Pat. And I thank you. You can be sure now that no one's going to ask you any more questions about sex."

Pat hefts her bag to her shoulder and they head back for the institute. Sam tells her about how backwards he was, compared to her, doing his required premed courses as an undergraduate (Princeton, '72). As they walk Pat watches the waves rip crookedly to shore. Never has she missed Joshua as much as she does now.

The four of them pile into the shiny gray Mercedes parked in the circle drive just outside the front entrance. Pat and Sam sit in the back. Wagner drives. And Shelley, introduced as "support" (the designation given on the institute photo-badge pinned to her dress), rides shotgun with a laptop in her lap and a radio clipped to one shoulder. (Overkill, Pat thinks, noting the cellular phone in the dash.) It is Sam's idea that Pat would feel more "comfortable" with a woman present during meetings that are not "one on one." At lunch he told the story of how he had had his "consciousness raised" a couple of years back, when, dining out, he had overheard a group of women talking at a nearby table. One of them had told how she had been in an elevator that morning with six men, the lone woman for a twenty-floor ascent, and of how creeped-out she had been. The others had then chimed in with similar tales. The conversation, Sam said, had "struck" him. He said that before then he had always assumed women felt unsafe with single men rather than a crowd, since by his logic a woman could always count on at least one man to come to her rescue against the depredations of another. . . . Wagner and Johns had rolled their eyes, but agreed to assign Shelley to "chaperon duty" (as they keep calling it). Shelley looks and acts so Vanna White, though, that Pat has so far taken little "comfort" in her presence.

The car is comfortable and she knows she should be glad for the chance to get out, but Pat is in such an aftermath of confusion that all she can think is that a) it is weird to be going out driving when she is really basically a prisoner, and b) her parents would not approve of the car. As they pass through the outer set of gates she fantasizes flinging open the door and running, and yelling that she's being held prisoner against her will. But at once the idea strikes her as crazy. She imagines that anyone who happened to be around to hear (and there are only cars in this neighborhood, certainly no pedestrians that she's yet spotted) would assume her to be a paranoid schizophrenic and simply ignore her claims. She thinks that is how she herself would likely react were she in their shoes.

They drive south down La Jolla Boulevard. Pat snatches glimpses of the water as it repeatedly enters and leaves their line of vision. They are going to Hillcrest, they told her. Supposedly to look for Joshua.

She has the feeling that what just happened on the top deck was important. Certainly it upset Wagner. If only she could have some time to herself to *think*. But the wine at lunch and all these *people* constantly surrounding her make it just about impossible.

Lying on the chaise lounge, headphones feeding her a much-needed hit of Sinéad's power passion, she fell asleep. Stuck in that hospital isolation unit, she hadn't slept much during the night. And she wasn't used to drinking wine at lunch. The Big Boys were all inside, having a meeting. (She could just guess about what.) Shelley, nearby, sat at a white metal table, under an umbrella, tapping a keyboard—presumably keeping her under surveillance. Still, closing her eyes and listening to Sinéad, she could almost believe she was lying in the sun at Torrey Pines Beach. The wind felt the same on her skin, and the air smelled of the same salt sea. It was, therefore, *natural* that she fall asleep and dream . . . about Joshua.

In the dream they were on Torrey Pines Beach after dark, lying on Joshua's old chenille bedspread. The remains of a wood fire smoldered nearby. The pounding rhythm of the surf engulfed them, the way it sometimes did. And Joshua's hands were caressing her balls and penis, and his tongue was sliding between her labia, making her close to crazy with sensation. She pressed her hands against the sides of his head, tight. And then slipped her index fingers into his ears. She thought she might be making a lot of noise, but Sinéad kept belting out *Nothing compares, nothing compares to you*, again and again and again.

"Pat!" a voice—not Joshua's—dragged her out of the dream.

"Jesus God it's gross! It makes me sick to my stomach, kind of like that creepy feeling I got in sophomore English class, having to look at Mrs. Anderson's flat-as-a-washboard no-titness from two to three o'clock every fucking afternoon. Only this, man, this is really, really *sick*!"

That was Wagner talking, Pat discovered when she opened her eyes. He was staring at her, shaking his head staring staring staring as if she were the Gorgon and he couldn't take his eyes away though the sight of her was killing him. Really foul stuff kept coming out of his mouth. Major Misogyny—until Sam, after telling him to "Cool it man," went over to him, grabbed him by the lapels, and warned that if he didn't "chill out" he'd be "yanked from the case."

Pat had no idea what had set Wagner off. But then Dr. Johns said: "Don't you believe in wearing underwear, young lady?" Pat gaped at him, and first wondered how he knew, and then grew suspicious that they had somehow peeked under her skirt while she was sleeping. "If modesty doesn't concern you, perhaps you might be interested to know you're just asking for a bladder infection," he went on. "And if there's one thing women are always getting besides yeast infections, it's bladder infections." And he *tsked-tsked* at her in that you're-so-disgusting way all adults, no matter their ideological persuasion, have.

"How do you know I'm not wearing underwear?" Pat demanded of him.

Sam came over to her and bent to whisper in her ear. "Your erection is showing."

Astonished, she looked down at her lap and saw her skirt flare up into a point, then as suddenly drop flat. The movement, she noticed, coincided with one of those delicious new genital sensations that had been introduced in the dream. Preoccupied with this revelation, she said (somewhat absently), "It's just that none of my underwear fits right, and larger sizes don't work because then they're too big everywhere else and just slide off."

Pat understands what happened up to this point. Gazing out the window, observing that they are accessing the San Diego Freeway, she can't help but smile at the memory of her having created such a humorous sight, *viz.*, her penis popping up and down, basically out of control. (How much easier, she thinks, not having to worry about the signs of one's sexual arousal showing. This new experience is a little like the kind of practical and psychological hassle you go through when you first start menstruating, or when your breasts are growing and you have to worry about bras, cup-sizes, straps, and the embarrassment of bouncing and all that. . . .)

No, it's what happened next that she doesn't understand. Actually, it was perfectly *natural* for her to put her hand over it—to hide it from view (and to keep it under control). Maybe it was the greasy white look on Wagner's face, or the pursed lips on Baldie's and the echo of Sinéad's voice endlessly repeating *Nothing compares, nothing compares to you . . .* (*not* from her tape player, which had long since shut off). But when she put her hand on it, it reminded her of putting her hand on Joshua's—maybe because it was through cloth, as she'd always felt his? But also, the pressure of her hand had caused a wonderful, shimmering sensation that ran through her entire body. . . . And so, smiling (she remembers that she was, because her whole being had in that moment been illuminated with joy), not thinking, she just started rubbing it, gently, with one finger. . . .

Except, of course, that Wagner had then gone *berserk*. And Sam said, "Pat, hey, *cool* that—if you'll just think for a second how you'd feel if *we* did that in front of *you*!"

Which had made her *giggle* (she still doesn't know why)—and say to Baldie off the top of her head, "I guess Freud was wrong, hunh? When he said that little boys feel threatened with castration when they discover that a woman or a girl doesn't have a penis. Because if that were true, wouldn't men feel less threatened when they saw that a woman did have a penis?" At which Wagner, cursing, screaming at her to "shut your mouth," charged her. And then suddenly Sam and Shelley were pulling her out of the chaise lounge and hustling her off to the bathroom, Sam all the while lecturing her about "behaving" herself and threatening her with "fifty-seven different kinds of hell to pay" if she didn't.

What stymies her is that the whole thing makes her want to laugh—and masturbate (both sets of genitals). Never has she in front of another person touched herself in a sexual way. Previously the idea would have horrified her. So why isn't she mortified at having been caught in the act by four people?

When they pass the exit to Interstate 8, Pat speaks for the first time since getting into the car. "Hey, I thought we were going to Hillcrest?"

"We are," Sam says, "but we're going to stop at your place first." He stretches his arm along the back of the seat. "So, tell me something, Pat."

Pat makes a face and turns almost sideways to stare out the window, to put her back to him. She hates it when men use their arms and legs to mark territory in that fake-casual way.

"I've been wondering, given what you said earlier about your reasons for not going to Berkeley or Santa Cruz," Sam plows on anyway, "whether you've told your parents about what's happening to you."

Pat freezes. Most of the time she lay awake in the hospital bed last night had been spent debating whether or not to tell them. Her first thought had been that they would make a big deal about it, would get lawyers, possibly the ACLU, maybe even involve the press. Which would turn her into a freak. And her parents and their collective would probably get hassled, her father's record dragged out. (SEX FREAK'S FATHER SHOT OFF TWO TOES OUTSIDE ARMY INDUCTION CENTER DURING VIETNAM WAR! HISTORY OF FAMILY INSANITY! WAS IT IN THE GENES ALL ALONG?) The winery could get blacklisted, or people might come to associate it with a mysterious virus, thereby washing twenty years of hard work down the tubes. . . .

"Did you even tell them you were seeing Joshua?" Sam presses. "Or are you so estranged from them that—"

Pat rockets back in her seat. "My relationship with my parents is none of your fucking business!" she blazes at him. All that seemingly *casual* conversation on the beach, about college choices, about how *weird* it was that someone who'd taken UC summer courses at Santa Cruz during her last two years in high school, someone with test scores as exceptional as hers, would go to a place like UCSD when Berkeley would obviously be glad to have her: all that was simply a fishing expedition.

Sam leans slightly forward and puts his hand on Shelley's headrest. "Could you take down a note for me, Shelley?"

Shelley flicks on the laptop (which Pat hadn't thought could be used literally in one's lap), flips the screen upright and makes several keystrokes. "All right, Dr. Hardwick, I'm all ready to go. Shoot."

Sam checks his Casio. "Two-twelve P.M. Subject continues to display signs of escalating aggression. Take blood sample immediately on return to institute to have testosterone levels checked. Speculation that t-production has surged since lunch. End note, Shelley." Sam settles back. "And thanks."

"Hah, hah, hah, that's really really cute," Pat jeers, just barely holding onto her temper. But that scene in the bathroom . . . She supposes that's what he means by aggression. Well if he thinks he can bamboozle her into believing such raging-hormone shit . . .

"I'm serious," Sam says.

Wagner swings the car off the freeway onto Fifth Avenue. "The sooner she has her operation, the better," he rumbles—then hits the horn in irritation at another driver's braking before giving a turn signal.

A lump rises in Pat's throat. Without thinking, she touches her hand to her lap. Though she was eager enough to get rid of it all only a few hours ago, the thought of losing these new sensations stuns her. They can't *make* her have it all removed, can they?

Whether they can or not, she vows that they won't. And it comes to her, for the first time, that it is all she has left of Joshua.

• • •

Ulrike had left a letter in the usual place. Acutely aware of Sam's gaze, Pat pounces on it. The entire crew has swarmed into the cottage, like locusts ready for a good chomp. "What are you doing?" Pat shouts at Wagner when she sees that he's seated himself at her desk and is going through the drawers. Hadn't they seen there was nothing to find when they searched the place last week?

"You let us in yourself, honey," Wagner says, unperturbed. "But don't worry. We won't *take* anything."

Pat rounds on Sam, who's still watching her (probably with designs on the letter). "You tricked me," she accuses.

"Go pack your bag," is all he says.

Shelley follows her into the bedroom, like a shadow. Thinking of how easy it would be to "lose" the letter, Pat stuffs it down the front of her shirt.

When they'd pulled up alongside the "court" of cottages, Sam had told her they were there so that she could pack "a few things" that would make her "stay at the institute more comfortable." Always thinking of her comfort, that man. What a guy! "For how long are you people holding me?" she nevertheless demanded. "I told you what you wanted to know. *I* kept *my* side of the bargain."

"Bargain?" he repeated, as though incredulous. But then he sidled close and half-whispered, "It'll just be for a couple of days, Pat. So that we can run a few more tests. And make sure the virus doesn't kick anything else up at you. The institute's more comfortable than the hospital, isn't it? Anyway, I've no doubt you'll be returning to classes on Monday. So if I were you I'd just relax, and enjoy the beach and the food and whatever else we can do for you." And then he leaned past her and opened the door.

Instead of getting out, she said, as though the idea had just occurred to her, "This is crazy, Sam. You know? It's not like this virus is *deadly*. You don't even treat people infected with HIV like this!"

"We don't *know* that it's not deadly," he said very gently. "And more importantly," he went on, his eyes agleam with sudden excitement, "you're the only one known to have it. Imagine if we'd gotten hold of the first case of HIV before it had been trans—" But there he stopped, as though realizing he was giving away more than he'd intended.

Pat throws a few things into a suitcase and heads for the bathroom. The door's got a bolt, and this she at once slides home. Relieved to be alone at last, she settles on the floor against the door and pulls out the letter.

Monday evening

Pat—

There's so much I have to tell you. (Though I don't know if you'll even get this—that's how little idea I have of what the eff is going on.) First, regret to say I'm off to L.A. as planned. Feel bad about leaving town, even for three days when god knows what your situation really is. But I don't think there's anything here I can do straight off, and then of course my parents have paid a lot for the workshop. . . . Suspect I'll be too worried to get much out of it. If so, I'll exit prematurely.

Hope you won't be pissed at me when I say I did a stupid thing, namely blabbed out some stuff about Joshua before I realized I shouldn't. (Me and my big mouth.) I said, for one thing, that you'd been staying over with him regularly. I also told how you met him at the Quel. (It was their GREAT interest in that that made me wake up, sorry to say.)

I really feel rotten about this. I mean, I don't even know what it is you have. THEY seemed to think it was ultra-dangerous. Why didn't you tell me, Pat O'Pat? Don't you know I care too much to be scared off? If you had AIDS I'd be sad, sure, but not PHOBIC for christsake. ('Course, I suppose

I could still turn out to have this thing—otherwise
why would they have taken a blood sample. And
then we'd be in the same boat together, right?)

Never mind, as you-know-who always said . . .

Now. The Second Big Thing. God, Pat, I agonized like mad over this one. But I finally decided
to do it. I called your parents, and told them about
the men who questioned me and took my blood.
I mean, it sounds like SOMEBODY should know
where you are. Since they wouldn't tell me, or let
me talk to you on the phone much less visit, how
the hell do I know if you're all right? To my nose,
the whole thing stinks like rotten fish. And anyway,
if you're seriously ill, they need to know. I mean
hell, Pat, you may not like them being so political
and all, but you're close, still, in spite of the differences. Considering how my folks are—busy in their
respective remarried lives, not all that interested in
the detritus of divorce. . . . Anyway. The bad thing
is, I knew only your gynecologist's name. Couldn't
tell them anything else. But they're flying down here
tomorrow. Probably they'll find you before you find
this letter.

Anyway. If I don't hear from you by the time I'm
back, I'll join forces with your parents and tear this
damned county apart looking for you. (And that's a
PROMISE.) If only, though, I had your address. . . .
(But then I might as well wish we were both tele-
pathic, right?)

Hang in there kid—
U.

Knuckles hit the door, making it rattle against Pat's
back. "Pat?" Shelley calls. "Are you all right? You've been
in there a long time."

Feeling sick to lose this small scrap of not-aloneness,
Pat rips the letter into shreds, drops the shreds into the bowl

and flushes. Ulrike hadn't known when she wrote the letter that she tested out negative. What the hell could she be thinking and feeling? And if she knew? What would she think *then*? Sharing a cottage with *that*?

Pat opens the medicine chest and pulls out the toiletries she wants to pack. Seeing the tube of Chap Stick makes her think of lipstick and the old trick of writing messages on mirrors. But neither she nor Ulrike wears lipstick. Or uses eyebrow pencil or mascara. Her eyes rove the shelves. . . .

This time a fist lays into the door. "Pat?" Sam shouts. "I want some voice contact, woman. And now! Or we'll come in through the window!"

Pat unscrews the cap on the tube of toothpaste. "You wouldn't fit!" she yells back. And then she quite carefully dabs GLEASON INST. OFF LA JOL BLVD, BEACHFRNT on the plain metal surface lining the inside of the cabinet door.

"What the hell are you doing in there, taking a bath?"

"No, of course not. I'm too horny for that!" Pat shouts back—but then spoils it by dissolving into giggles.

"Shit, man, she's *masturbating*!" It's Wagner's voice, right beside the door. Pat imagines the three of them crowded against it, competing for a place to lay their ears.

Very very gently Pat clicks the cabinet door shut. Then she checks the bowl to make sure the paper all flushed, gathers up the toiletries, slides the bolt back, and flings open the door. She's disappointed when only Wagner falls into the room.

Sam hustles her out to the car. "Surely you must have some memory of how you got from your house to his?" he says when Wagner asks for instructions.

Pat sighs; she studies her nails; she puts her hand to her throat. "Really, I don't. It was always dark. And we were on a motorcycle. From a motorcycle everything looks the same, nothing looks familiar. As I said before, it was one of those residential sections, somewhere in the vicinity of the zoo."

Sam leans his head back against the seat. "Liar," he mutters. But instead of trying to strike another bargain with her, he simply tells Wagner to drive to the other side of the park, near the zoo. They will "pick up the trail there," he says.

All the time he's watching, waiting, for something to show in her face. A facial twitch or a verbal slip are their only chances of finding Joshua. Which is why she's going to keep her nose glued to the window, out of sight, and her mouth shut whenever Joshua is mentioned.

Joshua's kisses on her neck, and the soft stroking of his hand on her belly, wake her, and his special smell fills her with recognition and joy. For a few seconds, in the dark, she's confused. Her senses tell her she's in Joshua's bed, and that Joshua himself is lying beside her, his hands and lips caressing and kissing her. But as she comes fully awake she knows that cannot be. She has a very clear and distinct memory of going to sleep in the room they'd given her in the Gleason Institute, of lying in a proper bed made with starched hospital sheets. Yet the sheet now covering her body is soft, unstarched cotton, and reaching out over the edge of the bed she can knock the wood floor with her knuckles. And when she strains to hear the ocean, she hears instead a car passing, as she had not done either while sitting up in bed reading or lying flat with the lights out, trying to go to sleep.

But she's so happy to have Joshua back she gives herself over to the delight of feeling, smelling, tasting and touching him, without trying to decide whether she's dreaming, hallucinating, or somehow really with him. She murmurs his name between kisses, and it becomes an incantation she chants again and again and again in honor of the dream, hallucination or miracle she wants the incantation to preserve.

It's when he's pulling the nightgown over her head that she realizes he's completely naked. No underwear, no pajama bottoms, no sweat pants keep her now from touching him. And how strange and delicious it is, taking in through her fingers such riches, warm and mysterious and slippery to the touch, folds and bulges and odd textures to stroke and penetrate. "Do you like it? Are you glad?" Joshua whispers, bringing the first words (other than names) into the night.

"It's beautiful," Pat whispers back. "But will you let me see?"

Joshua switches on the reading lamp he keeps on the floor next to his mattress and focuses the light on the wall. They stare for a long time into one another's eyes. "I'm sorry I had to leave for a while," he says finally. And then he lies back and spreads his legs wide.

Pat examines him with amazement. (Is this what *she* looks like?) She's aware that she has no live experience of male genitalia with which to compare it, but she knows this is the way it's *supposed* to be. At last, she thinks, she knows what is wrong with human beings. Sexual dimorphism, it is obvious, has been nothing but a disaster!

"I just couldn't stand it any longer, being around you while I was waiting," Joshua says. The smooth full lips under his mustache are curved into a smile, in amusement at the intentness of her examination, she thinks. "I guess I should have told you in advance, so that you wouldn't have exposed yourself to that doctor. But I was afraid you'd be horrified if you knew. And so I just couldn't." Joshua takes her hand. "I hope you're not mad at me for not asking you first?"

Pat imagines herself drowning in his dark liquid eyes. "I'm so happy to see you," she says. She ignores the hard knot forming in her stomach, she keeps herself from thinking much about his admission that it is he who's caused her to change. "And I love it, the way I am now. Though at first I hated it and felt like a freak, now I wouldn't give it up for anything." She frowns. "Except, maybe my freedom."

Joshua gestures at the room around her. "You don't need to worry about that," he says. "Haven't you noticed, I've sprung you?"

She glances around at the dimly lit walls, at the window exactly where it is supposed to be, at the dust bunnies dancing in the slight draft coming in through the window, at the cracks in the ceiling and even the cobweb in the corner where it has been allowed to remain for months undisturbed (since Joshua does not believe in killing spiders that aren't poisonous). She *knows* she's not at the Gleason Institute, she *knows* she's not dreaming. She peers at Joshua speculatively. If he could induce her body to grow a second set of genitals, perhaps "springing" her while she's asleep isn't such an impossible feat to have pulled off. He does look beautiful lying there, staring up at her. And his body is so . . . *there*.

She takes his hand and brings it to her mouth. "They're just dying to remove everything they think doesn't belong there," she remarks between kisses to his palm. "But I won't let them, Joshua. Just as I wouldn't let them find you." Almost breathless, she turns his hand over and kisses the back of it knuckle by knuckle, and then licks and sucks his index finger.

For the next couple of hours they don't stop to talk. It's all so fantastic Pat wants to do it again and again in every combination she can think of. Later, though, when they are lying quietly, drifting almost into sleep, her mind resumes work. "What a shame we can't both screw one another simultaneously," she says, sighing. "Don't you think that would be *neat*?"

"In most things human, precise complementarity is disastrous," Joshua observes, as though stating a universally acknowledged truth. "Hadn't you noticed? Also, though in theory it would be nice, geometrically it would be a little like trisecting the angle." Pat giggles at the image, and Joshua joins her. "But we call *this* symmetrical equivalence. Given this sexual arrangement, we can all get pregnant, can all impregnate, can all even do it solo, through artificial insemination. Though of course since it wouldn't be too good for the collective gene pool, self-impregnation is virtually taboo."

"Like incest," Pat says, then thinks that "doing it solo" would really mean that the same genes would be reproduced, rather than a possible slew of recessives. So the analogy doesn't quite hold up. But this *we* that Joshua refers to, as though a whole community of persons are as he is himself and has made her to be . . . It is time, she thinks, to pin him down. "Who *is* this 'we' you're referring to?" she asks him. "Are you saying there are others like you?" She has, since he admitted he had changed her, been thinking that his chromosomes must have mutated, and have mysteriously developed the power to cause hers to mutate, too. But then there's the mystery of how he got her from the institute to his room (and without waking her, yet). . . .

Joshua props himself on an elbow and gazes down into her face. "If I told you any of it, you'd think I was handing you a *National Enquirer* special."

That cracks Pat up. And so she has to tell him the conversation she overheard, in which Sam said that when he started reading the file Lewis had faxed him, he'd thought it was a hoax, *National Enquirer* style. "So," she concludes, "I don't think you have to worry about my dismissing it out of hand, considering how improbable *this*—" she gestures at his and her own genitals—"is."

"First, there aren't many of us left here." Joshua's face grows sober. "Which is why I broke the rules and got involved with you. I was born here—on this planet, I mean—but this is not where my people come from. Before I was born, a subset of our constellation—this is hard to explain, I'm not sure what the best English equivalences are. By constellation I mean something remotely like a guild, or association—but no. The thing is, it's more like a tribe, to which a certain kind of work has been allotted. . . ." Joshua frowns. "But 'tribe' must sound primitive to your ears, and it's not that. . . ." He fidgets with the top hem of the sheet. "Well, a number of us, from the group that is meant to do comparative sorts of studies— sort of a combination of your disciplines of anthropology, sociology, psychology, history and philosophy with quite a lot of the sciences thrown in—anyway, a group of us arrived here about one hundred years ago. Humans are especially interesting to us because they're physiologically very similar—except that they're sexually dimorphic." He smiles, almost shyly, and blinks his so-sweet brown eyes slowly at her. "You can't imagine how weird my people find it that most of the large animals on your planet are sexually dimorphic. Though actually, I probably can't imagine how weird it is to them, either, since I was raised here, and so have been used to it all my life."

It's all coming so fast. It's fantastic, but one part of her, the part coldly watching, doesn't feel all that surprised. Still, she knows she should be astounded and disbelieving (even after all that has happened to her). "You're saying you—your family or whatever—are from *another planet*!" she exclaims. And the watcher inside her thinks of how he told her nothing about this before, of how he did not warn her that her body would be changing (much less ask her permission to change it). . . .

He half laughs; his eyes meeting hers get even shyer. "You see, I told you. Anyway, the problem is that most of us have died. Which we weren't supposed to do. I mean, ordinarily our lifespan is several of your centuries. But disease and all sorts of accidents have been a problem." He shrugs. "I suppose if my constellation had realized that before the window-for-transit next opened humans would develop the capacity for destroying the planet any number of ways, we probably wouldn't have come. Anyway, we're stuck here. And those few of us born here who have survived are in need of mates. But of those available to my age-cohort all are forbidden me, because they are too closely affinial. And so I knew that if I wanted to have a child I'd have to mate with a human to do so. And though it's forbidden to mate with humans . . ."

It wildly elates her to think that not only did he choose *her*, but that he went against his own people in doing so. She grabs his free wrist. "You're saying you broke your people's laws when you got involved with me?"

His smile is so warm it touches even the watcher. She wonders how he rates with his own people, and whether they will accept what he has done. "Well, yes. But I think it will be all right. Because, you see, there are so few of us left here. And the travel window won't open until after I've passed the age at which I can bear children."

Pat flops onto her back and stares up at the dimly lit ceiling. "I can't handle this. You're saying *you* want to get pregnant by *me?*"

Joshua nods. "I suppose that sounds strange to you—because you think of me as a male. But remember, I'm no more a male than you are."

She turns her head and gestures. "But your mustache and beard. And you don't have developed breasts."

"All secondary characteristics, Pat. I chose them when I elected to present myself as a male. Since one must choose one or another on this world. And we've learned the hard way it's too risky to present as females. Too many times those of us presenting as females have been sexually attacked—and discovered. In addition to being less vulnerable to rape, men have greater mobility and access than women. It's simply safer for us to look like men."

"Does that mean I'm going to be growing out a beard, too?"

Joshua laughs. "Only if you want to."

She shakes her head. "I don't see how. Controlling hormones and all that . . ."

"It's easy. I'll show you." He leans over and kisses her lips very lightly. "Well, what do you think? Am I a liar or a lunatic?"

Pat throws her arms around him. "A charmer," she retorts. "I'm completely taken in." Or almost, the watcher murmurs. Because how can you really trust someone who has lied so massively, who chooses manipulation over honest discussion and decision-making? Half smiling, she strokes his flat furry stomach and tries to imagine it swelling under her hands with the persistent fullness of pregnancy. (With *her* child.) She kisses his shoulder. "There's just one thing. . . ."

He withdraws a little to look into her face. "What's that?"

"Will you please just say the words, 'I want to have your baby'?"

Joshua's eyes gleam. "Pat, darling, I want to have your baby," he repeats with utter gravity.

Pat laughs hysterically. Now *that*, she thinks, is true *National Enquirer*. But when she finishes laughing, she sits up so as to be more serious. "Another thing," she says, "that I absolutely have to know. How can we be here in your room? When I first woke I thought I must be dreaming, or maybe hallucinating. How *could* we be *here*?"

Joshua sits up, too. "I can't tell you. The strictures against showing our technology to humans are even more serious than those forbidding me to mate with you." He frowns. "Which reminds me. Pat, you must not ever have sexual intercourse with another human, or give others your blood." He gestures at her genitals. "It would spread, you know."

"I know." She bites her lip. More decisions he's making for her, about what to do with *her* body? "I'm not sure I like your deciding for me that I'm going to be permanently monogamous." She frowns. "But wait a minute, that's not how you changed me, is it. Because we never did have intercourse. So how *did* you do it?"

Joshua hesitates a few seconds before answering. "You remember that time you cut yourself chopping onions?"

Pat shakes her head. "No, not really . . ."

"Well you did. It was, I think, in January. And I kissed and licked the cut." His lips pressed tightly together. "Because I forgot. It completely slipped my mind that I could change you that way—though all the while I was being so excruciatingly careful in our sexual relations. . . ."

Pat's stomach drops. After maybe half a minute she asks in a very small voice: "You mean you didn't *mean* to?" So he *didn't* specially choose her?

Joshua sighs. "I'm afraid not." His eyes meet hers. "But I'm glad I did. My people are scattered all over the world—mostly in Asia. A person gets lonely. And, as I said, now I'll be able to bear a child."

Pat nods slowly. So it was an accident. But he came back for her anyway, didn't he. And surely that counts for a lot. . . .

Dawn is breaking when they finally settle down with the intention to sleep. In the morning, she thinks (even as she's watching the walls lighten), she'll call the collective, and they'll tell her where her parents are staying. They'll raise hell for her, and the bastards won't be able to touch her. All of her genitals will be left intact, of that she is determined. And they will not reincarcerate her. Next Monday she'll start classes, right on schedule. They don't *know* it's a virus. And whether it should be considered harmful or not is in any case a social, not a medical, issue.

Lying with her head on Joshua's chest, drifting off to sleep, she thinks how easy it would be to spread the virus. His people are here to study humans' innate perversity. It seems only fair to take advantage of her privilege, to spread the wealth around to others. She would be a traitor to her own kind if she didn't. So what if she spoils Joshua's and his people's research project? Humans did not ask to be studied. And what could be a more massive violation of privacy than to treat an entire sentient species as research subjects without their knowing consent?

Drifting to the edge of sleep, Pat imagines Wagner pregnant. Would it change even his kind? But how could it not?

A little fear scrapes up that cold pit in her stomach again. Joshua won't approve when he finds out. And Sam will know who's responsible. But she struck no "bargains" with either of them. And Joshua did not even ask her first. And besides, the privilege Joshua's bestowed on her confers its obligations. She may not choose to bear a child in her womb like Joshua, but she can be another kind of mother, mother to an age, mother to the Age of the Hermaphrodite. . . .

At nineteen, yet.

When Pat drops off to sleep she's smiling. It's a big job, changing the world. But she's ready for it.

The Saints

Bonita Kale

I N THE COLD WIND OF THE ALTIPLANO, TWO MEN HUDDLED down in striped ponchos. One of them looked measuringly at the clouds over the surrounding mountains. "Rain very soon."

Benjamín glanced down the steep, winding path below. He saw a woman hurrying along behind a small boy as agile as a llama. From above, they looked like a hat with a skirt following a hat with legs. You could not see how very tall the woman was, but hair the color of dried corn husks stuck out from under her hat and identified her. "Should we tell the Aqlla?"

A shrug. "Let her pray to her book. That will keep her dry."

Benjamín laughed, but called out to the woman, "Aqlla! Rain soon!"

Her pale face tilted up to him for a moment; then she waved and continued on her way.

• • •

Eleanor had known from the beginning that "Aqlla," said in the mocking tone of the village men, was no compliment. But over the six years she'd worked in this backward bit of Peru, she had become accustomed to the name, which was Quechua for a holy woman, a consecrated virgin, a sort of ancient Inca nun. A virgin Eleanor might be, but to be called a nun was a trial for a staunchly Protestant missionary of the Fellowship of God church. But she put up with it, and it had become a more or less friendly nickname that all the villagers used.

She was grateful for the warning, but she couldn't go home now. Maybe by the time Reyna's baby had come the rain would be over, and Eleanor wouldn't have to stay the night. Her own hut was no more luxurious than any other in the village, but at least she could be alone in it.

She scratched her itching palms. Above and below her lay sloping fields of potatoes, guarded by tall wooden crosses. And under many of the crosses, Eleanor knew, lay buried some sort of *huaca*—a holy object, a special stone or a shell. The crosses represented the rankest superstition, and they chafed at her. She called the boy ahead back to her. "Let me tell you a story about Jesus as we go."

The birth went smoothly. Taught by her mother, Eleanor had been handling simple deliveries such as this since she was sixteen. She prayed all through it, in the familiar way that was like talking to a friend: "Here's the head; thank you, Lord, it's presenting just right. Let it be healthy, Lord. Oh, God, that's nice, very nice. As if her body knows just what to do. It should, after five other times. Lovely, lovely . . ." Eleanor's careful, clean fingers didn't dare pat Reyna's less-than-clean leg, but she smiled encouragingly. "Good, good—here it comes! What a beautiful little boy! Thank You, Lord!"

God was the only one here she could talk to in English.

Eleanor laid the baby on a square of sheeting she'd brought, and cut the cord. Reyna and her sister were talking—one sleepy, the other excited. Eleanor caught the afterbirth in a bowl and checked it—all complete.

She sighed heavily, and lifted her eyes to where the mother was already suckling her newest child. "God has given you a beautiful son," she said in Quechua. Then, washing Reyna gently with warm water, she gave what she thought of as "the Lecture"—the talk she always gave about keeping the baby warm and reasonably clean, and above all, the necessity of *rest* for the mother. In planting season, she was sometimes tempted to omit the Lecture, because she knew the mother would be out in the fields the next day, or at best the day after.

"What have you got to keep the baby warm?"

Reyna lifted a corner of her threadbare blanket. The small lantern made the back room only a little less cold than outdoors. The child needed more covering, and so did the mother.

Eleanor gave a swift, appraising glance around the stone hut. In the front room sat Reyna's husband, Chepo, with their two other living children, plus a litter of guinea pigs being raised near the fire. Chepo's poncho seemed less worn than the others, though it too had been patched many times. Eleanor held out her hand. "Give me your poncho," she said peremptorily.

He did not seem to believe her.

She repeated it more slowly, knowing her accent was strong. When he still didn't move, she lost her patience. "A grown man should not fear the cold!" Stepping over a child's legs, she bent and tugged at the poncho.

He gave up, as Eleanor had known he would. From the day she had overpowered a drunk father by force and torn his warm poncho off his back, few had dared deny her what her babies needed.

Besides, he most likely had a fiesta poncho put away somewhere. And if not—"It's for Your baby, Lord."

She wished she could as easily bully the mother into resting. Even if she stayed home, Reyna was apt to think cooking and spinning more important than rest. The baby would be slung on her back, and nursed when he cried, but would Reyna, herself undernourished, be able to feed him and work also?

The rain had almost stopped, and it wouldn't be dark for an hour. Eleanor bundled up her pieces of sheeting, now bloody and dirty, and left gratefully for her own hut.

Should she have tried to get Reyna to commit herself to Jesus? They were more likely to agree in those moments after childbirth, when they were tired and grateful, but such conversions often didn't last. Still, Eleanor felt a vague sense of not measuring up to the evangelistic standards her parents had set. *They* would never let a moment for conversion slip by, even if it had to be done over and over again.

In the hut she had left, Reyna cuddled her baby and talked sleepily with her sister. "That Aqlla is a saint."

Chepo, wrapped in his fiesta poncho, grunted from the other room. "Oh, yes, she's a complete Virgin Mary. Takes my poncho . . . If that's the way they grow them in America, it's no wonder they don't get married."

"She does have a temper," Reyna admitted.

Her sister giggled, and Reyna smiled. They were remembering their neighbor, Victor, falling down drunk at a fiesta, and Eleanor, a head taller than he, tearing the poncho off his feebly resisting body.

"But she went back to him, remember, after she saw to the baby," said Reyna. "She went back, and helped him get home so he wouldn't freeze in the night."

"Scolding him all the way." The women laughed again.

Eleanor knew she should be more patient. She thought about it as she shivered through an all-over sponge bath in water so cold it made her hands ache. She studied her feet and hands carefully. They looked all right, but they'd been feeling strange lately, itching and tingling. She hoped she hadn't picked up a parasite.

She rinsed her cloths in her bath water, wrung them out, and set them in fresh water on the fire. At this altitude, it took a good two hours of boiling for her to feel the cloths were clean. Having stolen a few minutes of the fire to heat up Sunday's soup, she sat sipping it, a blanket wrapped around her, slowly growing warm.

She really ought not to get so angry. But it exasperated her unbearably to see the villagers clinging to beliefs that could never help them, when she had the Word they needed right in her hand.

She patted her old Bible, then picked it up and opened it at random. Of course, she didn't believe in omens, but it was amazing how often the Word of God had relevance.

The book opened at Ezekiel: "Also, thou son of man, the children of thy people still are talking against thee." Well, it might be so, but Eleanor couldn't say it was much help.

She tried another spot on the same page: "And lo, thou art unto them as a very lovely song of one that hath a pleasant voice, and can play well on an instrument: for they hear thy words, but they do them not."

She closed the Bible slowly, stroking it. It was true. Nothing she could say to the people seemed to get through their rock-hard combination of Quechua and Catholic superstition.

She had always known that Catholics, with their pope and saints, were practically idolaters. But the Quechua Indians carried idolatry to an extent she'd never imagined, lighting candles and bringing food for the dead, spending their few *soles* on elaborate clothes for statues of saints. At the same time, they were making sacrifices to their heathen idols. At several little stone cairns, Eleanor could be almost sure of finding a bit of llama fat, or a few coca leaves, left to propitiate some god or other, even the mountain itself, which some of the villagers called Apu, Lord.

And those processions! Every fiesta brought out the village's prized statue of San Juan, John the Baptist, life-sized, gaily painted. Normally, it wore a dark red robe, but for fiestas, it was dressed up in white and gold and blue, like a girl going to a dance.

She had tried to explain to the villagers that San Juan, the real San Juan, had died long before their grandfathers were born. They nodded and said Yes, they understood, and the next moment were bragging about the beauty and miracles of "*our* San Juan" as if he were some Inca rock to protect them from harm. "He has a special look in his eye," said Reyna. "You can tell he understands when you speak to him."

In her worst moods, Eleanor put herself to sleep imagining how it would feel to break that statue into bits.

Once there had been four people in this mission; three had transferred out. And the church missionary board, disturbed at having a single woman alone, kept edging closer and closer to calling for her return.

Tonight, she felt so gloomy that she pulled out an ancient copy of *Life* that had somehow found its way to the altiplano. She had been saving it for a mood like this. She scratched her palm absently as she read.

The next day, the rain was gone and life seemed worth living. The sun might even get hot. Eleanor tucked a Quechua New Testament in her pocket, and joined the villagers trotting an hour downhill to the nearest market town.

Eleanor loved the quiet of an ordinary market day. At fiesta time, flutes and drums and horns would play, people would shout and dance and sing. But today, people moved in near silence along the pre-Columbian stone pavement, studying the wares laid out on blankets, bargaining in low voices. Heads in dark felt hats nodded thoughtfully. The sun was warm on Eleanor's back, and the smells—of dust, of donkey, and of people—were warm, too.

Peacefully, she strolled around, letting her eyes roam over the bright shawls and blankets. She might buy some soup greens and dried potatoes, maybe a guinea pig if the seller would kill it for her.

Then she saw the image vendor sitting on the ground. He was a muscular, middle-aged man with only one eye, but that eye seemed to call her. He had a few shawls for sale, and a few pots. Beside them, he had laid out on a red blanket, held down by stones at the corners, two neat rows of plaster saints—perhaps a dozen in all. They were fetching things, like dolls, painted with care in bright colors. Some were almost a foot high, some only half that.

His wares stole Eleanor's peace. She bent over and peered at the saints. Tentatively, she picked one up, a small Virgin in a blue robe, with a halo painted red and yellow.

She studied it in mounting fury. Someone would pray to this—this *thing*—and rely on it in time of trouble, instead of on the Word of God. Eleanor hefted it gently. Its paint was cool and slick, and it weighed hardly anything. To Eleanor's faith, it was hateful. But to her hand, it felt like a doll from her childhood. She wanted to lay it down tenderly, so as not to hurt it.

"How much?" she asked.

The vendor's single eye met hers. "For you . . ."

Her hand was in her pocket; now she took it out, empty. "Not 'for me.' How much?"

The seller paused. An eyebrow rose over the empty socket. "Four *soles*."

She hesitated only a moment before reaching into her pocket. "Four *soles*." No meat this week. But the small bright Virgin was hers.

She tucked it away, glad for her skirt's large pockets. She didn't want to be seen carrying a statue of Mary.

Also in her pocket were several small cards. "Here," she said, handing one to the man. She had copied a verse on it, in Quechua. "This is for you."

He stared at it, then at her. He could not read, of course.

"It says, 'I am the Way, the Truth, and the Life. No one comes to the Father but by me.' "

"Thank you," said the seller, without interest.

"It is the words of Jesus, of El Señor."

"Ah, El Señor. I have one here." And he held up a small crucifix.

"No," she said. Anger swept over her as if the spirit of her father had come to give her strength. "No, you don't. You have *nothing*!" She paused to catch her breath and her patience, and tapped the card the man held. "El Señor, Jesus, lived long ago. This is one of the things he said."

She snatched her Testament out and shook it in his face. "And *this* is what else he said! Everything you need to know is in *here;* what is not in the Bible, you do not need!" She made a broad, dismissive gesture toward the images on the blanket. "And *these* things are not in the Bible!"

His eye seemed to sparkle at her. "You bought one, Mamacita."

Eleanor's raised voice had attracted a small crowd, some of them from her own village. She could smell *chicha*, the corn beer of the Indians.

Carefully, smoothing the pages, she put the Bible away. This wasn't how she had planned her demonstration, but maybe it would do.

"Do you know why I bought this little statue?" she asked, trying to control the shaking in her voice. She took the small Virgin from her pocket, fighting the feeling that she was betraying a living thing, and held it high.

"Do you know why I bought this child's toy? I bought it to do *this*!" Kneeling, she gritted her teeth and slammed the statue against one of the rocks that held the salesman's blanket down. The plaster broke, crumbling. A blue arm rolled off one way, a pink head the other. Eleanor stood with a feeling of triumph, and held high her plaster-dusted hand, containing the disintegrating remnants of the saint's blue dress.

"Do you see that?" she cried. Her father would be proud of her, she knew. "Do you see that inside of this thing is only plaster and dust? This is not a saint—this is a plaything for children!"

The group of people around her stood in shocked silence for a moment. Then two or three women bent down to pick up the pieces of the statue. "For shame!" they cried. "To break the poor little Virgin—for shame!"

"But it is not the Virgin!" Eleanor cried. "It is only a piece of plaster!"

"Because she is plaster, does she deserve to be broken?" asked one man, and a woman chimed in, "Is it her fault she is not a big fiesta Virgin? She would have helped you, if you had asked her, but instead you have killed her."

For a moment, looking at the people around her, Eleanor was frightened. They looked as angry as if she had slapped one of their children.

"I don't ask dolls for help," she cried. "I don't pray to toys!"

"No," said a small man, smiling. It was Benjamín, from her village. "You pray to your book. And your book helps you well—so well that you have no husband, you have no children, and you were as sick as anyone in the last influenza."

Eleanor was shocked into silence, and now the people were laughing. Any danger she might have been in was over, as was the chance to do any good.

Benjamín grabbed her by the arm. "Come on, Aqlla," he said in an exasperated way. "Time to go home." He searched the market with his eyes. "Josefina! Take the Aqlla home."

His wife obeyed, but her eyes promised reckoning.

After the first hour of climbing, Josefina heard Eleanor sigh, and knew the Aqlla was no longer angry. Walking uphill at a high altitude is hard enough without sulking at the same time.

Josefina had a question. With the sunshine warm around them, this seemed as good a time as any to ask it. "Why do you stay here?" she said. "We make you so angry; why don't you go home?"

"I don't want to leave," said Eleanor, grabbing a tuft of grass to help herself up a steep bit.

"We are glad to have you here," said Josefina. "You know *I* am glad." She shifted the child on her back. She and her child would both be in the village's small grave-yard, if Eleanor were not here. Her mother had told her so, and she knew it was true. "But for you—you help us all the time, and you don't ask for money, and people laugh at you, and you get angry—I think you would cry if you were like us, but you never cry. Why do you want to stay?"

She heard Eleanor stop climbing, and she looked back over her shoulder. Eleanor was staring at the mountain above them, and the icy white mountains across the val-ley, clouds hiding now one peak, now another. Perhaps, Josefina thought, she should not have mentioned the cry-ing. But all the village knew the Aqlla never cried.

The blue eyes, like the painted eyes of a saint, looked into hers. Josefina wondered sometimes, how such pale eyes could see. Then Eleanor's mouth twisted, and she shrugged. "I don't know why I want to stay," she said. "I just do." She gestured at the glaciated mountains and the deep blue sky behind the clouds. "Maybe because it's so beautiful."

Josefina bent and patted the sloping side of the moun-tain, then tipped her hat to it. "Apu Alpamayo likes having you here, I think."

Eleanor sighed.

"And you can pray to your book—we don't mind."

"I don't worship Your Word, Lord," she prayed fran-tically in her hut that night. "I don't pray to my Bible. I only hunt for You in it." She ruffled the pages urgently, peering at them in the dim firelight. "But I can't *find* You!" With a grunt, she stood and hurled the book across the room. It slammed against the wall with its soft leather binding bent, and dropped to the dirt floor.

Eleanor fell to her knees and grabbed it. She smoothed

its thumb-indexed pages and pressed its cover into shape. "I'm sorry. I'm so sorry."

She scratched at her palm and noticed a small smear of blood.

Eleanor delivered babies, checked children for worms, sewed up gashes and set bones. Her hands and feet continued to itch, and her palms bled slightly, though she could find no mark on them.

She bandaged them carefully. "It's nothing," she told the villagers. "Only to protect my hands." But the slow seepage didn't stop.

One day she found her feet bleeding, too. Wonderful. She could have wept with rage. Instead, she clenched her jaw and gave God an almighty scolding. "How *dare* You, Lord? You know what they'll say in the village! Do You want them touching me for healing, Lord? Is that what You want? I'm to be one more blasted idol—one more stone *huaca*, one more plaster saint? Is that the idea? You should be ashamed!"

She wrapped her feet up, apologized to God, Who was used to it, and told the villagers her sandals hurt her. Every night, she soaked and boiled the rags.

She continued to bleed. Anemia would help nothing, so she bought a few nails at the market and put them in her soup pot. "Lord, I *don't* want to leave here!"

But she bled through the rags more and more quickly. Whether that was because she was bleeding more, or because the rags were wearing thin, she did not know.

It was Josefina who found her out, walking in without warning late one afternoon when the Aqlla's hands were unwrapped. Eleanor grabbed a bandage, but Josefina was quicker than she. Gently, she held Eleanor's hand, staring at the drops that welled from the unwounded palm. The blood filled it like a cup and at length it overflowed. And still drops came, one at a time, falling to the ground.

Josefina looked up at Eleanor. Saints, one thought,

were calm beings, but this one had a deep terror in her
eyes. When Josefina bent to kiss her bleeding palm, Eleanor
yanked it away.

Talking was useless. Even the baby on her back knew
that, and was silent. Josefina picked up the discarded bandages and herself rewrapped Eleanor's hands. Then, since
she was not to kiss the saint on the hand, she kissed the
woman on the forehead, and went away.

That year was blessed. The harvest was magnificent;
even the corn, which had to be tended like prize roses
at that altitude, grew abundantly. The potatoes were the
largest ever seen. Eight babies were born, and all lived,
and all their mothers had milk. The sheep grew thick wool
and gave birth to twins. The llamas prospered. Someone
saw six vicuña on the high *puna* where vicuña hadn't
been seen since the day of the oldest woman's great-
grandmother.

Uneasily, Eleanor noted changes in her village. When
the villagers drank, the first drops had always been flicked
with a finger onto the ground. Now, the drops always
seemed to fly in her direction. If the men still mocked
her, they did it when she wasn't around. Even the women
treated her more respectfully. Eleanor missed the bawdy
jokes that somehow brought her inside the community
of village women. She gave up trying to deny what had
happened to her, though she still kept her hands and feet
bandaged. "It is an illness," she said. "It has no meaning.
No, it does not hurt."

Corpus Christi came in June, when most of the harvest was in. This year, the whole village seemed to look
forward to it. Eleanor heard none of the usual complaints
about the expense or the bother of stopping work for
a fiesta.

But the more cheerful the villagers seemed, the gloomier Eleanor felt. They would be taking the statue of San Juan
out of its tiny chapel again, and dressing it up, and carrying

it on their shoulders to the market town. Like parents at a Beautiful Baby contest, each village would study the other statues. "We could make flowers like that for our San Juan," they would say, or, "They have put a bird at the feet of their Virgin! Whoever heard of a bird with the Virgin?"

And then they would pray to the images. Not through the saints to God, nor even through the images to the saints, but *to* the images. And she could do nothing about it, nothing! She could do nothing at all for them, only heal them when she could and love them always.

For alone in her hut, sipping hot tea and soup that tasted bitter—perhaps it was time to start a new pot— Eleanor admitted that she loved the people of the village, more, even, than she loved the white mountains and the blue sky and the bleak, bare landscape. The people—they were why she wanted to stay.

Fretfully, she rubbed her stiff neck. Her semiannual report was written, but she knew it was unsatisfactory. By no twist of the truth could she make her fifty or sixty families, all stubbornly set in their ways, sound like promising ground for a mission. She would go to the fiesta in the morning, and she would find someone to take her report to a town with mail service. Eventually, an answer would reach her, and it would say, "Come home."

The day had not been especially hard, but Eleanor was exhausted. In another moment, she was asleep.

Josefina and her husband Benjamín, Reyna and her husband Chepo, slipped through the doorway into the hut where Eleanor lay sleeping heavily. "She will not like it," Josefina said.

"Is she a saint, or not?" demanded Chepo.

For answer, Josefina and Reyna untwisted Eleanor's bandages. Chepo crossed himself when he saw the bloody hands and feet.

"But what will we dress her in?" asked Reyna. "Her clothes are so old and worn—and such dismal colors."

After a moment, Josefina said, "She can wear my fiesta skirts. I will wear my old ones."

"And my black shawl," said Reyna. "A saint should be dressed properly for a procession."

And Benjamín patted her leg. "Our saint," he said. "Our bad-tempered scold of a saint."

Eleanor was moving, floating, in the midst of a sense-deadening din. Drums, flutes, horns, voices. People all around, shouting, shrieking, weeping, looking up at her. Looking up, because she was floating above them, their heads at the level of her feet. And they were all, men and women, bareheaded, as if for a religious procession.

It was a dream, no doubt. She had dreamed of floating before. It was pleasant, really, in spite of the noise. Ahead of her, she saw the familiar back of the statue of San Juan; ahead of that, yet other statues, borne on platforms carried by other shoulders. Oh, well, that explained it. It was a fiesta.

But she still didn't know why she was riding above the crowd. She noticed a bitter taste in her mouth. Could the villagers finally have persuaded her to try their *chicha*, or even the coca leaves they chewed? That might account for the floating sensation.

Rather bumpy floating. And what was she sitting on? She looked before her and saw a mass of pink and blue and yellow. It took her a measurable time to recognize it as a pile of paper flowers, such as some villages used to decorate their saints.

She was sitting on a platform, being carried, with paper flowers in front of her. She couldn't see her feet; her view was blocked by billowing, embroidered layers of skirts.

Oh, this *must* be a dream. Why should she be carried in procession, dressed in Josefina's treasured fiesta clothes?

Then she noticed her hands—unbandaged, naked before all these strangers. Blood dripped onto her skirts, shiny and red, brighter than the colored threads of Josefina's embroidery. And all the crowd looked on. Eleanor's humiliation was a small thorn-prick through her confusion.

In defense, her hand searched for a pocket and a Bible. Even after she realized she had neither, she continued to pat her skirts vaguely. She struggled to recall some consoling Bible verse, but the noise of the crowd disoriented her. All she could think was, "Thou shalt not make unto thee any graven image. . . ."

But I don't, Lord. Do I?

She looked at the people around her. All strangers? No—some were from her own village. Benjamín. Reyna. There was Josefina, struggling to keep her balance in the mob. She looked up at that moment, and Eleanor caught her eye.

"Josefina!" she tried to call. But if her voice made any sound, it was drowned in other noise. She reached out a hand, feeling strangely light and stiff.

Josefina crossed herself.

As nothing else had, that gesture reached Eleanor. *No!* Of all the stones and crosses and statues they could worship—*No!*

Where are You? she cried silently, fumbling again for a Bible in a nonexistent pocket. She had to stop what was happening, but how could she, when even to move was difficult?

Eleanor wrung her hands in despair at her own inadequacy. To her surprise, her right index finger broke off. "Oh . . ." she said, looking at it sadly. It was white plaster inside.

But perhaps this was her chance. She held the broken-off finger high for the crowd to see. "Plaster!" she cried. "It's only plaster!" But no one seemed to hear.

"Listen to me!" she shouted, but they would not listen. They were dropping to their knees now, and crossing themselves, reverencing her.

Stupid people, how she loved them.

"You fools!" Her jaw felt stiff. "Josefina! You know I'm not a saint!" But Josefina had knelt with the rest.

"No," Eleanor whispered, and slumped back in her chair. "Please, Lord—*please*, isn't it time to wake up now?"

It was the only time in her life she heard an answer to prayer.

Yes.

Eleanor's arms dropped to her sides, palms open to the crowd. The broken finger fell from her grasp.

She breathed out, and the crowd was gone.

"Our saint," murmured Chepo, raising his eyes humbly. He was overcome with awe and, for some reason he didn't understand, relief.

"Santa Elenora is very beautiful," said Reyna. "We must have a fine robe made for her for the next fiesta."

"She would not like it," said Josefina. "This is an angry saint." She did not know why she said that, but when her husband nodded, she knew she was right.

Blood continued to well from the saint's plaster hands, and many in the crowd touched the drops. Some looked hopefully up at her face, wishing, perhaps, to find there a sign of her love for them. But, as always, no tears fell from the painted eyes.

The Best Lives of Our Years

A. R. Morlan

. . . sociologists of the time predicted initially that if there was to be any so-called "positive" effect of the Esperme Virus Plague (EVP) in 2007, with its resulting drop in the male birth rate (down 59 percent in North and South America from 2007 to 2009 alone and dropping between 45 percent and 70 percent worldwide, with Africa and the South Pacific-Australia-New Zealand areas experiencing the most significant decreases in live male births), it would involve the overall shape of future civil and world wars. While there remained no doubt—thanks to Operation Desert Storm in the preceding decade—that women were capable of waging war, under the circumstances of EVP (and the eventual barring of all fertile males from active combat in 2012), it *was* believed that those women already in positions of power in government and the military would be more likely to rely strongly on negotiations rather than overt military action in potentially explosive diplomatic and territorial situations, due to their innate maternal and familial

protection instincts (which, after EVP, were
exacerbated by the added need to protect the ever-
dwindling male members of society), with all previous
notions of women's rights, equality of the sexes,
and rejection of the "Mommy Track" to be cast aside
by those women now experiencing the onus of possible
human extinction within the next 200 to 300 years.
(According to the initial projections of
Dr. Olivier Dreyfus, discoverer of the first strain
of EVP; those figures are currently undergoing
intense worldwide scrutiny.)

Unfortunately, sociologists—like practitioners in any
speculative field—can be wrong. . . .

—Dr. Coriane Katan, *The War of All Mothers*
(New York: Doubleday/Warner, 2085)

i

red

I DIDN'T LOOK AT THE LETTER AS I FISHED IT OUT OF
the narrow slot of the opened post office box; that Tyvek
envelope they send the notices in says it all, the second your fingers touch the damned thing. After ten years
behind the window, I've seen enough draft notices stuffed
into the 'router's bags to just about know those suckers
by *smell*. By the almost antiseptic sort-of-plastic stink of
them; the odor of bandages and suitcase linings and those
little rain bonnets with the flimsy ties that always broke
when Grandma tried to take them off in a hurry. And the
reek of the plastic kits they issue to new recruits, the War
Bags designed to be worn Velcroed around a waist, or
around a thigh or upper arm if your waist is ballooned
from within by child.

Enough of the returning War Bags come through the
post office for me to know their scent as intimately as I
know the odor of my own menses. That slightly acidic,

slightly *warm* redolence which somehow manages to per-meate the oversized Tyvek envelope they stuff the War Bags in after plucking them off the bodies of the fallen.

So . . . trusting my nose, and my fingertips, I wasn't about to waste my eye's time by reading my own name on the draft notice. It's always been a *given*, I suppose, that I'd be called; Tashia is five, and Alan still makes his deposits at the *s*'bank on a monthly basis (thanks to me taking the filled, vacuum-bottle-protected vial to the *s*'bank myself—His *Uniqueness* hasn't ventured out of the flat since '16 or so; he's still got the raz from the last time he got *s*'mugged, and won't go *near* any woman other than me bearing a *s*'vial in her hand).

At least he hasn't gone full-blown EVP; they can still use his *s*' in the banks, or so the credits for withdrawals he gets in the mail tell me. I know more about his payments than he does—I do every step of his banking except for signing the backs of his checks—so even without my P.O. check, they'll be set should I have to go.

When I go, now. I resist looking at the letter during the sub ride home; just the presence of it in my bag is enough. I know without bending down to smell it that it is already stinking up my bag, infecting all my civilian personal things with that syntho-blood aroma. Across from me, another 'muter's paper is folded in her hand so that I can read the inner frontpage headline, the one closest to the spine of the paper:

WAR IN MANDELIA CLAIMS 15,000 U.S. TROOPS

Another war-euphemism, like "fallen" for the dead, this one out-stripping the Penta-Pret's propaganda depart-ment. "Claims," instead of *kills*. Like war is someone who plucks up the footgroaners, collecting 'groans like seashells on a tide-washed beach, claiming the best ones for her store of soldiers. Like, "This here 'groaner is mine, I've *claimed* her."

Maybe "envelopes" would be a better word for what

war does to 'groaners. The envelope taketh you away, the
envelope giveth you back.

The 'muter folds her paper yet again, to swatting
size, and gets off at the stop before mine. Through the
opposite window, I see her (young, thin, hair puffed 'n'
piled, suit 'n' tie improbably bright olive) slide through
the crowd, waving her paper like a scythe. I try to imagine
someone like her getting a draft notice, showing up at the
'cruitment center, losing that piled puff of hair with just
a few swipes of the razor, standing in line with gov'issue
uniform parts in hand. . . . Midway through the scenario, I
give up. 'Muters in suit 'n' tie are just too valuable back
home, got to keep the corporate machines clicking along.
Today's version of Joe College from Grandma's teenhood,
when the 'groaners were grunts, and only guys burned their
draft cards.

Minutes before my stop comes up, I try to picture
Alan going through the draft notice routine, but it's just too
improbable. No man goes farther into battle than having
his voice issue orders from a safe bunker miles from real
action. And those 'groaners are oldies, past worrying about
EVP further messing up the chances of the boy-*s*' making it
past the tough hide of the egg, past worrying about making
girl babies whose kid-machines are defective. And past
s'bank donation checks, too.

No, even if His *Uniqueness* back home were a *woman*,
like the other eighty-five percent of us in the world, I still
couldn't see him making it as a 'groaner. He'd have to
leave our flat first. . . .

My stop; elbowing past the 'muters and on-leave
'groaners and palm-outs huddled behind their "My man's
EVP, no *s*'deposits" signs, I reach the stairway leading
up to my street. More palm-outs; men in the last stages
of EVP—no-colored behind beard stubble, mucus running
out of their eyes, nostrils, past mosaic-parched lips, and
women whose clothes are cut away to show the scars where
they'd been de-repoed, de-kid-machined. I feel around in
my bag for the draft notice, wave it around, let them catch

a whiff of its reek. I walk the last block unimplored by the palm-outs.

In the lobby, I press the buzzer one-handed, peeling open the envelope's gummed flap with the other hand, pressing the notice against my thigh for leverage. The gov' seal is there, over the computer-standard greeting— "Dear Ms./Mrs. Ingram"—but I am buzzed through before I have a chance to read more. No voice confirmation, no Alan fearing some *s*'mugger will barge into the flat, knock him on his back, yank down his pants and *s*'rob him at knife-gun-fistpoint because she can't make a legal *s*' withdrawal due to being a (take your pick) felon, drugger or ex-'groaner mustered out for a non-repo-related infraction. Maybe he thinks they can smell the live *s*' on his breath as he speaks, I tell myself, riding the elevator to our floor. The 'vator is empty, for once; I have a clear view of myself in the round convex security mirror in the upper corner, a leftover from the days when women had to worry *about* men, rather than just worry *for* them. I take myself in, as I am now, freshly post-civilian: hair pulled back in P.O.-reg flowing tail, light-over-dark uniform, shoes thick-soled enough for stand-on-your-feet comfort. I still have the unfolded letter in my hand; it has a date for my arrival at the 'cruitment center, but I will look at that later on. For a few more precious seconds, this is *my* life.

For the space of time it takes the elevator to travel up, up to my floor, I am still a *woman*, in the old sense, as if any female today can *ever* be a complete woman anymore (considering how we're all mothers not only to our young, but to our spouses or whatever man we have to defer to at the job, on the streets, or wherever one happens to encounter a *unique* member of an increasingly female society)—each step I take is for *me*, not for the Pentagon-Pretties in their leather chairs and uniforms with pants and half-inch-long hair under their uniform caps.

The 'vator reaches my floor. Doors slide open, wait for a few seconds, then start to close again. Sliding side-ways through the diminishing open space, I catch a last glimpse of myself—hirsute, skirted, *female*—before the 'vator closes itself to me and descends to the lobby.

Smoothing the skirt against my legs as I walk, savoring the feel of air circulating around my moving limbs, I tell myself that Tashia will be fine while I'm gone; Alan is a good mother, and once I'm gone, he can have a messenger carry his *s'*deposit to the *s'*bank. They have men with vaccine-arrested (but not cured) EVP just for that purpose.

Not wishing to make Alan take an unnecessary trip down our hallway, I get my keys (already scent-tainted) out of my bag and begin to unlock the six deadbolts set into the edge of our door. Alan has never had to do this; he hasn't been out of the flat since we had the fifth and sixth deadbolts installed. Through the fine gaps where the door and the door frame don't seal perfectly, I hear an odd sound coming from within the apartment. Too even to be crying, too loud to be moaning—opening the door, I see something rippling *over* the nap of the carpeting within. Radiating out in a sunlike formation from a central bare spot. The low yet persistent noise is coming from farther down the inner hallway, but the bright-color ripples on the carpet have command of my attention for the moment.

Bending down, I run my fingers over one of the rays of color, feeling the strands separate under the pressure of my fingertips, splaying out against the carpet's springy fibers. Hair . . . still smelling faintly of mild shampoo, the kind Tashia uses—

A pound of footfalls coming toward me, coupled with Tashia's "*Mommy*," attacks my ears. Looking up I see Tashia's legs first, encased in *pants*, oh *God* wherever She is, a little pair of *overalls* like little *boys* used to wear, like Alan wore in the days when he was a child and actually saved in the hope that his own little boy would . . . and then I slowly raise my eyes, to take in her little-boy pullover shirt, the one with the blue and red rugby stripes and the little white collar—and instinctively *stop* looking after one glimpse of Tashia's head, of the whitish scalp

showing through the places where Alan's electric razor
clipped too close, leaving almost no stubble at all.

Tashia stops short of the spot where her hair is resting,
fanned out in an approximation of the shape of her head,
saying in a voice I hear only faintly, coming like static
through the pound of blood in my ears, "Mommy, Daddy
said it was gonna be like Hallo'*een*, but 'stead of candy
I was gonna get a big s'prise 'long as I closed my eyes
an' layed on the floor *there*—" she may've been pointing
at the rays of her hair, all I could see was red and black,
hazing before me "—only it buzzed and tickled and then
Daddy went 'way without giving me my s'prise—"

Fainter still, I hear Alan, babbling either to me or to
himself or to God, from somewhere down the hallway,
"—fixed it, don't you *see*? They don't take little *boys*, not
for the war, little boys are too rare, too *unique* . . . saved
the bibbies, and the shirt, *knew* I'd have a boy someday,
little *boy*, with a buzz cut like I'd get every summer . . .
'fore little boys were *special*, and never left home any,
any more. Like their Mommies do . . . see, Tash's a *boy's*
name, and little boys don't go away . . . *they'll* never look,
never check, boys are too *special* have to protect the *sper*—
keep *it* safe, from the dis-*ease*—"

And Tashia . . . my *girl*. My *Na*tashia, she doesn't
care that she's dressed like a boy, or is shorn like a first-
day 'groaner in the 'cruitment center barber chair. *She's*
boo-hooing about not getting that "s'*prise*" Alan promised
her, *he's* congratulating himself for finally becoming a
boy-maker . . . and I glance down at my draft notice, praying for an early date of recruitment on that sane-smelling
form. . . .

ii

white

30.08.46 (*eleven hundred hours/thirty minutes*)

From: T. Sgt. Natashia Ingram c/o
            PSC Box 987760
            APO AP 96266

To: Captain Janet Ingram (Ret.)
            P.O. Box 5490342
            FDR Station
            New York, NY 10150-0342

Dear "Capt." Mom,

Got this machine* to myself for don't know
how long, so this will have to be brief. (* Usually
EVP'ers are chained to it!)

Looks like the 'Delas are in retreat; their antique
SCUDs are no match for our MOAWs, but that could
change any sec, as you remember from your hitch
here. Wish I could be more specif; but the CO would
rip off both my tits if I said more (not that they don't
have pens to black out classified info!). Needless to
say, we're ███████████ , so don't expect to take the
gold ribbon off the doorknob any time soon!

Went to ███████████████ to see the Li'l General; your granddaughter weighs over fifteen pounds,
and measures over twenty-five inches long. Tall like
you. Should make a great captain eventually, *you*
know how the tall ones are automatically officer
material. (I don't think Gen. Boles would be what
she is today if she were a Size 6 Petite!) Wish
I knew who the gen-dad was; tried pulling in a
few favors, but all I've heard on the wire is that
he was (is?) of Mid-East descent, which is unusual,

since EVP hit harder there, 'specially since it split off into EVP I and II. Like Leia, the 'ner on ▮▮▮▮▮▮ always says, tho: "All gen-dads look the same . . . smooth, white, and bald as a rubber bulb on top." My CO calls 'em "loaded tampons," but considering that only ▮▮▮▮ 'ners in the squadron are carriers now, I'm inclined to think of 'em as *blanks*!

Don't know how you and the rest of the 'ners in your squad made it through the POW camps without monthly gen-dad blasts; it's still bad for the POWs, but they will go easy on a carrier. Might be *with-unique*, fresh source of gen-dad for *them*. One of our 'ners brought back some of *their* gen-dad (same make of blaster we use, only the bulb is softer, more like wet Tyvek) she'd 'vaged off a fallen; it was confiscated, tho, and ▮▮▮▮▮▮▮▮▮▮ so we won't know for a while if it took. Only hitch is wearing the gen-dad *belt;* the cold element in there sometimes leeches out, and causes chem burns. Last night, I had a dream about you and Dad; he was telling me what a good *boy* I was, only it wasn't like we were in the old apartment, but I was in a 'cruitment chair, getting my first shave, and you were just standing there with a draft notice in your hand. Not saying a word, just holding out your free hand as my hair drifted down, like you were catching leaves in the fall.

I wonder if that's how guys used to feel when they were drafted or enlisted. I can't picture it; the EVP's in the offices are all so old they're natural shine-heads. Got to thinking. When it came to the whole war process before EVP, were we women jealous of what the men were able to do in war, or secretly proud that we didn't really *have* to get in there and fight? Once there was EVP, was it then "put up or shut up" time? Tried to bring that up once, in the bunker, but for all of us, it was like trying to figure out what the world would be like without sunlight, after we'd lived all our lives *with* it. Sort of a fairy-tale life, where women took pills *not* to have children, and men wore rubber sheaths on their s'rods *stop* them from blasting the women, and not just to try and stop AIDS or EVP. I can read about it, talk about it, and know all the while that it was true, but for *me* it *wasn't*, period.

I *know* you remember what it was like. Just like you remember Dad before EVP, and him eventually dying from it like just about all the men who got it and didn't respond to the vaccine. I'd ask you, but I know I'd never get my answer.

You asked about the POW situation; we only see them for a short time, before they're shipped out to ████████. Looks like their army is treating the 'ners on their side 'bout the same as us, maybe a little worse. Some of the POWs that come through here are only twelve, maybe less. No hair down there when they're stripped for delouse. Don't know how they 'spect to get results from the gen-dads the youngest 'ners carry. Probably give 'em blanks.

Lights are flickering; happens every time a ████████████ flies overhead. Which means that ████ is coming back, either more POW or more wounded. Least I hope it's just wounded. I hate seeing what they do to the fallen 'fore our 'ners can get to them. Hacked, or ringed with burning tires and always split open if they're carrier due to evacuate soon. Most of the time they're totally *claimed* when we find them. Worse if they aren't; we have to ████████████ them.

I wonder, honestly, if even pre-EVP male 'ners had to do that. Even if you won't—or can't—answer.

Light's again, almost out, taking the keys of this thing with them. Insane to send electronic machines;

too susceptible to brown/blackouts. An EVP just tod-
dled up, wants *his* toy back.

Salutes and hugs,
Tash

04.09.46

From: Major Emi Takei c/o
PSC Box 976591
APO AP 96266

To: Captain Janet Ingram (Ret.)
P.O. Box 5490342
FDR Station
New York, NY 10150-0342

Re: T. Sgt. Natashia C. Ingram

Dear Captain Ingram,

It is my sad duty to inform you that on 31/08/46,
your child Natashia was injured/killed
in the line of duty during a MOAW missile attack on
her bunker .

Her War Bag will be sent to you under separate
cover, along with her Purple Heart and Bronze
Star .

Her daughter/son Diee will remain
in Army custody, per Property Regulation 5499872-
C, as outlined in the standard enlistment forms
Natashia signed upon joining the Army in
2034 . You will be informed of the child's
progress as she/he advances in military training.

Again, I am sorry to inform you of the inju-
ry/loss of your child. May God comfort you and look
down upon you in this time of sorrow, and may She
comfort your daughter Natashia .

With regret,

Maj. Emi Takei, C.O.
U.S. Army

Captain Ingram,

Please excuse the form letter above; it is regulation,
and you & I know reg is God around here. I knew
your daughter, and while she and I did not always
agree on principle (or procedure—a habit of hers
I seem to have posthumously inherited!) I found
her to be a *woman* with a questioning, insightful
mind—not a prickle-headed 'groaner blindly following orders (in my case, *touché*!) despite their logic
or their true necessity. Not that she ever disobeyed
any order given by myself or any of her superiors,
but Tash was aware of the purpose (or lack thereof)
behind day-to-day Army life, and chose to rationally
and intelligently question the *why* of this woman's
Army.

Would that I had had the answers she was so desperately seeking.

Maj. Emi Takei
(Soon-to-be-retired)

LIST OF CONTENTS:
War Bag, T. Sgt. N. C. Ingram

- Dog Tags
- Genetic-donor receptacle belt (empty of donor
  syringes)
- Diary (edited to conform to regulations 87943-
  A and -B)
- Emergency MRE's (three packets)
- African-American phrase book
- Misc. photographs (Infant Recruit D. M. Ingram-
  Hussam)
- Letter dated 30.08.46 (unmailed at time of death)

iii

blue

Norma was taking ears again. We were bunkering, cleaning out abandoned subter dwellings of the enemy fallen, burying those who'd been left by *their* evac units, but ears (and noses and lips—upper and lower) were off limits—unless your mother was a lieutenant colonel, and *her* mother was a *ma*-frucking-*jor*. Norma can fillet the whole frucking *hide* off an enemy 'ner and wear it over her uniform, if she wants. Claims she's a pre-EVP relation to ol' General Norm*an* S. hisself.

She *is* big enough.

"G'eee over *here*," Norma barked, stretching the "G'eee" out hard and fast, like when you give an order to a K-9'er.

I didn't know if that was her way of saying "Get" or a corruption of my name, Diee, but I sure as *fruck* wasn't answering. I may be an I.R. born to a draftee tech sergeant, raised in Mandelia's kibbutz-cum-boot camp, but I don't lick *any* lips. Upper *or* lower.

Staying where I was, I shook powdery grayish snow off a Mongol-English phrase book, watching Norma through lowered lashes as she raised the fallen 'Gol 'ner by the meaty scruff of her neck (her rounded yellow-brown head was covered with a quarter inch of stubble), took out her laser-knife from her parka, and with a hum and a flash of rod-focused light, the right ear, followed by the left, rested in Norma's wide palm.

"Lieutenant Ingram-Huss*am*, g'eee *over* here!"

I put the phrase book into the 'Gol 'ner's War Bag, taking the time to untangle the straps before approaching the earless corpse. Patting the Velcro male section onto the softer, female patch on the 'Gol's outside belt, then resting the straps across her body (I wasn't strong enough to lift her and secure the straps under the uniform back), I leaned back on my heels, asking, "What, Norma?"

Glaring, yet unable to protest (we shared the same rank), Norma said, "I think this one's a *he*."

"I think not, Lieutenant." Rocking back 'n' forth before I built up the momentum to rise in a long, fluid movement (loving Norma's narrowed eyes and puckered lips as I did it), I dusted semimelted snow off my pants before walking away from her, adding over my shoulder, "I don't see the wisdom in using a nonexpendable member of any society as missile-munchie."

Muttering "Thesaurus-tongue," Norma opened her parka pocket—the rasp of separating Velcro carried far in the cold, dry air—and hid her latest ear harvest.

Norma wasn't the first to call me that. Once I gained access to my mother's War Bag effects, after *her* mother died in '63 when I was seventeen, I started to talk (and *think*, which no one can ridicule) like her. My mother was one of the last voluntary lifers. Why she kept re-enlisting I never could figure out, even after reading her censored diary. Black lines, passages, all inked out to protect long-declassified information. What was left was her first weeks in boot, her first carrier term (aborted male EVP-positive), MRE gripes ("Mucus Regurgitated Everyday!") and her thoughts, about everything else.

Those passages I memorized; there's little room in a War Bag for your own gear, let alone someone else's. Also I don't have to worry about harvesters like Norma going through my bag should I die, and misreading my mother's words.

My mother came from a real family, something even Norma can't lay claim to. A mother who eventually had to work once EVP began *s'* busting every man on the planet; a father who started out full of male-bonding hope and wound up drippy-eyed and -nosed, curled in a ball in a room he hadn't left since he found out his wife had been drafted. And whose granddaughter would be born into army-sanctioned servitude, in a society that demanded each member do her duty—be it by serving the Pentagon machine, or by endlessly bearing future cogs for said machine.

Or, as my mother wrote:

> I guess being army-doc blasted beats trying to do it on your own, month after month, in the privacy of your home—the latter way means reporting back to the *s*'bank within a week of withdrawal, empty vial in hand, ready to pee on a strip of treated plastic. In the army, there's something in the latrine water— once you're a carrier, you know immediately. As long as you don't flush prior to rising.
>
> If you prefer being blasted so hard it feels like the tip of the gen-dad probe will burst out of your navel (I swear all medics have balls *some*where on them!) it is *surely* worth not having to pee on a wand of chemical-treated plastic!

I would've liked to have spoken to her. My mother. I've an old picture of her. Looked like every 'groaner since the War Protection Act of '12. Round bare head, squinting eyes from too much combat in the sun, tanned face, and a blur of a smile. Same as me, save for my naturally darker skin. Not much opportunity to tan in Mongolia come winter. It's always winter after those bomb "tests" over the Ukraines.

Norma—her ears safely hidden in her parka—was rooting around in the fallen 'Gol's uniform; the rending of fabric brought me back to reluctant reality.

I closed my eyes until I heard her whisper, "*Diee. G'eee over here . . . told* you."

Oh, God, it was true. They were sending men into battle. Some *how*, some *way*, the 'Gol's had a surplus of men, enough to sacrifice new sources of gen-dad. How many? I asked myself. Ten, fifteen percent? I've never lived in (never *known* of, period) a time where men made up more than five to seven percent of the North American population. And most other countries were worse off than the U.S. and Canada.

Norma was about to switch on her laser-knife when I opened my eyes and asked her to wait. Crawling over to the earless 'ner, I peered down at the patch of exposed flesh between Norma's circling hands.

It was and it wasn't like a gen-doc: the long thinness was right, but there were two lightly haired bulbs of flesh above. And it was all attached, seamlessly. It was real . . . and sadly defenseless. Pointing the laser-knife at it, Norma remarked, "Just think . . . a world's trouble centered around a little virus getting into such a little organ," as she used the turned-off knife to lift the s'rod from the rest of the body. The whole thing was so opaque I couldn't see where the *s'* was hidden. Even the bulbs were deflated.

Norma was clucking, moving the dead bits this way and that, while I sat back on my heels, rubbing my face and scalp with my palms, wishing my mother was here, now, with me, Norma, and the dead man.

A few weeks after I was born, she'd written in her diary:

It puzzled me as a child, and it still makes me wonder—when it came to EVP and men, which was the real enemy of womankind (as opposed to *hu*man kind) . . . EVP, or the male organs it attacked? And once the war on man's ability to reproduce himself (i.e., *man*) was waged—and all but lost—were we women attacking each other because of what had happened to the men, or because there were no longer any men to attack? Is that why the women's army (and navy, and marines, and air force, *and*—) became more stringent, more basic, more *butch* than the old army, navy, and so on ever were? When men waged war, they took the time to *not* wage war; time to take R & R for the sake of Rest and *Relaxation*, not Rest and *Recuperation* (what yours truly's doing now: feet up, hair growing in, womb free of gen-docs for at least three months). Do we wage war so vigorously, so joylessly, so grimly, because it's always been so, or because we must do it better than it was done before? And in our case, must "better" mean . . . *meaner*? Shiny-headed killing wombs-on-legs, with little sense of bonding, of comradeship— just one-upmanship and "we'll show *them*" attitude, all directed at the *unique* men we have to both protect and better?

I wonder—are we waging war for the sake of humanity, or to forsake hu*man*ity? To prove forever and ever that even if we can lick EVP—not that the female doctors seem as driven to conquer it as their (dwindling) male counterparts seem to have been— we're still the better "men"? That real men only need exist on any level as gen-doc donors?

Were we women so put down that we need to forever fight to prove how strong, how capable, how *indispensable* we were all along?

"Well, Diee, make up yer mind—off or on?" Norma's thumb rested on the knife's switch—and said knife was resting, "blade" up, under the limp *s*'rod of the fallen 'Gol. One flick of her thumb and the *s*'rod would be severed, two more knife flicks and the 'Gol 'ner would be as good as female. Good as *us*.

"*No*. Better put a marker by the claim, so's the docs at the base can check it—*him*—out later. Might be able to analyze the *s*'rod, and the bulbs."

Norma—puffed up with importance over finding the first *male* 'Gol 'ner in the history of at least *this* war— waddled out of the bunker, into the drifting snow outside, in search of a red flag marker. Alone in the empty-walled bunker, I started to roll up the 'Gol's bedroll—until something fell out at my booted feet. A book, filled with carefully printed lines, in phrase-book English, no doubt penned in hope that if he was taken prisoner the 'Gol could prove to us American 'ners that he was ready and willing to learn the American way, to side with us if necessary. I'd seen this sort of thing before: copybooks filled with stilted English phrases, some written over and over, schoolgirl-fashion.

But this 'Gol—this *guy*—had something different on his mind, aside from learning English:

> Morning of each day I sit, wait, as day become noon, noon become night, as I wonder "Why *I* fight? Why my mother? Why her mother? Must I fight harder, because I man in woman world?" I one of few men, but we grow in number. Women, they try hard next to me, more hard than with other woman. And always, I hide man-ness, other soldier tell me, "*They* know you man, they kill you harder." But they woman too—so, then, *my* women, they do same to *their* man, if any? If that so, who *is* enemy?

I slowly paged through the thin diary, looking for a name, an age, *some*thing to identify this man lying behind me. I didn't want to touch him again, couldn't violate his War Bag. All I found was "I" and "me." Perhaps that's all I needed to find.

For my mother, in her diary, never mentioned *who* she was, never needed to use her own name. She knew herself, or tried to, considering that she belonged to a generation born to alien roles, and to an alien situation which reversed the roles of the sexes.

Yet my mother knew of this lost past, and took the time to discover pasts lost well before that of her own mother was devoured by an invasive virus:

> I remember reading a sociology textbook, how back in the early 1900s, baby boys wore pink, because it was such a healthy, robust color, while girls were dressed in blue, a delicate, gentle hue. It wasn't until after one of the world wars—I forget which one, they were spaced so far apart then—that the

• • •

My mother died a couple of days after writing those words. Oh, she did write a letter to her mother, but it only skirted the questions gnawing at her, perhaps in deference to her mother's rank, more probably in deference to her own unfaceable fear. Yet hers was a war of equals, of women hurting other women. No fear of being killed faster and dying slower. My mother fought a war, not others not quite like herself.

" . . . *who* is *enemy?*"

Sitting by the earless 'Gol, his soul resting cloth-bound in my hands, I wish I knew the answer to his—and my—question. Just as I wish I knew who was doing the real moving—me, or my image on a snow-flecked earthen wall.

AUTHOR'S NOTE: The newspaper article mentioned in this work appeared in the Tuesday, July 30, 1991 edition of *USA Today*, and was written by Jack Kelley. The diary passages quoted were written by Hussam Malek Mohammad Mardy, to whom this work is dedicated.

Embodied In Its Opposite

John M. Landsberg

ARIGA COMES TO ME TODAY, AS ALWAYS, JUST AS Ragigara rises. I have learned little enough, but I know this: Cariga will come in the light of Ragigara. I understand little enough, but I understand this: Cariga responds to the pull of this little moon as if he were an ocean rising. I grasp at this vapid fragment of knowledge as if it could save my life, even though I have no idea why it is as it is, any more than I know why anything is as it is in this place.

"Cariga gara ra-agiga Ragigara aririri."

I could answer him in his language, but it wears on me. After twenty years it still wears on me. I know there are subtleties that are beyond the human voice, the human ear, and it irritates me to know that after twenty years I still sound like this to Cariga: "Me think moon good not good too." It is amazing, in fact, that I can make *this* much sense with the five sounds I *can* discern, and lacking even a beginner's grasp of the sixty-eight qualifying tonalities.

Ah, Whiting, get a grip. Don't let pettiness slip in now. You have carried yourself with dignity these hundred days. You have shown them that you have nothing about which to be ashamed, that you deserve, by the integrity with which you have accepted your punishment, to be acquitted. Don't hang it up in the last hour.

"The moonlight is charming, and yet cold, Cariga. I like it not quite as well as you do."

He makes a kind of a snort. The wide, curving nostril flares. It is not insulting, I think.

"You are bitter, Charles."

"I am not bitter, Cariga. Why should I be bitter?"

"Now you jest. Do you imagine your irony is beyond me?"

This sounds a bit belligerent, but it isn't. I think it is a syntactical formulation meant to belittle the speaker for the benefit of the one addressed.

"Thank you, Cariga." In this way I absolve him.

Now he unlocks the door, steps just inside, and intones:

"You are here."

There it is. Again. One of the simplest yet most baffling constructs, three elementary words capable of a thousand meanings. I hear it every day, yet I am seldom capable of taking it at more than its minimal intention, which is a form of acknowledgement that everything is all right now.

"Cariga, may we dispense with the small talk? This is the one hundredth day."

"Yes. The one hundredth day. But you are here!"

"Of course I'm here. Where else could I be but behind these damn bars?"

Cariga folds the hearing cone that occupies most of his midsection in upon itself.

"I'm sorry, Cariga."

"Charles, my good friend, you are here."

"You know, I'm da—" I stop myself and start again. "I have to admit I'm quite sick of hearing 'You are here.'

What I want to know is, when am I getting *out* of here?"

Cariga hunches the base of his eye stalks into a sort of volcano-like shape, and the stalks themselves quiver for a moment, looking not unlike lava spraying upward from the top of his head. I recognize it as a reaction of extreme sadness.

"What pains you, Cariga?"

"Your death is not as I expected."

"What the bloody hell *did* you—? Cariga, this is nonsense. I *have* to be acquitted."

"Yes, you do."

"Damn it all!" I grab my dinner plate and fling it against the far wall. It clangs annoyingly. "Then get me acquitted!"

Now, that's far too much. Unquestionably my nerves are beginning to crack. I have steadfastly refused, and I still refuse, to believe that they seriously intend to execute me, and yet there is only one hour left! A last-minute reprieve is, of course, the stuff of legend, but I can't help thinking my acquittal would have occurred long ago if it had ever been meant to happen.

"You can't do this. Cariga! Where is your sense of justice? I can't be put to death for such a triviality!"

Stupid words. Cariga does not deserve to hear them; he is not my jailer. He, in fact, seems to be the only one who cares. And I'm sure—although it's more than ironic to say I'm sure about anything at this point—that he doesn't have the power to have me released.

"This is the final hour. You will now experience your life on Ranaag."

"What do you mean?"

"In the final hour, the condemned are shown their lives. Some find an answer."

"You mean—a way to make amends?"

"An answer can be many things, Charles."

"I don't understand."

"When you awake from your life, you will be in the chamber."

• • •

Whiting hesitated in the doorway of the shuttle, then stepped down, his boot pressing the soil of Ranaag for the first time. It gave under his weight only as much as the soil of Earth would have. He turned toward the shuttle, but it was backing away, its wake whisking the dust around him. The little craft scurried up into the red clouds; in minutes it would meet the ship and be gone forever.

A whispering noise—he turned to see the welcoming committee gliding towards him. They seemed to be in a constant state of flux, absorbing and extruding three or four appendages every minute or so. When they encircled him, and he gazed up into those cavernous brown mouths, he marveled. *My companions.* For life.

They made noises. He had no understanding. They waited. He waited. Then one of them said: "Charles Whiting."

It startled him, even though he was expecting it.

"I am he. Thank you for your greeting." He pondered further: Would it be rude . . . ? Well, give it a try. "May I begin by asking how you speak so many human languages so well?"

Their bodies seemed to sway ever so slightly. Whiting stared at their pebbly brown skin and multicolored robes, and felt himself sway as well. After a moment, the group began to move. Whiting felt a warm touch at his back, startling him out of his reverie. He walked.

Was it the wrong question? What question would have brought a response? In time, he would learn. And someday he would give what he had learned back to his own world.

He kept a journal. On the first evening he wrote: "I wonder if I will learn all that I possibly *can* learn, at some time before my tour is up. It is difficult to imagine grasping everything there is to know about a race of beings and their planet in as brief a span as twenty years, but I mean all that

I, specifically *I*, am capable of learning. Will I be twiddling my thumbs one year from now, agonizing over the fact that this planet is too far off the beaten track and too economically unimportant to warrant more than a single junior ambassador, who can expect no planned contact for nineteen additional years?"

The first night, he slept surprisingly well, and when he woke, and realized how good a sleep it had been, he knew he had been exhausted both from the long trip and from his prolonged anticipation, an anticipation which had found its release in his being on the job at last.

On his first full day, he walked among them. They made no move to stop him from going where he pleased, nor did they make any overtures of expecting anything from him. He wondered at their silence, but clung to one basic assumption, that the indigenous people must be allowed to deal with the intruder in their own way, in their own time. His first question had been a failure. Now, no matter how much he longed to pose question after question, he would not approach them until they made some show of being ready.

He waited. He watched.

The city resembled adobe, all of a uniform reddish gray color. The interiors were decorated simply, with projections that descended from the ceilings like stalactites twisted into remarkable constructs—what appeared to Whiting to be free-form designs. Most of the buildings were pyramidal, with fewer and fewer rooms on each floor. In time he discerned that not only were there fewer total inhabitants on each higher floor of the residential buildings, but there were also fewer inhabitants per unit volume of space. In the places of business, the same rule applied. It seemed an obvious indication of social status. Perhaps he had learned something, but then again, he cautioned himself, he should never jump to conclusions.

On the third day, he was quite convinced that his meals would always appear at regular times, no matter where he was in the city. The food was, astonishingly, exactly like what he ate on Earth. He did not understand how this could be, but on the third day it was this simple puzzle that drove him to break his own silence and approach one of them in the street.

"Forgive me for speaking before being spoken to, but I am in great confusion. May I ask one simple question?"

"I am Cariga," the creature replied. "Thank you."

"Why do you thank me?"

"I am honored to be chosen."

"But I only want a bit of information."

"Anything."

If it was this easy, why had they not spoken to him earlier?

"How can you make food exactly like what I am used to on Earth?"

"Food is." Cariga inclined his head slightly.

"Food is what?"

Cariga glided away.

Before long, he found himself, by choice, retracing his own steps of days before. In the mornings, he would walk among the Ranaagans, then take breakfast, and then hike into the barren hills surrounding the city. The perspective from atop some of the higher promontories afforded him a chance to see just how isolated this group of beings really was.

Many Ranaagans spoke to him, but only Cariga made sure to talk with him every single day. To his great frustration, portions of every conversation seemed quite intelligible, while other portions were more baffling than the most subtle Zen paradox.

For example:

"How do you build these buildings?"

"A basic system of clay blocks. They range in size from the span of your hand up to the size of twenty of you in your entirety."

"What kind of device do you use to lift such large blocks?"

"Machines."

"What kind of machines?"

"Blocks can be lifted."

"Where are these machines?"

"They are not here."

"Then where are they?"

"Never can they be."

"If they can never be, how can you use them to lift blocks?"

At this point, his companion would quietly leave his presence. Whiting found this exit would occur whenever he made a direct question to any statement which seemed a non sequitur, a paradox, or a simple impossibility. If he did not question such a statement—such as when Cariga offered the non sequitur "blocks can be lifted" and Whiting did not pursue it—the conversation would continue. After six months, he clung to this observation as if it represented a true understanding of these conversations; in fact, however, two years later he still had no clue to the meaning of this simple piece of information.

Through the years, his routines bore him along like the steady flow of a great river.

On many days he thought, "I do this for you," an image of a woman filling his mind. She was the emblem of his task, the symbol of his determination to fathom the Ranaagans, to make the connection across the stars; in the depth of his loneliness he made a connection against the soft sheets, striving to bring what would some day be his hard-won understanding back to his beloved, his Earth, she of the flaxen hair and heavy breasts. He stroked himself; he strained in the intensity and severity of his mission until at last he fell into her arms, and spent his seed into the Ranaagan linen. He had chosen this. He would see it out.

Three years into his mission, he wrote in his journal, "Sometimes I think I would give my life to uncover a key that would unlock these mysteries—if I could only find a Rosetta Stone!—although I suppose the analogy is bad, because after all it's not language that's the barrier. The barrier has more to do with something like—I want to say a fundamental difference in outlook, but that seems ridiculously simple. When one doesn't even understand what it is one doesn't understand, well—I don't know how to get beyond that."

In a year that may have been his sixth, seventh, or eighth on Ranaag, a day came on which Cariga took him to an open field. Ranaagans of all ages frolicked about. Some of the younger ones played a game in which a suspended hoop of stone was battered by sticks, to no apparent purpose, although once in a while a cheer would rise from the group.

"What are they doing?" he asked Cariga.

"Playing."

"Why are they hitting the hoop with sticks?"

"The hoop sees more than the stick."

Whiting found he could, very easily, leave it at that.

"Do you enjoy watching them?" Cariga said.

"Yes," Whiting replied. "I enjoy it."

"Cariga, I have been here for eleven years now."

He spoke in Earth years, because Cariga always did so when speaking to him, even though, due to the length of the Ranaagan year, only four of them had passed since he had arrived.

"You are here," Cariga said.

"I think I understand less now than I did when I arrived."

"Are you not happy?"

"The strange thing is, I am happy. I have become so accustomed to pondering your race and not feeling that I understand you in the slightest, that it is almost a comfort to me to be in this perpetual confusion."

"Socrates said he was the wisest of men because he alone knew that he knew nothing."

"Cariga, you never cease to astound me."

"And you me."

One day Cariga came to him, dressed in a way he had never seen. His robes seemed to rise up against the pull of gravity; for the first time in twenty years, Whiting saw the legs of a Ranaagan. They were like a thicket of brambles, with hundreds of tiny endings where they caressed the ground.

"This is the year of twenty."

Twenty years, Whiting thought with sudden awareness. *Can it be that long?*

"Cariga," he said, gathering his wits, "I see you."

"Charles, you are here. Now be with me."

Cariga turned and glided quickly away. Whiting, frozen by astonishment, hesitated a moment before racing after his friend.

"Where are we going?" he asked breathlessly. "It's a special event, isn't it?"

"It must be."

"Don't you know?"

"I do know."

"Can you tell me where we're going?"

"The Palace."

Whiting stopped. "The Palace?"

Cariga moved on a few meters before stopping and returning. This, too, was astounding. Never had any Ranaagan responded to *his* choice of whether to move or not, or which direction to take.

"What is wrong?"

"Cariga, *is* something wrong?"

"Now *you* puzzle *me*, Charles. It is imperative that you come." Cariga turned and resumed his march.

Whiting had seen the Palace many times, but had never entered, if only because of his upbringing. It was silly, he knew; on Ranaag he was never barred from any building, but as a child, he had viewed Buckingham Palace as a place of mystery and privilege, and even as an adult, he would never have dreamed of setting foot inside without a special invitation from the King himself, or at the very least an invitation issued under the King's personal direction. And yet, although he had been imposing a standard of his own on the Ranaagans, he had gradually put the Palace out of his mind, had settled into a life of bemusement and routine, and not since his early months here had he ever given any thought to speaking with the rulers of this place. It was his sudden awareness of this failure of duty that so deeply shocked him now, more than even the abrupt summons to the Palace after so many years of being ignored.

Ranaagans in all manner of gaily colored finery lined the route. Whiting couldn't help being embarrassed by the attention, but it seemed best to say nothing to Cariga about it. He would simply carry himself with the dignity befitting an ambassador of Earth.

"Cariga!"

"What is it, Charles?" He did not slow down.

"I—I'm the ambassador."

"You are the ambassador."

"No, I mean, I'm supposed to be the ambassador, but I have no idea of protocol here. I—my God, I can't believe it—but I've been here twenty years and I feel I barely understand how to say hello."

"This is the year of twenty."

"Cariga, for God's sake, that doesn't help me. Can't you at least give me a clue what I'm supposed to say in greeting?"

Cariga hurried on in silence.

Whiting clenched his teeth and tried to will his frustration back into whatever dark mental recess had engulfed it for so long.

A guard stopped them at the main entrance. Cariga stepped aside. Whiting tilted his gaze up at the looming figure, who brandished a shield bristling with steely points.

"Charles Whiting," the guard said.

Whiting glanced at Cariga, who was impassive. He turned back toward the guard. "I—I beg your permission to enter the Palace, kind sir."

"By whose leave shall you enter?"

"The King requests my presence."

The guard stepped aside. Whiting caught his breath. Where were the paradoxes and conundrums?

Whiting waited for Cariga to move, but Cariga only inclined his head slightly backwards. Whiting stepped tentatively forward; Cariga followed.

They passed through the gates in this manner, Cariga following as if he were Whiting's servant.

Unlike most interior walls on Ranaag, here the walls undulated in unpredictable waves. Many surfaces were hidden behind a dense thatchwork of interwoven matter rather like twigs, although Whiting had never seen any trees or bushes on Ranaag. At almost every turning, a glass encased column of fire illuminated the way.

Whiting moved ahead, never uncertain of his direction, because a glow in the air preceded him. Fascinated, he moved deeper and deeper into the Palace. Cariga maintained a respectful distance a few feet behind.

When suddenly the glow vanished from the air, Whiting found himself in a great hall. He had no real idea of its size, because the walls appeared to be semitransparent, revealing a receding series of walls on all sides. What manner of illusion this was he could not tell, nor could he say which, if any, of the walls were solid.

Hundreds of Ranaagans filled the hall, many of whom were guards stationed along some of the multilayered walls, but others milled about, apparently those privileged enough to be present at this historic meeting. Some approached Whiting and offered greetings.

"I will say something important, Charles," Cariga said.

"What is it, Cariga?"

"The King will be here soon. Do not speak."

"Do not speak? But—"

"Welcome!" The hall fell silent at the sound of the King's voice. He stood atop a shallow staircase, encircled by three horizontal rings of white light suspended around his midsection like three huge, fallen haloes. Whiting gaped; suddenly he felt almost giddy enough to lose his balance.

"Hail Giracara!"

"Thank you, Cariga. Charles Whiting, it is good to see you at last."

"Your Majesty, thank you for receiving me."

The crowd seemed to gasp as one. The King turned and left.

"Cariga, I—"

"You spoke."

"Yes—I did. Cariga, I'm sorry, I know you told me not to, but I was overwhelmed by the moment."

The onlookers were unobtrusively, yet quickly, leaving the chamber.

"Charles, the King does not—receive—anyone." The word carried a distinct impression of distaste.

"Cariga, I am truly sorry if I've committed an error in protocol—you see, I knew something would go wrong if I had no coaching in these matters!—but of course I will apologize right away."

"You cannot. The King has lost face. He has been disgraced."

Four guards appeared and seized Whiting's arms.

"Cariga! I don't understand!"

The guards dragged him away.

•   •   •

Cariga visited him in jail on the first day following the trial.

"The sentence is death."

Whiting stared at Cariga between the bars, blinked, then backed away and sat on his bed. What could be the meaning of such an absurd and frightening statement?

"Cariga, what is the sentence?"

"The sentence is death."

Again Whiting could not grasp it.

"Cariga, I don't know why you have chosen to say such a terrible thing to me, but I will overlook it. Just tell me when I will be set free."

"Today is day one of one hundred days." Cariga summoned the guard, had him unlock the door, then swung it wide open and stepped into the cell. "Charles, you are here."

"Well, no matter. As you say, I am here, although if that means all is well, I can't say I fully agree. Yet if a hundred days is what it takes, then so be it." He smiled. "What a scofflaw I am, eh? Of course I didn't think it would cost so dearly to learn a bit about your protocol."

Cariga turned and walked away.

But of course, Whiting thought, there can be no real intention to execute me. They must intend to punish me with the threat of it, and with these hundred days' imprisonment, and if I bear my punishment nobly, surely I will be released.

"Cariga, will I see you again soon?" Whiting called. He felt himself tremble behind his smile.

The hundred days passed, each indistinguishable from the last.

Every day Cariga visited his cell, and there would always come a time when he would open the door, stand just inside it and announce, "You are here."

Whiting would stare at the open door and think, *I could easily run past him, escape in an instant.* And then he would invariably think, *But that would be dishonorable.*

• • •

Whiting awoke.

He was strapped, spread-eagle, onto a table. Electrical wires pinned his eyelids, fingertips, groin. Cariga looked down into his eyes.

"Your life was," Cariga said.

"Cariga, I didn't find any answer!"

"You think you were supposed to learn a way to right the wrong."

"Wasn't I?"

"I told you many times that you are here."

"That's right, you did, damn you! What good was that?"

Cariga trembled at the profanity, but did not shrink away. "All possible good."

"How could it be? It's just a simple, stupid, obvious truth. What does it even mean?"

Cariga paused, cocked his head. "You are not disgraced, Charles."

"What?" Whiting said.

"Many expected that you would choose to live by accepting disgrace, but I was not of them. I am glad I was right; if you had, we could not have stood your pain." Cariga paused, and brushed some of his arms down the front of his robe; it was a gesture of confusion. "But, Charles, I must have changed through knowing you. I rejoice—I *must* rejoice—that you chose to stay; how then do I find myself sad that you will not live?"

Whiting tried to answer, but his voice would not come; he was paralyzed by the realization of how he had forfeited his life, paralyzed even more by the fact of nearly understanding why it was so. He almost understood—he *almost understood* what Cariga had said. For the first time since he had come to this planet, he almost understood something, and with a suddenness like the shock that would soon fill the wires, he saw the closeness and the chasm—he saw the uncrossable, though minuscule, distance between himself and the ability to understand only this one simple, lethal, irony.

And this small vision awakened a larger relative. Something glimmered inside the paradox, some kind of meaning leered out at him from within the self-contradictory admixture of everything his life had been on Ranaag; some kind of truth called to him from within the pain and the freedom of learning not to want to understand, blended with the joy and the imprisonment of suddenly, now, wanting once again to *understand*.

He tried, but could not reach the gem that sparkled and winked amidst the brambles, he could not follow all the diverging paths back to the single spot where they intersected, and all of it, all crammed at once into one place—the one finite place that was his mind—was too profound an agony to bear for long, but the electricity came then, and was merciful.

Foreigners

Mark Rich

RELEASE CAME NOT AS I EXPECTED—BURDENED WITH fines, restrictions, armed guard, and list of warnings longer than my conscience. Instead I walked away entirely free. The doctors, inquisitors, and officials did not visit my cell in the morning as they usually did. Only the middle-aged woman named Ardis entered the cell, without a guard. She arrived with the breakfast tray consisting of nothing out of the ordinary with its simple roll, butter, dab of marmalade, and small red pot of black tea. I stared at the tray, trying to assess what was different. Had the commissary taken a second longer in arranging the items across the yellow plastic? Had the usual disarray of items proved unsatisfactory this day? The normally skewed angles of napkin, butter knife, and spoon—had they demanded straightening today? In my brief look at the tray I could see the kitchen help had thought to cut into a fresh lemon for the tea saucer, instead of reaching for a slice remaining from the day before. Or perhaps Ardis personally had overseen the assembly of this breakfast, even stopping to straighten its contents as she stood in the hall outside my cell. As she placed it on the immovable round table near the bed, she did so with greater care than usual.

"After you finish your breakfast you are free to go," she said. "You can go."

Our eyes locked for a second. Often at this time I had some witticism for her, or some ironic comment as to the morning, the lack of sunshine in my cell, or the predictable fare. I could think of nothing to say this time, looking into her face. I had tried to study that face during her brief visits at breakfast, lunch, and supper times, trying to delve beneath that outer layer of tiredness and distracted concern. To my thirty years she had perhaps ten years more, yet she had about her face the kind of perennial attractiveness that can bring out the admiration of men of any age. While I felt no more than a friendly warmth for her, that I could feel anything at all while boxed in this windowless cell kept some part of me alive that might otherwise have starved and died.

Yet I could say nothing. Our eyes met for a moment as she set the tray down.

"Will you be wanting anything else?" she said.

I shook my head, still unable to speak.

Ardis smiled at me and left, closing the door behind her as she had on all previous days. A faint hint of her flowery perfume remained in the air. I rose from where I had been sitting at the edge of the cot and walked to the door, taking the knob and turning it. The door opened. The motion of it swinging open at my touch had an unbearable novelty to it. I closed the door again and returned to my place on my cot to contemplate my breakfast. Ardis's words had altered everything. The cot I sat on no longer remained mine; moments before I would have said, "This is my cot, my tray, my cell." In bringing me my breakfast she had effectively taken it away. Suddenly the four walls, the dull white ceiling and green-brown carpet moved away from my grasp. Ardis had displaced me. I no longer belonged. I was "free"—a circumlocution. These things, this room, even Ardis herself, were all free of me. They had achieved freedom; I had gained uncertainty.

I must have eaten, for when I rose again I had emptied my tray, and I felt a certain physical satisfaction. In the bathroom I washed my hands, examined my face in the mirror, then washed it, and examined it again, expecting it to have changed through the washing. Too long a time spent under interrogation had brought on a distrust of that face. "*After all,*" I could hear an interrogator saying to me, "*might it not be that the brown hair, rounded nose, dark brown eyes, and pale lips do not as such exist? Could they not be providing the façade for a deeper, more mysterious truth?*" Yet the water did not change my face. Nor had the interrogations or drug therapies pierced behind that skin or hair or eyes. They were releasing me, an action which in essence said: "You are what you say you are, George Bringland. You are not an alien."

The question of whether to take razor, toothbrush, or soap—or even the towel—besieged me for a moment. I took the few items from the shelf I knew to be my possessions: a pocket watch which ticked loudly, a set of keys, a wallet with some bills, and a handkerchief printed with fish in a geometrical pattern of greens and blues. I decided to take the toothbrush and razor. Was I to take the clothes I was wearing? What clothes had I brought with me to this place? I could almost seem to remember.

The haziness of my memory brought a quick flash of guilt: *I am not of this planet*. The drug treatments had left my connections with my memories tenuous. That vague, shifting cloud that seemed to follow me: even to call it a memory seemed a twisting of the language. Those people whose faces, voices, and movements I could bring forth to the mind's eye—they were my parents? My childhood friends? My schoolmates? Were they true memories? They might all have been planted images.

Yet the interrogations had ceased. Those in white lab coats and suits of gray officialdom now turned to me and

said, "We were doubters, but now we believe. Go. Leave."
I could turn to that cloud behind me and finally re-establish
my claim: You cloud, are my memory. Stay with me. Be
with me. You are mine.

In the hallway I knew which direction to go to find
the front desk, where a young woman, perhaps not many
years out of high school, handed me a light jacket and a
well-wrapped bundle. I had seen her before, at the time the
investigators had apprehended me and brought me here.
How long ago that had been I was unsure.

"Good thing you came with your jacket," she said.
"Might be a little cool out there."

In the bundle, not a heavy one, would be the few extra
shirts, underwear, and pants the orderlies had brought me
each morning.

"I don't want these," I said.

"They're yours," she said.

"I don't want them."

She had light skin and hair, the latter curled and put
up in a fashionable manner. She glanced at me without
holding my gaze for any length of time: a skittish animal,
I thought.

"Do you want us to hold them for you?" she said.

"If you wish."

I imagined the investigators taking the bundle back
into their laboratory, analyzing the fibers and closely
inspecting each fold and stitch for some hidden message,
some revealing fact. I was suddenly pleased to be leaving
the clothes behind. They were a gift to the investigators,
who apparently otherwise got nothing from me.

"Thanks," I said.

Footfalls down the hall did not herald the approach of
Ardis, to my disappointment. I would have enjoyed saying
goodbye to her. Instead it was Drs. Roann and Pylckner.
Dr. Roann, a younger man with genial features, dark hair,
and a marked tendency to frown and stare, walked up the
hall in a slight hunch, momentarily caught in his own

thoughts. Older than her colleague, being perhaps in her early forties, Dr. Pylckner walked with strict deliberation toward me. I regarded her with wariness. The silver streaks in her hair seemed to continue onto her skin, which hovered somewhere between white and gray even on her smooth face, a cold set of planes in which her black eyes rested.

"George," she said. I could not remember her having not said "Mr. Bringland" before.

"Ardis tells me I can leave."

"She told you correctly." Dr. Pylckner stopped sharply in front of me and motioned to a small carpeted square near the front door where a set of cushioned chairs and couches sat in conspiratorial arrangements. Looking through the glass of the doors I found myself—or some part of myself, a neglected part—swept outside. Trees losing their leaves, rumpled lawns cold with the melting dews of frost, and a tattered brown horizon where a woodland had met the sky when I first arrived here: I had missed the summer.

"George, we wanted to speak with you before you leave, if you don't mind spending a few minutes more." Dr. Pylckner sat on the chair to my left, and motioned Dr. Roann to the chair opposite mine. "We understand the trouble we have caused you. Philip?"

At the cue, Dr. Roann nodded his head vigorously. "We have placed in your account an amount equivalent to twice what you might have earned had you held your job during your time here." A frown at me, then a stare. "Your rent has all been paid. We took care of the everyday bills, the things that, oh, bother us all. A paid vacation, you see. Even though you probably don't see it as a vacation." A short laugh from the man, and the beginning of a stare, and then his frown.

"What Philip is saying is that we are trying to ease you back into the world as gently as possible." Dr. Pylckner's voice was not one to reflect gentleness or understanding extraordinarily well. "Since we are unable to establish you as an alien, the law indicates we must let you go, with ample recompense."

I could feel her voice grow colder. The fact of autumn did not enter my brain from the evidence of my eyes, from seeing its signs through the glass doors, but from Dr. Pylckner's voice. A chill spilled down my left side. Rising, I took the coat in my hands and found the pockets where I could put the razor, toothbrush, and handkerchief I had clutched. I must have left the hairbrush.

"If you need anything," said Dr. Roann, "just let us know." He rose, frowning but less intensely than at other times.

"Of course," I said. "Thank you." I looked at the both of them, the one sitting and the one standing, and suddenly wondered if they were not partners only professionally but personally as well. Had they sequestered away a cot in some empty cell where they could enjoy each other? I could only imagine Dr. Pylckner descending clinically upon the prone Dr. Roann, expertly bringing him to life and as expertly placing herself upon him with firmness and measured vigor.

Thinking of Dr. Pylckner made me wonder. Was I involved personally with a woman? In removing me from the rest of larger society, had these governmental clinicians removed me from some more closely bound, sexually tied relationship as well? I could not remember. No one had visited me here; but likely no one had been permitted. Not even permitted to know, perhaps. I could not picture any face of importance.

Dr. Pylckner rose and offered her hand, which I shook.

"Goodbye," I said.

At the door, the policeman standing with relaxed watchfulness nodded to me. I walked past him to reach the sidewalk, the damp lawn, the parking lot, the air, the gray clouds, the silvery boles of the street lamps. I knew where I was. I was on the edge of town. I lived perhaps an hour's walk away. I wondered what form my new captivity would take.

•   •   •

"You've let your hair grow long," she said.

I stared at her. Joann. I had forgotten her. I had returned here, to the used bookstore, to see if I could again work a few hours. Memory of this woman had escaped me: too young, too vivacious, too stylish and too quick-tongued for me. Yet hadn't she tried to become close? And hadn't I begun to hunger for her? Were these true memories? Human memories?

She turned back to her customer and the punch-button cash register, then flashed me another glance.

"Lila's in the back. She said you'd be coming."

"Good," I said. "She knew more than me."

Joann let out her too-high laugh.

The stacks called me with their musty scent of cracking, glued spines and dust-seasoned pages. The scent brought forth a memory from the cloud of the past, one that seemed true. A famous poet, visiting the nearby university, had stopped in the bookstore and chosen a few old volumes. I had stood at the counter, prepared to ring them up and trying to think of some comment to make: what does one say to a poet? The man had picked up one of the books and widened it at the middle, sticking his nose into the crevasse formed by the opened pages, and breathed in deeply. "That's how I tell an old book," he had said.

Lila was sitting pondering cartons of newly arrived books in the back room. She smiled as I entered, apparently with genuine feeling. A small, needle-featured woman having a full head of curling black hair and today wearing her usual outfit of loose jeans and a thick sweater, she commanded the authority of a person twice her size, and somehow did so through her more personable qualities instead of the usual Leader-of-Men pretentions such as official dress, somber manner, or gravity of pronouncement. Lila had a direct manner I remembered liking.

"I have you down on the schedule, George," she said. "In fact I'm a little shorthanded today so if you want to

stay, then stay. No one's been doing fanatical alphabet-
izations since you left on vacation." She smiled widely
at me and let that hang in the air for a long moment. "I
know something else was up this summer, but the word is
'vacation' around here. Okay?"

"Sure," I said.

"Is everything okay really?" she said, switching from
her cheerful gear. "It was pretty strange, that you disappeared. I got a few creepy feelings."

"They thought I was an alien."

She laughed. "That was one of the stories that came
up. I guess I wouldn't know from your résumé, would I?
You've got your spotty job record, what with your constant
dropping out to go be the artist in the garret."

"You went back and checked?"

Lila looked at me with a brief worried glance before
relaxing her features. "We talked about it often, George.
Don't you remember? You've told me how you save up a
little and go off to draw and write in the countryside. I'm
glad you've stuck with this place as long as you have."

Her words made a certain sense. "My memories are a
bit slow catching up with me," I said. "They used drugs.
I've been through a lot this summer. My head's a mess."

"That's all right," she said. "I'm sure you can still
work your magic on the stacks. You're going to stay and
work today?"

"I will if you want."

"Good. I'll take you to supper tonight to welcome you
back. You up to it?"

I thought back to the strange place that my apartment
had become. "Sure."

As I turned to leave the back room, Lila said, "By the
way, Joann has a boyfriend."

"Is that supposed to register with me?"

"Doesn't it?"

The stacks welcomed me back: the dull colors of
the long rows of history, the strange bindings and ornate
characters in the foreign language section, the colored

and pictured spines of the travel and adventure volumes. I moved to check the small shelf of geology books, drawn there by some interior urge: the ancient and prehuman always fascinated me. The old volumes of Salisbury were there, and the series of mining reports from Utah. A few new books sat among them, including a survey of recent paleontological results. The book opened in my hands to a paper by H. Xian-guang which detailed a new early Cambrian genus, *Atrypella*, correlatable with British Columbian Burgessian fauna. Xian-guang wrote, "If the evidence is correct, we have encountered yet another new phylum in the early rocks of China."

I closed the book. New phyla: paleontologists delved back to one of the points of morphological divergence and identified different types, each of which they designated new phyla. Was it possible? Or were all the functional patterns of organization no more different from one another, deep down, than ladybugs and praying mantids were within the Insecta? Or than the ladybugs and the horseshoe crabs within the Arthropoda? In other words, why could not all those early patterns of organization, recognized by paleontologists as "phyla," have fallen into one, single, primordial phylum? Why should not natural groupings change through time as fluidly as the earth's crust and the contours of the seas and oceans through the earth's long ages? Or better yet, why shouldn't our criteria for groupings change across the ages we glance over?

I replaced the book wondering why these matters should concern me. Perhaps because a group of scientists had followed some hint that I belonged to not only a different phylum, but perhaps even a different kingdom of life from their own. Was it because of the lip service that the scientifically trained gave to Objectivity that they saw boundaries so clearly between their own world and some other? What made paleontologists base their careers on differences they saw between past and present organisms? What made the new government scientists stake out detention centers and isolate certain individuals as alien? Did the aliens exist only as perceptions? It was hard telling.

The alien craft seized by the government, even the one collected from a site near where I stood, were secreted away in chambers known only to the highest officers in the new anti-alien brass. Fenced off from artifacts that should have been made public, we all became foreigners in our own communities. We were barred opportunity for recognition: how many of us, had we had a chance to look on the wrecks and recognize them, would have rejoiced to finally be able to say, Yes, I am an alien, I truly am. We were forced into ignorance of ourselves, and of others. Everyone became an outsider.

Yet could this man, George Bringland, have arrived by ship even from overseas? I found it hard to imagine, even with that undependable fog of memory bequeathed to me by my summer of captivity. The government propagated the myth that alien replication of human form descended even to the level of DNA, and to the reconstruction of human-style language capacities and memory structures.

The prospect of such similarities did not disturb me. With such talents for mimicry, the aliens and the humans were surely closely related. Perhaps one of those early Cambrian arthropods that were so much more successful than the proto-chordata in those ancient seas, say whip-handed *Leanchoilia* or the odd carnivore *Anomalocaris*, that they developed extraordinary means of travel; imagine if they had developed means of spatial transportation so radical that they shifted themselves to another locale around another sun, only to return later to the home planet in the same form the humans bore, with the same basic structures within their cells. Why shouldn't they appear to be humans, when we appear to be them? Why shouldn't we be disturbed at the resemblance we bear to the descendants of lowly *Leanchoilia*, instead of being disturbed that they look like us?

"I'll be just a moment. I really worked up a sweat moving those boxes," she said, heading for the bedroom. "Pour yourself something." She closed the door behind herself.

At the closing of the door the light dimmed and I was in my cell again. A strap held me back on my cot and kept me from leaping up and running for the wall as I saw the door open and Dr. Pylckner enter. Even the lights to the hall outside had been dimmed. She shut the door behind herself and came closer, standing near the foot of the cot.

"You're a little sedated tonight," she said. "But not too sedated. Don't move so much so you disturb the wires on your forehead. Of course you have the straps there. They should do the job, shouldn't they."

She laughed without raising her voice, sitting in the chair she always sat on and bending over to unlace her shoes, then remove her socks. The whiteness of her coat, blouse, and trousers fell away quickly into the dimness of the room. Her skin seemed a silvery gray. She removed her underwear, stretched herself as though truly enjoying what she became without her clothes; I could almost hear an oddly modulating melody as she looked up at the ceiling and opened her mouth, and could see her as a celestial animal outlined by faint lines between glowing stars, raising her face to the moon and courting it with a high ululating song. She looked down then and stood there, naked, and moved toward the cot.

The door opened again. I returned to Lila's apartment. She emerged in a new flannel shirt, her hair slightly more organized. She moved directly to the kitchen without noticing my distraught state. I attempted to reassemble myself before she returned.

"You didn't pour yourself something?" she said, poking her head back in from the kitchen.

I managed an intelligible order of a drink.

"You know what this alien scare is just like," she said, settling beside me on the couch. She placed the two glasses of brandy on the table in front of us.

"What."

"This whole men and women thing. Make sense to you?"

I was feeling dazed, and shook my head. The brandy did not help, burning in my throat.

"The whole thing about men being afraid of women, and vice versa. I mean, imagine some of that Freudian shit. God, men wanting to go to bed with their mothers, in Freud's book, and being jealous of their fathers? Hell, society makes men so afraid of women their mothers are the only safe women. That whole *vagina dentata* thing, what's more alien than that image of a woman equipped with carnivorous equipment between her legs? People get so damned afraid of the most stupid things. The government is still mostly male and they've finally found a new post-liberation way of expressing their fear of women. They've come up with aliens. They're suddenly paranoid they'll go to bed with an alien instead of a human, and not even know it!"

"Which they've been doing all along."

"That's right! They should welcome the aliens and finally get around to admitting that there are no aliens."

I felt awkward and laughed, the first laugh I remembered.

"Sorry," she said. "I get heavy sometimes. But you know that." She laughed herself, and lifted her cup in a mute toast. This sip, the ice cubes had softened the bite of the alcohol and given the brandy a pleasant smoothness. I felt warmer.

"It would certainly help me," I said, "if there were no aliens."

"Why? They let you go, didn't they?"

At the Chinese diner I picked up each piece of vegetable with curiosity, the memory building within me of often having cooked similar food myself. The stylization of the decor extended to the cut of the celery, carrots, and bamboo shoots, sliced into even, quasi-geometrical shapes.

I remembered not to eat the blackened hot peppers dotting the dish.

"You lost a lot this summer, didn't you," Lila said, watching me eat. She looked down then and may have blushed. "I'm sorry. I'm too direct all the time. You're probably—I mean, this last summer isn't probably what you want to talk about." She played with her own food. "I should probably shut up, and just be your boss. You like being back at work?"

I laughed again, enjoying the sensation. "I don't know what I've lost and what I've gained. For a while I was an alien, drugged out and living in space. Maybe the government isn't trying to identify aliens but make them."

"You think they've made you an alien?"

"I didn't think I was before. Now I don't know."

"What if you are an alien?"

"I'll go into a concentration camp for humans when I get back to my home world." I thought about that statement, raising an interesting slice of mushroom with my chopsticks. "Or perhaps I am alien, and have passed the test that proved I'm an alien, and am now free to join the rest of the aliens in this big concentration camp of ours."

"There aren't any humans, then, if we're all aliens."

"We're looking for them."

"If the government was looking for humans do you really think they'd find any?"

"Perhaps some will come here from abroad." I ate the mushroom, then searched my plate for another. "It must be hard keeping the alien stock pure, with so many humans flooding into the country."

She laughed. "You're a sketch, George," she said, her face quickly sobering. "But why do you take your summer so lightly? I mean, you've lost a chunk of your life, and it seems like—well, that it's affected other things. You keep saying you don't remember things."

I chewed my food and regarded her, wondering how an alien would see her. Or, if my viewpoint was alien, then how a human would see her. She was showing concern, one of those strange pieces of luggage of the strictly human: compassion, concern, worry, anxiety. I could not feel these things, especially for myself. But I could feel other things which I could not express by any common word. For a moment I sensed a ball of light swelling below my lungs and expanding upwards and outwards—an invisible ball of light, for Lila gave no sign of seeing it or feeling its heat. I began feeling giddy, and recklessly wanted to drop my chopsticks and reach over for her hand, to see if it was a human hand. To me she looked like a human mate; but wrapped in my glowing ball I could not tell from what shores she had arrived. What was her evolutionary history? Had *Anomalocaris* played a part? Or had she come to me in a straight line from old chordate *Pikaia*? I felt the ball of light expand to touch her, then dissipate in the glow of the orange-tinted oriental lamps above us.

"I'm not sure it's that I don't remember," I said. "It's almost as though I have added memories to my old ones."

"But you don't feel angry at what happened to you? At losing a whole summer?"

"Did I lose it? I don't remember much of it. I've blocked out some, or they have done the blocking-out for me. But I think I still have it. I haven't lost it. Isn't it true that whatever I have done has become a part of me?"

"You're beginning to remind me of your old self, George. You once quoted something to me from Socrates a lot like what you just said."

The ball of light had not entirely dissipated after all, but remained about us, cutting us off from the rest of the restaurant and raising us up into the garlic-scented air where we hung peacefully.

"Did you know me well?" I said.

"Pretty well." She smiled. "It was getting to be a weird time when you disappeared. I was getting confused about Barry. You and I were getting to be real good friends.

We did a lot together. And you were distracting yourself with that kid Joann, and I always supposed it was because nothing could happen between you and me. Because of Barry."

"The government got me just in time. I was meddling in human affairs."

"Cut it out, George. You're as human as the rest of us."

"How do you know."

"I trust my feelings."

I laughed, somehow delighted. Our table having returned to its place among the other tables in the restaurant, I noticed the sound of laughter rising almost simultaneously from every table, as though a spark of knowledge could pass around and charge a wave of delighted laughter through a room full of disconnected people.

The walk was not long. If you started from the middle of town you could pass one park, three blocks of housing, two graveyards, and a last stretch of housing and a lone restaurant and its excessive parking lot before coming to the railroad. The autumn made the walk quicker: you walked to build heat, where in summer you loitered to avoid building it. Once on the railroad you walked north a quarter mile, passed under the overpass, and continued on to the place you could take a jaunt to the right if your eye saw the place to dodge down into the underbrush. The dirt track followed the west side of the creek through low scrub and beneath the tall box elders and maples. The water ran calm, unobtrusive, and dark. You could reach the bluff by two ways. Either you could turn left before the bend in the creek, or you could go ahead and round the bend, passing the shallows where the raccoons liked to beach the river clams, and following the water until it led you straight to the base of the bluff. Either way, you climbed through the grasses to a spot not at the top where bike trails had destroyed the carpet of living things, nor too far down the side. There, you sat looking across the creek valley to the bluff on the other side.

I was beginning to feel more at home in this world. It felt like mine. I began reunderstanding certain things, such as the tilt of the head of a jay before it launched itself raucously from a branch, or the rhythm-keeping of a broken bough bent into the water, bobbing slowly up and down with the current. As I climbed the hill, the pebbles embedded in the dirt of a small washed-out area spoke to me with familiarity between the rustlings and quick chatterings of autumn-dried grass blades and the occasional browned seed pods.

I stopped at the edge of the last rise of the hill and turned to sit facing the creek valley, lined with poplars in this section, across to the opposite rise. The day was ending, which made my object of contemplation more visible. By day from this spot no more than a dark smudge of wires, trucks, and low buildings would appear to the naked eye, merging with the yellowed blur of the field grass. Through a binocular one could see little more, only discovering the fine-marked tightness of the fencing around the compound, the indistinct bleakness of the cement-block cubicles, and the official colors on the pickup trucks and smaller vehicles. One might even see the surveillance cameras turning atop their poles.

But at dusk the site came alive. Officialdom loves a well-lit space. Lights grew in brightness with the darkness to mark the fence, the outer perimeter of the top of the bluff, and the separate buildings. Above them all, however, rose the high lamps situated around a wide patch of land at the center of the compound. This level patch was never allowed to fall into darkness, having risen to the status of religious relic: here, governmental priests might well have found the heel impression of a governmental deity. In a sense, they had. Here they had found the abandoned, stripped fuselage of the alien craft, identical in all essentials to others found around the country and, perhaps, the world. The government then sequestered it. A few unrevealing photographs appeared from the news services. Otherwise the public received nothing of these contemporary relics beyond the sight of protective compounds and a general air of mystery.

Whether the government had incited the alien scare, or if the furor had scientific basis, it was hard to tell. People shook their fists, at the government for upsetting the routine of their placid existences, or at the sky. I had not felt bothered by the scare, interested and amused more than alarmed by the prospect of genetically identical aliens among us. The government was doing memory tests on selected subjects, I had heard. Mainly drifters, eccentrics, and general old folk—people with ambiguous pasts, into which category I had figured we all belonged. Who looks back in time with a crystal clarity? Not I, said the dog. Not I, said the cow. Well, you better, said the hen. Meanwhile the new Department for Extraterrestrial Affairs illuminated these landing pads, setting them up to allow good night visibility from far, far above.

The darkness of early evening settled in comfortably. I saw a sign of movement on the opposite bluff: a sentry, I supposed. A truck came, stayed, and departed. Through my binocular I could see the motionless dried grass beneath the high spotlights. It was a place locked away from our time. The government, best refuge for forecasters of every stripe, sat around its electric fire in hopes of a vision of the future.

I breathed out into the cold air, briefly fogging the lenses.

The sound of a tom drum suddenly started beside me, startling me.

I dropped my binocular and jerked my head over to see a man beside me in the dark. In the starlight and glimmering of moonlight I could see him well enough. He appeared underdressed for the chill. His breath came out in a great cloud, his hands coming down again on the small drum held between his crossed legs. I had heard nothing of his approach. Even the ever-present rustling of dried grass should not have been enough to conceal his approach. His hands now hovered again over the drum, turning and feeling the air with slow movements before one of them darted down to strike sound out of the tight cover.

He threw back his head. opening his mouth and releasing a thin, high note. A chill ran down my spine. I could almost see the note arch up into the night toward the stars, then curve back to earth, an increasingly bright ember of fire. Its orange hue grew and deepened as it returned, and flashed white as it burst roaring onto the grass just below us on the hill. It remained there as a fire, yet not as a fire I could say I had ever seen before: within it, as though its light meant not combustion but vision onto another scene, I could see the spikes and first leaves of new plants rising within the brightness of the flame, some of them shooting up rapidly and producing fleeting, brilliant flowers.

The man beside me was drumming in a more regular pattern now. I turned to him again and saw in the light of the flames that a dull wooden mask covered his face, painted a dirty white only around the ovals of the eyes and mouth. It seemed to me natural. At that moment I could not have imagined him looking other than this, with hidden features and simple garb, and I wondered if I had experienced this all before.

As I turned back to look again into the flames with their rising, flowering plants, the man's voice started up, this time in low register, a deep buzz in his throat running beneath his words as though he could maintain an internal, unceasing breath rotating within his lungs, punctuated only occasionally by drops in pitch or brief cessations:

The world and the death of the buffalo
The cattle and the death of the world
The sunflower follows the sun
It watches it fall and disappear
Come foreign people
Ancient ways are but youthful ways of play to you
Wisdom is of the gun and horse

Your happiness is to make trinkets from stones
You would take metal and give metal for land
You would make all things bow to the metal of air
You would yourselves obey the metal of air
But it is less than air this metal
I hold your metal to the sunflower and it ignores me
I hold your metal to the corn and it dies
You would have us exchange all things for less than air
You would give up all for less than air
You would sacrifice even yourselves
You would become less than air
You would become your own foreigners
You have made us all foreigners
We are all foreigners
We are in a land bought for less than air—

The plants grew taller, of a height greater than a person, bursting at the tops with clusters of golden blossoms, petals stretching wide as if to greet all the radiations emanating from the dark vastness of the universe and striking down on this small spot of light on the bluff. The plants then became fewer, and shorter. One burst of knee-high flowers of white-tinted blue and violet preceded the falling away of the leaves as snow began falling around us. The fire died. The whiteness kept falling, the flakes appearing unreasonably out of the star-flecked sky. Then the snow, too, ceased.

I looked beside me and saw no trace of the man with the drum. In the thin layer of whiteness I saw a track of fox footprints that abruptly appeared beside me and trailed away out of the circle of white. Before me in the snow no sign remained of the fire, the grasses still tall and unblackened, and framed now in whiteness.

Perhaps they could afford only simple methods, or perhaps simple methods were the best. A succession of people in coats and formal jackets would enter the room accompanied by uniformed men bearing odd-shaped items encased in leather at their belts. Each person had a task: they would utter a word, move their hands in front of my face, inject me, or attach wires to my forehead and stretch them to sockets in the wall that led to some cryptic place of analysis. They placed objects in my hand, sometimes rough, sometimes smooth, sometimes painful. They altered the temperature of the room, placed water on me, requested me to defecate, spoke unintelligible words and phrases to me and watched my reactions intently, then flashed cards of random items: an automobile, a carrot, a flying saucer, a naked man, a chair, a telephone pole, a watermelon, a naked woman, a grasshopper, a head of wheat, a tank, the president of the country. Once they flashed the cards behind my head. One of the doctors would enter at regular intervals to ask how I was doing. "Fine," I would say.

Ardis would arrive with her tray, bringing me food. If I could see her without the room moving, and if I could focus normally, I would speak to her.

"They showed me that picture of you again," I said.

She *tsk*ed. "I have to talk to those doctors."

"You looked fine."

"They must have taken it when I was a young thing. I'm a bit more saggy these days. Actually I did ask them for a look at those pictures they show you. You're right. She looks in fine shape."

"Did you see the man?"

"A bit scrawny."

"Dr. Roann," I said. She laughed, and left.

Later the routines would begin again. Often I would see the pictures several times in succession, sometimes with slight variations. Once when they changed the pose of the naked woman I commented. "You noticed that, did you?" said the man, an oversized one with the accent of having come from farther south. "Yes," I said. "I always look at her closely." He wrote in his notebook. "I shouldn't tell you this, but they changed the card with the building in it. You didn't notice that one," he said, perfectly seriously. "No," I said. Afterwards I would be fed a pill. Someone

The Googleplex Comes and Goes

Del Stone Jr.

WHEN THE GOOGLEPLEX CAME TO OUR TOWN, BIRDS flew into windows; dogs swallowed their tongues; and Mrs. Van Randwyck, who read palms and saw the future, got into her car and drove away.

She never returned.

The Googleplex came to the business district, where it stomped flat a Baskin-Robbins ice cream shop, Alice Mason's Art and Framing Supply store, and the parking lot at Mr. Keplinger's funeral home, across the street from the Rexall drugstore. It stomped flat the people inside those places too.

Nobody was watching when the Googleplex came. Some people say they were, but they're the liars. Some say they can't be sure it ever really came. They just don't know.

The Googleplex could have come to any town. I think it could have come to the ocean, a hidden forest, to the deep canyons in the West, or the moon. It could have come to the earth's core, another planet, or the wan light of some anemic little star you couldn't see or wish upon.

It could have come anywhere.

But it came to our town, and for that, some people thought we'd been chosen.

Nobody knows what it was, or is, or will be. Neither the liars nor the disbelievers. Only Ricky-Richard. I think he might know. If it is possible for him to know anything.

Our town has a name, but does it matter? We live in so-and-so, where the Googleplex came. I had a boyfriend who was interviewed on CNN. His name was Ricky. Or Richard, depending on the company. Ricky-Richard was average in height, resembled a weightlifter who'd folded up his Soloflex machine years ago, and had eyes that drifted between blue and hazel . . . and a peculiar cow-lick at the front of his scalp that allowed him to flip his bangs over his forehead, as if a half arc of halo had been imperfectly fitted to his skull.

I say he was my boyfriend. We spent a lot of time together, intimate time, which I take to mean a relationship existed, or *exists*, because I don't know how any of this will resolve itself. I do know he liked old-fashioned carburetors and movies where Middle Eastern dictators are bombed into the Stone Age and loud, loud Top-40 music.

He was fascinated by the Googleplex. He had his theories and I suppose they were as valid as any, which at face value made him one of the liars. But he meant well.

He was the world's antidote for me. I loved him, but it was an alloy of love, flawed with uncertainties, because he was shy the way men are shy, and there was much I needed to know.

Old Mrs. Wertz, who lives three doors down from my apartment, swears she heard the Googleplex come. She said the building shook, the way it shook that day Mr. Hayward's grain silo went up in a ball of spontaneously combusted fire. She said the windows rattled in their panes and the plumbing twanged like an out-of-tune guitar, and a haze of dust descended from the sheetrock ceiling. Only the coming of the Googleplex could have done all those things, she said.

She's not lying. She's crazy.

She called me one night to say there was a large snake, an anaconda or a python, coiled around the street lamp post out in the parking lot, and it was eating children who came by, sometimes snatching them right off their bicycles.

She called me one night to say a flying saucer was hovering outside her bedroom window.

She called me one night to tell me what a fine boy Ricky-Richard was.

What did she know that I didn't?

The Googleplex moved only once. Some of the towns-people said they'd seen it move, but I'd never seen it move, except that once, just before it left, and even then I didn't actually see it move. I only saw that it *had* moved.

Sometimes Ricky-Richard said it was moving. On those nights when the girl behind the candy counter at the Palm Theater would slip us a Dr. Pepper and a tub of greasy popcorn "for the road," we'd sit in the gazebo at St. Andrew's Square in the middle of town and watch the Googleplex. Watch the night slide around it as if even the dark would shun something so strange. And Ricky-Richard would swear he saw it move.

It was too big to move, I think. Or it didn't move the way I think of things moving. If it had, there would have been earthquakes, tidal waves, plagues, fire from the sky. The planet would have tilted—if it'd moved the way I think of things moving. But it moved only once. And I think if I'd been watching it at that moment, I wouldn't have seen it move.

It was big. It stretched into the sky, sweeping into the clouds on impossibly thin, tapered stacks of crystal-like facets. Its geometry insulted physics as easily as its existence defied motive and its origin, explanation. People came to study it—people from universities and multinational corporations and military interests. They scraped at it with diamond-tipped drills and plastic explosives and nuclear detonators. They sniffed at it with gas-chromatic spectrolyzers. They tried to decide what kind of materials it was made of and the distribution of its stresses and its mass. They probed it fruitlessly with radar, sonar, microwaves, portable colliders, and radio signals.

They shook their heads. They said it was impossible. And then, like most of the others, they just gave up and went away.

They were also the ones who didn't know.

I didn't know if Ricky-Richard loved me or liked me or felt comfortable with the ritual of being with me. There were times, I think, when he loved me—truly loved me, the way a guy like Ricky-Richard can truly love something so miraculously simple as a Phillips-head screwdriver.

And he liked me. Most times he liked me, though again I can't know this for a fact.

He was a slave to convention and tradition and the appearance of those things. Or maybe he really believed in them—hell, I don't know. I just don't know. Love was important to him, I think, and companionship was essential, as was sex.

But sometimes I felt as though his understanding of those things never went beyond an appreciation of their mechanical function and their institutional value. He didn't hear the music or see the sunsets in a relationship, or if he did, they never made him cry. In fact, I never saw him cry—I never saw him wrestle with any strong emotion . . .

. . . except his fascination with the Googleplex.

I'm an educated person, but the Googleplex didn't fascinate me. Ricky-Richard fascinated me. I would come home from our dates exhausted and simultaneously exhilarated, as if our being together could have ignited some critical mass but hadn't yet and I'd dodged a catastrophe, another flirtation with annihilation. I was miserable when he was away and terrified when he wasn't, and I learned to need the narcotic effects of adrenaline.

But I could no more solve the riddle of Ricky-Richard than he could solve the riddle of the Googleplex. No diamond-tipped drills or radars or university exogeologists could have told me the things I needed to know.

Only Ricky-Richard could have. But he couldn't.

We went there often, to the center of town, where the Googleplex had come, mostly after the government had switched off the floodlights and taken down the fences and pulled out the troops. Somebody was always there— bearded scientists from such-and-such university or raving cultists or fat guys from Wisconsin with the wife and kids, driving Oldsmobile station wagons with flaps of fake wood trim hanging off. Ricky-Richard would pick me up in his Bronco—the paint was oxidized and the shocks were so worn out that for Christmas, as a joke, I bought him a package of Dramamine skin patches from the Rexall drugstore. He'd have the damn stereo throwing out as many watts or amps or whatevers that his cheap Technics speakers could swallow without exploding, so that when we got to wherever we were going I felt as though the molecules of my body had come unglued from one another and he'd have to carry me home in a Jell-O mold. Then we'd do whatever we had planned—sometimes a movie at the Palm, sometimes a stroll through the strip shopping center just off the interstate exit—and then he'd make some excuse to drive through town and we'd sit in St. Andrew's for awhile.

To watch the Googleplex.

Ricky-Richard would yell things at the guys who were working there. "It's a fork from outer space!" to the engineer types. "It's Jesus, and boy is he pissed!" to the cultists. "It's six-year-old Limburger and it still smells better than you!" to the Wisconsin plates.

No matter who came to look, he knew a lie to tell them.

But it seemed he never knew what to tell me, and his silence—rather, his inability to speak, to say anything—was just as incriminating as the taunts he had for the people who were trying to figure out the Googleplex.

If he could tell me now that he knew anything, anything at all, I'd know he wasn't lying, instead of simply hoping that was so.

Hope is a scary thing.

I think what drew people to the Googleplex, apart from its inexplicable strangeness, was the fact that somehow, some way, it seemed familiar. It was like poetry. Everybody had their own interpretations of what they saw in it, but always they described things that were rooted in the utterly mundane, comfortable reality of everyday life. For some, it was the likeness of Jesus Christ lurking beneath that multiplanar surface, watching them from every angle, like that photograph of Ronald Reagan crazy Mrs. Wertz has hanging on her living room wall just above the Magnavox. For others it was a vague artistic gesture dedicated to a sentiment irreducibly grandiose, like a Steven Spielberg movie only a lot less transparent. The engineer types and shade-tree mechanics thought it was some kind of machine. The geologists talked about crystalline couloirs and aretes and flying laccoliths. The quantum physicist sniffed for unified field theories, and the metaphysicians debated purpose. Vicars and cardinals and shamans said they knew the whats and the whys, and some of them tried to make money from their answers.

What did I think? I'm not sure. The Googleplex didn't fascinate me.

But I remember that, as a child, I had nightmares about just such a thing. It was always the same, this dream. The world was rendered in the frugal, dimensionless abstraction of cartoon stick figures, and everything was painted yellow, as if the architect of this dream was too chintzy to spring for process color. I'd be standing on a sidewalk. Across the street I'd see a Shelly Duval-style stick-figure girl. Her hair was drawn in tight curlicues, all five or six strands. She'd stop and pick a daisy that was growing next to the sidewalk: two leaves, five petals. I hadn't noticed it there before; it seemed to appear as she bent to pick it, as if her intent caused it to exist. Then she'd pluck the petals, one by one, until only a single petal remained. At that moment she'd look at me, and the most maliciously evil smile you can imagine would spread across her face—I still can't believe the simple crease of a line could carry so much meaning—and she'd pull the last petal.

Then the world would vanish in a spasm of darkness and hugeness so vast I'd wake up screaming.

Ricky-Richard and I discussed marriage, sort of, if you can forgive an indiscretion of syntax. He didn't ask, and he didn't command. All he said was, "We should get married," as in, "I should fix that flat on the Bronco" or, "My pants are too tight in the waist. I should lose a few pounds."

We were sitting in St. Andrew's, not at the gazebo but at one of the benches along the web of sidewalks that divided the park into six equal pie wedges. A rusty old gas light next to the bench was hissing, its mantel limned in bright yellow. Moths traced erratic maneuvers around the hood and occasionally thumped dustily against the lamp panes. A group of somebodies was gathered at the base of the Googleplex, pouring something cold and smoky onto its surface. I think they were trying to freeze off a chunk of it, the way doctors remove cysts. It smelled like insulation burning.

I didn't know what to say. I didn't know what to think. My body had built up a stiff tolerance for adrenaline, but now that the moment had arrived, all my theories did not fit the puzzle of reality: How will I give myself to a person I can't know? Marriage, for God's sake. I would come into Ricky-Richard's life and he into mine, and we'd clear little spaces for each other and conduct all the investigations peculiar to newlyweds, and when the novelty wore off we'd have kids and fight about money and he'd probably have an affair with the girl behind the candy counter at the Palm. And I'd go through withdrawal. All those days and nights when the light would take on the unyielding starkness of forever.

I'd always be trying to get him to talk to me, and I'd always be trying to figure him out. And just like now, he'd never see the things that made me different than everyone else in the world.

But still, I wanted it, and God help me, I thought maybe I could change him . . . or change myself. Maybe the clouds would part and some insight, some revelation of understanding, would shine down on us. Because I needed it—we needed it. Now I'm not sure Ricky-Richard can give it to me. I'm not sure he can do anything for me, or even for himself.

So I didn't say anything for a moment, and then the issue became moot.

Because that was when the Googleplex moved.

I was about to tell him, "Yes," or "Maybe," or, "I don't know," when the Googleplex moved.

Damn the Googleplex. Damn it to hell, whatever it was, or is, or will be. I hate the memory of it now, every bit as much as I hated it then. It moved and suddenly everything was forgotten, the night, the gas light, the moths, the ozone smell of liquid whatever, the question of marriage. Gone.

We were sitting on the bench, my thoughts teetering on an emotional high wire, when I sensed a subtle shift in . . . something . . . the way a party will sometimes slide to a halt, every conversation pausing simultaneously, and a self-conscious silence drops over the room so that everybody sort of smiles, looks guiltily at everybody else, and then laughs. I turned and looked, and the men who'd been working at the base of the Googleplex were gone. Their equipment was gone. My eyes followed the Googleplex into the night sky.

It had reoriented itself. It was facing a different direction, and it was stacked differently, the familiar planes and sharp edges and Escher angles now horribly unfamiliar. I couldn't believe what I was seeing. That much mass, displacing that much air . . . there should have been a sound, claxons hooting, angels gasping—*something*.

But there hadn't been. No warning, no cause for such a thing to happen, nothing I could see. It just moved.

The breath lodged in my throat. Everything seemed to stop, the way it does when lightning strikes a utility pole down the street and the power goes off. I couldn't say anything—I couldn't *think* anything, for a frozen moment.

Then I heard Ricky-Richard hiss, "Jesus fucking Christ," and I felt the muscles in his arm go rock hard, and then he jumped off the bench and ran a few steps, shouting, "Christ! Jesus fucking Christ!" And he turned back to me, his eyes unfocused and looking wild in the feeble gas light, and he shouted, "I told you! I told you the damn thing was moving. Holy shit! It moved!"

I slumped against the bench, my thoughts sorting out from confusion and fear to a slow burn of resentment. Ricky-Richard ran off to the base of the Googleplex, as if nobody had just vanished from there, as if the thing hadn't moved and we'd been talking about nothing more important than the weather.

As if nothing else at all mattered.

Things happened quickly after that. The government rushed troops in again and the fences went up and the Googleplex defied every attempt to illuminate it. The crowds returned and CNN interviewed Ricky-Richard. I thought maybe his recounting of events leading up to the Googleplex moving might jog his memory, but he handled the situation in his engaging and, for me, infuriatingly coy fashion, saying nothing that held any significance for me. Mrs. Wertz swore she felt the earth shift on the night the Googleplex moved, and I, for my own reasons, had felt the same thing.

But I knew she was crazy. It wasn't her fault.

The Googleplex remained in our town two more days and then it left.

Just as nobody saw it come, nobody saw the Googleplex go. It simply went, and in the process it sheared off the second floor of the Rexall drugstore building, cleaving it with a diamond cutter's sure precision. The cut was at a shallow angle, exposing part of the first-floor ceiling on the south face and leaving a four-foot segment of wall along the north face. Pipes, wiring, mortar, studs, and in some cases nails were severed so neatly they appeared to have been made that way.

Later, after the experts had radared and X-rayed and sonicized the building to death, I heard that the entire structure had been subjected to compression and torsion stresses associated with high-velocity impacts. If the building had been a person, it would have been somebody who'd seen something so awful that the pigment had been shocked from his hair and the calcium sucked from his bones.

The Googleplex was gone, but it had left riddles in the physical condition of the Rexall drugstore, and it had left something else. A tiny flaw in the shear, a kind of splash mark, a spike of matter like cooled solder protruding from the building's north end. It reminded me of those shafts on the Statue of Liberty's crown.

Fastened to the end of this spike was a small crystal.

We were sitting in the gazebo at St. Andrew's, watching the soldiers load their useless tanks and radar-controlled guns onto huge, flatbed trailers. The park gas lamps were burning, but the soldiers had set up huge klieg lights around the site where the Googleplex had come, and any illumination the gas lamps offered was obliterated by the incandescent hell of the kliegs.

The air dripped with the smell of diesel. The gazebo trembled against the roar of turbine engines.

Ricky-Richard had his feet up, his legs outstretched on the bench that rimmed the gazebo. He was leaning against me. He was watching the Rexall drugstore, where men in white suits and breathing masks were using dental instruments to pry up parts of the building and put them into government-issue Ziploc bags.

"I'm gonna get that thing," he muttered—to me, to the night, to no one in particular. He was talking about the fragment left by the Googleplex, if that's what it really is. I'm still not sure. But everybody had been talking about it. Everybody wanted it. Why, I don't know.

I didn't ask him how he intended to do that, especially when teams from Cal Tech and Fermilab and the National Security Agency, among others, hadn't been able to "get that thing." But with Ricky-Richard that didn't matter, because he had no intention of "getting that thing." He'd talk about it the next fifty years, and always it would be, "I'm gonna get that thing. You watch me. One of these days . . ."

The subject of marriage had not come up again since the night the Googleplex moved, and I saw an opportunity, and now I think I regret doing it but at the time it seemed right, so I said, "It's a beautiful crystal. Wouldn't it make a unique setting for a ring?"

He didn't turn to look at me but I could feel his astonishment, thrumming right up out of his posture.

"Are you out of your mind?" he said incredulously. "When I get that thing I'm gonna sell it for a million dollars . . . get me a decent truck, one of them Toyota four-by-fours with air conditioning and velour seats and a frigging CD player." He thought a moment and then added, "Maybe buy a house on the lake and tell that jerkoff Quiggins he can take his carpet and tile store and shove it up his no-wax ass." He chuckled mirthlessly. "Ring . . . I can get a ring at the Wal-Mart over in Sneads."

I don't know what I expected of Ricky-Richard, but it seemed he'd distilled into one brutally efficient sentence every question I'd ever felt about our so-called relationship.

I jumped up. He fell back and smacked his head against the hardwood armrest. I was angry, or maybe I was hurt, but some strong emotion was burning through me like current through a bare wire. I circled the gazebo's perimeter, hands on hips, and Ricky-Richard watched me with a puzzled expression, mystified and, I still believe, amused. And that's what did it for me. That was the catalyst. His happy-go-lucky, shaggy-dog reaction to my reaction. And in a single moment, like those near-death episodes where your entire life supposedly flashes before your eyes, I saw again a future of always grappling with his lack of understanding and his silent patronization, until the inevitable happened and I wore him down or he wore me down and one or both of us would simply cease to care anymore.

Looking back, I still can't believe I did this, but I marched across the street, into the furnace of light baking what was left of the Rexall drugstore, and I began climbing one of the aluminum ladders standing against the south face. Somebody tried to stop me but I jerked away and continued climbing. I thought I heard Ricky-Richard calling my name, asking me what the hell I thought I was doing and asking me to come down. Other people were shouting.

I got to the top and catwalked across exposed girders until I got to the part where the floor was intact, and I strode through the knot of white-suited figures cloistered around the spike. I think they were all too surprised to react, especially when I reached out and grabbed the crystal.

Something happened. When I touched it. Something went through me. Not one of Mrs. Wertz's pane-rattling earth tremors or an interstellar person-to-person call or a Christ presence full of compassion. But something very big, a vertiginous chasm, opened somewhere within me, like in my dream of the stick-figure girl at the moment she yanked that last daisy petal. Something that groped at my sanity and made me want to flee, anywhere, anyhow, something random and beyond understanding and very, very powerful.

Ricky-Richard muscled his way through the white-suited figures—I saw him in slow motion, it seemed, as if the world and everything I'd known and felt before had been culled to a set of trite, quaintly unimportant ideas. Ricky-Richard's expression was almost comically panic-stricken, and I remember thinking he was either frightened that I'd done something he'd never do himself . . . or maybe he was frightened for me. I wanted to believe the latter.

Whichever the case, he grabbed my wrist to jerk my hand away from the crystal and I felt something else move through me, a sensation as bottomless and transcendant as the first but different in a way I can't explain, and Ricky-Richard changed—faster than I was able to see it happen. His body went cast-iron rigid, and the curves of his flesh, the concavities, the dimples, the ropes of muscle and the fast-flowing currents of his hair and the glistening, always simple luster of his eyes, were suddenly planed over into sharp, angular surfaces, as if he'd been poorly sculpted by an artist accustomed to working in only straight lines. I couldn't move him. He was as irresistibly locked into place as the earth was in its orbit around the sun.

The white-suited figures stood back, speechless for a moment. And then they began shouting, and one of them moved toward me before another grabbed him and shouted, "Don't touch them! Don't touch them!" And as they ran clumsily around the exposed second floor of the Rexall drugstore building, I watched the glacier of horror in Ricky-Richard's face, and wondered again why he had done what he'd done.

They had to amputate my hand to free it from Ricky-Richard's grasp.

They spread inflatable mattresses on the ground below and suspended nets from the building, in case I fell, and then they raised a surgeon in a cherry picker because he couldn't do the job while leaning over the edge of the building. The doctor, who was wearing one of the white contamination suits, gave me an injection of something and taped the syringe to my arm, then gave me a hit off a pressurized gas canister that pretty well did me in. I drifted into sleep thinking I could stay this way forever, trapped in Ricky-Richard's unforgiving grip.

I awakened in a hospital. My arm throbbed, the waves of pain crushing my thoughts until the next shot mercifully arrived. At one point somebody tried to console me. There'd been no other choice, they said. They couldn't free my hand. Ricky-Richard was now part of whatever the Googleplex had been. Nobody knew what that was, except the liars, and I didn't care anyway because none of it had mattered or mattered now or would ever matter.

I just wanted to stop hurting.

It hasn't stopped hurting. My hand . . . no, make that my arm, my wrist—whatever—is healed. And I even have a prosthetic that looks real if people are polite enough not to stare.

But it still hurts.

I went to the second floor of the Rexall drugstore to look at Ricky-Richard yesterday. The afternoon was dark, the clouds hanging low and threatening, like the heavy, dust-covered draperies in Mr. Keplinger's funeral home. Some government types came with me—out of concern I might do something stupid, or mess up their experiments and instrumentation, I don't know. It doesn't matter.

Ricky-Richard was still there, of course. He hadn't

moved. He was still horrified or jealous or angry—even now that I've had a chance to study his expression and think about things, I can't decide which it is. Something about the straight lines sucks all the empathy from his features.

But he's no longer alone.

Perched on Ricky-Richard's shoulder, to the left of the now-eternal halo of cowlick, was a crystal-black crow gazing forever upon whatever passes for the destruction of Sodom to crows. And insects had crawled onto Ricky-Richard's arm or had landed on his forehead and were preserved in crystal as surely as Ricky-Richard's geodic gaze watched the space where I had lain. The government types pointed them out to me. They said if certain living things touched the "latticework"—that's what they called Ricky-Richard—without protection, they became what Ricky-Richard was. Not all living things, but some, and they didn't know why that was so. They had their theories of course, theories about brain hemispheres and functional-operational thinking . . . but these were just theories, really. Just like everything else.

And the hand—my hand. It still clenched the crystal, held in place by Ricky-Richard's carved-ice grip. And it still moved. It hadn't died and shriveled to some horrible, mummified-looking, wasted thing, as I'd expected. It was cleanly severed at the wrist, although the cut wasn't nearly so clean as whatever force had sliced off the second floor of the Rexall drugstore. It looked as though I could fit the stump of my arm against it and the flesh would rejoin, the bone and blood vessels and nerves and muscle tissue happily knitting themselves to my body as if none of this ugly business with the Googleplex and the crystal and Ricky-Richard had ever come to pass.

I didn't stay long. Just a few minutes. A rift in the clouds let the sun shine through and I felt the weight of the light press against me as my shadow crossed and flowed into Ricky-Richard's crystal statue, and I thought, God, God. How could I have done this?

• • •

Whatever the Googleplex was, I don't think it was evil. I'm not even sure it was meant to be understood. At least not by people.

But seeing my hand gave me the idea that I could still do something. It's this kind of thinking that gets people in trouble, all the compassion and cruelty and stupid inquisitiveness that human beings inflict on the world and each other—all of it with the best of intentions. I guess I'm no more sensible or intelligent than the next person, but I'm not dealing with logic in this situation. Sometimes, I think, faith requires its own morality, as do love and risk and all the things that give life purpose. So I've decided to take my chances, which is a scary thing.

As I said, watching my hand wriggle in Ricky-Richard's grasp gave me an idea. I think a kind of circuit is at work there, a perpetual loop of emotion or perspective that wasn't meant to be cut apart and labeled and stored in jars of formaldehyde. I don't have any way of proving that, but there comes a day when instinct has to take over. And it seems to me that if the right kind of influence came along, say a joining of hands, a concession to forgive what can't be known, the current or state of mind or whatever is running through that loop might ground itself out.

That's probably a stupid metaphor, but it's the best I can do.

So one of these nights, very soon, I'll be climbing the ladder again. I prefer not to think of this as a concession to foolishness but a renewal of my humanity. If I'm right I'll apologize to him, and if I'm wrong I'll turn the other cheek.

Meanwhile, nobody knows why the Googleplex came to our nameless little town. Nobody knows what it was, or is, or will be. Some say they do. They're liars.

But I think Ricky-Richard might know. Now, he might know. Ricky-Richard told lots of lies, about the Googleplex and other things, but he wasn't evil.

He was like me. He just didn't know.

But now, maybe like me, he has his answers in ways he could never understand. And the knowing is so much sweeter for that.

The Beauty Addict

Ray Aldridge

I CAME TO NOCTILE WITH THE OTHER TOURISTS, AND FOR much the same reasons: to walk the narrow stone streets of the old cities that ring the Opal Eye, to visit the misty beaches, to watch the Firefly Moon reflected in the strange waters of the Eye—and of course to see the sylphs, who, though they are not human, are still the most beautiful women in the human universe.

I arrived in late winter, when storms sometimes disturb the Eye's tranquility and the air is damp and chilly. I always travel during the low season, if it's not too uncomfortable. It's cheaper then, of course, and in the low season the real life of a place sometimes creeps out from beneath its tourist-trap façade.

The shuttle delivered me to a field outside the ringwall. With a handful of fellow travelers, I rode a conveyor into a high-ceilinged terminal. There I arranged for transport to the walled city of Crondiem and converted my currency.

The money-changer was an old woman with sharp yellow teeth and fuzzy white hair. "Here to claim a sylph, are you?" she asked, grinning ferociously. "A handsome young man like you?"

"No," I answered, rather shortly.

"Ah? Well, in that case I'll see you again, won't I?" She seemed to be controlling her laughter with difficulty.

I went outside to wait. Through the high wire and snip fields of the perimeter, I was lucky enough to glimpse a pack of huge gray ferokim, loping through the barren scrub. Not many ferokim survive in the wild these days. It was the relentless bloodlust of these predators which forced the original colonists to build their cities inside the Eye's protective ringwall.

Some say the ferokim and the sylphs are both subassemblies in the same alien biomachine.

We boarded a small electric bus for the ride under the mountains. As we rattled through the long dark tunnel which connects Crondiem to the universe outside the Eye, the interior lights came on, revealing an assortment of graffiti on the plastic ceiling. Most were of the sort commonly left by travelers—names and dates and home worlds.

Here and there I noticed more interesting inscriptions. In angry angular script: "The beauty of women deserves no praise!" Over this, in smeared purple ink: "Small hearts fear to look on beauty!" In little wry squiggles: "Love's like a well—good to drink from, bad to fall into."

In an artless scrawl:

Beauty is but skin deep
Ugly lies the bone
Beauty dies and fades away
But ugly holds its own.

In round emphatic capitals: "Beauty may die but it leaves echoes forever." In green spray paint: "The beautiful die easily," a sentiment countered by pink glitterline: "Not here!" Scratched with a knife: "Love is like war. You begin when you like, and leave off when you can." Again the pink glitterline refuted: "Not here!"

In a tiny fragile hand, almost illegible: "Here beauty makes the heart ache so strangely that it cannot stand to be cured of its pain."

Thus entertained by my morbidly literate predecessors, I finally emerged into the watery late-afternoon sunlight of Crondiem.

There are ordinary human women in Crondiem, of course, and some of them are wealthy, so that they can afford to buy the kind of beauty that the flesh tinkers and the gene-splicers sell. One of my fellow tourists was beautiful in this human sense: a sloe-eyed, long-limbed woman dressed in a colorful Jaworld caftan. She watched me through the artful tangle of her hair, a careful assessing smile on her rich mouth. I returned her look boldly; adventure is where you find it.

She seemed at first oddly reassured, but then her smile evaporated and she turned away. I was amused. Apparently she had taken me for a sylph seeker and was disappointed to find me a common lecher.

Then I saw my first sylph, and I forgot all about the Jaworld woman.

The sylph ran along one of Crondiem's narrow sidewalks, past dark old shops with diamond-paned windows. She seemed to be taking her exercise; she was naked except for sandals and a vermilion breast band. Sweat gilded her, in spite of the street's cool shadows.

Most healthy young women have lovely bodies; what was it about hers that so affected me? I can't really say, but I can still feel the amazement I felt then. Certainly every line was tautly perfect, every firm convexity, every sweet hollow—but that's not so unusual. Her skin was as white as fine porcelain and as flawless, her long hair a floating red glory. In that passing glimpse I couldn't see the color of her eyes. I felt a remarkably strong regret at this failure of observation.

Her movements struck me as inhumanly graceful, but otherwise it was impossible for me to believe that beneath that wonderful skin beat a strange six-chambered heart, that pale green blood ran through her veins, that she had once been a cold aquatic creature. That, one day, she would cast off her human semblance and return to the Opal Eye.

When the bus rounded the next corner and I lost sight of her, I realized that I had been holding my breath. I felt lightheaded, as if I'd been enduring some great pain, or enjoying some great pleasure. I happened to glance at the Jaworld woman, and saw that she was examining me with baffled anger. Then she made her face smooth and inviting, but after the sylph she seemed coarse and ordinary, and I averted my gaze. She muttered something caustic under her breath.

The bus reached my hotel, and I gathered my coat and satchel. As I passed the Jaworld woman, she looked up and said, "*You* should be especially careful." She spoke almost kindly.

My small room was high in the west wing of the Skelpin, an ancient and well-regarded hostelry two blocks above the seawall. My one window framed a tall narrow slice of Crondiem, its gray slate rooftops, its black stone walls, the deep-blue awnings at every window and door. I went to the window and threw open the casement. By leaning far out and to the right, I could just see a sliver of pearly dazzle—the surface of the Opal Eye.

"Every room has a fine view of the Eye," the travel agent had said of the Skelpin, and so it was, almost. No matter; I could move later if I wished. In this season, Crondiem would be full of empty rooms.

The room was furnished simply: a deep wingback chair covered in crinkled black leather, a capacious wardrobe, a wide bed with a carved headboard. I looked closely and saw that the carving was a tangled knot of the sea serpents that are rumored to swim the central depths of the Eye. Their tails thrashed, their reptilian eyes glared horribly.

The walls were unadorned white plaster, and an old-rose and umber rug covered the polished wood floor. A small bathroom adjoined.

I busied myself for a few minutes, unpacking my possessions and putting them away.

On an impulse, I erected my easel and clipped a sheet of multimem into its rack. The multimem's surface lit with a soft white glow, indicating its readiness to accept an image. I took up my colorwand and connected its lead to the neural plug implanted into my wrist.

I drew the sylph from memory, in swift grainy strokes of simulated chalk, blue-gray and russet and black. But when I was finished, all I had was a competent drawing of a beautiful young woman, lips pursed to draw breath, strong legs driving her along the street, high breasts ajounce with her motion, hair trailing behind her like a storm cloud on fire.

Nothing more.

Other artists had spoken to me of this frustration— that no mere image could record the quality that set the sylphs apart from real women. I touched the edge of the multimem, transferring the sylph's portrait to storage. A clean new surface invited me—but I put aside the colorwand and went down to an early dinner.

The dining room was empty except for a portly man who affected that aggressively urbane style that I associate with the folk of Dilvermoon. The waiter seated us as far apart as possible, for which I was grateful.

My Dilvermoon dealer is an example. "Ah, Hender, good simple Hender," he said to me on one of my rare visits to that artificial world. "Your purity, your severity, your unembellished literality . . . all these are balm to our overly analytical eyes. Never change!" I sometimes wonder if he realizes how offensively patronizing he is. If so I'm sure he thinks I'm too simple to notice. I don't suppose it matters. So long as my paintings continue to attract a profitable number of subscribers, he will continue to conceal his contempt.

I dined adequately, though the kitchen had just opened. The waitress set before me a clear soup, a salad of pickled vegetables, a plate of spiced prawns and sweet red peppers arranged in a crisp spiral, a covered dish of fluffy saffron rice. The wine was a delicate vintage from the sunny side of the ringwall, palest green and slightly astringent. None of the food came from the Eye, of course; the peculiar fluid that fills the Eye supports no terrestrial life.

I left the dining room in a state of pleasant surfeit.

Under the front portico the doorman offered to summon a covered rickshaw, but I said, "I'll walk a bit." I patted the easel I carried folded under my arm.

"As you like, sir," he said gravely.

The inhabitants of Crondiem tend to be short and dark, with large liquid eyes and strong white teeth.

After a few days in the city, it seemed to me that never had I known a people so inobtrusive, so skilled at receding into the background, or so private. I suppose such an intense inner direction is a racial necessity, in a city where sylphs walk.

That first evening, I went down to the waterfront. I descended several broad staircases and walked along the paved paths atop the sloping walls. Even in that season of cold winds, nightflowering vines spilled beauty down every stony surface. Their blooms were beginning to open and their fragrance sweetened the darkening air.

I came quite suddenly to a promontory that looked out over the Opal Eye, and stood transfixed.

Many places are beautiful, from a happy conjunction of light and shape and color. For example, old seaports—which in some ways Crondiem resembles—are favorite subjects of mine. Their human-built beauty often appears to have rubbed so long and so relentlessly against the adamant beauty of their settings that the two are a perfect fit.

But the Opal Eye transcends the ordinary beauty of such places in the same way that the sylphs transcend the beauty of ordinary women.

The sun was setting beyond the far side of the ringwall—that the city lies on the eastern edge of the Eye was another reason I had come here. Noctile's star is golden, but the long rays that struck through the high mist were red as copper. Below the mist, the milky waters supported a veil of opalescent colors—blue veined with shimmering crimson. Behind me the towers of old Crondiem made black shapes against a fading purple sky.

I found myself holding my breath, as smitten by the Eye's beauty as any other tourist.

I was almost angry. I shook my head and hurried down the last flights of steps to the seawall.

I came to the widow's pen, one of the subjects I had most wanted to paint, though I hadn't meant to start so soon. Ordinarily I like to take a few days before I undertake serious work—but the light was compellingly melancholy, a suitably chill breeze stirred tiny wavelets in the pen, and I was alone. And I was still full of the exaltation the Eye's beauty had poured into me.

I quickly set up the easel and multimem, plugged in the wand.

The light was changing rapidly. I swept the wand across the sheet, laying in the image almost photographically—from my eyes to the wand, unedited.

In the foreground, the black solidity of the stone quay. The widow's pen itself, with the weedy wall that enclosed it and the weathered marble gargoyles that perched on the wall every few meters, staring down at the widows. The glittering glass globes of the widows' grails, scattered across the pale translucent fluid of the Eye. The bodies of the widows themselves, indistinct shapes floating a half meter beneath their grails.

When I had seized the image, I began to change it a bit: the gargoyles stretched a little higher and their worn teeth grew a little sharper. Here and there a glossy eye rolled in a stone socket. The grails became even more fancifully ornamental, more elaborately bejeweled, and I sowed the Eye thickly with reflected light—of the city's yellow lamps, the fading sky, and the cold gleam of emerging stars. I imagined the widows' bodies a bit more clearly than reality showed them: here a perfect breast became visible, there the curve of an exquisite thigh. Their faces remained obscure, however, and their blurred hands where they grasped the hoses of their grails had become clumsy animal paws.

Night fell over the Eye, and I stopped.

I disconnected the wand and looked at my sketch, which glowed with a dim internal illumination. It was, I finally decided, not entirely bad. "Twilight at the Widow's Pen," I spoke, cuing the title recorder.

When I took my attention from the easel, I found that I was no longer alone. A slender figure, bundled in a long hooded robe, stood a few meters down the quay, looking down into the pen.

After a moment, she turned toward me. The hood shadowed her face, though it wasn't really dark, there beside the Eye's white shimmer. I was suddenly sure she was a sylph, and I felt a knee-weakening thrill. "Hello," I said.

Her voice was music—I had never heard anything so harmonious. "Hello," she said. "You are a painter?"

"Yes," I answered.

Her manners were impeccable; she didn't even glance at the easel until she had asked: "May I look?"

At my nod she stepped closer and examined the image. Her perfume was a subtler scent than the night-blooming flowers, but it was all I could smell.

"Interesting," she finally said, and my heart fell. *Interesting* is the word critics use when no better word occurs to them . . . and they wish to seem kind. Perhaps she did not mean it so, but I couldn't bring myself to thank her for the comment.

She extended an elegant hand. One long finger almost touched the sketch, just where a widow's lumpy paw neared the surface. Then she opened her hand and slowly turned it, as if to allow me to see its grace from all angles.

I felt an apology trying to thrust itself from my throat but I forced it back.

Finally she said in that wonderful voice, "Thank you. For showing me your work." She walked away down the quay, and even in the long robe, her movements seemed like a slow, perfectly measured dance.

"You're welcome," I said, long after she was gone.

Up on the heights behind me a lamplit procession wound down toward the water—the widows' retainers, come to fetch them to their night homes.

I glanced into the pen and saw a roil of spasmodic movement, as the widows began to wake from their drugged slumber.

For some reason my curiosity had temporarily evaporated and I decided I wasn't in the mood to witness their emergence, this first night.

I packed up my easel and hurried away, passing a small park where a few rickshaws clustered. Other tourists strolled toward the pen, talking in loud expectant voices.

Back in my room, I lay on the bed, thinking about my encounter with the sylph. In my memory, which has always been unusually faithful, I heard again her voice, watched her move. In what specific way had she differed from a real woman? I couldn't say; the difference was either too large or too small for me to grasp.

After a while I activated the room's holotank, which was rather cleverly disguised as an antique footstool.

The menu shimmered in the air, a list of the available functions. I chose in quick succession: INFORMATION, THE OPAL EYE, SCIENTIFIC RATIONALE.

The holotank showed me the face of Noctile as if through the port of an old-fashioned starboat. The tagline at the bottom of the image read: *Humankind's first glimpse of Noctile, seventeen hundred standard years ago.*

Noctile swelled, spun over to reveal the Opal Eye, a dazzling white circle in the brown and green flank of the world. The Eye's ringwall of black basalt outlined it. It was local noon, so the ringwall mountains cast shadows only to the north—soft gray lashes.

The viewpoint dropped toward Noctile's surface, and the Eye grew until it almost filled the tank. A secondary image area developed in the lower forefront of the tank: a woman's face. She began to speak in a soft well-modulated voice. "The Opal Eye of Noctile is one of the Thousand Wonders of the human universe. Current opinion among the experts of the pangalac worlds holds that the Eye is an artifact of unknowable age, purpose, and provenance.

"Some have suggested that the Eye is the result of a meteor strike; this theory is difficult to credit, given the precise symmetry of the Eye, its depth—several times its width—and the composition of the fluid which fills the Eye, which has no analog anywhere else in the human universe. A water-based medium, the fluid apparently derives its unique qualities from a variety of continuously interlinking polymers, a chemistry too complex for the present analytic capacity of human technology. The life forms this medium supports are equally baffling—"

I cut her off. I saw no point in adding to my own unscientific bafflement.

The top menu reappeared, and I selected for Crondiem: NIGHTLIFE.

A listing of bars, clubs, cafes appeared. Each carried a paragraph detailing the establishment's specialties: entertainment, food, drugs, clientele. Several after-hour clubs claimed sylphs among their habitués. I cued up one called Cold Blood.

The tank filled with a view of Cold Blood's elaborate main ballroom, a view which had evidently been recorded during the height of the season, because tourists jammed the dance floors and drug bars, all in that state of feverish revelry which occurs only when the population density of an enclosed space exceeds a certain critical point. The tourists appeared to be having a fine time, but none of the women who danced through the tank seemed beautiful enough to be sylphs.

I shrugged and cued another self-described sylph gathering place, called The Opal Tower, and discovered it to be a bordello. The activities here were far less frenetic. Men and a few women entered a cozy panelled room and, sitting in comfortable armchairs, made their selections from little flatscreens. A beautiful woman would come in and lead the customer away. The commentary implied but did not explicitly state that these women were widows, fresh from the pen.

The guidebooks I'd read before my journey had described such places; the naive customer would be dosed with Ecstasine before the consummation of the act, and would go home happy, remembering fondly the sylphs of the Opal Eye.

It was true that the widows sometimes took visitors to their beds. As long as they retained their human shapes, the widows had the same sexual needs as any human woman. Still, I couldn't believe there was any organized commerce in the widows' favors, since they were almost by definition very wealthy.

I smiled at the optimistic credulity of my fellow humans.

Where would the sylphs go if—and this was perhaps a large assumption—they desired the companionship of their own kind—or that of humans other than their husbands? As the sylphs reached the zenith of their beauty, as their husbands neared death . . . might they not seek diversion, a place to wait, away from their husbands' deathbeds?

Probably they wouldn't frequent any place that tourists went. They had little to fear from human impertinence or even violence, of course—their alien musculature made them many times stronger than any human. But I remembered the almost secretive manner of the sylph I had met at the pen. Was she typical of her kind? I could imagine her taking considerable pains to avoid the possibility of some ill-mannered person thrusting a holocam into her face.

I called up a three-dimensional wireframe map of Crondiem's cafe district. "Mark the businesses listed on the hotel's database," I instructed the tank.

Most of the spaces at the bases of the old buildings lit up, filling with pale green glows, in the midst of which floated the place's name and business in tiny red letters.

Here and there were gaps, where spaces obviously existed, unlisted. I cross-connected to the city directory and used a light pointer to query these gaps. Most were small shops unconnected to the tourist industry. Some were residences. Three queries brought only a *Data Restricted* response, and I made a note of these addresses.

I took my coat from the wardrobe and shut the window. I left my easel behind, which I suppose was the first sign that my purposes had shifted, if only slightly.

This time I accepted the doorman's offer of a rickshaw, which was pulled by a small deep-chested man. He wore an orange raincoat, a shapeless black hat, and an air of impenetrable aplomb. I gave him the first of my addresses and he nodded wordlessly. We set off at a brisk trot, the rickshaw's padded wheels making a subdued clunking sound over the cobbles.

A curiously fragrant pale fog filled the dark streets, a fog called by the guidebooks "the breath of the Eye." It limited visibility to twenty or thirty meters and made the city seem even more mysterious. It lent a special warmth to the gleams of yellow light that escaped the tightly shuttered windows. Sounds came oddly through the fog: the music of a dozen worlds, a shout of laughter, a rattle of crockery. I sat back against the rickshaw's clammy cushions and tried to commit the sensations to memory.

The cafe district was higher on the mountainside, above the finer hotels and the widows' palaces. Here the façades of the buildings were less impressive. The black stone was patched with crumbling concrete and the blue awnings were often faded and tattered.

Each of the cafes and bars was identified by a name carved over the doorway and by a small circular window of stained glass, no more than twenty-five centimeters in diameter, set into the wall just beside the door. Some of the little windows were dark; I presumed these establishments were closed, perhaps for the season.

I became fascinated by the images presented in these windows. At a bar called Webfoot's, the window showed a little girl with pink ribbons in her white-blond hair. She wore an angelic expression and had canine teeth so long they seemed to dimple the flesh below her collarbones. At The Armored Heart, the window was divided by a narrow vertical strip of green glass, on which a man with outspread arms was superimposed. The man smiled sadly with the left half of his face; the other half was a grinning skull. Mae's Original Grogshop displayed a pensive woman fishing. The arc of her fishing rod followed the circumference of the window; at the bottom a wide-eyed man struggled to extract a huge emerald-cut gem from his mouth.

I stopped to look closely at that one, and marveled at the intricate workmanship. Within that small space were hundreds of pieces, some no more than glimmering splinters, the lead channels no thicker than a pencil line. I put my fingers lightly to the glass, and felt the vibration of an insistent music.

When I returned, the rickshaw man raised his eyebrow. "Go on," I said.

The first address turned out to be a substation of the Tourist Police. From the rickshaw, I peered in through the open door. A man in an odd three-peaked leather hat watched me impassively from behind a high desk. A green lamp threw his hard face into a strong pattern of light and shadow.

I gave the rickshaw man the next address on my list and felt a certain relief when we had passed around the nearest corner.

He took me to a dark doorless opening. Long tongues of soot licked up the façade of the building—apparently this establishment had recently suffered a serious fire. The rickshaw man looked at me without expression. I was sure he knew what I was seeking, and I thought it odd that he didn't offer to take me there, or at least to some place that simulated what I wanted.

But I gave him my third address and he nodded placidly.

We went deep into a warren of alleyways, where few lights showed and the fog seemed thicker. I might have been worried had the guidebooks not so emphatically declared every part of Crondiem safe, no matter the hour.

We stopped before a wide steel-strapped wooden door. No name showed above the lintel, but a circular window glowed dimly.

"Will you wait?" I asked.

The rickshaw man nodded.

I went up to the doorstep, bent to examine the window. It seemed at first a simple rhythmic abstraction in various densities of opalescent white glass. Then again it might have been a wave pattern, as seen from high above the surface of the Eye—or perhaps from far below. It was quite lovely, in a subdued way.

I rapped at the door, and it swung open immediately.

The doorman was a Crondiemer who took my coat without a word, then waved me down the vestibule toward a low-arched opening. The universal sounds of a quiet little bar drew me forward—the clink of glasses, the mutter of conversation, the racking coughs of smokers. I heard no music.

I felt a growing excitement. Even if I found no sylphs here, I had at least found a place unknown to the other tourists, and like most travelers I prize that sensation of selfish discovery.

I stepped into a low wide room, dense with narcotic smoke and the sickly-sweet smell of raw alcohol. It was quite dark except for a pattern of red glowstrips set into the floor, which cast up a wan light. I had to pause while my eyes adjusted.

A long bar crossed the far wall, but no one stood at it. The few patrons sat at tables around the walls. I looked eagerly, but none seemed to be sylphs; the shapes were for the most part lumpish, slumped wearily over their drinks.

My eyes gained sensitivity, and I suddenly realized that I stood in a room of dying men. I knew who the patrons were, then, and why the bar that served them preferred not to advertise. They all watched me, for the most part with remote curiosity—though some still seemed sufficiently vigorous to summon a glitter-eyed resentment.

I moved toward the bar anyway. Were this place prohibited to tourists, the doorman would have turned me away. The disease from which the husbands suffered was not contagious—or so I thought then.

The bartender was a huge man, naked to the waist, displaying the shoulder tattoos of a Retrantic enforcer. He regarded me with no discernible emotion; it was as if a machine awaited my order. "Abraxas brandy . . . do you have it?" I asked.

He nodded, and lifted a dusty bottle from beneath the bar.

I breathed in the bright fumes gratefully and sipped. The bartender watched me drink with that same unnerving lack of expression, and I turned away, intending to find a table in the darkest corner.

I saw, of course, that all the darkest tables were taken. What had I expected, here in this place of ugly decline?

One of the men lifted his glass to me and called in a surprisingly strong voice, "Come, visitor from afar. Join me for a moment."

I felt a flash of gratitude and sat down across the table. I could not see him clearly, though I tried, peering into his shadowed features with what I would later remember as an unmannerly curiosity. After a moment, he laughed without rancor and touched the wick of a pseudocandle at the table's center.

The small yellow flame revealed a face not too terribly ravaged, at least by the standards of the guidebooks, which had contained distressing images of terminal husbands. He was very gaunt, and his hair had fallen out in irregular patches, but he had no open sores, no eroding tissue. His eyes were clear, and when he smiled, he revealed a full set of teeth.

"So," he said. "Are you properly repulsed?"

From his expression I understood this to be a joking pleasantry, so I smiled back. "I've seen worse," I said.

"You're a hardened soul." He shook his head ruefully, still smiling. "My name is Rondello. Gie Rondello, formerly of Silverdollar. And you?"

"Millen Hender, presently of Parsivalle." I took another sip of my brandy and tried to contain the questions I wanted to ask.

"Parsivalle, eh? A pretty world. Farms in the valleys, sheep stations in the highlands, right? What takes you away from your peaceable kingdom . . . and brings you to this vale of sorrowful delights? An unhappy love affair, perhaps? Business? Pleasure?" Rondello spoke as if genuinely interested.

I shrugged. "My love affairs have always been reasonably happy. I'm a tourist, of sorts—though travel is also my business, in a way."

He sat up, his movements obviously giving him pain. "Intriguing, friend Hender—if a trifle obscure. 'Of sorts,' you say. 'In a way.' Can you not be more specific?"

There was a mocking quality to his tone, though he seemed unmalicious. Still, I answered a bit shortly. "I'm a painter," I said.

"Not, I assume, of houses?"

I had to laugh. "Only when they're particularly picturesque. No, I travel about, making paintings of those sights that strike my fancy. Then I go home and wait to see if the paintings sell. It's not a bad job, I suppose."

"It sounds fine," he said. "Are you famous? Should I have heard of you?"

"Probably not," I said, a little wistfully. No artist, however prominent, ever feels sufficiently appreciated, and I was then quite obscure.

"An honest man," Rondello said. "And did you come to the Eye to see the sylphs?"

"Among other things."

"Ah! Have you seen your first sylph yet?"

"Yes, I think so." In truth I was sure I had seen two of them.

"And what did you feel, when you saw her?"

I just shook my head; I had no words.

"Yes," he said, his voice much softer. "I felt the same, the first time. You know, I didn't come to Noctile to become a husband. Are you surprised? No, actually, I came to splice data cables, a stolid contract craftsman with a wife and three dear children. I had a personality profile that supposedly protected me from suicidal flights of fancy. I was here for only three weeks before I realized I had to have a sylph for my own." He took a drink and sighed. "How long have you been here?"

"Since this afternoon."

"And you found us so quickly?"

I was embarrassed. "Actually, I wasn't looking for you. I'd hoped to find the place where the sylphs go."

He laughed again, a throaty chuckle. "Hender, you're an optimistic explorer. No such place exists; if it did, the tourists would soon ferret it out—no offense intended. We husbands get to keep our privacy because no great interest attaches to us. After all, we're dying, we're ugly, and we're fools. Besides, why would the sylphs gather in a bar? They don't drink, except for Eye water, and human drugs don't affect them."

"Don't they want to see their friends?" I asked.

"Friends? What friends? Sylphs don't have friends, they don't understand the concept. Hender, just because they look like women, talk like women, walk like women . . . even smell a little like women . . . don't make the mistake of believing that they *are* women. That leads to madness, to the kind of pain that burns us up." In his intensity, he had half risen from his chair.

I found it very strange, to hear a sylph's husband warn me against madness. Something of that must have shown on my face, because Rondello sat back and his face relaxed a little.

"Yes, yes, of course you're right. I should speak, eh? But what, after all, do you know about the extent of our madness?" He made a gesture that took in the room full of dying men. "Would it surprise you to know that we in this place have all lived much longer than is common for husbands? I myself have lived six years with my lovely one, and I expect to linger for several more before she kills me completely dead."

This was intriguing information. According to the guidebooks, the average husband expires only fourteen months after the day he accepts the sylph's devotion.

"You wonder how?" Rondello asked, still reading my face. "I'll tell you. We here are all cowards. We taste, but do not gorge, on our darlings. My own Lireeta, for example, is only a little more beautiful than the most beautiful human woman in the universe. Compared to the ripest of the sylphs—those whose husbands have lived in their embrace continuously, whose husbands are about to die—Lireeta is a poor plain little thing. Hah!" He took a deep drink and made a wry face.

I was fascinated. Gie Rondello must be a man of superhuman restraint, to so ration his appetite for beauty. In the many holodramas set in cities beside the Opal Eye, the man who takes a sylph embarks on an ever-accelerating headlong rush to destruction. In these plays the sylph daily grows more beautiful, more irresistible, the husband weaker and more desperate to be consumed—and in fact this is no dramatic exaggeration, this is exactly the usual course of events, according to the xenobiologists quoted in the guidebooks.

"How . . . ?" I began.

"How? We are cowards here, did I not say so already?

Phlegmatic souls, one and all, who can look on inhuman beauty and be . . . not too discontent that it is not more. We stay away from our homes, hiding in places like this—or keep separate apartments, if we're wealthy. We limit the times we find ecstasy with our darlings; I myself dare go to Lireeta's bed but once a week. At other times . . . we must be content with the memory of what love can be." He shrugged.

"I didn't know that was possible," I said.

"Oh yes, friend Hender, many things exist that the guidebooks know not! In fact, I surmise that a man with a sufficiently implacable will . . . such a man could taste the delights of a sylph and then, before death has gained too strong a grip on him, draw back, sever the connection, allow the sylph to return to her natural state in the Eye." He finished his drink and signaled the barman for another.

"At one time," Rondello went on, "I thought myself such a man. Vanity, vanity. I wonder how many other fools have begun with similar delusions."

A long silence ensued. Rondello was correct. Never are the guidebooks complete, for which we must be grateful.

Finally he spoke again. "There may be another factor in our longevity, though I wish I didn't suspect it. I think we here are all men with little natural beauty in our souls, so little that when the sylphs draw it forth and make it manifest, we can resist it for a while. Does that make sense? No, no, don't answer. I really don't want to know what you think about it."

He looked at me with an expression so remotely sorrowful, so alien, that I had to repress a shiver.

He spoke one more time. "You yourself must be very careful. An artist, a worshipper of beauty . . . you would be tinder to her flame, gone in a moment. Be very careful." He drew a long shuddering breath. "Well, you are a clever tourist, you've found something to write home about. Now it's time for you to go." He reached out and snuffed the pseudocandle, and I could no longer see his expression.

I went.

• • •

In the morning my head seemed thick with half-dreamed visions, and I had breakfast sent up to my room.

Over sweet pastry and Jaworld coffee, I leafed idly through my guidebooks, seeking a purpose for the day, a focus for my curiosity.

One book fell open on the carefully composed black and white image of a Meeting Beach, where men wait for the sylphs to emerge from the Eye.

I read: *Every city along the shores of the Eye has its own Meeting Beach, and many of these incorporate small masterpieces of early Settler architecture, preserved from the days when the original human colonists of Noctile still attempted to explain the strange phenomena of the Eye in religious terms.*

I closed the book and dressed for an expedition to the beach.

I chose to walk; my travels had recently given me little opportunity for exercise. I find that without that stimulation my eye grows a little cloudy, my hand a little unsteady. The beach was only three kilometers from the hotel and the drizzle had ceased for the moment.

When I stepped from the Skelpin's portico, the odd blue-green sky of Noctile showed in fleeting patches through a gray swirl of low cloud. The air was almost warm and the breeze a faint caress.

Crondiem lay in a sloping declivity between two great cliffs. To the north, the city ended abruptly against a vertical face that plunged two thousand meters into the Eye. But to the south, a shingle beach ran along the base of the cliff for a kilometer.

At the city's south portal, the colonists had erected an impressive gate. The black basalt pillars were five meters tall and supported a massive lintel stone, carved in the shape of a reclining naked woman. She smiled gently, holding her chin in her right hand, and in her left hand, which rested on the sweet curve of her hip, she held a small sickle.

The carving was quite magnificent, powerful and restrained. Clearly the folk of Crondiem had once been sensitive to beauty. I stopped for a few minutes, to make a quick sketch. The gate would make a fine narrative backdrop for a painting of a sylph—though perhaps none of them passed this way after the day they came from the Eye.

Beyond the gate a rough path led down to the beach, and I followed it.

A light wind fell down the heights and blew out over the Eye, flattening the surf into lapping wavelets. I walked along the beach, occasionally slipping in the coarse gravel. The Eye's fragrance seemed more intense here than in the city, and the sun shone down, warm enough to make me take off my sweater.

The men waited in a row of stone huts, small open-fronted buildings with high-peaked roofs. The guidebooks called them "shrines," and reported that in the early days, men had waited in them as a religious duty. Then the sylphs appeared more rarely, and their choice was interpreted as an oracle.

There were six shrines, each dedicated to a different Eye-dwelling creature: the milkfish, the great vindid eel, the frigate skimmer, the four-winged ray, the red pangoloid, the moonbug. The people of Crondiem still classified their clans by these totems, but the original religious impulse had long since evaporated.

The totems' carved likenesses still adorned the front gables of the shrines, even though now the men who sat within came from the faraway worlds of the human universe, and for reasons somewhat different from those that had moved the early settlers.

I strolled slowly along the beach in front of the shrines, staring, with the bright innocence of the casual tourist, at the three seekers currently in residence. Presently they waited in relaxed poses; high tide was still a half hour away. One had a folding lawn chair and an ice chest, the other two sat crosslegged on mats.

I decided to approach the best-equipped seeker, who sat inside the shrine dedicated to the vindid eel. He sipped from a canister of lager.

"Hello," I said, walking toward him, trying to keep my balance on the black pebbles.

He waved genially and I was encouraged to step under the overhang of his shrine.

At close range he seemed not to present the fevered aspect one might expect of a man who had chosen to die for love. He had an open florid face, a chunky broad-shouldered body, and blunt calloused hands. He wore a faded shipsuit and turquoise-studded silver bracelets. He had an air of phlegmatic competence. I took him for an engineer or a mechanic.

"Hello," I said again. "My name is Hender. I'm a painter, here to record the sights of Crondiem. May I speak with you?"

"Why not?" he answered, smiling. "So long as our conversation ends before the tide's high." He pointed to an obelisk set into the shingle, marked with rings to show the stages of the tide; twenty centimeters of white weed and blood-red barnacles still showed above the Eye's bright surface.

"Thank you," I said, but then I didn't quite know how to go on. I set my easel aside and sat on the shrine's front steps, wondering what I might ask this friendly madman.

"Well," he said. "I can introduce myself. I'm Kirm Dellant, formerly of Bron City on Tregaskis. Do you know it?"

Tregaskis is a mining world, harsh and unlovely, and Bron City its industrial capital. I nodded.

"So? Then, have a beer with me, in remembrance of that armpit of the pangalac worlds, which I will have the great privilege of never setting eyes on again." He fished a canister from his ice chest and handed it to me.

It was only moderately cool; apparently he had run

out of ice some time before. But I was thirsty from my exercise and I drank it gratefully.

Before I'd formulated a graceful way to present my curiosity, he spoke again. "I suppose you wonder what I'm doing here."

"Yes I do, in fact."

He looked at me sharply. "Usually the tourists don't come here; they don't want to see the sylphs as they really are. You're sure you're not here to claim a sylph yourself?"

"Oh no," I assured him. I must have looked quite shocked at his suggestion, because he laughed and relaxed.

"Good, good," he said. "Some who come to claim a sylph think there is some technique to it, something that can be learned. A way to make her choose you over the others. There's no such trick. You just have to wait, as patiently as you can." He patted his ice chest and winked.

"Why *are* you here?" I asked.

He finished his beer and flipped the empty canister over his shoulder to join a growing heap at the back of the shrine. Then he put his hands on his knees and leaned forward, regarding me with less geniality. "Do you find it so hard to believe . . . that a man like me might want to be loved by a beautiful woman?"

I shook my head, remembering what the dying husband had said, that a sylph never became a woman, despite appearances. "No. But the price . . . how can it be worth it?"

He shrugged and opened another beer. "I guess everyone who comes here has a different reason. I'll tell you mine, if you like." He glanced out at the tide obelisk. "In as few words as possible."

"Please," I said.

"All right. How old do you think I am? No need to answer; I'm almost eight hundred standard years old. That's a long life, isn't it?" He sighed. "In that time I've fixed a lot of broke-down mining machinery, a whole lot. I've drunk enough beer to float a starcruiser. I've been married fourteen times, most of them good marriages, and I have more children, grandchildren—great-great-great, whatever—than I can count. In all that time I never had a hobby for more than a week or two. Never wanted to travel. A man of limited imagination, you might call me.

"So when you've done everything that's in you to do, what do you do next? Sneak into a euthanasia parlor, when none of your doting descendants are looking? Not if you're me, you don't. Seems like a disrespectful way to kiss off a life as lucky as mine's been."

He chuckled and gestured out toward the Eye. "No, you try to think of something else, somewhere to go where no one will think to look for you, where finally you can do something completely different from the things you've spent your life doing. This *is* completely different, wouldn't you say?"

"I suppose so," I said.

"Of course it is!" he said fiercely. "Besides, have you *seen* any of those women?" He shook his head in wonderment. "Wouldn't *you* be willing to fuck a sea slug to get next to one of those women . . . I mean, if you didn't have to die for it, too?"

I took this for a rhetorical question and didn't answer. He gave me a glance of mild annoyance and didn't speak again for a while.

Finally he said, "So I saved up until I had the price of a ticket—it's not bad, because you only have to get it one-way." He chuckled and swigged at his beer. "And here I am."

Another question occurred to me, a rather impolite one. The guidebooks tended to focus on the more glamorous lives and marketably tragic declines of the wealthiest seekers, those who could buy palaces and grails for their widows. "How will you support yourself, after you're chosen? Have you saved up enough to live on?"

"No," he said, without apparent embarrassment. "The

widows provide rooms in their palaces, and food, for those who can't pay for their own keep. Why not? They can afford it."

I thought about that, and tried to imagine what went on in those rooms. He seemed to guess what I was thinking, and went on: "Yes, I won't live long. But what a way to go, eh? Locked up with the most beautiful woman in the universe. And they say the sylphs from the little rooms are the most beautiful of all—that on the day I die and she goes back to the Eye, even the Crondiemers will weep to see her pass.

"No grail for her, of course, but that's a custom I don't understand," he went on. "When you're dead, you're dead; what do you care if your sylph turns back into a sea slug?"

"I don't know," I said. "In fact, there's a lot here I don't understand." But I suddenly *did* understand the husbands' impulse to preserve the beauty they had created. What if I knew that all my paintings would turn to ash on the day I died? What wouldn't I do to preserve my life's work?

"Well," Kirm Dellant said briskly. "I can't chat any more. The tide is nearly in, so you'll have to go."

I got up. "Good luck," I said, rather uncertainly.

He nodded affably, but all his attention was on the beach, and on the pearly swells of the Opal Eye.

I went away, back toward the path to Crondiem. As I drew abreast of the last shrine, the one dedicated to the moonbug, I obeyed an impulse and stepped inside.

This was the most derelict of the shrines, and had collected a substantial windrow of rubbish. I stood at the front of the shrine and tried to imagine how it might feel to wait here for a creature who would take my life.

I looked out at the Eye and saw the sylph's alien head break the surface.

In a sort of shocked fascination I watched it emerge onto the beach, a creature a bit like a reptilian seal. Its skin was hard and white and showed the glitter of myriad tiny scales. It had two large violet eyes and an underslung maw. A fleshy dorsal fin began about halfway down its sacklike body, then divided at the point where its rear appendages joined the body. Bony pectoral fins pulled it over the pebbles, toward me, in a flopping gait that was unexpectedly swift.

Toward me? I don't know what I'd been thinking, when I'd stopped in the shrine. That the creature would somehow know that I was only a spectator, content to observe from a safe distance? I glanced at the other shrines, and saw angry faces turned toward me.

I ran away up the beach as fast as my legs could carry me. When I turned for one last look, the sylph was making for the shrine occupied by Kirm Dellant.

I felt oddly pleased that the mechanic was getting what he wanted, though I couldn't understand how he could do what he was doing.

According to the guidebooks, he would spend the coming night with his sylph, and in the morning it would walk to the city with him, on new legs.

When I returned to the lobby of the Skelpin, the deskwoman held up something and called to me. "Sir? A message left for you."

She handed me the wafer. "Who's it from?" I asked, surprised. Who knew I was in Crondiem?

She shrugged. "A messenger left it, sir, without explanation."

I went up to my room, still wondering, but when I got there I didn't immediately play the wafer. I lay on my bed, thinking about the seekers on the beach. Was the whole phenomenon only a new twist in that urge to death that some humans had always carried in their hearts? That seemed too easy an explanation, somehow.

After a while, I set up my easel.

I thought about what I had seen on the beach. I tried a quick study of the shrines, with their impatient inhabitants hunkered back out of the light like so many lurking predators. I made their eyes glitter and their teeth flash, and I painted the scene as if it were a day so overcast that all the color had seeped from the world, leaving only grays and black and cold umbers.

I didn't like the result much, but I cycled it into memory for future revision.

I attempted a view of the tide obelisk, striving at first for an entirely literal depiction. But as I worked, the surface of the Eye took on an unnatural curvature and resilience, as though it were the breast of a vast woman, and the obelisk, with its ring of blood-red barnacles, seemed a black spike driven into that perfect skin.

I discarded the image, a bit appalled at what had risen from the bottom of my mind.

Finally, I attempted an image of the sylph pulling itself from the sea, but this was even less satisfactory. I could not seem to make the sylph look like anything more than an ugly alien animal. So I reduced the sylph to a small element in the composition, framed by the arms of a man reaching out in supplication. This image I also kept for further work, but I had exhausted the creative impulse and I put away my easel.

I activated the holotank, at first intending to play my message, but then I ran through the menu until I reached an entry called SPECULATIONS. I cued it and sat back against the headboard.

The tank ran with random color and then cleared, to show the face and upper body of a field xenobiologist named Crandl. He had owlish eyes and a thin beard. He wore faded overalls and a thick coat of green sun ointment on his nose. He spoke earnestly from the cockpit of an armored skiff. "We don't yet have any reasonably defensible hypotheses to explain the . . . ah . . . peculiar interactions between human males and the so-called 'sylph.' The situation is complex in the extreme, further complicated by the fact that none of the humans involved has ever been willing to submit the course of their personal interactions to scientific scrutiny.

"However, if I may speculate . . . The sylph would appear to be an extreme example of a parasitic mimetic lifeform, a not too uncommon adaptation. One theoretical difficulty, in this case, is that during the evolutionary process which culminated in the sylph, humans could not have been present. Additionally, the sylph in its 'natural' form does not appear to possess sapience, whereas in its adapted form it appears to be at least as intelligent as a human being—though the sylphs have always resisted efforts to test their intelligence.

"The terminal deterioration of the sylph's so-called husband is another puzzling matter. During the sexual activities which appear to play an essential part in the sylph's transformation, cilia extend from special pores in the sylph's skin and penetrate the body of the human, to an unknown purpose. Nutrition does not seem to be involved, since the proteins of sylph and human are not only incompatible, but highly toxic, one to another."

Crandl shook his head. "We just don't know. . . ."

I cued the next item, a symposium of religious leaders.

A sleekly attractive woman, the Reverend Angeena Demirelle of the United Cosmic Congregationalists, spoke first. "It's clear that the events on Noctile are more than a metaphor, more than a glorious, miraculous demonstration of the great foundation of our belief: that love conquers all—even the fear of death!

"No, we feel sure that it is also a cosmic mechanism for the storage of love, that the Opal Eye is in simple truth no less than the beating heart of the universe, and that one day, when we have learned to love each other as the husbands love their sylphs, this great storage cell of loving energy will burst forth and flood the Universe with its warmth!" She sat back, apparently exhausted by her fervor, eyes shining.

The camera panned to the next participant, a slender man with a long sardonic face. The tagline identified him as Deacon Iramus Geater, of the Church of Man Militant.

He sniffed and made a shooing gesture, as if waving away a bad smell. "Clearly you are overwrought, Reverend Demirelle. Even more clearly, the end results of the perversions practiced on Noctile are a warning by the Universal Presence against the unevolved, unsanitary, and morally destructive practice of coupling with *women*." The deacon managed to invest that last word with a quality of shuddery horror.

He went on in more dispassionate tones. "Did Noctile not exist, it would have been necessary for us to invent it, as an object lesson for those to whom simple reason has no appeal."

An old man with a wry smile leaned forward into the camera's field. "Are you making a public admission, Iramus? Are the sylphs merely a theological weapon? If so, why did you confine them to the Eye? Why not seed them throughout the oceans of the pangalac worlds?" The tagline identified the old man as Roger Lakhoson, a representative of the Society for the Continuing Evolution of Humankind. The camera dropped and showed the old man's lower body, which had been replaced by a cluster of leathery tentacles, each clothed in a tube of orange silk.

The old man sat back and steepled his fingers. "Consider this paradox: How can a member of an alien species be more beautiful, more seductive, to a human man than any human woman? We hold that this could not be the case, were humankind evolved to its full potential. We must continue to experiment, to drive the engine of evolution—as events on Noctile clearly demonstrate."

I reached for the remote control, to shut this babble off, but then the camera shifted to the next person on the panel, one Nelles Asiuhn, identified as a logician associated with the Church of Secular Rationality, incorporated on Dilvermoon. She was a lean woman with charcoal-black skin and short ruby-red hair cut so that ridges of it spiraled out from her ears and merged in a crest atop her long skull. Her face was strongly chiseled and she wore a glittering blue topaz in one nostril. I wanted instantly to paint her portrait.

So I listened as she began to speak. "We have examined a great number of speculations on the so-called sylphs of the Opal Eye. The only one that makes any sense to us is this: As the Eye itself is an artifact, so too are the lifeforms within the Eye. But for what purpose were these creatures designed?"

She paused as if gathering her thoughts, but I had the impression that the pause was actually a skillful oratorical device, that she had spoken these words so many times that she could give her attention wholly to the style in which she spoke them.

She went on, in a lower and darker voice. "We believe the sylphs exist to store the memories and emotional resonances of the men they seduce. We think they were created by some vanished or currently absent race to appeal to just the sort of race that we humans are: sentimental, vulnerable to beauty, vulnerable to a carefully crafted illusion of love—a species for which love can transcend the fear of death.

"Apparently the population of sylphs in the Eye is stable; no juvenile specimens have ever been found, no evidence of breeding. The same sylphs come from the Eye over and over again, learning more and more, returning to the Eye to shed their human forms and recuperate. And indeed the sylphs of today are more beautiful than they were in the early days, more sophisticated in their simulation of humanity.

"We see no malice in this mechanism," she said. "The husbands must die that the sylphs may reenter the cycle and eventually find another source of memory— but the husbands are volunteers. We feel that humanity as a whole has nothing to fear from the engineers of the Eye. Therefore, we believe that the use of Transpirene is a counterproductive practice. It should be outlawed, the grails destroyed, and the so-called 'widows' returned to the Eye, there to continue their designed function."

She stared directly at the camera. "It is inherently dangerous for monkeys to tamper with machinery they do not understand."

At the bottom of the tank was a definition-of-terms area, and I selected TRANSPIRENE. The data appeared in a simulated flatscreen on the near side of the tank. TRANSPIRENE: *A human recreational drug originally developed to allow human divers to breath water. Extremely expensive, since a specific and unique formulation must be designed for every single user. It was accidentally discovered that the drug, if tailored to the DNA of a sylph's husband, would—if taken by the sylph every day starting soon after the husband's death—arrest indefinitely the devolution of the sylph into its original form.*

I remembered the grails floating in the twilight milk of the Eye, and I selected GRAIL.

GRAIL: *A common term for the mechanisms which supply the so-called 'widows' of the Opal Eye with their daily requirement of Transpirene. Essentially a solar-powered synthesizer designed to float in the fluid of the Eye, each grail is an absurdly expensive and irreplaceable device, its programming tailored to the sylph it serves. Should a grail accidentally be destroyed or rendered inoperable, that sylph will swiftly return to its original form.*

I shut down the tank.

For a while I just lay there on the bed, enjoying the uncomplicated silence and the soft air that came in through my open window. I refused to think about the musings of my fellow humans. I was sure that there was some deeper, wordless significance to the Eye, and I resolved to cling to this romantic notion, even if this significance never became any clearer to me.

Finally I inserted the message wafer in the bedside reader. The little flatscreen showed a static image against a pale violet mist—a garland made from the elegant white pseudo-blossoms of a plant that floats free on the Opal Eye's surface.

A voice I remembered said softly, "Citizen Hender, I

am the person to whom you spoke yesterday—at twilight, by the widow's pen. You were kind enough to show me your work, and I mentioned our meeting to my husband. He would like to discuss the possibility of a commission. If you think you might be interested, please come to our home this evening, after you've dined."

The message ended. An elegant fluid signature appeared in the center of the garland: Madelen d'Osimry— and then an address.

Madelen lived on the first street above the seawall, where the finest palaces were.

Certainly I was excited by this invitation. However, the image of the sylph as it emerged from the Eye was still too fresh in my memory—and the recollection dampened my enthusiasm, just a little.

I fell asleep.

I finally woke at twilight, chilled by the wind that blew in through my window. I got up to close it, still groggy, trying to remember a dream.

The red-haired sylph I had seen from the bus had been trying to serve me a dish of curried milkfish, which I had refused, saying, "No, no, I'd like to try them, but they'd poison me. Really."

She was naked; she had discarded her vermilion breastband. Her loveliness was obscured only by the dish of milkfish, which she held toward me enticingly.

My loins still ached. There was more, but the details fled as I shook off the grogginess. It was a dream so obvious and banal in its meaning as to be almost an embarrassment to the dreamer.

I went down to supper, but I dined without noticing what I ate, so intrigued was I by the prospect of meeting a sylph in a social setting—such a thing was unusual. The typical husband felt no impulse to share the beauty of his sylph with anyone else.

I thought of Gie Rondello and his cronies. He had assured me that sylphs have no friends. I wondered if he were instead describing himself and the other husbands.

On my return to my room, I bathed and then dressed with unusual care. My old teacher, Anabade the Younger, once told me: "All true artists are vain. Artists who claim not to care about their appearance are not to be trusted. They probably lie about other things too."

At two hours after sunset, I presented myself at the address Madelen d'Osimry had given me—a narrow bronze gate in a tall basalt wall. A blue lamp illuminated the street number, and a flowery fragrance drifted over the wall.

Before I could press the buzzer, a soft voice came from the speaker. "Good evening, Citizen Hender. The servant will bring you to us."

The gate swung open to reveal an unusually plain Crondiem woman. She inspected me without expression. "This way, sir."

I followed her along a mossy brick path, through a garden which had once been beautiful. It had now an air of long neglect, the beds overgrown and weedy. The thorniest plants seemed to have retained the most vigor; a stiletto vine tore the sleeve of my jacket as we climbed up to a terrace.

I muttered something peevish, and the servant turned to give me a look of malicious amusement. "Take care, sir," she said, with relish. I wondered what she thought of me—no doubt the women of Crondiem had an unflattering opinion of men, especially the outworld men who came here to die. Did she take me for one of these? I shook my head uneasily.

At the top of the wide terrace steps, I turned and looked back. The view out over the pale surface of the Eye was magnificent—in the darkness the Eye was like a great snowy plain, and the lights of other cities twinkled along the black jagged band of the ringwall.

I turned back to the palace. Behind the line of glass doors that fronted the terrace, someone waited, silhouetted against the interior glow. I could not see her clearly, through the beveled glass of the doors, but there was an unmistakable grace in her posture.

I stood there for a moment, unmoving, afraid. "Come, sir," the Crondiemer said. "The mistress waits."

Finally I moved forward, but I was full of a mixture of anticipation and, strangely, regret . . . as though I were passing down a road in my life that I would never be able to walk again.

The servant held the door for me and I passed within.

Then I saw Madelen clearly for the first time.

There are some things that defy description, and yet make so strong an impression on us that we feel compelled to describe them, over and over—not only to others, but even to ourselves. Soldiers try to describe the hallucinatory sensations of war. Mothers try to describe the emotion of putting a newborn baby to the breast. Lovers try to describe the loss of their beloved ones. Saints try to describe the touch of their particular deities.

I can try to describe Madelen . . . though I am certain that even my fiercely held memory does not return her image adequately to me.

Her skin was a violet so pale it was almost white. Her hair was a torrent of translucent amethyst, cascading in shining ripples almost to her waist. Her eyes were huge and magenta, her lips a dark dark crimson. At that moment, her coloring seemed to me the most beautiful conceivable . . . and every other woman in the universe a muddy lump by comparison.

Broad cheekbones, upswept brows, a narrow chin below a wide mouth—these were details in a totality of such daunting loveliness that I had to look down.

She wore a simple white sleeveless dress, thigh-length, with a high silver brocade collar—but no jewelry. She wore a purple-pink nightvine blossom and a sprig of dusty-rose alyssum, pinned to a gather of fabric at her right hip. Any other adornment would have detracted from her perfection. Her dress was slit to

the waist on the left side, revealing her smoothly muscled thigh.

Her body seemed entirely human in its attributes, a
narrow taut waist, hips a little wider than was currently
fashionable, small round breasts, wide shoulders, graceful arms, a long elegant neck. Such a bloodless inven-
tory can give no useful idea of the effect she had on
me.

It occurred to me that her husband must be very
near death.

She wore the same perfume I had noticed by the pen,
and I wondered if it were a product of the perfumer's art,
or simply the scent of her body.

In the pangalac worlds, where anyone with a little
money can be handsome, one grows inured to ordinary
beauty. Hers was so extraordinary that when she said,
"Hello, Citizen Hender," my reply was a wordless gasp.

But I recovered somewhat, and said, "Pardon me; I
think I have a bit of a cold."

She accepted this excuse without a trace of mockery.
"I'm sorry . . . our climate isn't very pleasant, this time of
year. You should visit our city in the spring; it's much
nicer." She smiled, a bit wistfully.

This seemed such an incongruously human observation
that I could think of no reply, so I simply nodded.

"Well," she said, still smiling, "Byron would like to
meet you right away." She turned away and I understood
that I was to follow.

She walked toward a bright hallway. Her grace in the
clinging dress was even more mesmerizing than it had been
at the widow's pen, and I stumbled over the edge of a rug,
making something of a clatter while regaining my balance.
She didn't look back.

Of our passage through the palace, I can remember
nothing. Ordinarily I'd have been vastly interested in the
details of furnishings, decor, art objects—I've always been
fascinated by the very rich and their peculiar vulgarities.

I might as well have been following her through a featureless white tunnel; all I could see was Madelen.

But gradually other impressions seeped in, grew stronger. There was a stink: harsh chemicals and sickness. The lights dimmed. Madelen moved more slowly and her graceful stride developed an odd hesitancy.

Finally she stopped and so did I—after moving up to her side, desperate for a glimpse of her profile. She gave me a swift ambiguous glance, and then spoke. "Citizen Hender, my husband, Byron Osimry of Barramatta."

As I reluctantly looked away from her, I felt a flush of embarrassment, followed by a small shock of revulsion.

There wasn't much left of Byron Osimry. His remnants lay on a narrow life support table, invaded by tubes and sensor-wires, covered by a glossy black plastic sheet. It was as if a skeleton lay there, but a skeleton of some soft substance, collapsing. His face was concealed behind a skin-mask, and I wondered if the clever well-formed features on the mask had been Osimry's, before his decline. His eyes showed through the mask, greasy black bulges somehow more dreadful than everything else. I imagined how he must look under the sheet, a puddle of decaying flesh, the crumbling bones poking up through the rot.

I had a brief horrific vision: Madelen's loveliness pressed passionately against this living cadaver. I thrust the image from me instantly, before I could gag or shudder or otherwise reveal my reaction.

His body and head remained motionless while he spoke in an artificially generated voice. "Citizen Hender! Welcome to our home." He sounded incongruously vigorous.

I managed to nod politely and say: "Thank you, Citizen Osimry."

An awkward silence ensued, during which I fought the urge to look at Madelen, though I was conscious of almost nothing but her warm presence beside me.

"Well," Osimry finally said. "Madelen tells me you are an artist of ability. She spoke quite enthusiastically of the sketch you showed her. Of the widow's pen, wasn't it?"

"Did she?" I meant it to be a noncommittal pleasantry; it came out with a tincture of amazed delight.

"Yes, she did," he said, somewhat dryly. "How did you put it, dear? That Citizen Hender's painting caught 'something of the desolation and sterility,' I think you said."

There was some strong undercurrent here, some intractable emotional struggle that I didn't understand at all. I glanced at Madelen and her face was oddly taut—though the expression took nothing away from her beauty.

I was surprised that Osimry's dying body could hold such willful passion, but its existence made me wary. "Ah," I said stupidly. "Well, a preliminary sketch, you know."

"I see," said Osimry. "Did you bring a portfolio? May I see it?"

"Of course," I said, and turned to setting up my easel. "Will this be all right?" I asked, meaning the easel's location.

"That's fine. I've arranged matters so that my vision will be the last to go. For obvious reasons." His terrible wet eyes rolled toward Madelen.

I set the sheet of multimem in place, and activated it.

I gestured at the image. "A scene painted during my visit to Snow. You know of the ephemerals who once lived there? This was one of their portrait halls—now ruined, of course." The multimem showed a corridor drifted with snow. Along its mildewed walls a few tattered paintings hung askew, the whole scene framed by a sagging doorway. I was proud of the piece; through luck or unconscious skill the various angles formed a dark vortex, trembling on the edge of chaos.

Osimry said nothing. I went to the next image. "This is a court portrait of the Linean high executioner on the day prior to his retirement." It had been an unusual commission, but again I was pleased with the result. I'd managed to give the blue toadlike alien an almost human quality of dignified expectant sorrow—though I've never been entirely sure that was the appropriate effect. Aliens are alien.

"Fine work," said Osimry. "But have you no examples from our own little city?"

"Well," I said. "I've only been here a short time, and all I've got are rough sketches, really. I'm not proud of them."

"Nonsense, Hender," he said. "I'm sure they're wonderful—but I'll keep in mind that they're not finished work. Show us." There was an edge to the artificial voice, as if he would not remain so polite, were I so foolish as to thwart him.

I felt a sudden quiver of apprehension. It's always dangerous to deal with the very rich; they often refuse to recognize the limits that lesser folk must observe. Perhaps I had been careless to come here.

"If you like," I said finally. "Though as I said, I have only a few things." I removed the multimem that held my standard portfolio and replaced it with the sketchpad.

I showed the image of the carved gate above the Meeting Beach.

"Ah," he said. "So long ago, it seems now, that I walked beneath her. And yet, a very short time, by the count of the days. Another picture!"

I touched the multimem and recalled the sketch of the widow's pen.

He examined this for several long moments. Finally he said: "An expressive work, but I don't see the melancholy that Madelen described. It seems a rather peaceful image, to me."

Again I felt that undercurrent of conflict, but this time I didn't dare look at Madelen.

I brought up the sketch of the naked red-haired sylph.

He stared without reaction for a moment, then said: "A sylph?"

"I believe so," I said, a little stung by his doubtful tone.

"Some men are so small in spirit that they need the envy of others. So they send their darlings out into the streets." His voice fell low. "And yet, it's an understandable urge . . . if a crudely satisfied one, in this case. Tell me, Hender, do you like a challenge? Do you think you could succeed where so many others have failed? To make an image of a sylph that would convey her more-than-human loveliness?"

"The thought has crossed my mind," I said cautiously.

"Good! Show us more."

As soon as I displayed the sketch of the emerging sylph, as seen through the entreating arms of a seeker, Osimry's body quivered. I was astonished; I would have thought such movement impossible, in his decayed condition.

"Turn it off," he grated. "Turn it off!"

I shut down the multimem instantly. "I'm sorry," I said. "I meant no offense."

Osimry lay silent, his dreadful eyes fixed on me. So much silence passed that I wondered if he had died, and I was about to say something foolhardy when he finally spoke again.

"No," he said. "You did no more than I asked. But what you showed me was a true lie. Or a lying truth, if you prefer. Look at Madelen and tell me that she is only that *thing* you painted. Look!"

So I looked. She returned my gaze with a certain coolness, but no self-consciousness. Or resentment.

"I see your point," I said—but I wondered why we were speaking of her as if she were not here. Or as if she were some lovely inanimate object.

"Good. Good. I like your work, Hender, and besides, I'll be dead in a day or two, and how likely is it that another artist of any reputation will happen along before I turn into maggot meat?"

I was still watching Madelen, and I saw a sadness come into her face. Her mouth trembled and quirked down at one corner. I reluctantly returned my attention to Osimry.

I felt the necessity of saying something civilized, though in fact Osimry seemed dead already to me, a speaking corpse. But before I could frame any sympathetic remark, he went on.

"So. My commission is for a portrait of my darling Madelen, done to the best of your ability. Come again tomorrow night, at the same time, and begin." He seemed to regard the bargain as sealed, and I wouldn't have dared contradict him, even if I hadn't wanted so desperately to paint her.

"If I die before you're finished, I must trust you to complete the work." He paused, and those eyes showed a dull gleam. "Can I trust you?"

"I will finish the portrait, to the best of my ability," I said.

In some unseen way, he signaled the Crondiem servant, who appeared at my side, hands folded. Osimry spoke once more. "The serving woman will transfer a fee to your account; if it's not generous enough, speak up and we'll bargain. For now, goodbye. My beloved and I must make what use we can of these last hours." The eyes swiveled toward Madelen, and seemed to touch her with a dreadful expectation.

"Goodbye," she said, without turning to me.

"All right. Goodbye," I said, stomach churning with revulsion and thwarted lust. "Goodbye."

I followed the servant out, and somehow managed not to look back.

I felt no urge to return to my little room alone, so I hailed a rickshaw and went to Cold Blood, the club that claimed sylphs among its clientele.

There I drank Abraxas brandy and smoked green-gold Jaworld hashish until the universe took on a pleasantly casual quality.

I saw no sylphs, but after more smoke and more drink, the lack began to seem insignificant.

Presently a friendly young woman introduced herself and I invited her to sit with me. She was pretty and displayed a wry wit; I liked her. She told me she was from Amphora, a garden world, and that she and several of her demi-husbands had come to Noctile on a packaged tour.

Her demi-husbands had all gone off to the bordellos, hoping to bed a sylph, she explained. She was, she went on, quite a bit smarter than her men, much too smart in fact, to believe that the sylphs could be so easily bought. So she had stayed behind, to look for more realistic pleasures.

She told me all this with a certain unmistakable intensity, and her hand slipped gently up my thigh.

She had chosen wisely; I was bursting with frustrated sexual energy. When we got out of the elevator at my floor, I towed her down the hall toward my room, practically running.

Her enthusiasm seemed nearly equal to mine, however, and the night passed pleasantly. I don't remember a lot about it, except that she had tiny delicate fish tattooed on each muscular dimpled buttock. When she flexed them, the fish appeared to swim. "Fertility icons," she told me.

In the morning, she left without waking me.

It was—or should have been—an altogether satisfactory vacation liaison: intense, brief, and tidy. Still I felt a gnawing discontent, which made me angry with myself.

A long day lay ahead of me, and all I wanted was for the night to come as swiftly as possible. I might have slept it away; I was tired enough. But a strange energy still charged me, and I didn't think I could go back to bed.

I went down and had a light breakfast. Afterward I wandered the lobby, examining a dozen advertising holotanks ranged along the walls.

I stopped before one holotank to look at a woman who was almost beautiful enough to be a sylph. Perhaps she *was* a sylph—no recording medium was able to convey the intensity of a sylph's beauty, as numerous documentary makers had discovered to their despair and financial ruin. In any case, she was enthusiastically touting a pleasure cruise on the Eye. "Board the armored sailing catamaran *Flying Milkfish*, at the Old City Quay. Off-season fares now in effect. Sailings at 1000 and 1400 hours. Night cruises at 2500; sail under the Firefly Moon with someone you love, or someone you'd like to love."

The tank displayed a low-angle slow-motion visual: the Eye's waters peeling back in strangely viscid waves from the lean bows of the boat, as if it sailed through sweet condensed milk.

The woman's image returned, smiling brightly. "See the Opal Eye's weird lifeforms in their native habitat. See rays, pangoloids, moonbugs. Occasionally a vindid eel comes to the surface, or you may even be lucky enough to see a molting sylph."

A great ray leaped from the Eye, its white wings brilliant in a sunbeam. It fell with a thunderous crash, raising a welter of opalescent foam.

The woman spoke on: "All safety equipment provided. Snacks available. The opportunity of a lifetime—don't miss it."

"All right," I said. "I won't."

That morning I seemed to be the only passenger on *Flying Milkfish*. I chose a seat in the central nacelle, just forward of the wing mast. An armorglass canopy gave a panoramic view, while protecting the rows of seats from the dangers of the Eye, and each seat was equipped with a flatscreen and a headset.

The boat slid away from the pier and out through the breakwaters, propelled by silent jets, wing mast feathering into the wind. Once in open water the wing assumed an aerodynamic curve, and we shot off, parallel to the barren black cliffs, slicing through the pearly surface, throwing up rainbowing veils from each bow. The boat trembled like a living thing, pitching slightly as she crossed the quartering swell. It was a strangely exhilarating sensation, and I felt a bit less agitated.

"No wildlife today, I'm afraid." The voice came from the seat behind me; I hadn't heard the speaker approach.

I turned with a jerk, to see a small, somewhat wizened Crondiemer. He lounged back against the seat, rolling a cigarette from some sourly pungent vegetable matter.

"That's a shame," I said.

He lit his cigarette. It smelled even worse, and I was glad I had little tendency toward motion sickness. "Yes, the weather is wrong; today the things all stay deep in the white."

He puffed at his cigarette and watched me with oddly avid eyes, as though examining some eccentric wonder.

After a while his silent scrutiny made me uncomfortable, so I attempted conversation. "Are you the pilot?"

"You could call me that," he said. "But really she's all automated and doesn't need me. Sometimes I let her go out by herself. But not today."

He seemed to be offering me a conversational gambit. "Why not today?"

He laughed. "Because *you're* aboard, of course."

I was puzzled, and a little nervous. Did this strange person hold some grudge against me? I glanced out at the brilliant surface of the Eye. The aerated fluid was less dense than water; a human body would sink instantly, and be out of sight by the time it was a meter deep.

"Oh?" I said. "I'm just a tourist."

He made a snort of mild derision. "Just a tourist . . . who's going to get a crack at Osimry's Madelen."

I felt a flush of embarrassment and irritation. "What do you know about that? And what business is it of yours?"

"Oh, it's none of my business, but everyone in Crondiem knows about you and Osimry's Madelen. That you're to paint her picture . . . and so you'll be with her for some unknown length of time after Osimry croaks." He gave me a conspiratorial leer.

No suitable reply occurred to me, so I said nothing and looked out at the passing cliffs.

His voice was softer but tinged with bitterness. "I know what you outworlders think of the men of Crondiem. That our women have cut off our balls, that we have no appreciation for beauty." He cackled suddenly. "Well, it's true my woman might cure me with a knife, if she ever found out how much I do appreciate beauty. But she'll never find out; we've learned to live with the urges that kill you outlanders."

I found this a very strange confidence. All the other Crondiemers I had seen had seemed so impenetrably private, and I wondered why the pilot was speaking to me of such intimate matters. Perhaps he was just an unusually garrulous person. Or perhaps circumstances had taken me over some line, from tourist to participant in the life of the city.

"We can live with our urges . . . but we must also, if we're honest, admit to envy." He tapped ashes onto the deck. "Especially envy of you outlanders who come here and pluck the widows . . . ripe perfect fruit from our orchard." He sighed.

"I only mean to paint her," I said, finally.

He chuckled, a hard unbelieving sound. "Didn't you know that you can bed a widow in safety? It won't be quite as good as with a sylph you've made—or so they say—but it'll be good enough. Good enough, yes. And at least you won't die for it. Won't even make you sick. Didn't you know that?"

My throat was suddenly tight, for no good reason. "Yes," I muttered. "I knew."

Eventually he finished his cigarette and went away.

The boat's nervous roll and pitch no longer seemed pleasant. I looked about and finally noticed a small black button on the arm of my chair. On the button was a stick figure, bent over, one hand clutching its head, the other its stomach. A wavey line of stylized vomit hung from its featureless head. I pressed the button and felt the sting of a skinject as it sent some comforting drug into my finger. Thereafter I felt better.

After a further tedious hour of plowing the Eye, *Flying Milkfish* returned me safely to the pier.

My sightseeing impulses had evaporated. It's true that every destination has a thousand delightful aspects, and that these are most easily enjoyed by travelers—who can see them with fresh eyes. But Crondiem had taken on a singular meaning for me, and that meaning was all I could think about.

I went back to my room, to find that last night's sheets had been changed and the room restored to perfect order.

I took out my easel and attempted to involve myself in work—often when I work, I lose my sense of time and find that hours have passed unnoticed. But that afternoon, I was too conscious of the coming evening, and so I kept glancing at my watch. The work I did dissatisfied me.

I tried to paint Byron Osimry on his life-support table. I painted his face on two levels: the clear metallic features of the skinmask and—showing through faintly, as though the skinmask were slightly translucent—the corrupt flesh that must lie beneath. I exposed an eye rolling in a pit of decay, an edge of slimy bone, a maggoty wad of rotted cheek, with the black teeth glimmering through the stringy meat.

I fussed with the details of the life-support gear, transmuting the hoses into scaly reptiles and segmented worms. The feet of the table grew cloven hoofs. I arranged the bank of monitoring machinery so that the dials and gauges and touchscreens formed anthropomorphic faces, grinning and grimacing.

When finally I stood back to evaluate the picture, I saw that I had painted Osimry into some sort of medical damnation. It was a picture best suited to the frightening of children.

Instead of art, I had made propaganda. I could almost see the piece as a poster, to hang in the hallways of schools all over the pangalac worlds. The caption below would read: "Little boys, don't grow up and visit Noctile. Look what will happen to you!"

My first impulse was to delete the image—but I kept it. Perhaps I could make something of it; if not, I could always offer it to the poster makers. Not all propaganda is evil.

I spent the rest of the afternoon sitting beside my window, looking out at the roofs and awnings of Crondiem—and thinking about Madelen d'Osimry. Already it was hard for me to recall just how beautiful she had seemed, and I wondered if I had not been somewhat overwrought the night before . . . suggestible, enchanted by my expectations.

When twilight came I was too nervous to eat, so I took up my easel and went down to the widow's pen.

I arrived a little later than I had the first evening, and the servitors were standing along the seawall, holding towels and gowns, and padded cases for the grails. Their lanterns sat at their feet, throwing a yellow light. The servants seemed exclusively Crondiemers.

A little group of tourists, mostly men, waited across the road, making jovial conversation, and I moved away from them and found a spot along the seawall next to one of the guardian gargoyles.

The waters of the pen stirred and the first widow emerged, slowly climbing the steps from the pen to the seawall. She held the bubble of her grail cradled in one arm, and it was the grail that her servant saw to first, taking it in careful hands and settling it in its case.

The widow, when she had been relieved of her burden, fell to her hands and knees. A gout of white fluid poured from her mouth and nose, as she cleared her lungs, and then she coughed, her back arching with the effort. She made a sort of mewling moan.

I could hear her pant, like an exhausted animal.

After a minute she stood and took the towel her servant handed her. Her movements, at first somewhat uncertain, gained assurance, and she dried herself vigorously, ignoring the shouted invitations from the tourists. She wrapped a robe about her lovely body and strode off with the servant, bound, I suppose, for her palace.

Other widows were emerging by now, but I didn't stay to watch them all.

Were they all beautiful, the widows?

Yes, of course, though in the darkness their beauty was to some extent concealed.

But I remember not their beauty, but their brief helplessness, their pain. It was a spectacle tinged with some terrible *wrongness*, and I hoped never to see them again.

When I presented myself at the garden gate, the Crondiem woman let me in, glaring at me resentfully, without the amusement she had shown the night before—which I regarded as an improvement.

She took me to the terrace room, which I now saw to be tastefully furnished with well-kept green plants, white wicker, and brightly patterned cushions. It was a decor that would have been appropriate in any seaside bungalow on a hundred different worlds.

Madelen, wearing a long black robe and a crimson sash, was if anything more brilliantly lovely than before. I felt in her presence a shaky embarrassment for my earlier doubts.

"Hello, Citizen Hender," she said.

"Hello," I said, a bit breathlessly. "Please, call me Millen."

"All right," she said, without any mockery. It occurred to me that if her beauty were inhuman, her apparent lack of self-consciousness was also inhuman. A human woman might have been amused by the blaze in my eyes—or, perhaps, contemptuous.

"May I call you Madelen?" I asked.

"Of course," she said. "Byron won't see you tonight; he has so little strength left." Her eyes shone with tears, but didn't spill over. I felt a deeper astonishment. Were sylphs capable of love, as humans defined love? I had been assuming, for some reason, that the emotional currents all flowed one way: toward the sylphs.

"I'm sorry," I said.

She nodded. "It's the way things must go, I know. But it's hard." She attempted a small smile. "Well, would you like to begin? I'm to do as you ask, in every particular. Is this room suitable? We can bring in more light, if you wish."

I looked about. "The light's fine. Perhaps we could move a couch into this corner. Move the plants away." I indicated a spot where no prints or knicknacks corrupted the white walls and floor. "And could we put a white cover on the couch?" The thought of superimposing Madelen's perfection on that pastel print gave me a queasy stomach.

She nodded to the servant, who fetched a white coverlet and another Crondiemer. The two servants wrestled the couch over to the corner and spread the coverlet.

Madelen looked at me inquiringly. "Good," I said. "Will you sit?"

She sat on the couch, and her robe settled about her in graceful folds. I have painted many formal portraits, and usually the drape of a gown is a matter for endless fiddling. This instantaneous perfection was almost uncanny.

I set up my easel, plugged in my colorwand. "I'll just do a few quick studies," I said.

She nodded, and then gazed past me, out at the darkness of Noctile's night.

It should have been an elegant composition: the white wall, the black gown, the only color her pale violet skin and amethyst tresses, her eyes and mouth. And she was an excellent model, motionless and yet somehow still full of animation. But it took only a few minutes for frustration to set in. I would paint her face, her long hands, with as much intensity and skill as I possessed—and then I would look at her and see how sadly short of success I had fallen.

My frustration must have been obvious. Madelen spoke in a tone of sympathy. "Am I a difficult subject?"

I laughed ruefully. "You're very easy to look at, but very difficult to paint. Your husband was correct to call it a challenge; no one has ever really made a true image of a . . . of a person like you."

"You may call me a sylph; it's what I am. The term doesn't make me uneasy." She seemed quite matter-of-fact.

My curiosity ignited, became an overpowering impulse. "There're lots of questions I'd ask you, if I could."

She settled back against the couch. "Ask, Millen. My husband has directed me to do whatever you wish."

"I don't wish to make you uncomfortable."

She smiled. "I doubt you could ask me anything that would cause me unendurable discomfort."

For some reason, her confidence struck me as wholly, pathetically human. I suppressed a bizarre impulse to cry.

I looked down and tried to collect my thoughts. I was speaking to an alien creature, I was, I was. This was a *sylph*, a parasitic organism of unknown origins and purposes, not a woman. She had drained the life from Byron Osimry. And how many other men? If Osimry had friends, a family, then they surely considered this creature monstrous, a murderous demon.

Of course, she posed no danger to me; was that why I couldn't see her monstrousness?

"Well," I said finally. "What's it like, to be a sylph?"

"You haven't thought this through, have you?"

"What do you mean?" I heard a defensive tone in my voice, though there was no mockery or accusation in her face.

"Millen, you've asked what it's like to be me. If you were to ask any other person the same question, would you expect to get a useful answer? I don't know what it's like to be anyone but Osimry's Madelen. Do you really expect to understand what it's like to be anyone but Millen Hender?"

"I suppose not." Perhaps I at first thought her more knowable, less complex, *because* of her inhumanity. I saw what an essentially human opinion that was. "Then, would it be any easier to tell me how you differ from me? Or any other human?"

"You've rephrased the same question, Millen," she said—a little sadly. "As far as I know, in my human phase I'm as human as you are."

"Really? How can that be?"

"How not? My personality comes only from the men I've lived with, nowhere else."

I considered. "That's not how humans arrive at their characters."

"Isn't it? You're a product of your ancestors, physically and culturally. I'm my husbands' product—their ancestors' genes and cultures." She looked away, out at the pale glow of the Eye. Her suddenly pensive mood seemed to intensify her beauty to an unbearable degree. I had trouble finding my breath. "True," she went on. "I evolved through intermediaries—but to an extent, so did you. Had you no teachers?"

"Yes," I said. "But some of my teachers—and half of my ancestors—were women."

She smiled and gave me a mischievous glance. "And do you think men cannot understand what it is to be a woman? What a curiously archaic idea. The similarities between human men and human women are far more significant than their differences; has this not been the accepted wisdom for thousands of years, since before humans first fared to the stars? A man may become a woman and a woman a man, without any calamitous psychic adjustment. Aren't such changes the cheapest tricks in the gene-splicer's repertoire?"

"I suppose," I said.

"Haven't you heard of Helida Jones, the former saint of FemLife Church? She came to the Eye to take a sylph, on the premise that she could do anything a man could do. She waited on the Meeting Beach for over a hundred years, eating raw cornmeal and drinking recycled water—that's when she was canonized. But one day she threw up her hands and went to the gene-splicer and became a man. Then, of course, Helida claimed a sylph and died, but not before FemLife revoked his sainthood." Her eyes showed a lazy twinkle; I couldn't tell if she was joking.

A silence followed. I was content just to look at her. I had forgotten the colorwand I held in my hand, and I was on the way to forgetting our conversation when she spoke again.

"Millen," she said. "I know I teased you about your question. But, tell me: What is it like to be you?"

I was slow to respond; my thoughts were wandering in a sort of delicious reverie, sufficient to itself. "Me? Actually, I don't think of myself as having much of a personality. I like it that way; I try to be a clear unflawed lens, something for beauty to shine through, neither tinted nor warped."

"That's very ambitious."

I flushed, embarrassed by my foolish posturing.

"No," she said. "I didn't mean it as a criticism. So, what is the shape of your lens?"

"Shape?" I thought about that. "A human one, more or less. So other humans can look at my pictures and see something of the same things I've seen, with their human eyes. That's the best I can do, I suppose."

"Ah," she said, and somehow it wasn't the meaningless polite noise it would have been in most mouths. Though I can't explain how it was different.

Another question occurred to me. "You mentioned your human phase. How are you different, in your *other* form?"

"It's a better question, Millen, but I can't give you a very useful answer, I'm afraid. The scientists say we're not sapient, and they're probably right. I remember nothing about my life in the Eye, except . . ." Her face lit.

"Except that I think it's joyful. Wordless, thoughtless— but joyful."

This seemed so strange that I wanted to ask more questions, but then the Crondiem servant, eyes bulging, rushed into the room with an important message, which she whispered into Madelen's ear.

Madelen's face twisted and she rose. "Excuse me," she said, and left the room, practically running.

More than an hour passed before she returned. I had gone out to the terrace and was leaning against a stone balustrade, looking out over the Eye.

She had approached silently. "Millen?" she said, and I jumped.

She stood a few meters away, her face shadowed, hands folded together at her waist.

"Yes," I said.

"Byron Osimry is dead," she said, her voice trembling slightly.

I wasn't sure what I should say. After all, she *had* killed her husband, even though he had been a willing victim. Finally I settled for empty convention. "I'm sorry," I said.

"Thank you," she said. "Would you mind if we didn't resume until tomorrow? We have plenty of time. I'll call you at your hotel."

"Of course," I said. "Of course. I'll just fetch my easel."

She turned as I passed her, so that the light from the terrace room fell on her face. I was astonished to see that her cheeks were wet. Her eyes were rimmed with a delicate pale green, the color of her blood.

I walked home through the dark safe streets of Crondiem, full of an oddly pleasurable confusion.

My time here had proven eventful, far more so than I'd imagined in my most optimistic dreams. Not only had I met a sylph and talked with her, I was being paid to paint her portrait. No reasonable person would dare ask more from fortune than I had already received. Still . . .

But when I thought of taking Madelen to bed, my eagerness no longer burned as simply, as hotly, as it had before our talk. Before I knew her, a little.

People, even inhumanly beautiful people, even alien people, are always more complicated when they cease to be symbols and become persons. I realized that for better or worse, she had become a person.

I slept dreamlessly and long, waking late in the sunny morning. I ate in my room, and then, obeying a superstitious impulse, transferred the images from my current multimem into a courier wafer and posted it to my home world. Things happen, I told myself.

At least those few paintings were safe, however inept they might be. No matter what happened.

Her message arrived just before noon; she asked me to come to the palace at my convenience.

I rushed from the hotel a few minutes later, somewhat unkempt, hair still wet, shirttails out. I noticed odd stares from the hotel staff. Perhaps I imagined it, but the looks seemed both contemptuous and envious, a strange combination.

When the serving woman let me through the garden gate, I started up the path to the terrace at a near trot.

"Sir!" said the Crondiemer sharply. "Osimry's Madelen waits for you in her personal garden. This way, if you please."

She pointed along the wall, away from the terrace.

I followed her to a crosswall of ancient pink brick. She knocked at a lozenge-shaped wooden door.

"Come," said a perfect voice, and the servant swung the door open. I stepped inside and the servant closed the door, leaving us alone.

Madelen sat on a bench of grey stone, wearing a loose white caftan. Her hair was pinned up in an artful tousle. "Hello, Millen," she said.

"Hello," I said. I stared at her, marveling that her

beauty had grown no less shocking. After a moment, it occurred to me that I was staring rudely. With an effort I turned my eyes to my surroundings.

Her garden was a small shady oasis of order in the midst of the overgrown main garden. The walls were obscured by masses of viny green, flowers shut tight, waiting for the night. A hanging fountain in the shape of a droll face with a long tongue peeked out from the vines on the far wall. Water ran down the tongue and splashed into a semicircular pond. A cluster of cerise water lilies brightened the dark water, and silvery shapes darted beneath the pads.

A flame tree with an elegantly twisted trunk leaned above her bench, and along the walls were beds of aromatic herbs, their lacy foliage a hundred subtle shades of gray-green.

"Do you like it?" she asked.

"Very much," I said.

She patted the bench beside her. "Sit, please."

I did. Her nearness made my head swim, but I attempted a semblance of detachment, gazing at the little pond as if in serene contemplation.

"I see you have your easel," she said. "Would you like to paint me here? Is the light appropriate?"

I made a show of glancing about. "Fine. The light's fine, Madelen."

"Good. How long will it take? The painting?"

I felt a sudden stab of anxiety. "I don't know. Why? How long do I have?"

"Oh, you have as much time as you need. But in a week, or at most ten days, I must go to the widow's pen, and thereafter you may only paint me by artificial light. The sun is too harsh for the widows; it makes the skin slough. And once damaged, we're never the same. Our human template is gone." Her eyes became melancholy.

I took little note. "You mean, I may paint you for as long at it takes?"

"For as long as it takes." The melancholy deepened

for a moment, then seemed to glimmer away in a look of wry amusement. "My husband so ordered, and I must obey."

The guidebooks had described this absolute obedience as "the least human of the sylph's attributes."

I felt a sudden uneasiness. "Will you tell me something? If your husband hadn't so ordered, would you have permitted me to paint you? Would you have had any interest at all?"

"Perhaps," she said. "But in any case, you're a pleasant person, Millen. Your presence isn't so very onerous. What if I had happened across some boorish oaf of an artist? I understand such artists are not uncommon." Her eyes smiled, a little. "Of course, had you been an oaf, I'd not have mentioned you to Byron."

"Ah," I said foolishly. After a moment I got up and assembled my easel. I walked around the perimeter of the garden and finally selected a vantage that included the fountain and pond, just visible behind Madelen.

I plugged the colorwand's lead into my wrist.

"Millen," she said. "Byron instructed me to ask: Would you prefer to paint me clothed or naked?"

My throat closed, so that I could barely speak. "Would you be comfortable naked? The day is cool."

"Not for me. My comfort range is wider than yours." She stood and released the caftan's shoulder fastenings, so that it fell to her feet. She wore nothing beneath. She picked up the caftan and lay it across the bench.

With some small corner of my mind I thought: She knew this would happen, so she wore a garment that would leave no marks on her skin.

But mostly I stared, at that moment empty of all but admiration. I've said that most healthy young women possess lovely bodies, but looking at Madelen, I began to wonder if I had been absurdly undiscriminating.

She faced me, hands at her sides, completely at ease and without a trace of coquetry. Still, an almost unendurable pulse of lust shivered through me, and I was grateful for the easel and its multimem sheet, which concealed some of the evidence from her—though I'm sure my face shouted wordlessly.

I cast about for something innocuous to say, and of course didn't find it. "What other," I asked, "instructions did your husband give, regarding me?"

She sat gracefully. "He said I was to give you anything you wanted."

"Anything?" I asked stupidly, full of breathless anticipation.

"Yes. So long as you don't ask me to contravene any of his other instructions."

"What would those be," I said, feeling an odd panic, like a child offered some coveted treat, only to have it snatched away.

She sighed. "I must go to the pen, I must keep my human body, I must live here in our home a part of every night."

"But anything else, anything that doesn't interfere with that?" I was only dimly aware of how I must have sounded.

She didn't seem at all resentful. "Anything, Millen."

I felt dizzy. I looked at her glorious body and I wanted more than anything to ask her to lie down on the bench. To let me touch her everywhere, to experience her with all my senses—not just my eyes. To explore the textures of her skin, to taste her, to hear the sounds she might make. To join myself to her perfection.

But I didn't. Perhaps I feared the actuality would fall short of my expectations. Or that it would be a coercion, a kind of rape. Or at least that I might be committing a somewhat sordid act of self-deception, no different from purchasing the services of one of those imitation sylphs who sold themselves in the Crondiem bars.

No. None of those things. What I truly felt was a hope that if I could make myself wait, she might come to me willingly.

And if not . . . there would be other days, other nights.

I was ashamed of that last thought, so I shook my head and activated the wand.

"How shall I pose?" she asked.

"Sit comfortably," I said.

So she did, and I painted her. I can still remember almost every detail. She sat, back straight, shoulders back and breasts outthrust, long fine hands on smooth thighs, her legs slightly open, feet firmly planted on the bricks, a small smile on her face. Her head was tipped to the side a bit, so that her exposed neck assumed a delicate curve. She watched me with a curious intensity, though perhaps it was only a reflection of my own fierce attention.

By the time the light had waned, I had achieved a painting of a handsome woman who in every detail resembled Madelen d'Osimry. But was not.

I was heartsick, so full of frustration that I wanted to smash my easel.

She came to stand beside me, still naked. So strong was her air of innocent interest that I for a moment forgot to desire her.

"It's fine work, Millen. Is this really how you see me?" She spoke with apparently sincere admiration. She had the same sweet scent as the breath of the Eye, and I felt a little dizzy.

"No," I answered. "You're far more beautiful than this. I've failed."

She patted my arm and went to put on her caftan.

Watching her dress, my lust returned, hotter than before. Watching a woman dress is a far more intimate act than watching her undress. When a woman dresses before you, it implies that you have been with her when she was naked, and that whatever happened between you has left her comfortable with your regard.

Though in Madelen's case, I don't think she ever felt any uneasiness when she was naked. Perhaps that was due to her perfect, unassailable beauty—or perhaps it was evidence of her alien origin.

•   •   •

She insisted that I have supper at the palace, and so I did. Her cook made no great effort to please me; the meat was overcooked and the salad limp. But I was strangely happy, to be sitting across a vast ebony table from Madelen, chewing tasteless food and watching her sip a goblet of pale fluid brought fresh and cold from the Opal Eye.

There was a fairy-tale quality to the evening, as if I dined with a beautiful princess, one perhaps recently liberated from the bondage of a cruel wizard. The moment seemed to contain all the eccentric baroque glitter of such stories. I certainly found myself in a place I had never imagined, in the company of a mysterious being. I felt possibilities crowding around me—anything could happen.

This odd contentment kept me from speaking during the meal, and she seemed not to mind my silence.

After, she took me out on the terrace. The serving woman brought a padded bench, a fleecy coverlet, and a silver goblet of hot spiced wine.

We sat on the bench together, almost touching, facing away from the Eye, looking up to the black heights of the ringwall behind Crondiem. We shared the coverlet across our laps.

I sipped the wine, holding the warm goblet in both hands.

A few minutes passed. Then the Firefly Moon rose gloriously over the ringwall.

This was one of the sights I had come to Noctile to see. Several hundred years past, a consortium of Noctilians had built a robotic smelter and mass driver on the planet's single moon, which had since launched several million large reflective foil disks into tumbling eccentric orbits around the moon.

"It's pretty, isn't it?" said Madelen.

The moon swam in a glittering pink cloud. "Yes," I said. It *was* pretty—but no more than pretty. It lacked the heartbreaking irresistible beauty of the Eye. Or of Madelen.

After a bit, she spoke again. "Do you remember when you first came to paint me? You said you had a lot of questions for me."

"Well, I did. I do."

"Ask," she said. "Anything."

I thought about that night, and her eyes, when she had returned to me after her husband's death. "Did you . . . ? This is a terrible question to ask, but . . . did you love your husband?"

"Oh yes," she said, without hesitation. Her mouth trembled.

"He was a good man, then?"

"I don't know, really. He was very good to me, but that's almost invariably the case with sylphs and their husbands." She smiled. "People can mistreat their lovers or they can mistreat themselves. Sylphs are both, in a way. It seems to keep us safe. Anyway, Byron never spoke about his past. He always said that his life began when I came from the Eye." Her face was tender, soft with remembrance—and I felt a pang of unreasonable jealousy.

Partly to change the subject, and partly, I suppose, to be cruel, I said: "I watched a symposium the other day, on the tank in my room. They were arguing about the origins and purposes of the Eye. What do you think?" As soon as I spoke, I regretted my words.

She turned slowly toward me, her smile gone. "I have no certain knowledge. But I can speculate, if you wish. Obviously, I'm a parasite. But to what purpose? That's the question, isn't it?"

"I'm sorry," I said. "I really am sorry, Madelen."

"You mustn't be," she said. "No, I'll tell you what I think. I think I'm an artifact, made by the same ones who made the Eye. An organic machine. Put here to collect noble souls—though why, why, I don't know. I can't imagine." Her great eyes were tragic and she didn't look away and I thought I might die from shame.

"Millen," she said. "How can you help wondering

about these things?" She put her arms around me, as if I were the one who needed comfort.

Her closeness drove away all thought. I almost stopped breathing, so intense was my absorption in the sensations of the moment. She laid a hand on my chest and said, "Slow down your heart, Millen. I don't want to be responsible for exploding it."

I raised a trembling hand and touched, with my fingertips, the valley between her breasts. Her skin was warm, and her alien heart pumped in a slow complicated rhythm.

She kissed me, her lips soft and a little sticky, her breath sweet with the fragrance of the Eye. She tugged urgently at the buttons of my shirt.

No matter how long I live, no matter what happens to me, I'll never forget the hours that we spent there. On a palace terrace, overlooking the Opal Eye. Under the Firefly Moon.

I satisfied all my curiosities. I learned all the textures and tastes and scents of her miraculous body. I believe I gave her pleasure—though surely I couldn't possibly have given her as much pleasure as she gave me.

Her smile came back, and she laughed. Her laugh was as lovely a sound as I ever hope to hear.

Dawn glimmered above the ringwall. We huddled under the coverlet; I was astonishingly tired, and happy to the same amazing degree.

"Come to my room, Millen," she said, rubbing her face against my shoulder. "It's in the tallest tower of the palace. There's a fine view of the Eye. We can sleep away the day in my bed, if you like."

"All right," I said.

She pulled me to my feet, wrapped the coverlet around me. "Wear this. The servant will fetch our clothes later." She walked before me, naked and graceful, and led me through the palace.

In a small room at the base of her tower was a glass case containing a grail. I should have noticed how she ignored it, how she rejected its existence as she passed, but I was drowsy. Stupid from a surfeit of joy.

"Is this yours?" I asked, stopping by the case.

She stopped, reluctantly, and came back to stand beside me. "Yes," she answered, in a small dim voice.

"It's lovely," I said. The quartz globe containing the synthesizer concealed the machinery behind faceting so complex, so subtle, that the crystal seemed to waver on the edge of dissolving into pure light.

"Not to me," she said, more strongly.

I finally noticed. Still I spoke stupidly. "You don't want to be a widow?"

"How could you think that?" she said, a bit wildly. "Who wouldn't want to spend her days floating in the widow's pen, sucking up preservatives? Who wouldn't want to spend an endless life in this palace, alone, never changing, never healed of, of . . ." She stopped, and tears ran down her cheeks. I saw that they were as clear as any human woman's tears.

"Alone?" I said. "I won't leave until you tell me to go."

Her face crumpled. "Oh. Oh dear. How can I make you understand. You're a fine person, Millen, but you can never be Byron Osimry."

"No, of course not—"

She interrupted. "May I tell you what I think about evil? Please? Well then . . . I suspect Byron was once a harsh man, who did terrible things to gain his wealth. Before he came to Noctile and I came to him.

"This is what I think evil is: It's the result of an unevenness in the soul. The cruel person suppresses compassion and gives cruelty free rein. The hateful person looses hate on the universe, and keeps love imprisoned. But at the bottom of every soul, no matter how cruel and hateful, love and compassion survive, chained.

"I knew Byron's soul, down to the bottom, in all its hidden brilliance and beauty—because he gave it to me. I could never know yours that way, though I'm sure yours is just as beautiful. Or more beautiful, even . . . it doesn't matter."

"Oh," I said numbly.

She wiped at her eyes. "You've been very kind, Millen. I'm grateful; I needed you, and you eased my heart for a while. But you're not Byron, you're not my darling, who didn't mean to be cruel." She looked at the grail with a loathing so intense that I stepped back.

Then she turned back to me, and her eyes emptied of everything. "He gave me his soul. Then I murdered him."

I put my hand on her arm, but she shrugged it away. "I think my makers meant to be cruel. No machine, even a machine of flesh and blood, ought to feel such pain, simply because it has done its work.

"I know why we are made this way, I do, but it's still not right. The pain exists to drive us back into the Eye. Back into the Eye's forgetfulness." She paused and drew a shuddering breath. "My makers underestimated human cleverness, didn't they?"

I couldn't answer.

She took my hand, finally, and led me up a spiraling staircase, to her little room at the top of the tower.

There was only one window, as narrow as the one in my hotel room. She pulled me toward it. I looked down at the Eye, and saw that the widow's pen was just below us.

Beautiful women were shuffling wearily down the steps into the white fluid of the pen, holding their grails in careful hands.

Madelen made a choked-off sound of distress and pressed her face into the hollow of my shoulder. I put my arms around her; I could do that much.

We slept in her bed, but it was no longer the slumber of happy exhaustion that might have been.

I dreamed that we lay together in a very small place, in a dim shifting light, on a hard narrow bed. Propped on my side, I watched her with my customary willing fixity, as she slept.

Tears seeped from beneath her eyelids and moistened the curves of her cheeks. I had to look away, so I looked at her breasts—a reasonable diversion.

But then her uptilted nipples began to weep white droplets—milk with the fragrance of the Eye. The milk ran down her flanks and pooled under her. Her nipples bubbled like springs, and with the illogical smoothness of dreams, I found myself floating in sweet whiteness.

Madelen was gone, her essence melted into the fluid that held me. I was content for a while, but then I realized I hadn't breathed in a long time. I opened my mouth and tasted the milk, and understood that I was drowning in the milk of sorrow.

I woke without thrashing, propelled from sleep smoothly and abruptly.

I got up without disturbing Madelen, and wrapped a cotton robe around me. I stood beside her bed and looked down at her for a long time, filling my eyes with as much of her beauty as they could hold.

She slept on her belly, right arm curled under her head. One long leg had escaped the covers.

I bent close and examined the way her amethyst eyelashes caressed the pale skin beneath them.

I think I was hoping she would wake. But she didn't.

I went down the spiraling stairs. Selfishness and sorrow clamored at me, but I ignored their voices, and thought of nothing, nothing at all, holding nothing inside me but the weak sweet impulse that had driven me from her bed.

When I reached the room where her grail waited, I picked up a melt-stone planter and smashed the case.

I crushed the grail, pounding on it until its globe collapsed and spilled all its precious innards. A thin brown fluid dripped down the plinth. It smelled of bitter decay.

I dropped the planter, just as the Crondiem serving woman ran into the room.

She stopped dead and her hand went to her mouth.

"I'm done," I said.

Madelen came down the stairs. The look on her face when she saw the ruined grail was all I'd hoped it would be. But even as that glorious smile was curving her mouth, she said to the serving woman: "Call the Tourist Police."

The servant trotted away.

"Thank you, Millen," she said. "Goodbye. Goodbye."

I could manage only a jerky nod. What could I have said? She waved and went into the hall. I could hear a soft patter—her bare feet hurrying away.

After a while, I went out to the terrace. I saw her run the last few steps to the seawall. When she launched herself from the wall in a clean dive, there was something unforgettably exultant about the arc of her body.

The Eye closed over her and she was gone.

When the Tourist Police arrived, they were at first uncomprehending and then coldly enraged. They confiscated my easel and the multimem that held Madelen's last images.

They put me on the first shuttle available, and told me that I would never be welcome on Noctile again.

I believe that she did it to save me, that she knew how vulnerable I would be when she was gone. The Tourist Police assured me of a speedy departure from Noctile.

As I watched Noctile dwindle in the shuttle's aft port, I felt a growing certainty that we had exchanged some degree of love.

At home, I found the message wafer containing the early sketches from Crondiem. With my memories of Madelen and the sketch I had made of Byron Osimry, I fashioned a painting that pleased me—though of course it held only a ghost of her beauty.

Wearing her black gown, she stands beside Osimry's life-support table. Her fine hand lies gently on the unpleasant shape of her husband's dying body. His mask is only a vaguely human smudge in the shadows.

Her perfect face holds a grave sorrowing acceptance.

If you look very closely you can see, reflected in her wonderful eyes, the tiny distorted image of a man at an easel.

In Medicis Gardens

Jean-Claude Dunyach
translated by Dominique Bennett

THEY MET AGAIN THREE YEARS LATER IN MEDICIS GARdens. He was walking quickly with small, even steps, thinking small, even thoughts, as he crunched along the sand and gravel of the straight and even path. She was seated on a stone bench, a dog-eared book in her hands. Above her head, the umbrella pine seemed to sway gently in tempo with her breathing.

They never should have been able to catch sight of each other. To preserve their privacy, the path would only have had to curve a bit more, or a hedge grow higher around the bench to conceal anyone seated from the eyes of intruders. But at that time in the morning the Gardens were virtually deserted, and the mad architect who reigned over Medicis had not yet brought all the machinery to life. The lawns and walks lined with ivy-covered trees did not care to reshape themselves for the occasional passerby. Dawn had wiped the memories of the statues and the fountains. Each blade of grass looked the same as the day before, or shyly tried to grow a little more. The Gardens seemed, for the time being, to be in the unpredictable hands of chance.

And so they met. The noise of his steps on the gravel startled her and made her look up. He stopped, surprised to see her there. They stared at each other. He recognized her, she not.

When he sat down beside her on the stone bench, she shrugged her shoulders resignedly and put her book face open on her knees to look at him. His first words completely nonplussed her.

"Fancy meeting you here!"

She took another look at him, this time more closely. Brown eyes, regular yet nondescript features, and a smile which was beginning to falter a little. Impossible to remember. She cautiously delved into the gloomier regions of her memory as she searched for clues. Perhaps he was one of her passing loves, someone she had clung to for a few hours during that black period three years ago. Her instinct nevertheless whispered *no*. She shook her head.

"I don't know you."

"You don't remember me?" (His voice was incredulous, his smile fading.) "You really don't remember."

The name he added after a few seconds of silence was hers.

The book slid off her lap and fell at her feet. He bent down to pick it up and held it out to her, not daring to place it on her knees. They half looked at each other out of the corner of their eyes. She took the book and snapped it shut.

"Thank you."

A curtain of branches, grown out of their common desire, closed around the bench and the path gradually disappeared under a carpet of dead leaves. The Garden slowly woke up and prepared to embrace the innumerable strollers who, in love with solitude, had to be carefully isolated from each other by subtle maneuvers, so that each one was under the happy illusion that he had a vast area all to himself. Oblivious of the underground activity all around them, they remained silent for a while. He broke the silence first.

"I can understand that you don't want to talk to me anymore. I'm going. But don't try to tell me you've forgotten me; you don't have the right to do so."

He made as if to get up and go but she held him back by his sleeve.

"Please. Oh come on, wait!"

She bit her lips and then whispered,

"If I knew you at one time, I now have absolutely no recollection whatsoever. My memory is not intact. I sold bits of it three years ago."

She brushed away the fringe of dark hair covering her forehead. A scar scribbled its way along her hairline, the trademark of the memory dealers. He had already seen wounds of this kind displayed like signatures on fractured skulls. He knew.

When he got up to go she made no attempt to hold him back. The leaves on the path rotted underfoot. He disappeared into the distance, with the unconscious gait of a sleepwalker, dead leaves scattered all around him.

They should never have met again, but the Gardens had, by some incomprehensible quirk, memorized the circumstances of the encounter during their artistic restructuring, in order to replay them at will. A few days later he sat down next to her without a word. The scenery had not changed, and once again she had not recognized him.

She was rereading the same book. The bookmark was only a few pages further on and she constantly referred to the passages she had just read, already fading in her memory. Those who erase too many of their memories have trouble acquiring new ones. Facts and sensations eagerly endeavor to clutch at the slippery wall of neurons, but the contact is short-lived.

They replayed the scene of their last encounter with few variations. He already knew most of her replies; she invented them as she went along. He occasionally acted out of character, but she did not notice in the slightest.

They chatted longer than the first time. The Gardens wrapped their shadowy shawls around them, cloaking them in darkness which was quite in harmony with the dubious clarity of their words. Thus hidden, they had little difficulty in becoming more intimate and talking about themselves.

"You know my name. But I don't remember you."

"That's normal. I became buried forever in the depths of your brain when they took your memories."

She blushed a little.

"It's because of you that I did that?"

"Maybe. Probably."

They remained silent for a time. She opened her book and flicked away a fly hovering over a pleat of her skirt. He looked at her tenderly. After they had parted, he had cherished the impossible dream of starting anew with an ideal woman, her memory scrubbed clean of all misunderstandings. His wish was granted, as she had forgotten the circumstances of their breakup, and he himself only asked for them to be banished for all time from his memory. Nothing seemed to block their renewed intimacy. He braved placing his hand on hers and realized his mistake too late. She shut her book and walked off, leaving him petrified on the bench.

He slept badly that night and went to work via a huge detour, to avoid the Gardens. At nightfall he walked through them but met no one.

A week later, the gravel paths led him inexorably to the bench and its occupant. He stuttered a few excuses and then realized from her uncomprehending expression that she had no recollection of their last encounter. His worry slipped away and he risked a smile. Two hours later he had reestablished contact.

It became a habit of his to meet her there nearly every evening, to try to mend the fabric the memory dealers had torn apart. The moments he spent away from her undid the tapestry of their common memories. He patiently took up needle and thread during the next encounter, often starting from scratch. He became very skilled at this game, and succeeded after a few sentences in reestablishing the necessary intimacy for their talks. But she never retained what he said for more than a few days.

To know how much information she had forgotten since their last meeting, he had only to look at the book she persisted in reading. When the bookmark was in the same place he knew he had wasted his breath. The story, their own as well as that of the characters in her book, had not progressed. Sometimes, however, she had moved on a few pages and remembered his name or face. On those days she greeted him with a hesitant smile and did not seem to find it strange that he sat down beside her. But then a few days afterwards she would move the bookmark back to the beginning of the chapter and start the story afresh, and he was forced to also.

The bitterness of those moments was compensated by the tranquil sweetness of the time he spent chatting with her. The stage set that the Gardens raised around them was virtually unchanging, as if they were living in a barricaded area between the reality of the town and the easily adaptable decor of the Gardens. But every morning the machines wiped out all traces of the day before, and scattered the dead leaves they had trodden on.

She did not seem to notice, but it disturbed him not to be able to leave his mark on the memory of the Gardens, for want of marking that of his companion. His mind alone classified and retained the archives of the moments gone by, and he sometimes even doubted his own notion of time. At anguished moments like these he left her without even saying goodbye, or else scared her away by jumping steps in their accessory sequence, eager as he was at long last to come to the point.

As time passed, he came earlier and earlier. As soon as he was finished at work, he was in the Gardens, walking resolutely along the straight path that seemed to stretch away to infinity before him. The pools greeted his arrival with spouts of water, and the statues corrected their postures as he passed. He sat down on the bench and she shut her book with a gesture which was by now quite familiar.

On All Souls Day, he spent the whole day with her. Her memories of the day before were still intact, and she welcomed him by moving aside to make room for him. There was no sign this time of the book; it was unintentional, perhaps, but he preferred to consider it a good omen.

The morning passed like a dream, in haphazard chatting, with the past as the major topic of conversation. He had the time to tell her everything: their relationship, their separation, and then the long periods of tenderness interspersed with disagreements, like smooth beaches bracketed by rocks. She didn't know whether to believe it or not, but every one of his words rang in her ears like a forgotten melody. The story was too beautiful; it had to be true.

Towards midday he suggested they have a picnic, and brought out a salad dressed in vinegar, cooked ham, and bread with olives. They spread out a blanket at the foot of the umbrella pine and put the wine to cool in a sculptured basin. A flock of sparrows crossed the sky heading south, and the breeze caused the dry leaves to whirlpool upwards. The minutes ticked by at their own pace, as if the intervention of the memory dealers had created an air pocket in reality, into which a never-ending present came rushing.

After the meal, they remained stretched out on the grass, and he spoke to her about Venice. A glorified Venice, cleansed of any impurity that could spoil the images in her memories. He thus relived in her company an adventure as rich as the original, all the while keeping careful control of his meanderings. Unconsciously he distorted the landscapes of their communal life, in the same way the Gardens distorted themselves around them.

"We got to know each other during Carnival. You know that's when the town drains its canals and emerges briefly to enjoy its former splendor. The temporary dikes isolate the inner lagoon from the sea. The greedy mouths of the pumps gulp down the muddy water, causing palaces to appear out of the depths and disturbing the celebrated service given by the octopi in the sea-green depths of the basilica.

"Think back. We were staying on one of those hotel-gondolas, several hundred meters long, propelled by old mechanical gondoliers. They row smoothly and regularly, the flat of their oars the size of a porch. We slowly crossed the lagoon, lulled by the murmur of the songs issuing from the lungs of the loudspeakers and the lapping of the water thickened with mud.

"Occasionally two gondolas came side by side and the gondoliers, like wader birds with their black bodies and beribboned aigrettes, greeted each other with a great show of reverence, in a parody of courtship which passed over our heads entirely.

"It was so easy to fall in love aboard such boats. The fancy dress we wore was made only to be taken off, our masks barely disguised our wish to be recognized, we were only dressed to sheathe our bodies in a delectable gift wrapping which could be opened, oh so easily.

"We didn't, however, meet up on the deck with its ebony floors. We got to know each other in the town itself."

Carried away by his tale, he turned towards her to ask:

"Do you remember?"

And she shook her head, heartbroken, but happy nevertheless to hear their story for the first time.

"I was walking, dressed in a dark cowl and with a scythe in my hand. St. Mark's Square was littered with fish out of the water, gasping. A troupe of idle harlequins was throwing them pigeon seeds, and deriving great amusement from their ridiculous parodies of broken-winged flyers. I appeared amongst them in my reaper's outfit to threaten them with my scythe. They laughed and bombarded me with seeds, giving the dying fish a respite.

"A vision of Venice had invaded my mind, a Venice wrenched out of the water and likewise suffocating in the icy air. I fled towards the Rialto without looking back. You ran behind me hitching up your bright red skirts, and you spoke to me:

" *'Who are you?'*

" *'Me? I am Death!'*

"You laughed and we ambled together aimlessly along the seaweed-covered back streets, our arms around each other's waists, looking for somewhere dry where I could take off your dress.

"On the banks of the Grand Canal, the remaining workers had almost finished scraping away the silt which clothed the ancient palaces. The huge photographs, which they used to cover up the places where the damage was too extensive, were gradually being spoiled by mold, the hues of which blended nicely with the eerie decor. In the black mirror of water the cracked palaces seemed to watch themselves, fascinated by the serene slowness of their fall.

"You spoke to me then about a Venetian artist who had spent part of his life taking photos of his town, extracting as he did so all of its substance and forever imprisoning it in the depths of his black room. Only water could play that role now and, like the photograph's developer, reveal the true beauties of the Venice it held captive.

"We walked on and on, and I listened to your voice. You spoke a lot at the time, or maybe I was a better listener than I am now. You'd had the most fantastic nightmares in Venice, and you related them to me in low tones while looking fearfully at the statues of the Virgin, watchful in their grottoes. You told me that one day, even by scratching away the layers of mud, it would be impossible to reach the stone. The whole of Venice would be dissolved in the sea, leaving a mere dark and ugly fossil. On that day, man would destroy the dikes for good and let the currents in the ocean depths sculpt an even more beautiful city, which no one would ever see.

"We only went back to our floating hotel the next day. A Ghetto Nuovo chapel had sheltered us with its bare walls and faded frescoes. Your pale skin was highlighted by the purple of the chasubles, piled in haste on the slab of the sacristy.

"You're not shocked, I hope? It all comes back to me, I am telling you about it with the same spontaneity we felt at the time. I see that you're blushing, you who never blushed very often. How can you be moved by the recital of deeds of which you have not the slightest recollection? And what if I were lying?"

Leaning on her elbow, she smiled without replying, her eyes vague and distant. A gust of wind snatched at her dress, lifting it momentarily and revealing her thighs. He was moved by the sight. Their hands interlocked for a moment, then she withdrew hers gently. *Not now*, the line of her mouth seemed to whisper, *tell me more about Venice.*

"During the days that followed, we often explored the abandoned palaces, aboard a raft stolen from the town guards. I sank my scythe into the murky water with a delicious sense of wickedness, and the ripples of our wake lapped against the wainscoting of the thick walls. Doubled over, we explored ceremonial chambers transformed into damp caves. The strands of our hair brushed crystal chandeliers forever statuesque in their stalactite robes of seaweed and silt.

"Once the floor gave way under my pole, and the water gurgled away. The room emptied, so we left the sunken raft to open the door of the neighboring lounge, which retained its water like a lock. The waves carried us further and further across inundated rooms. I didn't know your name at the time, I only learned it when the carnival was over. Our costumes had for some time become totally unrecognizable, the mold and mud stains had transformed us into ghouls, or ghosts. The last dance of the harlequin troupe was quite macabre, with a kaleidoscope of diamond-shaped colors twinkling occasionally from the harlequins, who had never left the gondolas.

"Our hotel weighed anchor last of all. We stayed on the bridge crowded with silent pierrots, watching the town grow dark once again. The sky was violet. A titanic storm spread out its electrical embroidery above our heads, and Venice seemed to duck down into a wet shell, which clamped down on her like an oyster on its pearl.

"You pointed out to me the solitary lantern which shone at the windows of the Palazzo Cavalli. One of the former noblemen of the town undoubtedly had chosen to sink with her like the captain of a lost ship. The mechanical gondolier turned his expressionless face in that direction and saluted the man with a flourish of his boater before bending over his oar once more. A few minutes later we touched ground again at Lido.

"In the train which took us to Rome, we stripped ourselves of the remaining festive rags which we wore to put on, once again, our normal day-to-day uniforms. I found out that you were discreet and modest, and living a virtual hermit's existence in an attic. The contrast between these facts I learned from your information card, and the image I had gained during my exploration of you and Venice, made me want to see you again. A few weeks later we were living together and the conclusion of our story becomes easy to imagine."

She savored the silence which followed his last words, then nodded to thank him for keeping the circumstances of their breakup to himself. Thus the adventure remained sufficiently impersonal for her to convince herself quite effortlessly that the characters he had just described carried on their relationship elsewhere.

He kissed her on the corner of her mouth, catching her quite by surprise and bringing her down to earth. She turned her head towards him, astonished to see a face she had only just met so close to her own, a face that nevertheless occupied all her thoughts at the present moment. She was no longer alone on the narrow bench that stretched from the recent past, of which she was hardly aware, to the future, which she could hardly imagine. This frightened her. Her mouth twitched away and the second kiss slid along her cheek and got lost in her hair.

"No please. I don't want to."

The Gardens rustled an ocean of agitated leaves around them. They drifted to the ground, landing on the blanket as if on a raft.

"Why not?"

"I don't love you. Don't interrupt me, listen. I don't love you: I can never love anyone again. You need time for that and I no longer have enough, you know that. Whatever happens, I will have forgotten everything by tomorrow."

His fingers traced the line of her neck.

"I shall never let you forget me again."

And till the rising of the sun, his lips signed his rediscovered love on her virgin flesh, while the realm of Medicis prepared its next metamorphosis.

The next day, he ran along the paths to meet her, but the bench was empty. He waited until nightfall, and on the days that followed he waited again, but without success. For a whole week he awaited her return, book in hand, always taking care to leave her usual place free, so that she could be where she was used to sitting. The crack of a dead branch or a footstep on the gravel from an invisible stroller distracted him from his reading every time. He had trouble following the thread of the story and often backtracked, just like the person he was now waiting for. When darkness prevented him from deciphering the letters he shut his book and stayed a few minutes longer, looking vaguely ahead before leaving the Gardens.

The following Monday, he saw her again sitting on the bench, and he hurried towards her, relieved. She looked at him with her pale eyes reflecting no more than polite indifference, and the words he had prepared died on his lips. He sat down beside her and watched in silence while she dutifully reread the first pages of her never-ending book.

When he finally decided to speak to her, evening was just about to fall and they only exchanged a few words. He nevertheless had the time to ask her the reason for her absence, and the reply made him smile bitterly. She had caught a cold, in circumstances of which she had not the slightest recollection, and she had stayed in bed till her recovery. Unable to control his emotions, he preferred to be the first to leave.

She remained on the bench to enjoy the last warm hours of autumn, after the days she had spent cooped up in her room. She thought back, briefly, to the man who had just left her, regretting they'd not had more time to talk together. He was attractive, despite his abashed air, and resembled one of the characters in her novel.

He needed a week to accept that she had once again forgotten the day they had spent together. He could always resort to renewing his acquaintance with her each time, as in the past, but that no longer satisfied him. Several times he found the strength of will to avoid entering the Gardens, but, quickly, his steps led him back to the bench and to her. Their story threatened to continue indefinitely, like the desperate flow of the tides that had finally drowned Venice.

Finding no solution, he decided, in despair, to make her hate him. He tailed her along the paths like a flasher, drooling at the mouth, the flaps of his coat wide open. The next day she welcomed his attempts at conversation as if nothing had happened. Then he understood that nothing definitive would ever be possible between them until she recovered all of her mind, and the faculty of memory.

He emptied his bank account, went round to all his friends and acquaintances to borrow money from them. In

one week he had amassed enough for his plan. Without
wasting any more time he made an appointment with the
League of Memory Dealers, and arrived one morning at
the entrance of their private building to buy back the past
of his companion.

When he came out, the wet claw marks of tears
streaked his face. Her memories had been sold the week
following their extraction, almost three years ago. They
had evaporated without a trace in the anonymous mind
which had bought them. Too much time had since gone
by, and no one could help him anymore.

He went back to the Gardens two weeks later. In the
meantime he had knocked on all the doors he could think
of to ask for help, receiving the same cruel reply from
each of them. There was nothing anybody could do—his
companion's memory was lost forever. He gave back all
the money he had borrowed, and left the town to think.

When he came back, he took a day off and entered
the Gardens as soon as the gates opened. A fine drizzle
brought life to the green of the lawns, and added a sheen
to the flowers whose petals were already strewn all over
the ground. The trees waved their branches to get rid of
the leaves which still clung to them, and the smooth trunks
of the birches tried on their winter wardrobe. He drew
the collar of his coat tighter to protect himself from the
wind, and told himself he was crazy. Autumn was finished,
she wouldn't come back anymore. It was too cold to sit
motionless on a bench in the open air.

He nearly turned around. Spring was so far away and
the Gardens changed so often. After their initial encounters
he would have welcomed her disappearance with a somewhat cowardly relief. Now he hurried toward their meeting
place, worried by the idea that he would probably have to
make inquiries throughout the town to find her, with no
guarantee of success.

He hurried along the freshly raked paths without worrying about the decor surrounding him. Along the way the
pools emptied and the statues made faces without attracting

his attention. Indifferent to his anguish, the mad architect
practiced his morning scales on the vegetable keyboard of
the Gardens.

The bench was empty and his heart sank momentarily,
but then he suddenly caught sight of her on a side path. He
stopped and pretended to engrave his initials on the bark
of a tree, to give her the time to sit and take out her book.
Then he sat down beside her, and replayed the scene of
their meetings from the beginning.

Patiently, repeating each sentence as often as was necessary, he told her everything. She listened with growing
surprise to this stranger who spoke so well of her, and who
moved her in a way she had difficulty in understanding.
She received the news about the definitive loss of her
memories quite serenely.

She said:

"That was not really the answer, you know. I would
have been transported back three years all at once, and
you would have lost me. Now we can live together and
begin everything again each morning, without worrying
about the rest."

"I've thought about that, but it won't work. I can no
longer live at your pace. You have no past, and virtually
no future. You are a prisoner on a cramped island whose
coastline no ship ever reaches. I'm caught in the present,
but I also remember yesterday and I'm already thinking of
tomorrow. I make my plans and so I drift away from you
little by little. We can't grow old together because you've
forgotten what it is to grow old. And I won't have the
courage to tell you, over and over again every morning."

She remained silent for a moment and drew nearer
to him.

"I've made up my mind," he whispered. "I'm going to
sell part of my memories, and then I'll join up with you."

Without giving her the time to protest, he took the
book she had put away in her bag and opened it. On the
front page and on every blank page and beginning of a
new chapter, he arranged a meeting with her. He scribbled

heady words over every page, and filled the margins with promises. She helped him find the words which would touch her most of all, and composed the perfect love letter to herself. When they had written on all the available space he drew his face close to hers and whispered,

"Now look at me, and look closely. Engrave my features on your mind. So what if you forget them, maybe an inkling will remain, and you'll remember me in that way."

The umbrella pine fluffed out its protective canopy and, till nightfall, they remained pressed tightly against each other like two shipwrecks, isolated from the rest of the world by the ocean of their tears.

He visited the memory dealers very early the next morning and waited for their offices to open. He had no difficulty whatsoever in selling his story, and even allowed himself the luxury of bargaining with them, with a kind of desperate greed which surprised even himself. Before signing he read the contract several times over, but was unable to retain a single word.

An hour and a half later he left the building, and with his mind still numb, he carefully explored the crater in his memory. Just as on coming out of the dentist's, when the tongue tentatively probes the cavity of a torn-out tooth to make sure it is no longer there, so his mind continually thought back, flying over the abyss of his absent memories. He stood still on the pavement, disoriented, not knowing where to go. The passersby looked at him with sympathy, but no one came to help.

He walked on briefly and sat down on stone steps to try and gather his thoughts. A feeling of irreparable loss overwhelmed him little by little. He fought back, but with no real success. His confused brain tried to find the information that would enable him to understand his present situation, but the key links seemed strangely absent. He examined the problem from every angle without finding the answer. Maybe his mind would sort itself out later.

An envelope was peeping out of his pocket. He opened it and found a check for a large amount, with a signature like the one scarring his forehead. He put it into his wallet and went on his way, crossing the narrow streets of the town and automatically going towards Medicis Gardens.

The quiet paths led him towards the bench, and the trees waved their naked branches to welcome him upon his return. He walked on in silence, and the sound of his steps reverberated in his empty mind like the echo of other steps, traces of which had long since disappeared.

A girl he had never seen before closed her book when she saw him, and gestured hesitantly in his direction. She stopped when their eyes met, and looked down for fear of having made a mistake. He carried on walking without looking back, and went through the gates and out. Sadly, the Gardens wiped him forever from their mind.

The young girl turned to her book with its scribbled annotations, worried at the idea of missing this strange meeting of which she had not the slightest recollection. She unconsciously moved to make room on the bench and sat back. Someone, no doubt, would eventually turn up.

The Woman Who Loved Pigs

Stephen R. Donaldson

FERN LOVED PIGS, BUT IN ALL THE VILLAGE OF SARENDEL-on-Gentle she may have been the only woman who did not own one.

The Gentle's Rift down which the river ran was at once fertile and isolated. The wains of the merchanters came through in season, trading salt by the pound and fabric by the bolt for wheat and barley by the ton; there were no other visitors. And the good people along the river wanted none—especially after they had listened to the merchanters' tales of the larger world, tales of wars and warlocks, princes and intrigues. Their lives in the Rift were like the Gentle itself, steady and untroubled. Whether poor or comfortable, solitary or gregarious, the villages and hamlets had only four essential activities—their children, their farms, their animals, and their ale. Pleasure produced their children, work in the fields and with the animals produced their food, and ale was their reward.

Among the fields and meadows, cows were precious for their milk, as well as for their strength at the plow. And pigs made better meat. For that reason, sows and porkers were common.

It may have been because they were raised for meat—because they were such solid creatures, and so doomed—that Fern loved them, although they were not hers.

In Sarendel she knew them all by their size and coloring, their personalities and parentage. Recognizing her love, they came to her whenever they could. And she adored their coming to her as though she were a great lady visited by royalty.

Yet she took nothing which was not granted to her, and so she returned them. Before she returned them, however, she pampered them as best she could in the brief time her honesty allowed her, tending their small sores and abrasions, offering them the comfits and comforts she was occasionally able to scavenge for them, scratching their ears when she had no treats to offer. She wept for the porkers and flattered the sows. Since she had no language of her own, their throaty voices were articulate enough for her; she knew how to warm her heart with their snorts and grunts of affection.

When they strayed among the hills, she could divine where they were, and so she was able to recover them. When they misplaced their piglets, she found the young and brought them home—her ear for the thin squeals of the lost was unerring. When the sows suffered farrowing, she came to them from wherever her scavenging took her, bringing poultices and caresses which eased the piglets out.

The good people of Sarendel could not comprehend the sounds which came from her mouth, but they understood the importance of gratitude and kindliness in a small village. When Fern had performed her small services for the creatures she loved, the farmwives and alemaids to whom they belonged thanked her with gifts of food which did more to keep breath in her body than the sustenance she scavenged.

Indeed, in gratitude one of her fellow villagers would almost certainly have given her a pig, had she been capable of raising it. Alas, that steady nurturance would have been beyond her. In a village where poverty was common but active want was rare, Fern was destitute. If Yoel the aleman had not allowed her a disused storeshed to serve as her hovel, she would have had no place to live. If the farmwives had not given her scraps of weaving and discarded dresses, she would have had no clothes. If Sarendel-on-Gentle had not granted her the freedom of its refuse, she would have lacked food more than she had it. Her parents had been poor—her father a farm laborer, her mother a scrubwoman—able to feed and clothe and shelter her, but little more; and they were long dead. From dawn to dusk she was friendless as only those to whom words meant nothing could be, comforted only by the affection of the sows and porkers.

If she had owned a pig—so the village believed—she would have fed it before she fed herself; and so she would have died.

Even with only herself to keep alive, no one would have been surprised to find her dead one morning among the fields or beside the river. Her life was a small thing, even by the ordinary standards of Sarendel-on-Gentle. The village in turn was a small thing along the verdant Rift. And the Gentle's Rift itself was a small thing within the wide world of Andovale, where princes and warlocks had their glory.

No one took note—or had cause to take note—when Fern of Sarendel-on-Gentle was adopted by a pig.

He was not a handsome pig, or a large one. Indeed, she saw as soon as she looked at him that he was dying of hunger. His brindled skin showed splotches of disease, as well as of scruffy parentage. Stains and gashes marked his grizzled snout. One eye appeared to be nearly blind; the other was flawed by a strange sliver of argent like a silver cut. In the early dew of dawn, he shouldered his way into her hovel as though he had traveled all night for many nights to reach her, laid himself down at her feet, rolled his miscolored eyes at her weakly, and began at once to sleep like the dead.

Fern had seen that sleep only once before—a sleep without the twitches and snuffles, the unconscious rootings of a pig's dreams. She had no measure of time, and so she did not know when it was, but on some prior occasion she had found a lost sow far from the village. The sow had broken her leg crossing a stream bed. The disturbance of the rocks and mud showed that she had struggled for hours, perhaps for days; then she had lost heart. She was asleep when Fern found her, and Fern could not rouse her; she slept until she died.

Fern understood instantly that the pig now asleep at her feet was like that sow—brokenhearted and near to dying.

As she looked at him, however, an image formed in her mind. It was unfamiliar because she was a creature of instinct and did not think in images.

Rueweed.

Rueweed and pigsbane.

Also carrots.

Rueweed was poison to both pigs and cattle, as everyone knew. And pigsbane was presumed to be poison, for the simple reason that pigs refused to eat it—and pigs were known to be clever in such matters. Nevertheless Fern did not hesitate. The images which had come into her head were like the voiceless promptings that told her when one of the pigs of the village was in need of her. She did not question them any more than she questioned why this pig had come to her—or where he had come from.

She had seen Meglan, one of the farmwives, working in her carrot patch yesterday. Perhaps there would be carrots in Meglan's refuse-tip today. And Fern knew where to find rueweed and pigsbane.

Hurrying because a pig had come to her for his life, she clutched the scraps which served as her cloak around her and ran from her hovel.

Along the one street which passed over the hills and became Sarendel-on-Gentle's link to the other villages of the Rift, past both alehouses, into a little lane which separated thatch-roofed shacks from more prosperous homes of timber and dressed stone, she made her way in a scurry of haste. An observer who did not know her would have thought she looked furtive. However, the villagers were accustomed to her crouching gait and her habitual way of keeping to the walls and hedges as if she feared to be accosted by someone who might expect her to speak, and so she passed as unremarked as a wraith among the dwellings to Meglan's home on the outskirts of the village.

Apparently unaware of Meglan spading her vegetables outside the house, Fern went directly to the refuse-tip beyond the fence and began rooting in her human fashion among the farmwife's compost.

Meglan paused to watch. She was a kindly woman, and Fern's haste suggested extreme hunger. When she saw how Fern pounced on the remaining peels and tassels of yesterday's stew, the farmwife unthinkingly pulled up a fresh handful of carrots, strode to the fence, and offered the carrots over the rails to Fern.

Too urgent to be gracious, Fern snatched the carrots, snuffled a piggy thanks, and scuttled away toward the hills as fast as her scrawny, unfed limbs could carry her.

Pigsbane. Rueweed. Meglan's generosity had already fallen into Fern's vague past, in one sense vividly remembered, in another quite forgotten. In her present haste she could not have formed any conception of how she had come by so much largesse as a handful of fresh carrots. Her head held nothing except rueweed and pigsbane and the need for speed.

It did not occur to her to fret over the fact that centuries of habitation had cleared all such plants away around the village for at least a mile in any direction. She did not fret over facts. They simply existed, unalterable. Yet she was afraid, and her fear pushed her faster than her strength could properly carry her. A pig had come to her, heartbroken and dying. She did not understand time, but she understood that when the pig's broken heart became cold death it would be a fact, as unalterable as the location of pigsbane and rueweed on the distant hillsides. Therefore she was afraid, and so she ran and stumbled and fell and ran again faster than she could endure.

Scarcely an hour had passed when she returned to her hovel, clutching the fruits of her scavenging in the scraps of her clothes. Sweat left streaks in the grime of her cheeks, and her eyes were glazed with exhaustion; she could have collapsed and slept and perhaps died without a moment's pause. Nevertheless she was still full of fear. And when she looked at the pig sprawled limp and hardly breathing in the dirt of her hovel, new images entered her mind.

She had no fire for heat, no mortar and pestle for grinding; she made do with what she had. First she tore the pigsbane to scraps. Scrubbing one stone over another, she reduced the scraps to flakes and shreds. Then she set them to soak in a bowl of water.

Shaking with tiredness and fear, she broke open the leaves of rueweed and rubbed their pungent odor—the tang of poison—under the pig's snout.

With a snort and a wince, the pig pulled his head back and blinked open his eyes. One of his eyes was unquestionably blind, but the other flashed its slice of silver at her.

At once, Fern set her bowl of soaking pigsbane in front of him. In relief rather than surprise—how could she be surprised, when all facts were the same to her?— she watched him drink.

When he had emptied the bowl, she gave him the carrots.

That was all she could do. If she had understood time, she would have known that she herself had eaten nothing for at least a day and a half. Her fear and strength were used up. Curling herself against the pig's back to keep him warm, she sank into sleep.

She did not think of death. Her heart was not broken.

Sleep was a familiar place for her, full of colors which might have been emotions and the affectionate snuffling of sows suckling their young. But after a time the colors and sounds became more images, and these were not familiar.

She saw the silver cut of the pig's eye rising like a new moon over the night of her mind.

She saw herself. How she knew it was herself was unclear, since her only knowledge of her appearance came from reflections in the moving waters of the Gentle, yet she did know it. And she knew also that it was herself beaten and weary, nearly cold with extinction.

Although the image was of herself, however, it did not disturb her. She gazed at it the same way that she gazed at all the world, as a fact about which there were no questions.

A crimson hue which might have been vexation or despair washed the image away, and another took its place.

In this image, she rose from her hovel and went to the nearest alehouse. There she scratched at the rear door until the aleman opened it. Then she dropped to her knees and made supplicating gestures toward her belly and mouth.

This image did disturb her. It came to her clad in the yellow of lament. She was Fern. She accepted gifts, but she did not ask for anything which was not hers. The image of pleading sent tears across the trails of sweat on her sleeping cheeks.

Nevertheless the thin sliver of argent in her mind and in the pig's eye bound her to him. He had come to her, adopted her: she was already his. When she awoke, she pulled her scraps of clothing about her and crept weeping along the street to Jessup's alehouse, where she scratched at the door behind the building until he answered. Filled with yellow and tears, she fell to her knees and begged for food with the only words she knew—the movements of her hands.

From his doorway Jessup peered at her and frowned. He was not known for Meglan's unthinking generosity. Stern and plain in all his dealings, he had used his father's alehouse to make himself wealthy—as such things were measured in Sarendel—and he liked his wealth. He made good ale and expected to be paid for it. Farmers and weavers, potters and laborers, men and women who wished to drink their ale today and settle their scores tomorrow were strictly required to take their custom to Yoel's alehouse, not Jessup's. In some other village, in some other part of Andovale, Jessup would have closed his door in Fern's face and thought no more about it.

But here, in Sarendel-on-Gentle, beggary was unknown. Jessup had not learned to refuse an appeal as naked as hers. Fern herself *was* well known, however: both her destitution and her honesty were as familiar as the village itself. On this occasion, her plight was as plain as emaciation and grime, tears and rags could make it. And finally, at Jessup's back door there were no witnesses. No one would see what he did and think that he had become less strict.

With a black scowl, he retreated to his kitchen and brought out a jug of broth, a slab of bread, and an earthen flask of ale, which he thrust into Fern's unsteady hands.

Snuffling grief instead of thanks, she returned to her hovel.

She did not want to eat the bread or drink the broth and ale. She felt that a violation had taken place. She had been hurt in some way for which she had no words and no understanding. She took nothing which was not granted to her. But as soon as she re-entered her dwelling the brindled pig fixed his eyes upon her. He could scarcely lift his head; he clearly had no strength to stand. His exhaustion was as profound as hers, and as fatal. The danger that he would starve had been only briefly postponed. And the scabs and splotches which marked his hide were plain signs of illness rather than injury. Yet he fixed his eyes upon her—the one blind, the other flawed with silver—and she found that she could not refuse to eat. Did she not love pigs? And had he not come to her in his last need?

Held by his gaze, she chewed the bread and drank the broth. With a pig's cleverness she knew that the ale was too strong for her, so she did not touch it. Instead she poured it out in a bowl and set it under his snout so that he could have it.

When he had consumed it all, he drew a shuddering breath which she interpreted as pleasure. And that in turn pleased her more than any amount of food or drink for herself.

Together they slept again.

So Fern became a beggar—and so her pig's life was saved. Each time she slept, the images came to her: more scratching at doors, more supplication. And each time she awoke she acted on them with less sorrow. The loss of her honesty had become a fact, unalterable. Instead of grieving, she used the strength of new sustenance to scavenge for her pig. She was able to roam more widely, root more deeply. She found grains and vegetables for him, as well as herbs from which she concocted healing poultices and balms. Steadily, if slowly, he drew vitality from her care and began to mend.

After several nights, the images stopped. They were no longer needed. In their place, her head was filled with the soothing cerulean and emerald which she had always gained from the affection of pigs, and occasionally she heard sounds—silent except within her head—which might have been, *My thanks*. She felt the gratitude in them; but the sounds themselves meant nothing to her, so at last she concluded that they were the pig's name, and she took to calling him "Mythanks." That was the first word she had ever spoken, the only word she knew. She hugged him morning and night, and caressed him whenever the mood came upon her, and whispered fondly in his ears, "Mythanks, Mythanks," and her regret for the woman she had once been became vague with the uncertainty of all time.

When perhaps a fortnight had passed, Mythanks was well enough to join her in her scavenging. Although he

was still weak, he trotted briskly at her side, scenting
the air and scanning the vistas like a creature which had
come to a new world. Uncharacteristically for a pig, he
sniffed and snorted at every grass and herb and shrub
they encountered as though he were teaching himself to
know them for the first time. He surveyed the hillsides as
though he were measuring distances and possibilities. He
shied away from passing herd-dogs and farmers as though
they might be his enemies, despite the fact that no one
in Sarendel-on-Gentle would harm a pig—until the time
came to slaughter the porkers and the aging sows. And
when the herd-dogs and farmers were gone, he rubbed
his bristled back against Fern's legs with a pig's desire
for reassurance.

Because he was not yet fully hale, he could not roam
far; and so the day's scavenging found him less food than
he wanted. This worried Fern. She thought she saw a look
of discouragement—or was it calculation?—in Mythanks'
strange eyes. However she petted and coddled him, he did
not nuzzle her fondly, or fill her head with the hues of
gratitude. He had adopted her. He was her responsibility,
and her care of him was inadequate. When a tear or two
of remorse caught and spread on her muddy cheeks, he
ignored them.

But the next day he went with her while she begged.

Prompted by her instinct to creep from place to place,
calling as little attention to herself as possible, she had
taken her unwonted supplications to a different villager
each day. After the gift of carrots, she had not dared
return to Meglan. Certainly she had not approached Jessup
again. Rather she had been to Yoel's alehouse, then to
widower Horrik's tannery, then to Salla and Veil among
the farmwives, then to Karay the weaver and Limm the
potter; and so to a new benefactor on every occasion.

On this occasion, however, Mythanks had his own
ideas. Directly, as though he had lived in Sarendel all
his life and knew it well, he led Fern back to Jessup's
alehouse.

Wordlessly alarmed, she could not put her hand to the door at the rear of the alehouse. Jessup's sternness frightened her. If she had not been so near to starvation on that first day, she would not have dared come here at all. She could only watch and wince as Mythanks lifted a foreleg and scratched at the door with his hoof.

When Jessup opened the door and saw her, he did not take the sight kindly.

"You!" he snapped. "Begone! Do not think you can take advantage of me a second time. All the village is talking about your beggary. You have acquired a pig, and now you beg. Did you beg him as well, or have you fallen as low as theft? I would not have fed you so much as once, but I believed that you were honest. I will not make that mistake again."

Fern understood none of his words, but his tone was plain. It hurt her like a blow. Cringing, she tried to shrink down into herself as she turned away.

Mythanks snorted once, softly, and fixed Jessup with his eyes, the one blind, the other flawed by silver.

Jessup made a noise in his throat which frightened Fern more than shouts and abuse. To her ears, it was the strangling gurgle of death.

As if he were stunned, Jessup moved backward into the alehouse and out of sight. Then he returned, carrying a bushel of barley and a large basket overflowing with bread and sausages. These he set at Mythanks' feet without a word. Backward again, he re-entered the alehouse and closed the door.

Mythanks sniffed the barley, looked over at Fern where she crouched in alarm, and snorted a pig's laughter.

Fern was astonished. She had never seen so much food. "Mythanks," she murmured because she had no words with which to express her surprise, "Mythanks, Mythanks."

At once his laughter became vexation. New sounds formed in her mind. *My name is not Mythanks, you daft woman. It is Titus. Titus! Do you hear me? TITUS!*

"Ti-tus." Staring at him, she tried the word in her mouth. "Ti-tus. Titus." In her amazement, she failed to notice that she had understood him.

Blue pleasure and green satisfaction came into her head as she said his name. *That*, he replied, *is a distinct improvement.* But her instant of comprehension had passed, and she had no idea what the sounds meant.

"Titus."

Hardly aware of what she did, she set the basket of bread and sausages on his back, steadied it with one hand, then propped the bushel of barley on her hip and returned to her hovel.

That day they feasted and slept. And the next morning Titus nudged her awake with his snout. When she met his blind and piercing gaze, she heard more sounds in the silence of her mind.

It is time we began. Bread and sausages will feed your body, but they will do nothing to nourish your intelligence. I **must** *have intelligence. Also you are filthy—and filth wards away help. There are many lessons that a pig could teach you. Today we will make a start.*

This meant nothing to Fern. The sounds came from him—she accepted that as a fact—but they communicated less than the grunts of pigs. Nevertheless she hugged him happily because he seemed so brisk and whole. Yesterday's fear and surprise were forgotten. She was simply glad that Titus had come to her, and that she had been able to help him, and that she knew his name.

Never mind, he said while he nuzzled her neck. *Perhaps you will understand me in time. For the present, you are willing. I will make that suffice.*

Again he fixed her with the argent sliver of his good eye, and now in images she saw herself leaving her hovel and walking to a secluded bank of the Gentle, where she removed her shreds of clothing, immersed herself in the water, and scrubbed herself with sand until her skin became a color which she had never before seen in her own reflection.

It is a risk, he said as she rose to obey the image. *Change attracts attention, and attention is dangerous. But I need help. We must begin somewhere. Cleanliness will do much to improve your place in this misbegotten pigsty of a village.*

"Titus," she answered, dumbly pleased. "Titus."

Snuffling encouragement, he accompanied her down to the Gentle.

The image he had placed in her mind amazed her entirely, but her compliance did not. She had accepted her obedience to him as a fact. And she was not afflicted with modesty. Her impulse to cower, to avoid notice, grew from other fears than bodily shame. So it was not a hard thing for her to do as Titus directed. Hidden by the overarching boughs of a thirsty willow at the river's edge, she set aside her scraps and entered the water.

Here the Gentle was cool but not cold, and it had worn a fine sandy bottom for itself off the hard edges of time. Under Titus' watchful eye, Fern splashed and bubbled and rubbed until the color of her skin and the feel of her hair were transformed. As she did so, she was filled with a light blue pleasure as quiet and steady as the water. And the blue deepened to azure—she did not know or ask why—when the pig said to her like a promise, *Someday, you will ask me what loveliness is, and I will tell you.*

Next he gave her an image in which she scrubbed her clothes as she had cleaned herself. Washing them did not make them whole, but it did give them a gentler touch on the unfamiliar tingle of her skin.

At last she rose from the water as if on this day she had been made new.

As she dressed, two of Yoel's small sons scampered past the willow, looking to avoid the chores which Nell alewife their mother had in mind for them. They may have seen Fern or they may not; in either case, their attention was elsewhere. Nevertheless she crouched instinctively against the bole of the willow, so that whatever the boys saw would be as unobtrusive as possible.

At once the pleasure in her head changed to the hue of vexation. Perhaps all the colors of her mind were no longer hers, but now belonged to Titus.

Blast you, he muttered, *you have too far to go. And I am helpless.*

Almost as if he wished to punish her for her timidity, he urged her to scavenge all day for wood. And the next day he pushed her to accost one of Yoel's small sons while the boys played truant from Nell's chores. Fern herself did nothing except to put out her hand to pause the boy as he ran, and that was enough to make her heart beat in her throat. Titus did the rest. After he had gazed at the boy for a moment or two with his silver-marred eye, he turned away. Snorting in satisfaction, he led Fern back to their hovel.

Because she loved his satisfaction, she hugged and caressed him and fed him barley-mash. When Yoel's small son and two of his brothers arrived at her storeshed a short time later carrying a firepot full of flame, her ability to grasp that they might have been doing the pig's bidding had already faded. She understood them only because the farmwives sometimes sent her a firepot as an act of kindness, knowing that she had no other flame to keep her alive if the night turned bitter across the Gentle's Rift.

Before she lost her honesty, she had been able to accept gifts. But now kindness dismayed her. She cowered away from the children as though they frightened her.

The youngest boy set the firepot in the dirt beside Fern's woodpile. Staring at her, he asked, "Is she sick, then?"

"You're daft," the middle brother snorted with the contempt of his greater age. "That ain't sick, that's clean."

"Cor!" breathed the oldest. "Who'd have thought she looked like that?" Then he flushed and ducked his head.

While Fern tried to sink out of sight against the wall, Titus stepped in front of her. Standing proudly in the center of the space as if the hovel were a mansion and his, he fixed his eyes on each of the boys until they all nodded in turn. Then he dismissed them with a grunt and a jerk of his head.

"Titus," Fern murmured because she had no other name for her dismay. "Titus."

He looked at her. As if her distress were a question, he said, *Yes, they would be easier—for a time. But then they would begin to fear me, and then I would be lost. However, I seriously doubt that any of these clods and clowns is capable of fearing you. And the children even less than the adults. So I will ask only children for help—and only for you. The rest must be kept between the two of us.*

Seeing that she was not comforted, he nuzzled at her until she came away from the wall to scratch his ears. Then he added, *I will take it as a personal triumph if you are ever able to say* **yes** *to me of your own accord.*

Yes, Fern thought to herself. Yes. It was a strange sound. If it had been the name of a pig, she would have understood it. As matters stood, however, the sound could only trouble her with hints of significance; it could not reach her.

Never mind, he told her again. *For today we have gained enough. When those whelps return, we will cast our net wider.*

She heard sadness in his voice, and so she hugged him with all her strength, seeking to reassure him.

You or no one, Titus whispered to her embrace. *You must suffice. I have no other hope.*

The boys did not return until evening. While Fern and Titus warmed themselves beside her unaccustomed fire—which she built and tended and kept small according to the images he placed in her mind—hands tugged at the burlap curtain that served as her door, and children entered her hovel. During the day the three had become five, and two of them were girls. They came to her carrying small sacks and tight bundles of herbs.

Here her acceptance of facts failed her. Herbs? For her and Titus? Children did not do such things. Her vague experience of time did not contain those actions. Typically children ignored her; on occasion they teased and tormented her; sometimes they were as kind as a warm breeze. But they did not bring her gifts of witch hazel and thyme, rueweed and coriander, sloewort and marjoram and vert. And Titus had not prepared her with images. Whatever she knew and needed in order to live seemed to totter when Yoel's familiar sons and daughters offered her herbs.

In order to grasp what had happened, to accommodate it so that it could be borne, she had to make a leap across time; for her, a profound leap. She had to connect the fact that Titus had looked into Yoel's sons' eyes at some point in the imprecise past with the fact that these children had come here now with herbs. This was a leap greater than understanding that a sow broached in farrow must be helped to release her piglets. It was a leap greater than knowing that the farmwife who offered her a cloak after she had eased the birth pangs of the farmwife's sow did so in thanks. Those events were self-contained, each within its own sequence. But *this*—

As though he sensed her distress, Titus began to fill her head with images.

One of them showed her herself as she nodded in thanks and smiled for the children; it showed her rising from the protection of the wall to surprise them with her cleanliness, and to touch each of them gratefully upon the cheek, and to let them know that it was time for them to return home.

But she obeyed without noticing what she did: her attention was on other images, images which explained what the children had done. In those images, he spoke to them, and they complied. When they brought the herbs he needed to her hovel, they were acting on his instructions.

Yes, Titus told her firmly, almost urgently, as soon as the children were gone, *there* **is** *a connection. You guessed that, and you were right. You do not understand time, but you can understand that it is no barrier to sequence. If you touch the flame, will you not be burned? If Jessup at the hearth of his alehouse touches the flame, will he not* be burned, even though you do not see it? If I ask you to bathe, do you not go to the river and cleanse yourself? It is not otherwise with these whelps, or with time. One thing will lead to another because it must.

Yes, Fern repeated because that was the only sound she recognized. Yes, Titus.

She meant neither *yes* nor *no*, but only that she knew no other response. Nevertheless she saw clearly what he gave her to see: he had spoken to the boys as he spoke to her, silent and silver; those sounds conveyed images to them, which they had heeded; obediently they had hunted the hills for herbs and brought them to her, telling no one what they did. Again and again the events played through her, showing her the links between them, until she fell asleep; sleeping, she dreamed of nothing else. And when she awakened, the connection had become secure.

Across time, and against all likelihood, Yoel's children had brought these herbs because Titus had asked it of them.

At her side, Titus snored heavily, sleeping as though he had been awake all night to weave images. He did not rouse when she scratched his throat; dreams and images were gone from her head.

But the connection remained.

"Yes," she said aloud, although he did not hear her. The sound *Titus* meant this pig. The sound *Yes* meant the connection. One thing will lead to another because it must.

She had no idea what all these herbs were for, so she left them where they lay. After a fine breakfast of bread and sausages and clear water, she spent the morning hunting wood; then she returned to her hovel to find Titus awake at last.

About time, he snorted. *Did you think I gathered all these herbs for my health?* But the hue of his mood was reassuring, and the images he wove for her had an itch of excitement in them.

She set to work promptly under his watchful gaze. When she had built up her fire from its embers, she turned

to the gifts Yoel's children had brought. In a bowl of water
she mixed marjoram *(Not too much)*, vert *(Just so)*, coriander and thyme *(More than that, more)*, and sloewort *(Only
a pinch, you daft woman, I said only a **pinch**)*. This she
settled in the flames to boil, and as it heated she crushed
rueweed *(Better if it were dry, but it will have to serve)* and
a little witch hazel into a smaller pot. Once she had ground
the leaves as fine as she could, she stirred in enough water
to make a paste with a smell so acute that her nose ran.

Wipe it on a rag, not your hand, he told her imperi-
ously. *You already need another bath*. However, he gave
her no images to compel her. His attention was on the bowl
steaming among the coals.

At his behest, she stirred the herbs vigorously while
they boiled; then she pulled the bowl from the flames and
set it in the dirt to cool.

Hints of green and blue and a strange, raw crimson
flickered at the edges of her mind while she and the pig
waited. Titus was excited, she felt that. And expectant,
awaiting another connection. And anxious—

Anxious? Was it possible for the connection to fail?
Had he not told her that one thing will lead to another?

Because it must, he finished brusquely. *Yes. But it is
possible to misunderstand or misuse the sequence. And it
is possible for the sequence to be obstructed. It may be
that you are too stupid, even for me.*

His tone saddened her, but she did not know how to
say so.

Instructed by images, she stirred the herb broth again,
then scooped a measure of the thick liquid into a broken-
rimmed cup—the last container she owned. New images
followed. Titus showed her drinking from the cup, showed
her face twisting in disgust, showed her spitting the broth
into the dirt. Then, so vehemently that her head rang and
her limbs flinched, he forbade her to do what she had just
seen. Instead she must swallow the broth, no matter how
it gagged her. After that she must dip one finger into
the paste of rueweed and witch hazel, and place a touch

of it upon her tongue. That would cure her need to gag.

He was Titus, the pig who had adopted her; he was her only connection in all the world. She wished to shy away from the broth, but she did not do so. Thinking, *Yes*, with her peculiar understanding of the word, she gulped down the contents of the cup.

It felt like thistles in her throat; it stung her stomach like thorns and immediately surged back toward her mouth. Her face twisted; she hunched to vomit. Yet Titus' images held her. Obeying them, her finger stabbed at the paste, carried it to her tongue.

That flavor was as acrid as gall, but it accomplished what he had promised: instantly it stilled her impulse to gag. Her body felt that it had suffered another violation; however, the sensation faded swiftly. By the time her heart had beat three times, she was no longer in distress.

The pig rewarded her with a vivid display of pleasure and satisfaction, as bright as the sun on the waters of the Gentle and as comforting as dawn on her face. *Well done*, he breathed, although she did not know those words. *You are indeed willing. The fault will not be yours if I fail.* Then he added, *As you grow accustomed to it, it will become less burdensome.*

"Yes?" she murmured, asking him for the sequence, the connection. Without words or knowledge, she wished to comprehend what he did.

Now, however, he did not appear to understand her.

He required her to drink the broth again at sunset, and again at dawn and noontime. And when the sun had set once more, Yoel's children returned, bringing four or five of their young friends as well as more herbs and firewood. They also brought bread and carrots, corn and bacon, butter and apples and sausages and beans which they had appropriated from their parents' kitchens. Now Fern was not a beggar: she was a thief. But she did not see the connection, and so she was not disturbed by it. Instead she was simply gladdened that she did not need to abase herself for so much good food.

For perhaps another fortnight, Titus impelled her to do nothing new or strange. Indeed, her life became simpler than it had ever been, so simple that she hardly regarded its unfamiliar ease. Apparently he was now content. Three times a day she drank the broth and touched her tongue with the paste. Often she bathed in the Gentle. And she stopped pressing her bones against the wall when the children—at least a dozen of them now at various intervals—came to her hovel. More than often, she smiled; once she was so filled by pleasure that she laughed outright. The rest of her days and nights were spent sleeping with Titus, roaming the hills with him, caressing and cozying him, or perhaps watching the games and play of the children, and then studying the images in her mind while Titus showed her the sequences which explained what the children did.

She owned a pig, and she was happy. Only her lack of self-consciousness prevented her from knowing that she was happy. If other pigs needed her, she failed to hear their cries or feel their distress. And they no longer came to her when they succeeded at wandering away from their homes. But her knowledge of time was still uncertain, and she did not notice the change.

Of course, the village noticed. With the selective blindness of adults, the farmers and farmwives, the weavers and potters declined to recognize the surreptitious activities of their children; but they had all known Fern long enough to mark the change in her. They saw her new cleanliness, her new health; they saw the gradual alteration in the way she walked. When she raised her head, the brightness in her eyes was plain. And all Sarendel could hardly fail to observe that wherever she went she was accompanied by a pig which belonged to no one else.

Strange things were rare in Sarendel-on-Gentle. They were worthy of discussion.

"A beggar!" Jessup protested in his taproom. "That pig has made her a beggar, I swear it."

"Be fair, Jessup," rumbled widower Horrik, the tanner. He was a large man with large appetites. He still missed his wife, but because of Fern's cleanliness he had begun to see her in new ways, ways which did not altogether distress him. "She was only a beggar for a short time. Was it as much as a fortnight? Now she lives otherwise."

He looked around the taproom, hoping that someone would tell him how Fern lived.

No one did. Instead, Meglan's husband, Wall, said, "In any case, Jessup, you must be sensible." To counteract his softheartedness, Wall placed great store on sense. "The creature is only a pig—and not a prepossessing one, you must admit. How can a pig make her do anything?"

Jessup might have retorted sourly, Because she is daft and dumb. She cannot care for a pig with her own wits. However, Karay the weaver was already speaking.

"But where does he come from?" she asked. "That's what I wish to know. Pigs do not fall from the sky—or climb the sides of the Rift. No village is nearer than Cromber, and that is three days distant for a man in haste. At their worst pigs do not wander so far."

Wall and the other farmers nodded sagely. None of them had ever heard of a pig lost more than three miles from home.

Like Wall's, Karay's question was unanswerable. Glowering blackly, Jessup muttered, "I mean what I say. You mark me. That pig is an ill thing, and no good will come of him." He had no name for the silver compulsion which had caused him to give bread, sausages, and barley to Fern. "If she no longer feeds herself by beggary, it is because she has learned a worse trick."

"Be fair," Horrik said again, and Wall repeated, "Be sensible." Nevertheless the men and women gathered in the taproom squirmed uncomfortably at Jessup's words. All Sarendel had heard the tales of the merchanters on their annual drive down the Rift, tales of intrigues and warlocks and wonders. The villagers could adjudge with confidence any matter which was familiar along the Gentle, but who among them could say certainly what was and what was not possible in the wider world?

No more than a day or two later, the wider world offered them an opportunity to ask its opinion. Unprecedented on a white horse, with a rapier at his side and a tassel in his hat, a man entered Sarendel-on-Gentle from the direction of Cromber. In the center of the village, he dismounted. Stamping dust from his boots and wiping sweat from his brow, he waited until Limm the potter and Vail farmwife came out from their homes to greet him; until every child of the village had arrived as if drawn by magic to the surprise of a stranger; until Yoel and Jessup had left their alehouses, Horrik his tannery, Karay her weaving, and the other farmwives their kitchens and gardens to join the crowd he attracted. Then he swept off his hat, bowed with a long leg, and spoke.

His eyes were road-weary and skeptical, but he smiled and spoke cheerfully. "Good people of Sarendel-on-Gentle, I am Destrier of the Prince's Roadmen. Lately it has come to Prince Chorl the lord of all Andovale that his domain would profit if its many regions and holdings were bound together by a skein of tidings and knowledge. Therefore he has commissioned his Roadmen to travel throughout the land. It is the will of my Prince that I spread the news of Andovale down the Gentle's Rift, and that I bear back to him the news of the Rift's villages and doings.

"Good people, will you welcome me in Prince Chorl's name?"

Yoel tugged at his leather apron. Because he was an affable man who had shown during the visits of the merchanters that he was not chagrined by strangers, he sometimes spoke on behalf of the village. "Surely," he replied in a slow rumble. "We welcome any man or woman who passes among us. Why should we not? We mean no harm, and expect none." He might have added, We do not require the bidding of princes to extend courtesy. However, his good nature worked against such plain speaking.

Instead he continued, "But I fear I do not understand. What manner of news is it that you seek?"

"Why, change, of course," Destrier replied as though he found Yoel's affability—or his perplexity—charming. "I seek news of change. Any change at all. Change is of endless interest to my Prince."

Yoel received this assertion with some concern. "Change?" He dropped his eyes, and a frown crossed his broad face. Around him, people shifted on their feet and looked away. Children stared at the Roadman as though he might begin to spout poetry. At last Yoel met Destrier's gaze again and shook his head.

"We are as you see us—as we have always been. Along the Gentle we know little of change. Surely the other folk of the Rift have said the same?

"However, it is of no great moment," he went on more quickly. "You are road-weary, no doubt thirsty and hungry as well. I must not ask you to remain standing in the sun while I ask you to explain in what way your Prince believes we might have changed. Will you accept the hospitality of my alehouse?" He gestured toward it with an open palm. "Your horse will be cared for. We have no horses here, as you surely know, but the merchanters have taught us how to care for their beasts."

At once Wall stepped forward to place a hand on the reins of the Roadman's mount. "I have a stall to spare in my barn." During the visits of the merchanters, he often profited in a small way by tending their horses.

Smiling with less cheer and more skepticism, Destrier bowed and answered, "My thanks." To Yoel he added, "Aleman, I will gladly accept a flagon and a meal. I do not mean to overstay my welcome, but if you will house and feed me until the morrow, you will earn Prince Chorl's gratitude."

"In plain words," Jessup muttered softly to the farmwife standing near him, "the Prince's Roadman does not propose to pay for his fare. Let Yoel have his custom—and my gratitude as well."

If Destrier heard this remark, he did not acknowledge it. Instead he followed Yoel to the alehouse.

In turn, a good half of the villagers—Jessup among them—followed the Roadman. They desired to hear the tales he would tell of the wide world. And his talk of "change" had made them apprehensive; they wished to know what would come of it. The rest of Sarendel's folk herded their children away and returned to their chores.

While these events transpired, Fern and Titus knew nothing about them. Together they had roamed farther than usual, and they came home late for her midday dose of herbs. However, during the afternoon some of the smaller children made their way to her hovel with the tidings.

The pig responded as though he had been struck. Fern saw flashes of anger and fear in the air as he turned his one blind eye and his marred one commandingly on the children. Unfortunately, they were too young to give a cogent account of what had happened. Strangers and strangeness caught their attention more than names or words. One child remembered, "Roadman." Another babbled of "Prince Chorl." But none of them could say what brought a Roadman to Sarendel, or what Prince Chorl had to do with the matter.

Fools, Titus snorted bitterly. *Guttersnipes. Children. Why has that meddling prince invented Roadmen? And what damnable mischance has brought this pigsty to his attention?*

Curse them, I am not ready. I need more time.

In a voice so harsh that Fern was shocked by it, he cried, *I need more* **time!**

"Yes," she murmured incoherently, trying to console him. "Yes, Titus."

The pig turned on her. Thin silver ran like a cut into her brain.

For an instant, she saw an image of herself approaching Yoel's alehouse, entering it to witness what was said and done. She saw herself hearing voices and remembering what they said, remembering words—But before it was complete the image frayed away, tattered by despair.

You will understand nothing, he groaned. *And they will not allow a pig to enter.*

I must—I must—

He did not say what he must.

But when he had fretted Fern to distraction through the afternoon and evening, his fortunes improved. Late enough to find her yawning uncontrollably and barely able to keep wood on the fire, more children came to her hovel and nudged the curtain to announce themselves. When they entered, she recognized two of the older boys, one Yoel's tallest son, the other Wall and Meglan's boy, who was nearly of a size to begin working in his father's fields. She knew without knowing how she knew that their names were Levit and Lessom.

Titus jumped up to face them. With the familiarity of frequent visits, they dropped to the dirt beside the fire. Fatigue and excitement burned on their faces; their eyes were on a level with his. As if they no longer noticed the oddness of what they did, they spoke to the pig rather than to the woman.

"They told us not to go," Lessom panted, out of breath from running. "We are too young for ale, and we had no business there. But we sneaked into the cellar— Levit knew the way—and found a crack in the floorboards where we could hear. Cor, my legs hurt. We stood for hours and hours. Do all grown men talk so, of everything and nothing in the middle of the day, as if they had no work—"

Titus stopped the rush of words with a flash of his eyes. *Slowly,* Fern heard. *Be complete. I must know everything. Begin at the beginning. Who is he? Where does he come from? What does he want?*

Every line and muscle of the pig's body was tight with strain, as though he were about to flee.

"He is Destrier," Levit offered, "Prince Chorl's Roadman. He said Prince Chorl commissioned the Roadmen to carry news everywhere in Andovale. He said he wants to hear the news from all the villages in the Rift. And he told tales—"

"Cor, the tales!" Lessom breathed. "Better than the merchanters tell. Is it true that there are wars—that warlocks and princes fight each other for power beyond the Rift?"

No! Titus grunted. *Warlocks do not fight princes. The ruling of lands requires too much time and attention. Any warlock who neglects his arts for such things becomes weak. Warlocks reserve their struggles for each other.*

What "news" does this Roadman want?

"Change." Levit's eyes were as round and solemn as a cow's. "He said he wants news of change. Any change. For Prince Chorl."

Impelled by the pig's tension, Fern added more wood to the fire.

Titus held the boys with his gaze. *Now pay attention*, he insisted. *Make no mistake. My life depends on this. What did they tell him? Your fathers—all those self-satisfied clodhoppers who talk of everything and nothing when there is work to be done—what did they tell him?*

Did they betray me? Have I been betrayed?

Levit glanced sidelong at Lessom. "Your father talked about the weather. I've never heard so many words about wind and sun. The weather! I thought I would die of impatience. I wanted to hear what the Roadman would say."

"Yes." Lessom was too excited to take offense. "And your father repeated everything everyone has ever known about brewing ale."

Levit nodded. "And then Karay mentioned every birth or death in, Cor, it must have been ten years. My knees were trembling before the Roadman so much as began his tales."

Continue.

"But the tales were worth it," Lessom said, "were they not?"

Again Levit nodded.

"You say that warlocks do not fight princes," Lessom

continued, "but the Roadman said otherwise. He spoke of a time when the enemies of Andovale mustered a great army of soldiers and warlocks to march against Prince—"

"Prince Chrys," Lessom put in.

"—Prince Chrys, and were defeated by—"

Titus stopped him. *Old news. Ancient history. That war is why warlocks no longer meddle in the affairs of princes. Preparing for war, the warlocks of Carcin and Sargo neglected their true arts. They made themselves weak, and so were defeated by the warlocks of Andovale. In magic, those who do not grow must decline.*

Hearing another connection, Fern thought softly, Yes.

But, *Think!* the pig was saying. *This Roadman did not ride the length of the Rift to relate old news. He must have spoken of more recent matters—events which have transpired since the last visit of the merchanters. Tell me that tale!*

Titus' vehemence disconcerted Levit. "He spoke of a war among warlocks," the boy began. "But Prince Chorl was also involved—" He broke off as though he feared to displease the pig.

That *one*, Titus demanded.

"He was called Suriman," Lessom began abruptly. The small cut of silver in the pig's gaze seemed to take hold of him. His body tightened in ways which distressed Fern. From the corners of his mind he brought out the Roadman's tale just as Destrier had told it. "That was his title—men do not speak his name. He was a prince among warlocks, ancient in magic as well as years. That he was called Suriman shows the respect in which he was held by all his brother warlocks. When the masters of magic gathered in council, he was often the first to speak. When Prince Chorl or the other lords of Andovale needed either the help or the counsel of a warlock, they often approached Suriman first. Indeed, it was Suriman himself who devised the means by which the warlocks of Sargo and Carcin were defeated.

"Yet there were some in Andovale, warlocks as well

as ordinary men, who spoke ill of Suriman behind his back. They were thought jealous or petty when they hinted that he practiced his arts in ways which the masters of magic in council had proscribed many generations ago. They said—though they were not believed—that he had violated the foremost commandment of the councils, which is that the study and practice of magic is the responsibility of warlocks and must not be imposed on ordinary men against their will. If a warlock requires a man for experimentation or study, he must perform his researches upon himself, or upon some other warlock, not on men who can neither gauge nor accept—and certainly cannot prevent—the consequences.

"Those who spoke ill against Suriman said that he had performed his studies upon ordinary men, making some less than they were and others more, but always depriving his victims of choice in his researches. By so doing, he had gained for himself powers unheard of among warlocks for many generations. Thus his might, his stature, and his very title were founded upon evil."

Titus snorted in disgust, but did not interrupt.

"At first, those who spoke ill against Suriman were ignored. Then they were criticized and scorned. From time to time, one or another of them died, perhaps because they erred in their own experimentation, perhaps because they were punished for their indiscretions, perhaps because Suriman himself took action against them. Such deaths belonged to the province of warlocks, however, not to the jurisprudence of princes, and the masters of magic found Suriman faultless in them.

"But Prince Chorl had a daughter. Her name was Florice, and she was renowned throughout Andovale for her beauty, her sweetness—and her simplicity. In truth, she was not merely simple. She was a child of perhaps eight or nine years in a woman's body, unfit for a woman's life. For some time this was a cause of great grief to Prince Chorl. But when his grief was done, he cherished her for her beauty, for her sweet nature, and also for her simplicity.

Therefore she was unwed—and unavailable. The Prince kept her as a child in his household, both protecting and loving her for what she was."

Abruptly, Fern found that she could see Prince Chorl's daughter—a woman clad in white as pure as samite, with silken hair, eyes like sunshine, and a form which Titus might have called *lovely*. Her image in Fern's mind was as precise as presence. Yet Fern knew more of her through the colors of the image than from the image itself. They were the hues of a complex and insatiable hunger.

"So she would have remained," Lessom related in Destrier's tones, "until old age claimed her, if she had not caught Suriman's eye. To Prince Chorl's amazement, and all Andovale's astonishment, Suriman asked to wed Florice.

" 'No,' said the Prince in his surprise.

" 'Why not?' Suriman countered calmly. 'Do you fear that I will not cherish her as you do? I swear by my arts that her sweetness and happiness are as precious to me as my life, and I will find great joy in her.'

"Dumbfounded, Prince Chorl seemed unable to think calmly. 'It is absurd,' he protested. 'You do not know what you are asking. You—' Because he was not thinking calmly, he turned to his daughter. 'Florice, do you wish to wed this man?'

"Florice gazed at Suriman and smiled her sweetest smile. 'No, Father,' she said. 'He is bad.'

"Neither the Prince nor Suriman knew how to respond to such a remark. However, the warlock was less disconcerted than his Prince. Laughing gently, he said, 'Really, my lord, I am too old to be a jilted suitor. I have lost my appetite for appearing foolish. Please permit me to remain as your guest for a season. Permit me to speak to your daughter for a few minutes each day—in your presence, of course. If you see nothing ill in my comportment toward her, perhaps you will not believe that I am "bad." And if at the end of the season she does not desire me, I will accept my folly and depart the wiser.'

"This proposal Prince Chorl accepted. He is not to be blamed for his mistake—although he blames himself mightily. Suriman was held in high esteem throughout Andovale. And those who spoke ill against him could prove nothing."

The colors in Fern's mind were ones of hope and possession, of a grasped opportunity. She could not imagine why Titus showed them to her: they were simply a fact, as all his images were facts—or became facts. Perhaps they came from him involuntarily or unconsciously while he heard Destrier's tale in Lessom's mouth.

"Yet if the Prince erred, he did not err blindly. He made certain that Suriman had no contact with Florice outside his own presence. And he watched her closely while Suriman spoke with her, studying her dear face for understanding. Before a fortnight passed, he saw that her face had changed.

"Tightness pulled at the corners of her mouth, straining her smiles. Her eyes lost their forthright sweetness and turned aside from her father's gaze. She asked questions which the Prince had never heard from her before. 'Father, why do men and women marry?' 'Father, why do you treat me like a child?' By these signs, he understood that his loved daughter was in peril."

The image Fern saw conveyed satisfaction and excitement, whetted desire. Nevertheless, unbidden, she made a connection which did not come to her either from the image or through its colors. Rather it came from her own emotions—and from her growing sense of time.

Yes, she thought, not in acceptance, but in dismay. What she saw on the face of the Prince's daughter was violation.

Florice was not willing.

Perhaps Titus wished her to understand this, so that she would understand what followed.

"Yet Suriman was Suriman, respected everywhere. Prince Chorl felt that he could not send the warlock from his house. Instead he took other precautions. In secret he

summoned one of the warlocks—a man named Titus"—
again the pig snorted—"who was known to think ill of
Suriman, and he told Titus of his fears. He give Titus the
freedom of his house, and charged Titus to find proof that
Suriman wrought evil against Florice.

"With Prince Chorl's support and assistance, Titus did
as he was charged. Before another fortnight was ended,
Florice announced to her father her settled intention to
wed the warlock who courted her—and Titus announced
his accusation that Suriman had flouted the most urgent
commandment of the councils, that he had betrayed Florice
by using his arts to alter her to his will.

"Consternation! In an instant, the peace of Andovale
became chaos and distress. Flinging defiance at her father,
Florice sought to flee the house with Suriman." Fern saw a
hunger on her face which echoed the hunger of the colors
surrounding her—a hunger she had not chosen and could
not refuse. "Prince Chorl countered by imprisoning her,
his daughter whom he cherished. Suriman attacked her
prison, wreaking havoc in the Prince's house, and was only
prevented from freeing Florice by the foresight of Titus,
who had prepared defenses against the greater warlock—
and had also demanded the attention of the council in what
he did. The masters of magic gave Titus their aid until they
could learn the truth of his accusations, and so Suriman's
onslaught was beaten back. Even as the masters of magic
met in council to examine Titus' proofs, Suriman ran.

"Inspired by his loathing of the crimes he attributed
to Suriman, Titus had found sure proof. With gossamer
incantations and webs of magic, he had followed Suriman's
movements throughout the Prince's house. He had traced
Suriman daily to the kitchens where the delicacies which
Florice most loved were prepared. And in the foods she
was given to eat he found the herbs and simples, the
poisons and potions, which Suriman would need to make
Florice something other than she was against her will.

"Outraged, the council declared anathema on Suriman
and went to war against him.

"He was mighty—oh, he was mighty! He could stand alone against any half-dozen of his peers. And his dark tower where he studied his arts was mightily protected. But all the masters of magic in Andovale moved against him. They brought out fire from the air to crack his tower and drive him forth. Then he fled, and they gave chase. He took refuge in castles and towns. They scorched the very walls around him until he fled again. He hid himself in forests and villages. They shook the stones under his feet, so that he could not stand, but only run. And at last, on one of the farms at the end of the Gentle's Rift, they brought him to bay.

"The masters of magic do not speak of the final battle, but it was prodigious. In desperation, Suriman wove every power and trick at his vast command. Warlocks fell that day, and some never rose again. When the fire and passion had ended, however, Suriman lay dead among the wreck-age of the farm. The beasts had scattered, and the fields were blasted, but the council had triumphed.

"That is to say, the masters of magic believed that they had triumphed. Suriman's corpse lay before them. Only Titus insisted that the evil was not done—Titus and Florice. Crying in wild hunger, the Prince's daughter claimed that the warlocks were too little to kill a man of Suriman's greatness. And Titus, whom loathing for Suriman had made cunning, spoke of texts and apparatus in Suriman's tower which pertained to the transfer of intelligences from one body to another. He told all who would hear him that Suriman could have escaped the last battle cloaked inside another man, or even concealed within a beast. If what he said were true, then Suriman might well remain alive— and might return.

"So the council watches for Suriman constantly, seek-ing any sign that the most evil of warlocks yet lives. And Prince Chorl watches also. His daughter is little better than a madwoman now, sorrowing over the loss of the man who changed her, and because the Prince blames himself his anger cannot be assuaged.

"All considered," the Roadman concluded his tale in Lessom's voice, "it has been a tumultuous time. Surely you have felt it here? Magic and battles on such a scale have repercussions. Has nothing changed at all—nothing out of the ordinary? Do not the cows talk, or the pigs sprout wings? Has no thing occurred which you might call strange? Is everything truly just as it has always been?"

With a gasp, Lessom sagged as the pig's gaze released him. Titus turned his eyes on Levit.

Now think! he demanded. *Make no mistake. What answer was this Roadman given?*

Yoel's son appeared to search his memory. "They were silent," he said slowly. "I could not see them, but I heard their boots on the floor, and the benches shifting. Then Horrik said, 'You came. That was strange. We have never seen a Roadman before.'

"Everyone laughed, and the Roadman with them. After that my father took Destrier to a room for the night, and people left the alehouse. I heard nothing else."

Think, Titus grunted urgently. *Nothing was said of me? Of Fern? Did not that clod-brain Jessup speak against me?*

Levit glanced at Lessom. "Nothing."

Lessom nodded and echoed, "Nothing."

For a time, the pig did not speak. Both boys slumped on the dirt, wearied by Titus' coercion. Beside them Fern tended the fire uncomfortably; she wanted sleep, but she was full of a fear she could not name. Images of Florice seemed to resonate for her like wind past a hollow in a wall, as though they might convey another connection; yet the connection eluded her. Such things were matters of time, and her grasp on them remained imprecise.

Then Titus snuffled, *Ah, but they squirmed. I can see it. They dropped their eyes and twisted in their seats. And this Destrier noticed it. He was sent to notice such things.*

Hell's blood! I must have time!

Like Titus, Lessom and Levit needed time. Their parents would not speak kindly to them for staying out so late. Yawning and shuffling, they left the hovel.

But Titus continued to fret. He paced the floor as though his hooves were afire. Fern tried to rest, but she could not be still when the pig she loved was in distress. "Yes?" she murmured to him, "yes?" hoping that the sound of her concern would comfort him.

No, he retorted harshly. *You do not know what you are saying. It is not enough.*

As though he had judged and dismissed her, he did not speak again that night.

The next morning, however, he ventured out early to watch Prince Chorl's Roadman ride away from Sarendel-on-Gentle. And when he returned to the hovel, he was full of grim bustle. *I must take action*, he informed her. *Any delay or hindrance now will be fatal.* And he showed her an image which instructed her to prepare a double—no, a treble—portion of the herbs and paste with which he fed her thrice daily.

She obeyed willingly, because he instructed her. When his concoctions were done, she bathed thoroughly; she combed out her hair and let the sun dry it until it shone. Then, guided by images, she draped her limbs with her scantest, most inadequate rags.

Cold, she thought when she saw how ill she was covered. A moment later, she thought another word which might have been, Shame.

Shame? The pig's disgust was as bright as fire. *Shame will not kill you. My need is extreme. Extreme measures are required.* Nevertheless he allowed her to remain concealed in her hovel while he roamed the village; when he returned, they remained there together until the sun had set.

By that time Sarendel had newer, more personal news to replace Destrier's unexpected visit. Meglan's husband, Wall, had fallen ill. According to the children who brought the tale, he writhed on his bed like a snake, vomiting gouts of bile and blood, and his skin burned as though his bones were ablaze. Meglan and her children were beside themselves, fearing his death at any moment.

Meglan? Fern had little impression of Wall, but Meglan farmwife was vivid to her. Meglan's kindnesses, of which Fern had known many, came to her through veils of time—carrots and shawls, cabbages and sandals and smiles. She felt tugging at her the same concern, the same impulse to respond, which she had often felt for Sarendel's pigs.

Good, Titus said. *Such concern looks well.*

And he showed her an image in which she went alone to Meglan's home, bearing small portions of her broth and paste. Alone she knocked at the door until she was answered. Alone she repeated Meglan's name until Meglan was brought to her. Then, still alone, she spoke to Meglan. In words, she explained how the broth and paste should be administered to save Wall.

Alone?

Spoke? In words?

Explained—?

Fern flinched against the wall of the hovel as though Titus had threatened to strike her.

I will teach you, Titus replied patiently. *If you are willing, you will be able to do it.*

"No," she protested in fright.

Come now, Fern, Titus went on, filling her mind with the colors of calm. *You will be able to do it. I have made you able. Did you not hear yourself speak just now? That was a word. You know both "yes" and "no." And you know names. Each new word will be a smaller step than the one before—and you will not need many to save Wall.*

Alone? she cried fearfully.

If you love me, you will do this. Meglan will have no tolerance for pigs at such a time.

Fern did not know how she understood him; yet she comprehended that he needed her—and that his need was greater than she could imagine. With her crumbling resistance, she gestured toward the rags she wore.

You will feel no shame, he promised her. *There can be none for you, when you do my bidding.*

There: another connection. Through her fright and distress, an involuntary excitement struck her. She had always contrived to cover herself better than this; but now she did not because Titus had instructed her. His bidding— She acted according to his wishes, not her own.

Other connections trembled at the edges of her mind, other links between what he wished and what people did. However, his urgency and his steady promises distracted her. While she readied her small portions of herbs and paste, he taught her the words she would need.

When she left the hovel, she went in a daze of fear and shame and excitement. No, not shame—*There can be none for you, when you do my bidding*. What she felt was the strange, uneasy eagerness of comprehension, the unfamiliar potential of language. Ignoring how her breasts and legs showed when she walked, she crossed the village and did as Titus had instructed her.

She was almost able to recognize what she gained by wearing her worst rags. They caught the attention of the farmer who opened the door, a friend of Wall's; they trapped him in pity, embarrassment, and interest, so that he was not able to send her away unheard. Instead, he went to fetch Meglan, thinking that Meglan would be able to dismiss Fern more kindly.

And when Meglan came to the door, Fern astonished her with words.

"I know herbs," said Fern, slurring each sound, and yet speaking with her utmost care, because of her love for Titus. "These can heal Wall. A spoonful of the broth. A touch of the paste on his tongue. Four times during the night. His illness will break at dawn."

Meglan stared as though the sounds were gibberish. All Sarendel knew Fern did not speak; she could not. Then how could these sounds be words?

But Titus had taught her one more: "Please."

"Please?" Meglan cried, on the verge of sobs. "My husband whom I love dies here, and you say, Please?"

Fern could not withhold her own tears. Meglan's

grief and the burden of words were too great for her to bear. Helpless to comfort the good farmwife—and helpless to refuse her pig—she could only begin again at the beginning.

"I know herbs. These can heal—"

Another woman appeared at Meglan's shoulder, a neighbor. "Is that Fern?" she asked in surprise. "Did I hear her speak?"

Grief twisted Meglan's face. If Fern could speak, the farmwife could not. Taking both broth and paste, she turned her back in silence and closed the door.

Fern went weeping back to her hovel.

Titus had no patience for her nameless sorrows. When she entered the hovel and stumbled to the scraps and leaves which she used as a pallet, he fixed her with his eyes, compelling her with silver and blindness until he had seen what was in her mind.

After that, however, his manner softened. *It was hard, I grant,* he told her. *But you have done a great thing, though you do not know it. The next steps will be less arduous. That is a better promise than the one I gave you earlier.*

Then he nuzzled and comforted her, and filled her head with solace, until at last she was able to stop crying and sleep.

While she slept, new connections swam and blurred, seeking clarity. She had gone to Meglan because Titus bade her. She had bathed her body and combed her hair and donned her worst rags on his instructions. She had prepared new stores of broth and paste at his behest. Were all these things connected in the same way? One thing will lead to another because it must. Had the pig foreseen Wall's illness? Was time no barrier to him, neither the past nor the future?

For a moment, as if time were no barrier to her as well, she seemed to see through the veils of the past. She saw that the ease and comfort and companionship of her life were new—that her life itself had changed. How did it come about that all her needs were supplied by children who had taken no notice of her until Titus adopted her?

What had he done? He had filled her with images. And she had done his bidding. One thing will lead to another— Did the children also find images in their minds, new images which instructed them in Titus' wishes?

These connections were like the surface of the Gentle. They caught the sun and sparkled, gems cast by the water, but they were too full of ripples and currents to be seen clearly.

And they vanished when the pig awakened her. *It is morning*, he informed her intently. *You must be prepared to speak again soon.* His concentration was acute; his eyes seemed to focus all of him on her. *Hear the sounds. They are words. When I have given them to you, they will be yours. At first, they will be difficult to remember. Nevertheless they will belong to you, and you will be able to call on them at need.*

Words? she thought. More words? But he left her no opportunity for protest. When she tried to say, "No," he brushed that word aside. *It will become easier, I tell you*, he snapped. *And I have no time for subtlety.*

She surrendered to his bidding scant moments before a tentative scratching at her door curtain announced a visitor.

Held by his gaze, she spoke the first of his new words.

"Enter."

Expecting children, she was filled with chagrin when she saw Meglan come into her hovel. Only the strength of her love for her pig—or the strength of his presence in her mind—enabled her to rise to her feet instead of cowering against the wall.

Meglan herself appeared full of chagrin. Fern could look at the farmwife because Meglan was unable to look at Fern. Her gaze limped aimlessly across the floor, lost among her pallid features, and her voice also limped as she murmured, "I know not what to say—I can hardly face you.

My husband is saved. You saved him—you, who speaks when none of us knew you could—you gave no hint—You, whom I have treated with little concern and no courtesy. You, who came in rags to offer your help. You, whom I have considered at worst a beggar and at best a half-wit. You and no other saved my husband.

"I cannot—I do not know how to bear it. You deserve honor, and you have been given only scorn.

"Fern, I must make amends. You have saved Wall, who is as dear to me as my own flesh. Because of you, he smiles, and lifts his head, and will soon be able to rise from his bed. I must make amends." Now she looked into Fern's eyes, and her need was so great—as great as Titus'—that Fern could not look away. "I will tell the tale. That I can do. I will teach Sarendel to honor you. But it is not enough.

"I have brought—" Meglan opened her hands as if she were ashamed of what they held, and Fern saw a thick, woolen robe, woven to stand hard use and keep out cold. "It is plain—too plain for my heart—but it is what I have, and it is not rags. And still it is not enough.

"If you can speak—if you are truly able to speak—please tell me how to thank you for my husband's life."

Fern, who had never owned a garment so rich and useful, might have fallen to her knees and wept in gratitude. To be given such a gift, without begging or dishonesty—! But Titus' need was as great as Meglan's. He did not let her go.

Instead of bowing or crying, she answered, "Thank you." The words stumbled in her mouth; they were barely articulate. Yet she said them—and as she said them she felt an excitement which seemed like terror. "I helped Wall because I could. I do not need tales."

That is safe, Titus commented. *She will talk in any case.*

"Or gifts," Fern went on. Belying the words, she gripped the robe tightly. "Yet it would be a kindness if I were given an iron cookpot and a few mixing bowls."

Damnation! Titus grunted. *That came out crudely. I must be more cautious.*

Ashamed to be begging again, Fern could no longer face the farmwife. Because Titus required it, however, she gestured at her fire and her few bowls. "My knowledge of herbs is more than I can use with what implements I have. If I could cook better, I could help others as I have helped your husband."

Tears welled in Meglan's eyes. "Thank you. You will have what you need." Impulsively, she leaned forward and kissed Fern's cheek. Then she turned and hurried from the hovel as though she were grieving—or fleeing.

There. Titus sounded like Jessup rubbing his hands together over an auspicious bargain. *Was that not easier? Did I not promise that it would be less arduous? Soon we will be ready.*

For the second time, Fern felt her own tears reply to Meglan's. "No." She had no recollection that she had ever been kissed before. Her surprise at Meglan's gesture startled another surprise out of her—an unfamiliar anger. "No," she repeated. Almost in words, almost using language for herself, she faced the pig's strange gaze and showed him her shame.

Titus shook his head. *You did not beg.* Now he sounded condescending and desirous, like Horrik the tanner. *You answered her question—a small act of courtesy and self-respect. Consider this.* He showed Fern an image of Meglan coming to the hovel to offer gratitude, carrying not a robe but a cookpot and some bowls. *Would you have felt shame then?* he asked. *No. You were not shamed by the gift she chose to give you. It is only because you named your own need that you think you have done wrong.*

But it was not wrong. It was my bidding.

Perhaps we will have enough time. Perhaps you will be able to save me. Take comfort in that, if you cannot forget your shame. Perhaps you will be able to save me.

As I saved Wall? she almost asked. *Was that not also your doing?*

But she lacked the language for such questions. And the pig distracted her, nuzzling her hand to express his affection and gratitude, wrapping her mind in azure and comfortable emerald; and so the connection was lost.

After that, her life changed again. The roaming and scavenging which had measured out her days came to a complete end. Feeling at once grand and unworthy in her new robe, she sat in her hovel while Titus went out alone and came back; while children supplied her with food and water and firewood and herbs; while first one or two and then several and finally all of Sarendel's good people came to visit her. Some scratched at her curtain and poked their heads inside simply to satisfy their curiosity or resolve their doubt. But others brought their needs and pains to her attention. Meglan's tale had inspired them to hope that Fern could help them.

Red-eyed from sleeplessness, and strangely abashed in the presence of a woman whom she had scarcely noticed before, Salla farmwife brought her infant son, who squalled incessantly with colic. Had the boy been a pig, Fern would have known what to do. However, he was a boy, and so it was fortunate that Titus stood at her side to instruct her. (*A bit of the paste, diluted four times. Mint and sage to moderate the effect. There.*) When Salla left the hovel, she added her son's smiles and his sweet sleep to Meglan's tale.

And later Salla brought Fern the gift which Titus had told Fern to request—a mortar and pestle, and a set of sturdy wooden spoons.

Horrik came, bearing an abscessed thumb. After Fern had treated it with a poultice which she had never made before, he lingered to stare and talk like a man whose mind drooled at what he saw. Yet he did not take it unkindly when at last Titus succeeded at urging her to dismiss him. Smiling and bowing, the tanner left; still smiling, he brought to her the gift she had requested, a keen flensing knife.

Karay's daughter had been afflicted with palsy from birth. The weaver was so accustomed to her daughter's infirmity that she would not have thought to seek aid, were it not for the strange fact that Fern could now speak. Perhaps if a mute half-wit could learn language and healing, a palsy could be cured. So Karay set her forlorn child in the dirt beside Fern's fire and asked bluntly, "Can you help her?"

In response, Fern prepared a broth not unlike the one she ate herself, a paste not unlike the one she had given Salla's infant. "And ale," she added. "Mix in ale. Let her drink at her own pace until she has drunk it all."

Once Karay had seen that this rank brew indeed put an end to her daughter's palsy, she gave Fern a curtain of embroidered velvet to replace the hovel's burlap door. And also, because she was asked, she delivered to Fern a cupful each of all the dyes she used in her weaving.

Herded by his angry wife and four angry daughters, Sarendel's blacksmith entered her hovel, carrying so much pain that he could hardly move. He had fallen against his forge and burned away most of the flesh on one side of his chest; his wife and daughters were angry because they feared that he would die. Fern gave him a salve for healing, herbs to soften the hurt, and other herbs to resist infection.

When her husband began to mend, the blacksmith's wife at last allowed herself to weep. She cried ceaselessly as she brought Fern several small flakes of silver.

A farmer was given a cure for gout; he expressed his thanks with a lump of ambergris which he had treasured for years without knowing why. Over her father-in-law's vociferous objections, Jessup's eldest son's wife asked for and received an herb to ease the severity of her monthly cramps; her gratitude took the form of two pints of refined lard. One of the blacksmith's daughters believed that she was unwed because her beauty was marred by a large wen beside her nose; when Fern supplied her with a poultice which caused the wen to shrink and fall away, she— and her father—gave Fern an iron grill to hold Meglan's cookpot.

In the course of a fortnight, Fern seemed to become the center of all Sarendel-on-Gentle, the hub on which the village turned. Children cared for her needs, and adults visited her at any hour. Resplendent in her new robe—of all the gifts she had been given, this one alone warmed her heart—she sat in state to receive all who came to her. With Titus at her side, as well-fed and well-tended as herself, she made new concoctions and spoke new words as though those separate actions were one and the same, bound to each other in ways she could not see. She no longer cowered against her walls in fright or chagrin. Instead she gave her help with the same unstinting openheartedness which she had formerly shown only to pigs. Helping people made her love them. She disliked only the gifts she was given in thanks, never the efforts she made to earn that thanks.

Her life had indeed changed. This time, however, she recognized the change for what it was. She neither chose it nor resisted it, but she saw it. And when she watched the change, comparing it to what her life had once been, she made new connections.

She understood why she could speak, why she could understand the people around her and reply, why she could prepare complex salves and balms, why she could look her fellow villagers in their faces. It was because of the broth and paste which Titus caused her to eat three times daily. Those herbs had wrought a change within her as profound as the change in her life.

One thing will lead to another because it must.

And she understood that she did not deserve Sarendel's gratitude for her cures and comforts. That was why gifts gave her no pleasure, but only sorrow. She healed nothing, earned nothing. Like her new ability to speak, all the benefits she worked for others came from Titus: the credit for them was his, not hers.

She did not resent this. The pig had come to her in his extremity, and she loved him. Nor could she wish the lessons he had taught her unlearned. Nevertheless she grieved over her unworth.

In addition, she understood without knowing she understood that Titus himself caused a certain number of the hurts she treated. Too frequently to be unconnected, his forays away from her hovel coincided with the onset of injuries and illnesses in the village. The same powers with which he had raised her from her familiar destitution, he used to create the conditions under which Sarendel needed her.

He was trying to speed the process by which she accumulated gifts.

This troubled her. It offended her honesty more than begging; it seemed a kind of theft. But she did not protest against it. Other, similar connections crouched at the edges of her understanding, waiting for clarity. When she grasped one, she would grasp them all.

Ready, she thought to herself, using words instead of images. We must be ready. We are becoming ready.

We are, Titus assented. She could hear pride and hope in his voice, as well as anger and more than a little fear.

Before the end of another fortnight, Sarendel had learned to accept Fern in her changed state; the village had begun to live as though she had always been a healer rather than a half-wit. And Titus had finished accumulating the gifts he required.

Now she noted the passing of time. Around her the seasons had moved along the Gentle's Rift, turning high summer to crisp fall. Hints of gold and crimson appeared among the verdure; at their fringes the leaves of the bracken took on rust. Slowly the labor of tending fields and beasts eased. Soon would come a time she dreaded, a time she now knew she had always dreaded—the time when porkers were slaughtered for food and hide and tallow. She did not fear for Titus in that way: because he was hers, no villager would harm him. And yet she feared for him now, just as she had always feared for the porkers.

True, she could hear his own fear in the way he spoke. But she also saw it in the tension of his movements, in the staring of his flawed eyes; she smelled it in his sweat. It confirmed her apprehension for him when she might have been able to persuade herself that she had no reason for alarm.

One sharp fall morning, he poked his snout past her hovel's velvet curtain, scented the air—and recoiled as though he had been stung.

Hell's blood! he panted. *Damn and blast them!*

An unnamed panic came over her. She surged up from her pallet to throw her arms about his neck as though she believed that she could ward him somehow. He shivered feverishly, hot with dread.

"Titus?" She needed words for her fear, but only his name came to her. "Titus?"

He appeared to take comfort from her embrace. After a moment, his tremors eased. The confused moil of images and hues which he cast into her sharpened toward concentration.

Now we must hurry in earnest, he breathed. *There is a stink of princes and warlocks in the air. That damnable Roadman has betrayed me, and I have little time. As I am, I can neither flee nor fight.*

Oh, Fern, my Fern, if you love me, help me. Give me your willingness. Without it, I am lost.

"Who?" she asked with her face pressed to his neck. "Who comes to threaten you?"

Princes, warlocks, does it matter? he snapped back. *They are frightened, even more than I—therefore they will be enough. They would not come if they were not enough. I tell you, we must **hurry**!*

She could not refuse him. She gave him a last hug, as though she were saying farewell. After that, she dropped her arms and seated herself by the fire.

"Then tell me what to do."

She seemed to take his fear from him; he seemed to leach all calm and quiet out of her. The words and images which he supplied to instruct her were precise and unmistakable, as clear as sunlight on green leaves; yet her hands shook, and her whole heart trembled, while she obeyed. She was Fern of Sarendel-on-Gentle, a half-wit who loved pigs. What did she know of language or time, of magic or warlocks? Nevertheless Titus needed her, as he had needed her once before, and she did not mean to fail him.

Throughout the day she labored under his guidance, trying to do several things at once. As she heated her new cookpot until the iron shone red, she also ground rueweed and fennel and sloewort and garlic and vert and silver flakes to fine powder; at the same time, she gripped the lump of ambergris between her thighs to soften it. While she warmed lard to liquid in one of her mixing bowls, she also kneaded the ambergris until it became as workable as beeswax. And when her hands were too tired for kneading, she busied herself dividing her powders into ever more meticulous quantities and combining them with pinches of dried dyes.

Children came to scratch at her curtain, but she sent them away without caring whether she was brusque. She would have sent all Sarendel away. Horrik the tanner came as well; he seemed to want nothing more than an opportunity to sit and look at her. But she told him, "No," calling the word past Karay's heavy curtain without raising her head from her work. "If you meant to speak to me, you should have done so long ago." She hardly heard herself add, "I am too far beyond you now."

Morning lapsed to afternoon; afternoon became evening. Still she worked. Now her hands were raw and her arms quivered, and sweat splashed from her cheeks to the dirt. Fire and red iron filled the hovel with heat until even the slats of the walls appeared to sweat. The smells of powders and dyes in strange combinations made her head wobble on her neck. But Titus did not relent. His instructions were unending, and she labored with all her willingness to obey them.

At last he let her pause. While she rested, panting, he surveyed her handiwork, squinting blind and silver at what she had done.

Now, he announced distinctly. *Now or never.*

With the hem of her robe, she mopped sweat from her face. Fatigue blurred her sight, so that she could no longer see the pig clearly.

"Have they come yet?" she asked in a whisper. "Are they here?"

I cannot tell, he responded. *Even a pig's senses cannot distinguish between those scents and what we do.*

But it does not matter. Whether they are poised around us or miles away, we must do what we can.

Fern, are you ready?

Because all his fear was hers, she countered, "Are you?"

To her surprise, he filled her mind with laughter. *No*, he admitted, *not ready at all*. Then he repeated, *But it does not matter. For us there is only now or never.*

"Then," she repeated in her turn, "tell me what to do."

Now his instructions were simple. She obeyed them one at a time, as carefully as she could.

The lump of ambergris she divided in two parts, each of which she molded with her fingers until it was shaped like a bowl. Into these bowls she apportioned the powders she had prepared, the mixtures of herbs and dyes and metal. Using Horrik's knife, she pricked at the veins in her forearm until enough blood flowed to moisten the powders. Then quickly, so that nothing spilled, she cupped one bowl over the other to form a ball. With water warmed in a pan at the edge of the fire, she stroked the seam of the ball until the ambergris edges were smeared together and sealed.

Good. Titus studied her hands while she worked as though he were rapt. His breathing had become a hoarse wheeze, and sweat glistened among the bristles on his hide. *The ball. The lard. My water dish. And some means to remove that cookpot from the fire.*

Fern flinched at the thought. The fatal glow of the iron seemed to thrust her back. She was not sure that she could go near enough to the pot to take hold of it.

A shaft of anger and fear broke through Titus' calm; he grunted a curse. But then, grimly, he stilled himself. Reverting to images, he made her see herself taking two brands from her dwindling woodpile and bracing them under the handles of the cookpot to lift it out.

She picked up the brands, set them in front of her beside the half-full water dish, the lard, and the amber-gris ball.

The pig stood facing her as though nothing else existed—as though all the world had shrunk down to one lone woman. He had told her more than once to hurry, but now he gave her no instructions, and did not move himself.

Fear crowded her throat. "Titus," she breathed, "why do you delay?"

Like you, he told her, *I am afraid.*

After a moment, he added, *Do you remember your first name for me? It was Mythanks. At the time, I was not amused. But now I consider it a better name than Titus.*

So swiftly that she could not distinguish them, images rang through her head. In one motion, she rose to her feet and dropped the ball into the cookpot.

Ambergris hit the red iron with a scream of scalding wax. But before the ball melted entirely away, she snatched up the lard and poured it also into the pot.

Instantly the smoke and stench of burning fat filled the hovel. The walls seemed to vanish. Tears burst from Fern's eyes. She could no longer see Titus.

She could see his images still, however. They guided her hands to the brands, guided the brands to the cookpot; they made her strong and sure as she lifted out the pot and tilted it to decant its searing contents into the dish.

Gouts of steam spat and blew through the reeking smoke. Nevertheless Titus did not hesitate now. The potion would lose its efficacy as it cooled.

Plunging his snout into the fiery dish, he drank until he could no longer endure the agony. Then he threw back his head and screamed.

Fern cried out at the same instant, wailed, "Titus!" She had never heard such a scream. The pain of cattle was eloquent enough. And pigs could squeal like slaughtered children. But this was worse, far worse. It was the pure anguish of a pig and the utter torment of a man in one, and it seemed to shake the hovel. The walls bowed outward; smoke and stink filled the air with hurt.

And the scream did not stop. Shrill with agony and protest, it splashed like oil into the fire, so that flames blazed to the ceiling. The smoke itself caught fire and began roaring like the core of the sun. Conflagration limned each slat of the walls and roof, etched every scrap and leaf of her pallet against the black dirt. The scream became fire itself. Flames ate at Fern's robe, her face, her hair. In another instant it would devour her, and she would fall to ashes—

But it did not. Instead it seemed to coalesce in front of her. Flames left the walls to flow through the air; flames drained off her and were swept up into the center of the hovel. The fire she had made lost heat. Her pallet ceased burning. Every burst and blaze came together to engulf Titus.

At the same time, another fire burned in Fern's head, as though she, too, were being consumed.

Outside her, beyond her, he stood in the middle of the floor, motionless. Like wax, he melted in the flames. And like wax, he fed the flames, so that they mounted higher while he was consumed. From his pig's body they grew to a pillar which nearly touched the roof. Then the pillar changed shape until it writhed and roiled like a tortured man.

Abruptly, he stopped screaming.

The fire went out.

A deep dark closed over Fern. The smoke and stench blinded her with tears; echoes of flame dazzled her. She could see nothing until he took hold of her arms and lifted her to her feet.

Lit by the last embers of her fire, a man stood in the

hovel with her. Clad only in a faint red glow and shadows, he released her arms and stepped back so that she could see him more clearly.

He was tall and strong. Not young—she saw many years in the lines of his face and the color of his beard. Prominent cheekbones hid his eyes in caves of shadow. Beneath a nose like the blade of a hatchet, his mouth was harsh.

Looking at him, she was hardly able to breathe. She knew him without question—he was Titus, the pig who had chosen her, the one she loved—and the sight of him struck her dumb, as though he had stepped out of her dreams to meet her. Was he handsome? To her, he was so handsome that she quailed in front of him.

"Fern," he murmured softly, "oh, my Fern, we have done it." His voice was the voice she had heard in her mind, the voice which had taught her words—the voice which had changed her life. "We have *done* it."

Before she could fall to her knees in hope and love and astonishment, another voice answered him. As hard as the clang of iron, it called out, "*But not in time!*"

"Damnation!" A snarl leaped across Titus' face; embers and silver flashed from his hidden eyes. His strong hands reached out and snatched Fern to him as though he meant to protect her.

In that instant, a bolt like lightning shattered the hovel. Argent power tore the air apart. A concussion too loud for hearing knocked the walls to shards and splinters, and swept them away. Embers and rags scattered as though they had been scoured from the dirt. Fern was kept on her feet amid the blast only by Titus' grasp. She clung to him helplessly while her home ceased to exist.

Then they found themselves with their arms around each other under the open sky at the edge of the village. This was the spot where her hovel had stood, but no sign of it remained: even her iron cookpot had been stricken from the place. Dimmed by glaring coruscation, a few stars winked coldly out of the black heavens.

A circle of fire the color of ice surrounded her and Titus. It blazed and spat from the ground as though it marked the rim of a pit which would open under their feet. At first it was so bright that her abused eyes could not see past it. But gradually she made out figures beyond the white, crystal fire. On the other side of the ring, she and Titus were also surrounded by men and women on horseback, as well as by the people of Sarendel-on-Gentle.

She saw Jessup and Yoel there, Veil and Nell and Meglan, Horrik and Karay, all the folk she had known throughout her life. Only the children were absent, no doubt commanded to their homes with the best authority their parents could muster. The strange, chill light seemed to leach the familiar faces of color; they were as pallid as ghosts. Their eyes were haunted and abashed, full of shame or fear.

Among them towered the riders. These figures also were spectral in the icy glow. Nevertheless they masked their fear and betrayed no shame. Their eyes and mouths showed only anger and determination, an unremitting outrage matched by resolve.

Fern had never seen such men and women before. Their armor and cloaks and caps, their weapons and apparatus, were outlandish, at once regal and incomprehensible. Yet she seemed to recognize them as soon as she caught sight of them. There was Prince Chorl—there, with the blunt forehead, the circlet in his curling hair, and the beard like a breastplate. He was accompanied by his lords and minions, as well as by his daughter Florice—her plain riding habit, wild hair, and undefended visage made her unmistakable. And among the others were Andovale's masters of magic, come to carry out the judgment of the council against one of their own.

All of them had ridden here for no reason except that the people of Sarendel had squirmed when Destrier had asked them about change. And those people had squirmed because they had known of a change which they had not wished to name. Out of loyalty or pity, they had declined to mention that she, Fern, had been adopted by a pig none of them had ever seen before. And yet their very desire to protect Fern had betrayed the man who now held her in his arms. He was snared in this circle by his enemies because of her.

She did not ask how she knew such things. She knew a great deal which had been vague to her before: the fire which had transformed Titus had altered her in some way as well. Or perhaps in his desperation for her help he had altered her more than he intended. She made connections easily, as though the pathways of new understanding had been burned clear in her brain.

One among the riders was fiercer than the others; his rage shone more hotly. He lacked the sorrow which moderated Prince Chorl's anger. Alone of the warlocks—the men who bore apparatus and periapts instead of arms were surely warlocks—he rode at his Prince's side, opposite Florice. He appeared to command the ring of riders as much as the Prince did.

"So, Suriman," this warlock barked across the fire, "you are caught again—and damned as much for new crimes as for old. How you escaped us to work your evil here, I do not fully understand. But we are prepared to be certain that you do not escape again."

Suriman? Fern thought. Suriman?

The man in her arms loosened his embrace so that he could bow. If he felt any dismay at his nakedness, he did not deign to show it. His lips grinned sardonically over his teeth, and silver glinted like a threat in his eye. "My lord Prince." His voice was as clear and harsh as the night. "My lady. Titus. You are fortunate to catch me. In another hour I would have been beyond the worst that you can do."

Fern felt a pang around her heart. "Titus?" she asked aloud. Connections twisted through her, as ghostly and fatal as the riders. "You said *your* name was Titus."

"He is called Suriman because we do not speak his

name," the warlock barked. "I am Titus. If he told you his name is mine, that is only one lie among many."

"Titus?" Fern asked again. Surrounded by cold fire, she sounded small and lost. Ignoring the warlock, she faced the man who had been her pig. Unprotected from the cold, he had begun to shiver slightly. "Titus?"

He did not look at her; his gaze held the Prince and the warlock. When he spoke, his voice cut like a whip. "Her name is Fern, Titus. You will address her as 'my lady.' Regardless of your contempt for me, you will show her courtesy."

Fern flung a glance at this unfamiliar Titus in time to see him flinch involuntarily. All the power here was his— and still he feared his enemy.

Prince Chorl lifted his head. His eyes were as deep as the night. "Show her courtesy yourself, Suriman. Answer her."

For a moment, the man hesitated. But then, slowly, he turned in Fern's grasp so that he could face her. Again his eyes were hidden away in shadows. Yet he seemed abashed by her needy stare, as if he were more vulnerable to her than to any of the circled riders.

Tightly, he said, "I am Suriman."

She could not still the pain twisting in her. "Then why did you teach me to call you Titus?"

His brows knotted. "I feared such stories as the Roadman told. I thought that if I gave myself another's name I was less likely to be betrayed—and what name would protect me more than the name of the man who most wished me dead? But I misjudged you, my Fern. I misjudged your willingness. If I had known then what you are now, I would have risked the truth."

At his words, anger stirred the ring. Flames of ice leaped higher, as though the warlocks fed them with outrage. And Titus cried in a loud voice, "*Willingness?* She is not *willing*. She is a *half-wit*—the poorest and most destitute person in all the Rift. These folk love her—they do not speak against her—but at least one of them has told us what he knows."

Fern did not doubt that this was Jessup. The other villagers ached to have no part in her downfall. Yet they could not turn away. Fire and fury held them.

"We can surmise the rest," Titus continued. "She had no *choice,* Suriman. You took her life from her without her consent. You altered her for your own purposes, not knowing and not caring what she wished or desired. She is not willing because she chose *nothing.*"

Suriman did not shift his gaze from Fern. She felt the appeal in his eyes, although she could not see them.

"That is false," he said softly. "She is willing because she *is,* not because I made her so. She was willing when I found her. She loves pigs, and I was a pig. She would have given her life for me from the first moment she saw me."

Then the Prince's daughter spoke for the first time. In a voice made old by too much weeping, she protested, "But *I* was not willing. When you first asked to wed me, I knew your evil. I told my father of it as best I could. You did not heed that, or anything I might have desired for myself. Now I crave you, I cannot stop desiring you, and I chose none of it.

"Was that not a crime, Suriman? Have you not betrayed me? Tell me that you have not betrayed me."

Like Suriman's fire, Florice's pain burned through Fern, making new connections.

He turned to face this accuser. "I did not betray you, my lady," he answered. He seemed to hold the lords and warlocks at bay with harshness. To Fern, he looked strong enough for that. "I failed you. The distinction is worth making. If I had not failed, you would have craved me utterly. Prince Chorl would have lost a half-wit daughter, and all Andovale would have gained a great lady. You would have been as willing as my Fern is now, and you would have regretted nothing.

"It was my folly that I could not win your father's trust—and his that he asked this Titus to act in his name."

Titus reared back to launch a retort, but Fern stopped him by raising her hand. All her attention was focused on Suriman; she hardly noticed that Titus had stopped, or that all the ring fell silent as though she were a figure of power.

"I was not willing."

Suriman swung back toward her like a man stung. "Not?" The word was almost a cry.

If she could have seen his eyes, she might have told him, Do not be afraid. I must say this, or else I will say nothing. But they remained shadowed, unreadable. She knew nothing about him except what he had chosen to reveal.

"You made me a beggar." Her voice shook with fright; she felt overwhelmed by her own littleness in the face of these potent men and women. Yet she did not falter. "Oh, I helped you willingly enough. As you say, I love pigs. But in all my life I have taken nothing that was not mine. That shamed me."

"We would have died!" he countered at once, urgently. "You lacked the means to keep us alive. It is not a crime to ask for help—or to need it. Do you think less of me because I came to you when I was in need?"

She shook her head. "But Jessup did not choose to feed us the second time. The children did not choose to feed us. You chose for them. You cast images into their minds which they did not understand and so could not refuse. You made me a thief."

"A thief?" Suriman sounded incredulous—and daunted. "You stole nothing!"

"But I lived on stolen things. I grew healthy and comfortable on stolen things. The fault is yours—but you feel no shame, and so the shame is mine."

"What are you saying?" His voice came close to cracking. "You did not know the food was stolen because you could not comprehend it." He had another nakedness which signified more than his lack of garments. "It was beyond your abilities to see consequences which did not take place before your eyes—and you could not remember them when they were past."

"I do not say this in scorn, Fern. You simply were not able to understand. And now you are. I have given you that. You accuse me of a fault which would have meant nothing to you if I had not given you the capacity to see it."

His need touched her so deeply that tears came to her eyes, and the ring of fire blurred against the dark night. And still she did not falter.

"But you could see it," she replied. "You knew all that I did not, and more besides. You knew me—you saw into my mind. You saw the things which shamed me. And yet you caused the children of this village to go thieving for my benefit."

As though she had pushed him beyond his endurance, he snapped back, "Fern, I was *desperate*. I was a *pig*, in hell's name! If I did not die on the road to be devoured by dogs, I would be slaughtered in the village to be eaten by clods and fools!"

At the same time, she heard his voice in her mind, as she had heard it so often when he could not speak.

Fern, I implore you.

"So is the lady Florice desperate," she answered him. "So am I."

Florice could no longer keep silent. "Yes, desperate, Suriman—as desperate as you were. I am desperate for you, though it breaks my heart. But more than that, I am desperate to understand.

"What is this *willingness* you prize so highly? Why must you extract it from women who can neither comprehend nor refuse? You do not desire us as women—you desire only tools, subjects for research. Why must you make us to be more than we were, when what you wish is that we should be less?"

Suriman did not turn from Fern. He concentrated on her as though the circle of riders and villagers and fire had ceased to have any import. When he responded to Florice, his words were addressed to Fern.

"Because, my lady, no woman but a half-wit is able

to give herself truly. You say I do not desire you as women, but I do. If I had not failed, you would have lost your flaws—the limitations which prevent you from sharing my dreams and designs—but you would have retained your open heart, your loveliness of form and spirit.

"If that is a crime, then I am guilty of it." Finality and fear ached in his tone. "Do what you came to do, or leave me be. I am defenseless against you."

At the same time, his silent voice said beseechingly, *Oh, my Fern, tell me I have not failed.*

"We will," Titus announced loudly. And Prince Chorl echoed, more in sorrow than in anger, "We will.

"I care nothing for your protests or justifications, Suriman," the Prince continued. "We are not here to pass judgment. That has been done. Our purpose is only to see you dead."

"Dead," the warlocks pronounced. "Finally and forever."

"Yes," growled the lords and minions on their mounts.

The silver fire leaped up, encircling Suriman more tightly.

"Do not harm Fern!" a farmwife cried out. It was Meglan. Fern could no longer see her: all the villagers were hidden by flames of ice. "She has done nothing wrong!" Then, abashed by her own audacity, she pleaded more quietly, "My lords and ladies, if you say that he is evil and must die, we do not protest. We have no knowledge of these matters. But she is ours. There is no harm in her. Surely you will not hold her to account for his crimes?"

Titus might have answered, but Prince Chorl stopped him with a gesture. "Good woman," he replied to Meglan, "that is for her to say. Until now, she has made no choices. Here she will choose for herself.

"My lady Fern," the Prince said across the fire, "the warlock at your side is condemned for precisely such crimes as he has committed against you. Knowing what he has done, and having heard his answers, would you stand between him and his punishment? Or will you stand aside?"

Fern had been changed by fire. Even now, she could not stop making connections which had never occurred to her before. She had said what she must: that was done. Now she took the next step.

Letting go of Suriman, she backed away.

"No!" At the sight of her withdrawal, he flinched and crouched down as though his destruction had already begun; he covered his face with his hands. Spasms of cold shook and twisted his naked limbs.

To abandon him wrung her heart. Softly, so that only he might hear her, she murmured, "My thanks."

He must have heard her. A moment later, he lowered his arms and drew himself erect. For the first time in the ring of fire, she saw his eyes clearly—the one almost blind, the other marred by a slice of silver. Shivers mounted through him, then receded. He could not smile, but his voice was gentle as he said, "I regret nothing. You were worth the risk. You have not asked me what loveliness is— in that I was wrong, as in so many other things—but still I will tell you.

"It is you."

Because he did not try to compel her with images or colors or supplications, Fern answered, "Yes."

"*Suriman!*" Florice wailed in despair.

She was too late. The masters of magic had already raised their periapts and apparatus, summoned their powers. In silence the white fire raged abruptly into the heavens: mutely the flames towered over the ring and then crashed inward, falling like ruin upon the warlock.

He did not scream now, as he had when he was transformed. The force mustered against him surpassed sound. As voiceless as the conflagration, he writhed in brief agony while retribution and cold searched him to the marrow of his bones, the pit of his chest, the gulf of his skull. Then he was lifted out of the circle in a swirl of white embers and ash. The fire burned him down to dust, which the dark swallowed away. Soon nothing remained of him except the riders in their triumph, the shocked faces of the villagers, and Florice's last wail.

As though bereft of language, images, and will, Fern sprawled on the ground with her face hidden in her arms. Her heart beat, her lungs took air. But she could not speak or rise or uncover her face—or she would not. At Prince Chorl's bidding, two of his minions and one of the warlocks came forward to offer their assistance. Meglan, Karay, and others had already run to Fern's side, however, and they spurned help. Unexpectedly dignified in the face of lords and magic, Meglan farmwife said, "She is ours. We will care for her."

"I understand," said the Prince sadly. "But I give you this promise. At any time, in any season, if you desire help for her, only send to me, and I will do everything I can."

"And I," Florice added through her grief. "I promise also."

Titus was too full of fierceness and vindication to find his voice; yet he nodded a promise of his own.

When the riders were gone, Meglan and the others lifted Fern in their arms. Like a cortege, they bore her to Wall's house, where a clean room with a bed and blankets was made ready for her. There she was comforted and cosseted as she had once cared for Sarendel's pigs. Unlike the pigs, however, she did not respond. She lay with her face covered—as far as anyone knew, she slept with her face covered. And before dawn, she left the house. Meglan searched for her, but to no avail, until the farmwife thought to look out toward the refuse-tip beyond her garden.

There she saw Fern scavenging.

After Meglan had wept for a time, she bustled out to the village. She told what she had seen; men and women with good hearts—and no knowledge of warlocks—heard her. Before Fern returned from her scavenging, a new shed had been erected on the exact spot of her former hovel. A new curtain swung as a door; a new pallet lay against one wall; new bowls and cups sat on the pallet. And the bowls were full of corn and carrots, cured ham and bread.

Fern did not seem surprised to find her hovel whole. Perhaps she had forgotten that it was gone. Yet the sight of Meglan and Horrik, Veil and Salla, Karay and Yoel standing there to greet her appeared to frighten her. With a familiar alarm which the village itself had forgotten, she cowered at the nearest hedge, peering through her hair as though she feared what would happen if she were noticed.

In rue and shame, the villagers left the hovel, pretending that they had not noticed her. At once she took the fruits of her scavenging inside and closed the curtain.

From that moment onward, her life in Sarendel-on-Gentle became much the same as it had been before she had been adopted by a pig. From dawn to dusk she roamed the village refuse-tips and the surrounding hills, scavenging scraps and herbs and storing them against the coming winter. The changes which marked her days were few—and no one spoke of them. First out of kindness, then out of habit, Sarendel's folk gave her as many gifts as she would accept. The children learned to ignore her; but if any of the younger ones thought to tease or torment her, the older ones put a quick stop to it. As the days became fortnights, even Horrik forgot that he had once desired her. And she no longer seemed to know or care anything about pigs. Her love for them had been lost among the stars and the cold white fire. By slow degrees the present became so like the past that men and women shook their heads incredulously to think the continuity had ever been disturbed.

In this way she regained the peace and safety which had been lost to her.

If the villagers had looked more closely, however— if Fern had worn her mud-thick and straggling hair away from her face, or if she had not ducked her head to avoid meeting anyone's gaze—they might have noticed one other change.

Since the night when she had transformed her only love from a pig to a man, just in time to see him caught and taken by his doom, one of her eyes had grown warmer, brighter, belying her renewed destitution. The other bore a strange mark across the iris, a thin argent scar, as though her sight had been cut by silver.

The Story So Far

Martha Soukup

WE GREW UP IN THE SAME SMALL TOWN, IN THE SAME short story.

A first glimpse of classroom. Blinds raised, a sunny day. Mrs. Zelinski appears, short, gray, plump, pulling down a map with a stick with a hook at the end. In another moment she is wearing a plaid cotton dress, and it is ugly.

I am sitting at a desk among two dozen other murky students, but I do not know who I am yet. I only know Mrs. Zelinski, talking about Argentina, which hooks down to a point at the bottom of the map, and Dennis.

Then Dennis looks across at Sylvia, and I see her for the first time. Sylvia happens before I do, but only by an instant, because Dennis sees me sitting on the other side of her, so that I am there when we first see that she is beautiful.

Sylvia is beautiful. She is beautiful in the way few people are in their first rush of adolescence, which explains to me for the first time that that is how old we are. In this way I learn: Mrs. Zelinski's dress, tan and gray plaid, hitched up on the right where it catches in the belt, is ugly. Sylvia's blond hair pushed over to one side, Sylvia's skin so fair it glows, with no trace of the acne I know now I have, Sylvia's soft blue dress gliding down around her new breasts and her long legs crossed at the heels, under her chair—these are beautiful. There can be no doubt Dennis is struck with an awkward awe at the sight of her.

Dennis glances past her for a moment at me and I blush. I know he doesn't even see me (now I know my name is Emmy Cluff, and I am small and flat and forgettable) past the fleeting notice that I am a little pale mouse next to Sylvia. Still, Dennis has looked straight at me, and I blush and look down at the top of my desk. I do not care about Dennis, but I have to blush.

Mrs. Zelinski's stick crashes on her desk and Dennis is no longer looking at me. Now I don't have to look at my desk, so I look up, first to see Argentina, pale green on the map against the robin's-egg Atlantic Ocean. And then I look over at Sylvia.

She winks at me. Dennis is stammering at Mrs. Zelinski and doesn't see. Mrs. Zelinski says something and Dennis looks embarrassed. I am thinking, why do I have to have a dumb name like Emmy Cluff? I wish my name were Sylvia.

Mrs. Zelinski says something else, and that is the last I see of Mrs. Zelinski or the seventh-grade classroom.

It is a summer game of softball. I think more has happened between, but it is the next time I am in the story. I stand on the sidelines watching Dennis come to the plate. He is bigger now. While he hits his bat on the plate, I sneak a look down at myself. I am bigger too, but not much bigger in the place I am looking. I look around and see Sylvia, on the other sideline. She is wearing shorts that show how long and slim her legs are. I am in baggy blue jeans and a dull blue blouse.

There are other kids with names here, mostly on Dennis's team, but I can feel that they won't be very important to the story, and most of the kids don't even have names.

Dennis strikes out. He comes over to the side. Sylvia is laughing with another boy on the team. Dennis walks up to me.

"What are you doing Saturday?" It is the first time I really hear his voice, which is medium-deep and sounds like it's getting deeper. It is only the second scene that I have been alive.

"I have a clarinet lesson," I say. Do I play clarinet?

"No, I mean Saturday night," Dennis says.

I blush again, which is annoying. This story does not have much subtlety. "Nothing, I guess," I say.

Dennis glances over at Sylvia, who is laughing loudly enough to hear from here. If the look is meant to be surreptitious, it misses, so it probably isn't. "Want to go to a movie?"

I feel the blush burn harder. I want to shout *Stop that!* I say "Okay," which is all that's required of me, because there isn't a break, exactly, but the doorbell rings and I have parents, hovering over me in the front hall of our house.

My mother rushes to the front door and lets Dennis in. My dress is too tight in the ribcage and I guess too short, too. It shows I don't have many opportunities to dress up. As Dennis comes in I sneak a look at my parents. They are both short, plump, with brown hair the color of mine, my father's thinning and my mother's held round about her head with too much hair spray. They aren't much of a job of imagining parents.

As Dennis comes up to take my arm in an oddly courtly gesture, I wonder if he notices the gaps in the story, or if being the center of attention is enough to keep his mind occupied. I want to ask.

"Is the movie downtown okay?" he asks.

"Sure," I say. I walk to the door with him, feeling heavy. I must weigh twenty pounds more than I did in the first scene. My mother beams.

The movie playing is a second run of something. Of what, I'm not sure: I watch the screen but I see only random shapes, a shadow of something that is either a car chase or a dancing scene. Dennis cranes his neck over the balcony railing. I sit back, squinting my eyes against the darkness. I'm still taller than he is. I can see where he's looking: down in the main section, in front, over to the left. She is with the boy from the softball game, and she is pulling his head over to kiss him.

I shake my head in admiration. Right in front of the theater like that. Anyone else would hide in back, in the balcony. The longer I am alive, the more of the story's assumptions I understand. Now I know that Sylvia does not have a good reputation, and that Dennis doesn't dare talk to her. I wonder why this story seems to define girls by what boys think of them.

Then I realize the only reason the story has Sylvia kissing the other boy in plain sight is for what Dennis will think about that. I worry: Does she want to kiss the boy? Does she understand it's a show for Dennis? Does she enjoy it anyway?

I'm thinking about that when Dennis puts his hand up my blouse, and I push it away once and then do not. I am not thinking about his hand. It's the way the story goes, his hand groping randomly over me, and I can't do anything about it but think. I wonder what Sylvia thinks as she puts her tongue in the softball boy's mouth. I wonder if anyone thinks besides me. I hope Sylvia does.

Now it's a dance. Banners over the gym floor say JUNIOR PROM. I'm in a different dress, but it still feels tight. I glance down to see that I'm straining at the front of it. Must be a recent development, har har.

I am far from the center again, standing by the bleachers. It's more focused in the center of the gym, and it takes me no time to pick out Dennis, dancing with Sylvia. Her hair is longer and ripples like a waterfall when she moves. The story is dim where I am, and I find I can ripple my fingers in imitation of that watery shimmer, on purpose. I wonder if her hair feels like water. I run my fingers through my own hair.

Sylvia laughs. "What in the world are you doing?"

I drop my hands, startled. Dennis is still far away on the gym floor, arguing with some boys. Sylvia is grinning at me.

"Trying to make my hair like yours," I blurt.

The words come out exactly the way my thoughts are in my head. That's a surprise. I realize this isn't part of the story; the story continues with the boys slowly circling each other on the dance floor.

"It isn't, though," I say, a little more careful with these words, these words I am controlling myself. "It just hangs there." As long as Dennis doesn't see or hear us, I can really talk. "This is stupid, but—can I touch your hair?"

Sylvia looks slantwise at me. She doesn't say a word. I'm afraid she's really just a prop in the story after all, and I feel sadder than I'd learned how to feel before.

She takes my hand.

The argument across the gym is becoming more animated. I see one of the boys is the boy from the softball game and the movie. Sylvia's hand is warm and dry. Mine feels clammy. I am embarrassed, fascinated, as she raises my hand. I feel my pulse against the warmth of her skin.

The boy from the softball game is hitting Dennis in the face. The rest of the boys stand like statues.

Sylvia pulls my fingers through her hair. It is soft and smooth, but it isn't water and it isn't magic, it's hair, like mine. I like that.

I say, "I wish I could dance like you do."

"Oh, *dancing*," she says, dismissing it. "That's just for the story. What I *do* is think. You do that, too."

She smiles and I think she is going to touch my face when the boy from the softball game comes and takes her away, just like that. Dennis appears, a bruise around his mouth, his eye beginning to swell. "Let's leave," he says, and I realize I came to the dance with him. I want to wave goodbye to Sylvia, but my fingers cannot move that way when Dennis is looking at me. Instead they go up to touch his mouth, gently. He winces.

"I'm sorry," my voice says. "I should have told you Ralph was looking for you."

"It's a free country," he grumbles. "People can dance, can't they? Can't people do what they want?"

I don't know, I want to say. Can I?

"Of course," I say. "Could you take me home now? This is a stupid dance anyhow." He takes my hand to lead me from the gym. His fingers trap mine. They do not pulse with possibility. I look for Sylvia in the parking lot as we get into the car and the scene ends, but she is nowhere to be seen.

I am driving down the central part of town. I see Dennis and Sylvia walking along the sidewalk. Dennis seems to catch a glimpse of the car I am driving. He pulls Sylvia into an ice-cream shop. I want to try out how fast the car can drive on the expressway but

I am crying on the front steps of my parents' house. "The scholarship didn't come through," I say. "You know my parents can't afford to send me to the school you're going to." Tears feel weird. There is a teasing little breeze: it catches them in cold stripes down both sides of my face.

"I won't go. I'll take classes with you at the community college." Dennis has a brave look on his face, but his eyes look trapped. Does he want to stop the plot to see what happens, too? I want to ask him. I try. I open my mouth.

"Don't be stupid," I say. "You have to go. You'll learn all sorts of things. You'll be an engineer. And you'll meet lots of girls as beautiful as—prettier than me. You'll probably end up living in Paris or something, and

I'll stay in the suburbs." I guess this is a fight. I don't like the way I fight. I don't seem to do it in a very straightforward manner.

"I won't," he says. "I'll come back."

"You won't," I say. If he doesn't, is the story over for me? I know this is Dennis's story, though I wish it were Sylvia's. But not mine. If the story's spotlight were on me all the time, I wouldn't have been able to say what I wanted, to talk to Sylvia in the gym. She liked that I thought my own thoughts.

"I will," he says. "I'll marry you, Emmy."

I cry harder, which seems pretty stupid. Then my face is dry and we're in a jewelry store and I say "It's the most beautiful ring I ever saw, Dennis!" He kisses me. I see Sylvia through the store window. She puckers up and squoonches her eyes shut, making fun of the way Dennis kisses. She winks at me and skips away.

Dennis didn't even see her.

That's interesting.

The long train of my dress catches and pulls on the red carpet. I am taller than my father now, walking beside me, but he doesn't look any different or more formed than he did last time.

"Dearly beloved," the minister says.

Dennis puts another ring on my finger. He kisses the bride.

I throw the bouquet at the reception. Sylvia catches it. I try to catch her eye but everything is moving too fast.

He is carrying me into a hotel room. I am in bed. My clothes are gone. He gets on top of me. His legs are heavy on mine and he smells of sweat. He murmurs unintelligibly.

The scene breaks.

Dennis comes home. He's been doing things, but I don't know what, and I can't ask. I'm just in the apartment, which isn't much different from my parents' house except it's smaller.

"How was your day?" I ask. I know the story's been moving since the wedding. I can feel it. I wish I knew if Sylvia is still part of it.

"Fine," Dennis says. Then he makes a smile and says "Fine, honey." And he puts his mouth on top of mine and bends me back. That's that.

"The doctor said there's no reason I shouldn't have children," I'm telling Dennis. "He said just relax."

"Do you ever relax?" Dennis mutters. How would I know?

I bring him a dinner I must have cooked. Pot roast. I put it in front of him and he doesn't say anything. He just eats it. I don't say anything either. I don't think I like being married. My scenes are shorter and there's less for me to look at. I wonder if things will change, or the story will just end, or my part in it will end. I wonder if I'll know it when my part in the story is over, or if I'll just stop.

"A person can see who he wants to see, can't he? It's a free country, isn't it?" Dennis is shouting at me.

This marriage must not be very pleasant.

Sylvia walks by the front window and waves at me. I'm surprised she's there, and I want to go see her. But Dennis is still shouting.

"Don't let me stop you," I say in a low mean voice. Why should I sound angry? What is Dennis to me? He has made me blush, and marry him, and he bent me back in bed, but that doesn't touch me. I just have to say the things I have to say. We have not been in groups of people, so I could think my thoughts in the background while he interacts with someone else, not since the wedding. It all moves too fast now. I have to try to figure things out in the little moments between shouting and tears.

"I won't!" Sylvia is back outside the window. She

lifts her fingers and makes antennae behind the back of Dennis's head, where only I can see. She puts her hands on her hips, pretending to shout, and points and shakes her fist. I feel a huge laugh inside me, watching Sylvia clown out of the corner of my eye.

"That's fine. Don't expect me to hold dinner," I say in the same low voice. Dennis turns and Sylvia ducks instantly out of sight. He goes to the door. I stand frozen, scowling, laughter trying to explode out of me.

He slams the door and laughter does explode from me. I choke and shriek with it. Tears run down my face. I lean against the window, gasping for breath, watching Dennis sneak into a little red sports car. Sylvia sits behind the steering wheel. Dennis doesn't look back, but Sylvia turns and raises her eyebrows at me. I wave with both hands at her and dance around like a maniac. The car drives away, and I laugh for another minute, standing in the living room without Dennis there or anywhere around, just laughing, alone, laughing so hard that for several moments I don't stop being there, even without Dennis, his needs, his story.

That is the only time I laugh for a long time. My scenes stay short and angry. I suspect most of Dennis's story is somewhere else. Maybe with Sylvia. I am happy to think she's out there, somewhere, maybe clowning behind his back, but I never catch a glimpse of her. Fighting with Dennis was tedious the first time, but it's all that happens for me.

And I can't steal any more time for myself. When Dennis goes, I try to hang on. I promise myself a reward if I can do it. The problem is, I can't think what I could give myself. I think Sylvia must know something I don't. She was there that time, when Dennis didn't know it. How did she do that?

Somewhere within a scene break we have moved to a house, but it's the only thing that's changed. Dennis may be a little older. I probably am, too, but there are no mirrors in the rooms in which we fight.

This is the best I can do:

"You are a shrew," Dennis says.

My hands are wrapped loosely inside a big dish towel. "Who made me one?" I say. Inside the towel, I dance my fingers around crazily. He doesn't know I'm doing it.

Dennis is stomping away to the door, and I have seen this before, and before, and before.

When his back is to me I drop the dish towel and twirl around three times on my toes—in the few moments before he gets to the door and it's over again.

"I called her," I say to him. I called someone? I want to cheer. It's different. I have an active role in this fight.

"Who?"

"Your tramp," I say. I think that means Sylvia. I wish it hadn't happened off scene. I wish it was something I had done, rather than something I tell Dennis about. "I invited her for dinner."

"My god, Emmy, you didn't. There's nothing going on between us and you know it, and you're going to throw some kind of hysterical scene!"

"I don't see how you can have any objection to inviting one of your friends for dinner. I'm always alone and starved for company in this house." I wish this were true. I am always with Dennis, only with Dennis. I don't exist alone. "Maybe now you'll stay home for dinner one time."

"You're not going to do this," he says.

"She'll be here in half an hour. I have to finish making the gravy," I say. I go to the kitchen and stir brown stuff in a long flat pan on the stove. There is a heavy silence from the living room. It's very much like being alone. I like the feel of the wooden spoon in my hand. It feels more and more real as I move it through the thick brown sauce. I can feel the wood grain against my palm. I hold it firmly, its growing reality, thinking about nothing but the spoon.

I take the gravy off the stove when the doorbell rings and go to join Dennis, greeting Sylvia at the door. I can tell when I see her that we are all older. Maybe ten, maybe fifteen years older. She's beautiful.

"Hello, Emmy," says Sylvia. Her voice is a little lower than it was in the gym.

She hands me her coat. Her dress looks like one of the ones in the lingerie catalog I was shouting at Dennis about many scenes back. Then I don't look at her. I want to, but my face turns away. "Hello, Sylvia," I say flatly. "Dinner's almost ready."

"Maybe we can catch up on old times while it finishes," she says in a voice just as flat. Dennis looks upset. Sylvia and I walk back in the house to the den.

My heart is beating hard as I shut the door behind us. I am afraid the scene will break. My hands lock the door and it makes a loud click, loud enough to be heard down the hall. I can hear the floor creak from Dennis's step. He often paces when we're about to argue.

I turn to Sylvia. She whoops a whispered whoop and throws her arms around me in a hug that knocks my feet off the floor. "Time!" she whispers, picking me up. "We have time!"

"How much time?" I whisper, rubbing my sore bottom, a part of myself I think I've never felt before. "How long can this scene last until we have to go out there again?" Then, "*Slut!*" I shout. I pick up a lamp and throw it at the wall. It shatters loudly.

Sylvia giggles. Her high cheeks flush with merriment. "We're having a fight in here," she whispers. "How ridiculous!—Do you know the trick?"

"The trick?" I say, confused.

"To make time last."

I don't know what she's talking about.

"When he's not paying close attention to you, when the story's not paying close attention to you—when he's not *looking* at you, it doesn't matter what you're doing," she says. I make shapes with my fingers, remembering. "So it doesn't matter how much time *you* think is passing. You can decide for yourself how much time it is."

She grins. "Once when he went to the bathroom, I took the whole stereo apart. To see how it worked. When I decided I was finished and he came out, it all went back together again. I took a bicycle apart once too. It was easier to figure out." She's talking very fast, like she's stored things up to tell me. "I think I stole an hour, or two hours, just while he was taking a leak. I probably could have taken more, but there just wasn't anything to do once I had all those pieces laid out. Hotel rooms are boring. Haven't you done anything like that?"

"I'm never alone in a room," I say. "It's a fight, and another fight, and another fight. Nothing in between."

"No. Not even once?"

"Once I laughed, all by myself," I say, remembering.

"Tell me what you've done. Tell me what you've thought."

I tell her about my part of the story, what it's like to be the shrewish wife to a person I don't really know, how I've tried to fit the story together from the little pieces I've seen and decided it wasn't good or fair. I am too embarrassed to tell her how often I think about her.

"Excuse me a second," whispers Sylvia. She knocks over a leather chair and squeals a loud outraged squeal: "*You—!*" The floor creaks again outside.

I sit on the floor against the overturned chair. I clutch my knees and start to cry. The tears feel natural, and bitter.

"Hush," says Sylvia. "Hush." She kneels down next to me. She puts her arms around me. "Hush, honey, hush." She brushes my hair back with her fingers. I reach out to feel her own long, gold hair. It is soft and heavy. She kisses a tear off my cheek. I reach my hand down behind her neck.

Sylvia is so strong, the sort of person you know you can only admire. I start to pull away. She catches my hand.

"You're real," she whispers. "You see things. You think things. You're so beautiful." She brings my hand up and kisses my fingers. She kisses me on the lips. I find the way her dress unfastens, and I pull it away to see what all of her looks like. I run my hand from her neck down to her hip, along the warm curves of her side. She moves her arms gracefully, pulling my blouse up.

I want to tell everything and leave nothing out. I do not mean to leave anything out when I say: I do not now do anything that I have not thought to do. What Sylvia does is what she thinks of herself. It feels beautiful. It feels real. And I stop waiting for another creak outside the room. I forget for a long time that there is an outside the room.

We lie there together a long time, breathing quietly and not having to do anything we don't want to, most of the time. Once I have to slap my hands together hard, and Sylvia has to cry out. Her eye swells and starts to turn dark underneath.

"I wish I got hurt instead of you," I whisper.

"It doesn't hurt."

Finally I start to drowse, and that must be when time starts fast again. Dennis has forced the door open, and I am standing with my hand raised to Sylvia. There is a smirk on her mouth, but her eyes are kind and searching. She looks like she wants to tell me something. Dennis shoves me and takes Sylvia out of the room. I don't think he's coming back in this scene. I will myself not to go away. I will being alone in this room.

I sit beside the overturned leather chair and feel it, its grain different from the wooden spoon, different from Sylvia's skin. I compare the feeling of all three textures, wood and leather and skin, and I love them all. I stroke the chair and

Dennis doesn't talk to me now. There are no fights. There is silence. Bits of silence in fast patches, as he enters and leaves, enters and leaves, once or twice glowers through breakfast or dinner. In the silences, I think about my memories, and at the moments of his leaving I practice making time for myself out of his inattention.

I learn how. I make a lot of time.

I duck into the room in which Sylvia and I were together when we had the fight for his benefit, and I fix it up. I take the curtains off the windows so all the sun comes in. I don't worry about privacy, because there is never anyone outside the window, though I keep looking. I put the leather chair in the middle of the sunlight, so that it is warmer than a person, soft in the sun. I take books off the shelves to read them, but there are no words inside; so I take their bright jackets off and put them on the walls. Later I sneak in the kitchen scissors and cut the jackets into colorful shapes, flowers and birds and bright red mouths. I cover the walls with paper kisses.

I'd like to write in the empty books, but all I know is the story I am in, and I don't even know most of it. Just what I see from where I am.

The parts of the story I am in become more fractioned, more disjointed. Dennis walks into the room, throws his jacket on a chair, and walks out. Dennis shouts at me that he cannot take off work for a vacation. Dennis comes home late, drunk, and does not say a word. Dennis ages faster, scene by scene. The story must end when he dies, if not before that. Time is precious. I make my own hours for every few seconds of time with him.

In my time, I cut the curtains in my room into long shreds and sew them together to make a huge floral robe that swirls around me when I move. I exercise my memory: I remember seeing a boy sail a paper airplane in the first moments of my life, and I tear pages out of books and fold them until I get something that flies. The failed shapes I hang by thread from the ceiling so they won't have to be failures. When the weather is warm so I can open the window (one day it will be spring, the next winter, the next summer) they swing against each other, rustling.

Always I tire, lose my concentration and find myself in another fragmentary moment with Dennis.

He is reading the paper one time when I see a little red car drive by. It has dents and rust on it. I see Dennis see the car, too; his eyes flick up, and then he looks back down at the paper. Dennis shows no emotion now.

The instant he looks down I run into the kitchen and out the back door, where I've never been before. The back yard is an expanse of hazy green, without detail. I run around the house and wave frantically at the back of the car.

Sylvia pulls over, out of the view of our front window. I climb in. She is wide and round now, her hair more gray than gold. She looks good. I hug her.

"I've missed you," I say. "I've taken a lot of time for myself. I've fixed up the room. You'll think it's silly. Come and see."

"I've had no time since I saw you," she says. "One little bit with Dennis telling me it was over, but that was it—that was the one moment I've had since I was here last. I think I'm out of the story."

"I thought you *were* the story! I thought that was it—Dennis going back and forth between the two of us."

She shakes her head. There is a little gray curling around one ear. I want to touch it, so I do. "I don't think it has anything much to do with either of us. I think it has more to do with his job, now, and I'd bet he's selling secrets. Now that he doesn't have a home life or a mistress, I think he'll go further and further until he's caught."

"His job? I don't know anything about it! What could be interesting about that?"

"Who knows? We're just peripheral to it all."

I am angry. "All this mucking about to make a life for him, and it doesn't even have anything to do with us!"

"Poor Dennis," says Sylvia.

"Poor Dennis?"

She shakes her head. "He's so trapped."

"So are—"

She puts both arms around me and holds me, her breath in my hair. "We have room to make up parts of ourself. Room to live, in the cracks of this story. What does he have? Does he get to wonder? We can't even ask him. He can't even tell us." Her voice is rich with sympathy. I remember all over again how fine a person she is. I snuggle against her, feeling peaceful.

Later, when I ask, she gets out of the car and dances with me. There is no one on the street, no one on the sidewalk. She dances barefoot on the featureless grass, bending and reaching, slowly, with a kind of dignity that is new. Her body is mature, full, now. We dance to no music with the wind in our faces. Then we lie on the grass and look up. "I never saw clouds before," I say.

"Look closely," she says. "I think the story's almost over. You may never see them again." I turn on my elbow to her, but she is looking up at the sky. "You may never see me again, either."

"No!" I cry. "That can't happen—I've hardly seen you!"

"Things end." Blue sky reflects in her eyes. "This has been the best part. With you."

"Stories can be told again." If I say it firmly, I might believe it.

She smiles with her mouth and glances at me. "This isn't our story. We stole what we have." Her mouth quirks sideways and she looks back up. "When this story gets told again it's just Dennis's sad little life, starting high and selling out until he ruins himself. No happy ending. If he doesn't get one, why should we expect to?"

I want to cry, but I can tell she is close to it herself, and Sylvia is not a person who likes to cry. I lean over her and kiss her neck, in her favorite spot.

Time does not stretch forever. In the end Sylvia is back in the car driving out of sight, and I go back to the living room behind Dennis's back. I think I see a flash of light from her bumper as I hear the sound of her engine fade away. There has been no goodbye. She never saw my room.

Dennis folds his paper. "I have to go to the office."

"On a Sunday?" my voice says. None of the loss of Sylvia I feel in it: the tired resignation of a wife nagging her husband for the thousandth time.

"Things are complicated, all right?" he snaps. Suddenly I know it is almost over. Shaken, I forget to steal time.

Dennis is home, ashen, something terrible happening he won't talk about. I know Sylvia was right and I will never see her again. She is gone. Soon I will be too.

The phone rings and Dennis answers it, panic and wheedling, not words, audible in his muttering. I leave him on the phone and go back into my room. Lopsided paper birds fly under the ceiling. My robe is spread across the chair. If Dennis came into this room, would everything that is mine in it vanish?

It will all vanish soon anyway.

I look out the window, wanting to see her car. The road is not visible from here.

Now I cry, the first time I have ever really cried, myself, not Dennis's little wife Emmy in the story. I pull my flower robe up around my face and sob, silently. Dennis must not hear me. It could break the last time I can make my own time.

I cry until I get angry. I did not decide on my life. I did not write it. I tear off the robe and start yanking hangings from the ceiling, furious that they are all I have done with my life, furious that Sylvia never even saw them, furious that they are foolish. I think if she did see them, she'd laugh at them. I can hear her laughter in my mind.

But my mind can't make it mocking. Even when she made fun of Dennis, there was nothing hurtful in it.

I think of Sylvia, laughing. I'm the only one who knew her, and soon I will be gone. The story could be told again with nowhere any trace of me, of Sylvia. Only Dennis and the fleeting images of women in his life. Only Dennis's story.

I barely knew Sylvia, but knowing her made her more real, as her knowing me freed me. My anger falls away. My frustration falls away. Sylvia found ways around the limitations. I remember her laugh.

I push the leather chair over to the writing desk. My body has gotten older and the chair is heavy; I sweat doing it, and like the feel of my sweat. I open the drawer and find some pens. I take down two books and open the first one to a fresh, white piece of paper, clean, like Sylvia's grin. I gather my memories around me, with the cutouts and the hangings and my tattered funny robe. They all belong to me.

I write on the cloth cover of the first book, "The Story So Far." I write on the cover of the second, "The Further Adventures of Sylvia and Emmy." In the first book, I begin:

"We grew up in the same small town, in the same short story. . . ."

When I finish this story, I will start the new one.

Suicidal Tendencies

Dave Smeds

Mother

MY DAUGHTER KILLED ME TUESDAY MORNING.

I opened my front door and there she was in the hallway, armed with a wood axe.

"Cheryl—" I blurted.

"Hi, Mom," she said, and swung the axe.

My ribs made a funny sound. *Chock*. The noise reminded me of a dropped watermelon striking a tile floor. Suddenly all the thoughts that come with death burst forth in my head. Memories. Fear. Denial. *It's going to miss, it's going to miss*. But it had already struck, and I was sliding quickly into shock.

My left knee banged against the doorsill; the right collapsed altogether. My face swung down over a puddle of blood. It seemed odd to discover this red, wet liquid soaking into my welcome mat. It didn't register that the torrent originated from the vicinity of my left lung.

I suppose I felt a lot of pain, but my nanodocs have edited out the memory. It must have hurt, because my mouth popped open and stayed that way. I couldn't say a single word. Just as well, I suppose, considering the language I would have used had I been capable.

Cheryl whacked me on the spine next. I sprawled over the threshold. I guess I must have died at about that point, because the next thing I knew my ethereal self manifested up near the ceiling. I had a bird's-eye view as Cheryl brought the axe down like Paul Bunyan on my neck. My head bounced down the hallway and came to a stop against the potted fern by the elevator.

Cheryl regarded my decapitated body. The damn kid didn't even have the decency to turn green. She sighed, tossed the axe and her bloodstained clothes into the recycler, cleaned herself up, generated a new outfit from my wardrobe player, and left the apartment. She stole the barrette from my hair on her way to the elevator.

My ethereal self haunted the corridor, still too connected to the flesh to disappear into the Big White Light. Below me the nanodocs initiated resuscitation.

The big choice must have been whether to put my head back on my body, or my body back under my head. The docs chose the latter, probably because rebuilding the brain would take all that double-checking. I agreed with the choice—not that my condition allowed me to have any input.

Molecule by molecule, the docs stole material from the mess on the apartment threshold and funneled it down the hallway. A grainy stream, looking for all the world like a parade of sugar ants, gathered at my neck.

Once they got going, the docs worked quickly. My spine formed, only to vanish under layers of connective tissue, nerves, muscle, and fat. The corpse in the doorway dissolved steadily. The docs didn't neglect the blood in the carpet and the welcome mat; raw material was raw material.

Something pulled at my ethereal self. I descended.

I awoke to the tickle of a fern frond against my eyebrow. Instinctively I reached for my throat. No seam. Of course not.

Someone was standing beside me.

I jerked into a sitting position, hands up to guard my head. Then I saw who it was.

"Oh. Hi. Joan."

I extracted the words with invisible forceps. I guess part of me wasn't convinced my vocal cords would function.

My neighbor surveyed me as if she were a Mark Twain schoolmarm. Never mind that her body morph presented her as a stylish, if a bit voluptuous, nineteen-year-old blonde. Her carriage betrayed that she was really a prune-faced, four hundred-year-old gossip.

"Your daughter again?" Joan asked. Her eyebrows drew together, broadcasting sympathy, yet somehow that concern did not extend to helping me up.

"Yeah. My daughter." I didn't offer specifics. Joan was bound to make up something even more embarrassing than the truth, no matter what I told her. Might as well not give her grist for the mill. At least she probably hadn't seen the axe.

"The kids today—they just aren't like we were." The eyebrows stayed drawn.

Count on Joan for a handy cliché. Yet to my dismay, I had to agree with her this time.

"Got to run. Drop by later if you need to talk," Joan said, putting on her confidant hat.

Sure, Joan.

Once she was gone, I climbed to my feet. My reflection shimmered in the brass of the elevator door. My hair hung in disarray. If someone had shouted "Boo!" right then, my head would have fallen off again. I stumbled into my apartment, closed the door, and sagged onto my sofa.

Cheryl, Cheryl, Cheryl. Sixty-one years old and still acting like four.

The clock in the entertainment console advanced to 9:22 A.M. Twelve minutes had passed since Cheryl had arrived at my door. That alone told me how careful the nanodocs had been as they repaired my tissues, edited the pain out of my memory, made safety checks, and kick-started my autonomic functions.

I'd been killed, one way or another, five other times in my life. But used to it or not, I could barely rise from the sofa.

I grabbed my kimono off the floor by the front door. My hand fit right through the rents over the left breast and center of the back. I tossed the garment into the recycler and coded the wardrobe player to generate another in the morning. Same style, but I altered the sash to lavender. No way could I stand to wear a red one for a while.

I stank. The docs had put back every particle of my body, right down to the thin layer of perspiration that had burst from my skin the instant the axe swung.

I stepped into the cleanser. My skin tingled as the scrubbers vacuumed out my pores and dissolved the carpet lint in my hair. Feeling distinctly better, I sat down at my dining table and ordered it to create a pot of hot chamomile tea. Only after the first cupful—when I was damn good and ready—did I ask the Link to put me in touch with Cheryl's therapist.

"You were right," I said as soon as Ellen's virtual self materialized in one of my dining chairs.

"Matricide?" she asked.

"A regular tribute to Lizzy Borden," I replied. Ellen listened intently to the description of the assault. Like many psychologists, she affected the appearance of a studious person just entering classic middle age, complete with crow's feet at the outer corners of her eyes, an extra freckle or two on the cheeks, and strands of gray in her auburn hair. All these centuries since eternal youth became the norm, it's still easier to take advice from someone who projects an aura of maturity and experience.

I wondered what sort of morph she wore during her private time. Preadolescent, maybe?

"Well," Ellen said. "I wish she'd proven me wrong. At least you weren't taken totally by surprise."

I thought of the swinging axe. Not taken by surprise? I shuddered. She'd forewarned me that Cheryl would *try* to kill me, but that didn't mean I was prepared for the attempt to succeed, or for it to be done so . . . vividly.

"I don't know if I can go through this again," I said. "You should have seen her face."

Ellen placed her phantom hand on top of mine. Strangely, it soothed me. Any other person would have acknowledged the intangibility of the Link and not bothered to reach out. She seemed to know it was what I needed. It was an example of why she'd reached adept level in her profession.

"What would you ordinarily have done if you didn't have me to call?" she asked.

I saw what she was getting at. "I would have called Cheryl and asked her what the hell was up."

The psychologist nodded. "And she knows that. We've got to show her that the rules have changed."

"I know. I didn't really think she'd resort to murder, though."

"She's never had to before." Ellen leaned back. "You know, it's not too late to change the plan. I could still petition for a personality remorph. It would be easier on everybody."

My fingers tightened around the teacup. "Not easier for Cheryl."

Ellen pursed her lips. "Actually it would be. Once it's done, the new Cheryl would thank us."

The new Cheryl. I cringed, thinking of someone I'd known who'd had a personality remorph. "No," I said. "I can't. Not yet."

Was that approval in the psychologist's pensive smile? "Then we'll have to work it through. I'll talk to her today. I don't expect much, though. You should expect to be killed at least one more time."

I blanched. "I understand."

Ellen prepared to blink out. "Anything more?" she asked.

I sighed. "I feel like a terrible mother."

Ellen waited until I was willing to meet her glance straight on. "On the contrary. The problem is that you've been too good a mother. She needs just the opposite right now."

I bit my lip, and pretended that I accepted that.

Daughter

"Your mom still hasn't called, has she?" Giselle asked.

I pretended not to hear. Jacques was getting ready to jump. I focussed on that.

We were high in the Cascades, at the brink of a gorge. Scoured by glaciers and attacked by snow melt, the cliff below us was fissured and crumbling—not the smooth, tall, granite precipice type that attracts imagemakers and tourists. Steep, but nicely off the beaten track—we could usually get wilderness permits good at the site for an hour every week.

I could feel Giselle's smug grin, even if I didn't look at it. I yawned, projecting nonchalance. Not that it would fool anyone. Giselle knew me better than that.

Jacques leaped. He hit ass first on a shelf about fifty feet down, probably breaking his pelvis. It slowed him down, but he regained enough momentum to tear open his viscera on a jagged projection a hundred feet below that. He bounced against the cliff, through brush and over ledges, losing parts of himself, and slammed to rest near the outcropping we all called Buffalo with an Attitude.

"Not bad," Giselle commented. "He was probably conscious until that last series of boulders." We both knew that meant a lot to Jacques. He preferred to leave his memories unedited. No pain, no gain.

"Coming with me?" Giselle sprang onto a rock at the very edge of the drop.

I shrugged. "Nah. I'll wait another minute or two."

"Oh, Cheryl," she taunted. "If she hasn't called by now, she's not going to. You always expect so much."

"Why don't you give yourself a Tabasco sauce enema?" I asked.

She mocked an expression of deep offense. I glared at her. Her scowl transformed into a crooked smile, still a bit smug, but laced with a certain amount of empathy.

Giselle and I operated from the same foundation. She, Jacques, and I constituted half of the sixty-something-year-olds in all Oregon. She knew what it was like to be a kid born in a society of Old Farts. Except for us, everybody alive had been around ever since nanotechnology had eliminated aging. None of them knew what it was like to grow up among immortals. When they'd been young, their elders had politely croaked, opening up the good jobs, the good home sites, providing at least a chance to excel in some aspect of life. Giselle and I had met at Reed College, had tried to compete in classes with students back for their seventh or twelfth or twentieth degrees, and had joined the local chapter of the Suicidals together.

"Parents," Giselle said, sighing. She had both a father and a mother, a fact I thought rather quaint. "Fuck 'em."

She leaned farther and farther back, until the slightest breeze would have committed her to the plunge. She gazed downward over her shoulder. The anticipation stiffened her nipples until headlights formed along the front of her pullover sweater.

"Oh, look," she said. "The coyotes are back."

I peered down. A small pack of the animals circled near the base of the precipice. They yapped and whined, searching for pawholds in the scree. Obviously they smelled the blood and intestines with which Jacques had decorated the side of the mountain. My best guess said they wouldn't be able to reach the spot where most of the corpse rested.

"Poor puppies," Giselle said. "Do you think it's the same bunch as last time?"

"Naturally," I said. Though we hadn't been here for a month or so, the three of us visited often enough that the critters had figured out the routine. Time before last I'd revived from a fall to see a young female and her litter scampering off with one of my legs; my nanodocs had to steal material from a nearby streambed to fashion the replacement. The park rangers would've given us hell if they'd found out.

Thrusting with her ankles, Giselle sailed clear of the cliff. Her trajectory, unlike that of Jacques, guaranteed she wouldn't snag on anything on the way down.

"Choke on thiiiiiisss," she screamed at the coyotes as she picked up speed.

She impacted quite fabulously on a shelf of jagged rocks well below Jacques's partially repaired body. Even from my vantage point many hundreds of feet above I could see her brains spray, anointing the granite with a shade distinctly lighter than the crimson that smeared everything else.

Suicide Number 6,327 for her. She was one ahead of me, but I'd soon fix that.

Yet I waited. It was stupid. Giselle was right. If Monica had been going to call, she would have. But shit, all my dear mother had to do was say a few words to the Link and her virtual ass could sit itself down beside me, even for just a minute. Was that really too much to expect?

I stared at the high peaks jutting up above timberline to the north, kicked a pebble over the edge, and got ready to follow it.

"Call for you, Cheryl," said the disembodied voice of the Link. "It's Ellen Branson."

Just fucking great. Well, I could refuse it, but she'd only keep bugging me. "Put her through," I said.

Dr. Branson's image materialized beside me. She sat in an invisible chair, her hair unruffled by the mountain breeze. She looked around, noticed the bodies below, and gave me that professional frown of concern she so carefully cultivated.

"I talked to your mother an hour ago," she said. "Your stunt didn't impress her."

"It wasn't supposed to impress her," I said. "It was just supposed to get her attention."

"You're lucky she doesn't file a complaint with the Net. They've just increased the community service time for murder and other misdemeanor assault, you know."

"I'm real worried about it," I quipped.

"You'll miss work. You'll blow your commission and have to petition for another career."

"Another chance of a lifetime, thrown down the face of an Oregon mountain." I wobbled and pretended to lose my balance. I leaned out over the gorge for several seconds, smiled demurely at Dr. Branson, and straightened up. "Why should I worry, Doc? I've filed a suicide petition. Pretty soon I won't have to worry about anything. I'll be checking out. Permanently."

Dr. Branson massaged her forehead. "I've read your case history, dear. You've filed suicide petitions before. You have to refile every day for thirty days running before the Net will deactivate your docs. You always run out of steam before the end."

I kicked her in her intangible knee. "So what? This time it's real. I'm going all the way. You tell that to my mother."

She sighed. "But she knows it's not true. You're just waiting for her to make a fuss over you like she's always done. I think she's tired of that. I think she's leaving it for you to work it out on your own."

"I have worked it out. In five days, I get archived. All I want is for her to acknowledge that."

"Why should she? It's not her problem."

I blinked. Something about the matter-of-fact way Dr. Branson delivered her statement awakened my suspicions. I yelled so loudly it echoed across the gorge. "You're telling her to ignore me, aren't you?"

Doc folded her palms together. She didn't actually smile, but I felt like a victim of the Cheshire Cat anyway.

"Yes. I told your mother not to speak to you until you've cancelled the suicide petition."

"Keep your nose where it belongs," I said. "You're supposed to be *my* therapist, not Monica's. How the hell did I get reassigned to you? What are you, a journeyman, or a fucking apprentice?"

She didn't answer that last part. "I *am* your therapist, Cheryl. Why does that scare you? Why do you have to try to run back to Mommie?"

"Cancel link," I said. Dr. Branson's image popped out just as she opened her mouth to utter some more bullshit.

Mom couldn't keep it up. I knew her better than that. A lot better than any psychologist. I'd really thought the axe would do it, but if not—well, there were other ways.

I looked down to find Jacques, fully rebuilt, waving up at me. I waved back.

"That was nothing!" I yelled. "Take a look at this!"

I launched into the air. The bottom of the gorge raced up at me. On the rocks below, the coyotes licked their chops.

Mother

The transit pod dropped me off over on the west bank of the Willamette, in one of the old residential sections of town. I could tell just how long the neighborhood had been there because the trees and walkways still threaded among the houses in a vaguely gridlike pattern, following the courses of vanished streets. My assignment took me to a roomy old two-story Post-Quake Revisionist set on a full third of an acre.

I asked the Net to play back the job request while I inspected the house and its grounds. The resident must have had some job rating to have scored all this for himself. A programmer, maybe, or even a regional policymaker. Talk about perks. There wasn't even a co-occupant registered.

I wanted to tear my hair out. Here was I, a journeyman landscape architect for forty years, getting ready for my master certification, and the only housing the Net would grant me was an apartment. What I wouldn't give for my own yard.

I double-checked the instructions. They didn't make any sense to me. The yard's present motif was the ultimate in western Oregon xeriscaping. The flora and microfauna were not much different from what might have inhabited the neighborhood in the nineteenth, twentieth, or twenty-first centuries, or whenever this part of Portland had been settled. Someone, maybe even a maestro landscaper, had gone to a great deal of effort to create an environment perfectly suited to the house, to the city, and to the climate.

And I was supposed to change it?

I was still staring at the existing design, brows furrowed, when the occupant emerged. "Any problems?" he asked.

He was tall, blond, and muscular, the very epitome of maleness, yet he walked with a mincing gait. Maybe "he" was really a woman—the name on the job request was not gender-specific—but I didn't think so. A woman who goes to the trouble of adopting a male morph usually does not use it to project female body language.

"Actually, yes," I said. "This says you want lots of sun, but the foliage you've asked for is all deep-shade stuff. Hydrangeas, rhododendrons, azaleas. Your nanogardeners are going to have to compensate every summer to keep those thriving."

"Isn't that what they're there for?" he asked.

I opened my mouth to reply, but closed it. I could tell already that I wasn't going to win this one. "I'll just get started," I said evenly.

"Of course," he said, as if I'd had no choice but to comply. He lingered. Oh, God. He was going to watch. I hated that.

His grounds control box lay half-hidden under a honeysuckle vine by the side of the house. I opened up the programming port, identified myself, and set to work.

I deconstructed the broad ash and walnut trees around

the property line first, set the soil parameters for higher acidity and moisture, and assembled the new plants while the old ones dissolved. For ground cover I selected a Geary Classic strain of baby's tears—one of those with the aqua undertones—from the maestro's catalog of journeyman creations.

The resident pointed to a camellia bush. "I want that over by the steps."

"But—" I stopped short of explaining how that positioning destroyed the front yard's balance, but he seemed to guess what I would have said.

"Look, if this is that hard for you, I can request a new landscaper."

"That won't be necessary," I said with false cheerfulness.

"Fine," he said. "I've got an errand to run. I'll be back later for the fine-tuning."

A pod arrived for him and soon whisked him away. I was grateful.

Mother Nature was going to hate me for this day's work.

As I labored, the high cloud cover withdrew, heralding a gorgeous afternoon. Time passed quickly. That was a rare blessing. In the two days since Cheryl had come at me with the axe, I'd spent every moment of it obsessed over her. It was good to be able to focus on something else.

I was programming the sunscreens on a bed of primroses when a pod descended into the cradle at the end of the lane. I kept my back turned, not looking forward to another encounter with the resident.

The footsteps behind me stopped. No voice. I looked.

Cheryl stood there, holding a handgun.

It was one of those ancient models with a silencer—I never remember the brand names. She must have gone to a lot of trouble to get it. I don't know of many nanoplayers that permit creation of firearms. Perhaps she'd located an actual antique. The only time she ever showed real initiative was when she was up to no good. At least she wasn't going to flaunt the local noise abatement ordinance.

I ducked sideways. Too late. Three slugs tore into my chest. I fell on the tile walkway and threw up blood all over the winery harvest scene I'd just coded into the mosaic. As I tried to raise my head, I lost consciousness.

I woke up hanging upside down from a pod. Healed but disoriented, I slowly recognized the watercourse below and behind me as the confluence of the Willamette and the Columbia. We were heading east at a frightening rate of speed.

A rope held me tightly around one ankle, hemp gnawing into the skin. The acceleration and drag prevented me from reaching up to grasp it with my hands. I twisted around and saw Mount Hood expand to fill the horizon.

"Cheryl!" I screamed at the open pod door. "Stop it, Cheryl! This isn't going to get you anywhere!"

Cheryl leaned out of the hatch. Wind blasted her hair to one side of her face. She waved and cupped her hand to her ear as if to say, "Sorry, Mom. Can't hear you."

"Cheryl! I'll give you five seconds to knock this off. Otherwise I'm filing a complaint!"

I was lying. If I filed a complaint, the cops might interfere in ways Ellen Branson and I didn't want them to. But it was the only threat I could come up with on the spur of the moment.

Mount Hood took over the scenery. Snow turned to steam near the caldera. The pod slowed. I swung back and forth on the cord, trying desperately not to lose my lunch again, assuming the docs had put it all back in my stomach.

The vivid orange tones of the caldera spread across the landscape below me. The pod came to a stop.

"Oh, no. She wouldn't," I whispered. Sweat began to pop from every crevice of my body. "Cheryl! Don't you do it! Don't you *dare*!"

I could finally grab the cord. I started frantically climbing hand over hand.

Cheryl stuck her head out of the hatch of the pod, smiled, and released the cord.

I fell through surprisingly cool air toward the sea of lava. I knew I wouldn't just burn. I'd be vaporized. Sure enough. I landed, and that was that.

My ethereal self manifested high above the volcano. I watched Cheryl's pod fade toward the horizon.

Below, my physical self had not left even a dark spot on the molten rock. With it so thoroughly eradicated, nothing hindered the death process. The Big White Light emerged from a cloud and hung there like a second sun. It drew me upward.

The characteristic, ineffable calm of death chased away all concerns. The events of the life I was leaving rolled past me, memory upon memory, but with a peculiar distance, a detachment. I was removed from all worries, obsessions, emotional triggers.

The Light took me away to wherever it is that dead folks go. If anything happened to me on the other side, I can't remember it now. One instant I was rising toward the afterlife above a volcano, and in the next, I awoke in my apartment.

Naturally, as soon as the Net had verified that I didn't exist anywhere in the civilized universe, the nanomat in my bed had reconstituted me, using the scan it had routinely taken of me during the night.

I raised onto my elbows, serenaded by the sound of the mat's water reservoir refilling. *Now* the emotions came.

I put my hands over my face and shook. This was worse than the axe. I curled into a fetal position—an appropriate posture, all in all, considering that I had, in a sense, been reborn. The old Monica was dead, dead, dead.

Complete body annihilation is so rare in our culture that people forget that being shifted into a duplicate isn't quite the seamless continuance it's advertised to be. The body I currently inhabited didn't exactly match the one that had been fried in the volcano. It was a copy of a me that had existed several hours earlier.

My mental recall of my experiences was intact—those memories were part of my consciousness, carried with my ethereal self. But my new body lacked the subtle molecular alterations that my old body had undergone, and without those, I had no access to my short-term emotional memory.

I recalled nothing of what I had felt that morning. I knew I hadn't been pleased with the resident whose house I had landscaped, I knew I'd been scared when I'd fallen into the volcano, but now I scanned through those events as if they'd happened to some actress in a vid.

No matter that the missing emotions were those of job frustration, fear, and anger, they'd been mine. Now they were gone, killed as permanently as my whole person would have been had I been part of my grandmother's generation. It was only a little piece of death, compared to what Granny went through, but it brought back all the old terror of mortality with a vengeance.

"Access Link," I said, when I could stop trembling. "Branson, Ellen, psychologist. Priority interrupt."

In moments, Ellen's disembodied voice filled the room. "I'm with a client. Hang on a sec. I'll come to you."

She blinked in, saw me still lying on the nanomat, and flinched at my expression.

"Oh, dear. A total wipe?"

"You got it," I said weakly.

"Oh, I'm sorry, Monica. I didn't think she'd go that far. How in the hell did she—"

"A volcano."

"Oh." The therapist swallowed. "That would do it, I guess. This is no good. We have to shift our strategy."

"No more strategies," I said. "I believe her, Ellen. She's going to archive herself. I think I should make arrangements with her to be there." I huddled on the bed, wishing I were smaller.

"No. That's exactly the wrong tactic. She's sucked you in every other time, and it's only perpetuated the cycle."

"It's kept her alive."

"No," Ellen said. "I thought we'd been through that. We've got a dependency here that has to be shown for what it is."

I stared at Ellen through blurry eyes. How could she be so clear, so sure? I'd tried, really tried over the years to make Cheryl stand on her own. But when she did something dramatic, was it wrong of me to go overboard the other way and lavish her with attention until her mood passed? She was the only child I'd ever be permitted. If there was a dependency here, it was my fault. What if it were simply too soon in her life for her to grow up?

"What if you're wrong?" I asked. "What if she really does archive herself?"

She hesitated, and that really scared me. I'd never seen Ellen doubt herself. "You lose a daughter. I lose a client, and maybe my adept rating as well," she said softly.

"But you still think we should try?"

She nodded slowly. "I think it's a gamble we have to take."

Again the hesitation. But strangely, seeing that she was uncertain, too, pushed me past my own weakness.

"What's next, then?" I asked.

Ellen paced to the far wall and back. "We can't leave you exposed like this. We need to set up the time and place for the next confrontation. I want you to disappear for the next two days. Block the Link to incoming calls—all calls, just in case she gets one of her gonzo friends to access for her. Keep moving. Stay far away from home. But first, I want you to do some things here in the apartment. . . ."

Daughter

I'd waited long enough. Did she think I had forever? Early afternoon, the day before the Big Check-Out, I tried to raise Mom on the Link.

"Access blocked," the Link replied.

Son of a bitch. "Where is she?" I asked the Net.

"New Fisherman's Wharf, San Francisco, California. She is walking."

I marched out of my place and hailed a pod. I'd track her down, even if it meant sorting through all the tourists on S.F. Island.

Before I was airborne, I had a better idea. I rerouted the vehicle to Monica's apartment.

I made it to her front door and pressed my thumb against the lock. If my guess were right, Mom hadn't bothered to remove my DNA signature from the lock's database. She was terrible about those sorts of details.

"Monica is not at home," the door said.

So far so good. It wouldn't have spoken at all if it hadn't recognized me.

"I need to get in."

"Please wait," it said. I knew it was placing a call to Mom. I also knew the Link wouldn't put it through. A door query was too routine to override the block. "Monica does not respond."

"She's taking a little retreat," I said. "She asked me to look after the apartment for a day or so."

This apparently satisfied the door's guard program. It unlocked.

I meandered through the rooms. I hadn't been past the front room for two months, but the place was mostly the same. Other people might order their domiciles to redecorate themselves every week, but not Monica. Once in a while she'd move a wall, to create a more open feel, but she'd left things more or less alone ever since she'd moved out of the larger place we'd shared during my childhood. The Japanese rice paper scroll above the toilet had been there so long that it would have disintegrated had not the housekeeping programs restored it periodically.

I brewed some tea and strolled onto the balcony. A hummingbird stole nectar from a trumpet vine blossom not five feet away. The bird's ruby throat shifted momentarily to match the brassy tone of the flower—the city parks and rec department sure liked those chameleonic hummers— then the little thing rose up, perched in midair to regard me, and whizzed off so fast I couldn't track it.

Mom had generated the original of that trumpet vine when I was ten. What was that creator's name? Oh, yeah. Josef Rautiainen, one of the first Finnish horticultural maestros. Her hero.

Something about the apartment was wrong. The tea grew lukewarm while I puzzled it out.

I was drawn into the master bedroom. Gradually, by instinct, my gaze drifted to the large montage picture frame opposite the bed. Scenes of Mom's life filled the rectangles and ovals. I located the two portraits of her parents— one showing them in advanced middle age, just before the immortality threshold was reached; another of them restored to youth, as they looked on the day their ark left for Proxima Centauri. There were wedding shots of their parents, for whom nanotech didn't arrive in time. My great uncle, my mom's old friend Glorie, Monica herself at a university graduation and at tourist sites across the solar system—they were all here.

But where was the picture of me on my first set of roller skates? And the one of her nursing me when I was two months old?

I passed into the dining room. She'd always kept a drawing that I'd done at age six fastened to the food exchanger. She'd been amused by the artwork's scatological humor—I'd just figured out for the first time that the food the dining table created for us was a recycled version of what we put in the toilet.

No drawing. Not believing my eyes, I rushed into the workout room. I stepped on the mat and said, "Run routine thirty-seven."

A virtual of a svelte woman in a leotard appeared at the edge of the mat and began a regimen of exercises. I stared at her blankly. Routine thirty-seven should have been the recording of me, as a teenager, running through an entirely different set of calisthenics. Mom used to play it back quite often.

I stalked through the apartment, scanning right and left. I didn't have to search through much. Monica didn't like clutter; she knew she could always call up an object from its scan if she wanted it.

Nothing. Not a trace, not a single piece of evidence to show that she'd ever had a daughter.

That bitch. After all that talk she'd spouted at friends and relatives about how long she'd waited, about how exhaustively she'd searched the catalogs to find just the right sperm culture, and how she never would have gotten permission to have me if the Cassiopeia colony hadn't opened up, prompting the policymakers to rescind the birth moratorium for her age group.

She couldn't even wait until I was dead to erase me from her life.

I kept down the bubble that was trying to work its way up my esophagus. I relaxed my fingers, but they kept curling into fists. Mom was going to have *quite* a reception waiting when she got back.

Mother

"Good evening, Monica," said my door. "You have visitors."

I took two steps back toward the elevator. I had dreaded this moment ever since Ellen and I had confirmed that Cheryl had taken the bait. My heart pounded, threatening to bruise the inside of my rib cage.

"Shield at level ten," I said.

Normally I maintain my personal body shield on level two—just enough to keep gnats and flies from getting in my face. I don't like setting it so high that it stops bullets; the feedback makes me feel as if I'm moving through molasses. But I couldn't walk in there unprotected.

I pressed my thumb to the lock and shoved the door inward.

A body dangled from my chandelier, noose tight around her neck, blue tongue protruding from her mouth. Her jeans were wet at the crotch where the bladder had voided itself during strangulation.

It was not Cheryl. My offspring sat in a hammock chair at the far side of the living room.

"Hi, Mom," she said sweetly.

Cheryl rocked gently to and fro. Behind her the window broadcast a panoramic sweep of tropical island beach, dotted with coconut palms and bougainvillea. I recognized the flowers as a hybrid designed by Maestro Nathaniel Martin. I'd always hated the maestro's bizarre color combinations. I hated hammock chairs. Cheryl knew those things.

Something was odd about her looks, something I couldn't quite pin down. But I was too agitated to dwell on it.

I scowled at her friend in the noose. "Any others around?"

"Just Jacques."

I raised an eyebrow. She pointed at the closet.

I opened the door. The body of a man flopped onto my carpet, so stiff that he bounced like a mannequin and so brittle that he shattered three fingers. Frost rained out of his curly hair like a massive case of dandruff.

"Yesterday I called him a cold son of a bitch," Cheryl said. "So he decided to prove me right."

I checked the temperature coding for the closet, and found it set at minus 200°C. I ordered it back to normal. I didn't need a goddamn deep freeze in my home. Hadn't since nanotech had eliminated the need to store food.

"Oh, don't do that, Mom. He wants to stay dead the whole twenty-four hours."

I frowned, puzzled until I recalled that if a body is essentially intact but in a continually lethal environment—hanging from a noose and standing in a deep freeze would certainly qualify—the nanodocs hold off on repair until either the circumstances change or, at the twenty-four mark, they abandon the body and generate a new one from the person's latest scan. I suppose it could annoy Suicidals to go to all the trouble of killing themselves only to wake up a few minutes later.

"That's his problem," I retorted, and stepped over the corpsicle.

"Mom. You're so brusque."

It took concentration, but I made my next comment even more curt and dismissive—trying to play my role. "Don't tell me you recycled the gun? Couldn't you and your friends have used it on each other for target practice?"

"Oh, Mom, that's old. Jacques and I used to do that back in dorm days."

I folded my arms across my chest. "Is there something I can do for you today? Or are you going to keep cluttering up my apartment?"

"Sorry about that," she said, and shrugged. "It's day twenty-nine. When a person's got so few hours to live, what's wrong with raising a little hell?" She rocked the hammock chair until the ropes creaked in the hook.

"Give me a break, Cheryl. If you had any intention of following through with this suicide petition, you'd be off somewhere all alone, and you'd stop bothering those of us who have lives to conduct."

"Who have you been talking to? Dr. Branson? That sounds like her."

"Ellen has helped me realize what I should have done with you a long time ago. I've decided to take her advice."

I squinted at her, and finally pinned down what seemed strange about her looks. She wasn't wearing the morph she'd favored lately. She'd gone back to the one I had most often given her during childhood, the one which I suppose qualified most as her own. She hadn't used it much over the years.

"Dammit, Monica," she said, practically spitting out the comment. "I mean it this time."

"What is so bad about life, Cheryl? Why do you want to die?"

She stared as if I were crazy. "What's not wrong? The planet's overpopulated. The rules have all been around for hundreds of years. A nobody like me can't make a place in the world."

"You were eight years into an apprenticeship. You were making headway."

"C'mon, Mom. It was interior decorating. The only reason I got as far as I did was that no one could tell when I did a bad job. Sort of like therapy."

"It was something you stuck to. It was a sign of maturity. You can't expect to get to master if you don't stick with something."

"Right. Get to master. What're the averages now? Thirty years of apprenticeship, fifty years as a journeyman, and then being a master doesn't mean jackshit unless you're so outstanding and kiss so much ass that your peers declare' you an adept or a maestro. What the hell do eight years matter?"

"It's the longest *you* have ever lasted," I snapped.

Tears began to swim in the corners of her eyes. "You act like I mean as much to you as a turd you grunted out in the woods a hundred years ago. You don't care if I do it, do you? You brought me into this fucked-up world and now you won't even help me slide out. I'm *glad* I killed you!"

All I wanted was to stop here, and take her in my arms. But I forced the words out, though I was so cotton-mouthed they ripped my throat. "You're right. I don't care. I've given up, Cheryl. I hope you do it. I've made arrangements with the Reproduction Review Board. They qualified me for a new baby."

Cheryl blinked through her tears. The hammock chair ceased swaying and quivered to a stop. She stared at me open-mouthed. "You can't do that. Nobody gets more than one kid these days." The sarcasm and stridency had left her voice.

"Sure I can," I said. "Now that my request is on file, if you're archived any time before you turn a hundred years of age, I can get reproductive dispensation. You'll be categorized as an abortion."

I waited for her reaction. I hadn't raised my voice, and now I stood calmly, maintaining my stern glare, holding back the shuddering in my bones much like the crew of the *Enola Gay* must have poised while their bomb plummeted toward Hiroshima.

She didn't speak. She sat there wide-eyed, gulping air, tears streaming down her cheeks. Finally she whispered a single word, so softly I couldn't hear her.

I thought nothing was happening, until I noticed a faint, bitter-almond undertone to the aroma of sea salt and hibiscus wafting from the window. "What's that odor?" I asked. Suddenly my limbs sprouted lead weights.

"Cyanide," Cheryl said in an utter monotone. "I've got my filters set for it. How about you?"

Of course I didn't, because setting one's filters to that degree removes all scents from the air. I hadn't worried about poisons, since the nanodocs can usually render them harmless before they cause any suffering. But cyanide, as I recalled too late, is so fast that it's easier for the little machines to let a person die, wait for the air to clear, and then revive the corpse.

"So long, Ma," Cheryl said as stars flashed behind my eyes. Their light filled my vision, leaving me blind as my knees crashed to the floor. I was out before my head struck.

I woke up to the hiss of steam. Groaning, I rolled over to search for the source of the sound.

It was Jacques. He was enveloped in a cloud of mist. No doubt his docs were accelerating the thaw.

I scanned the room. Cheryl was gone, leaving her "friends" behind.

The first thing I did was toss the hanged girl over the balcony. Jacques followed, fingers and all. I didn't give a hoot what the neighbors thought of bodies on the lawn.

Then I sat down, right on the carpet, too drained to make it to a chair. The shuddering started.

I'd done it. Dr. Branson would be proud of me. I'd called Cheryl's bluff.

If it were a bluff.

The shuddering turned into sobbing. The tears burst out of me like rivers. My throat felt as if I'd swallowed thistles. I grabbed the end of the carpet and tried to wipe my face, but all that did was soak the tassels. I cried until I couldn't breathe, and then I cried some more.

When I could finally stand up, and later, when I could finally walk, I stumbled into my bedroom. I recoded the picture frame on the nightstand to the scene I'd kept there for the past half century or so: my daughter, blowing out the candles of her birthday cake as she turned four years old.

Daughter

Earth is glorious from a hundred miles up. At least, I've always thought so. Especially when I've exited my pod, told the craft to return to the planet, and I can just float there, suspended above that big blue sphere with nothing but a body shield, a cartridge of oxygen, and my surfboard to keep me company.

This was one vista I'd never shared with anyone, not even Jacques or Giselle. Oh, they knew about Earth surfing. After all, it had been a fad for centuries. Jacques had even told me about the portable scanner I could use to record and transmit my cusp-of-death configuration to the Net, so that when I was reconstituted my new body would remember as much of the emotional high of the experience as possible. The two of them indulged in the sport as often as I.

But never *with* me. This was my own, my favorite, my private means of suicide.

I hadn't activated the scanner this time. Why should I record experiences that weren't going to be plugged into a new body? This was *it*.

Oregon and the western coast of North America had just emerged from the terminator. Morning, the thirtieth day. If my eyesight were good enough, I could've spotted my mom down there.

Not that Monica mattered. She hadn't answered my Link call when I arrived up here. She really didn't care.

"Access suicide petition," I murmured.

The Net's clear tenor voice responded with shocking speed. "Suicide petition active. Day thirty. Upon your confirmation, your nanodocs will be disengaged and your scan will be transferred to archival storage."

Fog shrouded the Golden Gate. The jet stream poured its usual funnel of rain clouds across Puget Sound. The Willamette Valley warmed to the rays of the newly risen sun. I'd lost sight of Portland as dawn had doused the lights of the city. Now it hid in the greens and browns of the continent, as if it didn't exist at all.

What was one city in the history of a planet five billion years old? What was one more woman in the miasma of the human race?

No one would miss me. Just tag me as a fetus, aborted in its two hundred forty-ninth trimester. A statistic. Check me off the list—it's the only way left for humanity to make room for new folks, not counting spewing them into the colony worlds.

So big a planet. So little a me.

"Do you confirm?" asked the disembodied voice.

My surfboard itched for the press of my Velcro-soled boots. My mind filled with the memory of the heat glowing just outside my shield, the Earth looming below, larger and larger. No matter how many times I do it, the anticipation of death sends the tingle down my spine like ultimate sex, as dependable as a narcotic. And then there's the cool bliss of the Big White Light.

I wonder if there's a God? Is St. Peter pissed off at how few people have been streaming through those pearly gates lately?

Hey, Pete, here I come. Don't be lonely.

"Confirm petition," I said.

"Petition granted. Your nanodocs have been disengaged and your scan has been archived. Permanent suicide is now your option."

I licked my lips and took my stance on the board. With those ominous words, I had become the proverbial acrobat, treading the tightrope without a net. Sweat pooled at the end of my nose, prevented from dropping off by the proximity of my shield.

I aimed the board so that the tip obscured my view of Oregon. Too bad I couldn't target my mother's apartment—not that anything solid would make it far enough to create an impact crater. I wondered if she were awake yet. Wasn't much chance she'd stayed up late thinking about me.

So much ocean down there. The amniotic fluid of the whole planet.

My eyes widened. I cued the Net. "Access Reproduction Review Board database. Do you have a birth request from Monica Taylor, I.D. 555–94–1830–66–291?"

"Negative. No such request on file."

That sneaky bitch. She'd actually had me believing it.

Did it make any difference that she was bluffing? I was still up here, at the upper reaches of the atmosphere. I still had a decision to make.

Maybe I could hold off for a few weeks. With my docs out of commission, I could apply to become a Christian Scientist or a member of the Society of Mortals. Giselle had done it once. She'd said it was the most exciting period of her life, knowing she could really croak at any time, even by accident.

Mom would be left wondering exactly when I'd actually cash in. Or when I'd strike next. Or—

Who was I kidding? I was talking about only one thing here. Life was rearing its fuzzy little head in front of my carefully painted vision. I'd lost the moment. The worst part of it was, if I couldn't do it now, under these circumstances, when could I?

Probably never.

"Erase petition," I said, sighing. "Reactive docs and retrieve scan."

"Acknowledged."

I'd always thought I would do it someday. I always thought it was just a matter of time. Suddenly all those six thousand temporary suicides seemed like some hoary old game, a behavior based on a false assumption about myself.

I had no idea where to go from here. I didn't really like it. But I knew who I had to ask for advice. I had a hint I could reach her now.

I activated the Link. "Mom?" I asked.

Her voice came through quietly and clearly, unaccompanied by a visual. "I'm here."

Her hoarse, strained tone put an uncontrollable quiver into my smile. "Mom, can we talk?"

"Yes. If you'll let Ellen be there later on."

An image came into my head of Monica staying up through the night, pacing, asking the Net every five seconds if I'd cancelled the petition, unblocking the Link the instant I did so. My throat ached with a sweet, powerful tightness.

"Get some rest, Mom. I'll be there soon. I've got a couple of things to do first."

"I'll be here."

I smiled wryly at the big, beautiful planet that had given me so much shit, and would give me lots more. Only a crazy woman would go back. Sighing, I activated the scanner. Aiming the surfboard at the nightshrouded Pacific, I glided into the atmosphere. I made one hell of a meteor.

And within minutes, I was reborn.

The Mind's Place

Gregory Feeley

TSAI YEN'S SHIP REACHED COLD HARBOR IN GRAVEST extremity, dismasted, its lower deck awash, trailing sheets like a kite being dragged. The newfound land glimmered behind morning mists, whispering of unseen surf. Yen, dirty water swirling round her boots as she gripped a broken rail, called orders to her ill and weakened crew, who bent to haul about the battened sails, turning the great ship into the offshore breeze.

From the corner of her eye she saw Prasad, anachronistically attired in breeches and flapping blouse, standing high on the stern deck. She turned away.

The new continent emerged like a growing surmise through the fading mist, shoreline glistening before highlands still shrouded in fog. Monkeys, she thought, would inhabit the high branches of those mountain canopies, fur beaded with droplets from the lingering haze. But there would be no monkeys, something reminded her, no creatures remotely familiar from the lands she had traveled or read of. The landfall before her would offer only strangeness.

Four men worked the great rudder, trousered sailors with straining chests who slipped and bent as they dug their heels into the wet deck. The waterlogged ship turned sluggishly, swollen as a bruise. *I have brought my ship to shore*, Tsai Yen thought. The journey before them, the hardships and deaths that lay on the slopes ahead, would pass from her hands to others'; her responsibility was now discharged.

"Captain." Prasad had advanced to the edge of the stern deck, and stood looking down at the sloshing planks as though unwilling to set foot upon them. "A word with you, when you have a moment."

Yen looked unsmiling at the passenger, whose gaze seemed to fall upon the trash-bobbing waters of the main deck in what Yen briefly imagined was reproach. She nodded shortly, then climbed the ladder to stand beside him. The high ground was the captain's proper place, and Yen made a point of surveying the waters about her before acknowledging with a bare glance his presence.

Prasad too had been looking meditatively over the shrouded harbor. "A long passage," he remarked. Yen waited. "Do you feel then that you are nearing your destination?"

Yen looked at him as though he were being peculiarly obtuse, but something within her stirred. Prasad continued, "Your own voyage is not the ship's, and is not yet at an ending. But I am heartened to see you in harbor. Shall we go below?"

Yen tightened her lips, but made no objection as Prasad conducted her below, where she followed him through flooded compartments to drier ones and down a succession of corridors to the pastel cube of his office. The rolling swells faded, as did most of the ship's gravity. Prasad, his loose blouse now gone, settled with unnatural slowness into his chair behind a burnished expanse of desk.

"You seem to have weathered a great storm, which

speaks well of your confidence in the progress you have made. Do you feel you have steered to the proper shore?"

"Sailing by the stars," she said. "Mars in the Scorpion, red among red, and the northern Dipper steadfast as always."

"Interesting you should choose among the small body of constellations known to ancient China as well as the West. This conflation is in keeping with the design of your ship, that partakes of both the great junks that voyaged to Indonesia and the Greek galley."

Yen looked at him a bit sullenly, knowing what was to come. Prasad began to speak of the journey that was here before them, which he declined to call more real, but was real. They were embarked on a voyage through space, not sea, in a ship so great it resembled an island, borne by a sail vast as a continent sustained by a wind from the Sun that grew rapidly fainter with every kilometer traveled. They were going to a farther world than anyone had seen, the most distant real world in the Solar System, the outermost circle.

"Saturn is the farthest and slowest wanderer, although the Indian system admits *upagrahas*, or imaginary planets. No sailor acknowledges any such not visible in the sky."

"This world was not known to any culture's astrology," Prasad said patiently. "Saturn is the most distant planet known to any ancient civilization, although Uranus was recorded on a star chart a century before its discovery. We are going farther still."

She had, he explained, been outside the ship with a student crew. They were engaged in some minor repair which the mechs could easily do, but which would give them experience for the day when the ship reached its destination and great structures requiring all hands would be built. There was an accident—a chip of stone, hurtling along some unknowable orbit of its own, had drilled through her suit—and a pressure tank had burst. Yen had been flung from the ship by the spray of escaping gas, along a trajectory that would have taken her quickly beyond recovery had her fragmenting backpack not broken free several seconds later, spinning her about and into an elliptical orbit round the ship. By the time they had got her inside Yen was largely frozen, her helmet ruptured and her shattered skull exposed to space.

Yen listened without reaction to Prasad's recitation. Another culture, more careless of the integrity of the mind, would have had Yen's brain laced from birth with nanoprocessing structures, which would have preserved the entirety of her personality in several regions of her body, as well as elsewhere for safe storage. Such expedience would make treatment of her trauma routine: Yen would have woken up missing at most the last minutes of her memory, intact as a rebuilt toy.

Instead the *Centaur*'s physicians had induced her body to regrow its destroyed brain cells, a partially wiped slate which Yen and the wisdom of her body must restore in their own time. Yen had spent a year learning to walk and control her natural functions—such knowledge returned quickly, as though remembered in the flesh—and then to speak a language, in which she sometimes knew the words for unknown objects.

"Some of your friends are upset we are teaching you English, although that was your first language. That decision was presumably your father's, who was born of Australasian parents." Prasad looked at her closely and smiled. "Evidence of your sense of dual kinship to Chinese and Western culture emerges frequently. Do you remember what you look like?"

Yen considered and shook her head.

Prasad touched something behind his desk, and the wall to Yen's right became reflective as a mirror. Yen regarded her features, without recognition but unsurprised.

"Many people of course have mixed Asian and Western features. The crew of your sailing vessel, on the other hand, have always been wholly Chinese." Prasad began to speak of the injury she had suffered, likening it to a building that had been damaged in places to the very foundation, while elsewhere rooms and even window trim were untouched. "Structures of personality develop slowly, in established stages. To recreate early patterns that have been damaged or destroyed, while later ones continue to function unimpeded, can produce distorting effects."

"I am not distorted." This small flexing of will seemed to rouse Yen, a puff of wind to push a sail. Prasad looked impressed.

"No, you are healing," he said. "Old and newly replaced regions of brain are knitting, a very delicate process. This process of integration the mind must explain to itself, and it is using very old methods, archetypes and metaphors too deep to need learning. The voyage through unknown land is an image probably as old as humanity, a story that never stales."

Yen stirred restively. Possibly she remembered this point from an earlier session, for Prasad used it to shift into a discussion of the need to interact with the phenomenal world—he would not call it real—for a larger proportion of her waking hours. Yen could slip without drugs or mechanism into a deep and sustained reverie which her physicians, monitoring her closely, knew engaged her brain fully, a therapeutic workout that restored pathways effaced by trauma, rooting the mind in its own soil. Mindful of her rights, only gingerly would they step into these dereistic episodes, calling her gently back.

Prasad looked at her earnestly as he spoke, intent with the desire to convince. He was not going to compel her, she knew, and would be happy with evidence of progress. That she could easily give.

As though embarrassed, Prasad was being propitiatory. "Your nautical adventure, although prolonged, is not so far in its concerns from the greater voyage we are all engaged upon. The mind can create elaborate puns. Neptune, you may remember, is the name of the Roman god of the sea."

To this Yen said serenely, "The mind is its own place, and in itself Can make a Heaven of Hell, a Hell of Heaven."

Prasad looked surprised, and after glancing down at his lap for a moment said, "Milton. Interesting that you should remember that."

He conducted her, as always, to the corridor that would lead to the ship's minor axis, where Yen would ride down to her room. "Speak to the Onboard," he suggested, "or ask one of the pilots to explain things; they are all happy to talk to you. We are not without perils of our own here, enough for any voyager." As he spoke, Yen could hear gulls crying overhead, and the gently curving deck began to sway.

Sleeping quarters were below as in any ship, here at the bottommost levels where gravity was highest. Another therapist had shown her an animated display and explained how the hull of the *Centaur* did not spin fast enough to induce full Earth-level gravity, so that living quarters occupied two capsules at the end of long tubes like outflung arms. The therapist began to explain the nature of centrifugal force, but Yen had nodded impatiently, recalling the fact in her bones. She now rode an elevator downward, gaining mass and assurance as she descended.

Adults could spend only their sleeping hours here, while children enjoyed longer regimens in the full gravity needed for proper growth. Tsai Yen, growing as few did, had a bed for herself alone.

The elevator doors opened on shouts and a puff of warm air rich with humanity. The air of the living quarters, Yen remembered, tended to circulate more slowly unless blowers ran continually in the tubes. This bothered her not at all; the captain of a ship is no stranger to close smells.

A pack of children nearly collided with her as she rounded a corner, and the smallest, jostled by swerving companions, fell with full gravity's swiftness onto her bottom. Her expression of surprise had not yet puckered to a wail when she was hauled up and pulled from sight. Yen smiled briefly at the retreating footfalls, forgetting them at once.

Her room was a compact rectangle off a corridor reserved for unfamilied adults. As her treatment required Yen to spend at least fourteen hours a day in full gravity, the room was hers for all hours, while its neighbors were shared by pairs of women who never met. During the hours she spent in the main body of the ship Yen kept the compartment walls retracted into the deck so to add to the communal space, a courtesy Prasad had suggested.

At a spoken command the walls rose about her, glistening like a butterfly's still-damp wings. Yen waited until they had clicked against the ceiling, then touched her wallboard. "Tell me about a person named Milton," she said.

"First name or last?" the Onboard asked. Yen recited the line she had recalled. "John Milton," the system replied. "An English poet. What would you like to know?"

Yen thought. "Did he ever write of a sea voyage?"

The system considered this, then said,

Ay me! Whilst thee the shores and sounding seas
Wash far away, where'er thy bones are hurled,
Whether beyond the stormy Hebrides,
Where thou perhaps under the whelming tide
Visit'st the bottom of the monstrous world—

Yen interrupted for a clarification. The Onboard explained that the poem was widely regarded as a lament for a friend drowned at sea. Yen had the system recite it from the beginning, frowning as the invocation began to roll forth. At the mention of Neptune she started and interrupted, but the allusion, once explained, seemed meaningless. The poem contained nothing about journeying, but Yen, affected by its heroic language, asked the system for poems of that era that did dramatize sea voyages. The wall screen lit up with a long list of titles, none of them familiar. Only one had a title Yen readily understood, "The Castaway." She had the Onboard tag it for her reference file.

Supper was served for the present shift immediately after breakfast for the children, who were all on the opposite shift. Yen took a sticky seat along the back wall, instinctively maneuvering to face the door.

Diners glanced at her as they sat in small gatherings, some smiling or nodding. Yen felt uncomfortable with the attention of these people, many of whom had known her before the accident. She knew they harbored hopes that she might with recovery come to remember them, or renew lost acquaintances.

"Doctor Wu." The speaker had sidled up while Yen was looking in the other direction. A small man, wearing a coverall bearing the insignia of Life Support Sciences. He carried himself lightly, like a cat she had seen near the children's quarters. "I would like to speak with you, if I may."

Yen gestured across from her. "Sit down." The wise captain will listen to all officers.

"Don't bother trying to remember me; we never met." The man set down his tray, which bore only a cup of tea. The admission was at least refreshing, Yen thought, then reflected that it could, like the professions of past friendship, be untrue. "I'm Philip Tanaki."

Yen inclined her head slightly, seeing no reason to offer a name he already knew.

"You are well?" he asked, a bit stiffly.

Yen had learned that this was a courtesy, and replied by rote. "Yes, thank you. The physicians are pleased with my progress." She knew that she was not required to ask in turn, but did not care to sit for another interview, so made the requital expected of healthy persons. "And how are you?"

Tanaki smiled. "Oh, I am well. I take care." Yen sensed that he had touched on his subject, and looked at him steadily. "I fear you do not know how to," he continued. "There is much you do not now know, and you will hardly be told."

Yen was often lectured, but preferred discourses to questions. "Explain," she said.

Tanaki looked at her with appraising eyes. "What

do you already know of our world, our betrayal and our exile? Do you know we were sent beyond human frontiers because we defied the mechanization of the mind?"

Yen nodded. The shimmer of this resistance touched her, though she remembered few of the particulars.

"It was guilt at their crime that made our oppressors outfit this voyage rather than simply overwhelming us." The man's expression did not change, but Yen heard a tightening in his timbre. "The Constitution of the Circumlunar Catena sets forth clearly that the member habitats would retain sovereignty of internal policies. This principle was erected specifically to guarantee cultural diversity in the face of technological pressures. The majority disregarded this when it proved convenient; that is undisputed. All this is known."

"And what is not known?" asked Yen, watching his eyes.

Tanaki nodded slightly, approving the question. "Do you know about mites?—machines too small to see, that run on strong light or sugar, repair and reproduce themselves, and carry out complex orders programmed into them perhaps years earlier. Some are highly intelligent, and capable of executing missions requiring sophisticated evaluation and judgment. They are the basis for all industry off Earth—even this ship uses some.

"For fifty years scientists have been using nanoprocessing technology to tinker with the structure of the brain. The early steps were superficial—provide direct communication links, supplement memory stores, record neurological patterns that biomites can retrace in event of accident. Subsequent projects have been more ambitious: redesign the cerebral architecture to take advantage of materials smaller and faster than neurons; junk the principles that govern human thought so that it proceeds according to logic rather than stereotypy, which leads to egocentrism, chauvinism, and irrational aggression. I am using the language of such programs' proponents.

"The resulting creatures are not remotely human.

They have not sought to use their impressive powers against us—eliminating aggression produces impressive placidity—" (Tanaki assumed here an ironical tone) "—but they are nothing you would recognize as your race's children's children.

"The cultivation of these creatures is illegal in most nations, but many governments allow adults to tamper with their own minds. Children, of course, are permitted to grow up unmolested, but that is about to change. It has been widely noted that these children, if allowed to reach adulthood without having their minds radically deformed, evince a marked *rigidity*, an ossified preference for the way they are." Yen watched Tanaki let slip his pretense to objectivity. "So the Circumlunar Catena, in the fullness of its majority vote, has elected to develop the first program, I am quoting now, to establish Augmentation for all young children."

His eyes flashed. "Do you know what followed?" he asked.

"We rebelled, affirmed our right, and have left greater Earthspace to live as real humans."

"A negotiated exile. The Consortium of Earthly powers that funded and still owns much of settled space sided with the Catena, of course, but couldn't let it violate its obligations with impunity—Earth is crowded, and lives by the observance of law. And so we are traveling to the ends of the Solar System, in the largest craft ever built, dissidents and refugees as many settlers have been."

Yen enjoyed hearing this story, and let anyone who offered tell it to her in his own way, but sensed that this was prologue. "And so," she said. "Now tell me what is not known."

Tanaki ducked his head slightly, as though his words must pass to her unseen. "This is not the first ship to set for Neptune. The earliest probe flew past over a century ago, and robots have dived into the atmosphere and landed on Triton. That first flyby was launched out of Earth's atmosphere, because that represented the limits of space technology, and took twelve years to get there. Flights are now vastly easier; one was dispatched from Callistograd, by university students on a project."

"So?" she asked.

"So. New technology allows more comprehensive, cheaper flights. Why have there been only two missions to Neptune in twenty years?"

Yen stared at him.

"You could dispatch a probe from the Greater Jovian or even the Belt small enough to fit in a cigarette. Neptune is still an untrammeled world—there has never been a manned expedition after the Eurospace mission. Why should no one be interested?"

"A conspiracy, either to discourage missions or suppress their records."

Tanaki nodded, eyes agleam. "I do not believe we will find Neptune the unvisited edge of the solar system. Those we seek to escape have preceded us to our exile; worse, we carry them among us, the seeds of our undoing borne within our armor, nestled against our hearts."

Paranoid, she thought, wondering where the word came from. "Justify," she said.

Tanaki began to speak in the measured tone of one who has foreseen all possible objections. "Triton is valuable real estate—not now, but later, when settlements spread beyond Jupiter—and this ship will pass beyond other human jurisdiction. The outer Solar System is far larger than the inner; in two hundred years it will represent the undeveloped frontier of human space. Do you think the powers behind the Consortium would allow an independent sovereignty to set up shop on the edge of that lode?"

Yen thought about that. "Two hundred years is a long time."

"Not long enough to let you undo mistakes made early. The European empires that settled the New World . . . No, there are monitoring devices on board and awaiting us ahead. Control devices, too, if needed. Our ship is swarming with them, unseen. —That's induction, not deduction, but the logic holds," he said, too seriously.

Yen thought. The image of invisible mechanisms infesting the ship, drifting among the corridors like spores, intrigued her. "Would the Consortiumists not simply install such guardians in the brains of the *Centaur*'s governors, where they could exert influence undetected?"

"No, they cannot cross the blood-brain barrier—the technology that would permit biomites to alter neurological structures after being unwittingly ingested was never allowed to develop." Tanaki saw amused skepticism in Yen's eyes, and flushed. "We know that is true, else the Earth nations would have long since set such weapons against each other, and human civilization would be very different."

Yen nodded thoughtfully. "Have you presented your reasoning to the ship's authorities?"

"Fools, and worse. True knowledge of our sorry state must pass among those individuals able to penetrate the veil that swathes our understanding."

"I must go now." Yen stood suddenly, causing Tanaki to look up in surprise. His expression took on a sudden comprehension, and he turned his head slightly, as though to follow her gaze. Yen did not look at him as she carried her tray to the disposal chute and left the dining room.

The sheets were lifted dripping from the ship's wake and wrung before being spread to dry. Yen watched her sailors rub their bare arms and look toward shore, plainly thinking of freshwater streams where the salt could be washed from their skin. Too late, she thought; your landfall will only give onto a further journey, past this parched atoll, across seas where the sun rises smaller each morning.

The dockmaster did not like it, but could find no proscription in Yen's file against taking a walk. Nevertheless, she insisted on calling her physician, who was apparently startled but could offer no reason why Yen should not be allowed outside. "Yes, all the suits have guardians," the dockmaster said, her eyes still on Yen. "No change in air pressure at all, just gravity. Of course."

She tucked the phone back into her shirt pocket, still regarding Yen misgivingly, and brought a skinsuit out from beneath the counter. Yen wondered whether the dockmaster had seen her brought in from the accident, a bloody horror erupted from the purity of vacuum.

Yen shook the suit open and regarded it uncertainly.

"The suit will instruct you in its use," said the dockmaster. Yen looked toward the door opposite the one she had come through. The dockmaster saw her hesitate and threw up her hands. "Second left down the hallway," she cried. "If you remember so little, *please* listen to your suit."

Yen did as she was told, placing her clothes in the tiny room's locker and then listening patiently to the skinsuit's instructions. She stepped carefully into the bunched boots, and flinched for only a second when the suit began to swarm up her legs, the thin fabric curling round her toes like bathwater. None of this she knew, but none seemed unfamiliar.

The skinsuit was speaking to the airlock, a series of pips trilling in Yen's ear to inform her that systems were communicating on her behalf. "Evacuation commencing now," the suit told her. A millibar display appeared within the clear bubble that surrounded her head, its numbers whirling downward as air fled the chamber. Yen raised her arms, wondering if limbs moved more freely in vacuum.

A set of guardrails rose from the floor to enclose a square meter of deck, which slid open onto blackness. Yen leaned forward and looked down into space. With the skinsuit speaking reassuringly, Yen climbed down the inside of the rails, through the deck, and into emptiness. A lifeline attached itself to her belt as she slid through.

Yen let the line pay out as she floated free, drifting slowly from the ship under faint centrifugal force. The *Centaur*'s exterior partook of both spaceship and asteroid, carbon plate around the airlock hatch, rough rock elsewhere. One lifepod was visible from this vantage, a featureless capsule at the end of a long shaft. Yen studied it a moment, intrigued by the absence of scale: she could not tell whether it was twenty meters long or two hundred.

The slowly wheeling stars offered no referents: Yen could not discern the ecliptic, nor sense where the Sun lay behind her. The vista abruptly recalled her first excursion outside the ship, before the *Centaur* had achieved cruising velocity and retracted the lightsail. The micron-thin membrane had blotted the forward stars like an enormous gray world.

Yen tugged on the line to bring her around, and looked without emotion at the bright bead of the Sun. More interesting was a work party farther aft, walking with magnetized soles along a metal pathway. At Yen's command part of her helmet rippled, forming a magnified circle before her eyes. She watched the two women and three men stand about a ceramic housing, wondering idly which one was describing its features to the others.

Apparently one of them glanced up, for suddenly five heads were turned toward her. She hung motionless, seeing no reason to hail. After a few seconds some of them began waving, and abruptly her earphones spoke.

"—this channel? Hello, are you well?"

"Tell them I am fine," Yen instructed her suit, when she saw one of the men, mouth open in a tiny O, take several steps forward.

"Mei-ling!" A new voice. The mouth was moving.

The man abruptly leaped from the deck, sailing toward her in a straight line. Yen began to pull herself in on her lifeline. Seeing this, the man gestured, and a silver thread spun from his hand toward the ship. He jerked hard as the line struck and pulled tight, and swung round in a downward arc.

Watching him carefully, Yen drew herself back to the deck, activating her boot magnets with a word. She felt only a faint sense of hanging from her feet.

The man had come to deck several meters away, and

was approaching hesitantly. "Mei-ling, my darling, you so frightened me." His expression was crumpled, as though under hard deceleration.

Yen looked at him carefully. "I do not remember you."

Tears were streaming from his eyes, trailing upward across his brow.

He said, "I will always love you."

"That must have been an unpleasant surprise," Takeshita said, looking at her with some disapproval. "The poor fellow probably thought he was flashing back to the moment of your accident."

"I did not know this man was my lover," Yen said patiently. "If I should have taken care for his feelings, why did you not tell me his name?"

"We did not know Zhiang was your lover; do you think our records would contain such things? He certainly did not approach us during your convalescence with a claim on your attention."

Takeshita was toying absently with her fountain pen, a keepsake that resembled an antique rocket ship but was, she had told Yen during their first session, even older. Yen sensed the woman's irritation was not really directed toward her.

She asked, "Then his name is Zhiang?"

Takeshita scowled. "We still know nothing, can in conscience ask nothing. But the dockmaster reports that of the student crew outside at the time of your jaunt, the one who returned sobbing was one Engineer Zhiang." She looked at Yen. "You are free to take up the threads of your past relationships, which would doubtless prove healthier than courting autism."

Yen considered this, then decided to placate her physicians, lest their untoward concern become a nuisance. At the midday meal she introduced herself to the woman sitting beside her, who seemed startled and rather unnerved. Plainly she had once known Yen and was unsure how, or whether, to note their acquaintance. Yen relieved her of this by confessing her infirmity of memory and asking that her friend tell her all some day, which prompted a smile of gratitude Yen found oddly touching.

In the nursery Yen offered to assist with the infants, who were fed and changed by human hands only. Beleaguered parents, unhappy to be spending so much time at full gravity amid smells and noise, accepted her help without evident recognition. Yen watched others and worked clumsily, and afterward stood in the women's shower washing away the sour odor she brought with her. Around her steam-wreathed figures joked, not knowing her. She responded to a sardonic comment in kind, and was satisfied not to have provoked a stare.

That night Yen resolved to reward herself with a binge of dereism. Scarcely had she composed herself on the bed when the salt air touched her nostrils, a swell lifted her bunk, and the familiar network of creaks ran through the loose-planked ship like current down a branching of nerves.

Voices called overhead, feet drummed against deck. Yen rose, her gait adjusting automatically to the steady roll of the sea. A heft to the lift of the next swell, and the hiss of water against the side, told her that they were under full sail.

Yen started across the cabin, hindbrain alarm ringing. She had just realized what was wrong—breakers in the middle distance, their sound a half-heard susurrus—when a sudden blow threw her hard against the doorjamb.

A great tearing broke through the ship, felt more than heard as long timbers splintered inward. Yen fell sprawling to the corridor, which rose to hit her at a crazy angle. The ship slewed hard, its mass dragging round its impaled keel. Clamor exploded as furnishings and implements went flying.

Yen shoved past scrambling crew members onto the lower deck, which listed too strongly for one to stand unassisted. Men slid across the wet tilting boards as the ship ground hard against the unseen rocks. Those already climbing the rigging to cut free the sails grabbed wildly as the masts swayed; one fell with a scream to the quarter-deck.

From the pump well came the sound of water rushing in below, loud as a millrace. Yen fought her way over to peer down its depths, and looked up to meet the stricken expression of the carpenter. The ship canted further with a tremendous vibration underfoot and a sound like mountains grinding together, and the man lost footing and fell backward.

Drenched sailors were climbing up from below, eyes wild at the sight of daylight. Yen stared for a second, peculiarly struck by this superfluous bit of evidence that the ship was indeed sinking, within—she ascertained with a glance—a kilometer of the beaches. The sun had already vanished behind the mountains, and the clear sky was deepening toward the plum of this latitude's brief twilight.

"Captain!" The first officer, face bright with blood, hailed from the quarter-deck. "The boat is—" The officer pitched forward as the ship, which had pulled tortuously loose from the rocks and wallowed for a second, was struck against them by a seventh wave. Yen fell backward, slipping on the sluiced deck as she sought to recover and twisting her ankle with a sudden shocking pain. She slid helplessly across the streaming boards, striking a length of railing now tilted seaward with the ship. A burst of water enveloped her, and she felt the railing scrape across her back as she was carried over the side.

The sensation of falling was immediately punctuated by stunning impact, and Yen was carried underwater in a stream of bubbles. Her boots were pulling her down, and in panic Yen tore at them, shucking one but wedging her heel in the other. She kicked wildly as pressure mounted in her ears, then grasped the boot in both hands and twisted it almost to her waist, tearing loose the heavy heel and sole. Yen kicked for the surface, broke through and drew a spumy breath before a wave smacked her away.

She was repeatedly thrust under and swallowed a great deal of water, but Yen thrashed continuously and gulped air when she could. Her cotton trousers were growing heavy, and she pulled them off. A great swell lifted her, and for a second Yen saw the landing boat dangling over the ship's side, banging against its hull as the waves pounded the vessel.

She was being carried rapidly away from the listing ship, in the direction—she turned her head quickly—of the shore. The evening tide, she remembered, was incoming. Yen attempted to lift the hem of her blouse above the water in order to trap air in it, but the sodden silk clung to her legs and belly. She kicked hard, hearing the surf grow louder even as the shoreline vanished into the enfolding dusk.

When her feet scraped sand Yen rolled into a ball and let the next wave carry her into the shallows. As she waded toward shore her ankle sang out in pain, causing her to fall. She scrabbled and crawled the final distance, suddenly nauseated. Dragging herself past the high-water mark, Yen vomited gouts of water and fainted.

The cry of birds woke her shortly after dawn. Yen lifted her face from the sand, parched and suddenly aching. Scrapes and cuts covered her legs, and she pulled up her blouse to find her back marbled with bruises. The sleeve of one boot still sheathed her calf, the foot below it swollen as though straining to burst free.

The ship lay submerged to its stern deck, torn sails flapping on tilted masts. No sign of the landing boat showed on the water or shore, although the body of a sailor rolled with the surf a hundred meters down the beach. Yen crawled toward it, thinking to take the trousers. As she approached, however, it disappeared under a roll of foam and failed to emerge a second later.

When she turned, she found that the land behind her had changed. Yen knelt upon a blackened stump of island, not a hundred meters across. The sand beneath her was crumbling cinder.

She looked back. There was no harbor before her, no

foundered ship. A featureless sea stretched away in every direction.

Yen normally maintained no awareness of the irreality of her illusions until either she had grown replete with dreaming or one of her therapists came for her. The sundering of her reverie's fabric, however, sufficed to bring this realization to mind, and Yen promptly summoned the concentration to dissolve her fancy.

No, a voice somewhere said.

Yen turned, deeply startled, and began to stand. A sharp pain, fiercer than anything she had known since her accident, sent her tumbling to the ground. Frightened, she sought again to erase her surrounding figment, and was rewarded with a blinding headache.

She rolled onto her back, holding her head, and lay still. No voice came.

My mind is gone awry, she thought, shaping the words carefully. She had strained some internal strut and it had snapped, sending her falling. *I am on my bunk, my body is beyond danger.* The cinders seemed to bite into the cuts on her legs.

She attempted to put herself into a trance state, but her head ached with the effort. Angrily she turned to scan the shriveled isle, certain she was being balked.

"Who spoke?" she demanded.

Silence. Yen sat up and peeled away her blouse. Save for the ankle, which was swollen as though boiled, she appeared to have only numerous scrapes and cuts, many filled with sand from the vanished beach. She pulled herself down to the surf, where she bathed her reddened limbs in the salt-stinging water.

Shapes moved beneath the water, swifter than its sluggish stirrings. Yen stared into the refracted shallows, imagining arms weaving, the sidling of carp. The twinkling of light on the surface resolved into a human face, almost recognizable, and Yen was leaning interestedly forward when cold hands closed round her legs and pulled her under.

The water was instantly dark, the grit beneath her feet

gone. Yen writhed as hands swarmed up her chest, pinning her arms, covering her mouth. Something pressed against her ear, not a hand but—Yen didn't know how she knew—a pair of lips.

"Th'art not afraid?" The voice was insinuating, knowing. "Does thy courage surmount all fear, or is thy brain pan now too shallow for depths? 'Tis a poor broken mind knows not fear."

Her feet began to grow cold. A chill was working its way up her legs, an aching cold that resisted numbing. Yen twisted her hips as the chill touched her knees, then panicked as she felt the grip tighten around her shoulders. She wrenched her head sideways, felt something lose its hold and slide across her face, and bit down hard.

"You fight! Good! But you cannot beat me." The hands seemed to be lifting her to a region of light, for she could see them now, dead white fingers gripping her biceps, legs, chin. At once they broke apart, each digit a writhing larva, which immediately began burrowing into her skin. She opened her mouth to shriek and one was between her teeth, squirming for purchase and then in.

"Learn, now, to lose."

They were tunneling into her body, riddling her. She felt them passing through her skull, crisscrossing her with slender tubules.

"I am everywhere. I am in you."

Yen found breath at last for a scream which resounded as though shouted against a wall. She waved her arms, free of impediment. A fog of condensation was beading centimeters from her nose, and rapidly cleared as a jet of air hissed beside her ear to show an unbroken vista of stars.

"Are you distressed?" an affectless voice asked from within the confines of her helmet. "Your pulse is highly elevated, although no danger is apparent."

Yen bounced lightly against the end of her lifeline. Above her, the etched rockscape of the *Centaur* hung motionless in the dim light, its clean lines unbeguiled by fantasy: an anchor for all that surrounded it.

•   •   •

"There is more in the mind than we know," Prasad said. He was wearing a dressing gown, and Yen realized she did not know what hour it was. "Scientists long thought that the fundamental processing unit of human consciousness was the neuron, and believed that an entity with a hundred billion switches could match the complexity of the brain. Now that we know how much information is stored and processed in the microtubules of each neuron's cytoskeleton, we have become more cautious in discussing the fine structure of the personality."

Prasad peered at Yen, who looked back blankly. He changed his tone. "Much of your surviving brain tissue was traumatized, the neurological connections that wove it into mind destroyed. As new connections are slowly grown, data from numerous cytoskeletal structures are being restored to the whole. What your subconscious makes of this, I cannot know."

"This wasn't a dream," Yen said, voice fretful. "I left the ship."

"Yes. Perhaps you woke, chose to take another spacewalk, then lost memory of your last hour in a, well, a shifting of circuits. Or possibly you were indeed dreaming, not conscious of your actions, as you acted."

"You don't *know*?"

Prasad grimaced. "Medical information on brain trauma patients is not readily applicable, since most such patients are treated more intrusively than you. And consultations with leading authorities on Earth would be prohibitively expensive at the moment." He saw Yen's expression and shrugged. "Information exchange tariffs. Politics."

Yen stood. "You must find something before I venture out once more. This cannot be done to me again." She held out her hands, stared at the unscoured flesh, then thrust them into her pockets. "Good night, Doctor," she said, and left.

Several hours later a woman Yen's own age came to her room and introduced herself as Ann Chang. Yen recognized her face, although she could not say from where. She admitted that she did not remember Chang's repeated visits during her convalescence, which seemed to distress the woman.

"I have forgotten very little since my release," she said politely, "so should not forget you again."

Chang showed her an embroidered cushion and a bowl of artificial flowers beside her bed, which she said her friends had made for her while she was in hospital. "We should not have waited for you to visit us," she said in Chinese.

Yen leaned over to kiss her friend's cheek, a practice she had observed between young women in the family quarters. "You must tell me all I have forgotten," she said.

Chang took her to a dramatization of the flight of the *Centaur* that was being enacted for a class of young children. They reclined in darkness and watched a vault of space before them brighten as a stylized Sun swung into view. Mercury and Venus, much larger than scale, trundled around it as though riding the tracks of an orrery.

The narrator was explaining how the *Centaur* took advantage of a ballistic phenomenon called the Four Body Problem to hurl its great mass out of the inner Solar System. Yen disregarded this, instead watching as the outfitted asteroid that was the *Centaur* fell toward the Sun, swinging round in a close perihelion that took it deep within the orbit of Mercury. Glowing like a coal, the empty ship was accelerated to thirteen gravities as it was flung back out, swerving around the outsized planets as though to avoid collision.

The children stirred restlessly as the narrator explained how "ejection to infinity" took place in the interaction of the four bodies. They were waiting for what came next: the enormous lightsail blossoming ahead of the speeding ship, unfolding across two thousand kilometers like a flattened moon. Under the solar pressure of the still-huge Sun, even the *Centaur*'s millions of tonnes were boosted to the velocity of deep-space flight, vividly enacted with musical accompaniment.

Yen had little interest in the drama created by the dispatch of the *Centaur*'s crew to catch up to their speeding vessel, but she watched the last stages of the ship's deployment—the extrusion of the twin living quarters, the firing of the rockets to induce spin—with deep absorption. The *Centaur* now corkscrewed like a bacillus toward the outer planets, its lightsail dimming with distance. Falling free, it receded from the viewer's sunward perspective as a triumphal score came up.

Yen and Chang remained seated as the children, exuberant in the amphitheater's low gravity, were at length herded out of the chamber. "Do you not remember our fast ferry from lunar orbit?" Chang asked. "How the ship smelled strange for weeks after we moved in? We were girls then, too young for skilled work, so they set us to wiping surfaces. You've forgotten *that*?"

Takeshita joined them for lunch, clearly unsurprised to find them together. People sitting around them nodded and smiled, pleased to see the solitary diner among company. At table Takeshita was less reserved; she discussed shipboard news, made little jokes. Yen found herself relaxing by degrees, and smiled when others did.

In her office later Takeshita showed her a tiny device, which resembled a pea trailing a centimeter of fine wire. "It would be placed in the sphenoid sinus, and gradually extrude filaments no thicker than axons into the pons, midbrain, and corpus callosum. This will allow us to monitor electrochemical activity more precisely than with exterior scanning devices."

Yen retained some memories of intrusive procedures during hospitalization. "Fine," she said. "What happens if I begin to wander?"

"You will be attended throughout your next reverie. We will merely have to wait until the recorder has established its connections, perhaps a day and a half. I think such a respite is well advised on other grounds as well. Can you refrain from 'voyaging out' for two days?"

Yen sat in her room yearning for open sky and salt breezes. She touched her wallboard and asked, "When did we last speak?"

"Two days ago, Shipday 3261."

Yen could only remember something about the sea. "What did we speak about?"

"Poems dramatizing ocean voyages."

Yen lay back. "Recite me one."

The Onboard was programmed to weigh available data when humans required them to make selections. "Obscurest night involved the sky, Th' Atlantic billows roared," it recited in a sonorous, accented voice.

When such a destined wretch as I
Washed headlong from on board,
Of friends of hope, of all bereft,
His floating home forever left.

Yen heard a hissing in the corridor, like the passing of one of the ship's larger machines. She dimmed the lights, letting the words roll over her.

. . . He long survives, who lives an hour
In ocean, self-upheld;
And so long he, with unspent power
His destiny repelled . . .

Something thumped against her door. Yen sat up, brightening the lights. A pool of water was seeping beneath the door.

"Onboard, what is happening?"

No answer. Yen opened the door. Several centimeters of water washed over her sandals and across the room. Outside the corridor was deserted, the deck rippling beneath a steady inflow of sea-smelling water from one end.

"No!" Yen waded into the corridor and struck her fist against the bulkhead. The deck began to tilt faintly, and Yen extended an arm to steady herself, then snatched it back.

A ghostly human form, the size of a child, shimmered faintly a few meters away. Yen started toward the figure, which was staring at her in surprise. "Tell me, boy," she began, but the figure vanished as a boom reverberated down the corridor.

Yen turned, and a blast of gunpowder-singed air struck her. The deck lurched underfoot. She stood with her legs spread, willing herself to hold fast. A foaming wave burst around the corridor and hissed toward her, and she turned and ran.

"Wu Mei-ling!" Philip Tanaki was waving from the common room, where a wooden stairwell spiraled up through an opening in the ceiling. She splashed her way across and started up after him, looking up into streaming sunlight. *This is not real*, she told herself. But the unpolished railing was hard to her touch, and ran a splinter into her trailing hand.

She followed Tanaki onto a pitching deck, racing clouds and hurled spray dashing at the afternoon sunlight. Her captain's blouse snapped in the wind, but Tanaki was wearing technician's overalls. "Why are you here?" she demanded.

"But I'm not. *You* are." And he touched a finger to her chest, which snapped as though with static electricity.

Yen stepped back, looking anxiously at the swirling deck. Its nearly submerged bulk was either that of the *Centaur* or of Yen's own command. Either way its chambers were filling, and the hull's imminent plunge would drag all nearby objects with it.

"If I die, it really means nothing," Yen said carefully. "This is a purely mental phenomenon."

Tanaki raised his eyebrows. "If that is so, you certainly don't have to convince me."

A burst of spray struck Yen in the face, stinging her eyes. "You know something," she said.

"I represent something *you* know."

"What?" The hull took a long roll, sluggish as it grew water-heavy. Yen started. "I'm getting out of here."

The lifeboat was banging against the stanchions that held it over the railing. Yen pulled the tarp off and began untying the ropes. Tanaki was beside her, undoing the second set. She ignored him as they lowered the boat, slid down the ropes and cast loose. Bubbles boiled alongside the hull, evidence of flooding compartments below, and they rowed quickly.

A greenish cast filled the twilight air, and Yen looked up to see Neptune emerging from behind the clouds. The huge orb seemed to watch with remote interest as the ship lifted its bow dripping from the water and slid slowly under.

The first wave hit the boat stern on, lifting the craft in a swell that Yen thought dizzily they might ride out until the second crashed over them. An oar struck her shoulder, and doubling over, Yen was thrown from the boat as it tipped.

Undertow gripped her as surely as hands, pulling her down in the wake of the plummeting ship. Blackness and pressure closed about her swiftly. *All right*, she thought. *Crush me to unconsciousness*.

Her head broke the surface, lambent with green light. Shouts, then hands lifting her under the arms. Dripping, she felt her feet dragged along a surface. The light of Neptune receded, yellowing into the disk of a doctor's lamp swiveled over her.

"Mei-ling, are you all right?"

A physician Yen remembered from her surgery was bending over her, two children and a young woman staring from behind him. Takeshita came running up, pushing her shirt into her waistband.

"Do you understand me?" The physician was speaking with exaggerated clearness. Yen felt a wave of nausea, which echoed in an aching skull. She realized with mortification that a trail of mucus was smeared across her cheek.

She wiped her face with a hand gritty from the floor, a detail too squalid for fantasy. "Happened again," she muttered. Yen raised her arms to be helped up, which the physician reluctantly took.

"Let's take her back to her room," Takeshita suggested. The two physicians supported Yen on either side, passing doorways filled with staring children.

"I warned you against that," Takeshita said when they were in Yen's room.

"Not my doing." Yen sat tiredly, wishing she had been taken up to the infirmary and lower gravity.

"Would you like an attendant? Perhaps a system to watch your vital signs, alert us and administer a sedative when you start to go."

Yen touched the bridge of her nose. "Sedation would stop this?"

"Perhaps not. I wouldn't want to try anything powerful." Takeshita had her recorder out. "You said you were listening to a poem: which?—No, don't answer; I'll query the system. Think of something else: Do you recall how much time seemed to pass?"

"Thirty minutes, perhaps. How much in real time?"

"I'll find out. Describe—no, better not. Concentrate on the here and now; did you already have those scrapes on your palms?"

Yen looked at her hands. For a second she thought she saw sand glint in the parallel abrasions, but could feel no granules under the skin. "I don't know," she said.

Takeshita stood. "I'd like to get you upstairs," she said. "We should run tests before you sleep."

The door slid open as Takeshita stepped toward it. She looked back at Yen, who rose slowly. Abruptly Yen froze, staring at Takeshita in horror.

"Is there something wrong?" Yen stood transfixed, unable to explain or resist her terror. "Mei-ling, are you all right?"

Takeshita's face began to run, melted wax dripping to disclose features contorted with intensity. "You *will* come," she said. Her hands darted forward, impossibly fast, to seize Yen's wrists in a grip of iron.

"No!" Yen was dragged through the door, into howling wind that pelted her with flying debris. "It's not true!" The wind vanished instantly, but Takeshita held her like a pincer, her face machined with resolve. People in the corridor stared and were at once transformed into gaping statues.

"They cannot help you," Takeshita said. "In real time you are strolling on your own volition, attracting no notice whatever."

Takeshita thrust her into an elevator capsule and slammed the door button. The capsule slid shut, leaving Yen abruptly alone. As it began to ascend Yen shook her head, staring about her. Do I wake or dream? she thought, pressing hands against either side of the capsule as though to force the nightmare from her.

The capsule door opened, strong hands grabbed her. Yen was pulled out through air that supported her like water. She dazedly realized that she had been conveyed from the ship's peripheries, realm of weight and hard falls, into the bodiless empyrean of the core. The surrounding dome appeared lit from all sides, abolishing shadows.

She was spun about to face a visage intent beyond emotion, a stylized mask of swirling frown lines and purposeful curves. It seemed to fill her field of vision.

"You have ventured beyond prudence," it said in a voice from a well, the lineaments of its mouth bending like strata. "From here no travelers return."

"I'm not a captain," she whispered. "I'm an engineer. My name is not Tsai Yen."

Yellow eyes narrowed, pinning her in the beam of their scrutiny. "Pretender," the creature said. Disdain rolled off it in great waves. She felt herself withering in the blast, shame filling her consciousness like some noisome gas.

Something brushed against her sides and arms, and

she looked down to see tendrils sprouting around her, vegetable tips wavering as though questing for light. The talons that grasped her had grown still, and shoots were curling over them like a jungle overwhelming a stone idol. When she managed to turn back toward the terrible visage, there was nothing before her but a tangle of stirring fronds.

She reached out, grasped a handful and pulled herself forward. The tendrils were interweaving themselves, forming a spongy lattice that yielded but would not tear. An odor, faint but ubiquitous, surrounded her as she moved through the growth, which she realized smelled unpleasantly of her own self. She cringed at this, but sought to calm herself, pressing her fist briefly over her pounding heart. "I'm not here," she reminded herself, looking nevertheless about her as though fearful of being heard.

The tangle was growing denser, and could be pushed aside only with effort. Despite the lack of gravity, she persisted in imagining the foliage beyond her reach as an overhead canopy, which now seemed to be drawing close as the surrounding space grew darker. She attempted to draw back, then jumped as thorns pricked her: the vines were hooked like brambles, impeding retreat. Turning in bewilderment, she found herself pathless in the matrix of branching filaments, as though lost in a wild wood.

Movement flickered through the interstices of vine, although they had grown too thick to stir in what air current managed to reach them. She pressed carefully forward, pushing aside a raveled mass to disclose a small clearing before her. An indistinct figure stood in the center, its back to her. A chill spilled under her breastbone as it began to turn.

"I see you there," it said clearly. She froze, certain she could not be seen across the meters of shadowed copse. The figure was facing her, but it was difficult to see. When she tried to focus on its face she had a confused impression of familiar images she could not identify, then found herself looking elsewhere.

The creature was coming forward, straight toward her. "I can see you see me. Indeed, your perceptions can be modified by feedback, to present a more pleasing aspect." The image rippled as though glimpsed through water, then contracted rapidly into the figure of a slender woman wearing a chiffon dress that would cause problems in this gravity. The apparition smiled prettily, but the image did not hold; patches began crumbling from her face like cake.

"I do not see you," she said steadily. "You are a figment, a hallucination produced by injured synapses."

The figure smiled. "Less, and more. Would even damaged circuits behave at total random?"

"Nothing you do can have any real effect." Yen said this confidently, but quavered as the woman stepped forward, her face blurring like static. She stepped back against a resilient thicket, terribly afraid.

The foliage separating them melted away, and the figure, expression gaining clarity as it approached, gazed at her without love. "Would-be hero," it said. Its face, roiling as though too charged to take stable form, was suddenly and briefly her father's. "Play at being captain. *Make believe*."

She tried to avert her gaze but could not. The figure was graven stone, robed as though to pronounce judgment. Solemnly it raised an enormous sword. As she watched in horror, the stern expression became animated, as though lit from within by malign fire. She leaped backward just as the sword slashed at her. "Why don't you *die!*"

She kicked desperately, and the blade sliced across her shoulder. Pain burst into her consciousness, blowing out all thought like a candle. She tried to run, but found herself unable to turn. Scrabbling backward on hands and legs, she watched helplessly as the swordsman approached, the blade swinging back and forth like a scythe. "You have done *nothing*," he said, his features rippling to resemble her physician's, an old teacher's, her supervisor's. "You are a *failure*."

"I'm sorry!" she screamed. Abjectly she collapsed

before him, awaiting the final blow. A shadow fell over her.

"Wu Mei-ling." The voice was different, higher. She raised her head and squinted at the face looming over her. "Are you all right? I have to talk to you."

The man squatted before her, reaching to grasp her shoulders as she sat up. He was a young Asian of middle height, callow and intent. His skin was blemished, and his breath smelled of a recent meal.

"You know the secret," he said, excitement in his voice. "Only a scant few have penetrated the veil."

She drew back slightly, raising an aching arm to brush his aside. "Please leave me alone," she muttered.

The man persisted. "It's important that you understand."

She attempted to push herself away, then looked into his face for the first time. In its fatuous depths every failure, every presumption and disappointment of her life shone forth in mute appeal, a mirror of her soul in sallow flesh.

"Get away!" she cried, striking out in panic. Somehow he was holding her wrists, calling faint entreaties as she struggled to get free. His expression, hair falling before wild eyes, held a vacancy that seemed to pull at her, a swirling void that sang *Here you truly belong.*

"No!"

Blindly she struck out, smashing hard into his nose with the heel of her hand. She felt cartilage give but could not halt the swing of her other hand, nor prevent the first from striking again as she fell upon him, screaming and pummeling.

Forces were swirling around her like air fronts, pulling at her arms. She fought frantically, slamming his head against the ground before being dragged away by forms that glimmered like mist. Shocked voices reached her as she sank to her knees, and she turned from a welling nausea to see her tormentor, his face a red ruin, disappear behind crowding backs.

Hands grasped her as she slumped forward, cheek coming to rest against the oil-smelling deck: reality's grainy substrate, the bottom of the monstrous world.

Takeshita turned her display screen round and adjusted its angle, smiling hopefully as its beam fell upon Wu. "You can see it here," she said. Sitting across the desk with her hands inert in her lap, Wu looked up without interest.

"Electric potential, nothing more. The healing process affects the conductivity of thin fronts of tissue, too slightly to interfere with cognition." The disposition of colors across a screen's glowing model of the brain shifted slightly. "Here is the normal configuration." Takeshita shifted the picture back and forth between the two images, as though to impress on Wu the reality of her recent disorder.

"Residual charges build up in the cytoskeleton of neurons adjoining these areas. Eventually they seek discharge, escaping along pathways of least resistance like spilling water." Takeshita was looking at her concernedly, and after a moment she swung the display down into her desk. "There is no question of the hallucinogenic effects this would produce. We will explain this at the hearing, and that will be that."

Wu attempted to raise her hands in acquiescence, a sardonic gesture common among young people, but she brought it off clumsily and let them drop again. Her hands, encircled above the wrists by thin golden hoops, moved as though through heavy liquid. The cuffing had been done by judicial order, for her case was still pending.

"Mei-ling, please look at me."

Reluctantly Wu raised her eyes to his steady gaze. "Mei-ling, those episodes are over. Your medication will prevent these electrochemical corrections from happening while you are awake, and they will soon take their proper place among the mental housecleaning of sleep. Nor will these fugitive impulses continue to activate long-dormant memories. Do you still remember those swatches of schoolbook poetry?"

Wu shook her head.

"I am sorry about Philip Tanaki. The man was a nuisance, a malcontent nurturing paranoid theories with which he bothered others. It was simply bad fortune that he encountered you in the passage well and persisted after you. Even in your delirium you must have realized the threat his attentions posed."

"I understand."

"You will feel better with time, believe me. I do not want to prescribe antidepressants; it is normal for you to be unhappy with those neurosuppressors round your hands. We will take care of them. In the meantime you shall heal, although slowly. But it will come."

In the observation deck Wu looked out upon the forward stars, sharper than they ever shone through the clouded lens of atmosphere. The desk spun slowly to counter the ship's rotation, so the convex wall of stars appeared as it might from a true spaceship's bridge. She swayed slightly in the zero gravity, her soles clinging to the textured floor.

No voyages sang in her skull, and Wu gazed placidly upon the immensity before her, as though awed by its expanse of emptiness and disorder. The appearance of stillness was illusion. Something inside her was counting, and with every iteration a minute cellule appeared, each one taking its place in complex and perfect order like the poised atoms in a crystal. Wu regarded them mount precisely about her, like a prisoner watching herself being bricked into a wall.

Slowly she disappeared, yet remained in a fashion: the outline of a cave painting preserved in the flux of a greater, more intricate dance.

The flux was potential, its pattern a germ. The *Centaur*'s prow cut through waves of aether like the hardened husk of a seed, borne surely by tides toward the soils of a stranger shore.

Ah! Bright Wings

Howard V. Hendrix

SITTING AMID ALL HIS ELECTRONIC MEDIA PARAPHER-nalia, Manny Shaw seemed every inch the unhealthy overage technoweenie. On first meeting him, one might almost imagine that a time-lapsed video of his life would look something like this: Pre-teen Manny, ruddy-cheeked and crew-cut and 20/20-visioned, sits down at his first computer; the years swiftly pass and the screens about him multiply as he clacks endlessly away at a keyboard, until finally even the keyboard has transmogrified beyond recognition and Manny has grown pale and paunchy and thickly bespectacled, his long hair streaked with early-middle-age gray in the unremitting light of the screens.

Manny, however, did not see himself or his life that way. When he sat down at his workstation in his small cabin in the San Bernardino Mountains each day, he was back in the hypersaddle again, riding the range on the final frontier. He was an artist of light and logic, a vir-tual shaman hunting and gathering in the forests of the byte—and he had designed his virtuality to reflect just that.

No cold Neon New Jerusalems or cybernetic Cities of God for him, thank you. His virtual integrated reality was an unspoiled Late Pleistocene wonderland inhabited by mammoths and bison and reindeer and horses and aurochs and God only knew what all else. Manny had downloaded the original VIR program from a netfriend who happened to be an anthropologist—then modified the Upper Paleolithic Man template-scenario for sight, sound, tactiles, and force feedback to suit his own needs. His handle in the net was "Electric Shaman," and—though he knew little enough about historic and prehistoric shamanism—it was what he had become.

His system up and running, Immanuel Shaw, Great White-Noise Hunter, surveyed each day the Mandelbrot mountains and fractal forests of his heuristic happy hunting grounds and was content. From video and virtual games he had learned long ago that the great value of simulations lay in their being faster, cheaper, and more forgiving of error than the realities they represented. He'd come to see not only virtual games but also cartoons, stories, plays—maybe even religious rituals—as simulations in some deep sense. He'd put his theoretical "slant" to good use and had, over time, gained some reputation as a free-lance imagineer of virtual games and expert training programs.

The Game Preserve: that was his own private, punning name for this virtuality where he did his designing and occasional hacking. Here, programming problems and infosphere opportunities manifested themselves as constellations in the skies of data by night, plants and animals by day, for his computers had ticked a virtual heaven round the stars, one synched to the time cycles of that other, slower, more expensive, more fatefully consequential reality. It was that reality which Manny had been less and less aware of lately, particularly since Diamond Thunderbolt Interactive had become his major client and begun to demonstrate an insatiable desire for revision in so much of the code he was sending them.

DTI was a new and fairly small virtuals company. Manny had yet to see any of their products, but they paid very well and he was fairly sure they had no military or security tie-ins—avoiding such employment being Manny's one great ethical scruple. He'd been working long and hard on code rewrites one day when he decided to take a break from it all and putz around a bit in the data world the Game Preserve was capable of representing. Beside a lake of light reflecting its surroundings with digital precision, he came upon a bird of transcendent beauty—an ibis or crane or swan of some sort, white, with a crown of gold feathers radiating from its head. Viewing it from a distance, he only gradually realized that the bird was in distress. Zooming closer, he saw that it had been struck by something his VIR program was representing as an arrow, and that the bird was bleeding.

The white bird—actually the data construct of some obscure foundation for the arts—was no real concern of his, but he was so impressed by the beauty of the thing and the pathos of its situation that he gently took hold of it and set about removing the arrow, which turned out to be a wedge of code intended to kill the construct. Removing the arrow took time, but as he worked to untangle bird from arrowhead he thought the code seemed familiar— like something adapted from one of those "bookworms" or "tapeworms" the book-banners were so fond of using to destroy library text files.

By the time he'd removed the arrow and gotten the bird patched up enough that it could fly again, it was twilight in both virtuality and reality. As night fell he released it, watching it rise up and up on its wings until it disappeared among the early stars, perhaps becoming a cross-shaped constellation, though he could not be sure.

Realizing the lateness of the hour, he clocked out of his system with a sigh. Perhaps he had wasted this day to no purpose, but the fact that he had found and addressed someone else's difficulty—not for any benefit it might bring him, but merely for the pure challenge of

it—was something that made him feel his effort was not
in vain but very, very worthwhile. He planned to search
for the bird again the next day—after his DTI work was
completed, of course.

Thonk thonk thonk thonk!

Manny's eyes shot open. The bright-eyed skeleton
on one of his ancient (but mint condition) Grateful Dead
posters stared blissfully back at him from the far wall of
his bedroom. Disoriented, it took him a moment before he
realized that the ungodly banging that had wakened him
was the sound of someone knocking at the front door of
his cabin. Flopping over onto his side, he stared through
one bloodshot eye at the readout on his digital alarm clock.
8:03 A.M.

"Coming!" he shouted hoarsely as he rolled out of bed
and into some clothes, wondering as he made his way to the
door who could possibly have come all the way out here
to annoy him. Usually only door-to-door religious fanatics
had dared brave the tortuous dirt road up from the main
highway—and ever since he'd hung that big pentacle in his
front picture window the religioids had left him alone.

Fools, he thought as he approached the door. They
didn't even know their own religious traditions. It was only
when the pentacle was hung upside down that it was a
satanic symbol; hung right side up it was a Judeo-Christian
emblem called Solomon's knot. Manny considered himself
a Druid (certainly not some simple-minded Satanist) and
his big five-pointed star was quite consciously hung right
side up. Even in that position, however, the pentacle was
enough to scare off the holy dolts—especially when, with
a flick of a switch, he could light it up with dozens of tiny
Italian twinkle-lights.

"Mister Shaw?" said the young woman at the door as
he opened it. Her wildly spiked blonde hair didn't much
fit the profile of a god-marketer, Manny thought. But what
about those white coveralls and sensible sneakers she was
wearing—some sort of new cult uniform, maybe?

"Yes?" Manny said cautiously.

"Hi." She extended her hand for him to shake. "I'm Cyndi Easter, the housekeeper from the agency."

"Housekeeper? Agency? I didn't—"

Stepping inside, she quickly handed him her work papers. He read them over. Letter of introduction, resumé, references, work assignment. According to the paperwork, Manny had been granted the services of a live-in housekeeper for a period of one year—at absolutely no cost to himself. Aside from the fact that it was utterly absurd, everything seemed to be in order.

"This isn't some kind of 'trial offer' scam, is it?" Manny asked.

"No, Mister Shaw," Ms. Easter said with a wan smile. "My services are completely prepaid for one year."

"But by whom?" Manny asked, suspicious. "Is this one of my mother's schemes?"

"I can't really say," Ms. Easter said thoughtfully. "You've been given a grant of some sort, but I'm afraid the grantor has requested anonymity."

Manny shook his head and sighed. He could make no sense of it. In the silence that opened up between them, he realized he was completely stymied.

"May I make a suggestion?" Ms. Easter asked, glancing about at Manny's living room, which suddenly began to look embarrassingly cluttered. "Why don't you go ahead and call the agency about me? In the meantime, I'll assume I'm going to be working for you, so I'll start tidying things up a bit here—fair enough?"

"I suppose," Manny said with a shrug as he picked up the phone and began punching away at the house-cleaning agency's phone numbers.

As Ms. Easter dusted and swept, Manny spoke on the phone to any number of agency flacks, but the story was always the same: Yes, the housekeeper's services really are being provided to you at no expense for one year; no, I'm afraid we cannot tell you who has paid for these services. Manny went round and round with them but they proved the most impervious and inscrutable bunch of bureaucratic sycophants he had dealt with since the last time he'd complained about an error in his credit report. Finally he hung up in disgust, pondering.

A live-in housekeeper. How had the amorphous They known that he had room for a live-in? How could They possibly have known that he had a guest room—and that, with the exception of his mother's rare visits, he almost never had overnight guests?

His mother . . . well, certainly their parting hadn't been particularly amicable the last time she'd visited, what with her madly screaming "How dare you tell your own mother we don't get along!" and him shouting back "See?! I rest my case!" The tension between his intrusive old Mum and her thirty-five-year-old bachelor boy was undeniable—but was that enough for her to set up something like this?

The more he thought on it, the more he convinced himself that this had to be an inside job. Furiously he rang up his mother, and furiously he demanded that she stop interfering in his life.

Despite his prolonged badgering, however, it gradually became clear that his mother really had no idea what he was talking about—either that, or she was a far better actress than he ever would have believed. By the time he got off the phone, he was more confused than ever, his last best lead having turned into a dead end. He thought of other, less likely possibilities—a hidden perk from DTI, perhaps? Not very likely. Ms. Easter said he'd been given a grant, but from someone who'd requested anonymity, another dead end. . . .

"I thought I might fix us some lunch," Ms. Easter said, peeking in on him, broom in hand. "Interested?"

"Sure," he said glumly. "Whatever you're having."

Waiting for lunch to be served, he thought of all the ways this housekeeper would prove an intrusion, or at the very least a distraction. No denying it, she *was* distracting—very pretty, even beautiful, in a waifish sort of way. But what had he to do with all that? She probably didn't have a brain in her head, and he had always been backward around women anyway. This would just be another case of the unending mismatch between him and the opposite sex.

Couldn't he still just turn down the offer of her services and send her back to the agency? Why not? Might it not be best to simply tell her "No"—as soon as possible?

Somehow, though, over the soup and salad Cyndi Easter made for lunch, Manny couldn't find it in him to tell her that she would have to go. Instead, he struck upon the plan of getting in contact with one of his bulletin-board acquaintances, who went by the *nom de machine* of "Dash Chandler" and fancied himself a sort of high-tech detective. Though he'd never met Dash in person, Manny had communicated with him over the net on several occasions—it was Dash who'd first informed him of the work available with DTI, as a matter of fact. Putting that same DTI work on hold again, Manny spent the afternoon over modem, piquing Dash's curiosity about his mysterious situation, then set the dubious investigator to the task of ferreting out all the information he could get on Ms. Easter, the agency she worked for, and most of all the identity of the anonymous grantor.

Yet for all his covert plans, Manny still could not tell the woman to leave over dinner, either. He felt a twinge when she brought in two suitcases from her battered car and took them into the guest room upstairs. In the flurry of the day's events he had quite forgotten the wounded bird of the day before. Once he finally managed to get back to the rewrites for DTI, he found himself trying to remember what he had forgotten, a disgruntled and grumbling lone hunter in his Pleistocene Eden—convinced his temporary memory loss was already ample proof that Cyndi Easter was distracting him.

As it turned out, Cyndi did have a brain in her head— was in fact quite intelligent, especially when it came to electronic media. When Manny expressed his surprise at her knowledge about such things, all Cyndi would say was that she had had some experience with electronic media during her student days.

Despite her occasional reticence and his initial dislike of having the private space of his home invaded this way, Manny found himself less and less disturbed by her presence in his house. Though he would not have liked to admit it, he actually began to enjoy having her around— and he had cause to hope the feeling might be mutual.

A sure sign of the change in their relationship was that one day over breakfast, when Cyndi had begun to razz him good-naturedly about how much time he spent in virtuality, Manny, instead of taking offense, invited her upstairs to his Game Preserve. After sitting her down and helping her into an old set of sensorium headgear and a connection suit he'd long since outgrown, he gave her a guided tour through the Pleistocene world where he worked.

As they moved through his VIR he spoke with excitement and pride about how lifelike his artificial environment was. Did she see the glittering of the birch leaves as the wind moved them against the sun? Did she smell the pine forests—and other scents not so pleasant? Did she hear the deer in the brush? The bleating of the wild sheep and goats? The lowing of the aurochs? The thunder of the wild horse herds? Even the call of the occasional woolly mammoth or shaggy rhinoceros as it moved through the dwarf birch and willow tundra, nearer the edge of the northern ice? Did she see how it was a mindscape, a universe of valuable information for the person who could interpret it—the ice signifying more than just ice, the aurochs more than just aurochs, every cloud and plant and bird and beast pregnant with meaning?

Yes, yes, she assured him, she saw it all.

"Electronic Eden," Manny said proudly as he switched off the system at last. "Sight, sound, tactiles, scent atomizers, force feedback, the works. Well? What do you think?"

"Interesting," Cyndi replied, smiling her Gioconda smile as she removed the sensorium headgear and zipped herself out of the connection suit. "But I know what really happened in Eden. Your 'virtual integrated reality,' impressive as it is, is only a pale shadow of that."

"Oh really?" Manny said, staring at her crookedly. She knew "what really happened in Eden"—*that* sounded ominously like the prelude to a chapter-and-verse Bible-thumping. He had wanted to impress her, and it unsettled him a bit that she took it all so easily in stride—almost as if she were long familiar with such technological wonders as those he'd just shown her. "You were there, I suppose?"

"If you've been there, you can get there," she said with a shrug, "but you can get there only if you've been there."

She had to turn and hurry about the housework then, but during those idle moments when he rested from his work the riddle she had left him kept him intrigued (in a tangential sort of way) all day long. They discussed it again that night at dinner, over the Chardonnay she had purchased when she'd gone shopping two days before.

"You're not going to like what I'll have to say," Cyndi said when he asked her what she had meant. "You'll think I've got strange ideas."

"Try me," Manny replied, sipping at his wine.

"Okay then. VIR is dopertronics, like all that tech. Sensorium expansion via electronics rather than hallucinogenics. When R. Gordon Wasson back in the summer of 1955 became one of the first modern white men to experiment with the *Psilocybe* mushroom, he said that in his initial visions 'the landscapes responded to the command of the beholder: when a detail interested him, the landscape approached with the speed of light and the detail was made manifest.' Responsive landscapes, Manny. Sound familiar?"

"Virtual reality," Manny said quietly.

"Bingo. Virtuality's another plug-in drug, like TV. Another attempt to remove the boundaries between things conceived in the mind and things perceived by the senses, kind of like what happens in hallucinations. A very useful technique, in its own way. But all its depth is on the surface."

"And it was deeper in Eden?" Manny said, slowly swirling the wine in his glass, wondering why his maid should be familiar with the distinction between mind creations and sense perceptions, between concepts and percepts. . . .

"Certainly. Deep in. Right inside the brain." Cyndi took another sip of her wine. "Did you ever think about what the 'fruit of the tree of the knowledge of good and evil' might really be?"

He shrugged.

"I'm not particularly religious—at least not in that direction."

"Neither am I," said Cyndi, finishing her wine. "But I suspect it was a hallucinogen—or, more properly, an entheogen."

"*What?*" Manny shook his head. The more wine they drank the more their conversation seemed to proceed by non sequiturs. "I don't follow you. What's an entheogen?"

"Something that allows God to be generated within. But since context is everything with mind-altering substances, you get out of them what you want out of them, what you want out of yourself. When the mindset of the person ingesting the substance is directed toward communion with the divine, when the setting in which the substance is ingested is relaxed and calm, odds are good that the experience will be positive and revelatory. When the mindset is escapist, the setting paranoid and self-destructive—as it to some degree always is when you're inside a culture caught up in a drug persecution hysteria—then the entheogen is reduced to a hallucinogen, to a drug that destroys rather than enlightens. The story of Eden was about that too. Have you ever heard the phrase 'ontogeny recapitulates phylogeny'?"

"Of course," Manny said, surprised again to hear such a phrase coming from his housekeeper. "It's from embryology."

"Right," Cyndi said slowly, choosing her words carefully. "But I think it applies to myths and primordial stories too. Mythology recapitulates prehistory. Maybe not completely, and maybe not completely accurately, but the old stories retell, in capsule form, the prehistory of the human species. The story of Adam and Eve is a story of consciousness—'knowledge of good and evil'—flashing on as a result of eating or ingesting something. Before they took and ate, before ignition of cognition, Adam and Eve and all our ancient ancestors would have known only the ignorant bliss of bees or pocket calculators. But after they took and ate, they took and ate again and the consciousness process became self-sustaining. The happy homeostasis of the biological brain gave way to the innovative chaos of the developing mind, and they were gone from Eden for good."

Manny's head began to spin—not just from the wine, either. What was someone obviously educated—someone who could correctly toss off a word like "homeostasis"— doing, working as his housekeeper? Before he could formulate this question, though, Cyndi was speaking again.

"Think about it," she said, leaning forward. "I've seen your virtual Pleistocene upstairs and the old Grateful Dead memorabilia all around here—so you must have at least an inkling of what I'm talking about. The distribution of psychoactive compounds in plants is so widespread, so ubiquitous, that it's highly unlikely that any animal, in the wild, will fail to encounter such a compound."

Manny nodded. Images of poppy capsules, coca leaves, hemp buds, cacti, little brown or big red mushrooms, morning-glory seeds, jimson weeds, nutmegs, Polynesian kawa, East Indian betel, ergot-infected grasses—inside his wine-lubed mind they all drifted up brief and glittering as evanescent bubbles.

"Since the women's work of foraging provided seventy percent of the food base for early humans," Cyndi continued, "women would have likely encountered such substances before men did—*Eve eats the apple first.* As you know, much of the prehistory of humanity took place during the Pleistocene ice ages, so the climate over most of the inhabitable Northern Hemisphere was subarctic: fir and birch forests, like in your virtual. The mycorrhizal associate of the birch tree—the 'world tree' for many northern peoples even today—is a particular mushroom, *Amanita muscaria*, which, depending on the strain, looks like a golden or a red *apple* before its cap fully opens.

"That particular mushroom was a favorite of sibyls and shamans. In the alchemy of myth, the hallucinogenic mushroom growing at the base of the world tree became the fruit of the tree of knowledge; the fibers of the mushroom's hyphae, its mycelia, became the snake wrapped round the tree; Woman gathering the mushroom became Temptress; Man accepting the fruits of her labor became Poor Mind-Expanded Schmuck who can't go home to ignorance again. Presto! Tens of thousands of years of prehistoric shamanic practice, mythically transformed into a warning about how the desire to 'be like God' brought sin and death into the world."

Manny stared at her, dumbfounded.

"But what were the shamans and sibyls after in the first place?" was all he could think to say.

Cyndi sat thoughtfully for a minute, staring at her empty wine glass, then seemed to remember something.

"*Chaos*," she said suddenly, impatiently augmenting her words with emphatic gestures. "Look. In the brain the release of neurochemicals controls the 'gain,' the ability of neuron systems to amplify signals both in terms of the number of neurons involved and number of action potentials involved. Gain is 'set' by the brain and depends upon how interested an animal is in receiving particular sensory input. When gain is set high enough, a small stimulus can excite large numbers of neurons into simultaneous activity—prime chaotic situation. Chaotic systems are self-organizing and self-regulating—a great way to generate new ideas. But it's even more than that. Contact with psychoactive substances initiated the chaotic neural behavior that gave rise to the self-aware thinking process itself. The goal was hallucination, but the result is civilization."

Cyndi stopped short, as if she'd said too much already. She corked the wine bottle firmly, but the pouring out of her words couldn't be explained or excused by the wine alone. She stood up abruptly and began clearing away the dinner dishes, but it was already too late. Manny's maid had just told him that civilization was a shared hallucination, and he found her more distracting than ever. He wanted to know more about her—much more. But the next instant he recalled her reticence about her electronic media experience, and then he did not feel comfortable with the idea of asking her directly about her past. No, not comfortable at all.

How to learn more about her then? He had once heard or read somewhere that "truth in circuit lies"—that the indirect route was, at times, the best path to take. Hoping that Cyndi Easter's truth might reside in the circuits of some computer somewhere, he prodded his bulletin-board acquaintance to get moving on his investigation.

Dash Chandler's information on Cyndi Easter, once Manny downloaded it, was both more and less surprising than he'd expected. Dash had been unable to dig up any dirt on the housekeeping agency and still had nothing on the source of the anonymous grant, but he had discovered that, during the most recent lightning war, when the Federal Emergency Management Authority had invoked its little-known martial law powers for dealing with "civil unrest," Ms. Cyndi Easter had been one of the hundreds of thousands of political dissidents who had been arrested and sentenced by secret trial to internment in old military bases turned detainment camps.

Eventually, when the war was over, she'd been released in one of the General Amnesties, but in her chosen field she had been blacklisted and had to begin all over again. That was the confusing part: In her former life Cyndi had been a filmmaker by trade, and apparently had been arrested for making an unreleased video documentary called *The Five-Million-Day War*. Manny assumed it was a work that the authorities considered politically subversive, yet in the scant unclassified references to it that Chandler had been able to dig up the video was constantly condemned in terms of its "immorality" and "effect on young people." The murkiness of the situation was only worsened by the censorship of the documents Dash had been able to obtain— censorship apparently aimed at protecting a shadowy something called Project Medusa Blue, which was in turn part of a still more shadowy entity called the Tetragrammaton Program.

Reading over the downloaded material, Manny had the uncomfortable feeling that something extremely dangerous lurked in those shadows. In his Pleistocene virtuality, every time he tried searching out information regarding Tetragrammaton or Medusa Blue he quickly ran into the great glacial ice sheets of heavily protected power-elite data. There was no way through that.

Later the same day, he got a most uncharacteristic message from Dash: "Search into Easter redflagged me in lots of security banks. Countermeasure probes sparking up everywhere. Getting hot. Fly low and under radar, buddy! If things get too hot, I may need to crash at your place for a while. Can do?" Manny felt torn. He had not communicated with Dash that often, but something didn't sound quite right about the message—its tone, its phrasing, something. At the same time, he felt more than a little responsible for the situation Dash found himself in. Finally, with some hesitation, Manny sent his address and a message back to Dash that if things got tricky, then yes, Dash could drop in on them. In his heart, though, Manny hoped such courtesy would not become necessary—unexpected house guests always complicated matters, as he knew all too well already.

But he could worry about all that later. Right now there was a larger question: Who was Cyndi that a probe into her identity should still arouse such attention? As much as Manny disliked the idea, he would have to go directly to his source.

"Cyndi," he said as they rinsed the dinner dishes one Wednesday evening. "Tell me about *The Five-Million-Day War*."

For the first time since she'd moved in, Cyndi looked startled and taken aback, and Manny felt obscurely embarrassed.

"You ran a search on me. You could have told me, you know," she said, an edge of anger and violation in her voice. She stood hunched over the sink, water dripping slowly from her wet hands until, recovering her composure, she sighed deeply. "Then again, I could have been more forthcoming about my past, too. So now you know. I'm a 'political.' You'll be wanting to terminate my employment, I suppose?"

"On the contrary," he said, shaking his head, "I'd be tempted to give you a raise—if I were paying you to begin with. I'm on your side. I thought you knew that."

"How am I *supposed* to know that?"

"I showed you my VIR program."

"So?"

"You didn't really see everything, then. Come upstairs, and look again."

They made their way up the staircase, Cyndi following somewhat reluctantly. In moments they were geared up and in the system once more.

"I didn't choose the Ice Ages for my virtuality just to fulfill some electronic back-to-nature fantasy," Manny said over his throat mike. "But this virtual does catch the sense of an open frontier—and what threatens that openness. Which is exactly what I wanted."

Swift as thought they surged over the terrain, forests and meadows blurring into tundra. At last they arrived at the walls of the great ice sheets, kilometers high, wreathed in mists and snowstorms. Manny zoomed in on and freeze-framed one of the snowflakes. Before their eyes the deeper geometry of the snowflake revealed itself: cold crystalline planes of code, complex cryptographic protection.

"Every snowflake that falls in here is a Solomon's knot, a pentacle with a pentagon around its heart," Manny explained. "Each one represents the five-way interlock of government, military, media, weapons corporations and intelligentsia think tanks—all freezing off access to another piece of data, another piece of the truth. I've seen how much snow is falling, Cyndi. I know how fast the ice sheets are advancing all over the infosphere. I've known it for years, but I've always kept moving round the margins to avoid getting caught. For you to end up in a FEMA concentration camp, something about your documentary must have hit the Abominable Snowmonster head on. I can understand all that. What I can't understand is what people were up to back when the government was gutting the Bill of Rights. Everybody must have been asleep, or looking the other way."

Out of the corner of his eye, Manny saw something like the flicker of a white wing, but when he looked again he saw only Cyndi's face, digitized and projected into the Pleistocene beside his own.

"Actually," Cyndi said quietly, over the throat mike dangling from her own sensorium headset, "everybody was busy fighting the same drug war that's been going on for at least ten thousand years. For my documentary I did a hell of a lot of book research into the history of mind-altering substances throughout the world, and everywhere the same process of suppression has come into play. Five million days is just a number. Whether the goal of the process is to control informational substances or information itself, it's all a part of the same long suppression. The war to confine the opened mind has been going on for a long, long time."

As the wind and snow began driving down at them, they pulled out of virtuality. Once they had returned to the hallucination called reality, they left Manny's work area and walked—quietly, thoughtfully—to the bottom of the stairs. They decided to just keep going, walking together out of the house, beneath the darkening sky as the first stars began to appear.

"How much do you know?" Cyndi asked at last, over the sound of their feet crunching on gravel.

Manny told her what he knew, and what he wanted to know. About Project Medusa Blue. About Tetragrammaton. Cyndi laughed hollowly.

"Tetragrammaton is a four-letter word for God. YHWH, JHVH. Yahweh. Jehovah. Maybe it was some program director's idea of a joke. But what Tetragrammaton really is is a program for the development of a mind/machine linkage, in order to make possible the creation of an information density singularity."

"A what?"

Cyndi laughed quietly again, less hollowly, less cynically.

"A mathematical model for opening a gateway into the fabric of spacetime," she said mechanically, as if quoting from long familiarity words that would never be her own. "The model would be indistinguishable from an actual gateway—the virtual and the real would coincide. If someone ever pulls it off it could mean much-faster-than-light travel to any point in the spacetime continuum—"

"But what's that got to do with Project Medusa Blue?" Manny asked. Around him the breezes were cool this evening, scented with pine after the heat of the day. The stars above him were brighter and clearer every minute. "And what does either of them have to do with you?"

"Medusa Blue is phase one of Tetragrammaton. To reach the critical levels of information density needed to generate a singularity, you have to use computers and AIs, but the right kind of chaos is the key for the gateway to infinity and we can't design chaotic acausality into machine systems. An acausal machine is a contradiction in terms. The human element has to enter the equation because that kind of chaos is the primary way the brain differs from artificial intelligences. If the singularity is to form and the gateway into infinity is to open, the machines need chaos. Consciousness, visions, dreams. Hence the quest for direct mind/machine linkage, an interfaceless interface."

"And Medusa Blue was part of that?" Manny prodded.

"Medusa Blue was a psi-power enhancement project aimed at computer-aided apotheosis—"

"Say what?"

Cyndi smiled in the darkness.

"Taking the consciousness, the soul, the god within, out of the body and putting it into the machine."

Manny shivered, then wondered if it was only the breath of the night wind that was causing him to do so.

"Sounds like psychic vampirism," he said. "Like soul-catching."

Cyndi looked at him, surprised.

"That's a very good way of putting it. Of course the scientists working on the project wouldn't speak of it that way—that would sound far too metaphysical for government work. In the documents of Project Medusa Blue an out-of-body experience is called an 'emergent delirium' and the Sight is a 'cognitive preperception,' but they're still aware that such arcane experiences are their best hope for putting a soul in the machine."

She stared vaguely away through space and night for some time before she spoke again. Night birds called in the woods as the two of them padded softly along, the gravel of the roadbed having degenerated to graded hardpan.

"They must have been good at screening out their feelings with words and categories," she said at last, wondering. "How else could they have had no qualms of conscience when they began secretly administering experimental entheogens to women in their first trimester of pregnancy—in the hopes that their babies might develop 'unusual talents'?"

They stopped and stood, then sat on a fallen log beside the road. The pellucid skies above, the dark woods and road around them, the strangeness of the conversation—it began to work on Manny's thoughts.

"Is all this true?" he asked hesitantly. "Sitting here in the dark listening to you, I'm beginning to wonder whether we'll be momentarily kidnapped by space aliens or arrested by federal agents dressed in dark suits and wearing sunglasses at night. If this is all real, how do you know so much about it?"

She looked at him squarely, unflinchingly.

"I wouldn't believe it myself," she said, "if it weren't for the fact that what I am and what my mother became are both products of Project Medusa Blue."

The words poured out of her then, mostly coming too fast for him to remember in any fashion more exact than phrases colored with great and varying emotions. Bitterness that the same government that blindly prohibited its citizens and soldiers from knowingly experimenting with drugs had itself experimented on its soldiers and citizens without their knowledge or consent, covertly administering to them LSD, BZ, dozens of others, including (in Cyndi's mother's case) KL 235, ketamine lysergate—"gate," in the argot of the experimenters.

"In the name of some scientific approximation to truth and national security," Cyndi said, the flow of her words slowing slightly, distilling for a moment into a pool of bright sharp bitterness, "the covert operators had payrolled my mother's ob-gyn to pump women with a supposedly 'uterotonic' biochemical extracted from an obscure South American fungus, *Cordyceps jacinti*. They turned my mother into a gatehead and long-period schizophrenic—and for what? All the children of Medusa Blue turned out to be only latent talents at best, and their families and their own upbringings were crippled and distorted almost beyond recognition. Just like mine."

The fast flood of words began again. Manny gathered that, by the time the history of Medusa Blue began to leak out, Cyndi was seventeen and had watched her beautiful mother drift in and out of madness for years. She had vowed to learn everything she could about what had been done to her mother and others, and to expose the whole dark business to the world. Seven years later the outcome of that vow had been the independent production of *The Five-Million-Day War*, an exposé of the hypocrisy of power which told her mother's story within the larger historical context of what Cyndi called the Long Suppression, the war to confine the opened mind.

But her work had never been released; it had been pulled from distribution, "market censored" before it could even be shown, and Cyndi herself taken off to internment. It was the final anguish, the final hypocrisy, the final painful irony. The government that had seen to it that an illegal informational substance would be administered to Cyndi's mother and to her daughter in the womb now had also seen to it that Cyndi's attempt to tell about the results of that experiment, her attempt to convey her information on the story of suppression, would itself be suppressed—and all in the name of protecting the young, the children.

By the time she had finished telling of it, Cyndi was crying tears of bitterness, tears of anguish, tears of frustration and despair. Manny found himself cradling her head against his shoulder and crying with her, for her— and for himself and the whole world of suffering that human beings had made for each other. Around them the night wind grew cold at last, coaxing them out of their commiseration, up and onto the road again, arms about each other's waists and leaning against each other, dabbing at their eyes and their noses and clearing their throats all the way back to the cabin, where they could not untangle themselves to go to their separate beds in separate rooms but fell in each other's arms into one bed to make love with all the awkwardness of tenderness and all the power of vulnerability.

They did not speak of falling in love—almost as if calling it by name might frighten it away. Instead they talked about neurotransmitters and chocolates, phenylethylamine and theobromine, scientific words to conjure the impossible into the merely improbable. Love ain't nuthin' but PEA misspelled, they joked—but the joke had its own sweet, dark, enigmatic bite.

Manny began to spend more time out of virtuality. First it was just conversations with Cyndi, then it was long walks together with her in the mountains, sometimes collecting mushrooms. He lost weight, grew less pale and paunchy, and his health improved overall. His bank account alternately suffered and benefited: his freelance infogathering was his bread and butter, so less time working meant less cash flow, but since he was less virtually obsessed he wasn't spending as much on the newest programs and hardware either. One day out of curiosity he checked to see if Dash was still manning his modem line, and was obscurely relieved to find that the line was being manned and the person on the other end was very curious about what Manny'd been up to. Manny only stayed on line long enough to send hello and exchange some pleasantries, for he had other things to do.

A new equilibrium, a steadier state, seemed to be developing in his life. He found he even had the temerity to come down from the mountains and brave Los Angeles's swarming hordes for a chance to take Cyndi to the Grateful Dead retrospective at the L.A. County Museum of Art. The exhibit soft-pedaled the role of hallucinogens in Dead art and in the Dead's early popularity generally, but the program was authentic enough to serve as a focal point for a gathering of the countercultural tribes. Cyndi loved it all—the vendors, the impromptu percussionists drumming and rhythm driving endlessly around the La Brea Tar Pits, the barterers, the hawkers, the endless paraphernalia.

She even went so far as to shed her usual neo-nihilist white plumage to purchase and put on a tie-dyed skirt and blouse of many colors which, on her, seemed more abstract than tie-dyed, a quasi-chaotic piece of wearable art that looked—all at the same time—like an Impressionist rendering of a vivid floral print, a crystalline Cubist shattered rainbow, and an organicist assemblage to which every bird of every paradise had contributed its most brilliant feathers.

Manny, so used to seeing her clothed in white, found the new ensemble remarkable—but all the more remarkable for Cyndi's being dressed in it.

Away from the human warmth and bright colors of that gathering, however, the glaciers crept on, the snow-fields grew, the ice sheets advanced. Manny began to find more and more of what looked like his DTI gaming code in the military simulations he managed to come across. He started to wonder whether Diamond Thunderbolt Interactive might not be a front company for another DTI—something like Defense Technologies International, maybe? And did they only share acronyms, or other information as well? His delaying on DTI work became more obstinate. When Diamond Thunderbolt informed him that the company was "no longer interested" in his work, he'd almost half expected it.

Without his major client, Manny found it more and more difficult to earn a living hunting and gathering information in his virtual Pleistocene. He began to wonder if DTI had managed to blackball him when other potential employers began requiring that he come down and take a piss test in person at some corporate headquarters in Orange County. He was clean enough, or could test clean in minutes (there were products on the underground market for that), but the principle of the thing bothered him. It was all too clear a proof that the ice was moving faster, further and further down from both poles.

In the Game Preserve snow seemed to be falling everywhere. The landscape was becoming less and less responsive to his needs as a hacker hunter-gatherer—making it increasingly difficult for him to pay his bills, to even keep food on the table. If he only had this image analyzer, or that cryptographic lock breaker, Manny lamented to Cyndi, he could drive the ice back a bit, bring on an interstadial spring. But such specialized equipment and underground programs all cost money—which he did not have. Months passed. Head in his hands, Manny began to despair.

"Maybe I can help," Cyndi said one day, determination in her voice. Perhaps she had seen too much of how the money worries were tearing at him, at them, and the pain of it had forced her to a difficult decision. "Let me have some time alone in your workspace. I'll need absolute concentration, so *do not* interrupt me. Just leave the door shut and don't open it. I'll come out when I'm ready."

"What are you planning to do?" Manny asked, raising his head from his hands at last.

"Maybe something," Cyndi said, "or maybe nothing. I won't know until I try, and I can't try unless I have that time alone."

Reluctantly Manny agreed. The next morning Cyndi was up early, rummaging in her bags and about the house. By the time Manny was fully awake, Cyndi had laid out on the kitchen table some seeds and what looked at first like little pieces of wood—but which, on closer inspection, appeared to be dried fungus of various types. Some of them looked like dessicated versions of specimens they'd picked up on their walks.

"What's all this?" Manny asked.

"A New World witch's brew, if you like," Cyndi said levelly, preoccupied. "What the Mayans in the *Popol Vuh* called *kakuljá,* the 'lightningbolts.' " She picked up a specimen from a pile of larger dried gill mushrooms. "*Kakuljá hurakan,* Lightningbolt One-Leg—a particular strain of *Amanita muscaria.*" Picking up a much smaller dried gilled mushroom in her right hand and then a seed in her left, she continued: "*Chipi kakuljá*—dwarf lightningbolt, a *Psilocybe* fungus. *Raxa kakuljá,* green lightningbolt, seeds of the *Ipomaea* morning glories. Together they form the trinity that the Maya called the Heart of Heaven." She picked up a last mushroom—an unfamiliar one that looked like a shriveled brain. "And one last lightningbolt that the Maya knew nothing about—a fourth lightningbolt, *Cordyceps jacinti,* the source of KL 235."

"But what's it all for?" Manny asked, obscurely disturbed by the ritual unfolding before him.

"To get there from here," she said, picking up the materials she'd selected and walking off toward Manny's virtuality workspace. Manny followed.

"And 'there' is—?"

"Elsewhere," she replied, opening the door to the workroom. "Maybe elsewhen. Don't look so worried. I thought you were the Electric Shaman—right? Now we'll see if electric shamanism is real after all—or only virtual."

She closed the door behind her.

Manny paced nervously for a bit before the door to the Game Preserve—then, sighing, went downstairs. What was she up to? What should he do about it? Anything? He'd given his word that he wouldn't interrupt. . . .

He decided he was in need of distraction. Sitting down on the living room couch thinking he might watch some brain-deadening TV, he noticed a tape on the coffee table that he'd never seen before. One of Cyndi's, maybe? With a shrug he popped it into the VCR.

White noise, then images. A cold sharp winter morning—someplace in the Midwest? He turned up the sound. The rusty-swing honking of distant geese singing the sun up over the rim of the world. In the sharp air the only other sound was the flapping of a large flag in front of a garment factory. A man and woman walking along, their feet scrunching over the snow. They do not look or carry themselves like actors.

"Funny thing about that flag," the man says. "Every time management is ready to announce a new wave of layoffs, they put a bigger flag on the flagpole out front."

"Pretty soon," the woman says, nodding, looking up at the banner lolling in the wind, "the flag'll be too heavy for the wind to lift or the pole to hold."

"The factory will be closed, before then."

"Maybe they should switch to making flags."

Not more than fifty feet above them, wild geese fly in a vee right down Main Street.

More white noise then. Odd stuff, Manny thought. Not the usual mass audience fare, at any rate. He fast forwarded until he was out of the electronic snow again.

Pounding music. Camera-eye soaring down a double helix endlessly, knocking off a purine here, adding a pyrimidine there. The helix suddenly becoming twisting coiling shining Asklepian snakes, or maybe just one vast snake, one serpentine shining Babel tower stretching above and below, a Möbius Caduceus Ouroboros swallowing its own tail forever, eternity in love with time, in love with itself. A woman riding on the back of the great jewel-scaled snake through a doorway to infinite horizons.

More white noise. Stranger and stranger, Manny thought. He fast forwarded again.

"Those substances weren't just poisons," said a woman captioned DR. EVITA CALDERON, PSYCHONEUROIMMUN-OLOGIST. She would occasionally get up and walk to a display board while her interviewer—Cyndi!—took notes. "The mammalian brain, including that of humans, evolved in such a way as to be sensitive to chemicals that occur outside the body—because such sensitivity had positive adaptive value. There was an adaptive advantage for those creatures whose central nervous systems evolved in such a way as to be influenced by the presence of biological compounds found in their environment—compounds in materials likely to be consumed as food—that would sooner or later exert some kind of influence on the animal's nervous system. The evolution of the human brain proceeded in such a way as to deliberately take advantage of psychoac—"

White noise blotted out the screen again before Dr. Calderon's image reappeared.

"—okay?" she continued. "In the brain there are these dense collections of nerve cell bodies, called nuclei. Neural fibers arising from the dorsal and median raphe nuclei of the brain stem are dispersed throughout the brain, as well as having direct contact with structures in the limbic system and the frontal cortex. These cells receive input from the spinal cord reticular formation, a neuronal network that receives inputs from the entire somatosensory system."

"They've got their little dendrites on the pulse of body activity, as it were?" Cyndi asked.

"Right," Dr. Calderon said, smiling politely, "but they also have fibers that branch back upon themselves, their axons synapsing on their own dendrites. These neurons release a monamine chemical, 5-hydroxytryptamine, also called 5-HT or serotonin. 5-HT acts as an inhibitory neurotransmitter. The neurons of the brain have a set level of activity and if left on their own they would discharge at some variable chaotic rate. But the neurons are not left alone—specialized neurons in the brain secrete 5-HT which inhibits their normal activity. The brain is like a car with its accelerator welded to the floor, and the speed at which the brain operates is controlled by the chemical brake pedal, 5-HT."

More white noise yelled out of the set before the image abruptly stabilized to show Dr. Calderon once more.

"—lysergic acid derivatives, usually thought to be the most potent known psychoactive agents, are found in various members of the *Convolvulaceae*—morning glory family—and in the *Claviceps*—ergot fungi. Psilocin and psilocybin in mushrooms and mescaline in peyote cacti are cross-tolerant with the lysergics and all of them are 5-HT antagonists, the lysergics binding to the 5-HT neurons at their feedback sites, while the mushroom and cacti products block the effects of 5-HT at receptor sites. The 5-HT antagonists take the foot off the brake pedal, resulting in enhanced neural sensitivity throughout the entire brain and the sort of spontaneous neural activity characteristic of chaotic systems. Small stimuli lead to a cascading effect and things are perceived differently, information is processed differently. The well-ordered and rhythmic brain processes of breathing and digestive regulation are supplemented by new chaotic processes of cognition. Experiences take on new meanings, the world is understood in fundamentally different ways. Under the influence of these substances some have claimed to see beyond what mortal eyes can see, to travel backward and forward in time, to visit other planes of existence—"

White noise, then a snippet of the credits—"The director wishes to thank the Kitchener Foundation for the Arts, without whose support this film would not have been possible"—then white noise and only white noise after that, all the way to the end of the tape. Manny pondered. This fragmented material—was it outtakes from *The Five-Million-Day War*? The only surviving remnants of that work, perhaps? Or just video notes for some other project Cyndi had worked on?

Manny watched the material again. Something about that arts foundation sounded familiar, but he couldn't put his finger on it. He went up to the locked door of his workspace. Leaning close to the door, he heard only a continual low roaring—the white noise of mountain streams in spring, of wind upon water, of the far subatomic flux of eternity magnified millions of times. Of Cyndi there was no sound at all—not a chair squeaking, not a breath in or out.

Turning from the haunting, indecipherable sound, Manny walked downstairs and outside. He strode into an autumn afternoon, deciduous oaks blazing up in a last flame of color before bare-branched ashen winter—all against the stolid relentless green of the conifers. A Steller's jay called raucously and dropped onto the dirt road before him, a rowdy thing of black topknot and blue feathers and hard bright little eyes, blue-painted Pict punk of the forest screaming away from him as it took wing once more. Crows flapped and cawed, chickadees flashed and flitted. In the shadows of the woods larger animals moved, or their ghosts. So much of the natural matrix out of which human beings had come was gone. In the shift from wild to civilized, from raw to cooked, from real to virtual, something must be lost, he thought, though he had technophile net acquaintances who said that all that was lost was ignorance—that extinction was only the loss of one kind of information in the generating of another. Shaking his head slowly, he walked on and on.

Night was falling by the time he returned to the cabin. The door to his workroom was still locked, but as he stood

outside contemplating his next move the servomotors of
one of his printers in the hall began to hum, spewing out
pages of information. The other printer, behind the locked
door, also seemed to be feeding out, from the sound of it.
He walked over to the hall machine and looked through
the hard copy. Cities and jargon: New York NYSE Dow
NASDAQ; Tokyo Nikkei JAZDAQ; London FT-SE 100-
share index; Frankfurt DAX; Sydney Ordinaries; Taiwan
weighted index; Hong Kong Hang Seng index; Manila
Composite; Singapore Straits Times industrial index—the
list went on. It took him a moment before he realized
that he was looking at selected stock quotations for and
from markets around the world. It took him even longer
to realize that they were quotations from one week into
the future—big winners and big losers, those varying most
from their previous performances.

He heard the door of his workspace unlock and saw
Cyndi step out of the Game Preserve. He noted momentarily that she looked haggard—very pale and frail and tired,
as if from an ordeal recently passed—but as the realization
of what the hard copy data in his hand might mean dawned
upon him, he became thoroughly preoccupied with it.

"Is this for real?" Manny said, trying to keep the
excitement out of his voice.

"I think so," Cyndi said warily, an odd gleam in her
tired eyes. "When I get all the way there, all the way to
elsewhere, I'm usually pretty sure about what I've seen.
Only one way to find out. Put some money down. I've
got a bit saved up, and you've got some old computer
hardware and that entertainment center with the TV and
the CD and the VCR—"

Manny was reluctant at first, and even when he did finally
agree he would only sell off his entertainment gear—none
of his computer or virtuality systems, no matter how old and
underutilized they were. He claimed that infotechnologies
had virtually no resale value. Cyndi nodded dully, handed
over her money to him, went to bed complaining of a
headache and fever, and slept for nineteen hours straight.

By the time she woke, Manny had sold the entertainment center through the nets and added the newly generated money to Cyndi's savings, brokering the accumulated funds as surreptitiously as he could in case anything went wrong and someone tried to trace the money to its source. Never good at keeping secrets, Manny worried and fidgeted and hoped and dreamed restlessly for the next six days. When on the fourth day Dash flagged him in the net with a "Long time no hear from" message, Manny abruptly gave in to the temptation (compounded of equal parts anxiety and braggadocio) to broadly hint to Dash about the scheme he and Cyndi had embarked on. Cyndi, however, seemed calm all along, as if still recovering from the ordeal of her mysterious time alone. Even the revealing of "their" secret did not faze her very much.

On the evening of the seventh day electrons representing money flooded into Immanuel Shaw's accounts, and Dash Chandler came tumbling after, a thin wiry man with a large misshapen nose and long hair who appeared on the cabin doorstep breathless and agitated but most of all madly curious. They had never met before in person and, after perfunctorily introducing himself (both his net handle of Dash Chandler and his rather unfortunate given name, Mark DeLepper), their new acquaintance launched into a series of questions.

"What are you people up to here? First you send me stumbling onto all that hush-hush Project Medusa Blue stuff and now you've got this coming down! A handful of aces on all the exchanges! How'd you do it? Bugger the automated trading systems?"

With a glance Manny turned that question over to Cyndi, but she was reluctant to answer. With a glance of her own she conveyed much unspoken information back to Manny, which he read extravagantly: Suspicion; We don't even know whether this person is who he says he is; Everything he's saying might be a cover story; Maybe he's been sent to trap us; If Dash isn't his real name, maybe Mark isn't his real name either; Maybe he's fake all the way through and all the way back; How do we know we can trust him? Manny in turn shot her a "You're being paranoid" grimace. Seeing it all, Dash/Mark grew truculent.

"Look," he began, "haven't I sacrificed enough for you people already? People I don't even really know! Things have gotten too hot for me to be anywhere near my home terminal—at least for a while. Manny told me what he was up to, so I kept a neighborly eye out. The program probes were starting to fire back in *your* direction, Manny m' friend, so I diverted them to me, tracked you down and out, then blanked all my connections. I've had to burn all my bridges, give up my livelihood and disappear! Protecting you people! The least you could do is explain to me what the hell is going on."

Cyndi tried, despite her unwillingness, her unease at having to bare her soul to a virtual stranger, even if that stranger was someone Manny seemed to have taken an almost instant liking to. Slowly, hesitantly, she spoke of time as a "structure of possibility" and of her ability to move around in that structure while under the influence of certain entheogens. How she could look beyond the screens separating days, look through the spacetime static, deep into reality's white noise as if it were the snow on a TV set jammed between channels—and see there not just meaningless randomness but something more, a shifting pattern behind it. A more subtle level of order.

"I felt like I was surrounded by glass walls," she said. "Like I was in a glass diving bell ringing in the depths of an infinite ocean. Around me waves were cresting and troughing over the sea of static. An island of darker light appeared before me, expanding and contracting, like an amoeba, big and fluid and grainy. Appearing and disappearing at the center of vision. Flows everywhere—crepuscular, corpuscular. Like biology-class videos of capillary action. Swarming and shuttling leukocytes and erythrocytes, all moved by the thudding of a distant heart.

"I saw swirling depths, dimensions beyond dimensions, jewels and flowers and faces floating—and worming spinning curling gray-white snow maggots sweeping back and forth, endlessly devouring everything with such mindless ferocity that I had to look away. When I focused again everything was moving faster, happening so much faster, like I was flying down amid quantum flux, worming my way through the dreamtime soil of eternity, the gravitational bed in which the threads of spacetime grow, from which fruit each of our days, a mushroom on the mycelium of time—"

Manny and Dash stared at her uncomprehendingly. She tried to sum up.

"At that point I rose into pure white light. I had gotten *there,* I was being *elsewhere.* I could see the time lines branching and branching, weaving and knitting in patterns of fantastic complexity. I was less a person than a place through which strings and threads of light and information were passing. I could see the information I wanted, weave the threads of probability into a whole that made sense. Maybe it was 'buggering the automated trading systems,' as you put it, but I don't think so. I think I was just seeing what was happening there and then, in another possibility structure, an elsewhere outside the here and now."

The two men looked at her in silence for quite a while.

"Let me get this straight," Dash said, clearing his throat. "You did a bunch of drugs, sat in front of some snowed-out screens, mind-traveled and brought back stock quotes from a week into the future—?"

"No," Cyndi said, bristling at Dash's obtuseness and blatant insensitivity. "Not 'drugs' the way you're thinking of them, and not in front of white-noise screens. The entheogens were for triggering chaos in my mind, to open it out beyond its usual boundaries. I'd programmed Manny's screens not to white noise but to channel-switch at greater than flashcut speeds—as an information trigger for going elsewhere. The stock data I found is already there, is already here, if you can see into the chaotic patterns—"

Manny cut Cyndi off—and in so doing preempted Dash.

"All I know is, it works," Manny said. "We're thirty thousand to the good—ten thousand for each of us, if we choose to divvy it up that way. Dash, or Mark, or which-ever—since you're out of your place on our account, stay with us for a while! We should be celebrating our good fortune, not analyzing it to death!"

So, in the midst of the impromptu party they threw for themselves, it was decided: Cyndi moved her things into Manny's room, and Dash took up residence in the spare bedroom, and no one thought to question it further—at least not aloud.

The first snow of the season fell early not long after, and everything was warm and cozy for a time. Manny bought the image analyzers and codebreaking equipment that he felt would help him push back the ice sheets, and he and Dash had some success in bringing at least a small interstadial spring to the virtual Pleistocene. They were able to thaw their way through the glaciers in spots, and the money began to flow in again—all from hacking, for Manny had by now left game and simulation designing almost completely.

But "flow" wasn't good enough, when it came to money. With Dash to goad him on, Manny's appetite for ever newer and more sophisticated technologies explod-ed—a satellite uplink, an untraceable global phone-call-rerouting program, a gigaflop holographic virtual representation system—the wish list grew daily. What was needed was not flows of cash but floods, torrents of capi-tal. Manny lingered longer in virtuality with Dash, skip-ping meals and forgetting sleep as he tried to open wider the great cash spigot in the virtual sky.

Cyndi worried quietly, on occasion spoke grimly about his obsessiveness, but Manny felt he was doing just fine. Just dedicated to the work, was all. He still went out walking or running with Cyndi almost every day—and, though his hair and beard had gotten grayer and longer, Manny still looked leaner and stronger than he had in many years. Dash never joined them on their jaunts in the out-of-doors, always insisting that if humans had been intended to stroll about in the woods, the forest would have come equipped with benches every hundred paces. Manny often sensed that there was more to it than that—a certain unspoken enmity between Cyndi and Dash? some odd sort of jealousy?— but he let it go, never enquiring further.

Not long after Manny circuitously asked Cyndi to marry him (yes, she had agreed, and quietly they had set a date in May—a painstaking decision for two long-single people), he began, with some hesitation, to nudge her toward another of her entheogenic ordeals. He remembered vaguely how much the previous one had fatigued her, but that memory was overwhelmed by his mounting desire for the newest tools of his trade.

Cyndi was reluctant. Manny explained that he and Dash weren't able to cut through the ice quickly enough, deeply enough, or permanently enough—but once they'd bought the new software and hardware they wanted, he assured her, they'd be able to move about at will and everything would fall into place. Dash had already located two prospective buyers who would pay quite well for "advance information"—particularly info concerning the big multinational military/industrial firms.

"Come on," Dash prodded, annoyed by Cyndi's reluctance. "How bad can it be? You yourself called it an ecstasy."

"I also called it an ordeal," Cyndi said, frustrated with Dash's perpetual obtuseness and the "dumbing down" effect his presence was having on Manny. "It is an ecstasy in the ancient Greek sense—an *ekstasis*, an out-of-body experience. Ecstasy is not fun. Weaving possibilities is draining at the deepest level, at the very core of the soul."

Cyndi's arguments had no effect on Dash, but that was somehow appropriate since his arguments had no effect on

Cyndi either. Manny, however, listened to them both, and still he urged her to do it—for him. With all her misgivings intact, Cyndi agreed to undergo her ordeal once more.

"All right," she said pointedly, in the direction of both men, as she stood at the door of the workspace. "For you, Manny. Always everything for you."

This time the continual low roaring from behind the door persisted for two days straight and Manny had begun to worry in earnest when finally the printers in the hall and workroom hummed and spat out pages with the information Dash's buyers lusted after. Cyndi emerged from the workroom at last—slowly, ghostly pale and weak. Without a word to either of the men, she walked down the hall and collapsed into bed, where she slept fitfully, feverishly. Manny made her soups first, then sandwiches and more substantial fare.

After five days Cyndi's health began to improve. Manny was glad, not least because playing Florence Nightingale wasn't exactly his strong suit. Throughout the seven days that she was bedridden, Manny told her of all the wonders her latest ordeal had allowed them to accomplish. The money from Dash's buyers had flooded in—not by the tens but by the hundreds of thousands. With the new equipment he and Dash had purchased, they were already making more permanent progress against the glaciers, keeping the ice off long enough so that, in every place the snows had recently melted, his now-gigaflop virtual had begun sending up these surrealistic "snowplants"—lurid red-pink alien-phallic saprophytes half a meter tall. Listening to Manny's excited descriptions, Cyndi had smiled wanly, and not, perhaps, without some sadness.

Again, all went well for a time. Manny bought his first hovercar and he and Cyndi disappeared for a camping trip in the Mojave the first weekend in December—Dash refusing any thought of "roughing it" in the desert as firmly as he refused to join them on their walks in the mountains. Their weekend was a much-needed space taken out of time. The only odd note came when, one evening after they'd returned to the tent from a day of hiking, Cyndi's thoughts turned to darker matters.

"If anything ever happens to me," Cyndi said, taking a card from her stuffsack and handing it to Manny, "get in touch with these people. Call them as fast as you can."

"Cyndi dear, don't be morbid. Nothing's going to happen to you," Manny said, then glanced at the card. "Kitchener Foundation for the Arts. That name's familiar. Who are these folks, anyway?"

"An anticensorship group," Cyndi said quietly, sitting back on her elbows in her sleeping bag, "trying to make whole cloth from the tatters of the First Amendment. The foundation is a complex trust that's a beneficiary of another trust, which is in turn a beneficiary of another trust, et cetera, et cetera. The trust's guardians helped bankroll my documentary, and I'm pretty sure their political action committee wangled me my place in the internment amnesty. I think their influence probably helped get me work with the housekeeping agency too."

"You mean you don't know?"

Cyndi shook her head.

"I don't know how up front they can be about any aid they give me. Something about laws governing fiduciaries."

Manny nodded, though he had little enough idea what she was talking about. The whole setup sounded byzantine, labyrinthine, and paranoid in the extreme. Something about it itched at the back of his mind, like the clicking into place of the final piece of a puzzle that he no longer had any desire to solve. He glanced at the card in his hand again.

"Well, I doubt we'll be needing their help any time soon. But I'll keep the card, for your sake."

They returned to Manny's cabin blissfully relaxed, content, and satisfied. Their ease was short-lived, however. Almost as soon as they walked through the door, Dash—who seemed to have become the voice of all the household's lacks and wants and needs—began croaking on about More Money! The data they'd been freeing from the ice had apparently come to the attention of the state and corporate security apparats. The NSA and Interpol and FBI and WorldWackenhut all had begun sending out counterintelligence probes. Manny's operation was still in the clear, but if things kept heating up they'd all have to shut down and flee the country. The only option, as far as Dash was concerned, was a direct strike to the security infostructures themselves—and that would require covert channels on a "black" satellite, a teraflop-capable virtual system, and much, much more. He had already located interested groups to bankroll them if they could first provide specific and highly detailed advance information on the much-rumored "chilldown," the consolidation of state and corporate security systems into a single global network.

Cyndi said nothing. Dash said much, and he had Manny's ear completely.

"We can strike a great blow against the state," Manny was saying before long. "This'll bring freedom to the electronic frontier *permanently*."

In Manny's mind it all quickly became a Grand Crusade: a noble quest which would, not coincidentally, also allow him to make an incredible financial killing and get away clean, retiring gloriously from the young guns' world of the nets to live out the rest of his days with Cyndi, safe and secure on some moderately priced private island.

About this rose-colored vision of the future Cyndi would not comment. Three days before the shortest day of the year—and long before Manny's utopian rhetoric had even begun to scale the hyperbolic heights to which it might have risen—a snowstorm swept into the mountains and Cyndi sequestered herself in the virtual workroom, saying not a word as she left, only staring sadly at Manny, glaring hard and piercingly at Dash. It was enough.

A day of the continual low roaring behind the door, a night, a second day and night. Outside, the snowstorm continued. By midmorning of the third day, Dash and Manny had taken to pacing in the hall outside the locked workroom—Dash impatiently, Manny worriedly. At noon an agonized cry sounded from inside, at the same moment that pages began to feed out of the printers. Dash ran toward the printer in the hall, carefully eyeing all that it was printing out. Manny ran to the locked workroom door in a panic.

"Cyndi! Cyndi! Are you okay? What's wrong?" The only reply to his shouting was a moaning sound, barely audible over the continual low roar. In a frenzy Manny tugged at the locked door, then took a quick step back. With his right foot he kicked savagely at the door, his foot slamming into wood beside the doorknob. With a splintering and cracking sound the door flew open, swinging all the way on its hinges, bouncing against the wall and rebounding halfway back. Dash came up behind him. When Manny pushed the door wide again, the scene that confronted him was one he wished he had not seen to believe.

Images flooded and surged from all the screens, all the walls, and from the holographics in space. The air roared and whirred. On the floor lay Cyndi but also not Cyndi. Electric-bright white light feathered off of her, off her torso and lower body, off her arms like luminous wings, made her hair stand about her head like a radiant crown of golden feathers. She seemed an otherworldly creature compounded equally of bird and woman and pure light, yet at that brightness emanating from her she tore convulsively, like an angel sick of holiness and grace. Watching her pulling the diffuse light into glowing threads with her bright-winged hands, hearing the new information spitting out of the printer as she did so, Manny at last understood why Cyndi had always emerged drained and weary. She had been weaving possibilities *out of herself.*

The brightness about her connection suit died, the printer stopped, the virtual Pleistocene returned to all the screens, snow falling fast and heavy as ashes from a million crematoria. Manny fell to his knees and cradled Cyndi in his arms, her head lolling weakly against his shoulder. She could not rise from where she had fallen, could barely hold her head up. Her eyes looked dull, burnt out. The printout trailed across her lap and out.

"Too much—can't fill your need," she said weakly. "Over there too long. Can't come back. Can't hold on. . . ."

Manny started lifting Cyndi.

"Dash!" he called out, but the other man was gone from the doorway. Faintly he heard the front door slam downstairs. "Mark! I need your help."

Outside, Dash's car started and ground away over the snow.

"Dash!" Manny called out, bewildered, confused.

"Don't," Cyndi said, her breathing growing labored. "Dash . . . Tetragrammaton operative. Suspected it—"

She coughed—a horrible racking, choking sound. Manny tried to hold her up more comfortably, so she could breathe.

"Oh God, oh God, I'm sorry," he said, a sob breaking into his voice. "My lust for all those damn technofixes— look what it's done!"

She raised her hand lightly to his cheek.

"I love you, Manny. They wanted me . . . out of the picture. But to get me they had to tell you how to get free. You're free."

"But you—" he began, trying to unzip her from the connection suit and drag her.

"No," she said quietly. "Leave me connected. It's the only way . . . I can get free."

"How?"

"Almost there," she said hoarsely, her eyes kindling to final bright delirium. "Catch my soul. . . ."

She fell into silence then, the dying of her light falling with the light going out of the shortest day of the year. Manny cradled her for hours. He stared blankly at the printout draped into and out of her lap: sharp shining paper, down which ran a thin inexplicable line of red, a bloodsoaked thread woven into the center of a bolt of luminous white silk. Like her last words it haunted him, raised in him questions both terrible and beautiful. On the screens and beyond the windows, the snow in its falling gave no answers.

In worlds more and less illusory, time appeared only to pass. He was free, but he made a phone call anyway. The sheltering dark wings of the Kitchener Foundation closed around him, carrying him to safety for a time.

When he was out on his own again he found the snow was still falling, but slower, lighter, like feathers from a great molting of the universe. As the snowfall surged around him Manny felt as if he were walking through fields of white feathers. Before him, a wounded bird with a golden crown rose up and he followed after, headed into a world of light.

As she flew, the bird's wings flared into every color, turned snow to rain and rebuilt shattered rainbows, printed flowers upon the world, returned feathers to all the birds in all the paradises through which she passed until, high in the sky, she became a gathering of stars, bright wings spreading just beyond the finite Now's unbounded edge, her heart—enflamed, enfeathered, enflowered, encrystalled—indistinguishable from the heart of heaven itself.

Falling into the same heart of the same sky, Manny saw it was his own heart as well, and he felt that he had come safely home at last.

Vox Domini

Bruce Holland Rogers

IN A CANYON OF BLUE SANDSTONE, A MAN IS DIGGING A
hole. It's a deep hole, long and narrow. It could hardly
be anything other than a grave.

There's a stream flowing nearby. Above the canyon
walls, the sky is tinted orange with dust, the color of the
setting sun. The wind is blowing hard up there. In this
region of the planet, the wind always blows hard at sunset.
But down here in the canyon, at the base of these high blue
walls, the air hardly stirs.

There is no sound but the soft snick of the shovel
cutting through the sand.

Mohr half opened his eyes when he felt Boursai wiping
his mouth again. The cloth was cold and rough, but Boursai
was gentle with it.

"That's better," Boursai said. "Isn't that better?"

Mohr tried to turn his back on Boursai, but he was
still too drugged, too weak. All he could manage was to
turn his head and face the other way.

The light coming through the open doorway was brilliant. The blue cliffs and canyons looked washed out and unreal in the distance. There by the door were the remains of the yellow hexes, tiny cracked shells like dead insects. And between the doorway and the cot where Mohr was lying was the still-damp spot where Boursai had tried to scrape the floor clean.

"Do you want some water to drink?" said Boursai. "It will wash away the bitterness from your mouth."

But not from my soul, Mohr thought. And then he thought to himself, *Shut up. Stop thinking.*

Mohr heard water trickling from one of the jugs, and then Boursai was in front of him again with a cup in his black hands.

"Take it. Drink."

Mohr closed his eyes and gestured toward the door.

"Gabriel, drink it."

Mohr tried to lift his arms to tap a message into his wrist communicator, but he couldn't manage it. He flicked his wrist impatiently toward the door again.

"I'll go soon enough, Gabriel," said Boursai. "But I must attend to some things first. You've been letting things go around here." He held out the cup. "You need to take better care of yourself and your trees. You've been neglecting your trees, Gabriel."

Mohr tried again to bring his right hand to the keyboard on his wrist. This time he managed to type in a message by feel. Boursai leaned forward to read it. It said: FUCK TREES.

"You don't mean that. They'll die. Your trees need you, Gabriel."

Mohr keyed in another message. It said, GO AWAY. DONT CALL ME GABRIEL. GO.

"It's a good name," Boursai said. "It was the angel Gabriel who brought God's words to the prophet, and . . ."

Mohr tried to tune him out. He didn't want to hear more talk of God and the prophet, and he didn't want to hear his name again. Gabriel. His adopted name, the name the Catholics had given him. The name for the fool who had wasted years and years listening for the voice of God. Gabriel. The name Tireen had liked so much. Mohr felt his body stiffen, his heart accelerate. Tireen. Damn Boursai for that, for making him think of Tireen.

Summoning all his strength, Mohr lifted his arm to knock the cup from Boursai's hand.

He keyed the communicator to display GO AWAY and to keep scrolling those words across its screen. Then he closed his eyes and slept.

When Mohr woke, Boursai was not in the room, but Mohr could hear him moving outside in the compound. The wind had come up, blowing so hard that it had to be midafternoon.

Boursai moved for a moment to where Mohr could see him framed by the doorway. The man stood swaying in the wind like some tall, black sapling. On his back he carried a water tank, and in one hand he held the dripping nozzle.

Mohr sat up slowly, making the cot creak. His head throbbed, and his body felt as though it were made of rags. He looked around the room. Everything had been ordered, tidied up. Even the litter of empty hexes by the door had disappeared. Mohr reached into the breast pocket of his fatigues.

There was nothing there.

He patted the pocket to make sure, then pushed himself up from the cot and shuffled to his footlocker. It was unlocked. He *never* left it unlocked. He touched his neck, feeling for the string that held his key. It was gone.

Hands shaking, he threw the locker open. The bag had been right on top. But not anymore.

The empty water tank scraped on the ground outside. Boursai came in, ducking through the doorway.

Mohr punched keys on his wrist. Then he shook the word at Boursai. WHERE?

Boursai stepped close. Too close. Mohr turned his

face away and keyed in, GET AWAY! His hands were shaking. WHERES STASH?

Boursai, arms extended as if to catch him, said, "Careful! You shouldn't be on your feet so soon."

Mohr started to key something in, then stopped. This was taking too long, punching one key at a time. He half walked, half stumbled past Boursai to the com-link sitting beside his sink. He switched it on and typed in: "If I fall, it's my own business! If I want to goddamn take a fistful of hex and goddamn die, that's my own business! Where the hell is my stash?"

Boursai stood just close enough to read the screen. "I took them away," he said. "I put them somewhere."

Mohr glared at Boursai as he typed in: "I suppose you think you're doing me a favor! I'm an addict. Hex is something I need!" He held down the word-repeat key so that the screen filled with, "need! need! need! need!"

"I'll give them to you," Boursai said quietly. "I'll give you one a day."

Mohr closed his eyes. His hands felt rubbery. "Thief!" he typed. "What did the prophet say about thieves?"

"I'm sure you know the words of the prophet as well as I do," said Boursai.

"Did once. Trying to forget such crap. Give me my hexes."

Boursai's answer was a soft, "No."

Mohr brought his trembling hands to his face, then raised them in a frustrated, angry gesture. *Why are you doing this to me*?

"All men are brothers," said Boursai.

Mohr spun back to the keyboard. "Bullshit! All men are brothers, the beloved children of God? Hah! God's gone, Boursai! God's in hiding!"

"It's a wondrous universe, Gabriel. Even if God is remote." Boursai thought for a moment and said, "Isn't this planet proof to you of God's benevolence?"

Mohr shook his head. He had heard this argument

before. Not from Boursai, but from other recruits to the Planters Corps. Onazuka's World did seem like a godsend to some. It was a world with an Earthlike atmosphere but with almost no native life forms, the perfect place to colonize. But how had this wonderful situation come into being? Onazuka's World had evolved over billions of years, just like the Earth. Artifacts and bones only a few hundred years old showed that there had been a rich and varied biosphere here, the product of an evolutionary process that was just beginning to produce toolmakers. In fact, it seemed there were several toolmaking species. And then, just centuries before the first humans set foot on this world, a massive meteor collided with the planet, cloaking it in dust. The planet froze. When the dust settled out and the surface warmed again, few native species came back. It was as though the world had been made and wiped clean for humanity to colonize with Earth life.

"Benevolence?" Mohr tapped in. "A God who murders a world for our convenience is benevolent?"

"If you are as cynical as you seem," Boursai said, "then why did you enlist in the Planters Corps?"

Because, Mohr thought, I wanted to get out of the Live Free Cluster, out of all of the clusters, if I could find a way. I wanted to make planetfall. Any planetfall. And because the recruiter showed me the biggest bag of yellow hex that I had ever seen and said the magic words: *Signing bonus.* But what he typed was, "None of your damn business. Give me my hex and get out!"

"You're a good planter," Boursai said. "Until recently, you've always been very careful with your trees. Whenever I came to see you, you would be at work."

That's because they'll send me back to Onazuka City if I don't do a good job, Mohr thought. Or back to the clusters. But he had no stomach for explaining things to Boursai. "Come on!" he typed. "Give me my hex and get out! Out! I want to be left alone!"

Mohr turned to look at the other man. He could read the thought in Boursai's eyes: If I'd left you alone today, you'd be dead. But Boursai didn't say this. He didn't have a chance, because at that moment his wristwatch began to sing in Arabic. His electronic muezzin was calling him to prayer. He excused himself and went outside, consulting the display on his wrist to see what sector of the sky he should face for his obeisance to Earth, to Mecca.

Mohr staggered to the door to shut it behind the man, but instead he leaned in the doorway to look out at the blue cliffs, to think of the canyons where he sometimes planted his trees. The coolness of those streams. The solitude.

While Boursai prayed, Mohr thought of Tireen again, and something stabbed at his heart.

Long ago, when Mohr had gone to the Holy Cluster of the Catholic Church, an old woman named Sister Sarah Theresa had been assigned to instruct him. She was little more than a body suit stretched over bones, and her hair was too white and too thin to hide her skull. She was, secretly, a heretic.

The stabbing in his heart made Mohr think of her now. "It's like a worm in your heart, Gabriel," she had told him. They were floating in the zero-g cathedral—so many religions put their holy places in the hubs of their clusters, as if weightlessness put them closer to God. Mohr and Sister Sarah Theresa were in the apse, looking at the statue of the Son of God and Man. Stars wheeled slowly by in the windows behind the Savior's head.

"The catechism teaches that there is no guilt," the old woman said, looking around to see that she was not overheard. They were, in fact, alone in the cathedral. "They say now that there is only Affective Spiritual Dissonance." She chuckled. "They water God down until there is nothing left but psychology." Then, more seriously, she pointed a bony finger: "There *is* guilt, Gabriel. It's like a worm eating away at your heart from the inside. God can take away that worm, but you have to confess. You have to speak aloud what sin you have committed, in the hearing of another human being."

"Why must it be spoken?" Mohr had asked her.

"Because that's the only way to release what's in your heart. That's the only way God will hear you. Speak aloud what you have done—you can't just think it or write it. It's still in your heart, then. You have to confess. The heart and the tongue are connected. When you confess, you poison that worm in your heart with truth."

Boursai was finishing his prayer, and Mohr felt the stab in his heart once more. He remembered the way that Tireen had clawed at his hand on the airlock button, then on the override switch. He remembered the look in her eyes. The disbelief. He remembered what the vacuum did to her face. Guilt is a worm. Guilt is a worm. Confess, Gabriel Mohr!

But he would have to use words for that, wouldn't he? Spoken words. That's what it would take to confess.

He reached into his pocket out of reflex. If only he could shut off this chatter in his head, these memories! His knees had weakened, and as he slid toward the ground, he felt Boursai's grip seize him. Touching him. Boursai was touching him.

Mohr pulled away, felt the bile rising in his throat. But his stomach was empty. He only gagged. He thought, half amused, *It's nothing personal, Boursai, you thieving bastard. It's just that I can't stand human beings.* He smiled weakly.

"Come back inside," Boursai said. "Lie down." He offered his hand to help Mohr up. Mohr looked at the hand. No, his reaction to Boursai was more than his ordinary revulsion. There was something about Boursai that made him cringe.

Mohr got to his feet without help. He went back to the com-link. "You're the problem, Boursai. When you don't come around, I need one hex a day, maybe two. But you visit and I take four, I take five or six." He pounded the counter next to the keyboard. "Leave me alone! Give me my hex and go!"

"I will go," Boursai answered, "but I cannot return your drugs to you."

Mohr picked up an empty water jug and hurled it. It went wide of Boursai's head.

"I am sorry for this," Boursai said.

Mohr waved angrily as if to say, *Just get the hell out!*

The door closed. Mohr waited a few minutes, then went outside. The wind gusted and Mohr flinched. He didn't like wind. In the clusters, he had never felt more breeze than the gentle exhalations of the ventilation shafts.

Boursai was already a small figure striding near the horizon.

Mohr went back inside and checked under the convex bottom of one water jug, and then reached into the space between the counter and the wall, and then checked the hole he had hollowed out from the dirt floor and covered with a stone. They were all there, his emergency stashes. Boursai hadn't found any of them, probably hadn't thought to look.

First Mohr refilled his breast pocket, then put a hex between his teeth and cracked it. He inhaled through his mouth, felt the warmth travel down his throat, into his lungs and body. Then he spit the empty yellow shell onto the floor.

He looked at the bag and felt his pocket. This supply wouldn't last long. He'd have to convince Boursai to return the rest. What was it with that man, anyway? Why did he insist on coming around here? He had his own compound to attend to, his own trees to get into the ground. Maybe Boursai was lonely. It was just the two of them for a hundred miles in any direction. So what? It wasn't Mohr's fault if Boursai couldn't take a little solitude.

Mohr closed his eyes, and Tireen's face floated up from his memory. Damn Boursai. Damn him! Mohr cracked another hex.

The sun wasn't quite setting when Mohr turned on his com-link and opened a channel to Boursai. Mohr hardly ever turned his unit on, but now he had a reason. He couldn't stop thinking of that bag of hex.

"Boursai," he transmitted, "bring back my property."

The red contact light came on as Boursai turned on his machine miles away and received the message. And his reply came an instant later: "You took an overdose."

"That's my damn business," Mohr wrote, then wiped it out and replaced it with, "I need the stuff."

"You think you need it."

"I *need* it, Boursai. Return it!"

"Why? Why are you convinced you need to poison yourself?"

Mohr stared at the screen for a moment. If Boursai knew even half of Mohr's story, the ways people had changed him, the things they had done to him, the things *he* had done. . . .

"It may make you feel good for a little while," Boursai's message continued, "but it could kill you. It almost did."

That was the idea, Mohr thought. Poison wasn't such a bad idea. If Boursai only knew. . . .

"You've got to adjust to this world, Gabriel."

Adjust! That's what he had done more than anyone else he knew, adjusting to one cluster after another. The only place he really hadn't tried to fit in was Holdham, his home cluster, and the only reason he couldn't fit in there was because he happened to be curious about the wrong things! "Where do you get those ideas, boy?" his instructors asked him. And when he told them, they'd say something like, "Those entries ought to be wiped from the encyclopedia. That's ancient history. Useless stuff."

No one else on Holdham was interested in religion. Holdham was a poor cluster, one that barely clung to existence by making its organic cycle as efficient as could be. "There's no room for nonsense in Holdham," his teachers said. "If you can't count it, it isn't real. Spend your time studying Life Support. That's your religion."

But there were questions Mohr wanted answers for, questions that were only half-formed in his mind. Since no one on Holdham even thought the questions were worth asking, he applied to emigrate.

It wasn't easy to get out. The Holdham Cluster saw Mohr as an investment. Not only was his body a storehouse of valuable organics, he was the product of long schooling as a Life Support engineer. But he insisted, and they had to let him go. The laws of the Great Swarm applied to every cluster. Every person had the right to choose another cluster in the Swarm.

The Catholics were the first to take Mohr in. They paid the cost of ferrying him from the Holdham Cluster to their own. Most of the religious clusters would pay this expense, happy to have a convert.

Boursai's words were still on the screen: "You've got to adjust to this world, Gabriel."

"I have adjusted," Mohr typed. "I've adjusted to so many worlds that my head spins. I've adjusted to life on two dozen different clusters, damn it, but I still need my yellow hex!"

He felt uncomfortable having typed this much, and he hadn't revealed anything new. Boursai had already figured out this much about Mohr's past. Mohr thought of breaking the link, but then he thought of the yellow hex Boursai had taken. His only hope of getting it back was convincing Boursai of his need.

"Tell me about that," Boursai prompted.

Nosy bastard, Mohr thought. And then he thought, All right. Maybe—it wasn't likely—but maybe it would even do him some good to write about these things. Some of these things, anyway. There was a lot he would have to leave out.

"If I tell you more, will you return my hex?" he typed.

"I will do what I believe is proper."

"Hell of a guarantee," Mohr wrote, but then he continued: "All right, I'll make you see why I need what I need. And then you'll have to do the right thing."

"That is what I have promised: the right thing."

"When I was young," Mohr typed, "I did some wandering. I started with the Holy Cluster, but I didn't get what I wanted from the Catholics."

Mohr stared at that last word, thinking of the huge, ornate collection of pods and corridors and great rooms that made up the Holy Cluster.

"What were you looking for?"

"You figure it out, Boursai. Anyway, they weren't it. They weren't anything like the believers I had read about in some encyclopedia. The Catholics were so rational that they weren't godly. They weren't passionate in their beliefs. Their faith was cold and scientific, infected with technologies. It was more psychology than religion. You didn't go to confession to expiate your guilt, as I had read. No, you went to a Process Group to work out your Affective Spiritual Dissonance. God wasn't even in the loop. What mattered in atonement was not that you would make yourself at one with God, but with yourself."

"Faith is tested," came a message from Boursai, "and men speak openly of their doubts. In this way are religions transformed."

"Transformed to the point of meaninglessness," Mohr fired back. Then he froze. He looked back at what he had already written. He was putting down more than he absolutely had to, was feeling more caught up in this than was safe. He had never told his story, the whole story, to anyone. But he couldn't just end the transmission, not with his yellow hex hanging in the balance.

He could at least abbreviate what he wrote, not be so detailed. "So I left," he wrote, "and tried elsewhere. I went to the Wahabi Cluster and the Cluster of the All. I tried the Chen Buddhists, the Sikhs, the Baptists and the Bleeders and the Templars of the Void. I lived in the clusters of the Sufis and the Jews. Each time, I held out hope that the answers would be waiting for me at my next destination. Each time, I was disappointed."

"Was your soul unnourished in every place? Did you feel no rumor of God in your heart?"

It was strange that Boursai had put it that way, for that was just the thing Mohr had decided he was looking for: a rumor of God, some whisper of God's voice. A personal revelation. In the face of religions watered down by reason, he wanted direct contact with the divine. He demanded it. Yes, he wanted a rumor of God.

But what he wrote on the com-link was, "God is a lie. But I ran after that lie. I ran to the City of God. For the Citizens of God, God wasn't mere philosophy or a therapeutic tool."

Yes, in the City of God, Mohr remembered, God was still great and absolute and revered. God was God. But He was also a hoax.

Mohr wrote about the City of God haltingly. He didn't really want to remember all of this, but it was the experience that explained his addiction, that would make Boursai return that plastic bag full of oblivion. He thought for a bit, wrote a sentence, thought, and wrote a sentence more.

The first thing the Citizens of God did when he arrived was shoot him full of muscle relaxant and wheel him into surgery. They knocked him out and put a cochlear receiver in his head. All without asking him, almost before they asked him his name.

"The implant," they told him as he came out of surgery, "will teach you obedience to God." And then they taught him the catechism of the Citizens of God while he was still woozy from the drugs.

Obedience was everything to the Citizens—obedience to God's commands. The core of their doctrine was this: God summons each mortal to serve Him, but we are usually so distracted that we hardly hear His voice, and when we do hear, we are too willful to obey. Because of this, God does not call most mortals again, but consigns them to eventual oblivion.

Only those who listen carefully for God's word and prepare to obey Him without thought will know the "release of obedience," the joy of serving a divine master. And so life in the City of God was a continuous drill in servitude.

Several times a day, Mohr would hear a voice in his head, a command spoken directly into his cochlear nerve. In the morning, it would tell him where to report and what to do for the day's labor.

"That part was easy," Mohr wrote for Boursai. "What was difficult was the other half of the day, the evenings in the Hive."

The Hive was a matrix of glass-walled rooms in the hub—the weightless center of the City of God. From any room, you could see the six adjacent rooms, and other rooms beyond each of those, stretching on and on until imperfections in the glass made the farthest rooms dissolve into a milky haze.

The voice in Mohr's head would tell him at dinner where he was to report—which cell number. He would undress in his quarters and proceed naked, with all the other Citizens, to his cell. There he would find one or more other Citizens, and the voice would command him again. Sometimes he would be commanded to perform some sex act, or to float at a distance from the other Citizens in the cell, not touching them, not touching himself, while he watched couples or trios in the neighboring cells having sex. Sometimes he was commanded to beat someone. Sometimes he was beaten. Once he was told to push a needle and thread into his palm and draw the thread all the way through his hand. He did it. He'd have done anything. This was the path to God.

"Then one night," Mohr wrote, "I was ordered to beat a man with my fists. Without hesitation, I hit him in the face, time after time. He let himself be bloodied. We would drift toward one another, and then the force of my blow would send us apart. We'd push off from the walls, drift together again, and I'd hit him again. He never raised his hands to stop me. His face was swelling. His lips were split, and the air was red with droplets of blood. I could taste his blood with every breath I took, and the thought came to me that this was madness. So I left the cell. Though the man begged me to go on hitting him, to test his obedience to God, I left the cell."

The wind gusted outside and the walls of Mohr's shelter shook. The wind would stop soon with nightfall. He kept typing: "I went to the elders and I told them that I was going to leave the City of God, that I was returning to my home cluster of Holdham. But they refused me.

" 'You can't stop me,' I told them. 'The laws of the Swarm provide that I may go.'

"And they said, 'What are the laws of men compared to the will of God?' And they told me to return to the Hive, to go back and bloody that other Citizen some more."

But he didn't go back. He went to his sack in the dormitory and crawled into it. The voice inside his head ordered him back to the Hive, but he refused to get out of the sack. He no longer believed that the City of God could be the path to the divine.

"I refused. They were having none of my apostasy, though," Mohr wrote. "I was trying to escape, but there were a hundred thousand souls in the City, a hundred thousand tools for making me see that escape was impossible. So first, the implant shut up, and then the two biggest men I had ever seen came to the dormitory and beat me while I was still in my bag, beat me until I crawled out and went back to the Hive as they told me to. And in the Hive, they beat me some more. It's strange, but I felt it much more when I was taking the punishment for punishment alone, not as a step along the path to God. The blows stung as never before."

Mohr stopped for a moment to stare at what he had written. He stared long enough that Boursai queried, "Still there?"

The story was getting closer and closer in time to Tireen. Mohr realized his breathing had become fast and shallow. But if he got the hexes back, they would protect him from the memories he was getting so close to. So he continued, trying to write too fast to think about what he put down: "It wasn't just the beatings. I was used to that. But my whole life in the City changed. The voice stopped speaking to me. I didn't know what to do next, and my actions produced unpredictable results. Whatever I did, some person near me was commanded to do something to me—to give me pleasure or pain, and I would never know which to expect. I would follow the others to work, find a job to do, and try to do it, and some guy would cuff my ear one moment, then pray aloud for me the next. The woman next to me might jab my side with a tool or reach inside my body suit to fondle me. If I enjoyed what she was doing, she might continue or she might bite me. If I stayed in bed, I might get a slap or a kiss. I might be beaten or seduced. I never knew what to expect. I had no control over how people treated me. And so the sight of another human being began to sicken me with anxiety."

He stopped typing and stared at the screen. Was it helping to write these things down? No. Sister Sarah Theresa had been right. A confession had to be spoken aloud. As it was, he was just making himself feel more and more vulnerable. But he still could not turn off the com-link when he thought of what Boursai had and how much he wanted it back.

"You going to give me my hex?"

"Tell me what happened in the City of God."

"They broke me, Boursai. They broke me. When the elders had me carried to their chamber, I begged them to let the voice speak to me again, to order my life once more."

Words on the screen could not say it. They could not represent what had been done to him. For a while he stared at his hands while the wind rattled his shutters and sand hissed against the outer walls of his quarters.

"I see," prompted Boursai.

Not half of it, Mohr thought. He wrote, "People make me sick. All people. I want to be alone. All the time alone."

"But how did you escape them?" Boursai wrote.

"They let me go."

Boursai's reply was long in coming.

"But why? Wouldn't they expect you to go to the

authorities, to notify the Court of the Swarm? And haven't you done so?"

"That's my story," Mohr wrote, "or all that matters." He thought of Tireen clawing at his gloved hand, then trying to get her helmet from him. That look. The change in her face, blood boiling under her skin . . .

Writing all of this down was a stupid mistake. Mohr reached into his pocket for a hex.

"Give me my hex," he typed. "It's mine."

Boursai's reply was a question: "Did you ever hear the voice of God?"

Mohr closed his eyes, made no move to reply. When he opened his eyes, there was more from Boursai: "I ask because that is the thing I hope for," the message said. "I hope that one night, when I am on the edge of sleep, God will say to me, 'Momoudu Boursai, there is no God but God. I am He, and Mohammed is my prophet.' "

Mohr typed: "You're a fool. Give me my hex."

"So you never heard the voice of God."

Oh, but he had. He had heard the voice of God all right!

"I heard a voice in my cochlear implant. Not the usual voice. A deeper voice. I was supposed to believe it was God. It told me to go to the Live Free Cluster and make money any way I could. It told me to buy organics and ship them back to the City of God. I was to enrich the elders, all for the greater glory of God." And now he'd really had enough of this. He had told Boursai all he was going to. "Give me my hex, damn you!"

"Well," Boursai replied, "a message from an imposter does not preclude the existence of God."

Mohr felt flayed open, exposed by what he had written. He was furious with himself for letting Boursai lure him into this exchange. He pounded the keys: "Give me my hex!"

The wind was calming a little, and raindrops sounded on the corrugated roof. It was always like this: strong wind in the early afternoon, then calm, then wind again near sunset and rain at night. The weather on Onazuka's World, a planet with no axial tilt, was as reliable and monotonous as the ventilation cycles in a cluster.

Boursai: "I do not wish for you to suffer."

"My hex, damn it!"

"No matter what the elders did to you, no matter how they broke you down, you are still a human being. You still need other people. Some day, you'll have to come to terms with this."

"Bastard! Thief!"

"You will run out of them eventually. I have the bag before me, now. How long will they last? How will you possibly get more?"

"I need them! I NEED THEM!"

"I will bring them to you. And I will stay away. May you find peace, Gabriel Mohr."

Mohr took a deep breath of relief and turned off the com-link without formally logging off. Then he put his face in his hands and shook. This had been a trial. But it was worth it if Boursai would now give back his hexes and stay the hell away, as he had promised.

There were, of course, important things that he had left out of the story. He hadn't told Boursai how he had lost his voice. It had no physical cause, his speechlessness. It was his own act of defiance. If God would not speak to Mohr, Mohr would not speak to God. Or to anyone. He would turn his heart and mind to stone.

God had let him search through the clusters, let the corrupt elders break him like an animal, and still God had not whispered one syllable into Mohr's ear, had not dropped one hint, had not said simply, "I am."

The elders in the City of God seemed unsurprised by this loss of speech. Perhaps they were pleased that they had driven Mohr's voice from him. They gave him his wrist communicator.

Mohr also hadn't told Boursai about Tireen, his wife in the City of God.

Once the elders were convinced that Mohr had been thoroughly conditioned, once they were sure that he thought the new voice in his cochlear implant was truly the voice of God, they assigned him to maintaining the hull of the cluster. Perhaps one day, they told him, if God commanded it, he might be made a missionary, might leave the City of God. But for now his task was to work on the hull, to learn its construction and drill himself on how to repair it should some rare piece of debris come hurtling across the void and strike the home of God's obedient servants.

They gave him a wife, assigned Tireen to him like some cell partner for the Hive.

Mohr went to his door, opened it, and stood listening to the rain. If he'd found wind difficult to adjust to, he had found rain instantly to his liking. He stood outside and felt it fall on his head.

What would Tireen have thought of rain?

And why had he trusted Tireen? She wanted so much for him to trust her, but that should not have been enough. How did he overcome his revulsion, let her touch him? That had been a mistake, letting someone get close to him like that.

She was dangerous, this woman they had given him. She whispered things into his ear, his right ear, for she said that the implant could hear what was said in the left one. She whispered her doubts, her certainty that the City of God was a hoax, a sham that made the elders rich and enslaved the Citizens. She whispered to him her hopes of escaping, of being made missionaries and running away when they had the chance.

Sometimes he was certain that she had been assigned as his wife to trick him, to make him reveal his own doubts and longing to escape. So he did not answer the things she said to him, did not key in any reply on his wrist communicator. But if he was sometimes certain she planned to betray him, he was at other times just as certain that he could trust her, that she meant the things she whispered. But even then he would not answer her with even a glance of encouragement. He was afraid for her. He was afraid that the elders would find out that her faith was pretended, and then they would break her as they had broken him.

But, of course, the thing that had finally happened to her was far worse.

"We must pretend absolute obedience," she whispered in the darkness of their sleeping cell. "Absolute devotion."

As Mohr recalled these things, he found himself taking another yellow hex from his pocket. Hexes numbed him generally, but worked especially on his speech centers. They turned off his inner voice, separated him from memories.

No, he hadn't told Boursai about Tireen, about how he had trusted her so much that one time as he lay in her arms he found himself whispering, uttering words into her ear. He broke his promise to never speak again by telling her that he was with her, that they would escape together, that they would make a life somewhere else and never even remember the City of God. He gave her his word, his spoken word. And she gave him a conspiratorial smile.

And then, an hour later, standing in the airlock together, he looked at her and saw her otherness, saw what a stranger she was. And he was sure, as she helped him to attach his helmet, that she would betray him. She had contrived to make him speak. She would tell the elders that he was not really mute, that he was a blasphemer who spoke of defying them. And the consequences of that? They would return him to the Hive. They would try again, try harder than before, to break his will completely.

Mohr had activated the vacuum. The airlock sensors knew that Tireen's helmet wasn't attached to her suit, so he had had to hit the override, too.

And Tireen, not believing, did nothing at first. Then she was clawing at his hand on the switch, grappling for her helmet. The expression on her face, before her face was something else altogether . . . the expression of fear and bewilderment . . .

No, he hadn't told Boursai about Tireen. And he
hadn't told him, either, why he had taken a handful of
yellow hexes and cracked them open, one at a time, inhaling one after another until he could scarcely move, could
scarcely remember who he was, but still went on cracking
and inhaling. It had been because Boursai had insisted on
visiting, had returned time after time to Mohr's compound,
no matter how unwelcome Mohr tried to make him feel. It
was because Boursai talked and talked about God and the
beauty of Onazuka's World and doubt and faith and all
the things that Boursai was liable to talk about whether
you answered him or not. And Mohr had found himself
liking this man. Even as the thought of being within fifty
yards of another human being made him queasy, he found
himself liking Boursai. And he began to imagine Boursai's
face smashed in with a shovel.

Mohr cracked the hex he was holding. There was
time enough for one more memory before the hexes covered over his mental past. He remembered the first thing
he had felt when he was coming to. The overdose had
almost killed him. He had stopped breathing. And now
he remembered the feel of Boursai's breath filling his
lungs, breathing him back to life. The man's hot, wet
breath. And *that* made him reach for one more hex now
to crack between his teeth. And then one more. And then
just one more after that.

When he awoke the next morning, the bag of hex was
there on the ground outside his door.

*In a canyon of blue sandstone, a man is digging a
hole. It's a deep hole. It's a grave.*

*There's a stream flowing nearby. The water is tinted
green with algae, an indigenous species. One of the few.*

*The man digs in silence. There's the sound of the
shovel cutting the blue sand. The sound of his breathing.
But there's no birdsong. The man is not accustomed to
birdsong, anyway, but one day there will be birds in this
canyon. And soon, very soon, there will be the buzzing of*

bees, bees imported from a long way off, light-years away, brought here to pollinate the trees. But for now, silence.

At first, Mohr was afraid that Boursai would come visiting in spite of his promise to stay away. For a week, he cracked yellow hex after yellow hex as he constantly scanned the horizon, always expecting Boursai's distant silhouette. But Boursai was a man of his word. When he said he would stay away, he stayed away.

Finally, Mohr tapered off on the hexes and paid attention to his work. He had neglected the trees in his nursery too long, and some of them were dying. He worked hard to get them transplanted and to pamper them once they were in the ground. There wasn't an hour of daylight when he didn't have either his shovel in hand or the water tank on his back. It felt good to work, good to feel the weight of the shovel as he carried it here and there. He worked, in fact, like a man who cared about what he was doing. But what he truly cared about was having something to do that kept his mind from the tiny worm that was eating at his heart.

Sometimes he caught himself gazing in the direction of Boursai's compound, thinking that perhaps he could trust the man enough to tell him about Tireen, to finally poison that worm. To even speak the words aloud. But then he'd think of God, smug and distant, listening, too, to the confession, eavesdropping as Mohr bared his soul. If God existed, God would know already what Mohr had done, but he would not speak of it, not mention it aloud. And whenever Mohr thought of Boursai now, he remembered Boursai's breath filling his lungs, and he'd have to fish a hex from his pocket and crack it in his teeth.

Why did he kill Tireen? That he had suspected her of setting him up, of preparing to betray him, seemed only part of the answer. So he sometimes found himself thinking that thought when his mind was briefly clear of yellow hex. Why did he kill her?

The elders had wanted to know the same thing. Why did you kill her?

BLASPHEMER, he had keyed onto his wrist.

"Did God command you to kill her?"

He shook his head. I COULD NOT BEAR THINGS SHE SAID. LIES. BLASPHEMER

It was easier to lie in writing, much easier than saying the words aloud. And they believed what he said. They made him a missionary to Live Free Cluster, where he was to win not souls, but wealth. Any way he could, he was to earn money, to buy organics for the City of God. And he obeyed. He stole. He sold his body, repelled though he was by the bodies of others. He did whatever it took to get enough money to keep them happy and to set just a little aside. He bought yellow hex, a lot of it. And when he had enough money he paid a drunken medtech—a real surgeon was beyond his means—to fish out the cochlear implant with a stimwire. That finally shut up the day-and-night whisperings of the false God in his ear. It was when he was healing from this, unsure if his hearing would return, that the Planters Corps recruiter had found him.

As Boursai continued to stay away, Mohr's life returned to the comfortable rhythm he had known before. He concentrated on getting his trees into the ground and on listening for the hum of the ground skimmer that came to resupply his nursery. If he could, he would make for the cliffs and hide himself in the canyons until the skimmer crew had unloaded the trees and resupplied his larder. But if he was too far from the canyons, or if the skimmer surprised him, he would have to endure the conversation, the questions of the crew while he worked alongside them to speed their departure. They would ask him again why they could never reach him on his com-link, and he would key a sentence or two onto his wrist about how the com-link had been down, but he had managed to fix it himself. Or he would say that he had just forgotten to turn it on. And on almost every visit, one of the crew members would ask, "How do you stand it out here? Don't you get lonely?"

Mercifully, such visits were rare, and Mohr could always count on the crew's being in a hurry to finish the day's run and get back to Onazuka City with its closed-in spaces full of people.

Alone again at dusk, he could listen to the rain falling on his metal roof, crack a hex, and drift into silence. No people. No memories. No worm gnawing at his heart.

Then one morning, as he was digging a hole, Mohr heard his name in the still air: "Gabriel!" He looked up to see Boursai striding toward him like some impossibly tall bird, hallooing from the shimmery distance and waving his hand.

Mohr felt in his pocket for a hex.

"I'm sorry," Boursai called out as he drew near. "I'm sorry, Gabriel, but I had to come. There's something I have to tell you about, something I must show you."

Mohr spit the empty yellow shell onto the ground. He held the shovel between himself and Boursai, and he tried to look as unwelcoming as he could.

"If I had a choice, Gabriel, I would stay away. But someone has to know about this. And who else can I tell? Who else can I trust?" Boursai was gesturing wildly as he spoke. Mohr had never seen him in any state but calm and peaceful. Now Boursai moved his arms like some excited stork in a windstorm.

So Mohr keyed the word WHAT? onto his wrist, and Boursai stepped close enough to read it.

"You must come with me. Come, and I'll show you."

Boursai was already turning to lead him away, back in the direction of Boursai's compound. Mohr looked at the hole he was digging, at the sapling that needed to go into the ground. Then at his own compound of squatty buildings.

Boursai wasn't waiting for him, nor looking back.

Hell, he thought. He cracked a second hex, breathed in through his teeth, and then ran on his drugged, rubbery legs to catch up. He brought along his shovel. He was so used to having it in his hand that he didn't think of leaving it behind.

It was an hour and a half to Boursai's compound, and they didn't stop there. Boursai kept leading him on toward the cliffs to the west, cliffs much like the ones near Mohr's own compound. There were canyons here, too, Mohr discovered, and Boursai led him into one of these.

What Boursai wanted to show him was a spring, a six-foot depression in the blue rock. It was ringed with moss that Boursai himself must have planted.

Mohr made a gesture that said something between, "This is it?" and "So what?"

"Look down into it," said Boursai. "Look carefully."

Mohr bent closer to the water. All he could see was a scattering of blue stones at the bottom of the water. What did Boursai expect him to see?

One of the stones moved. Mohr squinted, looked closer.

Again something moved, but now Mohr could see that it wasn't a stone. Mixed in among the stones, blue like the surrounding rock, were a few tentacles or worms of some sort.

"Indigenous life form," Boursai said excitedly, as if he had invented the thing and not merely discovered it.

Mohr nodded slowly and keyed in, so? It was meant to stand for many things: So what? So why bother me about it? So why not just radio it in if it's such a big deal?

"I had to show it to you," Boursai said, "because if I told anyone else, they might try to stop my little experiment." He began to unbutton his fatigues at the collar. "I drank water from this spring before I saw there was something living on the bottom, you see."

He opened his shirt.

Mohr almost spoke. He almost said, "Name of God." Instead, he only mouthed the words and keyed in, WHAT?

"I don't know what it is," Boursai answered. He touched the thick, raised welt that stretched across his chest, and something beneath his skin twitched and wriggled. "But whatever it is, it's growing. See this?" He traced what looked like a vein that went from one end of the welt, up his neck, and on to the place where his jaw joined his skull. There it stopped. There was another such vein or filament on the other side of his neck.

Mohr felt his stomach twist, and he dug deep in his pocket for another hex. Cracking it, he keyed in: GO TO ONAZUKA CITY. GET IT OUT!

Boursai read the message and said, "No."

DISEASE! Mohr keyed in. PARASITE!

"No," Boursai said softly. "It's nothing like that. I feel calm, Gabriel, more calm than you can imagine. It's as though . . . Gabriel, it's as though God has touched my mind to tell me to trust this, that this is meant to be."

CALM, Mohr punched out, BECAUSE DRUGGING YOU. COMMON IN PARASITES. STRATEGY. PRODUCE TOXINS TO DRUG HOST, BLOCK FEAR, STOP PAIN.

Boursai said, "Perhaps you are right. But then you must look at it this way: What are the chances that a parasite would evolve on this world with a chemistry compatible with mine? Our species evolved light-years from one another, beyond contact or influence, so how could we be compatible? How, without the mediation of God?"

MADNESS, Mohr wrote. YOURE TAKING TOO BIG RISK.

"It's a miracle, Gabriel. So I'll wait to see what develops. I'll be all right, if that is the will of God. Whatever God wills."

WHYD YOU BRING ME HERE? WHYD YOU SHOW ME THIS?

"Why didn't I just use the com-link or write this down in my log? So that someone else has seen the spring. So that there is a witness in case . . . in case it is the will of God that I should die. And also, Gabriel, I had to tell someone. I just had to speak of it. Can a man make a secret of something like this? Can he carry something like this only in his heart? I had to tell someone."

GO ONAZUKA CITY. GET HELP. Mohr gestured as though he were tearing the thing from his own chest and flinging it away. Then he keyed in, DIDNT HAVE TO SHOW ME. DAMN YOU! He let Boursai read this last message, but then picked up his shovel and turned before the man could reply and started to walk out of the canyon.

Damn Boursai. Damn him! he thought. Boursai had given him the burden of a secret, and, damn it, he felt as he had with Tireen, knowing about the things she whispered to him, the blasphemies that were dangerous to both of them. But this was dangerous only to Boursai himself. No, that made no difference. It was an unfair burden. He didn't want Boursai to die. In spite of everything, his longing to be utterly alone, he didn't want Boursai to die. Not like this. Not with some foul parasite eating away at his flesh. . . .

Stop it! he commanded his inner voice. *Shut up!* And he took two yellow hexes from his pocket and cracked them both at the same time.

It was past noon when he got back to his own complex. He went out to where he had been planting the tree, but he just stood looking at the hole, the tree, and then the small, white sun overhead. A breeze tousled his hair. Before long, it would be a wind, and he would want shelter from it. He worked some more on the hole, dug it deeper than it needed to be and put the tree into it. While he packed the sandy soil around the roots, he tried to concentrate on what he was doing, tried not to think.

But it was no good. Thoughts of Boursai, pictures of what he might look like when the thing in his chest was finished with him, kept creeping into his mind. *Damn him!* He threw the shovel to the ground and walked away, leaving the tree only half planted, exposed to the wind. It didn't matter. He didn't care.

God damn that man!

Back in his quarters, he emptied the hexes from all his hidden stashes into the one bag. That at least made his supply look a little bigger. And then he put two more hexes between his teeth. He would shut up the voice inside his head if it took a dozen.

• • •

The next day was a little better. He was able to work, at least. But he found himself looking again and again toward Boursai's compound. He was afraid, his guts knotted with fear.

It was like the fear he'd once felt for Tireen.

And damn Boursai once more! Why, when he thought of that man, was he endlessly thinking of Tireen?

What would happen to Boursai? How large would the thing in his breast grow to be?

Dig like a machine, Mohr told himself. *Dig. Don't think. Just dig.*

All day he was like that. And the next day, and the day after. He would think of Boursai and of Tireen and he would tell himself to work harder, always harder, until his back ached and his arms shook with fatigue. But he could not resist at some point reaching for a yellow hex, and the first one made it easier to reach for the second.

Finally, he felt he must act. He must do *something*.

He picked up his shovel and set out for Boursai's compound. What he would do when he got there, he was not sure. Was he only going to see that Boursai was all right? Or to tell Boursai about Tireen, to burden Boursai as Boursai had burdened him? He didn't know. He just had to go. He shouldered the shovel and walked.

Boursai was not there.

Mohr walked twice around the compound, gingerly opening the doors of the nursery and of Boursai's living quarters. He was not there. Not in the toolshed, not anywhere in sight among the saplings that dotted the land.

He looked toward the canyon mouths that opened in the cliffs. He thought of the spring. Boursai would be there, perhaps, next to the water with the writhing blue things. Doing what? What would Mohr see if he went that way?

Mohr shuddered, imagining Boursai's body covered with twitching welts that hatched, releasing blue worms that wriggled their way back to the water. Or worse. It could be even worse than that, and Boursai would be smiling, drugged by the worms into feeling fine. *Whatever God wills*. What a mistake Boursai was making, to trust the will of God, to trust that *thing* inside his body. To trust anyone or anything at all.

Boursai was going to die. The thing would kill him. That was what came of trusting.

Mohr ran, still carrying the shovel, toward the spring. When he could no longer run, he loped until he could run again. He had brought no water with him. His throat seemed to swell with thirst, but still he hurried on to the mouth of the canyon, into the blue shadows, toward the spring.

When he rounded the corner where he thought the spring was, he thought he saw Boursai stretched out on the ground, covered all over with blue worms. And he called out, "Boursai!" His voice cracked. "Momoudu!" The sound of his voice echoed back from the canyon walls.

Then he saw that it was not Boursai at all, but only a pile of stones colored a little darker than the ones around them. This was not where the spring was. He had to go farther up the canyon.

He wiped the sweat from his forehead and went on. When he found the spring, Boursai was not there.

Mohr sat to catch his breath. He looked at the waters of the spring. Two words he had called out, the two words of Boursai's name, and his throat was hoarse from shouting. And his throat felt thick with thirst, too, but he would not drink here. Nor from the stream below. He would rather die of thirst.

The blue tentacles waved in the basin of the spring.

Mohr shuddered. He looked around one more time for Boursai, and then he went home.

Eventually, it was Boursai who came to him. It happened late at night, after the winds had died and the rain was only starting. Boursai's voice startled him out of sleep.

"Gabriel," it said again as he lay in the dark, listening. The rain tapped lightly on his roof.

Mohr went to the door without turning on the lights. Boursai was standing away from the buildings, silhouetted against the stars that shone through a break in the clouds.

"I bring you news of paradise," said Boursai. He stood too far away to read Mohr's wrist communicator, so Mohr just stood silently, waiting for whatever came next.

The rain continued to fall, tapping on the metal roof and whispering on the ground. The two men stood for a long time in the darkness, listening.

"It is the end of loneliness, this thing I carry in me," Boursai went on. "And you are lonely, aren't you, Gabriel?"

Again there was only the sound of the rain. Boursai lowered himself to the ground. "I hear the voice of a god, now," Boursai said. "Not Allah, not the all-powerful, all-knowing, but an eternal voice. A wise voice. I am never without it." And then he told the story of what the thing in his chest had become.

It was not long after Mohr had come and seen the spring that Boursai began to feel lightheaded and a little ill. Still, he was confident that he had made the proper choice to let the parasite, or whatever it was, continue to grow. In spite of his physical queasiness, he still felt that things were as they were meant to be, that however things turned out, it was the will of God.

The welt was growing thicker by the day, and so were the cords that ran up the sides of his neck. Sometimes Boursai would touch them and feel them throbbing with a pulse that was not his own.

Then one night, he woke with the feeling that someone was watching him. It was no mere uneasiness. This was an almost physical sensation, a certainty that there was another presence with him in the room. In a panic, Boursai switched on the light.

There was no one else in the room, of course. The light shone brightly into every corner, onto the secure latches of the shutters and the door. But even as he assured himself that there was no one else in his quarters, the sensation of being watched did not go away. If anything, it intensified. Was there someone or something outside, peering through a crack in the shutters? No, it was closer than that. There was another being quite near. Inside this room, inside this . . .

Then it dawned on him. Inside his body. There was another mind with him, inside his head.

And with a certainty that defied explanation, Boursai understood that the second mind in his body was discovering the same thing he was: *There is another here. I am supposed to be alone, but there is another.*

Following that thought came this one: *We must go to the water.*

Which meant, of course, the spring.

"So that is what I did, Gabriel. I went to the spring, and the voice inside my head told me to drink. Not by cupping my hands and drawing the water up, but by putting my mouth into the water, drinking like an animal. And when I did this, the thing that was inside me emerged part way—"

Mohr stiffened at those words. *How?* he wondered. *Where did it come out?*

"—and it stretched itself into the water, and the being in the spring reached up to meet it. They touched. They knotted around one another, and they spoke without sound. It was a chemical exchange, I think, one brain trading information with another, and it lasted a long time. I could not rise . . . without pain."

The clouds had closed behind Boursai, so that Mohr could no longer see even his silhouette. He was just a voice floating in the darkness.

"Perhaps I am making you afraid," Boursai said. "You must understand. This is a miracle, a blessing."

And he went on to tell Mohr about the thing that lived in the spring. The blue tentacles were only a small part of it, the tongue-tip of an enormous creature with many mouths, many tongue-tips stretching out to taste the world.

Deep below the rock was the main part of its body, winding through the underwater passages of Onazuka's World. From springs here and there, its tentacles emerged to feed, to reproduce, and to communicate. But the being consisted mostly of neurons. It was a huge, everlasting mind, and it had been the source of all animal intelligence on the planet before the cataclysm of the meteor.

"The part of it that lives in my breast," Boursai said, "is like a remote unit. It has a mind of its own, this thing inside of me, a mind as complex as mine. But when I drank at the spring, it drew upon the intelligence, the knowledge of the greater being beneath the ground. What the greater mind knows, the smaller mind may know by touching it. And so it received an education, this thing inside of me, while I drank at the spring."

The rain fell a little harder now, and the sound of it on the roof was not so gentle.

PARASITE, Mohr keyed in, but Boursai could not see the glowing letters.

"I carry with me the experiences of a thousand generations," Boursai said. "What each individual mind learns in its life, the great mind receives and remembers."

Again Mohr thought of the thing emerging somehow from Boursai. Any way that he pictured that happening, it sickened him.

"It thought I was just an animal, Gabriel. It sought to give me a mind, to give me intelligence and direction. But since I already have my own mind, my own volition, it does not struggle with me. It does not command. It asks. It wants me to bring food to the spring, wants me to feed the greater one, which has hungered so long."

WANTS TO ENSLAVE YOU, Mohr keyed in.

"No it doesn't," Boursai said. He had moved close enough to read the communicator. The hair rose on Mohr's neck.

"I control my body," Boursai went on. "We are two minds in one body. This being is my partner, my companion. Not my master."

Mohr tapped a message out: WHY DO YOU COME AT NIGHT?

"Gabriel," answered the voice in the darkness, "this is a miracle. My companion shares my body, shares my life. It knows the wisdom of the ages. Inside my body with me, how can it be my enemy? How can it be anything but a brother to me, a closer brother than any man can be? When it speaks, I feel as though God speaks to me. And I am like the prophet, receiving the holy word, opening my heart."

Again: WHY DO YOU COME AT NIGHT?

"I know it is not truly the voice of God, but this thing stands in God's place. Perhaps God speaks to me through it, in some fashion. I am at peace, Gabriel. For me there is no loneliness." Boursai's voice was much nearer now. "Gabriel, there is an end to your fear. There is release from suffering. Come to the spring with me. Come drink at the spring."

STAY AWAY! Mohr keyed in.

But the voice came even closer, softened to a whisper in his ear, his right ear, so that he remembered the sound of Tireen's whisper. "All men are brothers," Boursai said, "and how much more deeply they may come to know this! Gabriel, I would see you healed!"

For a moment, Mohr was frozen with the memory of Tireen. Then he shook himself and stumbled backward through his door. He turned and made for the light switch by his cot. He tripped, went sprawling.

"I mean you no harm," said the voice outside. "It is up to you, Gabriel. You must choose what you will."

Mohr switched on the lights inside and out. Then he rummaged through his footlocker until he found the hand torch. He went to the doorway, but Boursai was not within the glare of the compound lights. He walked to the edge of the compound and flipped the torch to life. The powerful beam cut through the intensifying rain as he swept it over the flat ground beyond the compound lights. Left, right, in every direction he cast the beam, there was no sign of Boursai.

Mohr walked the perimeter of the compound twice to make sure, directing the light into the shadows of his buildings, then out into the surrounding dark. Boursai was gone.

He went in, took a yellow hex from the bag, and stood looking at it for a moment, reminding himself that he had a choice. He always had the choice of not using. And they were almost gone now. The bag that had looked like an endless supply was almost empty. Maybe, he thought, he should start to ration them. Then he set the shell between his teeth and bit down.

For the rest of that night, Mohr did not sleep. He went from shutter to shutter, to the door and back to the shutters, checking the latches. Now and then, he cracked another hex.

He needed to do something, but he didn't know what it was. He tried to think about it, tried to decide, while he was in a nonverbal stupor, a haze of yellow hex. As his supply grew smaller and smaller, he grew more and more desperate. But he still didn't know what to do. He tried cutting back on hex, but then there were all of these thoughts and memories flooding in.

He thought of Tireen. He kept seeing his gloved hand on the airlock switch, on the override.

He thought of Boursai, who really did believe that this was a miracle, the thing that had happened to him. And maybe it was. Maybe having that thing living inside your chest, stretching its tendrils into your brain, maybe that was as close as you could ever come to communing with God.

He thought of the worm gnawing at his heart. It twisted and turned inside of him, and he needed to confess, to finally tell someone, anyone, about Tireen. Boursai. He could tell Boursai.

Then he remembered the sensation of Boursai's breath filling his lungs. The hot moisture of Boursai's lips. He remembered how, coming to, he had turned away from Boursai, felt the sandy floor on his cheek, and vomited.

He thought of what it would be like to never be alone again. *Never.*

Thinking these things drove him back to the yellow hexes. He took the last four, and they washed the words from his head. And in that wordless haze, he acted. He shouldered his shovel and walked to Boursai's compound.

Boursai saw him coming from a distance, and he disappeared into his quarters. When Mohr arrived, Boursai had wrapped a cloth about his face so that only his eyes showed. It was afternoon. The wind was blowing and sand was in the air.

"Do you want to come with me to the spring?" Boursai asked.

Mohr nodded.

"Why don't you leave your shovel here?" Boursai said.

Mohr put it down, but felt strange without it. He picked it up again.

"Too used to carrying it?" Boursai said. Mohr could hear the smile in his voice. "Very well. Come."

They walked wordlessly to the spring, but all the time they walked, there was some thought, some urge that was swimming up through Mohr's mind, trying to rise through the fog of yellow hex. There was something he wanted to say, something he wanted to speak aloud. He was grateful for the hex. It kept the words down. At the same time, he could feel it beginning to wear off.

When they arrived, Boursai knelt and gazed into the water. Mohr leaned on his shovel and did the same, peering over Boursai's shoulder. Boursai took a bundle from inside his clothes and unwrapped it. It was grass seed. With a stone and water from the spring, Boursai pounded the seeds into a mealy mass which he then dropped into the water. The blue tentacles squirmed, wrapped around the coarse dough, and disappeared into the depths of the spring.

"I have so little to give it," Boursai said. "It is hungry.

It has had only itself to feed on, eating its own great body, swallowing some of its memories, its wisdom as it did so." He stared into the water where the tentacles were now reemerging. Then, almost whispering, he said, "Go on, Gabriel. Drink."

Mohr shook his head.

"I thought you came to drink."

Again, Mohr shook his head. A word formed on his lips. A name. *Tireen.* But he made no sound.

"What is it?" said Boursai. "Something is wrong, isn't it?"

Mohr's hands were shaking. The fog of yellow hex was lifting.

"It's the drug, isn't it?" said Boursai. "You've run out."

Mohr nodded.

"We'll talk," Boursai said. "We'll go back to my compound and you can use my com-link. But first . . ." He looked at the spring and began to unwind the cloth from his face. For a moment, however, he paused. "There is a price one must pay for this miracle," he said. He let the last of the cloth drop.

There were slits beneath his eyes, jagged-edged openings with something wet and blue shining from inside.

He dropped the cloth at the edge of the spring. "It is a small price to pay, Gabriel." And he bent toward the water. Blue tendrils slithered from beneath his eyes like snakes, and the tentacles in the water twisted upward to meet them.

"Tireen," Mohr said aloud. Boursai jerked with surprise at the sound of his voice, but he couldn't rise. The tentacles held him in place, and they seemed to keep him from speaking, too.

"There's something . . ." Mohr said. His voice was thick. His whole body was shaking now. The yellow hex had worn off completely. "There's something I . . ."

He felt sick. It was hard to breathe. And how could he say it, what words could he use? "I . . . Tireen . . ." With both hands he raised the shovel, shaking with frustration. "A thing I did. Didn't mean to . . ." He shut his eyes and felt himself bring the blade down hard on Boursai's neck. Once. Twice. Again and again. He opened his eyes, but kept raising the shovel and bringing it down.

Boursai pulled free of the tentacles for a moment, and the next blow caught him in the face. And the next one.

Mohr didn't stop for a long time. When he did, he said, "Tireen," in an impossibly high voice. He bit his lip and squeezed his eyes shut. It didn't matter what he said now. There was no one to hear him.

There was a tree growing not far up the canyon, a tree that Boursai had planted himself. At its base, Mohr began to dig.

In a canyon of blue sandstone, a man is digging a hole. It's a deep hole, long and narrow. It could hardly be anything other than a grave.

There's a stream flowing nearby. The sky is tinted orange with dust, the color of the setting sun. The wind is blowing hard up there. But down here in the canyon, at the base of these high blue walls, the air hardly stirs.

There is no sound but the soft snick *of the shovel cutting through the sand.*

When the hole is long enough, and wide enough, and deep, the man goes to where the body is. The dead man is tall, his skin black except where it is marked with blood. On his battered face are two slits beneath his eyes, and two blue tentacles stretch up from these, twisting and turning in the air. The man raises the shovel and lets it fall again, but the blue worms still twist, still reach for something they can't find in the air.

The man leans on the shovel and is sick.

Why, he wondered as he pulled Boursai into the hole. Why?

Even with his wounds, even with the blue things still

waving beneath his eyes, Boursai was beautiful. Why had Mohr killed him?

How could Boursai be dead?

It was the yellow hex, he thought as he shoveled.

No, it was seeing him with those parasites in his face, seeing him reduced to a slave, to an animal.

Or was it the blue tentacles he wanted to kill, the things that had taken Boursai over?

He filled the trench and scattered the pile of sand that remained. Walking home, he absently reached into his breast pocket, but of course there was nothing there.

His hands shook for a few days, and he sometimes found himself looking in the places where he remembered hiding an extra hex or two even though he had already looked there two or three times before. But that anxiety, that nervous searching, was all that he suffered with the withdrawal. There were no convulsions, no hallucinations, no headaches.

He didn't sleep, but that had another cause. Sister Sarah Theresa's worm of guilt kept him awake, gnawing at his heart.

No. Not one worm. Two.

He would lie awake and think of three things: the airlock, the sound of Boursai's gentle voice, and the thing that still lived in the spring, that abomination, that horror.

To never be alone again, what could be worse than that?

Days passed. Mohr cared for his trees as if in a trance. As he worked, Boursai's face would float into his awareness. Or Tireen's face.

When Mohr slept, it was fitfully. He would wake to hear the sound of Tireen or Boursai whispering into his ear, then would realize it was only the rain.

He hardly ate. Sometimes he would stand under the sun and stare for an hour at the blue cliffs, and finally he began to understand.

He had spoken to each of them. Then he killed. He

had broken his pledge to seal his heart from God and from all others.

If he hadn't killed them, who knows what might have come flooding out of his soul? All his fear. All his loneliness. All his longing for God, a God who had sealed His heart against him. Mohr was not worthy of even a divine whisper.

He longed to speak of these things. If only he could tell someone what he had done, and why. He would stand before the com-link an hour at a time, hand trembling on the switch. Then he'd go outside to stare at the blue cliffs, kick at the dust, chew his lip for a while before he returned to hold his hand above the com-link again.

He stopped caring for the trees and they wilted in his nursery, shriveled under the white sun of Onazuka's World.

If he wrote it down, if he transmitted his confession, what would they do? They would try to help him. They would put him somewhere to watch him, to change him, somewhere close to lots of other people. Bodies all around. Other men breathing the air that he was breathing.

Another man's breath filling his lungs.

The airlock switch.

Boursai lying alongside the trench, eyes half closed and the thing in his chest still throbbing with life.

The twin worms eating at Mohr's heart, digging, burrowing, poisoning his blood.

"When you confess," said Sister Sarah Theresa, "you are poisoning that worm with truth."

He looked one more time, turned the compound inside out. There were no forgotten hiding places, no last stash of yellow hex.

So one afternoon he walked to Boursai's compound, and from there to the spring. He watched the repulsive twisting under the surface. Then he bent toward the water.

It was weeks later that he was lying on his cot, tracing the welt on his chest with his finger. He felt a presence.

Some shadow sat at the edge of his mind, looking in on him. He could feel that it was surprised to see him here, astonished to find his head already occupied.

Mohr shuddered. But he tried to ignore the coldness in his gut, the feeling of being flayed open, hopelessly exposed.

It wasn't words that he heard then, but the thought came to him so clearly that it might as well have been spoken. It was an urge, an insistence: We must go back to the water.

The thing inside of him would know his thoughts whether he voiced them or not, but Mohr answered aloud. "I know," he said. His throat felt thick. He did not like the sound of his voice. He coughed and spoke again, "Back to the water. Yes, I know." He felt ill, but he fought the feeling.

The airlock. The shovel.

"But first," Mohr said, "there is something I have to tell you."

The Erl-King

Elizabeth Hand

THE KINKAJOU HAD BEEN MISSING FOR TWO DAYS NOW. Haley feared it was dead, killed by one of the neighborhood dogs or by a fox or wildcat in the woods. Linette was certain it was alive; she even knew where it was.

"Kingdom Come," she announced, pointing a long lazy hand in the direction of the neighboring estate. She dropped her hand and sipped at a mug of tepid tea, twisting so she wouldn't spill it as she rocked back and forth. It was Linette's turn to lie in the hammock. She did so with feckless grace, legs tangled in her long peasant skirt, dark hair spilled across the faded canvas. She had more practice at it than Haley, this being Linette's house and Linette's overgrown yard bordering the woods of spindly young pines and birches that separated them from Kingdom Come. Haley frowned, leaned against the oak tree, and pushed her friend desultorily with one foot.

"Then why doesn't your mother call them or something?" Haley loved the kinkajou and justifiably feared the worst. With her friend exotic pets came and went, just as did odd visitors to the tumbledown cottage where Linette lived with her mother, Aurora. Most of the animals were presents from Linette's father, an elderly Broadway producer whose successes paid for the rented cottage and Linette's occasional artistic endeavors (flute lessons, sitar lessons, an incomplete course in airbrushing) as well as the bottles of Tanqueray that lined Aurora's bedroom. And, of course, the animals. An iguana whose skin peeled like mildewed wallpaper, finally lost (and never found) in the drafty dark basement where the girls held annual Hallowe'en seances. An intimidatingly large Moluccan cockatoo that escaped into the trees, terrorizing Kingdom Come's previous owner and his garden-party guests by shrieking at them in Gaelic from the wisteria. Finches and fire weavers small enough to hold in your fist. A quartet of tiny goats, Haley's favorites until the kinkajou.

The cockatoo started to smell worse and worse, until one day it flopped to the bottom of its wrought-iron cage and died. The finches escaped when Linette left the door to their bamboo cage open. The goats ran off into the woods surrounding Lake Muscanth. They were rumored to be living there still. But this summer Haley had come over every day to make certain the kinkajou had enough to eat, that Linette's cats weren't terrorizing it; that Aurora didn't try to feed it crème de menthe as she had the capuchin monkey that had fleetingly resided in her room.

"I don't know," Linette said. She shut her eyes, balancing her mug on her stomach. A drop of tea spilled onto her cotton blouse, another faint petal among faded ink stains and the ghostly impression of eyes left by an abortive attempt at batik. "I think Mom knows the guy who lives there now, she doesn't like him or something. I'll ask my father next time."

Haley prodded the hammock with the toe of her sneaker. "It's almost my turn. Then we should go over there. It'll die if it gets cold at night."

Linette smiled without opening her eyes. "Nah. It's still summer," she said, and yawned.

Haley frowned. She moved her back up and down against the bole of the oak tree, scratching where a scab had formed after their outing to Mandrake Island to look for the goats. It was early August, nearing the end of their last summer before starting high school, the time Aurora had named "the summer before the dark."

"My poor little girls," Aurora had mourned a few months earlier. It had been only June then, the days still cool enough that the City's wealthy fled each weekend to Kamensic Village to hide among the woods and wetlands in their Victorian follies. Aurora was perched with Haley and Linette on an ivied slope above the road, watching the southbound Sunday exodus of limousines and Porsches and Mercedes. "Soon you'll be gone."

"Jeez, Mom," laughed Linette. A plume of ivy tethered her long hair back from her face. Aurora reached to tug it with one unsteady hand. The other clasped a plastic cup full of gin. "No one's going anywhere, I'm going to Fox Lane,"—that was the public high school—"you heard what Dad said. Right, Haley?"

Haley had nodded and stroked the kinkajou sleeping in her lap. It never did anything but sleep, or open its golden eyes to half-wakefulness oh so briefly before finding another lap or cushion to curl into. It reminded her of Linette in that, her friend's heavy lazy eyes always ready to shut, her legs quick to curl around pillows or hammock cushions or Haley's own battle-scarred knees. "Right," said Haley, and she had cupped her palm around the soft warm globe of the kinkajou's head.

Now the hammock creaked noisily as Linette turned onto her stomach, dropping her mug into the long grass. Haley started, looked down to see her hands hollowed as though holding something. If the kinkajou died she'd never speak to Linette again. Her heart beat faster at the thought.

"I think we should go over. If you think it's there. *And*—" Haley grabbed the ropes restraining the hammock, yanked them back and forth so that Linette shrieked, her hair caught between hempen braids—"it's—*my*—turn—*now*."

They snuck out that night. The sky had turned pale green, the same shade as the crystal globe wherein three ivory-bellied frogs floated, atop a crippled table. To keep the table from falling Haley had propped a broom handle beneath it for a fourth leg—although she hated the frogs, bloated things with prescient yellow eyes. Some nights when she slept over they broke her sleep with their song, high-pitched trilling that disturbed neither Linette snoring in the other bed nor Aurora drinking broodingly in her tiny shed-roofed wing of the cottage. It was uncanny, almost frightening sometimes, how nothing ever disturbed them: not dying pets nor utilities cut off for lack of payment nor unexpected visits from Aurora's small circle of friends, People from the Factory Days she called them. Rejuvenated junkies or pop stars with new careers, or wasted beauties like Aurora Dawn herself. All of them seemingly forever banned from the real world, the adult world Haley's parents and family inhabited, magically free as Linette herself was to sample odd-tasting liqueurs and curious religious notions and lost arts in their dank corners of the City or the shelter of some wealthier friend's up-county retreat. Sleepy-eyed from dope or taut from amphetamines, they lay around the cottage with Haley and Linette, offering sips of their drinks, advice about popular musicians and contraceptives. Their hair was streaked with gray now, or dyed garish mauve or blue or green. They wore high leather boots and clothes inlaid with feathers or mirrors, and had names that sounded like the names of expensive perfumes: Liatris, Coppelia, Electric Velvet. Sometimes Haley felt that she had wandered into a fairy tale, or a movie. *Beauty and the Beast* perhaps, or *The Dark Crystal*. Of course it would be one of Linette's favorites; Linette had more imagination and sensitivity than Haley. The kind of movie Haley would choose to wander into would have fast cars and gunshots in the distance, not aging refugees from another decade passed out next to the fireplace.

She thought of that now, passing the globe of frogs. They went from the eerie interior dusk of the cottage into the strangely aqueous air outside. Despite the warmth of the late summer evening Haley shivered as she gazed back at the cottage. The tiny bungalow might have stood there unchanged for five hundred years, for a thousand. No warm yellow light spilled from the windows as it did at her own house. There was no smell of dinner cooking, no television chattering. Aurora seldom cooked, Linette never. There was no TV. Only the frogs hovering in their silver world, and the faintest cusp of a new moon like a leaf cast upon the surface of the sky.

The main house of the neighboring estate stood upon a broad slope of lawn overlooking the woods. Massive oaks and sycamores studded the grounds, and formal gardens that had been more carefully tended by the mansion's previous owner, a New York fashion designer recently dead. At the foot of the long drive a post bore the placard on which was writ in spidery silver letters KINGDOM COME.

In an upstairs room Lie Vagal perched upon a windowsill. He stared out at the same young moon that watched Haley and Linette as they made their way through the woods. Had Lie known where to look he might have seen them as well; but he was watching the kinkajou sleeping in his lap.

It had appeared at breakfast two days earlier. Lie sat with his grandmother on the south terrace, eating Froot Loops and reading the morning mail, *The Wall Street Journal* and a quarterly royalty statement from BMI. His grandmother stared balefully into a bowl of bran flakes, as though discerning there unpleasant intimations of the future.

"Did you take your medicine, Gram?" asked Lie. A leaf fell from an overhanging branch into his coffee cup.

He fished it out before Gram could see it as another dire portent.

"Did you take yours, Elijah?" snapped Gram. She finished the bran flakes and reached for her own coffee, black and laced with chicory. She was eighty-four years old and had outlived all of her other relatives and many of Lie's friends. "I know you didn't yesterday."

Lie shrugged. Another leaf dropped to the table, followed by a hail of bark and twigs. He peered up into the greenery, then pointed.

"Look," he said. "A squirrel or cat or something."

His grandmother squinted, shaking her head peevishly. "I can't see a thing."

The shaking branches parted to show something brown attached to a slender limb. Honey-colored, too big for a squirrel, it clung to a branch that dipped lower and lower, spattering them with more debris. Lie moved his coffee cup and had started to his feet when it fell, landing on top of the latest issue of *New Musical Express*.

For a moment he thought the fall had killed it. It just lay there, legs and long tail curled as though it had been a doodlebug playing dead. Then slowly it opened its eyes, regarded him with a muzzy golden gaze, and yawned, unfurling a tongue so brightly pink it might have been lipsticked. Lie laughed.

"It fell asleep in the tree! It's a—a what-you-call-it, a sloth."

His grandmother shook her head, pushing her glasses onto her nose. "That's not a sloth. They have grass growing on them."

Lie stretched a finger and tentatively stroked its tail. The animal ignored him, closing its eyes once more and folding its paws upon its glossy breast. Around its neck someone had placed a collar, the sort of leather-and-rhinestone ornament old ladies deployed on poodles. Gingerly Lie turned it, until he found a small heart-shaped tab of metal.

KINKAJOU
My name is Valentine
764-0007

"Huh," he said. "I'll be damned. I bet it belongs to those girls next door." Gram sniffed and collected the plates. Next to Lie's coffee mug, the compartmented container holding a week's worth of his medication was still full.

The animal did nothing but sleep and eat. Lie called a pet store in the City and learned that kinkajous ate insects and honey and bananas. He fed it Froot Loops, yogurt and granola, a moth he caught one evening in the bedroom. Tonight it slept once more, and he stroked it, murmuring to himself. He still hadn't called the number on the collar.

From here he could just make out the cottage, a white blur through dark leaves and tangled brush. It was his cottage, really; a long time ago the estate gardener had lived there. The fashion designer had been friends with the present tenant in the City long ago. For the last fourteen years the place had been leased to Aurora Dawn. When he'd learned that, Lie Vagal had given a short laugh, one that the realtor had mistaken for displeasure.

"We could evict her," she'd said anxiously. "Really, she's no trouble, just the town drunk, but once you'd taken possession—"

"I wouldn't *dream* of it." Lie laughed again, shaking his head but not explaining. "Imagine, having Aurora Dawn for a neighbor again. . . ."

His accountant had suggested selling the cottage, it would be worth a small fortune now, or else turning it into a studio or guest house. But Lie knew that the truth was, his accountant didn't want Lie to start hanging around with Aurora again. Trouble; all the survivors from those days were trouble.

That might have been why Lie didn't call the number on the collar. He hadn't seen Aurora in fifteen years, although he had often glimpsed the girls playing in the woods. More than once he'd started to go meet them, introduce himself, bring them back to the house. He was lonely here. The visitors who still showed up at Aurora's door at four A.M. used to bang around Lie's place in the City. But that was long ago, before what Lie thought of as The Crash and what *Rolling Stone* had termed "the long tragic slide into madness of the one-time *force majeur* of underground rock and roll." And his agent and his lawyer wouldn't think much of him luring children to his woodland lair.

He sighed. Sensing some shift in the summer air, his melancholy perhaps, the sleeping kinkajou sighed as well, and trembled where it lay curled between his thighs. Lie lifted his head to gaze out the open window.

Outside the night lay still and deep over woods and lawns and the little dreaming cottage. A Maxfield Parrish scene, stars spangled across an ultramarine sky, twinkling bit of moon, there at the edge of the grass a trio of cottontails feeding peacefully amidst the dandelions. He had first been drawn to the place because it looked like this, like one of the paintings he collected. "Kiddie stuff," his agent sniffed; "fairy tale porn." Parrish and Rackham and Nielsen and Clarke. Tenniel prints of Alice's trial. The DuFevre painting of the Erl-King that had been the cover of Lie Vagal's second, phenomenally successful album. For the first two weeks after moving he had done nothing but pace the labyrinthine hallways, planning where they all would hang, this picture by this window, that one near another. All day, all night he paced; and always alone.

Because he was afraid his agent or Gram or one of the doctors would find out the truth about Kingdom Come, the reason he had really bought the place. He had noticed it the first time the realtor had shown the house. She'd commented on the number of windows there were—

"South-facing, too, the place is a hundred years old but it really functions as passive solar with all these windows. That flagstone floor in the green room acts as a heat sink—"

She nattered on, but Lie said nothing. He couldn't believe that she didn't notice. No one did, not Gram or his agent or the small legion of people brought in from Stamford who cleaned the place before he moved in.

It was the windows, of course. They always came to the windows first.

The first time he'd seen them had been in Marrakech, nearly sixteen years ago. A window shaped like a down-turned heart, looking out onto a sky so blue it seemed to drip; and outside, framed within the window's heavy white curves, Lie saw the crouching figure of a young man, bent over some object that caught the sun and flared so that he'd had to look away. When he'd turned back the young man was staring up in amazement as reddish smoke like dust roiled from the shining object. As Lie watched the smoke began to take the shape of an immense man. At that point the joint he held burned Lie's fingers and he shouted, as much from panic as pain. When he looked out again the figures were gone.

Since then he'd seen them many times. Different figures, but always familiar, always fleeting, and brightly colored as the tiny people inside a marzipan egg. Sinbad and the Roc; the little mermaid and her sisters; a brave little figure carrying a belt engraved with the words SEVEN AT A BLOW. The steadfast tin soldier and a Christmas tree soon gone to cinders; dogs with eyes as big as teacups, as big as soup plates, as big as millstones. On tour in Paris, London, Munich, L.A., they were always there, as likely (or unlikely) to appear in a hotel room overlooking a dingy alley as within the crystal mullions of some heiress's bedroom. He had never questioned their presence, not after that first shout of surprise. They were the people, *his* people; the only ones he could trust in what was fast becoming a harsh and bewildering world.

It was just a few weeks after the first vision in Marrakech that he went to that fateful party; and a few months after that came the staggering success of *The Erl-King*. And then The Crash, and all the rest of it. He had a confused memory of those years. Even now, when he recalled that time it was as a movie with too much crosscutting and no dialogue. An endless series of women (and men) rolling from his bed; dark glimpses of himself in the studio cutting *Baba Yaga* and *The Singing Bone*; a few overlit sequences with surging crowds screaming soundlessly beneath a narrow stage. During those years his visions of the people changed. At first his psychiatrist was very interested in hearing about them. And so for a few months that was all he'd talk about, until he could see her growing impatient. That was the last time he brought them up to anyone.

But he wished he'd been able to talk to someone about them; about how different they were since The Crash. In the beginning he'd always noticed only how beautiful they were, how like his memories of all those stories from his childhood. The little mermaid gazing adoringly up at her prince; the two children in the cottage made of gingerbread and gumdrops; the girl in her glass coffin awakened by a kiss. It was only after The Crash that he remembered the *other* parts of the tales, the parts that in childhood had made it impossible for him to sleep some nights and which now, perversely, returned to haunt his dreams. The witch shrieking inside the stove as she was burned to death. The wicked queen forced to dance in the red-hot iron shoes until she died. The little mermaid's prince turning from her to marry another, and the mermaid changed to sea foam as punishment for his indifference.

But since he'd been at Kingdom Come these unnerving glimpses of the people had diminished. They were still there, but all was as it had been at the very first, the myriad lovely creatures flitting through the garden like moths at twilight. He thought that maybe it was going off his medication that did it; and so the full prescription bottles were hoarded in a box in his room, hidden from Gram's eyes.

That was how he made sure the people remained at Kingdom Come. Just like in Marrakech: they were in the windows. Each one opened onto a different spectral scene, visual echoes of the fantastic paintings that graced the walls. The bathroom overlooked a twilit ballroom; the kitchen a black dwarf's cave. The dining room's high casements opened onto the Glass Hill. From a tiny window in the third-floor linen closet he could see a juniper tree, and once a flute of pale bone sent its eerie song pulsing through the library.

"You hear that, Gram?" he had gasped. But of course she heard nothing; she was practically deaf.

Lately it seemed that they came more easily, more often. He would feel an itching at the corner of his eyes, Tinkerbell's pixie dust, the Sandman's seed. Then he would turn, and the placid expanse of new-mown lawn would suddenly be transformed into gnarled spooky trees beneath a grinning moon, rabbits holding hands, the grass frosted with dew that held the impressions of many dancing feet. He knew there were others he didn't see, wolves and witches and bones that danced. And the most terrible one of all— the Erl-King, the one he'd met at the party; the one who somehow had set all this in motion and then disappeared. It was Lie's worst fear that someday he would come back.

Now suddenly the view in front of him changed. Lie started forward. The kinkajou slid from his lap like a bolt of silk to lie at his feet, still drowsing. From the trees waltzed a girl, pale in the misty light. She wore a skirt that fetched just above her bare feet, a white blouse that set off a tangle of long dark hair. Stepping onto the lawn she paused, turned back and called into the woods. He could hear her voice but not her words. A child's voice, although the skirt billowed about long legs and he could see where her breasts swelled within the white blouse.

Ah, he thought, and tried to name her. Jorinda, Gretel, Ashputtel?

But then someone else crashed through the brake of saplings. Another girl, taller and wearing jeans and a halter top, swatting at her bare arms. He could hear what *she* was saying; she was swearing loudly while the first girl tried to hush her. He laughed, nudged the kinkajou on the floor.

When it didn't respond he bent to pick it up and went downstairs.

"I don't think anyone's home," Haley said. She stood a few feet from the haven of the birch grove, feeling very conspicuous surrounded by all this open lawn. She killed another mosquito and scratched her arm. "Maybe we should just call, or ask your mother. If she knows this guy."

"She doesn't like him," Linette replied dreamily. A faint mist rose in little eddies about them. She lifted her skirts and did a pirouette, her bare feet leaving darker impressions on the gray lawn. "And it would be even cooler if no one was there, we could go in and find Valentine and look around. Like a haunted house."

"Like breaking and entering," Haley said darkly, but she followed her friend tiptoeing up the slope. The dewy grass was cool, the air warm and smelling of something sweet, oranges or maybe some kind of incense wafting down from the immense stone house.

They walked up the lawn, Linette leading the way. Dew soaked the hem of her skirt and the cuffs of Haley's jeans. At the top of the slope stood the great main house, a mock-Tudor fantasy of stone and stucco and oak beams. Waves of ivy and cream-colored roses spilled from the upper eaves; toppling ramparts of hollyhocks grew against the lower story. From here Haley could see only a single light downstairs, a dim green glow from behind curtains of ivy. Upstairs, diamond-paned windows had been pushed open, forcing the vegetation to give way and hang in limp streamers, some of them almost to the ground. The scent of turned earth mingled with that of smoke and oranges.

"Should we go to the front door?" Haley asked. Seeing the back of the house close up like this unnerved her, the smell of things decaying and the darkened mansion's *dishabille*. Like seeing her grandmother once without her false teeth: she wanted to turn away and give the house a chance to pull itself together.

Linette stopped to scratch her foot. "Nah. It'll be easier to just walk in if we go this way. If nobody's home." She straightened and peered back in the direction they'd come. Haley turned with her. The breeze felt good in her face. She could smell the distant dampness of Lake Muscanth, hear the croak of frogs and the rustling of leaves where deer stepped to water's edge to drink. When the girls turned back to the big house each took a step forward. Then they gasped, Linette pawing at the air for Haley's hand.

"Someone's there!"

Haley nodded. She squeezed Linette's fingers and then drew forward.

They had only looked away for an instant. But it had been long enough for lights to go on inside and out, so that now the girls blinked in the glare of spotlights. Someone had thrown open a set of French doors opening onto a sort of patio decorated with tubs of geraniums and very old wicker porch furniture, the wicker sprung in threatening and dangerous patterns. Against the brilliance the hollyhocks loomed black and crimson. A trailing length of white curtain blew from the French doors onto the patio. Haley giggled nervously, and heard Linette breathing hard behind her.

Someone stepped outside, a small figure not much taller than Haley. He held something in his arms, and cocked his head in a way that was, if not exactly welcoming, at least neutral enough to indicate that they should come closer.

Haley swallowed and looked away. She wondered if it would be too stupid just to run back to the cottage. But behind her Linette had frozen. On her face was the same look she had when caught passing notes in class, a look that meant it would be up to Haley, as usual, to get them out of this.

"Hum," Haley said, clearing her throat. The man didn't move. She shrugged, trying to think of something to say.

"Come on up," a voice rang out; a rather high voice with the twangy undercurrent of a Texas accent. It was such a cheerful voice, as though they were expected guests, that for a moment she didn't associate it with the stranger on the patio. "It's okay, you're looking for your pet, right?"

Behind her Linette gasped again, in relief. Then Haley was left behind as her friend raced up the hill, holding up her skirts and glancing back, laughing.

"Come on! He's got Valentine—"

Haley followed her, walking deliberately slowly. Of a sudden she felt odd. The too-bright lights on a patio smelling of earth and mandarin oranges; the white curtain blowing in and out; the welcoming stranger holding Valentine. It all made her dizzy, fairly breathless with anticipation; but frightened, too. For a long moment she stood there, trying to catch her breath. Then she hurried after her friend.

When she got to the top Linette was holding the kinkajou, crooning over it the way Haley usually did. Linette herself hadn't given it this much attention since its arrival last spring. Haley stopped, panting, next to a wicker chair, and bent to scratch her ankle. When she looked up again the stranger was staring at her.

"Hello," he said. Haley smiled shyly and shrugged, then glanced at Linette.

"Hey! You got him back! I told you he was here—"

Linette smiled, settled onto a wicker loveseat with Valentine curled among the folds of her skirt. "Thanks," she said softly, glancing up at the man. "He found him two days ago, he said. This is Haley—"

The man said hello again, still smiling. He was short, and wore a black T-shirt and loose white trousers, like hospital pants only cut from some fancy cloth. He had long black hair, thinning back from his forehead but still thick enough to pull into a ponytail. He reminded her of someone; she couldn't think who. His hands were crossed on his chest and he nodded at Haley, as though he knew what she was thinking.

"You're sisters," he said; then when Linette giggled shook his head, laughing. "No, of course, that's dumb:

you're just friends, right? Best friends, I see you all the time together."

Haley couldn't think of anything to say, so she stepped closer to Linette and stroked the kinkajou's head. She wondered what happened now: if they stayed here on the porch with the stranger, or took Valentine and went home, or—

But what happened next was that a very old lady appeared in the French doors that led inside. She moved quickly, as though if she slowed down even for an instant she would be overtaken by one of the things that overtake old people, arthritis maybe, or sleep; and she swatted impatiently at the white curtains blowing in and out.

"Elijah," she said accusingly. She wore a green polyester blouse and pants patterned with enormous orange poppies, and fashionable eyeglasses with very large green frames. Her white hair was carefully styled. As she stood in the doorway her gaze flicked from Linette and the kinkajou to the stranger, then back to Linette. And Haley saw something cross the old woman's face as she looked at her friend, and then at the man again: an expression of pure alarm, terror almost. Then the woman turned and looked at Haley for the first time. She shook her head earnestly and continued to stare at Haley with very bright eyes, as though they knew each other from somewhere, or as though she had quickly sized up the situation and decided Haley was the only other person here with any common sense, which seemed precisely the kind of thing this old lady might think. "I'm Elijah's grandmother," she said at last, and very quickly crossed the patio to stand beside the stranger.

"*Hi*," said Linette, looking up from beneath waves of dark hair. The man smiled, glancing at the old lady. His hand moved very slightly toward Linette's head, as though he might stroke her hair. Haley desperately wanted to scratch her ankle again, but was suddenly embarrassed lest anyone see her. The old lady continued to stare at her, and Haley finally coughed.

"I'm Haley," she said, then added, "Linette's friend." As though the lady knew who Linette was.

But maybe she did, because she nodded very slightly, glancing again at Linette and then at the man she had said was her grandson. "Well," she said. Her voice was strong and a little shrill, and she too had a Texas accent. "Come on in, girls. *Elijah*. I put some water on for tea."

Now this is too weird, thought Haley. The old lady strode back across the patio and held aside the white curtains, waiting for them to follow her indoors. Linette stood, cradling the kinkajou and murmuring to it. She caught Haley's eye and smiled triumphantly. Then she followed the old lady, her skirt rustling about her legs. That left Haley and the man still standing by the wicker furniture.

"Come on in, Haley," he said to her softly. He extended one hand toward the door, a very long slender hand for such a short man. Around his wrist he wore a number of thin silver- and gold-colored bracelets. There came again that overpowering scent of oranges and fresh earth, and something else too, a smoky musk like incense. Haley blinked and steadied herself by touching the edge of one wicker chair. "It's okay, Haley—"

Is it? she wondered. She looked behind her, down the hill to where the cottage lay sleeping. If she yelled would Aurora hear her? Would anyone? Because she was certain now that something was happening, maybe had already happened and it was just taking a while (as usual) to catch up with Haley. From the woods edging Lake Muscanth came the yapping of the fox again, and the wind brought her the smell of water. For a moment she shut her eyes and pretended she was there, safe with the frogs and foxes.

But even with her eyes closed she could feel the man staring at her with that intent dark gaze. It occurred to Haley then that the only reason he wanted her to come was that he was afraid Linette would go if Haley left. A wave of desolation swept over her, to think she was unwanted, that even here and now it was as it always was: Linette chosen first for teams, for dances, for secrets, and Haley waiting, waiting.

"Haley."

The man touched her hand, a gesture so tentative that for a moment she wasn't even sure it was him: it might have been the breeze, or a leaf falling against her wrist. She looked up and his eyes were pleading, but also apologetic; as though he really believed it wouldn't be the same without her. And she knew that expression—now who stared at her just like that, who was it he looked like?

It was only after she had followed him across the patio, stooping to brush the grass from her bare feet as she stepped over the threshold into Kingdom Come, that she realized he reminded her of Linette.

The tea was Earl Grey, the same kind they drank in Linette's kitchen. But this kitchen was huge: the whole cottage could practically have fit inside it. For all that it was a reassuring place, with all the normal kitchen things where they should be—microwave, refrigerator, ticking cat clock with its tail slicing back and forth, back and forth.

"Cream and sugar?"

The old lady's hands shook as she put the little bowl on the table. Behind her Lie Vagal grinned, opened a cabinet and took out a golden jar.

"I bet she likes *honey*," he pronounced, setting the jar in front of Linette.

She giggled delightedly. "How did you know?"

"Yeah, how did you know?" echoed Haley, frowning a little. In Linette's lap the kinkajou uncurled and yawned, and Linette dropped a spoonful of honey into its mouth. The old lady watched tight-lipped. Behind her glasses her eyes sought Haley's, but the girl looked away, shy and uneasy.

"Just a feeling I had, just a lucky guess," Lie Vagal sang. He took a steaming mug from the table, ignored his grandmother when she pointed meaningfully at the pill bottle beside it. "Now, would you girls like to tour the rest of the house?"

It was an amazing place. There were chairs of brass and ebony, chairs of antlers, chairs of neon tubes. Incense burners shaped like snakes and elephants sent up wisps of sweet smoke. From the living room wall gaped demonic masks, and a hideous stick figure that looked like something that Haley, shuddering, recalled from *Uncle Wiggly*. There was a glass ball that sent out runners of light when you touched it, and a jukebox that played a song about the Sandman.

And everywhere were the paintings. Not exactly what you would expect to find in a place like this: paintings that illustrated fairy tales. Puss in Boots and the Three Billy Goats Gruff. Aladdin and the Monkey King and the Moon saying goodnight. Famous paintings, some of them—Haley recognized scenes from books she'd loved as a child, and framed animation cells from *Pinocchio* and *Snow White* and *Cinderella*.

These were parceled out among the other wonders. A man-high tank seething with piranhas. A room filled with nothing but old record albums, thousands of them. A wall of gold and platinum records and framed clippings from *Rolling Stone* and *NME* and *New York Rocker*. And in the library a series of Andy Warhol silk-screens of a young man with very long hair, alternately colored green and blue, dated 1972.

Linette was entranced by the fairy-tale paintings. She walked right past the Warhol prints to peruse a watercolor of a tiny child and a sparrow, and dreamily traced the edge of its frame. Lie Vagal stared after her, curling a lock of his hair around one finger. Haley lingered in front of the Warhol prints and chewed her thumb thoughtfully.

After a long moment she turned to him and said, "I know who you are. You're, like, this old rock star. Lie Vagal. You had some album that my babysitter liked when I was little."

He smiled and turned from watching Linette. "Yeah, that's me."

Haley rubbed her lower lip, staring at the Warhol prints. "You must've been really famous, to get him to do those paintings. What was that album called? The Mountain King?"

"The Erl-King." He stepped to an ornate ormulu desk adrift with papers. He shuffled through them, finally withdrew a glossy pamphlet. "Let's see—"

He turned back to Haley and handed it to her. A CD catalog, opened to a page headed ROCK AND ROLL ARCHIVES and filled with reproductions of album cover art. He pointed to one, reduced like the others to the size of a postage stamp. The illustration was of a midnight landscape speared by lightning. In the foreground loomed a hooded figure, in the background tiny specks that might have been other figures or trees or merely errors in the printing process. *The Erl-King*, read the legend that ran beneath the picture.

"Huh," said Haley. She glanced up to call Linette, but her friend had wandered into the adjoining room. She could glimpse her standing at the shadowed foot of a set of stairs winding up to the next story. "Awesome," Haley murmured, turning toward Lie Vagal. When he said nothing she awkwardly dropped the catalog onto a chair.

"Let's go upstairs," he said, already heading after Linette. Haley shrugged and followed him, glancing back once at the faces staring from the library wall.

Up here it was more like someone had just moved in. Their footsteps sounded louder, and the air smelled of fresh paint. There were boxes and bags piled against the walls. Amplifiers and speakers and other sound equipment loomed from corners, trailing cables and coils of wire. Only the paintings had been attended to, neatly hung in the corridors and beside windows. Haley thought it was weird, the way they were beside all the windows: not where you usually hung pictures. There were mirrors like that too, beside or between windows, so that sometimes the darkness threw back the night, sometimes her own pale and surprised face.

They found Linette at the end of the long hallway. There was a door there, closed, an ornate antique door that had obviously come from somewhere else. It was of dark wood, carved with hundreds of tiny figures, animals and people and trees, and inlaid with tiny mirrors and bits of glass. Linette stood staring at it, her back to them. From her tangled hair peeked the kinkajou, blinking sleepily as Haley came up behind her.

"Hey," she began. Beside her Lie Vagal smiled and rubbed his forehead.

Without turning Linette asked, "Where does it go?"

"My bedroom," said Lie as he slipped between them. "Would you like to come in?"

No, thought Haley.

"Sure," said Linette. Lie Vagal nodded and opened the door. They followed him inside, blinking as they strove to see in the dimness.

"This is my inner sanctum." He stood there grinning, his long hair falling into his face. "You're the only people who've ever been in it, really, except for me. My grandmother won't come inside."

At first she thought the room was merely dark, and waited for him to switch a light on. But after a moment Haley realized there *were* lights on. And she understood why the grandmother didn't like it. The entire room was painted black, a glossy black like marble. It wasn't a very big room, surely not the one originally intended to be the master bedroom. There were no windows. An oriental carpet covered the floor with purple and blue and scarlet blooms. Against one wall a narrow bed was pushed—such a small bed, a child's bed almost—and on the floor stood something like a tall brass lamp, with snaky tubes running from it.

"Wow," breathed Linette. "A hookah."

"A what?" demanded Haley; but no one paid any attention. Linette walked around, examining the hookah, the paintings on the walls, a bookshelf filled with volumes in old leather bindings. In a corner Lie Vagal rustled with something. After a moment the ceiling became spangled with lights, tiny white Christmas-tree lights strung from corner to corner like stars.

"There!" he said proudly. "Isn't that nice?"

Linette looked up and laughed, then returned to poring over a very old book with a red cover. Haley sidled up beside her. She had to squint to see what Linette was looking at—a garishly tinted illustration in faded red and blue and yellow. The colors oozed from between the lines, and there was a crushed silverfish at the bottom of the page. The picture showed a little boy screaming while a long-legged man armed with a pair of enormous scissors snipped off his thumbs.

"Yuck!" Haley stared open-mouthed, then abruptly walked away. She drew up in front of a carved wooden statue of a troll, child-sized. Its wooden eyes were painted white, with neither pupil nor iris. "Man, this is kind of a creepy bedroom."

From across the room Lie Vagal regarded her, amused. "That's what Gram says." He pointed at the volume in Linette's hands. "I collect old children's books. That's *Struwwelpeter*. German. It means Slovenly Peter."

Linette turned the page. "I love all these pictures and stuff. But isn't it kind of dark in here?" She closed the book and wandered to the far end of the room where Haley stared at a large painting. "I mean, there's no windows or anything."

He shrugged. "I don't know. Maybe. I like it like this."

Linette crossed the room to stand beside Haley in front of the painting. It was a huge canvas, very old, in an elaborate gilt frame. Thousands of fine cracks ran through it. Haley was amazed it hadn't fallen to pieces years ago. A lamp on top of the frame illuminated it, a little too well for Haley's taste. It took her a moment to realize that she had seen it before.

"That's the cover of your album—"

He had come up behind them and stood there, reaching to chuck the kinkajou under the chin. "That's right," he said softly. "The Erl-King."

It scared her. The hooded figure in the foreground hunched towards a tiny form in the distance, its outstretched arms ending in hands like claws. There was a smear of white to indicate its face, and two dark smudges for eyes, as though someone had gouged the paint with his thumbs. In the background the smaller figure seemed to be fleeing on horseback. A bolt of lightning shot the whole scene with splinters of blue light, so that she could just barely make out that the rider held a smaller figure in his lap. Black clouds scudded across the sky, and on the horizon reared a great house with windows glowing yellow and red. Somehow Haley knew the rider would not reach the house in time.

Linette grimaced. On her shoulder the kinkajou had fallen asleep again. She untangled its paws from her hair and asked, "The Erl-King? What's that?"

Lie Vagal took a step closer to her.

"—'Oh father! My father! And dost thou not see?
The Erl-King and his daughter are waiting for me?'
—'Now shame thee, my dearest! Tis fear makes
     thee blind
Thou seest the dark willows which wave in the
     wind.' "

He stopped. Linette shivered, glanced aside at Haley. "Wow. That's creepy—you really like all this creepy stuff. . . ."

Haley swallowed and tried to look unimpressed. "That was a *song*?"

He shook his head. "It's a poem, actually. I just ripped off the words, that's all." He hummed softly. Haley vaguely recognized the tune and guessed it must be from his album.

" 'Oh father, my father,' " he sang, and reached to take Linette's hand. She joined him shyly, and the kinkajou drooped from her shoulder across her back.

"Lie!"

The voice made the girls jump. Linette clutched at Lie. The kinkajou squealed unhappily.

"Gram." Lie's voice sounded somewhere between reproach and disappointment as he turned to face her. She stood in the doorway, weaving a little and with one hand on the doorframe to steady herself.

"It's late. I think those girls should go home now."

Linette giggled, embarrassed, and said, "Oh, we don't have—"

"Yeah, I guess so," Haley broke in, and sidled toward the door. Lie Vagal stared after her, then turned to Linette.

"Why don't you come back tomorrow, if you want to see more of the house? Then it won't get too late." He winked at Haley. "And Gram is here, so your parents shouldn't have to worry."

Haley reddened. "They don't care," she lied. "It's just, it's kind of late and all."

"Right, that's right," said the old lady. She waited for them all to pass out of the room, Lie pausing to unplug the Christmas-tree lights, and then followed them downstairs.

On the outside patio the girls halted, unsure how to say goodbye.

"Thank you," Haley said at last. She looked at the old lady. "For the tea."

"Yeah, thanks," echoed Linette. She looked over at Lie Vagal standing in the doorway. The backlight made of him a black shadow, the edges of his hair touched with gold. He nodded to her, said nothing. But as they made their way back down the moonlit hill his voice called after them with soft urgency.

"Come back," he said.

It was two more days before Haley returned to Linette's. After dinner she rode her bike up the long rutted dirt drive, dodging cabbage butterflies and locusts and looking sideways at Kingdom Come perched upon its emerald hill. Even before she reached the cottage she knew Linette wasn't there.

"Haley. Come on in."

Aurora stood in the doorway, her cigarette leaving a long blue arabesque in the still air as she beckoned Haley. The girl leaned her bike against the broken stalks of sunflowers and delphiniums pushing against the house and followed Aurora.

Inside was cool and dark, the flagstones' chill biting through the soles of Haley's sneakers. She wondered how Aurora could stand to walk barefoot, but she did: her feet small and dirty, toenails buffed bright pink. She wore a short black cotton tunic that hitched up around her narrow hips. Some days it doubled as nightgown and daywear; Haley guessed this was one of those days.

"Tea?"

Haley nodded, perching on an old ladderback chair in the kitchen and pretending interest in an ancient issue of *Dairy Goat* magazine. Aurora walked a little unsteadily from counter to sink to stove, finally handing Haley her cup and then sinking into an overstuffed armchair near the window. From Aurora's mug the smell of juniper cut through the bergamot-scented kitchen. She sipped her gin and regarded Haley with slitted eyes.

"So. You met Lie Vagal."

Haley shrugged and stared out the window. "He had Valentine," she said at last.

"He still does—the damn thing ran back over yesterday. Linette went after it last night and didn't come back."

Haley felt a stab of betrayal. She hid her face behind her steaming mug. "Oh," was all she said.

"You'll have to go get her, Haley. She won't come back for me, so it's up to you." Aurora tried to make her voice light, but Haley recognized the strained desperate note in it. She looked at Aurora and frowned.

You're her mother, you bring her back, she thought, but said, "She'll be back. I'll go over there."

Aurora shook her head. She still wore her hair past her shoulders and straight as a needle; no longer blonde, it fell in streaked gray and black lines across her face. "She won't," she said, and took a long sip at her mug. "He's got her now and he won't want to give her back." Her voice trembled and tears blurred the kohl around her eyelids.

Haley bit her lip. She was used to this. Sometimes when Aurora was drunk, she and Linette carried her to bed, covering her with the worn flannel comforter and making sure her cigarettes and matches were out of sight. Linette acted embarrassed, but Haley didn't mind, just as she didn't mind doing the dishes sometimes or making grilled cheese sandwiches or French toast for them all, or riding her bike down to Schelling's Market to get more ice when they ran out. She reached across to the counter and dipped another golden thread of honey into her tea.

"Haley. I want to show you something."

The girl waited as Aurora weaved down the narrow passage into her bedroom. She could hear drawers being thrown open and shut, and finally the heavy thud of the trunk by the bed being opened. In a few minutes Aurora returned, carrying an oversized book.

"Did I ever show you this?"

She padded into the umber darkness of the living room, with its frayed kilims and cracked sitar like some huge shattered gourd leaning against the stuccoed wall. Haley followed, settling beside her. By the door the frogs hung with splayed feet in their sullen globe, their pale bellies turned to amber by the setting sun. On the floor in front of Haley glowed a rhomboid of yellow light. Aurora set the book within that space and turned to Haley. "Have I shown you this?" she asked again, a little anxiously.

"No," Haley lied. She had in fact seen the scrapbook about a dozen times over the years—the pink plastic cover with its peeling Day-Glo flowers hiding newspaper clippings and magazine pages soft as fur beneath her fingers as Aurora pushed it towards her.

"He's in there," Aurora said thickly. Haley glanced up and saw that the woman's eyes were bright red behind their smeared rings of kohl. Tangled in her thin fine hair were hoop earrings that reached nearly to her shoulder, and on one side of her neck, where a love bite might be, a tattoo no bigger than a thumbprint showed an Egyptian Eye of Horus. "Lie Vagal—him and all the rest of them—"

Aurora started flipping through the stiff plastic pages, too fast for Haley to catch more than a glimpse of the photos and articles spilling out. Once she paused, fumbling in the pocket of her tunic until she found her cigarettes.

YOUTHQUAKER! the caption read. Beside it was a black-and-white picture of a girl with long white-blonde hair and enormous, heavily kohled eyes. She was standing with her back arched, wearing a sort of bikini made of playing cards. MODEL AURORA DAWN, BRIGHTEST NEW LIGHT IN POP ARTIST'S SUPERSTAR HEAVEN.

"Wow," Haley breathed. She never got tired of the scrapbooks: it was like watching a silent movie, with Aurora's husky voice intoning the perils that befell the feckless heroine.

"That's not it," Aurora said, almost to herself, and began skipping pages again. More photos of herself, and then others—men with hair long and lush as Aurora's; heavy women smoking cigars; twin girls no older than Haley and Linette, leaning on a naked man's back while another man in a doctor's white coat jabbed them with an absurdly long hypodermic needle. Aurora at an art gallery. Aurora on the cover of *Interview* magazine. Aurora and a radiant woman with shuttered eyes and long, long fishnet-clad legs—the woman was really a man, a transvestite Aurora said; but there was no way you could tell by looking at him. As she flashed through the pictures Aurora began to name them, bursts of cigarette smoke hovering above the pages.

"Fairy Pagan. She's dead.

"Joey Face. He's dead.

"Marletta. She's dead.

"Precious Bane. She's dead.

"The Wanton Hussy. She's dead."

And so on, for pages and pages, dozens of fading images, boys in leather and ostrich plumes, girls in miniskirts prancing across the backs of stuffed elephants at F.A.O. Schwarz or screaming deliriously as fountains of champagne spewed from tables in the back rooms of bars.

"Miss Clancy deWolff. She's dead.

"Dianthus Queen. She's dead.

"Markey French. He's dead."

Until finally the clippings grew smaller and narrower, the pictures smudged and hard to make out beneath curls of disintegrating newsprint—banks of flowers, mostly, and stiff faces with eyes closed beneath poised coffin lids, and one photo Haley wished she'd never seen (but yet again she didn't close her eyes in time) of a woman jackknifed across the top of a convertible in front of the Chelsea Hotel, her head thrown back so that you could see where it had been sheared from her neck neatly as with a razor blade.

"Dead. Dead. Dead," Aurora sang, her finger stabbing at them until flecks of paper flew up into the smoke like ashes; and then suddenly the book ended and Aurora closed it with a soft heavy sound.

"They're all dead," she said thickly; just in case Haley hadn't gotten the point.

The girl leaned back, coughing into the sleeve of her T-shirt. "What happened?" she asked, her voice hoarse. She knew the answers, of course: drugs, mostly, or suicide. One had been recent enough that she could recall reading about it in the *Daily News*.

"What *happened*?" Aurora's eyes glittered. Her hands rested on the scrapbook as on a Ouija board, fingers writhing as though tracing someone's name. "They sold their souls. Every one of them. And they're all dead now. Edie, Candy, Nico, Jackie, Andrea, even Andy. Every single one. They thought it was a joke, but look at it—"

A tiny cloud of dust as she pounded the scrapbook. Haley stared at it and then at Aurora. She wondered unhappily if Linette would be back soon; wondered, somewhat shamefully because for the first time, exactly what had happened last night at Kingdom Come.

"Do you see what I mean, Haley? Do you understand now?" Aurora brushed the girl's face with her finger. Her touch was ice cold and stank of nicotine.

Haley swallowed. "N-no," she said, trying not to flinch. "I mean, I thought they all, like, OD'd or something."

Aurora nodded excitedly. "They did! *Of course* they did—but that was afterward—that was how they *paid*—"

Paid. Selling souls. Aurora and her weird friends talked like that sometimes. Haley bit her lip and tried to look thoughtful. "So they, like, sold their souls to the devil?"

"Of course!" Aurora croaked triumphantly. "How else would they have ever got where they did? Superstars! Rich and famous! And for what reason? None of them had any talent—*none* of them—but they ended up on TV, and in *Vogue*, and in the movies—how else could they have done it?"

She leaned forward until Haley could smell her sickly berry-scented lipstick mingled with the gin. "They all thought they were getting such a great deal, but look how it ended—famous for fifteen minutes, then *pffftttt!*"

"Wow," Haley said again. She had no idea, really, what Aurora was talking about. Some of these people she'd heard of, in magazines or from Aurora and her friends, but mostly their names were meaningless. A bunch of nobodies that nobody but Aurora had ever even cared about.

She glanced down at the scrapbook and felt a small sharp chill beneath her breast. Quickly she glanced up again at Aurora: her ruined face, her eyes; that tattoo like a faded brand upon her neck. A sudden insight made her go *hmm* beneath her breath—

Because maybe that was the point; maybe Aurora wasn't so crazy, and these people really *had* been famous once. But now for some strange reason no one remembered any of them at all; and now they were all dead. Maybe they really were all under some sort of curse. When she looked up Aurora nodded, slowly, as though she could read her thoughts.

"It was at a party. At the Factory," she began in her scorched voice. "We were celebrating the opening of *Scag*—that was the first movie to get real national distribution, it won the Silver Palm at Cannes that year. It was a fabulous party, I remember there was this huge Lalique bowl filled with cocaine and in the bathroom Doctor Bob was giving everyone a pop—

"About three A.M. most of the press hounds had left, and a lot of the neophytes were just too wasted and had passed out or gone on to Max's. But Candy was still there, and Liatris, and Jackie and Lie Vagal—all the core people—and I was sitting by the door, I really was in better shape than most of them, or I thought I was, but then I looked up and there is this *guy* there I've never seen before. And, like, people wandered in and out of there all the time, that was no big deal, but I was sitting right by the door with Jackie, I mean it was sort of a joke, we'd been asking to see people's invitations, turning away the offal, but I swear I never saw this guy come in. Later Jackie said *she'd* seen him come in through the fire escape; but I think she was lying. Anyway, it was weird.

"And so I must have nodded out for a while, because all of a sudden I jerk up and look around and here's this guy with everyone huddled around him, bending over and laughing like he's telling fortunes or something. He kind of looked like that, too, like a gypsy—not that everyone didn't look like that in those days, but with him it wasn't so much like an act. I mean, he had this long curly black hair and these gold earrings, and high suede boots and velvet pants, all black and red and purple, but with him it was like maybe he had *always* dressed like that. He was handsome, but in a creepy sort of way. His eyes were set very close together and his eyebrows grew together over his nose—

that's the mark of a warlock, eyebrows like that—and he
had this very neat British accent. They always went crazy
over anyone with a British accent.

"So obviously I had been missing something, passed
out by the door, and so I got up and staggered over to see
what was going on. At first I thought he was collecting
autographs. He had this very nice leather-bound book,
like an autograph book, and everyone was writing in it.
And I thought, God, how tacky. But then it struck me as
being weird, because a lot of those people—not Candy,
she'd sign *anything*—but a lot of the others, they wouldn't
be caught dead doing anything so bourgeois as signing
autographs. But here just about everybody was passing this
pen around—a nice gold Cross pen, I remember that—even
Andy, and I thought, Well this I got to see.

"So I edged my way in, and that's when I saw they
were signing their names. But it wasn't an autograph book
at all. It wasn't like anything I'd ever seen before. There
was something printed on every page, in this fabulous gold
and green lettering, but very official-looking, like when
you see an old-fashioned decree of some sort. And they
were all signing their names on every page. Just like in a
cartoon, you know, 'Sign here!' And, I mean, everyone had
done it—Lie Vagal had just finished and when the man saw
me coming over he held the book up and flipped through
it real fast, so I could see their signatures. . . ."

Haley leaned forward on her knees, heedless now of
the smoke and Aurora's huge eyes staring fixedly at the
empty air.

"What was it?" the girl breathed. "Was it—?"

"It was *their souls*." Aurora hissed the last word,
stubbing out her cigarette in her empty mug. "Most of
them, anyway—because, *get it*, who would ever want *their*
souls? It was a standard contract—souls, sanity, first-born
children. They all thought it was a joke—but look what
happened." She pointed at the scrapbook as though the
irrefutable proof lay there.

Haley swallowed. "Did you—did *you* sign?"

Aurora shook her head and laughed bitterly. "Are you crazy? Would I be here now if I had? No, I didn't, and a few others didn't—Viva, Liatris and Coppelia, David Watts. We're about all that's left, now—except for one or two who haven't paid up. . . ."

And she turned and gazed out the window, to where the overgrown apple trees leaned heavily and spilled their burden of green fruit onto the stone wall that separated them from Kingdom Come.

"Lie Vagal," Haley said at last. Her voice sounded hoarse as Aurora's own. "So he signed it, too."

Aurora said nothing, only sat there staring, her yellow hands clutching the thin fabric of her tunic. Haley was about to repeat herself, when the woman began to hum, softly and out of key. Haley had heard that song before— just days ago, where was it? and then the words spilled out in Aurora's throaty contralto:

> "—'Why trembles my darling? Why shrinks she
>   with fear?'
> —'Oh father! My father! The Erl-King is near!
> 'The Erl-King, with his crown and his hands long
>   and white!'
> —'Thine eyes are deceived by the vapors of night.' "

"That song!" exclaimed Haley. "He was singing it—"

Aurora nodded without looking at her. *"The Erl-King,"* she said. "He recorded it just a few months later. . . ."

Her gaze dropped abruptly to the book at her knees. She ran her fingers along its edge, then as though with long practice opened it to a page towards the back. "There he is," she murmured, and traced the outlines of a black-and-white photo, neatly pressed beneath its sheath of yellowing plastic.

It was Lie Vagal. His hair was longer, and black as a cat's. He wore high leather boots, and the picture had been posed in a way to make him look taller than he really was. But what made Haley feel sick and frightened was that he was wearing makeup—his face powdered dead white, his eyes livid behind pools of mascara and kohl, his mouth a scarlet blossom. And it wasn't that it made him look like a woman (though it did).

It was that he looked exactly like Linette.

Shaking her head, she turned towards Aurora, talking so fast her teeth chattered. "You—does she—does he—does he know?"

Aurora stared down at the photograph and shook her head. "I don't think so. No one does. I mean, people might have suspected, I'm sure they talked, but—it was so long ago, they all forgot. Except for *him*, of course—"

In the air between them loomed suddenly the image of the man in black and red and purple, heavy gold rings winking from his ears. Haley's head pounded and she felt as though the floor reeled beneath her. In the hazy air the shining figure bowed its head, light gleaming from the unbroken ebony line that ran above its eyes. She seemed to hear a voice hissing to her, and feel cold sharp nails pressing tiny half-moons into the flesh of her arm. But before she could cry out the image was gone. There was only the still dank room, and Aurora saying,

" . . . for a long time thought he would die, for sure—all those drugs—and then of course he went crazy; but then I realized he wouldn't have made that kind of deal. Lie was sharp, you see; he *did* have some talent, he didn't need this sort of—of *thing* to make him happen. And Lie sure wasn't a fool. Even if he thought it was a joke, he was terrified of dying, terrified of losing his mind—he'd already had that incident in Marrakech—and so that left the other option; and since he never knew, I never told him; well it must have seemed a safe deal to make. . . ."

A deal. Haley's stomach tumbled as Aurora's words came back to her—*A standard contract—souls, sanity, first-born children.* "But how—" she stammered.

"It's time." Aurora's hollow voice echoed through the chilly room. "It's time, is all. Whatever it was that Lie wanted, he got; and now it's time to pay up."

Suddenly she stood, her foot knocking the photo album so that it skidded across the flagstones, and tottered back into the kitchen. Haley could hear the clatter of glassware as she poured herself more gin. Silently the girl crept across the floor and stared for another moment at the photo of Lie Vagal. Then she went outside.

She thought of riding her bike to Kingdom Come, but absurd fears—she had visions of bony hands snaking out of the earth and snatching the wheels as she passed—made her walk instead. She clambered over the stone wall, grimacing at the smell of rotting apples. The unnatural chill of Linette's house had made her forget the relentless late-August heat and breathless air out here, no cooler for all that the sun had set and left a sky colored like the inside of a mussel shell. From the distant lake came the desultory thump of bullfrogs. When she jumped from the wall to the ground a windfall popped beneath her foot, spattering her with vinegary muck. Haley swore to herself and hurried up the hill.

Beneath the ultramarine sky the trees stood absolutely still, each moored to its small circle of shadow. Walking between them made Haley's eyes hurt, going from that eerie dusk to sudden darkness and then back into the twilight. She felt sick, from the heat and from what she had heard. It was crazy, of course, Aurora was always crazy; but Linette *hadn't* come back, and it had been such a creepy place, all those pictures, and the old lady, and Lie Vagal himself skittering through the halls and laughing. . . .

Haley took a deep breath, balled up her T-shirt to wipe the sweat from between her breasts. It was crazy, that's all; but still she'd find Linette and bring her home.

On one side of the narrow bed Linette lay fast asleep, snoring quietly, her hair spun across her cheeks in a shadowy lace. She still wore the pale blue peasant's dress she'd had on the night before, its hem now spattered with candle wax and wine. Lie leaned over her until he could smell it, the faint unwashed musk of sweat and cotton and some cheap drugstore perfume, and over all of it the scent of marijuana. The sticky end of a joint was on the edge of the bedside table, beside an empty bottle of wine. Lie grinned, remembering the girl's awkwardness in smoking the joint. She'd had little enough trouble managing the wine. Aurora's daughter, no doubt about that.

They'd spent most of the day in bed, stoned and asleep; most of the last evening as well, though there were patches of time he couldn't recall. He remembered his grandmother's fury when midnight rolled around and she'd come into the bedroom to discover the girl still with him, and all around them smoke and empty bottles. There'd been some kind of argument then with Gram, Linette shrinking into a corner with her kinkajou; and after that more of their laughing and creeping down hallways. Lie showed her all his paintings. He tried to show her the people, but for some reason they weren't there, not even the three bears drowsing in the little eyebrow window in the attic half-bath. Finally, long after midnight, they'd fallen asleep, Lie's fingers tangled in Linette's long hair, chaste as kittens. His medication had long since leached away most sexual desire. Even before The Crash, he'd always been uncomfortable with the young girls who waited backstage for him after a show, or somehow found their way into the recording studio. That was why Gram's accusations had infuriated him—

"She's a friend, she's just a *friend*—can't I have any friends at all? Can't I?" he'd raged, but of course Gram hadn't understood, she never had. Afterwards had come that long silent night, with the lovely flushed girl asleep in his arms, and outside the hot hollow wind beating at the walls.

Now the girl beside him stirred. Gently Lie ran a finger along her cheekbone and smiled as she frowned in her sleep. She had her mother's huge eyes, her mother's fine bones and milky skin, but none of that hardness he associated with Aurora Dawn. It was so strange, to think that a few days ago he had never met this child; might never have raised the courage to meet her, and now he didn't want to let her go home. Probably it was just his loneliness; that and her beauty, her resemblance to all those shining creatures who had peopled his dreams and visions for so long. He leaned down until his lips grazed hers, then slipped from the bed.

He crossed the room slowly, reluctant to let himself come fully awake. But in the doorway he started.

"Shit!"

Across the walls and ceiling of the hall huge shadows flapped and dove. A buzzing filled the air, the sound of tiny feet pounding against the floor. Something grazed his cheek and he cried out, slapping his face and drawing his hand away sticky and damp. When he gazed at his palm he saw a smear of yellow and the powdery shards of wings.

The hall was full of insects. June bugs and katydids, beetles and lacewings and a Prometheus moth as big as his two hands, all of them flying crazily around the lights blooming on the ceiling and along the walls. Someone had opened all the windows; he had never bothered to put the screens in. He swatted furiously at the air, wiped his hand against the wall and frowned, trying to remember if he'd opened them; then thought of Gram. The heat bothered her more than it did him—odd, considering her seventy-odd years in Port Arthur—but she'd refused his offers to have air conditioning installed. He walked down the corridor, batting at clouds of tiny white moths like flies. He wondered idly where Gram had been all day. It was strange that she wouldn't have looked in on him; but then he couldn't remember much of their argument. Maybe she'd been so mad she took to her own room out of spite. It wouldn't be the first time.

He paused in front of a Kay Nielsen etching from *Snow White*. Inside its simple white frame the picture showed the wicked queen, her face a crimson **O** as she staggered across a ballroom floor, her feet encased in

red-hot iron slippers. He averted his eyes and stared out
the window. The sun had set in a wash of green and deep
blue; in the east the sky glowed pale gold where the moon
was rising. It was ungodly hot, so hot that on the lawn the
crickets and katydids cried out only every minute or so,
as though in pain. Sighing, he raised his arms, pulling his
long hair back from his bare shoulders so that the breath
of breeze from the window might cool his neck.

It was too hot to do anything; too hot even to lie
in bed, unless sleep had claimed you. For the first time
he wished the estate had a pool; then remembered the
Jacuzzi. He'd never used it, but there was a skylight in
there where he'd once glimpsed a horse like a meteor
skimming across the midnight sky. They could take a
cool bath, fill the tub with ice cubes. Maybe Gram could
be prevailed upon to make some lemonade, or he thought
there was still a bottle of champagne in the fridge, a
housewarming gift from the realtor. Grinning, he turned
and paced back down the hall, lacewings forming an iri-
descent halo about his head. He didn't turn to see the
small figure framed within one of the windows, a fair-
haired girl in jeans and T-shirt scuffing determinedly up
the hill towards his home; nor did he notice the shadow
that darkened another casement, as though someone had
hung a heavy curtain there to blot out the sight of the
moon.

Outside the evening had deepened. The first stars
appeared, not shining so much as glowing through the
hazy air, tiny buds of silver showing between the unmoving
branches above Haley's head. Where the trees ended Haley
hesitated, her hand upon the smooth trunk of a young birch.
She felt suddenly and strangely reluctant to go further.
Before her, atop its sweep of deep green, Kingdom Come
glittered like some spectral toy: spotlights streaming onto
the patio, orange and yellow and white gleaming from the
window casements, spangled nets of silver and gold spilling from some of the upstairs windows, where presumably

Lie Vagal had strung more of his Christmas lights. On the patio the French doors had been flung open. The white curtains hung like loose rope to the ground. In spite of her fears Haley's neck prickled at the sight: it needed only people there moving in the golden light, people and music. . . .

As though in answer to her thought a sudden shriek echoed down the hill, so loud and sudden in the twilight that she started and turned to bolt. But almost immediately the shriek grew softer, resolved itself into music—someone had turned on a stereo too loudly and then adjusted the volume. Haley slapped the birch tree, embarrassed at her reaction, and started across the lawn.

As she walked slowly up the hill she recognized the music. Of course, that song again, the one Aurora had been singing a little earlier. She couldn't make out any words, only the wail of synthesizers and a man's voice, surprisingly deep. Beneath her feet the lawn felt brittle, the grass breaking at her steps and releasing an acrid dusty smell. For some reason it felt cooler here away from the trees. Her T-shirt hung heavy and damp against her skin, her jeans chafed against her bare ankles. Once she stopped and looked back, to see if she could make out Linette's cottage behind its scrim of greenery; but it was gone. There were only the trees, still and ominous beneath a sky blurred with stars.

She turned and went on up the hill. She was close enough now that she could smell that odd odor that pervaded Kingdom Come, oranges and freshly turned earth. The music pealed clear and sweet, an insidious melody that ran counterpoint to the singer's ominous phrasing. She *could* hear the words now, although the singer's voice had dropped to a childish whisper—

—" 'Oh Father! My father! And dost thou not hear
'What words the Erl-King whispers low in mine ear?'
—'Now hush thee, my darling, thy terrors appease.
'Thou hearest the branches where murmurs the
    breeze.' "

A few yards in front of her the patio began. She was hurrying across this last stretch of lawn when something made her stop. She waited, trying to figure out if she'd heard some warning sound—a cry from Linette, Aurora shrieking for more ice. Then very slowly she raised her head and gazed up at the house.

There was someone there. In one of the upstairs windows, gazing down upon the lawn and watching her. He was absolutely unmoving, like a cardboard dummy propped against the sill. It looked like he had been watching her forever. With a dull sense of dread she wondered why she hadn't noticed him before. It wasn't Lie Vagal, she knew that; nor could it have been Linette or Gram. So tall it seemed that he must stoop to gaze out at her, his face enormous, perhaps twice the size of a normal man's and a deathly yellow color. Two huge pale eyes stared fixedly at her. His mouth was slightly ajar. That face hung as though in a fog of black, and drawn up against his breast were his hands, knotted together like an old man's—huge hands like a clutch of parsnips, waxy and swollen. Even from here she could see the soft glint of the spangled lights upon his fingernails, and the triangular point of his tongue like an adder's head darting between his lips.

For an instant she fell into a crouch, thinking to flee to the cottage. But the thought of turning her back upon that figure was too much for her. Instead Haley began to run towards the patio. Once she glanced up: and yes, it was still there, it had not moved, its eyes had not wavered from watching her; only it seemed its mouth might have opened a little more, as though it was panting.

Gasping, she nearly fell onto the flagstone patio. On the glass tables the remains of this morning's breakfast sat in congealed pools on bright blue plates. A skein of insects rose and trailed her as she ran through the doors.

"Linette!"

She clapped her hand to her mouth. Of course it would have seen where she entered; but this place was enormous, surely she could find Linette and they could run, or hide—

But the room was so full of the echo of that insistent music that no one could have heard her call out. She waited for several heartbeats, then went on.

She passed all the rooms they had toured just days before. In the corridors the incense burners were dead and cold. The piranhas roiled frantically in their tank, and the neon sculptures hissed like something burning. In one room hung dozens of framed covers of *Interview* magazine, empty-eyed faces staring down at her. It seemed now that she recognized them, could almost have named them if Aurora had been there to prompt her—

Fairy Pagan, Dianthus Queen, Markey French . . .

As her feet whispered across the heavy carpet she could hear them breathing behind her, *dead, dead, dead.*

She ended up in the kitchen. On the wall the cat-clock ticked loudly. There was a smell of scorched coffee. Without thinking she crossed the room and switched off the automatic coffee maker, its glass carafe burned black and empty. A loaf of bread lay open on a counter, and a half-empty bottle of wine. Haley swallowed: her mouth tasted foul. She grabbed the wine bottle and gulped a mouthful, warm and sour; then coughing, found the way upstairs.

Lie pranced back to the bedroom, singing to himself. He felt giddy, the way he did sometimes after a long while without his medication. By the door he turned and flicked at several buttons on the stereo, grimacing when the music howled and quickly turning the levels down. No way she could have slept through *that.* He pulled his hair back and did a few little dance steps, the rush of pure feeling coming over him like speed.

" 'If you will, oh my darling, then with me go away,
My daughter shall tend you so fair and so gay . . .' "

He twirled so that the cuffs of his loose trousers ballooned about his ankles. "Come, darling, rise and shine, time for little kinkajous to have their milk and honey—" he sang. And stopped.

The bed was empty. On the side table a cigarette—she had taken to cadging cigarettes from him—burned in a little brass tray, a scant half-inch of ash at its head.

"Linette?"

He whirled and went to the door, looked up and down the hall. He would have seen her if she'd gone out, but where could she have gone? Quickly he paced to the bathroom, pushing the door open as he called her name. She would have had to pass him to get there; but the room was empty.

"Linette!"

He hurried back to the room, this time flinging the door wide as he entered. Nothing. The room was too small to hide anyone. There wasn't even a closet. He walked inside, kicking at empty cigarette packs and clothes, one of Linette's sandals, a dangling silver earring. "Linette! Come on, let's go downstairs—"

At the far wall he stopped, staring at the huge canvas that hung there. From the speakers behind him the music swelled, his own voice echoing his shouts.

" 'My father! My father! Oh hold me now fast!
He pulls me, he hurts, and will have me at last—' "

Lie's hands began to shake. He swayed a little to one side, swiping at the air as though something had brushed his cheek.

The Erl-King was gone. The painting still hung in its accustomed place in its heavy gilt frame. But instead of the menacing figure in the foreground and the tiny fleeing horse behind it, there was nothing. The yellow lights within the darkly silhouetted house had been extinguished. And where the hooded figure had reared with its extended claws, the canvas was blackened and charred. A hawkmoth was trapped there, its furled antennae broken, its wings shivered to fragments of mica and dust.

"Linette."

From the hallway came a dull crash, as though something had fallen down the stairs. He fled the room while the fairy music ground on behind him.

In the hall he stopped, panting. The insects moved slowly through the air, brushing against his face with their cool wings. He could still hear the music, although now it seemed another voice had joined his own, chanting words he couldn't understand. As he listened he realized this voice did not come from the speakers behind him but from somewhere else—from down the corridor, where he could now see a dark shape moving within one of the windows overlooking the lawn.

"Linette," he whispered.

He began to walk, heedless of the tiny things that writhed beneath his bare feet. For some reason he still couldn't make out the figure waiting at the end of the hallway: the closer he came to it the more insubstantial it seemed, the more difficult it was to see through the cloud of winged creatures that surrounded his face. Then his foot brushed against something heavy and soft. Dazed, he shook his head and glanced down. After a moment he stooped to see what lay there.

It was the kinkajou. Curled to form a perfect circle, its paws drawn protectively about its elfin face. When he stroked it he could feel the tightness beneath the soft fur, the small legs and long tail already stiff.

"Linette," he said again; but this time the name was cut off as Lie staggered to his feet. The kinkajou slid with a gentle thump to the floor.

At the end of the hallway he could see it, quite clearly now, its huge head weaving back and forth as it chanted a wordless monotone. Behind it a slender figure crouched in a pool of pale blue cloth and moaned softly.

"Leave her," Lie choked; but he knew it couldn't hear him. He started to turn, to run the other way back to his bedroom. He tripped once and with a cry kicked aside the kinkajou. Behind him the low moaning had stopped, although he could still hear that glottal voice humming to itself. He stumbled on for another few feet; and then he made the mistake of looking back.

The curved staircase was darker than Haley remembered. Halfway up she nearly fell when she stepped on a glass. It shattered beneath her foot; she felt a soft prick where a shard cut her ankle. Kicking it aside, she went more carefully, holding her breath as she tried to hear anything above that music. Surely the grandmother at least would be about? She paused where the staircase turned, reaching to wipe the blood from her ankle, then with one hand on the paneled wall crept up the next few steps.

That was where she found Gram. At the curve in the stairwell light spilled from the top of the hallway. Something was sprawled across the steps, a filigree of white etched across her face. Beneath Haley's foot something cracked. When she put her hand down she felt the rounded corner of a pair of eyeglasses, the jagged spar where she had broken them.

"Gram," the girl whispered.

She had never seen anyone dead before. One arm flung up and backwards, as though it had stuck to the wall as she fell; her dress raked above her knees so that Haley could see where the blood had pooled onto the next riser, like a shadowy footstep. Her eyes were closed but her mouth was half-open, so that the girl could see how her false teeth had come loose and hung above her lower lip. In the breathless air of the passageway she had a heavy sickly odor, like dead carnations. Haley gagged and leaned back against the wall, closing her eyes and moaning softly.

But she couldn't stay like that. And she couldn't leave, not with Linette up there somewhere; even if that horrible figure was waiting for her. It was crazy: through her mind raced all the movies she had ever seen that were just like this, some idiot kid going up a dark stairway or into the basement where the killer waited, and the audience shrieking *No!;* but still she couldn't go back.

The hardest part was stepping over the corpse, trying not to actually *touch* it. She had to stretch across three steps, and then she almost fell but scrabbled frantically at the wall until she caught her balance. After that she ran the rest of the way until she reached the top.

Before her stretched the hallway. It seemed to be lit by some kind of moving light, like a strobe or mirror ball; but then she realized that was because of all the moths bashing against the myriad lamps strung across the ceiling. She took a step, her heart thudding so hard she thought she might faint. There was the doorway to Lie Vagal's bedroom; there all the open windows, and beside them the paintings.

She walked on tiptoe, her sneakers melting into the thick carpeting. At the open doorway she stopped, her breath catching in her throat. But when she looked inside there was no one there. A cigarette burned in an ashtray next to the bed. By the door Lie Vagal's stereo blinked with tiny red and green lights. The music went on, a ringing music like a calliope or glass harp. She continued down the hall.

She passed the first window, then a painting; then another window and another painting. She didn't know what made her stop to look at this one; but when she did her hands grew icy despite the cloying heat.

The picture was empty. A little brass plate at the bottom of the frame read *The Snow Queen*; but the soft wash of watercolors showed only pale blue ice, a sickle moon like a tear on the heavy paper. Stumbling, she turned to look at the frame behind her. *La Belle et La Bête*, it read: an old photograph, a film still, but where two figures had stood beneath an ornate candelabra there was only a whitish blur, as though the negative had been damaged.

She went to the next picture, and the next. They were all the same. Each landscape was empty, as though waiting for the artist to carefully place the principals between glass mountain and glass coffin, silver slippers and seven-league boots. From one to the other Haley paced, never stopping except to pause momentarily before those skeletal frames.

And now she saw that she was coming to the end of the corridor. There on the right was the window where she had seen that ghastly figure; and there beneath it, crouched on the floor like some immense animal or fallen beam, was a hulking shadow. Its head and shoulders were bent as though it fed upon something. She could hear it, a sound like a kitten lapping, so loud that it drowned out even the muted wail of Lie Vagal's music.

She stopped, one hand touching the windowsill beside her. A few yards ahead of her the creature grunted and hissed; and now she could see that there was something pinned beneath it. At first she thought it was the kinkajou. She was stepping backwards, starting to turn to run, when very slowly the great creature lifted its head to gaze at her.

It was the same tallowy face she had glimpsed in the window. Its mouth was open so that she could see its teeth, pointed and dulled like a dog's, and the damp smear across its chin. It seemed to have no eyes, only huge ruined holes where they once had been; and above them stretched an unbroken ridge of black where its eyebrows grew straight and thick as quills. As she stared it moved its hands, huge clumsy hands like a clutch of rotting fruit. Beneath it she could glimpse a white face, and dark hair like a scarf fluttering above where her throat had been torn out.

"Linette!"

Haley heard her own voice screaming. Even much later after the ambulances came she could still hear her friend's name; and another sound that drowned out the sirens: a man singing, wailing almost, crying for his daughter.

• • •

Haley started school several weeks late. Her parents decided not to send her to Fox Lane after all, but to a parochial school in Goldens Bridge. She didn't know anyone there and at first didn't care to, but her status as a sort-of celebrity was hard to shake. Her parents had refused to allow Haley to appear on television, but Aurora Dawn had shown up nightly for a good three weeks, pathetically eager to talk about her daughter's murder and Lie Vagal's apparent suicide. She mentioned Haley's name every time.

The nuns and lay people who taught at the high school were gentle and understanding. Counselors had coached the other students in how to behave with someone who had undergone a trauma like that, seeing her best friend murdered and horribly mutilated by the man who turned out to be her father. There was the usual talk about satanic influences in rock music, and Lie Vagal's posthumous career actually was quite promising. Haley herself gradually grew to like her new place in the adolescent scheme of things, half-martyr and half-witch. She even tried out for the school play, and got a small part in it; but that wasn't until the spring.

With apologies to Johann Wolfgang von Goethe

The Death of John Patrick Yoder

Nancy Kress

L OOK AT THIS, JOHN," SARAH SAID. SHE PASSED THE
newspaper across the breakfast table to Yoder. "Your
obituary is in here!"

Yoder took the paper. Sarah's face roiled with barely
suppressed glee. She hadn't yet brushed her graying blonde
hair and it stood up in wavering peaks like underbeaten
whipped cream.

It really was his obituary: "YODER, JOHN PATRICK,
43. July 10. Survived by his wife Sarah (Pelletier) Yoder;
son Dale Richard Yoder; brother Samuel Donald Yoder of
Valdez; mother-in-law Dorothy Pelletier; aunts and cousins. No prior calling; private services."

"It's a mistake," Yoder said, with a stiffness that made
him feel uncomfortable. These days Sarah frequently made
him feel uncomfortable.

"Of course it's a mistake!" Sarah said. She broke into
whoops of laughter. "Otherwise, I would have thought they
were in bed with us last night!"

Yoder folded the paper and rose. Sarah's irreverent raucousness, which had seemed so free-spirited and honest twenty years ago, seemed that less and less. He picked up his briefcase. "I'll call the newspaper from the office."

"You do that," Sarah said. "Good morning, Dale. Your father's obituary is in the newspaper!"

"Ummm," Dale grunted. He scowled at his mother, the array of breakfast cereals on the table, the world. He was sixteen. Sarah's glee vanished; she hated Dale to be surly at table. They fought constantly. Before she could begin her maternal attack, Yoder made his escape.

On the drive to Zircon Corporation, his anger grew. How dare the paper print irresponsible obituaries from unconfirmed sources! Journalism had no standards anymore. What if business associates saw the obituary and assumed he was out of the running for accounts? What if Sarah's mother saw it? She'd have another heart attack.

By the time he reached the parking garage, he was in a rage. He parked the Mercedes, punched the elevator buttons, swung into his office under firepower. The phone lines were all busy. He cut off somebody else's call and dialed.

"*Tribune and Chronicle*. May I help you?"

"Give me the editor-in-chief!"

"I'm sorry, Mr. Strickland is unavailable at the moment. Can someone else help you?"

"Whoever writes the goddamn obituaries!"

He was transferred to a Ms. Stein. "This is John Patrick Yoder. My obituary appeared in your newspaper this morning, Ms. Stein, and I am not dead! Got that? I am not dead. Now I want to know two things—how the hell this happened, and what the hell you're going to do about it!"

"Just a moment, please," Ms. Stein said crisply.

"No, wait, don't you dare put me on—"

He was put on hold. Pachelbel's *Canon* started to play. He'd hang up. No, he wouldn't—that's what they wanted. He wouldn't hang up. They had no right to treat him this way! The *Canon* finished and Vivaldi's *Four Seasons* began.

"Mr. Yoder? I think I can answer your first question. The source of the obituary was the Gibson Funeral Home. The usual procedure is for the funeral homes to send in the obituaries and for us to print them unless there's some question about the source. We've worked with the Gibson people for years, and there's never been a—"

"Thank you," Yoder snapped. He didn't want the edge rubbed off his anger by irrelevant apologies. The Gibson Funeral Home was obviously the real screw-up. He looked up the number.

His secretary stuck her head in the door. "Mr. Yoder—"

"Not now, Tiffany!"

The head disappeared.

"Gibson Funeral Home, Norm Gibson speaking. May I help you?"

"You sure the hell can," Yoder said. "My name is John Patrick Yoder. My obituary appeared in the news-paper this morning and they say you gave it to them. But I am *not* dead! Got that? Now I want to know two things—how the hell this happened, and what the hell you're going to do about it!"

"We're sorry you're not the dead party in the obituary, Mr. Yoder. Please hold a moment while I check our records."

"Don't put—" The *1812 Overture* began playing.

Five minutes later the voice of Norm Gibson inter-rupted six cannons. "Mr. Yoder? I'm afraid there's been no mistake. The death certificate for John Patrick Yoder, forty-three, of Fourteen Fairview Lane, Mapledale, was sent to us by the Bureau of Contemporary Statistics downtown. The body is listed as 'unavailable,' which is what they do when it's a drowning kind of thing or when the body is donated for medical research or something like that. We write the obituaries for them and handle the newspaper end of things, on a retainer basis. We've never had any trouble with the system before." His tone implied that the trouble was with Yoder, not the system.

Yoder said angrily, "Well, obviously the system's not working so goddamn hot right now! What are you going to do about it?"

"We'll look into the circumstances, of course, and I'll get back to you personally. Will you be in town a week from Thursday?"

"A week from—Why the hell can't you call them up today? Right now?"

Gibson said gently, "You're not the only client the Gibson Funeral Home has, Mr. Yoder. Today alone—"

"I'm not the Gibson Home's client!" Yoder yelled. "I'm not dead! I'll call them myself!" He slammed down the phone.

Tiffany appeared in the doorway, looking scared. Her hair, which rose six inches above her forehead in a stiff topknot that reminded Yoder of Woody Woodpecker's, bobbed nervously. "Mr. Yoder . . . Ms. Robinson at Doyle, Dane is on the phone. She wants to know where they should send flowers for the funeral—the paper didn't say. She also wants to know who'll be taking your place as her contact at Zircon."

"I'm not dead," Yoder said, despairingly this time. Tiffany nodded loyally. Her topknot bobbed.

*Th-th-that's **all** folks* . . .

Yoder couldn't laugh.

He had never heard of the Bureau of Contemporary Statistics. "Downtown," Gibson had said. The government pages in the phone directory confused him; they were a mass of QuikReference listings, "please see" notations, and lengthy breakdowns by department of organizations Yoder also had never heard of. Finally he found it: "Bureau of Contemporary Statistics, McMillan Building." An answering machine put him on hold "until the first available operator becomes available." The machine played "Raindrops Keep Falling on My Head." Yoder got his coat and walked to the McMillan Building.

The Bureau of Contemporary Statistics was on the eighth floor. Behind a frosted glass door was a bleak room with a bare long counter, three wooden chairs, and travel posters of India stuck on the walls with Scotch tape. No one was there. Yoder called, "Hey! Can I get some service?"

An enormous black woman in a flowered muumuu waddled from a side door. Her hair was in cornrows. She wore four gold necklaces that made concentric circles on her chocolate skin.

Yoder knew he wasn't comfortable dealing with people of color. Not the blacks in Marketing or Legal, of course, the men in well-cut suits and the women in bright silk blouses and softly waved hair. They were just like anybody else. But people like this woman, whom Yoder now saw wore thongs instead of shoes even though this was a business office . . . he wasn't comfortable with these people. The reasons were complicated, and old.

"Yes?" the woman said softly. Her voice had a pleasant fuzziness to it, like the hand-torn edges of good stationery. The soft fuzziness did nothing to mitigate Yoder's anger, but of course he couldn't have dumped it on her in any case. Something to do with fairness. Or maybe it was noblesse oblige. She was so fat.

"This obituary," Yoder said. He'd brought along the newspaper. "See? That's me. But I'm not dead."

"Lemme see," the woman said in her fuzzy voice, even though he was thrusting the paper right at her. He gave her the whole thing and backed away slightly. She studied the page for a long time, squinting at it and bending over the counter. Her four necklaces jangled. Finally she said, "I check it out for you," and disappeared through the side door.

"I can't wait too long," Yoder called after her, but it was too late. He was on hold.

Ten minutes later the woman re-emerged. She held a sheaf of papers. Yoder jumped up from the closest of the uncomfortable wooden chairs. "Well?"

"No mistake, mon. You dead."

"What? What the hell—" Yoder restrained himself with difficulty. The gold jewelry was so fake. The thongs were so thongy. "How can I be dead? I'm standing right here in front of you!"

The fat black woman regarded him impassively. "You dead," she said softly. "The way we keep our records."

"The way you—what the hell are you talking about?"

She regarded him a minute longer, then seemed to come to some sort of decision. "Look, mon. This ain't the Bureau of Vital Statistics. This the Bureau of Contemporary Statistics. The measurements be different. By our measurements, you dead."

Yoder stared, dumbfounded. The woman sighed and laid her papers on the counter. "Here—look. It take three measurable signs to establish death. See what I got here? These your three death signs. 'Course, these be copies. The originals, they in the vault."

She set out six pieces of paper in three groups of two. Despite himself, Yoder stepped closer to look. He yelped and grabbed the first paper, crumpling it in his hand.

"That's a Zircon Private Data memo! How did you get that!"

The black woman didn't answer.

Yoder's position at Zircon, a Fortune 500 telecommunications company, was head of the Vehicular Assets Division, which controlled the company cars used by sales reps and service technicians. There were 2,106 company cars in the United States alone. The Private Data memo concerned Yoder's negotiation with a Big Three car manufacturer to trade in a third of Zircon's fleet before tough new federal laws regulating exhaust emissions raised the price of each car. Paired with this memo on the fat woman's counter was a newspaper picture of Yoder twenty-five years ago, in college, demonstrating against Dow Chemical's manufacture of pesticides.

His wedding picture was there, Sarah smiling with her unique combination of rowdiness and radiance. It was paired with a computer printout from Bud's Motel and

Hot Hut, listing a double room for J. Yoder and Carol
Sanderson at 1:42 in the afternoon.

His last confidential credit counseling report, noting
that he owed $38,000 in credit card debt and had discussed
Chapter 13 bankruptcy with the counselor, was paired with
a crushed paper flower. Yoder regarded the flower with
disbelief. It was the kind he used to sell in airports when
he'd been a Hare Krishna.

"How . . . You can't . . . These are . . ."

The fat black woman merely shrugged. Her furry
voice was very sad. "You soul-dead, mon. Rest in peace."

By lunchtime Yoder had a grip on himself. It was
simple, really. These people were crazy. They arranged
this elaborate hoax from some sort of compulsive delusion
about the world, some infantile pathology that refused to
recognize that people grew up, changed, accepted reality.
No one could remain an idealistic, faithful, socially moti-
vated flower child forever. If you did, the world stomped
on you. Hard. Yoder's decisions since his adolescence had
all been correct. Who in his right mind would *want* to be
a Hare Krishna now? That was only another kind of scam.
Only these poor benighted fools in the Bureau of Contemporary Statistics or whatever the hell it was couldn't see
this. They were stuck in some sort of time warp, acting out
pathetic fantasies that had taken on the grandiose arrangements of a Walden Two. The only appropriate response
was to pity them.

Having worked all this out, and much calmer now,
Yoder went to lunch.

At his favorite restaurant, a woman came up to his
table. She looked vaguely familiar, although when Yoder
ran through the categories of people he knew she didn't
seem to belong to any of them. Not a business associate,
not in that long print skirt and sweatshirt. Not a friend of
Sarah's, not with that humorless intensity. Not the wife of
a golfing buddy, not with that straggly brown hair. She
carried a bouquet of flowers.

"Hello, Johnny," she said solemnly, and he was staggered. How could he not have recognized her!

"Diane! After all these years, how many has it been now, let's see . . ."

She was uninterested in his social filler. She handed him the flowers and said softly, "I was sorry to hear of your loss."

"My . . ."

"I'll always remember that summer in Vermont, Johnny. I'm really sorry you're dead."

She turned and walked away. Yoder, open-mouthed, thought irrelevantly that if he hadn't recognized her voice, he would have recognized the walking-away view of her body. Diane! All that summer on the commune in Vermont they had made love outdoors: wildly, tenderly, as if the grass and trees and very air were recycling the sweet constant ache of desire in some sun-driven sexual photosynthesis. They'd got it on in the fields, on the roof, beside the tiny deep blue lake. *Diane* . . .

She had handed him flowers because he was dead.

By the time he reached the street, she was out of sight. He was left holding the bouquet, daisies and tiger lilies and buttercups like shallow yellow suns.

"Diane Harding?" Sarah said, a wary note in her voice. "The one you told me about? After all these years?"

"Yes," Yoder said. He sat on his deck chair, cradling a large Scotch and water. He hadn't wanted any dinner. Sarah leaned against the deck railing opposite him.

"I didn't know you ever saw her," Sarah said.

"I don't 'see her,' Sarah. I just happened to see her."

"How did she look?"

Yoder spoke before he thought. He was still incredulous. "Just the same. Not a day older. It was amazing."

"Lucky Diane," Sarah said acidly, and Yoder saw his mistake. But one of Sarah's virtues was generosity: she forgave him. "Still, the whole thing sounds odd."

"That's putting it mildly!"

Sarah scratched a mosquito bite on her thigh. There was a strange note in her voice. "So what are you thinking of doing?"

"I don't know. Forgetting all about it, I guess."

His wife regarded him meditatively. Then she grinned. "And I was going to go out tomorrow and buy a black veil."

"Sarah, it's not funny!"

"With flowing weeds to match. What exactly are weeds, anyway? It always sounds like widows are walking around covered in crabgrass. Or possibly buttercups."

"I'm glad you find this so amusing," Yoder said. He stood stiffly. Really, sometimes Sarah went too far. "I'm going to bed."

"I'll go with you," Sarah said, and gave him one of her roguish winks.

But it turned out that standing was the only thing he could do stiffly.

Long after Sarah slept, Yoder lay awake, staring at the ceiling, remembering Diane.

At 9:00 A.M. the next morning Tiffany stuck her head through the doorway. "Mr. Castle on line three, Mr. Yoder. I know you said not to be disturbed, but . . ."

"That's all right, Tiffany. You can always put Mr. Castle through." Castle was with the Big Three car manufacturer.

"John! Great news on this end!"

"I'm always in line for great news," Yoder said heartily. "Shoot."

"We can push through the vehicle delivery on the twenty-seventh, and the word from the Hill is that the President won't sign the Clean Air Act until Monday the twenty-ninth."

Yoder calculated rapidly. A two-day leeway was not his idea of great news. "Wonderful! That's terrific! The only thing is, I wonder if we might not be cutting it a little close? You know how it always is: If something can go wr—"

"Not at all!" Castle said. "It'll tick along like clockwork. Right under the wire. Legal is ecstatic."

If Castle's Legal was anything like Zircon's Legal, "ecstatic" would never describe them. But Yoder recognized from Castle's tone that this was a nonnegotiable. The twenty-seventh was the best he was going to get. Tone was everything.

"Fantastic!" Yoder said. "Bring me up to speed on the details."

He took rapid notes. Tiffany appeared in the doorway, waiting nervously until he was off the phone.

"Mr. Yoder . . . there's a man here."

"Who?"

"He won't give his name."

"Send him away." Salesmen with automotive accessories came with Yoder's job; salesmen who didn't give their names weren't worth bothering with.

"He says it's personal," Tiffany said. She ducked her head, and the woodpecker topknot swooped and bobbed. "He's a little strange, Mr. Yoder."

"Send him in," Yoder said. His throat felt dry. Now what?

"Hello, Jack," Tom Navik said. "Long time no see."

Yoder stood slowly and offered his hand. Tom grabbed him in a bear hug and burst into tears.

"Damn, Jackie-boy, I'm so damn sorry! I just heard yesterday!"

Tom had been his best friend from the fourth grade on. He had hunted frogs with Tom, hunted summer jobs, hunted girls, hunted colleges. He had hunted an AA group for Tom the day after Tom had thrown a two-hundred-pound off-duty policeman through the men's room door at Barber's Bar and Grill. He had visited Tom in the county jail, in the drying-out institute, in a succession of seedy boarding houses until they'd lost track of each other. Tom had been at the center of two decades of Yoder's life, the pick-up in its engine. There was nobody Yoder wanted to see less.

"Tom," Yoder said, crushed against Tom's stained down vest and torn T-shirt, "I'm not dead."

"Denial," Tom said. "A normal stage in the grief process. Don't fight it, Jackie-boy."

Yoder struggled free. "I'm not having a grief process!"

"I understand. When my mother died, I went through the same thing. It takes six months to a year to work through."

Yoder made a strangled sound.

"Look, I can't stay," Tom said. "I have a client waiting. I do life-trauma counseling, that's how I heard about you. I just wanted to stop by with my condolences. How's Sarah?"

"Fine. What's how you—"

"Great girl, Sarah," Tom said. "Well, take care, buddy."

"Wait! *What's* 'how you learned about' me? Is there some sort of list or—"

"Yeah, there is, but this time Diane told me. We stay in touch."

"Diane! Wait, Tom—"

"Mr. Yoder," Tiffany said, "Mr. Castle again on line two."

"Not now!" Yoder snapped. "Tom, do you see Diane? Wait a minute—"

"I'm *sorry*," Tiffany said huffily. "You just told me to put Mr. Castle through anytime."

"My client can't wait, either," Tom said. "Take care, Jackie-boy."

"Can we have lunch? No, wait, Tiffany, I'm sorry, I'll take the call, I didn't mean to snap at you—"

"Not today," Tom said, edging out the door. His sneakers were untied. "I'm having lunch with my mother."

"I thought you said your mother—"

"Hey, John!" Castle said heartily from the speaker-phone. "Can you call 'em, or what? Twenty minutes after I talk to you and we hit a snag. The fleet delivery can't happen until the twenty-eighth. But not to worry—I've fixed it up with the union for a Sunday volume delivery, and of course we'll eat the overtime ourselves. So everything's still Go."

"Bill, could I call you back? I'm firefighting on this end—"

"Sure, no problem. If I'm out, just keep trying."

But the elevator and lobby held only business suits hurrying to meetings.

Shaken, Yoder returned to his office and stared at the phone. After a long while he called home, but Sarah was out. He dialed his brother Sam.

Alaska was five hours behind; it was only 4:32 on Prince William Sound. Sam, who was with the EPA, had been there for nearly a year, working on a major oil-spill cleanup. Yoder hadn't seen his brother in three years. Ordinarily they had little to say to each other and so fell into childhood reminiscences that after a while only made both of them feel more like strangers.

Sam answered sleepily. "Hello?"

"Sam, it's John. Your brother."

"Hello? Hello?"

"Sam, it's *John*!"

"Is anyone there? Hello?"

"It's John!"

Sam hung up.

Yoder called in Tiffany. "I want you to dial this number and ask for Charlie. Right now, on my phone. Do it, please."

Tiffany looked at him oddly. She dialed Sam's number. Yoder could hear it ringing faintly. "Yes?" Tiffany said. "May I speak to Charlie? . . . Oh, I'm sorry. Please excuse the inconvenience." She hung up. "Mr. Yoder, you gave me the wrong number, there's no one there named— Are you all right, Mr. Yoder?"

"No," Yoder said shakily. "Yes. Thank you, Tiffany."

"Well, if you're all right . . . You had another call while your visitor was here. Mr. Selenski at Selenski Universal. He wanted to know who would be handling his account from now on."

Selenski Universal, despite the grandiose name, was a small, family-owned, rock-honest company that supplied discount tuneups and lube jobs for headquarters company cars. Tiffany didn't meet Yoder's eyes.

"Did any other service suppliers call?" Yoder asked.

"No, Mr. Yoder."

Maybe, Yoder thought wearily, Selenski was the only service supplier who read the obituaries. Or maybe he was on whatever official notification list reached Tom and Diane. It wouldn't have surprised Yoder. The Selenskis made a point of employing the handicapped. To Tiffany, peering at him anxiously, he said, "Tell Mr. Selenski I'm still handling the account. Tell him the obituary was a mistake."

"Okay," Tiffany said. "And Charlie, at this number— you want me to keep trying?"

"No," Yoder said. "It wouldn't do any good."

He went back to the McMillan Building on his lunch hour. The Bureau of Contemporary Statistics was open, but the fat black woman was not there. Behind the counter stood a tall thin man in his twenties with a stringy ponytail halfway down his back and wire-rimmed glasses. He wore torn jeans, a T-shirt that said ANIMALS HAVE RIGHTS, TOO, and a button proclaiming MALE FEMINIST. It occurred to Yoder that if he had indeed sold out, at least he was now spared the activist wardrobe.

"Can I help you?" Stringy Ponytail asked. Like the fat black woman, he had a kind, pleasant voice.

"I'm John Patrick Yoder. You declared me dead yesterday."

"I'm sorry," Stringy Ponytail said. "That must be hard, man."

"You don't really think it's hard," Yoder said harshly. "You think it's deserved."

Stringy Ponytail didn't deny this.

"So now I can't even talk to my own brother, is that it? Because he's on the side of the angels and I'm not? Well, answer me this—how come I could talk to Diane? And Tom? They could hear me, but Sam couldn't! Does that make sense?"

"For thousands of years people have thought that death made no sense," Stringy Ponytail said softly. He didn't deny that Yoder couldn't talk to Sam, or had talked to Diane. It occurred to Yoder that this guy probably never denied anything.

For just a moment he wondered how that would feel.

"Screw 'thousands of years'! Why can't my brother hear me on the telephone but you can in person?"

"I'm not sure," Stringy Ponytail said quietly. "Each death is different. But, hey, if it helps you deal with it, consider vampires."

"Vampires?"

"People can see them in person but not in a mirror, right? Sort of like your case. Technology, man." Stringy Ponytail shook his head regretfully. "We've really screwed ourselves up with technology."

"Well, what am I supposed to *do*, you bastard?" Yoder yelled. Vampires! Technology!

Stringy Ponytail fixed him with a steady stare. "Whatever you choose, brother. Whatever you choose."

"I don't want to be like you again, damn it!"

"We don't particularly want you, either," Stringy Ponytail said, and buried himself in a copy of *Garbage News: The Magazine of Recycling*. He didn't look up when Yoder left.

Halfway down the corridor Yoder turned back. "I want Diane Harding's number," he blustered as he strode into the Bureau. But the ugly little office was empty, the side door locked. A hand-lettered sign propped on the counter said BACK AFTER THE DEMONSTRATION ENDS.

Yoder didn't know there was a demonstration. Or what anybody might be demonstrating for.

At the commuter station on the way home, Yoder bought a newspaper. The demonstration was against nuclear power. Yoder was actually in favor of nuclear power; it seemed to him the only viable approach to future energy, despite the unsolved technical and disposal difficulties. His position was not a frivolous one. He had researched the subject, thought about it.

The governor had vetoed a bill reinstating the death penalty. Yoder was in favor of the death penalty, and had been since his aunt, his mother's sister, had been killed by a serial murderer while hanging up clothes in her own back yard. It seemed to Yoder that a society that genuinely valued life must be willing to demand its forfeiture for murder. Anything less was a false valuing of the victim's life. He had thought about this, too.

If you thought about things, and your thought yielded change of viewpoint, did that mean your soul was dead? If you'd rather live in a suburban tract house with decent schools than a rural commune without running water, did that mean you were bad karma? If you'd rather make a living to support your family than hand out paper flowers in an airport, did that mean you were plastic? Or did it just mean you'd grown up?

Anger billowed in Yoder. He yanked the paper open to the obituaries, looking for youthful deaths. ANDERSON, BARBARA, 39; SHOEMAKER, DOUGLAS, 53; BROWNLEE, EDWARD, 43, SUDDENLY . . . Where did these lunatics get off judging him? Who had that right?

"Fuck paper flowers," he said aloud, and a woman in a Donna Karan suit grimaced and moved away from him, wrinkling her nose. The nose-wrinkle suddenly angered him: Now he was being shunned by the righteous *and* the fellow damned. "Fuck you, too," he said to her, and when she turned to stare icily he saw that she was Diane.

Diane with her brown hair in a smart geometrical cut, her briefcase polished, her Charles Jourdan shoes.

"Diane! Wait, Diane, it's me—"

"If you take one step more towards me, buddy," Diane's voice said, "I'll scream at the top of my lungs."

Yoder backed away. His heart pounded. In a second she was gone.

Sarah waited for him in the living room, standing rigid beside the CD speakers, her eyes steely. A suitcase rested at her feet. For a dazed moment Yoder thought she knew about Diane, but that was crazy—there wasn't anything *to* know about Diane.

"Carol Sanderson called me today," Sarah said. "She told me you and she'd been having an affair for several months."

Yoder wished fervently that Sarah were not so direct. Directness was so hard to counter, so difficult to finesse. . . .

"She was crying," Sarah said, conspicuously dry-eyed. "Her mother sent her the obituary. She wanted to know if you'd sent her any last words."

"Oh my God," Yoder said.

"Precisely. How could you have an affair with a woman dumb enough to tell her mother about it?"

"I—"

"And dumb enough to think you'd have any last words for her that you'd send through your *wife*? God, Yoder, you sure can pick 'em."

For a moment Yoder had had some hope—the dry eyes, the raillery about his choice—but now it died. Sarah only called him "Yoder" when she was furious. And her calm furies were always the worst. How angry was she?

"Sarah, I don't know what to say, I—"

"At least *I* picked somebody with taste. Brad Ryan would never have called *you* just because he saw my obituary."

That angry. Yoder felt physical pain, as if someone had knifed him in the belly. Brad Ryan . . . Sarah watched him, icily. Like Diane at the station. Who wasn't Diane, and was. *Brad Ryan* . . .

"I'm not actually leaving you," Sarah said in a clear, hard voice. She kicked the suitcase at her feet. "After all, I'm just as guilty as you. Or maybe not quite as guilty—mine was just a one-nighter, after you'd been gone every night for three solid weeks. But we can compare guilts later, Yoder. Right now I'm going to a motel to think about what a schmuck you've become."

"Don't go," Yoder said. And then—suddenly, bizarrely, "I'm not dead!"

"Oh, yes, you are," Sarah said. "You just don't know it yet, you poor bastard."

Before Yoder could answer, Sarah gave a muffled shriek and clapped her hand over her mouth. Dale stood in the doorway, his gaze traveling coldly from one parent to the other, his eyes full of hate but his hair sticking up on the top of his head, exactly the way it used to do when he was a little boy and crawled trustingly into Yoder's lap for a bedtime story.

Yoder sat up all night. Sarah didn't return. Dale locked himself in his room. The next morning, as he left for school, Dale wouldn't answer anything Yoder said. In ninety seconds he was out the door.

Yoder kept dropping things as he dressed. His tie, his toothbrush, his belt. At the office, he couldn't concentrate. Tiffany peered at him worriedly, her topknot bobbing. Bill Castle phoned. "John! Great news!"

"Oh?" Yoder said cautiously.

"We don't have to worry about wrestling with the union for a Sunday delivery of the cars after all. I don't have to tell you how complicated they can make things! Instead we're on for delivery Monday the twenty-ninth, seven A.M. sharp."

"But . . . but Monday's the day the President signs the Clean Air Act—"

"Not till nine A.M.," Castle said jovially. "Absolutely

reliable inside information. The press will be there. We'll be safely under the wire."

"But you can't have seven hundred and two cars all delivered to twenty-three U.S. locations by nine Washington time—"

"No, that's the beauty of it!" Castle said. "We just get the transfer papers signed at seven! We'll come to your office, have a notary right there. Clean as cake."

"The regulations say physical delivery has to be effected by—"

"But this *is* physical delivery!" Castle crowed. "Physical delivery of the contract! Oh, it'll hold, John, it'll hold. I checked. Legal is ecstatic."

"I have to run this by a few people, Bill," Yoder said. "It's not what we've agreed to. McConaghie is on the coast today, but I'll track down his off-site meeting and—"

"Oh, of course, I know you have to run it by McConaghie. Probably Souder and Foss, too. But they'll go for it, John. I mean"—Castle's tone changed—"we really have no choice on this end."

Which meant Zircon had no choice either. It was far too late to reopen negotiations with another company. Yoder closed his eyes. McConaghie, the division president, would hold him responsible for this one.

"Catch you later," Castle said heartily. "Good talking to you, John."

"Tiffany," Yoder said, "get Mr. McConaghie's itinerary from Patty and find him for me. Keep trying till you get him. Hold all other calls. No, wait—I'll take any call from my wife." He paused. "And from a Diane Harding."

But neither one called.

At noon Yoder went to the McMillan Building. The fat black woman was back behind the counter, doing macramé. In two days she had gotten even fatter. Or maybe, Yoder thought, he himself had shrunk.

Yoder didn't introduce himself. "Where is Diane Harding?"

"We don't give out no information like that," the

woman said in her soft, furry voice. Today her muumuu was tie-dyed in pink and orange. Her hair was still in cornrows. The necklaces jangled.

Yoder said, not raising his voice, "I once taught people like you. An inner-city seventh grade, one hundred percent black. It was 1969 and I was fresh out of college. I thought that the right education could save the world."

"And did it?"

"On my third day, one kid knifed another. During spelling workbook. The fourth week, there was a riot in the classroom. Throwing desks, yanking loose the water fountain, shoving stuff out windows. I resigned."

"It be worse now," the woman said.

"I know. I mean, I don't know, but I read about it in the papers. I don't know what you people need."

The woman didn't answer this. She looked up from her macramé to gaze at Yoder. Her eyes were so sad, so soft, that he was startled. Hadn't he just insulted her? Hadn't he just revealed what a gulf he perceived between himself and people like her? Hadn't he just branded himself a racist, on top of everything else?

"Not everybody gotta live the same. The bureau ain't unreasonable," the woman said softly.

To which Yoder answered, in the same tone, "Your bureau is ruining my life."

"You got no life to ruin, Mr. Yoder. You dead," she said, her dark eyes liquid with old grief.

Sarah left a message on the answering machine to say she was spending a few weeks in Chicago with her sister Jane. Dale moved to a friend's house. He refused to talk to Yoder. "Look, pal," the friend's father said when Yoder raced over to their house, "maybe you better let it go for a while. Dale's pretty upset. He needs some time out, you know?" Yoder didn't know. The man's diction, his cheap jeans, the shabby clapboard house with yellow plastic ducks on the lawn, all enraged Yoder, but not as much as the man's gentle pity. Yoder called his lawyer. The lawyer said Dale was sixteen; he could legally leave home if he chose. There was nothing Yoder could do about it.

Every night Yoder sat alone, in the dark, drinking. The only phone calls on his answering machine were from the credit-card counseling agency, until one night he lurched in from work, punched on the machine, and heard Diane Harding.

"Johnny, this is Diane. Look, I'm not supposed to do this, but I am because . . . well, just because. Listen to me, Johnny. I wrote to Sarah. I explained things. Things about you, I mean, and how you were when we were kids together. Maybe it'll help. She didn't know you then. And now I want you to remember something. It's this: Not everybody has to live the same. You can be a grown-up and still be a good person. Just remember that, okay?" The machine beeped.

Diane had written to Sarah. *To Sarah.* Fingers trembling, Yoder dialed Sarah's sister in Chicago. "Gee, no, I'm sorry, John, Sarah's not in just now," Jane said.

"She never will be in when I call, will she, Jane?" Yoder said, and maybe something in his tone moved her because she didn't hang up.

"Listen, John—sell the beach house. You know Sarah never wanted it in the first place—you did. Sell the beach house and trade in the Mercedes and—oh, I don't know—cut down on the Louis XIV reproductions."

"Financial advice? I call to talk to my adulterous wife who's abandoned me and our son and you offer me *financial advice*?" Yoder cried.

"She didn't abandon Dale. He's out here with us," Jane said crisply, and hung up.

Yoder ripped the phone from the wall. Later, he had to go to an all-night discount store clear across the city to buy cable to rewire it. On his hands and knees before the phone jack, Yoder thought about how there hadn't been a phone in the Vermont commune the Summer of John and Diane. When Terry Jorgensen had overdosed, he'd nearly died because nobody could call for an ambulance.

When the phone was rewired, Yoder called his brother

in Alaska. Sam still couldn't hear him. He called the
Bureau of Contemporary Statistics, which he found quite
easily in the phone book. There was no answer, not even
from a machine. He called every Harding in the phone
book, nineteen of them, waking up several irate people but
not finding Diane. He called Tom Navik, but Tom's mother
said he'd gone to Texas with a legal advocacy program
for migrant workers. The mother sounded querulous and
irritated as she gave this information. But then, Yoder
remembered, she was, after all, dead.

Towards dawn he got back in his car and drove to
Lake Erie. The air was cold; the light was thin and skimpy.
But birds sang along the shore, and the untrimmed weeds
smelled like Vermont had: of wild thyme, and mint, and the
rough uncivilized smell of pine needles shaken in the wind.

The morning of Monday the twenty-ninth, Yoder was
at the office by 6:45. The sunrise edition of the *Tribune
& Chronicle* said in the "News Bites" section: PRESIDENT
TO SIGN CLEAN AIR BILL TODAY. Yoder's more immediate president, James McConaghie of the Zircon Business
Division, was not present; if the legal shit hit the press fan,
McConaghie could claim he hadn't been kept informed
of events in Vehicular Assets. Already hovering in the
lobby was Bill Castle, beaming heartily, with his lawyers
and assistants. He had brought with him the bank notary.
Yoder saw that it was Diane Harding.

It really was Diane. She wore a tailored skirt and sweater with a string of fake pearls and low heels, just the sort of
outfit a bank notary might wear. Her hair was in a not-very-
neat French twist. She gave no sign of recognizing Yoder.

"John!" Castle cried. "Good to see you! Where's the
entourage?" It occurred to Yoder that Castle *would* refer
to a set of lawyers, hardworking and underpaid assistants,
and corporate climbers as an "entourage," as if attached to
royalty.

"Coming right along, Bill!" John cried. "A bit nippy
this morning. Is this the notary?"

"Yes," Castle beamed. "John Yoder, Diane Harding. Now let's see, you know Todd Delancey—"

Before Castle could continue the introductions, Yoder interrupted. "Bill, I just have to check one little thing with Building Security. You know how careful we've gotten! Ms. Harding, would you come with me, please?"

He strode purposefully around the corner of the lobby, ignoring Castle's tiny frown. Diane followed. When they had rounded the corner, Yoder grabbed her hand and yanked open the door to a stairwell. "Come with me! Quick!"

For a terrible moment he thought she wasn't going with him. He suddenly remembered her threat at the commuter station: *I'll scream* . . . But then she slipped behind him through the doorway.

They ran down the stairwell two flights to the parking garage, to Yoder's car. He drove up the back ramp out the far side of the building. Neither of them spoke until they were on Main Street, heading east.

"Drop me at the McMillan Building, please," Diane said. "You're coming up on it fast. Right here . . ."

"No! We have to talk!"

"No, we don't," Diane said. Yoder turned his head at a red light and saw that she was smiling at him warmly, her eyes full of grace, her slim body bent curiously towards him, as if giving benediction. "We really don't. And I'm late, John."

"For what?" Yoder cried, but she was already out of the car. The light changed. Traffic behind him honked and he had to move forward. Diane waved gaily.

He drove to the lake. Wet grass clung to his wingtips, climbed the pants of his suit. He sat on a rock, not caring if it were damp, and tried not to feel afraid.

Just before nine o'clock he drove to a lakeside bar that had just opened, ordered a beer, and asked the sleepy bartender to turn on CNN. The President sat at his desk in the Oval Office, signing the Clean Air Act into law. Yoder finished his beer and called for a telephone.

"Tiffany? John Yoder here. Has my wife—"

"Oh, Mr. Yoder, it's terrible! Mr. McConaghie's been on the phone since I came in at eight, trying to reach you, and he's saying the most terrible things! There was nobody with authority to sign Mr. Castle's papers and by the time they found somebody it was too late and—oh, Mr. Yoder—"

"It's all right, Tiffany. Listen to me. Tell Mr. McConaghie I'll send a fax to the California office in a few hours. He can get it there, or have it refaxed to his hotel. Meanwhile, there's a picture of my wife on my desk, and a file in the lower right-hand drawer labeled 'Résumés.' Would you take them out and send them by messenger to my house? Right away?"

"Sure, Mr. Yoder. But I—"

"Thank you, Tiffany. I appreciate it. 'Bye."

The bartender eyed him grumpily. Yoder ordered another beer. He dialed the credit-counseling agency and left a message with his counselor. He called a real estate agent and told her he had a beach house for sale. He called the *Tribune & Chronicle* and put in an ad about the Mercedes. Then he dialed Chicago.

Sarah answered. "Hello, John."

"Sarah . . ."

"I saw it in the newspaper. You had it put in the Chicago papers, too, didn't you, so I'd see it? Lucky Jane's sister-in-law is pregnant."

Yoder had no idea what she was talking about. "Sarah—come home. You and Dale. You belong here."

"You know, I think we do," Sarah said sadly. "Although not because I want to belong with you. But we just *do*."

Yoder's throat felt too tight to say anything. But he managed, "I lost my job."

Sarah was silent a minute. Then she said, "How?"

"I didn't exactly lose it. I made it lose me. And I put up the Mercedes and the beach house for sale."

"Those are probably both good," Sarah said. Yoder

thought she might be crying. "I suppose it'll be hell in the short run, though. And damnation in the long run."

"Yeah. Sarah—"

"Dale saw it in the paper, too," Sarah said. "I'm not sure he'll ever forgive either of us, but at least he smiled. As long as you can make us smile, I guess there might be hope. Maybe."

"There is," Yoder agreed fervently, not knowing what he meant, or what she did, hearing only that she would come home. "Honey—Carol Sanderson didn't mean anything to me!"

"Well, that's part of your problem, isn't it?" Sarah said, her tone acid again, the old Sarah. "You meant something to *her*, and so it was pretty scummy of you to encourage hopes. You better call her and get things straight, John!"

"I will," Yoder said, his hopes rising. The old Sarah: acerbic, raucous, unpredictable, fair. His whole body yearned towards the phone.

"I'm hanging up now," Sarah said. "God, you're a pig. I love you, John Yoder."

"I love you, too."

Yoder finished his beer. It tasted salty. After a while he remembered Sarah's remarks about the newspaper. Something about Jane's sister-in-law pregnant? There was a copy of the *Tribune & Chronicle* farther down the bar. He turned to the "Births" section, but even before he had the flimsy pages folded back, it hit him what he would find. It had been in Tiffany's voice on the phone, in Diane's smile as she hopped out of his car into the horns and stinks of morning-rush traffic:

> BORN: Ashley Brittany Carter, g, to Mr. and Mrs. Robert Carter, 463 Elm St.
>
> Michael Nicholas DaCosta, b, to Mr. and Mrs. Francisco DaCosta, 618 State St., Rockport.
>
> John Patrick Yoder, b, 14 Fairview Lane, Mapledale.

Human, Martian —One, Two, Three

Kevin J. Anderson

ICE, THE COLOR OF SPILLED PLATINUM ON OCHRE DUST, extended from the breached pipeline. Water had spewed into the thin atmosphere and frozen in lumpy stalactites dangling from the pipe. Before long the solid lake would erase itself again, volatilizing into the Martian sky.

As she brought the crawler vehicle toward the pumping station, Rachel Dycek tried to assess the area of spilled ice. "Thousands of liters," she said to herself, "many thousands. A disaster."

She turned a sharp eye from the clinging scabs of ice on metal to the broken pipe itself. The thin-walled pipe was more than just breached; someone had torn it apart with a crowbar.

That almost piqued her interest. Almost. But Rachel didn't let it happen. Her successor would have to deal with this debacle. Let him show off his talents. He deserved the trouble. She no longer considered herself in charge of the Mars colony.

As she drove up, three *dva* emerged from the insulated Quonset hut beside the pumping station. The *dva*—from the Russian word for "two"—were second-stage augmented humans, surgically altered and enhanced to survive the rigors of the Martian environment. Rachel watched them approach; she recognized none of them, but she had done little hands-on work herself with the second stage. Only the first.

She parked the crawler, checked her suit's O_2 regenerator system, then cycled through the airlock.

"Commissioner Dycek!" the leading *dva* greeted her. He was a squat man covered with thick silver and black body hair, wearing loose overalls, no environment suit. Rachel looked at him clinically; she had spent a great deal of her time in UN hearings justifying every surgical change she had made to the *dva* and their more extremely modified predecessors the *adin*.

The man's nose and ears lay flat against his head to protect against heat loss, and his nostrils were wide sinks on his face. The skin had a milky, unreal coloration from the long-chain polymers grafted into his hide. His chest ballooned to contain grossly expanded lungs.

The other two *dva*, both females also wearing padded overalls, clung beside him like superstitious children. They let the man do the talking.

"We did not expect someone of such importance to investigate our mishap," the *dva* man said. His accent was thick and exotic; from the southern Republics, Azerbaijan or Kazakhstan most likely. He shuffled his feet in the rusty sand, kicking loose fragments of rock. "You see, it is much worse than we reported in our initial transmission."

Rachel stepped forward, turning her head inside the environment suit. "What do you mean, is worse? How much water was lost?"

"No, the loss is what you see here." The *dva* man gestured to the metallic sheet of ice. Wisps of steam rose from its surface. The salmon-colored sky had an olive tinge from the algal colonies that had proliferated in the atmosphere for nearly a century. Rachel saw no sign of the seasonal dust storm she knew to be on its way.

"Come with me," the man said, "we will show you what else."

As the *dva* man turned with the two women beside him, Rachel finally placed him and his ethnic group. Kazakh, from one of the abandoned villages around the dried-up Aral Sea. The Aral Sea had been one of Earth's largest fresh-water bodies until the early twentieth century, when it had been obliterated by Joseph Stalin. Trying to rework the desert landscape to fit his whim, Stalin had expended all that water to irrigate rice fields in the desert—rice, of all things!—until the Aral shoreline had retreated kilometers and kilometers inland, leaving boats high on dry land, leaving fishing villages starving and disease-ridden. The area had never recovered, and when the call went out for *dva* volunteers, many families from the Aral region had leaped at the chance to come to Mars, to make a new start. Even here on a new planet, though, they clung to their ethnic groupings.

Rachel followed the *dva* man. Her suit crinkled, unwieldy from its high internal pressure. The three *dva* led her to their hut and then behind it. Part of the back wall had been knocked down and then shored up. Bright scars showed where someone had battered his way in from the outside.

Under a coating of reddish dust and tendrils of frost, two iron-hard corpses lay on the ground. Rachel bent down to look at the wide, frozen eyes, the splotched, bloodstained fur, the ragged slashed throats.

With a grim smile, Rachel could think only of how the new commissioner, Jesús Keefer, was going to have a terrible blot on his first month as her successor. So far Keefer and the UN had kept everything cordial, a comfortable transition period between two commissioners who held nothing but outward respect for each other. But Rachel had been cut out of all responsibility, with nothing to do but twiddle her thumbs in the pressurized habitation domes until the supply ship came to take her back to Earth. After she had gone, Keefer would probably find some way to connect this event with something Rachel had done during her administration. He had to keep his own record clean, after all.

"We left this other one by himself." The *dva* man took her to the far side of the Quonset hut. "We did not want him tainting the soil beside our comrades."

The third body lay sprawled, arms akimbo, head cocked against a boulder as if the *dva* survivors had tossed his body there in disgust. Inside her helmet, Rachel Dycek let out a gasp.

"*Adin*," the *dva* man said, stating the obvious. First-phase augmented human.

"I thought they were all dead by now," Rachel said.

"Not all," the *dva* man answered, gesturing with his stubby hand at the exaggerated adaptations of the *adin*. "One other escaped."

The *dva* looked human—distorted to the point of the caricatures found in Western newspapers, but human nevertheless. But the *adin*, placed on Mars in an earlier stage of the terraforming process, had endured more extreme transformational surgery. The eyes were deep-set under a continuous frill that hooded the eyes to shelter them from cold and blowing dust; the nostrils were covered with an extra membrane to retain exhaled moisture. A second set of lungs made bulbous protrusions in the *adin*'s back, half hidden by this one's skewed position in the dust. The *adin*'s body lay naked in the freezing air.

"He came out of the darkness," the *dva* man said. The two women nodded beside him. "His comrade smashed the pipeline, and we were distracted by the screaming sound of the water. This *adin* came through the back wall of our dwelling and attacked us. He slashed the throats of our two comrades while they were still trying to wake up. We managed to club him to death."

Rachel noticed what she should have seen right away. Frozen blood trailed dark lines from the *adin*'s ears; his eyes had shattered. "Down here on the plain the air pressure must have been killing him. The *adin* were adapted for conditions much worse than this."

She heard faint sounds from the chemical O_2 regenerator system in her suit. It hissed and burbled as it made her air. She marveled at the irony of the atmosphere being too thick, the temperature too warm for the first group of Mars-adapted humans.

Rachel turned back to the lake of ice and the broken pipeline that stretched from the water-rich volcanic rocks of the Tharsis highlands. "Can you repair this yourselves?" she asked. She did not want to report back to the UN base if she didn't need to.

The *dva* man nodded as if it were a matter of pride. "We are self-sufficient here. But we hope there will be replacements for . . . for our lost comrades. We have much work to do."

Rachel made a noncommittal response. No more *dva* would be created, and both of them knew it. Though conditions on Mars remained worse than a bad day in Antarctica, tough unmodified humans would soon be making an earnest attempt at colonization, more than just the token UN base Rachel Dycek had overseen. Politics had changed, and the days of augmented humans—and their creator— were over.

"You will need to make your repairs with haste," Rachel said. "A Class-Four dust storm is on its way from the north and should arrive late today."

The *dva* women looked at her with sharp, deep-set eyes. The man nodded again and took a step backward. "Thank you, Commissioner. We already know about the storm. We can smell it in the air."

The response took her aback. Of course the *dva* would know such things just by living closer to the Martian environment.

Rachel herself had been concerned only with how

the storm would obliterate her own tracks, allowing her to disappear forever. . . .

The breached water pipeline had been a mere pretext for her to take one of the crawlers from the inflatable base. Everyone else had duties, and no one had complained when she volunteered to make the long trip. Now the *dva* would perform their repair tasks, and Commissioner Keefer would think Rachel had taken care of everything. She would be long gone before anybody suspected something might be wrong.

After cycling back through the crawler's airlock, she drove off toward the volcanic highlands and the mighty rise of Olympus Mons, leaving the *dva* behind with their spilled ice and their dead. She had no intention of ever returning to them, or to her base.

Even on the highest slopes, the Martian air tasted spoiled to Boris Tiban. His first inclination would have been to mutter a curse and spit at the ground, but he had learned decades ago never to waste valuable moisture in pointless gestures. All the *adin* had learned that in their first days on Mars.

Boris reached the opening of the cave and turned to survey the endless slope that stretched down to the horizon. The climb from the plains to the highlands had not even left him out of breath. With only a third of the gravity that his body had been born to, Mars made him feel like a superman. He belonged here at high altitudes, where he could still breathe.

Two of the other *adin* came out to greet him as he stood in the cave entrance. They appeared unkempt, un-human—as they had been designed to look. When they saw him alone, they hesitated. Stroganov asked, "Where is Nicholas?"

"Dead. The *dva* killed him." But the cause of death had been more than the *dva*. He and Nicholas had descended too rapidly, and the atmospheric pressure had maddened him with pain. Nicholas had begun to hemorrhage before the *dva* struck their first blow.

"Oh, Boris!" Bebez said. Her words sounded too human coming from the tight, insulated lips, the flattened face.

Boris leaned against his pointed metal staff, torn from the center of a transmitting dish, and closed his eyes. *Boris Tiban.* That was what they had called him in the camps in Siberia, decades ago on Earth before his surgical transformation into *adin.* Prior to that he had worked in the Baku oil fields near the Caspian Sea; his superiors had showed no mercy when a fire in his area caused a major explosion that destroyed a week's production of petroleum. Sentenced to Siberia, Boris Tiban had grown strong in the hellish winter wasteland, the harsh labor. And then they had snatched him away again, put him through rigorous selection procedures, made him sign forms written in English, a language he could not read, and then worked their black cyborg magic on him.

"Is Boris all right? Why doesn't he come inside?"

Boris had never heard Cora Marisov's voice in the rich atmosphere of Earth, but he imagined it had been deep and musical, not the shrill tones caused by the thin air. Cora herself must have been beautiful. She refused to leave the shadows now, especially now.

He stepped into the cave. "We destroyed one of the water pumping stations. It will do no good. Nicholas died."

Inside, the caves were comfortable, the air breathable. The dim light hid the traces of green lichen crawling over the rocks. Boris remembered how excited he had been, all the *adin* had been, when their terraforming efforts began to show results: the lichens, the algae, the changing hue of the sky. They had worked together in selfless exertion, tearing themselves apart to terraform the planet, to make it a better place for *themselves.*

The *adin* had been the first true Martians, feeling the soil with their bare feet, breathing the razor-thin air directly into their enhanced lungs. They had set out to conquer a world, and they had succeeded—too well. Now none of them could breathe the dense air below.

Cora came out, swaying as she walked. She went to him, and he embraced her. "I am glad you came back. I was worried."

Boris could not feel the details of her body against him. The long-chain polymers lacing his skin insulated against heat loss but also deadened the nerve endings. He felt like a man in a rubber monster suit from a ridiculous twentieth-century film about Martians. But like those costumed actors, Boris Tiban was human inside. Human!

With the death of Nicholas, only five of the *adin* remained of the initial 100. He, and Cora, and three others.

And Cora frightened him most of all.

Through the trapezoidal windowports of the crawler, Rachel Dycek could look out at the Martian sky and see bright stars even during the daytime. Twice a day the burning dot of Phobos swam from horizon to horizon, running through its phases—full, to quarter, to crescent, to new—though they were visible only in telescopes. The other moon, Deimos, seemed nailed to the sky, hanging in nearly the same place day after day, as it slowly lost pace with the planet's rotation.

The uphill slope of Olympus Mons was shallow, taking forever to rise up from the Tharsis Plain until it pushed itself clear of the lower atmosphere. The crawler vehicle made steady progress kilometer after kilometer.

The monotonous landscape sprawled out on all sides. Rachel felt small and insignificant, unable to believe the arrogance with which she had tried to change all this. She had been successful against a world; because of her work, adapted humans could live in the open air of Mars—but now her successors were tossing her aside as casually as if she had been the most miserable failure. That phase of the project was over, they said.

The terraforming of Mars had begun with atmospheric

seeding of algae many decades before the first permanent human presence on the planet. The algae latched onto the reddish dust continually whipped into the air, gobbled the abundant carbon dioxide, photosynthesized the weak sunshine, and laid the groundwork of terrestrial ecology.

Encke Basin, in the Southern Highlands, showed the great recent scar where the united space program had diverted a near-Earth comet into Mars. The comet brought with it a huge load of water, and the heat of impact measurably (though only temporarily) raised the planet's temperature. Encke Sea had volatilized entirely within seven years, further raising the atmospheric pressure.

But the terraforming had been an enormous and unending drain on Earth's coffers, siphoning off funds and resources that—some said—might better be spent at home. Fifty years had passed, and still no humans smiled under the olive sky or romped through the rust-colored sands as the propaganda posters had promised. Popular interest in the project had dropped to its lowest point. The beginning of a worldwide recession nearly spelled the end of a resurrected fourth planet.

No wonder the Sovereign Republics looked on Rachel Dycek as a national hero. With her secret work, she had succeeded in creating a new type of human that could survive in the harsh environment. Double lungs, altered metabolism, insulated skin like a living protective suit.

In a surprise move, suddenly there were people living on Mars—and they were Russians, Siberians, Ukrainians! The news shocked the world and catapulted Mars back into the headlines again.

Rachel Dycek and her team came out of hiding with their rogue experiments and raised their hands to accolades. A hundred human test subjects began eking out a living on the surface of Mars, breathing the air, setting up terraforming industries, ingesting the algae and lichens and recovered water. They transmitted progress reports that the whole world watched. They were called the *adin*, the first.

After months of interrogation by outraged—or perhaps envious, Rachel thought—investigative commissions from the world scientific community, she and her team had developed a second generation of Mars-adapted humans, the *dva*, who needed less drastic changes to survive on a world growing less hostile year by year.

All the enhanced males were given vasectomies before they were shipped to Mars; since they were not genetically altered, any children conceived by *adin* would have been normal human babies who would die instantly upon taking their first freezing, oxygen-starved breaths.

And finally, just five years ago, a "natural" human presence had been established on the surface, living in thin-walled inflatable colonies set up in canyons protected from the harsh weather. Rachel had been given the title of commissioner of the first Mars base as a reward for her accomplishments. She had watched as her *dva* workers paved the way on the highlands, remaking the world for humans to live on unhindered.

The *dva* project no longer needed her supervision, though; and most of the *adin* had abandoned their work and died out before Rachel ever set foot on the planet. Adapted humans were a short-term phase in the terraforming scheme.

Jesús Keefer, the UN Mars Project advisor, had come to replace her. Rachel's work on Mars was finished, and she had been ordered to go home. Keefer would not want her around, and Rachel's superiors had left her no choice. They would return her to Earth a well-respected scientist and administrator. She would fill her days with celebrity banquets, lecture tours, memoirs, interviews. Charities would want her to endorse causes; corporations would want her to endorse products. Her face would appear on posters. Children would write letters to her.

It would be pathetic. Everything would remind her of how she had been retired. Obsolete. Tossed aside now that she had completed her task. But Mars was her home, her child.

The crawler toiled up the lava slope of Olympus

Mons. Black lumps of ejecta thrust out like monoliths from the dust, scoured and polished into contorted shapes by the furious wind. On the sunward side of some of the rocks she could see gray-green smears of lichen, a tendril of frost. It made her heart ache.

Even in the one-third gravity her body felt old and weak. Returning to Earth—and the extra weight it would make her carry—would be hell for her.

Instead she had made up her mind to go to the highest point in the solar system, fourteen miles above the volcanic plain. *Make sure you finish up at the top*, she had always said. Olympus Mons stood proudly above most of the atmosphere, two and a half times the height of Mount Everest on Earth.

On the edge of the eighty-kilometer-wide caldera, Rachel Dycek would stand in her laboring environmental suit and look across her new world. Already she could see the bruised color of the northern sky as the murky wall of dust stampeded toward the southern hemisphere.

The crawler itself might survive—the vehicles had been designed to be tough—but the sandstorm would obliterate all traces of *her*.

Cora Marisov remained in the shadows of the lava tubes where the *adin* lived partly out of shyness, partly out of the revulsion she felt toward her changing body.

Fifteen years ago her eyes had been modified for the wan Martian sunlight. They had been dark eyes, beautiful, like polished ebony disks, slanted with the trace of Mongol features retained by many Siberians. Her Martian eyes, though, were set deep within sheltering cheekbones and brow ridges, covered with a thick mesh of lashes. She remembered her grandmother braiding her hair and singing to her, marveling at what a beautiful girl she was. Her grandmother would no doubt run away shrieking now, making the three-fingered sign of the Orthodox cross.

Cora made her way up the sloping passageway to where sunlight warmed the rocks. The wind picked up

as she stepped outside. The cramps in her abdomen struck
again, making her wince, but she forced herself to keep
moving. She used her fingers to collect strands of algae that
had clung to the flapping skimmer-screens that captured
airborne tendrils. The *adin* would cook the algae down,
leach out the dusts, and bake it into dense, edible wafers.

After greeting her upon returning from his raid, Boris
Tiban sat brooding in silence below, basking near the
volcanic vent. She thought of him as a rogue, one of the
legendary Siberian bandits, or perhaps one of the exiled
revolutionaries. It had taken her a long time to grow
accustomed to the abomination of his body, the lumpy
alien appearance, the functional adaptations tacked onto
his form.

She recalled her emotions the first time they had made
love, more than the usual turmoil she felt when lying with
a man for the first time. This was no longer a man, but a
freak, with whom she grappled in a charade of love.

He had taken her under the dim sun, inside a sheltering
ring of lava rock that reminded her of a primitive temple.
She lay back in the cold, red dust but could not feel the
sharp rocks against her padded back. When Boris held her
and caressed her and lay his body on top of her, she could
enjoy little of his touch. Too much of her skin's sensitivity
had been surgically blocked.

Thin wind had whistled around the rocks, but she
could hear Boris's breathing, faster and faster, as he pushed
into her. Her external skin may have been deadened, but
she squirmed and made a small noise deep in her throat; the
nerves inside had not been changed at all. They moved and
grabbed at each other, making an indentation in the dust
that looked afterwards as if a great struggle had occurred
there.

They had nothing to worry about. The Earther doctors had made sure they were all sterile before dumping
them on this planet. Sex was one of the few pleasures
they could still enjoy. Cora and Boris had made love
often. What did they have to lose? she thought bitterly.

A hundred of the *adin* had set out to establish new lives on Mars. Eight had died within the first week when their adaptations did not function as expected; more than half succumbed within the first year, unable to adapt to the harsh new environment.

As good workers, they had transmitted regular reports back to Earth, at first every day, then every week, then intermittently. With a forty-minute roundtrip transmission lag, they could transmit their report and be gone again from the station before the Earth monitors could respond. Boris had liked using the delayed messages to taunt and frustrate. The Earthers couldn't do a damned thing about it.

After three years, cocky with invulnerability, Boris had spoken to the remaining *adin*. The Earthers had abandoned them on Mars, he said, to sink or swim depending on their own resourcefulness. Earth wanted to watch a soap opera, the quaint outcasts' struggle for survival. Finally Boris transmitted an arrogant refusal to do terraforming work anymore, and then destroyed the station. He had taken the metal spire from the tip of the dish and kept it as his royal staff.

By that time, only thirty *adin* remained. They moved to higher altitudes where the climate was more comfortable, the air thinner and easier to breathe.

Within a Martian year, the first *dva* arrived. They had been planned to replace the *adin* all along. . . .

Now, her arms laden with wind-borne algae strands, Cora turned and listened to an approaching mechanical noise, tinny in the thin air. She looked down the slope and saw the human crawler in the distance, raising an orangish-red cloud behind it.

Cora stumbled back down into the cave, but already the other *adin* had heard it. Boris leaped to his feet from where he had been brooding; his body glistened with diamonds of frozen vapor. He held the pointed staff in his hand and peered out the window opening. The other three *adin* hurried to him.

No one paid attention to her. She couldn't be much help to them right now anyway.

Cora slumped down against the rough rock wall, breathing heavily and sorting out the algae strands. She felt tears spring to the corners of her eyes as she patted her swollen belly—the last great practical joke of all.

The crawler helped Rachel choose the best course. She opted to follow a gaping chasm that spilled down the slope of Olympus Mons, possibly extending to the base of the towering cliff that lifted the volcano from the Tharsis bulge. The chasm was one of the only landmarks she found on the vast uphill plain. It suggested days long past when liquid water had spilled downhill from melting ice. Or perhaps the enormous shield volcano had simply split its seams. She knew little about geology; it was not her area of expertise. If she had been a geologist on Mars, her specialty would never have become obsolete.

Gauges showed the outside air pressure dropping as she ascended. The wind speed picked up, bringing gusts that carried enough muscle to rattle the crawler. She had been climbing for half a day. The distant sun had passed overhead and dropped to the northwestern horizon. Behind her reeled two parallel treads, marking the path of the crawler. They would be erased when the storm hit, certainly before anyone thought to come looking for her.

With a momentary twinge of guilt, Rachel hoped the *dva* at the pumping station would be all right, but she knew they had been trained—and made—to survive the weather conditions of this new transitional Mars.

Ahead Rachel saw areas that looked like ancient volcanic steam vents, lava tubes, and towering jagged teeth of black rock rotten with cavities formed by blowing dust. It looked like an extraterrestrial Stonehenge guarding a gateway to a wonderland under Mars. Long sunset shadows stretched like dark oil spilling down the slope.

And then figures stepped away from the rocks,

emerging from the lava tubes. Human figures—no, not quite human. In the fading light she recognized them.

Adin.

She saw three at first, and then a fourth stepped out. This one carried a long metal staff. Her heart leaped with amazement, awe, and a little fear. Rachel's first impulse was to turn the crawler around and flee back downslope to report the presence of this encampment of rogue "Martians." What would they do to her if they caught her?

But instead she stopped and parked the vehicle, locking its treads. So what might they do, and what did it matter? She sealed the protective plates over the windowports, then stood up. The recompressed air in her suit tasted cold and metallic.

Rachel had nothing to lose, and she wanted to know how the *adin* had fared, what they had done, why they had broken off contact with Earth. At least she would know that much before she died, and it would bring closure to her work. She had to find out for herself, even if no one else would know. She was probably the only one who cared anyway.

She cycled through the door of the crawler and turned back to key the locking combination. Rachel stepped forward to meet the *adin* survivors as they bounded toward her.

The Earther inside the suit looked fragile, like eggshells strung together with spiderwebs. She would never survive ten seconds unprotected outside.

Assisted by Stroganov, Boris took the captive woman's arm and lifted her off the ground. Her reflective suit, bloated from internal pressure, felt slick and unnatural in his grip. He noticed that the suit design had changed somewhat since he had last dealt with Earthers, when they had first deposited the *adin* on the Martian surface.

He and Stroganov carried their captive easily in the low gravity; oddly, she did not struggle. Boris set the woman down in the dimness of the lava tube and scrutinized her small body. Apparently nonplussed, she straightened herself and looked around the grotto. Through the faceplate of her helmet, Boris saw dark eyes and an angular face, salt-and-pepper hair. He discerned no expression of help-lessness and fear. He found it disconcerting.

"I recognize you," the Earther woman said. Her words filtered through the speaker patch below the faceplate in crisp textbook Russian straight from Moscow schooling. "You are Boris Petrovich Tiban."

Pleased that she knew him but also angry at where she must have seen him, Boris said, "You must have been entertained by our struggle for survival on this world, while you sat warm and cozy on yours? How often do they replay my last transmission to Earth, just before I dismantled the dish?" He rang his staff on the porous lava floor for emphasis.

"No, Boris Tiban, I remember you from my selec-tion procedures." She paused. "Let me see, Siberian labor camp, correct? You had been a worker at the Baku oil fields in Azerbaijan. Your record showed that you got into many brawls, you came to work drunk more often than not. During one shift you had an accident that started a fire in one of the refinery complexes. The resulting explosion killed two people and ruined a week's oil production."

The other three *adin* stepped away, looking at her in amazement. Bebez grabbed onto Elia's arm. Boris felt a cold shiver crawl up his spine that had nothing to do with the temperature of Mars. Flickers of memory brought him fuzzy glimpses of this woman, dressed in a white uniform, bustling down cold tile halls. "How do you know all this?"

The woman's response was a short laugh. She seemed genuinely amused. "I selected the final *adin* candidates myself. I performed some of the surgery. I *made* you, Boris Tiban. You have survived here because of the aug-mentations I added to your body. You should be grateful to me with every breath you take of Martian air." She turned around, flexing her arm. The suit made crinkling noises.

"I do not remember these others as well," she continued. "There were so many candidates in the first phase."

Boris felt the fury boil within him. It all came back to him now. "Doctor . . . Dycek—is that your name, or have I remembered it wrong?" She was provoking him, taunting him—perhaps she did not know him as well as she thought. Stroganov gawked at her, then at him; yes, he remembered her too, the smell of chemicals, the slice of pain, the promises of freedom, the exile on this planet.

Boris brought the metal staff up. "Maybe I should just smash open your helmet."

"Do what you will. I never intended to return anyway."

Boris stared into her dark eyes distorted by the transparent polymer. He could not say anything. She had made him helpless.

"Tell me why you are so angry," she continued. "We set you free of your labor camp. You signed all the papers. We gave you a world to tame and all the freedom to do it. Better to rule in hell than to serve in heaven, is that not correct?"

All the clever words tumbled in his throat, clambering over each other to come out. Where was the tough, charismatic leader who had conquered Mars? He had made his speeches over and over to the surviving *adin;* but now he had the proper target in front of him. He clenched his hand so tightly that he actually felt the nails against his thick, numb palm.

The anger finally burst out, and Boris shouted in a way that overrode all his training for shallow breaths and conservation of exhaled moisture. "You created us for Mars—and then you took Mars away!"

He gestured out beyond the cave walls. In his mind he held a picture of the growing lichen, the tracings of frost on the lava rock, the thickening air. Dr. Dycek looked at him through the faceplate. He saw a weary patience in her eyes, which made him even angrier. She did not understand.

"Why is she here?" Elia asked him. "Find out why she is here."

Boris looked down at Dr. Dycek. "Yes, why?"

"I am being replaced. I have no more work on Mars, and I am to be shuttled back to Earth."

Boris tightened his grip on her thin metallic suit. "So now you know what it feels to be obsolete yourself. We watch our world slipping away with each new *dva* establishment, with each water-recovery station, with every normal human setting foot on our planet! The time has come to send them a message they cannot ignore."

Dr. Dycek put her gloved hands on her hips. "I came up here to be swept away in the dust storm. They will never find my body. If you kill me it makes no difference."

"We could dump your body just outside of the flimsy inflatable base. They would find you then."

"Then someone would have to hunt you down," Dr. Dycek said. "Why bloody your hands? No need to add murder to your conscience."

Boris laughed at that. He felt easier now, more in control. "Murder? It is murder only when a human kills another human. *Mars* will be killing you, Dr. Dycek. Not me." He hefted the metal staff over his head, ready to swing it down upon the curved faceplate. She tilted her head up. "It is the way with all creatures: those who cannot adapt to their environment must die. So here, breathe the clear, cold air of Mars. It will be a grand gesture for the *adin!*"

"Oh Boris, stop!" It was Cora's voice, sounding annoyed. She made her way out of the shadows from the back of the cave. "I once admired your ways, but now I am tired of how you must make a grand gesture of everything. Tearing up our transmitter, sabotaging the *dva* pumping station, even blowing up the Baku oil refinery."

"That was all justified!" Boris snapped. But he watched Dr. Dycek's attention flick away from him as soon as Cora stepped into the light. Cora panted, then winced at internal pain.

"She's pregnant!" Dr. Dycek said. "How? That's impossible!"

For a moment, Boris thought her comment so ludicrous that he stifled a chuckle. *How?* Does a doctor not know how a woman gets pregnant?

"Even the best Russian sterilization procedures must not be one hundred percent effective," Cora answered.

Dr. Dycek's entire attitude altered. "Your baby will die if it is born up here! It will have none of your adaptations. Just a normal, human child."

"We know that!" Boris shouted.

"This changes everything. An *adin* having a child! The first human born on Mars!" Her voice rose with command as if they were her slaves—just as she had sounded in the *adin* training and therapy sessions back on Earth. "We will have to take you in the crawler vehicle back down," she said to Cora. "I can pressurize the cabin slowly so you will acclimate and tolerate the atmosphere below for a short time."

Boris felt his control of the other *adin* slipping like red dust through his fingertips. Stroganov and Bebez nodded, looking at the suited figure and ignoring him. Cora stepped forward, so intent with new hope and excitement that she did not try to hide her swollen appearance. "You can save my baby?"

"Perhaps. If we get you back to the base."

"This is good news, Boris!" Elia said. "We thought the baby would die for certain."

Boris released his hold on Dr. Dycek's arm and turned to face his four companions in the cave. "Yes, save the child! And then what? Then everything will be perfect? Then all our problems will be solved? No! Then the Earthers will know where we are. They will come here and watch us die off, one by one. They will make a documentary program about us, the failed experiment. Maybe it will be on worldwide *National Geographic*?"

He moved toward the cave opening to the deepening dusk outside. It was difficult for him to stomp in anger in the low gravity. "You are all fools! I can have more intelligent conversations with the rocks."

Boris Tiban stalked out into the air to stare at the brightening stars, at Phobos rising again in the east and the pinprick of Deimos suspended partway up the sky. He felt like the king of all Mars, a king who had just been overthrown.

Not even Boris's tantrum could disturb Rachel's concentration as she stared at the rounded abdomen of the *adin* woman. The survival of these augmented humans impressed her, but the simple miracle of this pregnancy that should never have happened amazed her much more. A pregnancy, the type of thing men and women had been doing for millions of years—but never before on this planet.

She and her medical team had seen no need to sterilize the female *adin*, a much more difficult operation than a vasectomy. Though Rachel had heard of men siring children years after they had had vasectomies, she and her team considered that possibility to be an acceptable risk. Russian medicine had somewhat low standards for "acceptable risks." Rachel could hardly believe it herself.

But the tight skin stretched over Cora's belly spoke otherwise. The thick *adin* fur wisped up and curled over, showing white patches where toughened skin had been stretched to its limits. Rachel reached out with a gloved hand to touch the bulge, but she could feel little through the protective material.

Cora seemed more preoccupied with excusing Boris's temper. "He is not always like this. He is strong and has kept us alive by our own wits for ten years now, but everything is running through his fingers. He lost our companion Nicholas two nights ago in a raid." She drew a deep breath. Her words carried a rich Siberian accent that evoked thoughts of wild lands and simple people. "These grand gestures of his always backfire."

Suddenly Cora's mouth clamped shut and she let out a hiss. She squeezed her eyelids together. The skin on her abdomen tightened until it had a waxy texture and was as hard as the rind of a melon. Her hands groped for something to grab onto, finally seizing a lump of lava. She squeezed the sharp edges until blood oozed from shallow cuts in her palms, freezing into a sparkling smear on the rock.

Rachel knelt beside Cora while the other *adin* came closer, showing their concern. Rachel had never had children of her own; she had been too preoccupied with her work, too driven, too dedicated. She had never regretted it, though—had she not done something far more important by preparing the first human to set foot on Mars?

Cora gasped out her next words after the spasm passed. "It's all right. For now. That has been happening for days. I can bear the pain, but I can concentrate on little else."

"You must not have the child here," Rachel repeated. She didn't know if the baby would be getting enough oxygen through the mother's bloodstream even now, but it certainly could not survive in the open air. "How frequent are the contractions?"

"I have no idea," Cora snapped in a voice filled more with pain and weariness than anger. "I don't exactly have a chronometer! Boris left all that behind when we came to the highlands."

"They are about every fifteen minutes," said one of the *adin*, Bebez. "You must get her away from here. Give her whatever help you can offer. The baby will surely die up here."

Rachel would have to give up her own pointless gesture of defiance, standing on the volcano top while the dust storm swept her away. But it seemed a ridiculous thing to do now, like something Boris Tiban would attempt. A grand gesture that would impress no one. Instead, she would accomplish something to hold up in front of Jesús Keefer's face.

Cora's infant would focus Earth's attention once again on the *adin* and the *dva*, and on Rachel's own efforts. She might even get a reprieve, be allowed to stay on Mars to study the remaining altered humans and how they adapted to their changing planet. But she felt she was doing this for something else as well. Better to save a life than to take her own.

"Let us go and save your child, Cora. My crawler is not far."

Cora stood up and Rachel touched her shoulder. The other three *adin* nodded their agreement, but made no move to help as the two women went to the door opening into the Martian dusk.

Outside, Boris Tiban was nowhere to be seen. The sky's green had turned a muddy ochre. The upthrust rocks were stark against the smooth slope of Olympus Mons.

The crawler was gone.

Leaving Cora to stand against a rock, Rachel ran over to where she had stopped the vehicle. The low gravity made her feel light on her feet. The wind ran groping fingers over her suit.

She found the crawler's tracks, already beginning to blur in the wind, then she came to a sloughed-off portion of the chasm wall where a large object had been toppled over the edge. Pry marks in the lava soil showed how Boris had used his metal staff.

As dread surged inside her, Rachel went to the brink of the gorge. More lava rock lay strewn a hundred meters below. In the gathering shadows of night, she could make out the squared-off form of her vehicle, out of reach far below.

In darkness, they used tough cables and harsh white spotlights to reach the bottom of the chasm. The *adin* had taken the equipment from the remaining cache of supplies they had brought with them when they had abandoned the Martian lowlands. Low gravity made the climb easier.

Cora allowed Stroganov and Dr. Dycek to help her over the roughest patches. She had to stop four times during the descent while cramps seized her body, demanding all her attention.

Over the past two days the cramps had clenched her stomach muscles, squeezing and pushing, then gradually loosening again. At first they had been intermittent, several an hour and then giving her a few hours' rest before they started again. But the pain grew worse, more regular, more intense, as her muscles lowered the baby, helped position it, started to open Cora up inside. Cora knew the baby could come within hours, or she could have to endure this for several more days.

She watched Stroganov jerk the thin cable as his spotlight shone down on the crawler vehicle surrounded by broken scree. He had never told anyone his first name, but clung to his family identity; he traced his lineage back to the first nobles sent by Peter the Great to conquer the wilds of Siberia.

The crawler had plowed a clean path down the cliff as it fell, and its low center of mass had brought it to a rest upright, though canted against a mound of rubble. As Stroganov played the light over the scratched and dust-smeared hull, Cora looked for the disastrous damage she expected to see.

"It appears to be intact," Dr. Dycek said. She squeezed Cora's shoulder and jumped the last few meters to the bottom of the chasm, landing with deeply bent knees. Her voice sounded thin and far away as she shouted through her faceplate. "This vehicle is tough, built to withstand Mars— as you were."

Dr. Dycek held out her hands for Elia to toss down one of the spotlights. From above, Cora tried to pay attention to the operation. Using the spotlight beam, Dr. Dycek climbed around the vehicle, inspecting the metal plates protecting the trapezoidal windowports. She rapped on one with her gloved fist, then held her fist high in satisfaction.

On her own initiative, Cora began the last part of the descent. Stroganov and Elia helped her until they all stood on the jumbled floor of the chasm. Loose boulders the size of houses lay strewn about. Cora looked up to the top of the cliff wall, a black razor-edge that blocked all view of the stars. Bebez had remained in the caves, and Cora saw no figure looking down at them.

They had called into the darkness for Boris to come and help them, but he had remained silent and hidden.

Dr. Dycek trudged up to them. "The door-lock mechanism is still functioning. The antenna is smashed, though, so we will not be able to let anyone on the base know we are coming." She paused. "From the dents around the antenna base, it looks to me as if Boris knocked it off himself."

The other *adin* said nothing. Cora nodded to herself. Yes, that was the way Boris would do it. He was so predictable.

Then her knees buckled as a new labor spasm squeezed her like a fist and sucked away thoughts of the outside world. Stroganov caught her and held her upright.

Dr. Dycek grabbed one of Cora's arms and began to stumble-walk her toward the crawler. "Come on. We have at least a day's journey before we get back to the base. Even at that, I cannot be certain this chasm will lead us anywhere but a blind end. But there is no other way. The crawler is down here, and we have no choice of roads. You have no time to waste."

Dr. Dycek hauled her into the tilted opening of the crawler's small airlock. Stroganov and Elia helped, each of the *adin* men squeezing Cora's numb skin in a silent gesture of farewell.

"The storm is coming," Stroganov said, sniffing the air.

"I know," Dr. Dycek answered. She made no other comment about it, but faced Cora instead. "We will get you inside and begin the slow pressurization of the interior. We have to make the atmosphere thick enough so the baby can breathe, in case it is born along the way."

Cora dreaded the thought of air as thick as soup and heavy as bricks on her chest, making an ordeal out of every breath—especially during the most exhausting hours of her life. •

She doubted the baby would wait until they reached the Earthers' inflatable base.

The airlock door closed behind them, leaving them in claustrophobic darkness. Already Cora longed for one last breath of the cold air on top of Olympus Mons.

As the southern hemisphere of the planet Mars entered its winter season, the falling temperature caused great portions of the atmosphere to freeze out. Water vapor and carbon dioxide piled up in layers to form a polar icecap. The resulting drop in air pressure sucked wind from the northern hemisphere down across the equator. Gathering force, the wind rushed to fill the invisible hole at the bottom of the world, picking up dust particles in a fist as tall as the sky.

The storm hit them three hours after they had left the *adin* encampment. Rachel could barely see as the roiling murk pounded and shook the crawler from side to side. The brilliant high beams of the vehicle's lights revealed only an opaque haze; the low beams illuminated no more than a shallow puddle of ground directly in front of her. Rachel squinted through the whirlwind, hoping to swerve in time to avoid the largest rocks or another gaping chasm. The walls of the crevasse sheltered them from the worst gusts, but vicious crosscurrents forced her to wrestle with the controls.

Rachel had no idea where the narrow canyon would take her, but she had to follow it. She wound her way along the crevasse floor, hoping it would spill out onto the Tharsis Plain or climb back up to the flat surface of Olympus Mons. She did not know where the nearest settlement would be, or if she would have a better chance heading straight for the main base facilities.

As they continued, Rachel increased the air pressure in the crawler, gradually acclimating Cora to the change. The muffled sounds of the scouring gale came through only as distant whispers. Her suit worked doubletime to absorb her perspiration. She no longer felt like someone who wanted to surrender.

A wry smile came to Rachel's face: she had never imagined she would be facing the dust storm in such a manner. Her planned suicide had seemed poignant and dramatic at the time, like a great hero going to meet doom—but now she realized that most people would have shaken their heads sadly and pitied her instead. They would have found her pathetic. They would have reevaluated all of her successes, used her final madness to brush aside the accomplishments and then forgotten about her.

She kept her mind focused on moving ahead, on the need to return to the main base, where she could show Jesús Keefer how important she still was to the Mars project. Keefer had always been impatient with the slow work of the *adin* and the *dva*, wanting instead to have humans scrape out a direct existence on Mars from the start.

But Rachel and her team had made it possible for the first humans to walk free on another world. No matter how the future changed, no one could alter that. Her work had resulted in the birth of the first Martian, a landmark event never before rivalled in human history.

Behind her on one of the passenger benches, Cora Marisov spoke little, gasping as another labor spasm hit. Rachel used the vehicle's chronometer to time them. They occurred about every four and a half minutes. Cora seemed oblivious to the storm outside.

"I think . . ." Cora said, gasping words that Rachel heard muffled through her helmet, "you had better find a place to stop the crawler. Park it. Shelter. I need you now."

Rachel slowed the vehicle and risked a glance backward.

Cora lay on the floor, her back propped against the curved metal wall and her legs spread as far apart as she could manage around the mound of her belly. Between her legs a gush of liquid spilled out, steaming and freezing in the icy air.

Her water has broken! Rachel lurched the crawler over to the canyon wall under what she could dimly see as an overhang. Now what would she do? Rachel was a doctor, no problem. No problem! But she had studied environmental adaptation, worked with cyborg enhancements. The closest she had come to witnessing birth was in staring at cells dividing under a microscope. It had been a long time since her basic training, and she had used none of it in practical situations.

She looked down the treads of the crawler and turned back to Cora. The pregnant *adin* woman looked up at her; Rachel hoped the faceplate hid her uncertainty.

"I may be able to help you now," Cora said, "but when the final part of labor comes, I will not be able to hold your hand through this."

The thought of Cora helping *her* in the emergency made Rachel stifle a raw-edged giggle, but Cora continued. "I helped my grandmother deliver two babies when I was small. Midwives still do much of that work in Siberia."

Rachel fought away her scattered emotions and stared into Cora's dark, slanted eyes. "All right, should I check to see how far you are dilated?"

"Yes. Reach . . . inside me. Then we will know how much time I have."

Rachel looked down at her clumsy gloved hand. She checked the external air pressure monitor; though the suit seemed more flexible now that the differential was not so great, she still could not survive unprotected in the crawler cabin. "I dare not remove my suit yet. There is not enough air for me. And the glove is too big as it is. I would hurt you."

Cora's eyes shut in a wince and her body shook. Rachel watched her body straining, the augmented muscles stretched to a point where they seemed to hum from the tension. Cora's fingers scrabbled on the smooth metal floor, looking for something to grasp. After a minute or two, the spasm passed.

Cora took five deep breaths, then brought her attention back to the problem. "We need to learn how long it will be. If I am not fully dilated, we might have enough time to reach your base. If I am, then the baby could come in as little as an hour."

Rachel drove the panic away and tried to dredge up alternatives from the thin air. "There are small cutting tools in the repair box, and some metal tape." She looked down at her suit. "I could cut off my glove, seal the sleeve around my arm with the tape. Then I could feel inside you."

Cora looked at her, saying nothing, as Rachel continued. "My hand would get numb in this cold, but I can raise the internal temperature here as much as you can stand."

"If you damage the suit, you will never be able to go outside until we reach your base." Cora closed her eyes in anticipation of another labor pain. "Perhaps you should keep driving. Hope we will find help within another hour or so."

Instead, Rachel made up her mind and went to the crawler's tool locker. In this storm, and with the distance yet to travel, they would never get to a safe haven in an hour. She had spent most of a day maneuvering the crawler up the smooth slope of Olympus Mons, making good time and seeing exactly where she was going. She had now been driving barely four hours, over rough terrain, unable to see for the past hour. They would never make it. Better to prepare here.

First, she wrapped the tape around her forearm as tightly as she could, making a crude tourniquet. Then she pulled up the slick fabric around her wrist and removed one of the small cutting tools from the locker. The tough suit material could resist most severe abrasions, but not intentional sawing. Keeping the metal tape at hand, she pulled in a deep lungful of air and sliced across the fabric.

Her ears popped as air gushed out. She could feel the wind and the cold pushing against her skin. The tourniquet could not make a perfect seal. She cut the gash longer, enough that she could pull her fingers out of the glove and thrust her hand through the ragged opening. With her protected hand, she wrapped more metal tape around her wrist where the suit material met the skin. She taped back the flopping, empty glove, then sealed the seam over and over.

Panting, Rachel tried to catch her breath as the suit reinflated. The chemical oxygen regenerator on her back hissed and burbled, adding to the ringing in her ears. Her head pounded, but her thoughts cleared moment by moment.

Cora squirmed on the floor in her own ordeal. Rachel knelt in front of her. "Cora? Cora, I am ready." She touched the *adin* woman's bristly coating of fur, the waxy texture of her polymerized skin. Rachel's hand felt crisp from the cold, then sensitivity faded as it grew numb. "Tell me what I should expect to feel inside you."

Cora blinked and nodded.

The placental water on the crawler floor had sheeted over with a film of ice, clinging in gummy knots to Cora's inner thighs. Rachel slowly felt the folds of skin between Cora's legs, dipped her fingers into them, then slid her hand inside.

At first the temperature felt too hot, like melted butter, in startling contrast to the frigid air. She forced herself not to withdraw. Her skin burned.

"Feel the opening deep inside. It is surrounded by a ridge," Cora said, biting off each word as she said it. "Tell me how wide it is."

"A little wider than my hand and thumb."

Cora bit her lip.

Rachel withdrew and grabbed the other woman's arm.

The biting cold of the air felt like acid on her wet hand. "Is that good or bad. I can't remember my training."

"Bad. No, good. That means this should be over much sooner. A few hours, perhaps."

The sound of the storm outside suddenly turned into a monster's roar, a grinding, crunching sound that pounded through the walls of the crawler. The rock outcropping above them came crashing down, tossing boulders and blankets of dirt.

Rachel fell on her side, clawing at the air; Cora rolled over and curled into a ball to protect her abdomen. Rocks pummeled the top of the crawler, bouncing and thudding. Reddish smears clogged the view from the main front windowports, blowing away in patches as gusts of wind tore it free of the smooth glass.

Rachel got to her knees. She felt herself shaking. The palm of her bare hand seemed to burn into the frigid metal of the floor. "Are you all right?" she asked Cora. The *adin* woman nodded.

The sounds of the avalanche faded into the roar of the storm, but then another, softer thump sounded on top of the crawler. Cora froze, and her eyes widened.

Rachel got up to go to the crawler's control panel. Luckily none of the falling rocks had smashed through the front windowports.

Then a face and shoulders appeared from above, hands reaching down from the roof of the crawler, brushing the dust aside. The face pressed against the glass, peering inside and grinning.

An *adin*. Boris Tiban.

In shock, Rachel caught herself from crying out. She smacked her hands down on the controls for the protective plates, which slammed over the windowports. The last thing she saw was Boris Tiban leaping aside in surprise, vanishing into the tangled murk of the storm. Then the metal clanged into place, leaving the crawler in dimness. The central illumination automatically stepped up, bathing the interior in a blue-white glow.

Cora stared wide-eyed at the sealed windowport. "Boris!" she muttered. She seemed to have forgotten about her labor. "He caused the avalanche. He must have been working at it ever since we stopped."

"Out in the storm?" Rachel could hardly believe what she had seen herself. "How could he survive without shelter?"

Cora shook her head; Rachel saw a smile on her lips. "He likes to do that, pit himself against the elements. He is proud of how he can cope with anything Mars throws at him. Tamer of Worlds—that is what he wants to be called. He does not like to see you domesticating this planet. Then he will be obsolete."

"I know what that feels like," Rachel muttered, then stopped. "But if Boris tries to kill me, he will also destroy you, and his baby. Does he not realize he will murder his own child?"

Cora hung her head, then shuddered with another spasm. Rachel adjusted the air compressors to increase the pressure inside the crawler more rapidly. When Cora recovered, she looked Rachel in the eye and kept her voice flat.

"He needs the baby to die. He has always planned on it."

Rachel opened and closed her mouth without words; she knew that behind the faceplate she must look like a dying fish in a bowl. "I don't understand."

Cora let her slanted eyes fall shut beneath the thick lash membranes. "His grandest gesture of all. He has been anticipating it for months. We have always known the baby would die at birth. I should never have gotten pregnant. That loss would be a direct fault of the Earthers. He has found a way to blame all of our troubles on you. He is good at that.

"When the baby dies, he will have all the reason he needs to strike back. It will be a catalyst, an excuse. Everything must be perfectly justified. Those are the rules by which he plays." She sighed. "No one ever thought someone like you would come."

Rachel struggled with the sick logic. "What will he do?"

"He plans to go to your inflatable base and destroy it. With his metal staff, he can tear holes right through the sides of the walls. He can run from one section to the next as fast as his legs will take him, striking and moving. He can do it. The alarms will send everyone into confusion. He can burst every module even after they seal themselves. The people inside will be trapped and he can pick them off one room at a time. The Earthers might repair some of the walls, but Boris can just strike again. He can wait longer than any of them."

"But what about you? He's trying to kill you now, too!"

"That is incidental. He loves me in his own way, but he sees the cause as more important. Just like a great revolutionary."

Rachel felt anger welling up inside of her. "Well then, I must make sure he has no reason to attack the base. Your baby will live." She patted Cora's bulging stomach with her bare hand and turned to look at the heavy metal plates covering the windowports. "We are safe here, for now."

Surrounded by the muffled whirlwind of the storm, Cora Marisov gave birth to a daughter. The crawler walls creaked and groaned as the wind tried to push in, but the shelter remained secure.

As soon as Cora's final labor began, Rachel had no choice but to begin pressurizing the crawler interior as rapidly as the pumps could bring in more air. Many of the intake vents had been clogged with dust from the storm and the avalanche, but the gauges showed the air pressure increasing.

Cora cried out with the effort of her labor, but also gasped, complaining about how difficult breathing had become. "Like a metal band around my chest! My head!"

"There is nothing for it. The baby must breathe when it comes." *No matter what it does to Cora*, Rachel thought. "You are strong. I made you that way."

"I . . . know!"

When Rachel had pulled the slick baby free, it steamed in the air, glistening with red wetness. "A girl!" she said.

Cora's mouth remained open, gasping to fill her lungs. The baby, too, worked the tiny dark hole of her mouth in a silent agonized cry of new life, but she could not find enough air.

Rachel moved quickly now. As she had planned, she shucked her suit and popped open the faceplate, letting the blessed warm air gush out. The shock stunned her, but she forced herself to keep moving, to plow through the black specks in front of her vision. A bright pain flashed behind her forehead. Moments later, a warm, thick trickle of blood came from her nostrils.

She grasped the loose end of the metal tape sealing her wrist to the suit. The grip slipped twice before her numb fingers clutched it and tore it off. She let out a howl of pain, releasing half the air left in her lungs. She felt as if she had just flayed the skin off her arm.

She had to hurry. Grogginess started to claim her, but she stumbled through the motions.

Shivering already, she stepped out of the empty suit, letting the metallic fabric fall in a rough puddle on the floor. She wore only a light jumpsuit underneath, clammy with sweat that froze in icy needles against her skin.

Rachel clamped shut the empty faceplate and grabbed up the baby. The infant skin, smeared with red from the birth, took on a bluish tinge as she tried to breathe. The umbilical cord, tied in a crude knot, still oozed some blood.

Cora found the strength to reach over and touch the infant one last time before Rachel slid the girl inside the loose folds of the suit and sealed her whispered cries into silence. She began pressurizing it immediately. The folds began to straighten themselves as air pumped inside.

Heaving huge breaths but still starving for oxygen, Rachel grasped the limp sleeve where she had cut off the glove and knotted it. Suit-warmed air blew from the edge, squirting onto her skin. Rachel clutched the roll of metallic tape and wrapped it around and around the end of the sleeve. The hissing noise stopped, replaced by the ringing in her ears. She crawled over to where regenerated air streamed into the chamber, but that helped only a little.

Cora, though, grew worse. "Can't inhale," she said. "Like stones on my chest. Breathing soup." She was too weak to cope with the increasing difficulty.

Rachel felt all her words go away as she looked at the exhausted new mother, at the mess of blood and amniotic fluid and afterbirth tissue on the crawler floor. This had not been clean and quick like the make-believe births shown in entertainment disks. It looked like some slaughter had occurred here. But not slaughter—new life.

Somehow, Cora got to her knees, wavered as she tried—and failed—to draw a deep breath, then crawled toward the airlock. "You must let me out. Dying. Need to breathe."

Rachel, dizzy from her own lack of air, tried to fight against confusion. "Not in the storm! Not right after the baby. You are too weak." But she knew Cora was right. If the *adin* woman had any chance for surviving, it had to be outside, not in here.

Cora reached the door and rested her head against it, panting. "Strong enough," she said, repeating Rachel's words. "You made us that way."

Rachel watched her open the inner door and haul herself into the airlock. The noise of the storm outside doubled. Cora looked at the sagging environment suit on the floor, focused on the squirming lump that showed the girl's movements, then raised her deep-set eyes to meet Rachel's. She looked intensely human and inhuman at the same time.

"I will tell Boris his daughter is alive. Safe." With great effort, she filled her lungs one more time. "He must face that. Adapt to new conditions—his own words." She raised her hand in a gesture of farewell, then sealed the door.

Somehow, her words about Boris Tiban did not reassure Rachel.

The noise of the storm muffled again, grew louder as Cora opened the outer door, then finally resettled into relative quiet. Rachel found herself alone with the newborn baby.

She had to push the crawler into overdrive to break free of the avalanche rubble. The vehicle groaned and lurched as it heaved over boulders, bucking from side to side. Rachel wished she had strapped herself in. Unsupported on the floor, the baby in the environment suit slid over to one corner and came to rest against a passenger bench. She could not hear the infant's cries over the sound of the storm and the straining engine.

"Come on!" Rachel muttered to herself, pounding the plastic control panel. The effort sent a wash of dizziness over her. Her jaws chattered in the cold. The back of the crawler rose up at an angle over the worst of the obstacles, then she found herself free of the rock slide.

She slid the protective plates aside so she could see her course, though the storm made that nearly impossible. Using less caution now, she increased the crawler's speed, trusting the vehicle to crush medium-sized rocks under its treads so she would not need to pick a path around them.

The chasm walls lowered and the floor widened within half an hour. She felt the urgency slackening as confidence grew; she would be out on the flat slope of Olympus Mons in a few moments, and she could use the guidance gear to choose the most direct course back home. She eased the crawler to greater speed.

She turned around to glance at the baby, to make sure it had not been injured.

Then Boris Tiban sprang out in front of the vehicle again and bounded onto its sloping hood. The dust swirled around him, but he seemed to draw energy from the storm. He hefted his metal staff over his head like a harpoon. The expression on his face made him look like a savage beast from the wilds of Mars.

Instinctively, Rachel ducked back. She did not think quickly enough to slam the protective plates over the windowports.

Boris brought the pointed rod down with a crunch in the center of the trapezoidal glass plate. A white flower of damage burst around the tip, and a high whine of air screamed out as he withdrew the staff. He brought the tip down again even harder, puncturing another, larger hole through the thick glass.

Rachel heard the wind's roar and a distant howl that might have been triumph from the *adin* leader. "Stop!" she shouted, expending precious air. She yanked back on the control levers, bringing the crawler to a sudden halt.

The lurch tossed Boris Tiban from his perch, and he rolled nearly out of sight a few meters away. He staggered to his feet, using the metal staff.

She slapped at the control panel. The brilliant high beams on the crawler stabbed out like an explosion of light. Boris froze, blinded. He wrapped a forearm over his eyes.

Rachel could have accelerated the vehicle then and crushed him under the tread. But she could not do it. She stared at him, listening to the scream of escaping air from the puncture holes. She had created Boris Tiban and exiled him here. He had survived everything Mars could throw at him, and she could not kill him now.

Still unable to see, Boris staggered toward the crawler, raising his staff to strike again.

Cora appeared out of the whirlwind, stumbling and off balance—but perhaps only due to the wind, for she looked stronger than she had when she departed from the crawler. She kept her back to the bright lights.

Boris seemed to sense her presence and turned. He blinked at her in astonishment. Before he could react, Cora snatched the pointed metal staff out of his hand. Delayed by surprise, he did not grab it back immediately. He turned, as if shouting something through the storm at her.

Then Cora shoved the staff through his chest. In the low gravity, her strength was great enough for the thrust to lift him completely off the ground. The spear protruded from his body, puncturing the second set of lungs that rose like a hump on his back. Then she tossed him away from her.

Rachel slapped the palm of her hand against the largest hole in the windowport, picturing herself as the legendary Dutch boy who put his finger in the leaking dike. Instantly she felt the biting cold and the suction tearing at her hand, trying to rip it through the hole. She screamed.

Cora had fallen to the ground outside, but she staggered to her feet and stood in front of the vehicle. She made frantic motions with her arms. Their meaning was clear: Go! Now!

Rachel tore her hand away from the windowport, leaving a chunk of meat behind that dribbled blood and slurped as it was sucked outside. A frosty red smear coated the white cracks in the glass.

Blood dripping from her torn palm, Rachel found the metal tape and pushed several pieces over the punctures in the windowport. The tape dug into the hole, pulled toward the outside. She added a second and then third strip of tape over the punctures, and then began to breathe easier.

Outside, red dust had begun to pile around the body of Boris Tiban. Already Mars hurried to erase all traces of the intruder. Boris had thought himself invincible because he could withstand the rigors of the harsh environment. But Mars had not killed him—a human had, an *adin* human.

Hours later, she continued on a straight downhill course. The slope of the volcano offered a relatively gentle road, scoured clean. The wind continued to hammer at her— such storms rarely let up in less than four days—but it no longer seemed such a difficult thing to withstand.

The layers of metal tape sealed the punctures in the front windowport, but air still hummed out. The compressors kept laboring to fill the crawler with air; the heaters warmed the interior as fast as the Martian cold could suck it away. Rachel hoped she could remain conscious for as long as it might take.

The indicators showed the general direction of travel, though the storm and the iron oxide dust in the air could ruin the accuracy of her onboard compass. Boris had smashed her antenna, so she could not pick up the homing beacons of any nearby settlements, nor could she send out a distress signal.

But if she continued down to the base of Olympus Mons, she might encounter one of the *dva* materials-processing settlements that tapped into leftover volcanic heat, unleashing water from hydrated rock, smelting metals. She had been squinting through the dust for hours—and hoping. She could barely hear the baby crying inside her suit.

Rachel thought her eyes had begun to swim with weariness when she finally saw the yellow lights of a *dva* encampment. The squat, smooth-curved walls made the outbuildings look like hulking giants. Much of the complex would be underground.

Rachel let herself slump back in the driver's chair.

She had made it back with the baby. She had returned to her world, when she had intended to be gone forever. Rachel felt a moment of bittersweet failure, wondering now if she could ever have stood alone and faced the onrushing wall of the storm, to let it carry her away into death. And what would have been the point? An empty gesture for no one but herself.

There was no use mourning the completion of a job well done. Strong people found new goals to achieve, new challenges to face. Weak people bemoaned the loss of great days. Beside her on the crawler floor, this new baby was trying to be strong, to survive against all odds. Rachel Dycek could be strong, too, stronger than Jesús

Keefer or the UN administrative council. *Adapt to the hostile environment, and defeat it*, Boris Tiban would have said. Humanity, in all its forms, would never be obsolete. Rachel would not be obsolete until she surrendered to obsolescence.

Ahead, the dim yellow lights of the *dva* settlement looked as welcoming as a New Year's tree. The cold air of Mars whistled outside the windowport of her vehicle, moaning as it tried to enter through the metal tape. But she would not let it harm her.

She had work to do.

What Continues, What Fails . . .

David Brin

BLACK, AS DEEP AS NIGHT IS BLACK BETWEEN THE stars.

Deeper than that. Night isn't really black, but a solemn, utter shade of red.

As black, then, as Tenembro Nought, which drinks all color, texture, substance from around it, giving back only its awful depth of presence.

But no. She had found redness of an immeasurably profound hue, emerging from that awful pit in space. Not even the singularity was pure enough to typify true blackness. Nor was Isola's own dark mood, for that matter—although, since the visitors' arrival, she had felt smothered, robbed of illumination.

In comparison, a mere ebony luster of skin and hair seemed too pallid to dignify with the name "black." Yet those traits were much sought after on Pleasence World, one of many reasons a fetch ship had come all this way to claim the new life within her.

The fetus might know blackness, Isola thought, laying a hand over her curved abdomen, feeling a stirring there. She purposely used cool, sterile terms, never calling it "baby," or a personalized "she." Anyway, when is a fetus's sensory innervation up to "knowing" anything at all? Can one who has never seen light comprehend blackness?

Leaning toward the dimly illuminated field-effect mirror, Isola touched its silky-cool pseudo-surface. Peering at her own reflection, she found at last what she was looking for.

That's it. Where light falls, never to emerge again.

She brought her face closer still, centering on one jet pupil, an inky well outlined by a dark iris—the universe wherein she dwelt.

"It is said nothing escapes from inside a black hole, but that isn't quite so."

Mikaela was well into her lecture when Isola slipped into the theater, late but unrepentant. A brief frown was her partner's only rebuke for her tardiness. Mikaela continued without losing a beat.

"In this universe of ours, the rules seem to allow exceptions even to the finality of great noughts . . ."

Isola's vision adapted and she discreetly scanned the visitors—six space travelers whose arrival had disrupted a quiet, monastic research routine. The guests from Pleasence World lounged on pseudo-life chaises overlooking Mikaela and the dais. Each sleek-furred settee was specially tuned to the needs of its occupant. While the three humans in the audience made little use of their couch amenities—only occasionally lifting fleshy tubes to infuse endorphin-laced oxygen—the squat, toadlike Vorpal and pair of slender Butins had already hooked up for full breathing symbiosis.

Well, they must have known they were coming to a rude outpost station, built with only a pair of humans in mind. Isola and Mikaela had not expected guests until a few months ago, when the decelerating starship peremptorily announced itself and made its needs known.

Those needs included use of Isola's womb.

"Actually, there are countless misconceptions about gravitational singularities, especially the massive variety formed in the recoil of a super-nova. One myth concerns the possibility of communicating across a black hole's event horizon, to see what has become of all the matter which left this universe so violently and completely, long ago."

Mikaela turned with a flourish of puffy sleeves toward the viewing tank. Winking one eye, she called up a new image to display in midair, above the dais. Brilliance spilled across Mikaela's fair skin and the visitors' multihued faces, causing several to flinch involuntarily. Isola smiled.

Titanic fields enveloped and deformed a tortured sun, dragging long shreds of its substance toward a spinning, flattened whirlpool—a disc so bright it searingly outshone the unfortunate nearby star.

"Until now, most investigations of macro black holes have concentrated on showy cases like this one—the Cygnus A singularity—which raises such ferocious tides on a companion sun as to tear it apart before our eyes. In galactic cores, greedy mega-holes can devour entire stellar clusters. No wonder most prior expeditions were devoted to viewing noughts with visible accretion discs. Besides, their splashy radiance made them easy to find."

Isola watched the victim star's tattered, stolen essence spiral into the planate cyclone, which brightened painfully despite attenuation by the viewing software. Shimmering, lambent stalks traced magnetically directed plasma beams, jetting from the singularity north and south. As refulgent gas swirled inward, jostling and heating, it suddenly reached an inner lip—the edge of a black circle, tiny in diameter but awesome in conclusiveness. The Event Horizon.

Spilling across that boundary, the actinic matter vanished abruptly, completely. Once over the edge it was no longer part of reality. Not *this* reality, anyway.

Mikaela had begun her lecture from a basic level, since some of the visitors weren't cosmogonists. One of these, Jarlquin, the geneticist from Pleasence, shifted on her chaise. At some silent order, a pseudo-life assistant appeared to massage her shoulders. Petite, even for a starfarer, Jarlquin glanced toward Isola, offering a conspiratorial smile. Isola pretended not to notice.

"Most massive noughts don't have stars as close neighbors, nor gas clouds to feed them so prodigiously and make them shine." Closing one eye again, Mikaela sent another command. In a flickered instant, the ostentatious display of stellar devouring was replaced by serene quiet. Cool, untroubled constellations spanned the theater. Tenembro Nought was a mere ripple in one quadrant of the starry field, unnoticed by the audience until Mikaela's pointer drew attention to its outlines. A lenslike blur of distortion, nothing more.

"Solitary macro-singularities like Tenembro are far more common than their gaudy cousins. Standing alone in space, hungry, but too isolated to draw in more than a rare atom or meteoroid, they are also harder to find. Tenembro Nought was discovered only after detecting the way it bent light from faraway galaxies.

"The black hole turned out to be perfect for our needs, and only fifty-nine years, shiptime, from the colony on Kalimarn."

Under Mikaela's mute guidance, the image enlarged. She gestured towards a corner of the tank where a long, slender vessel could be seen, decelerating into orbit around the cold dimple in space. From the ship's tail emerged much smaller ripples, which also had the property of causing starlight to waver briefly. The distortion looked similar—though on a microscopic scale—to that caused by the giant nought itself. This was no coincidence.

"Once in orbit, we began constructing research probes. We converted our ship's drive to make tailored micro-singularities . . ."

At that moment, a tickling sensation along her left eyebrow told Isola that a datafeed was queued with results from her latest experiment. She closed that eye with a trained squeeze denoting ACCEPT. Implants along the inner lid came alight, conveying images in crisp focus to her retina. Unlike the digested pap in Mikaela's presentation, what Isola saw was in real time . . . or as "real" as time got, this near a macro black hole.

More rippling images of constellations. She subvocally commanded a shift to graphic mode; field diagrams snapped over the starry scene, showing Tenembro's mammoth, steepening funnel in spacetime. An uneven formation of objects—minuscule in comparison—skimmed toward glancing rendezvous with the great nought's eerily bright-black horizon. Glowing traceries depicted one of the little objects as another space-funnel. Vastly smaller, titanically narrower, it too possessed a center that was severed from this reality as if amputated by the scalpel of God.

" . . . with the objective of creating ideal conditions for our instruments to peer down . . ."

Columns of data climbed across the scene under Isola's eyelid. She could already tell that this experiment wasn't going any better than the others. Despite all their careful calculations, the camera probes still weren't managing to straddle between the giant and dwarf singularities at the right moment, just when the black discs touched. Still, she watched that instant of grazing passage, hoping to learn something—

The scene suddenly shivered as Isola's belly gave a churning lurch, provoking waves of nausea. She blinked involuntarily and the image vanished.

The fit passed, leaving her short of breath, with a prickle of perspiration on her face and neck. Plucking a kerchief from her sleeve, Isola dabbed her brow. She lacked the will to order the depiction back. Time enough to go over the results later, with full-spectrum facilities.

This is getting ridiculous, Isola brooded. She had never imagined, when the requisition-request came, that a simple clonal pregnancy would entail so many inconveniences!

"... taking advantage of a loophole in the rules of our cosmos, which allow for a slightly offset boundary when the original collapstar possessed either spin or charge. This offset from perfection is one of the features we hope to exploit ..."

Isola felt a sensation of being watched. She shifted slightly. From a nearby pseudo-life chaise, Jarlquin was looking at Isola again, with a measuring expression.

She might have the courtesy to feign attention to Mikaela's presentation, Isola thought, resentfully. *Jarlquin seems more preoccupied with my condition than I am.*

The Pleasencer's interest was understandable, after having come so far just for the present contents of Isola's womb. *My anger with Jarlquin has an obvious source. Its origin is the same as my own.*

An obsession with beginnings had brought Isola to this place on the edge of infinity.

How did the universe begin?
Where did it come from?
Where do I come from?

It was ironic that her search would take her to where creation ended. For while the expanding cosmos has no "outer edge," as such, it does encounter a sharp boundary at the rim of a black hole.

Isola remembered her childhood, back on Kalimarn, playing in the yard with toys that made pico-singularities on demand, from which she gained her first experience examining the warped mysteries of succinct event horizons. She recalled the day these had ceased to be mere dalliances, or school exercises in propulsion engineering, when they instead became foci for exaltation and wonder.

The same equations that describe an expanding universe also tell of a gravity trough's collapse. Explosion, implosion ... the only difference lay in reversing time's arrow. We are, in effect, living inside *a gigantic black hole!*

Her young mind marveled at the implications.

Everything within is aleph. Aleph is cut off from contact with that which is not aleph. Or that which came before *aleph. Cause and effect, forever separated.*

As I am separated from what brought me into being.

As I must separate from what I bring into being. . . .

The fetus kicked again, setting off twinges, unleashing a flood of symbiotic bonding hormones. One side effect came as a sudden wave of unasked-for sentimentality. Tears filled Isola's eyes, and she could not have made image-picts even if she tried.

Jarlquin had offered drugs to subdue these effects—to make the process "easier." Isola did not want it eased. This could be her sole act of biological creation given the career she had chosen. The word "motherhood" might be archaic nowadays, but it still had connotations. She wanted to experience them.

It was simple enough in conception.

Back in the eighteenth century, a physicist, John Mitchell, showed that any large enough lump of matter might have an escape velocity greater than the speed of light. Even luminous waves should not be able to escape. When John Wheeler, two hundred years later, performed the same conjuring trick with mass *density*, the name "black hole" was coined.

Those were just theoretical exercises. What actually happens to a photon that tries to climb out of a singularity? Does it behave like a rocket, slowing down under gravity's insistent drag? Coming to a halt, then turning to plummet down again?

Not so. Photons move at a constant rate, one single speed, no matter what reference frame you use. Unless physically blocked or diverted, light slows for no one.

But tightly coiled gravity does strange things. It changes *time*. Gravitation can make light pay a toll for escaping. Photons lose energy not by slowing down, but by stretching redder, ever redder as they rise from a spacetime well, elongating to microwave lengths, then radio, and onward. Theoretically, on climbing to the event horizon of a black hole, any light wave has reddened down to nothing.

Nothing emerges. Nothing—traveling at the speed of light. In a prim, legalistic sense, that nothing *is* still light.

Isola spread her traps, planning tight, intersecting orbits. She lay in a web designed to ambush nothing . . . to peer down into nowhere.

"You know, I never gave it much thought before. The whole thing seemed such a bother. Anyway, I always figured there'd be plenty of time later, after we finished our project."

Mikaela's non sequitur came by complete surprise. Isola looked up from the chart she had been studying. Across the breakfast table, her colleague wore an expression that seemed outwardly casual, but studied. Thin as frost.

"Plenty of time for what?" Isola asked.

Mikaela lifted a cup of *port'tha* to her lips. "You know . . . procreation."

"Oh." Isola did not know what to say. Ever since the Visitor Ship announced itself, her partner had expressed nothing but irritation over havoc to their research schedules. Of late her complaints had been replaced with pensive moodiness. *So this is what she's been brooding about*, Isola realized. To give herself a moment, she held out her own cup for the pseudo-life servitor to refill. Her condition forbade drinking *port'tha*, so she made do with tea.

"And what have you concluded?" she asked, evenly.

"That I'd be foolish to waste this opportunity."

"Opportunity?"

Mikaela shrugged. "Look, Jarlquin came all this way hoping to requisition your clone. You could have turned her down—"

"Mikaela, we've gone over this so many times . . ." But Isola's partner cut her off, raising one hand, placatingly.

"That's all right. I now see you were right to agree. It's a great honor. Records of your clone-line are on file throughout the sector."

Isola sighed. "My ancestresses were explorers and star messengers. So, many worlds in the region would have—"

"Exactly. It's all a matter of available information! Pleasence World had data on you, but not on a seminatural variant like me, born on Kalimarn of Kalimarnese stock. For all we know, I might have what Jarlquin's looking for, too."

Isola nodded earnestly. "I'm sure of that. Do you mean you're thinking—"

"—of getting tested?" Mikaela watched Isola over the rim of her cup. "Do you think I should?"

Despite her continuing reservations over having been requisitioned in the first place, Isola felt a surge of enthusiasm. The notion of sharing this experience—this unexpected experiment in motherhood—with her only friend gave her strange pleasure. "Oh, yes! They'll jump at the chance. Of course . . ." She paused.

"What?" Mikaela asked, tension visible in her shoulders.

Isola had a sudden image of the two of them, waddling about the station, relying utterly on drones and pseudo-life servitors to run errands and experiments. The inconvenience alone would be frightful. Yet it would only add up to a year or so, altogether. She smiled ironically. "It means our guests would stay longer. And you'd have to put up with Jarlquin—"

Mikaela laughed. A hearty laugh of release. "Yeah, dammit. That is a drawback!"

Relieved at the lifting of her partner's spirits, Isola grinned too. They were in concord again. She had missed the old easiness between them, which had been under strain since that first surprise message disrupted their hermits' regime. *This will put everything right,* she hoped. *We'll have years to talk about a strange, shared experience after it's all over.*

The best solutions are almost always the simplest.

Within a sac of amniotic fluid, a play is acted out according to a script. The script calls for proteins, so amino acids are lined up by ribosomes to play their roles. Enzymes appear at the proper moment. Cells divide and jostle for position. The code demands they specialize, so they do. Subtle forces of attraction shift them into place, one by one.

It is a script that has been played before.

A script designed to play again.

The pair of nano-naughts—each massing just a million tons—hovered within a neutral gravity tank. Between the microscopic wells of darkness, a small recording device peered into one of the tiny singularities. Across the room, screens showed only the color black.

Special fields kept each nought from self-destructing—either through quantum evaporation or by folding space around itself like a blanket and disappearing. Other beams of force strained to hold the two black holes apart, preventing gravity from slamming them together uncontrollably.

It was an unstable situation. But Isola was well practiced. Seated on a soft chaise to support her over-strained back, she used subtle machines to manipulate the two funnels of sunken metric toward each other. The outermost rims of their space time wells merged. Two microscopic black spheres—the event horizons themselves—lay centimeters apart, ratcheting closer by the second, as Isola let them slowly draw together.

Tides tugged at the camera, suspended between, and at the fiber-thin cable leading from the camera to her recorders. Peering into one of those pits of blackness, the mini-telescope saw nothing. That was only natural.

Nothing could escape from inside a black hole.

A special kind of nothing, though. Nothing that had formerly been light, before being stretched down to true nothingness in the act of climbing that steep slope.

The two funnels merged closer still. The microscopic black balls drew nearer.

Light trying to escape a black hole is reddened to nonexistence. Nevertheless, virtual light can theoretically escape one nought, only to be sucked into the other. There, it starts blue-shifting exponentially, as gravity yanks it down again.

Between one event horizon and the other, the light doesn't "officially" exist. Not in the limiting case. Yet ideally, there should be a flow.

They had not believed her on Kalimarn. Until one day she showed them it was possible, for the narrowest of instants, to tap the virtual stream. To squeeze between the red-shifted and blue-shifted segments. To catch the briefest glimpse—

It happened too fast to follow with human eyes. One moment two black spheres were inching microscopically toward each other with the little, doomed instrumentality tortured and whining between them. The next instant, in a sudden flash, all contents of the tank combined and vanished. Space time backlash set the reinforced vacuum chamber rocking—a side effect of that final stroke which severed forever all contact between the noughts and this cosmos where they'd been made. In the instant it took Isola to blink, they were gone, leaving behind the neatly severed end of fiber cable.

Gone, but not forgotten. In taking the camera with them, the singularities had given it the moment it needed. The moment when "nothing" was no longer nothing but merely a deep red.

And red is visible. . . .

This was what had won her funding to seek out a partner and come here to Tenembro Nought. For if it was possible to look inside a micro-hole, why not a far bigger one that had been born in the titanic self-devouring of a star? So far, she and Mikaela hadn't succeeded in that part of the quest. Their research at the micro end, however, kept giving surprising and wonderful results.

Isola checked to make sure all the secrets of the vanished nano-nought had been captured during that narrow instant and were safely stored in memory. Its rules. Its nature as a cosmos all its own. She had varied the formation recipe again, and wondered what physics would be revealed this time.

Before she could examine the snapshot of a pocket universe, however, her left eyelid twitched and came alight with a reminder. Time for her appointment. Damn.

But Jarlquin had shown Isola how much more pleasant it was to be on time.

The temperature of the universe is just under three degrees absolute. It has chilled considerably in the act of expanding over billions of years, from fireball to cosmos. Cooling in turn provoked changes in state. Delicately balanced forces shifted as the original heat diffused, allowing protons to form from quarks, then electrons to take orbit around them, producing that wonder, hydrogen. Later rebalancings caused matter to gather, forming monstrous swirls. Many of these eddies coalesced and came alight spectacularly—all because the rules allowed it.

Because the rules *required* it.

Time processed one of those lights—by those selfsame rules—until it finished burning and collapsed, precipitating a fierce explosion and ejection of its core from the universe.

Tenembro Nought sat as a fossil relic of that banishment. A scar, nearly healed, but palpable.

All of this had come about according to the rules.

"We've liberated ourselves from Darwin's Curse, but it still comes down to the same thing."

The visitor made a steeple of her petite hands, long and narrow, with delicate fingers like a surgeon's. Her lips were full and dyed a rich mauve hue. Faint ripples passed across her skin as pores opened and closed rhythmically. A genetic graft, Isola supposed. Probably some Vorpal trait inserted into Jarlquin's genome before she was even conceived.

Fortunately, laws limit the gene trade, Isola thought. *All they can ask of me is a simple cloning.*

Over Jarlquin's shoulder, through the window of the lounge, Isola saw the starscape and realized Smolin Cluster was in view. Subvocally, she ordered the magni-focus pane to enlarge one quadrant for her eye only. Flexing gently, imperceptibly to other visitors across the room, the window sent Isola a scene of suns like shining grains. One golden pinpoint—Pleasence Star—shone soft and stable. Its kind, by nature's laws, would last eons and never become a nought.

"You see," Jarlquin continued, blithely ignorant of Isola's distraction, "although we've pierced much of the code of Life, and reached a truce of sorts with Death, the fundamental rule's the same. That is successful which continues. And what continues most successfully not only lives, but multiplies."

Why is she telling me this? Isola wondered, sitting in a gently vibrating non-life chair across from Jarlquin. Did the biologer-nurturist actually care what her subject thought? Isola had agreed to disrupt her research and donate a clone, for the genetic benefit of Pleasence World. Wasn't that enough?

I ought to be flattered. Tenembro Nought may be "close" to their world by interstellar standards, still, how often does a colony send a ship so far, just to collect one person's neonate clone?

Oh, the visitors had also made a great show of scrutinizing their work here, driving Mikaela to distraction with their questions. The pair of Butins were physicists and exuded enthusiasm along with their pungent, blue

perspiration. But Jarlquin had confided in Isola. They
would never have been approved to come all this way
if not also to seek her seed. To treasure and nurture it,
and take it home with them.

*As I was taken from my own parent, who donated an
infant duplicate to Kalimarn as her ship swept by. We are
a model in demand, it seems.*

The reasons were clear enough, in abstract. In school
she had learned about the interstellar economy of genes,
which prevented the catastrophe of inbreeding and spread
the boon of diversity. But tidal surges of hormone and
emotion had not been in her syllabus. Isola could not
rightly connect abstractions with events churning away
below her sternum. They seemed as unrelated as a sonnet
and a table.

Two pseudo-life servitors entered—no doubt called
when Jarlquin winked briefly a moment ago—carrying hot beverages on a tray. The blank-faced, bipedal
protoplasmoids were as expressionless as might be expected
of beings less than three days old . . . and destined within
three more to slip back into the vat from which they'd
been drawn. One servant poured for Isola as it had been
programmed to do, with uncomplaining perfection no truly
living being could have emulated.

"You were speaking of multiplication," Isola
prompted, lest Jarlquin lose her train of thought and
decide to launch into another recital of the wonders of
Pleasence. The fine life awaiting Isola's clone.

"Ah?" Jarlquin pursed her lips, tasting the tea. "Yes,
multiplication. Tell me, as time goes on, who populates the
galaxies? Obviously, those who disperse and reproduce.
Even though we aren't *evolving* in the old way—stressed
by death and natural selection—a kind of selection is still
going on."

"Selection."

"Indeed, selection. For traits appropriate to a given
place and time. Consider what happened to those genes
which, for one reason or another, kept individuals from

leaving Beloved Earth during the first grand waves of colonization. Are descendants of those individuals still with us? Do those genes persist, now that Earth is gone?"

Isola saw Jarlquin's point. The impulsive drive to reproduce sexually had ebbed from humanity—at least in this sector. She had heard things were otherwise, spinward of galactic West and in the Magellanics. Nevertheless, certain models of humanity seemed to spread and thrive, while other types remained few, or disappeared.

"So it's been in other races we've formed symbioses with. Planets and commonwealths decide what kinds of citizens they need and requisition clones or new variants, often trading with colonies many parsecs away. Nowadays you can be successful at reproduction without ever even planning to."

Isola realized Jarlquin must know her inside and out. Not that her ambivalence was hard to read.

To become a mother, she thought. *I am about to . . . give birth. I don't even know what it means, but Jarlquin seems to envy me.*

"Whatever works," the Pleasencer continued, sipping her steaming tea. "That law of nature, no amount of scientific progress will ever change. If you have what it takes to reproduce, and pass on those traits to your offspring, then *they* will likely replicate as well, and your kind will spread."

What came before? And what came before that?

As a very little girl, back on Kalimarn, she had seen how other infants gleefully discovered a way to drive parents and guardians to distraction with the game of "Why." It could start at any moment, given the slightest excuse to ask that first, guileless question. Any adult who innocently answered with an explanation was met with the same simple, efficient rejoinder—another "why?" Then another . . . Used carefully, deliciously, it became an inquisition guaranteed to provoke either insanity or pure enlightenment by the twentieth repetition. More often the former.

To be different, Isola modified the exercise.

What caused that? she asked. Then—*What caused the cause?* and so on.

She soon learned how to dispense quickly with preliminaries. The vast, recent ages of space travel and colonization were quickly dealt with, as was the Dark Climb of man, back on Beloved Earth. Recorded history was like a salad, archeology an aperitif. Neanderthals and dinosaurs offered adult bulwarks, but she would not be distracted. Under pestering inquiry, the homeworld unformed, its sun unraveled into dust and gas which swirled backward in time to be absorbed by reversed supernovas. Galaxies unwound. Starlight and cold matter fell together, compressing into universal plasma as the cosmos shrank toward its origins. By the time her poor teachers had parsed existence to its debut epoch—the first searing day, its earliest, actinic minute, down to micro-fractions of a second—Isola felt a sense of excitement like no story book or fairy tale could provide.

Inevitably, instructors and matrons sought refuge in the singularity. The Great Singularity. Before ever really grasping their meaning, Isola found herself stymied by pat phrases like "quantum vacuum fluctuation" and "boundary-free existence," at which point relieved adults smugly refused to admit of any prior cause.

It was a cop-out of the first order. Like when they told her how unlikely it was she would ever meet her true parent—the one who had brought her into being— no matter how far she traveled or how long she lived.

Subtle chemical interactions cause cells to migrate and change, taking up specialties and commencing to secrete new chemicals themselves. Organs form and initiate activity. All is done according to a code.
It is the code that makes it so.

Isola took her turn in the control chamber, relieving Mikaela at the end of her shift. Even there, one was reminded of the visitors. Just beyond the crystal-covered main aperture, Isola could make out the long, narrow ship from Pleasence, tugged by Tenembro's tides so that its crew quarters lay farthest from the singularity. The implosion chamber dangled toward the great hole in space.

"Remember when they came into orbit?" Mikaela asked, pointing toward the engine section. "How they pulsed their drive noughts at a peculiar pitch?"

"Yes." Isola nodded, wishing for once that Mikaela were not all business but would actually talk to her. Something was wrong.

"Yes, I remember. The nano-holes collapsed quickly, emitting stronger spatial backwash than I'd seen before."

"That's right," Mikaela said without meeting Isola's eyes. "By creating metric-space ahead of themselves at a faster rate, they managed a steeper deceleration. Their engineer—the Vorpal, I'q'oun—gave me their recipe." Mikaela laid a data-sliver on the console. "You might see whether it's worth inserting some of their code into our next probe."

"Mmm." Isola felt reluctant. A debt for useful favors might disturb the purity of her irritation with these visitors. "I'll look into it," she answered noncommittally.

Although she wanted to search Mikaela's eyes, Isola thought it wiser not to press matters. The level of tension between them, rather than declining since that talk over breakfast, had risen sharply soon after. Something must have happened. *Did she ask Jarlquin to be tested?* Isola wondered. *Or could I have said something to cause offense?*

Mikaela clearly knew she was behaving badly, and it bothered her. To let emotion interfere with work was a sign of unskilled selfing. The fair-skinned woman visibly made an effort to change tacks.

"How's the . . . you know, coming along?" she asked, gesturing vaguely toward Isola's midriff.

"Oh, well, I guess. All considered."

"Yeah?"

"I . . . feel strange though," Isola confided, hoping to draw her partner out. "As if my body were doing something it understood that's totally beyond *me,* you know?" She tapped herself on the temple. "Then, last night, I dreamt about a man. You know, a male? We had some on Kalimarn, you know. It was very . . . odd." She shook her head. "Then there are these mood swings and shifts of emotion I never imagined before. It's quite an experience."

To Isola's surprise, a coldness seemed to fill the room. Mikaela's visage appeared locked, her expression as blank as pseudo-life.

"I'll bet it is."

There was a long, uncomfortable silence. This episode had disrupted their planned decade of research, but now there was more to it than that. A difference whose consequences seemed to spiral outward, pushing the two of them apart, cutting communication. Isola suddenly knew that her friend had gone to Jarlquin, and what the answer had been.

If asked directly, Mikaela would probably claim indifference, that it didn't matter, that procreation had not figured in her plans anyway. Nevertheless, it must have been a blow. Her eyes lay impenetrable under twin hoods.

"Well. Good night, then." The other woman's voice was ice. She nodded, turning to go.

"Good night," Isola called after her. The portal shut silently.

Subtle differences in heritage—that was all this was about. It seemed so foolish and inconsequential. After all, what was biological reproduction on the cosmological scale of things? Would any of this matter a million years from now?

One good thing about physics—its rules could be taken apart in fine, separable units, examined, and superposed again to make good models of the whole. Why was this so for the cosmos, but not for conscious intellects? *I'll be glad when this is over,* Isola told herself.

She went to the Suiting Room, to prepare for going outside. Beyond another crystal pane, Tenembro Nought's glittering blackness seemed to distort a quarter of the universe, a warped, twisted, tortured tract of firmament.

There was a vast contrast between the scale human engineers worked with—creating pico-, nano-, and even micro-singularities by tricks of quantum bookkeeping—and a monster like Tenembro, which had been crushed into existence, or pure *non*existence, by nature's fiercest explosion. Yet, in theory, it was the same phenomenon. Once matter has been concentrated to such density that space wraps around itself, what remains is but a hole.

The wrapping could sometimes even close off the hole. Ripples undulating away from such implosions gave modern vessels palpable waves of spacetime to skim upon, much as their ancestors' crude ships rode the pulsing shock-fronts of antimatter explosions. The small black holes created in a ship's drive lasted for but an instant. Matter "borrowed" during that brief moment was compressed to superdensity and then vanished before the debt came due, leaving behind just a fossil field and spacial backwash to surf upon.

No origin to speak of. No destiny worth mentioning. That was how one of Isola's fellow students had put it, back in school. It was glib and her classmate had been proud of the aphorism. To Isola it had seemed too pat, leaving unanswered questions.

Her spacesuit complained as pseudo-life components stretched beyond programmed parameters to fit her burgeoning form. Isola waited patiently until the flesh-and-metal concatenation sealed securely. Then, feeling big and awkward, she pushed through the exit port—a jungle of overlapping lock-seal leaves—and stepped out upon the station platform, surrounded by the raw vacuum of space.

Robotic servitors gathered at her ankles, jostling to be chosen for the next one-way mission. Eagerness to approach the universal edge was part of their programming—as it appeared to be in hers.

Even at this range, Isola felt Tenembro Nought's tides tugging at fine sensors in her inner ears. The fetus also seemed to note that heavy presence. She felt it turn to orient along the same direction as the Visitor Ship, feet toward the awful blankness with its crown of twisted stars.

Let's get on with it, she thought, irritated by her sluggish mental processes. Isola had to wink three times to finally set off a flurry of activity. Well-drilled, her subordinates prepared another small invasion force, designed to pierce what logically could not be pierced. To see what, by definition, could not be seen.

The color of the universe had once been blue. Blue-violet of a purity that was essential. Primal. At that time the cosmos was too small to allow any other shade. There was only room for short, hot light.

Then came expansion, and a flow of time. These, plus subtle rules of field and force, wrought inexorable reddening on photons. By the time there were observers to give names to colors, the vast bulk of the universe was redder than infrared.

None of this mattered to Tenembro Nought. By then, it was a hole. A mystery. Although some might search for color in its depths, it could teach the universe a thing or two about futiginal darkness.

For all intents and purposes, its color was black.

"I thought these might intrigue you," Jarlquin told her that evening.

There was no way to avoid the visitor—not without becoming a hermit and admitting publicly that something was bothering her. Mikaela was doing enough sulking for both of them, so Isola attended to her hosting duties in the station lounge. This time, while the other visitors chatted near the starward window, the nurturist from Pleasence held out toward Isola several jagged memory lattices. They lay in her slender hand like fragments of ancient ice.

Isola asked, "What are they?"

"Your ancestry," Jarlquin replied with a faint smile. "You might be interested in what prompted us to requisition your clone."

Isola stared at the luminous crystals. This data must have been prepared long ago: inquiries sent to her homeworld and perhaps beyond. All must have been accomplished before their ship even set sail. It bespoke a long view on the part of folk who took their planning seriously.

She almost asked, *"How did you know I'd want these?"* Perhaps on Pleasence they didn't consider it abnormal, as they had on Kalimarn, to be fascinated by origins.

"Thank you," she told the visitor instead, keeping an even tone.

Jarlquin nodded with an enigmatic smile. "Contemplate continuity."

"I shall."

In school, young Isola had learned there were two major theories of True Origin—how everything began in that first, fragmentary moment.

In both cases the result, an infinitesimal fraction of a second after creation, was a titanic explosion. In converting from the first "seed" of false vacuum to a grapefruit-sized ball containing all the mass-energy required to form a universe, there occurred something called *Inflation*. A fundamental change of state was delayed just long enough for a strange, negative version of gravity to take hold, momentarily driving the explosion even faster than allowed by lightspeed.

It was a trick, utilizing a clause in creation's codebook that would never again be invoked. The conditions would no longer exist—not in *this* universe—until final collapse brought all galaxies and stars and other ephemera together once more, swallowing the sum into one Mega-Singularity, bringing the balance sheet back to zero.

That was how some saw the universe, as just another borrowing. The way a starship briefly "borrows" matter without prior existence, in order to make small black holes whose collapse and disappearance repays the debt again. So the entire universe might be thought of as a *loan*, on a vastly larger scale.

What star voyagers did on purpose, crudely, with machines, Creation had accomplished insensately but far better, by simple invocation of the Laws of Quantum Probability. Given enough time, such a fluctuation was bound to occur, sooner or later, according to the rules.

But this theory of origin had a flaw. In what context did one mean " . . . given enough time . . ."? How could there have been time before the universe itself was born? What clocks measured it? What observers noted its passage?

Even if there was a context . . . even if this borrowing was allowed under the rules . . . where did the rules *themselves* come from?

Unsatisfied, Isola sought a second theory of origins.

Black.

Within her eye's dark iris, the pupil was black. So was her skin.

It had not always been so.

She looked from her reflection to a row of images projected in the air nearby. Her ancestresses. Clones, demi-clones and variants going back more than forty generations. Only the most recent had her rich ebony flesh tone. Before that, shades had varied considerably around a dark theme. But other similarities ran true.

A certain line of jaw . . .

An arching of the brows . . .

A reluctant pleasure in the smile . . .

Women Isola had never known or heard of, stretched in diminishing rows across the room. Part of a continuity.

Further along, she found troves of data from still earlier times. There appeared images of *fathers* as well as mothers, fascinating her and vastly complicating the branchings of descent. Yet it remained possible to note patterns, moving up the line. Long after all trace of "family" resemblance vanished, she still saw consistent motifs, those Jarlquin had spoken of.

Five fingers on each clasping hand . . .

Two eyes, poised to catch subtleties . . .

A nose to scent . . . a brain to perceive . . .

A persistent will to continue . . .

This was not the only design for making thinking beings, star travelers, successful colonizers of galaxies. There were also Butins, Vorpals, Leshi and ten score other models which, tried and tested by harsh nature, now thrived in diversity in space. Nevertheless, this was a successful pattern. It endured.

Life stirred beneath Isola's hand. Her warm, tumescent belly throbbed, vibrating not just her skin and bones but membranes, deep within, that she had never expected to have touched by another. Now at least there was a context to put it all in. Her ancestors' images nourished some deep yearning. The poignancy of what she'd miss—the chance to know this living being soon to emerge from her own body—was now softened by a sense of continuity.

It reassured her.

There was a certain beauty in the song of DNA.

Perched in orbit, circling a deep well.

A well with a rim from which nothing escapes.

Micro-noughts, spiraling toward that black boundary, seem cosmically, comically, out of scale with mighty Tenembro, star-corpse, gate-keeper, universal scar. What they lack in width, they make up for in depth just as profound. Wide or narrow, each represents a one-way tunnel to oblivion.

Is it crazy to ask if oblivions come in varieties, or differ in ways that matter?

Rules were a problem of philosophical dimensions when Isola first studied origins.

Consider the ratio of electric force to gravity. If this number had been infinitesimally higher, stars would never grow hot enough within their bowels to form and then expel heavy nuclei—those, like carbon and oxygen, needed for life. If the ratio were just a fraction *lower*, stars would race through brief conflagrations too quickly for planets to evolve. Take the ratio a little farther off in either direction, and there would be no stars at all.

The universal rules of Isola's home cosmos were rife with such fine-tuning. Numbers which, had they been different by even one part in a trillion, would not have allowed subtleties like planets or seas, sunsets and trees.

Some called this evidence of design. Master craftsmanship. Creativity. Creator.

Others handled the coincidence facilely. "If things were different," they claimed, "there would be no observers to note the difference. So it's no surprise that we, who exist, observe around us the precise conditions needed for existence!

"Besides, countless *other* natural constants seem to have nothing special about their values. Perhaps it's just a matter of who is doing the calculating!"

Hand-waving, all hand-waving. Neither answer satisfied Isola when she delved into true origins. Creationists, Anthropicists, they all missed the point.

Everything has to come from somewhere. Even a creator. Even coincidence.

Mikaela barely spoke to her anymore. Isola understood. Her partner could not help feeling rejected. The worlds had selected against her. In effect, the universe had declared her a dead end.

Isola felt, illogically, that it must be *her* fault. She should have found a way to console her friend. *It must be strange to hear you'll be the last in your line.*

Yet, what could she say?

That it's also strange to know your line will continue, but out of reach, out of sight? Beyond all future knowing?

The experiments continued. Loyal camera probes were torn apart by tides, or aged to dust in swirling back-flows of time near Tenembro's vast event horizon. Isola borrowed factors from the visitors' ship-drive. She tinkered with formulas for small counterweight black holes, and sent the new micro-singularities peeling off on ever-tighter trajectories toward the great nought's all-devouring maw.

Cameras maneuvered to interpose themselves between one nothing and another. During that brief but time-dilated instant, as two wells of oblivion competed to consume them, the machines tried to take pictures.

Pictures of nothing, and all.

"To pass the time, I've been tinkering with your pseudo-life tanks," Jarlquin announced proudly one evening. "Your servitor fabricants ought to last as long as nine days now, before having to go back into the vat."

The visitor was obviously pleased with herself, finding something useful to do while Isola gestated. Jarlquin puttered, yet her interest remained focused on a product more subtle than anything she herself would ever design. Unskilled, but tutored by a billion years of happenstance, Isola prepared that product for delivery.

The second theory of origins had amazed her.

It was not widely talked about in Kalimarn's academies, where savants preferred notions of Quantum Fluctuation. After all, Kalimarn served as banking world for an entire cluster. No doubt the colonists *liked* thinking of the universe as something out on loan.

Nevertheless, in her academy days, Isola had sought other explanations.

We might have come from somewhere else! she realized one evening, when her studies took her deeply into frozen archives. The so-called "crackpot" theories she found there did not seem so crazy. Their mathematics worked just as well as models of quantum usury.

When a black hole is created after a supernova explosion, the matter that collapses into it doesn't just vanish. According to the equations, it goes . . . "elsewhere." To another spacetime. A continuum completely detached from ours.

Each new black hole represents another universe! A new creation.

The implication wasn't hard to translate in the opposite direction.

Our own cosmos may have had its start with a black hole that formed in some earlier cosmos!

The discovery thrilled her. It appalled Isola that none of her professors shared her joy.

"Even if true," one of them had said, "it's an unanswerable, unrewarding line of inquiry. By the very nature of the situation, we are cut off, severed from causal contact with that earlier cosmos. Given that, I prefer simpler hypotheses."

"But think of the implications!" she insisted. "Several times each year, new macro black holes are created in supernovas—"

"Yes? So?"

"What's more, at any moment across this galaxy alone, countless starships generate innumerable *micro*-singularities, just to surf the payback wave when they collapse. Each of these 'exhaust' singularities becomes a universe too!"

The savant had smiled patronizingly. "Shall we play god, then? Try to take responsibility in some way for our creations?" The old woman's tone was supercilious. "This argument's almost as ancient as debating angels on pinheads. Why don't you transfer to the department of archaic theology?"

Isola would not be put off, nor meekly accept conventional wisdom. She eventually won backing to investigate the quandaries that consumed her. Much later, Jarlquin told her this perseverance was in part inherited. Some colonies had learned to cherish tenacity like hers. Though sometimes troublesome, the trait often led to profit and art. It was a major reason Pleasence World had sent a fetch ship to Tenembro Nought.

They cared little about the specific truths Isola pursued. They wanted the trait that drove her to pursue.

Cells differentiate according to patterns laid down in the codes. Organs form which would—by happenstance—provide respiration, circulation, cerebration . . .

In one locale, cells even begin preparing for future reproduction. New eggs align themselves in rows, then go dormant. Within each egg lay copies of the script.

Even this early, the plan lays provisions for the next phase.

Normally, a pseudo-life incubator would have taken over during her final weeks. But the nurturist, Jarlquin, wanted none of that. Pseudo-life was but a product. Its designs, no matter how clever, came out of theory and mere generations of practice, while Isola's womb was skilled from trial and error successes stretching back several galactic rotations. So Isola waddled, increasingly awkward and inflated, wondering how her ancestors ever managed.

Every one of them made it. Each managed to get someone else started.

It was a strange consolation, and she smiled, sardonically. *Maybe I'm starting to think like Jarlquin!*

She no longer went outside to conduct experiments. Using her calculations, Mikaela fine-tuned the next convoy sent to skim Tenembro's vast event horizon, while Isola went back to basics in the laboratory.

What mystery is movement—distinguishing one location from another? In some natures, all points correspond—instantaneous, coincidental. Uninteresting.

What riddle, then, is change—one object *evolving* into another? Some worlds disallow this. Though they contain multitudes, all things remain the same.

Is a reality cursed which suffers entropy? Or is it consecrated?

Once more a flash. Two micro-singularities fell together, carrying a tiny holo-camera with them to oblivion. In the narrow moment of union, the robot took full-spectrum readings of one involute realm. The results showed Isola a mighty, but flawed, kingdom.

The amount of mass originally used to form the nought mattered at this end—determining its gravitational pull and event horizon. But on the other side, beyond the constricted portal of the singularity, it made little difference. Whether a mere million tons had gone into the black hole or the weight of a thousand suns, it was the act of geometric transformation that counted. Instants after the nought's formation, inflation had turned it into a macrocosm. A fiery ball of plasma exploding in its own context, in a reference frame whose dimensions were all perpendicular to those Isola knew. Within that frame, a wheel of time marked out events, just as it did in Isola's universe—only vastly speeded up from her point of view.

Energy—or something like what she'd been taught to call "energy"—drove the expansion, and traded forms with substances that might vaguely be called "matter." Forces crudely akin to electromagnetism and gravity contested over nascent particles that in coarse ways resembled quarks and leptons. Larger concatenations tried awkwardly to form.

But there was no rhythm, no symmetry. The untuned orchestra could not decide what score to play. There was no melody.

In the speeded-up reference frame of the construct-cosmos, her sampling probe had caught evolution of a coarse kind. Like a pseudo-life fabrication too long out of the vat, the universe Isola had set out to create lurched toward dissipation. The snapshot showed no heavy elements, no stars, no possibility of self-awareness. How could there be? All the rules were wrong.

Nevertheless, the wonder of it struck Isola once more. To make universes!

Furthermore, she was getting better. Each new design got a little farther along than the one before it. Certainly farther than most trash cosmos spun off as exhaust behind starships. At the rate she was going, in a million years some descendant of hers might live to create a cosmos in which crude galaxies formed.

If only we could solve the problem of looking down Tenembro, she thought.

That great black ripple lay beyond the laboratory window, crowned by warped stars. It was like trying to see with the blind spot in her eye. There was a tickling notion that something lay there, but forever just out of reach.

To Isola, it felt like a dare. A challenge.

What strange rules must reign in there! She sighed. *Weirdness beyond imagination . . .*

Isola's gut clenched. The laboratory blurred as waves of painful constriction spasmed inside her. The chaise grew arms which held on, keeping her from falling, but they could not stop Isola from trying to double over, gasping.

Such pain . . . I never knew . . .

Desperately, she managed a faint moan.

"Jar . . . Jarlquin . . ."

She could only hope the room monitor would interpret it as a command. For the next several minutes, or hours, or seconds, she was much too distracted to try again.

It is a narrow passage, fierce and tight and terrible. Forces stretch and compress to the limit, almost bursting. What continues through suffers a fiery, constricted darkness.

Then a single point of light. An opening. Release!

Genesis.

They watched the fetch ship turn and start accelerating. Starlight refracted through a wake of disturbed space. If any of the multitude of universes created by its drive happened, by sheer chance, to catch a knack for self-existence, no one in *this* cosmos would ever know.

Isola's feelings were a murky tempest, swirling from pain to anesthesia. A part of her seemed glad it was over, that she had her freedom back. Other, intense voices cried out at the loss of her captivity. All the limbs and organs she had possessed a year ago were still connected, yet she ached with a sense of dismemberment. Jarlquin had carefully previewed all of this. She had offered drugs. But Isola's own body now doped her quite enough. She sensed flowing endorphins start the long process of adjustment. Beyond that, artificial numbing would have robbed the colors of her pain.

The fetch ship receded to a point, leaving behind Tenembro's cavity of twisted metric, its dimple in the great galactic wheel. Ahead, Pleasence Star beckoned, a soft, trustworthy yellow.

Isola blessed the star. To her, its glimmer would always say, *You continue. Part of you goes on.*

She went on to bless the ship, the visitors, even Jarlquin. What had been taken from her would never have existed without their intervention, their "selection." Perhaps, like universes spun off behind a star-drive, you weren't meant to know what happened to your descendants. Even back in times when parents shared half their lives with daughters and sons, did any of them ever really know what cosmos lay behind a child's eye?

Unanswerable questions were Isola's metier. In time, she might turn her attention to these. If she got another chance, in a better situation. For now, she had little choice but to accept the other part of Jarlquin's prescription. Work was an anodyne. It would have to do.

"They're gone," she said, turning to her friend.

"Yes, and good riddance."

In Mikaela's pale eyes, Isola saw something more than sympathy for her pain. Something transcendant glimmered there.

"Now I can show you what we've found," Mikaela said, as if savoring the giving of a gift.

"What we . . ." Isola blinked. "I don't understand."

"You will. Come with me and see."

Tenembro was black. But this time Isola saw a different sort of blackness.

Tenembro's night fizzed with radio echoes, reddened heat of its expansion, a photon storm now cool enough to seem dark to most eyes, but still a blaze across immensity.

Tenembro's blackness was relieved by sparkling pinpoints, whitish blue and red and yellow. Bright lights like shining dust, arrayed in spiral clouds.

Tenembro Universe shone with galaxies, turning in stately splendor. Now and then, a pinwheel island brightened as some heavy sun blared exultantly, seeding well-made elements through space, leaving behind a scar.

"But . . ." Isola murmured, shaking her head as she contemplated the holistic sampling—their latest panspectral snapshot. "It's *our* universe! Does the other side of the wormhole emerge somewhere else in our cosmos?"

There were solutions to the equations which allowed this. Yet she had been so sure Tenembro would lead to another creation. Something special . . .

"Look again," Mikaela told her. "At beta decay in this isotope . . . And here, at the fine structure constant . . ."

Isola peered at the figures, and inhaled sharply. There *were* differences. Subtle, tiny differences. It was another creation after all. They had succeeded! They had looked down the navel of a macro-singularity and seen . . . everything.

The still-powerful tang of her pain mixed with a heady joy of discovery. Disoriented by so much emotion, Isola put her hand to her head and leaned on Mikaela, who helped her to a chaise. Breathing deeply from an infusion tube brought her around.

"But . . ." she said, still gasping slightly, " . . . the rules are so close to ours!"

Her partner shook her head. "I don't know what to make of it either. We've been trying for years to design a cosmos that would hold together, and failed to get even close. Yet here we have one that occurred by natural processes, with no conscious effort involved—"

Mikaela cut short as Isola cried out an oath, staring at the pseudo-life chaise, then at a waiter-servitor that shambled in carrying drinks, a construct eight days old and soon to collapse from unavoidable buildup of errors in its program. Isola looked back at the holographic image of Tenembro's universe, then at Mikaela with a strange light in her eyes.

"It . . . *has* to be that way," she said, hoarse-voiced with awe. "Oh, don't you see? We're pretty smart. We can make life of sorts, and artificial universes. But we're new at both activities, while nature's been doing both for a very long time!"

"I . . ." The pale woman shook her head. "I don't see . . ."

"Evolution! Life never *designs* the next generation. Successful codes in one lifetime get passed on to the next, where they are sieved yet again, and again, adding refinements along the way. As Jarlquin said—whatever works, continues!"

Mikaela swallowed. "Yes, I see. But universes . . ."

"Why not for universes too?"

Isola moved forward to the edge of the chaise, shrugging aside the arms that tried to help her.

"Think about all the so-called laws of nature. In the 'universes' we create in the lab, these are almost random, chaotically flawed or at least simplistic, like the codes in pseudo-life."

She smiled ironically. "But Tenembro Universe has

rules as subtle as those reigning in our own cosmos. Why not? Shouldn't a child resemble her mother!"

What came before me?
How did I come to be?
Will something of me continue after I am gone?

Isola looked up from her notepad to contemplate Tenembro Nought. This side—the deceptively simple black sphere with its star-tiara. Not a scar, she had come to realize, but an umbilicus. Through such narrow junctures, the Home Cosmos kept faint contact with its daughters.

If this was possible for universes, Isola felt certain something could be arranged for her, as well. She went back to putting words down on the notepad. She did not have to speak, just will them, and the sentences wrote themselves.

My dear child, these are among the questions that will pester you, in time. They will come to you at night and whisper, troubling your sleep.

Do not worry much, or hasten to confront them. They are not ghosts, come to haunt you. Dream sweetly. There are no ghosts, just memories.

It wasn't fashionable what she was attempting—to reach across the parsecs and make contact. At best it would be tenuous, this communication by long-distance letter. Yet who had better proof that it was possible to build bridges across a macrocosm?

You have inherited much that you shall need, she went on reciting. *I was just a vessel, passing on gifts I received, as you will pass them on in turn, should selection also smile on you.*

Isola lifted her head. Stars and nebulae glittered beyond Tenembro's dark refraction, as they did in that universe she had been privileged to glimpse through the dark nought— the offspring firmament that so resembled this one.

As DNA coded for success in life-forms, so did *rules* of nature—fields and potentials, the finely balanced constants—carry through from generation to generation of universes, changing subtly, varying to some degree, but above all programmed to prosper.

Black holes are eggs. That was the facile metaphor. *Just as eggs carry forward little more than chromosomes, yet bring about effective chickens, all a singularity has to carry through is* rules. *All that follows is but consequence.*

The implications were satisfying.

There is no mystery where we come from. Those cosmos whose traits lead to forming stars of the right kind—stars which go supernova, then collapse into great noughts—those are the cosmos which have "young." Young that carry on those traits, or else have no offspring of their own.

It was lovely to contemplate, and coincidentally also explained why she was here to contemplate it!

While triggering one kind of birth, by collapsing inward, supernovas also seed through space the elements needed to make planets, and beings like me.

At first, that fact would seem incidental, almost picayune.

Yet I wonder if somehow that's not selected for, as well. Perhaps it is how universes evolve self-awareness. Or even . . .

Isola blinked, and smiled ruefully to see she had been subvocalizing all along, with the notepad faithfully transcribing her disordered thoughts. Interesting stuff, but not exactly the right phrases to send across light-years to a little girl.

Ah, well. She would write the letter many times before finishing the special antenna required for its sending. By the time the long wait for a reply was over, her daughter might have grown up and surpassed her in all ways.

I hope so, Isola thought. *Perhaps the universe, too, has some heart, some mind somewhere, which can feel pride. Which can know its offspring thrive, and feel joy.*

Someday, in several hundred billion years or so, long

after the last star had gone out, the great crunch, the Omega, would arrive. All the ash and cinders of those galaxies out there—and the quarks and leptons in her body—would hurtle together then to put *fini* on the long epic of this singularity she dwelled within, paying off a quantum debt incurred so long ago.

By then, how many daughter universes would this one have spawned? How many cousins must already exist in parallel somewhere, in countless perpendicular directions?

There is no more mystery where we come from. Had she really thought that, only a few moments ago? For a brief time she had actually been *satiated*. But hers was not a destiny ever to stop asking the next question.

How far back does the chain stretch? Isola contemplated, catching the excitement of a new wonder. *If our universe spawns daughters, and it came, in turn, from an earlier mother, then how far back can it be traced?*

Trillions of generations of universes, creating black holes which turn into new universes, each spanning trillions of years? All the way back to some crude progenitor universe? To the simplest cosmos possible with rules subtle enough for reproduction, I suppose.

From that point forward, selection would have made improvements each generation. But in the crude beginning . . .

Isola thought about the starting point of this grand chain. If laws of nature could evolve, just like DNA, mustn't there exist some more *basic* law, down deep, that let it all take place? Could theologians then fall back on an ultimate act of conscious Creation after all, countless mega-creations ago? Or was that first universe, primitive and unrefined, a true, primeval accident?

Either answer begged the question. Accident or Creation . . . in what context? In what setting? What conditions held sway *before* that first ancestor universe, that forerunner genesis, allowing it to start?

Her letter temporarily forgotten, with mere galaxies as backdrop, Isola began sketching outlines of a notion of a plan.

Possible experiments.

Ways to seek what might have caused the primal cause.

What had been before it all began.

Roar at the Heart
of the World

Danith McPherson

I REMEMBER THE DAY THE WORLD CHANGED. NOT BY A date or a time or by any number. I remember it by the low voices of men in dusty boots who hunched over the table on our veranda and drank gin and tonic. I remember it by the dry wind through the weaving grass and the red-maned lion's roar. I remember because that day Africa changed. And Africa was my world.

"One man dead and a war begins." Young Mr. Finch tapped the side of his glass but ignored its contents. "South Africa seems so far away, and yet— If only they hadn't killed him."

"They were looking for an excuse," Mr. Kreshenko said, his Romanian inflection rumbled deep from a round chest. "Any would do, but they got about the best possible. The real reasons are more complex—economics, dignity, power, ego. So it has always been. This is only the lit match tossed onto the pile of straw."

Poor Mr. Finch. Thin and pale, he seemed unsuited to

the wilderness of the Kenyan highlands, newly reopened to foreign ownership a century after the remnants of the first settlers were expelled. "The blaze is out of control," he muttered. "What will we do when it reaches us?"

From my child-sized chair at my child-sized table set a short distance from the adults' furnishings I searched the horizon for the glow of flames. I sniffed the air for smoke. I listened to the animals for panic. A fire is a frightening thing in a land that gives water more by whim than by season. Beyond the veranda the night was black and still. I heard my dog Orion patroling the stable. In their boxes the horses dreamed of familiar things. In the hills a leopard circled its prey without a sound. They did not know of a fire. Not then.

I bent over my paper and finished covering the flaming yellow with black. Africa was like the drawing I made. A layer of coloured patches—red, blue, green, every pigment in the crayon box—then a dark layer covering it like the night. The wax sticks grew soft in the hot day. I kept them in a cool place and took them out after sunset. In the brittle light from the battery-powered torch I scratched off a design of hills and wattle trees, antelope and grasses. The colours beneath the black appeared in sudden vividness.

"Hah!" Mr. Haugen gave a single sharp laugh. "We'll be murdered in our beds by the natives, that's what."

I fussed with my crayons while I pulled the meaning from his thick German accent. The Romanian spoke like the ocean; I floated on the rolling rhythm. But the German ground out his words, and I had to pick through the rubble.

"Hush, you'll frighten the child." Finch touched me with a concerned look, quick as a feather.

"Frighten Lizzy?" my father said. He leaned against a post that supported the slanting roof of the veranda and swirled the liquid in his glass. "Lizzy stalks wild boar with the Nandi hunters. A little war won't frighten her."

No. I was not afraid. I was not afraid of the faraway

fire. I was not afraid of a war, barely knew what one was. There was history, of course, but Father had little interest in the past and I had less, having less past to be interested in. He told me nothing of wars, except that there had been some. I was too young to read the thick books wrapped in tooled leather. When I did read, it was about horses.

Togom told me about the many battles between the Nandi and the Masai. But that was different. They were both warrior tribes; it was their heritage to fight. Tribe against tribe. Not Black against White as in the war my father and his friends whispered about.

I preferred the stories of great hunts. A hunter armed with spear and shield against a lion was braver than human against human—be it with spears or guns. There was little challenge in an opponent who had the same kind of strength, the same weapons, the same thoughts as you, whether or not the skin was the same colour.

But a lion thinks differently from a human and a leopard thinks differently from a lion. Each animal is a separate challenge: That is the essence of the hunt.

"They can't force us out," my father said. "It's only an excuse to take back the land now that we've paid for it and spent four years proving we're not crazy, that it can produce."

"It isn't just the Kenyan government," Finch said. "England and all the other countries have told their citizens to leave. Burton," he said to my father, "you received your notice officially signed by His Royal Majesty the same time I did."

"And what would I do back in Germany?" Haugen asked the insects buzzing around the spots of light hanging from the bare rafters. "Can't raise coffee there. My older brother inherited the family vineyard. That's why I came here in the first place. Invested my meager inheritance in the land. Now they want me to leave. Burton, not to minimize your situation, but at least you can train horses anywhere, even back in England. You still have connections there."

My father's chin was set with a determination I knew well. "And what about the mill? I have contracts to deliver flour."

"There may not be anyone to deliver the flour to," the German said.

"Well," Finch said with forced vigor, "Diana and I haven't been here that long. We still have investments in London and a little money. Of course this isn't the way I planned . . ." He let it trail off. Nothing seemed to turn out as he planned. "You're staying then, Burton?"

I pretended absorption in my artwork. As if there was any doubt, I thought.

"Yes."

"Suspected you'd feel that way." Finch stared at the table cut from the cedar forest a short distance behind the house. "Burton, Diana and I talked it over. This war is going to be tough, no other way about it. And—I hope you won't think me critical—Elizabeth is beyond the age when most girls begin formal schooling. And you know that we adore her. We practically think of her as our own, especially since the baby—Diana and I would like to take her back to England with us, just until things are settled here or until you decide to come home. It makes perfect sense, really.

"Damn it," he said with more weariness than strength. "I'm trying to make it sound so noble, as if we'd be doing you a favor. Truth is, it would break Diana's heart to be separated from Lizzy. Mine too, I'm afraid."

My father showed no surprise. Since my mother died when I was two years old, people who wanted to take me away from him had lined up like mismatched beads on a string. Each argued that it was for my own good. I should have been too young, yet I remember every one.

A particularly ugly bead—one of my mother's aunts, I think, in a wide hat covered with impossibly large net flowers—proclaimed that with her social contacts and careful guidance I would "get on in the world very nicely" and probably "marry above my station." But her real thoughts were simple and close to the surface. She wanted a little princess buried in taffeta flounces to show off to her friends. As always, Father politely declined the offer.

No previous bead was as honest as Finch, few were as nice. Still, I was surprised when my father said, "I'll think about it."

What was there to think about? Of England I remembered only starched dresses, tight shoes, overly perfumed relatives in stuffy rooms, and boredom.

I belonged to Africa. Finch and his equally porcelain wife could no more uproot me, transplant me into British soil, and expect me to thrive than they could a bamboo tree. And yet I heard my father say, "I'll think about it."

The guests left. Kreshenko and Finch lived the farthest away on farms with a common border, their houses still kilometers apart. Haugen was our closest neighbor, but he lived on the other side of the wide Rongai Valley, quite a distance by road, a bit less cross-country. The headlights of their tough, battered vehicles caught the eyes of animals along the edge of the ruts that served as a road.

Do not move, I told them. The noisy motor-beasts will soon rumble past and be gone.

"If war was an animal, I would hunt it and kill it," I told Sayid that night when he tucked me into bed. The Somali served as housekeeper and nanny. He was one of the colours of Africa that I tried to capture in my drawings. Unknown to outsiders. Unseen unless you scratched the continent's surface. His face was grim in the pale glow from the lamp on the narrow table beside my bed.

"It would not let you, Lizzy. It is not a natural beast."

I leaned over the edge of my little cot and gave Orion's brown-and-white coat a pat good night. A fusion of hard muscle and simple mind, he stood waist-high to my child body. My father made him for me, so he was of no discernible breed. He sauntered to the end of the bed, respectfully avoiding Sayid, who was a Muslim and could not touch or be touched by a dog, and curled up on his rug. I didn't think of him as big, for as the years passed he seemed to shrink. But I suppose that my own growth caused it to seem so and that he was larger than most dogs.

Sayid pressed the button that turned off the light. He stepped out of the room, leaving a trail of spice and soft rustles. As every night since we have lived in this little house, he left the door tilted open the width of his hard, narrow body, so I would not be alone, so he could slip in if I cried out in my sleep. To my knowledge, I never did.

For a moment I listened to the animals—Orion at the foot of the bed, the horses in their boxes, the large cats prowling, the slim eland sleeping yet watchful for the cats. I never heard the smaller animals—the chickens in our coop, my pair of chameleons in their cage. Either the smaller animals spoke in voices too soft for my sense or their tiny brains made no noise.

Only rarely did I hear humans. Perhaps their thoughts were too deep within them and too complex. I especially never heard my father. Perhaps he could protect himself from my intrusion. Usually I had other ways of knowing his thoughts.

Because of the company, I had been allowed to stay up past my bedtime. Drowsiness crept in and enveloped me sooner than I expected, so I had no time to consider the adults' concerns about this faraway war. As was my habit every night, I consciously stopped listening. Otherwise the animals kept me awake with their triumphs of life and screams of death. I was instantly asleep.

In the morning before a proper dawn had the chance to announce the day I took my knife and spear and slipped out of the house with Orion at my side. The cool air bit my legs below the khaki shorts, nipped my arms exposed by the brief sleeves of my blouse. Soon my father would be up to begin the daily work with the racehorses. I wanted to be gone so he could not turn me back to my neglected lessons in grammar and arithmetic. Like the horses, I, too, had daily work.

In all other things my father allowed me the freedom

of a sprite, an independence that shocked the other farmers and gave Sayid nervous fits. But my studies were carefully monitored, and I received scoldings for hunting when my lessons had shown no progress. I was a child and endured them with a penitent bow, but without remorse or the resolve never to do it again.

The banks of solar panels sat expectantly beside the mill, tilted toward the point of sunrise, ready to power the machinery. Shiny solar flats, similar to the others but portable, leaned against the building. Each morning Kitau, one of the Kikuyu workers, set them up as needed to recharge the batteries for the lamp in my room and the torches that we relied on at night for the veranda and the stable.

Wheat stalks swayed in the field, each slim plant reaching above my head. Beside the golden spears, Father's prized patch of genetically enhanced maize rustled with health. Less tall than the wheat, its thick shafts supported a heavy crop that my father was already using as a wonderful excuse to plan a party for harvest. Farther up in the hills there was a cluster of coffee trees, the traditional crop of the area left over from the first wave of European settlers long ago. My father's nature rebelled at tradition, but I think their untended survival intrigued him. He fussed over the plot as if it were nature's equivalent of his maize.

I traveled over the hill and into the valley. Three hundred meters below, smoke from the Nandi village drifted up in thin lines that converged into one, then faded. I descended through the half light at the edge of day. The mongrel dogs yapped at my approach. They were ill-mannered and barked at everything. Orion refused to answer their coarseness with anything but silence. They shared an inherited memory; but because of his mixed genes, Orion felt no kinship with them.

Togom and Ruta ducked out of their huts and greeted me. They each wore a *shuka*. The single piece of cloth wrapped under one arm, sloped across the chest and back, and was knotted at the opposite shoulder.

Togom gave Orion a pat. The motion seemed a wasteful use of the strength stored in his lean muscles, but the
fluid body, like shadowed water, craved movement. "How
are the animals this morning?" he asked me in Swahili.

I wasn't fluent in Nandi, but Swahili was accepted as
a common language. The Kavirondo and Kikuyu workers
on the farm used it. I spoke it better than I did English,
which appalled the fragile Mrs. Finch. I could substitute
a few Nandi, Kikuyu, even Masai words if they fit my
purpose. "Nervous," I said. Did I describe them or myself?
Although it dominated my thoughts, I didn't say that my
father might send me away.

Togom, the village's *ol-oiboni,* spiritual leader, nodded. "The sun quivers, afraid to come out." His soul grew
from this land. He didn't need me to tell him how the
animals felt, so I knew it was a lesson. He recognized my
distraction. He wished me to stay alert, to push deeper into
my sensitivity.

Ruta shook his head. His shoulders were wide for a
Nandi's, and he carried more weight on his round chest
than Togom. But he was just as quick with a spear.
"*Mbaisa sana,*" terribly bad, he said. "This is not good
for hunting."

"Ahh, but we have Elisbet to tell them not to be
so, to say they die honourable deaths on murani spears,"
Togom said.

I knew the other message in his words. I am *ol-oiboni,*
he said, I can do much but this I cannot do: I cannot make
the animals hear me. Only you can do this, Elisbet.

Togom motioned. A girl no older than my eight years
dressed in a skirt of skins that brushed her ankles brought
three gourds of blood and curdled milk.

In the village there is no division between life and
ceremony, living and religion. Solemnly we observed the
pre-hunt ritual. We each took a gourd and drank in turn,
chanting praise to the blood of the bull. Togom first as
leader. Then Ruta. Then me, Orion respectfully sitting at
my feet.

The girl watched me because it was not allowed for her eyes to touch the men. Nandi women do not hunt. I'm sure she wondered how I dared to stand beside the strong warriors and drink warm bull's blood, how I dared to lift a spear against a boar. I had no answers for her unasked questions. Only that it seemed natural to hunt and that I wasn't afraid with Togom and Ruta and Orion.

Togom and Ruta hefted their spears and shields. Morning blossomed across the flat sky. In this part of Africa, so near the equator, the sky is very close to the earth. I imagined that when I grew as tall as a muran, I would be able to stand on Mount Kenya and stretch my fingertips to touch the blue.

We crossed a pasture crowded with indulged cattle. The uncircumcised boys who tended them watched covertly as we passed. When we cleared the worst of the slippery dung, we ran in single file. The floor of the long, winding valley is clogged with foliage and impassable from one end to the other. Togom led us up over the lip, then along the perimeter of the Mau Forest. We descended back into the Rongai as the sun rose. I listened.

Impala, eland, kongoni—all to the sides of us, all scattered. And below us—

"Boar," I said, trying not to let my excitement rattle my voice, trying to be a calm hunter. "But it is too quiet between here and there."

We reached the jumble of rocks where water trickled through the scarlet dust, turning it to sucking clay. In the heat, mist rose from the puddle that formed.

Mist. The Masai word is *E-rukenya*. Kenya.

The meager watering hole was always populated with sleek impala, eland, zebras. I saw nothing except the indentations of hooves and paws in the clay. I heard nothing.

Togom and Ruta froze, experience guiding them. In imitation, I stood still. Orion moved in front of me. He sniffed the ground, the air. His thoughts danced bright and expectant.

"*Simba*," I whispered. "Orion tells me this."

"Ahh," Ruta whispered back, "the one with the red mane who will not talk to you."

"It must be," I said.

"But you can talk to it," Togom said. "Say that today we do not hunt lion. Say that we hunt boar."

In my mind I repeated Togom's message to the invisible animal. I sent the thought across the crimsons and coppers of the clearing, into the tawny grass and skeletal brush that clawed the stones, not knowing if I was heard.

From the deep, cool shadow of an overhanging rock drifted a huge golden cat, a muted color of Africa silently revealed. It shook the cinnamon halo surrounding its head and flicked its cinnamon-tipped tail with impatience. The steady eyes evaluated Togom. Then Ruta. Then Orion. I cried to the dog to hold. The lion's stare was a challenge. Orion's every muscle tightened to spring. He was furious with me for the restraint.

The lion's eyes slid to me. The stare burned and chilled. "I know you," the eyes said, although I heard nothing.

The lion's eyes returned to Togom—muran, leader of murani, *ol-oiboni*. This beast had no time for lesser beings such as Ruta, Orion, and me.

Togom raised his shield and held his spear ready, but already he battled the lion with a returned stare. "He is furious with us for disturbing him," he said calmly, almost mockingly to shame the lion. I knew the cat did not speak to him. Togom read the animal's stance and breathing and eyes. Face to face with an adversary, he did not need my assistance. He understood the lion's thoughts because they were both warriors, both proud.

A lion saunters with a lazy economy, but it charges with speed and conviction. If the red-maned beast attacked, it would seriously rip apart or kill at least one of us. But it could not win. Together the two murani would bring it down. And in my youth I imagined that I could play a role in this, too. Certainly Orion, who saw all encounters with cats as great sport, would do his share. Still, the cold of one of us dead or nearly dead—

I repeated the message because it was all I could do. I was certain it heard, but I feared it did not listen.

The lion claimed a step of ground toward us. I held my spear ready. Now I saw wet patches on the lion's paws. Blood. It had a fresh kill nearby, one worth protecting if only to protect its honour.

I squinted against the sunlight to peer into the shadow behind the lion. A slain boar, the hide shredded by a dozen slashes, stained the crimson soil darker.

We will kill our own boar, I told the lion with false bravado. We are hunters, not hyenas who take from others.

I saw no change in the lion, but Togom quietly said, "Let us leave this place."

We moved away from the water hole. Ruta and I did not ask Togom how he knew that the lion had decided not to attack. The beast watched our cautious retreat, then went back to its kill.

Orion was especially valiant in our quest for a boar, putting all of his frustration over the lost cat into it. Ruta brought down a large one with his spear and Orion ripped out its throat, suffering a wound in the flank from one of the curved tusks. The dog's tough hide held scars from worse encounters, still I worried about the bleeding and possible infection.

We returned to the village with fresh meat, avoiding the water hole on the way. Dusk gently moved through the valley. One of Togom's wives met us and hurried us into his hut. The wise men of Togom's age group who served as a village council sat cramped and cross-legged around a freshly lit fire.

Room was made for Togom, Ruta, and me. The warm, moist smell of unbathed humans who had labored through a hot afternoon was stronger than the smoky odor.

I held a strange position in village life and politics. I am White, child, female. According to Nandi laws, these should have excluded me from the circle. Yet there seemed to be a rule that said uniqueness exempts one from the rules. I was accepted because of my differences. So, as I had done before, I sat with the old men.

"While you were hunting, *ol-oiboni,* a magistrate came from Nairobi," one of them explained intensely. "With him were two *askari* who did not look like *askari*. They were natives, true, but they behaved like mongrel dogs, not like police officers. Our young men must go into the militia, the magistrate said. He strutted through the village as if he had a right to be here and bothered the young men, even the uncircumcised boys, for their names and the names of their brothers. He will be back, he said, with many more *askari* to take the young men away, even if they do not want to go."

"I will go to this war," said the youngest of the old men—for sometimes in the village old had nothing to do with years—still full of uncooled fire. "I will show the bravery of the Nandi murani." He shook a fist as if it held a spear.

"Aiyee," Togom said, "this is not a war of spears. This is a war of weapons falling from the sky. It is no place for a true warrior. There is honour in a spear, in staring into the eyes of your enemy, in judging his character and acknowledging his bravery. There is no honour in bombs."

"What do you know of bombs?" he challenged.

Togom's face took on the glow of the new fire. His eyes transformed from the hard black of the warrior into the soft brown of the seer. He looked through the flames, through the earth to the world's core. "A great bomb has already fallen. Hate explodes from its depths. We feel the heat. Soon we will know the burning."

The old men made it law: No Nandi will fight in this war.

It was almost too dark to find my way home when the meeting ended. Togom walked with Orion and me up the valley slope to the top of the hill closest to our farm. I would have to hurry, and there was still my father's wrath to face.

Togom put a hand on my shoulder as he often did when he had something important to say, as if the weight of his hand paralleled the weight of his words. A rim of soft brown still circled his black eyes. He moved dreamily, and I wondered if the vision he had had in the hut moved with him at the edge of his sight.

He blinked several times before focusing on my face. "Elisbet, you must call to the animals. Tell them, do not go south, do not go west, do not go north. You must say, come to this valley. Kill only for food, not for territory. And do not kill until your hunger is very strong. The Nandi promise to do the same. Tell them, come close and be ready."

"Ready for what?" I asked, afraid he would tell me. My small, tired body trembled at the unknown image that circled his vision.

"Tell them."

Togom turned and walked unsteadily back toward the village. Limping from his wound, Orion did his best to guide me home in the closing darkness.

There is a human thing called a war that brings many dangers, I sent into the night to the animals. You must come to Njoro, to Rongai, because the *ol-oiboni* says it should be so. He sees many things that you and I cannot see. He knows many things that you and I cannot know. He thinks many things that you and I cannot imagine. Come close so you will be ready.

That night in my little bed the village drums woke me. I was too exhausted from the day's hunt to decipher their meaning. Just as quickly the rhythm lulled me to sleep.

The next morning I sneaked out of my room and headed for the village to find out about the drums. I made Orion stay at the farm to give his injury time to heal. He scowled at me in his wide-jowled way but obeyed. The pain meant nothing to him, he told me.

I am not going hunting, I assured him. My knife and spear are only for protection.

He remembered charging the boar, Ruta's spear sticking from its back like a narrow third tusk. He remembered clamping his teeth into the boar's throat and shaking his head until the flesh tore and warm blood sprayed across his face. He did not remember the tusk ripping a gash across his flank. I am a better weapon than a knife and spear, he told me through his memories.

With longing, he remembered the lion at the water hole, an opportunity missed because I held him back. You owe me a cat, he said.

Another time, dog, I told him with affection.

I took my usual path to the valley, reached the crest of the hill, and looked down, eager to see the comforting domed roofs of the huts around the circular clearing, the wisps of smoke.

I saw nothing but the valley floor thick with foliage. My breathing came so fast I could scarcely draw oxygen from it and I thought I might faint. Tears blurred my sight. How could they leave? I thought, when I really meant *How could they leave without me?* How could they move a village and close plants over the spot where it had been so there was no sign it ever existed?

They couldn't, my mind shouted in disbelief. They couldn't leave without me—

They couldn't. Of course. So simple.

I hefted my spear and boldly walked into the valley as I always did, straight through the thick growth that should have swallowed me but didn't. As I descended, the surroundings blurred. I stepped, uncertain if my foot would find the earth. It settled on cleared ground despite what my eyes told me. I stepped again. Again.

The grass and leaves reformed into familiar patterns and opened a trail at my feet. Before me a village snapped into existence with the sudden sound of barking dogs and the smell of cooked boar from yesterday's hunt.

Ruta greeted me with a wide grin and twinkling eyes, as if this was a joke meant just for me. "You have found us then, Elisbet. Our little trick did not fool you." Yet obviously he knew that it had, at least for a little while, and he took some delight in that.

I tried to laugh through the rags of my fear. "So this is what you did with the drums making such noise all night so no one could sleep. You have made yourselves invisible."

He proudly pointed out the boundary of the illusion. "It is a small thing for an *ol-oiboni* as skilled as Togom," he said.

I followed the ripple that circled the village like a great ring of heat. It was not a small thing. Not a small thing at all.

Four days later open trucks rumbled along the road from Nairobi. I was at the edge of the farm exercising Valiant Lady, a golden beauty with more loyalty than legs. Her tendons were weak, and she required easy handling. She had been custom-designed, the fertilized egg smuggled into Africa, then implanted into our roan mare. Father forbade me to go hunting until my lessons were satisfactory, and he punished my disobedience by placing this wonderful creature in my care.

He said nothing of Finch's offer to take me to England; but nightly during supper while we discussed each horse's progress and possible training strategies, I knew he thought about it. Thought about sending me away. Away from him. Away from Africa.

The noisy trucks were empty, which meant they expected to pick up something to haul back to the capital. I followed the caravan, staying to high ground. The vehicles bumped onto the cart trail that twisted into the Rongai, then stopped where Togom's illusion dissolved the road and barricaded the narrow entrance with phantom bamboo trees and thick vines.

A Black man dressed in blazing white shirt and shorts got out of the cab of the lead truck. He might as well have had MAGISTRATE stamped on him in bright letters. He fumbled with a map. The driver got out, pulling something with him. A large rifle, the kind for firing many bullets very quickly. Not a rifle to be used against animals but one to be used against humans. The man slung a strap over his shoulder to support the heavy gun. He strolled to the magistrate's side with an ease that said he was used to the extra weight and hardly knew how to walk without the additional appendage at his side.

I suspected that the men packed into the cabs of the other trucks also had such rifles and such walks.

The two studied the map for a long time. They poked fingers at it, gestured in confusion to the road and the hills. The gunman strolled a little way into the bush, then returned, rubbing his temple as if it ached.

They came to take the young Nandi men, to train them as soldiers to fight in the war that had begun in the far south and moved closer each day.

I watched them and knew that the war was already here.

The magistrate shouted orders. He and the gunman got back into the truck. Vegetation pushed as close to the trail as it dared, sometimes snaking over it with great bravado. There was no clearing large enough for a truck to turn around in. The entire caravan crawled backward along the cart trail like a segmented worm. The string of dust-caked vehicles had to back up all the way to the Nairobi road. And it would return to the capital empty.

I laughed, urging Valiant toward the farm. She shook her pure white mane and flicked her snowy tail, ready to do anything I asked.

Two days later in the grey morning, Kitau stumbled onto the veranda, panting like an ill-used steeplechaser. He and some of the other workers took turns going to Nairobi, so we had daily bulletins about the war.

Father and I were just about to go to the stables. Father, broad and beefy, supported the wiry Kitau and placed him in a chair. The young man's appearance with the sunrise spoke more eloquently of horror than his words ever could.

"*Bwana* and *Memsahib* Kreshenko," Kitau puffed out between gulps of air, "murdered." He glanced at me, then quickly returned his water smoothed-stone eyes to my father. "And their little ones with them."

I was only eight, but I knew both masks death wore, the natural and the tragic. I felt more rage at the injustice of murder than sorrow at the loss of the Kreshenkos.

Violence had moved north blindly. The animals' increasing distress had become an expanding roar in my head. Cats. Monkeys. Elephants. Rhinos. Zebras. They rushed like a stampeding zoo before the advancing guns and bombs. Some had been caught in bursts of fighting that flared like spontaneous combustion.

Humans have gone mad, they told one another. Humans have gone mad.

Father put his hands on his hips. He shifted his mouth as if he chewed a piece of tough meat. "Who did it? Their servants?"

"No, no," Kitau protested. "You must not think such a thing. For the servants are dead beside their master and mistress. Much was burned. It is the police who believe that this and other things were done to hide the identity of the murderers. In front of their clerk the police say it was activists from South Africa who wish once again to form the Mau, so they can drive out all Whites. They say they know this from other police. *Bwana* Kreshenko and his family are not the only Whites to be killed. The police say this in front of their clerk and their clerk says this to me."

"You ran all night?" It seemed unfair that the thoroughbreds in our stable rested comfortably while Kitau traveled from Nairobi to Njoro on foot. Father wanted the workers to take the horses, but they were experienced runners, not riders. They had more stamina, were more sure-footed in the uncertain terrain, and needed less rest than the products of royal bloodlines who still slumbered in their boxes.

Kitau nodded.

"That's dangerous."

The Kikuyu silently told my father that it was necessary, and my father silently thanked him.

"The Haugens?"

"Gone quickly more than a day ago. The servants bring many boxes to the city to send after them."

"Any news of Finch and his wife?" my father asked carefully, as if he suddenly had difficulty speaking.

"Safe. In Nairobi. That is the other message I bring. They leave tomorrow for England and say they would be most pleased to take little Elizabeth with them."

My world stopped. I closed my eyes, afraid to blink, afraid any movement would start time again and I would be on my way to Nairobi with a suitcase, wearing the dress from last Christmas that was too small for me but was the only one I owned.

My father looked at his boots. His shoulders lifted with the intake of a great breath, then sagged with decision. "No." A long word that hung in the growing heat. "Lizzy belongs here. I'll send word to the Finches. Kitau, get some food and rest. I'll have guards posted around the farm."

My world had movement and meaning again. I ran into my father's arms; they were suddenly low enough to catch me up and swing me to his chest. We held one another and let the horses wait.

That night snarls and screams woke me to the dark. At the foot of my bed raged a battle of teeth and claw. Orion and the red-maned lion.

I heard the lion carry the dog from the room in triumph. Heard Orion struggle and snap in the grasp of its jaws, taking away any dignity the lion had hoped for.

Sayid appeared with an electric torch, Father with the rifle that lately was never far from his hand. Together we followed a broken line of shiny blood while I followed Orion's anger.

I knew the dog twisted in the lion's jaws and was released. I knew he rolled, then gained his feet and faced the glittering eyes. To Orion's credit, he didn't challenge the lion's right to sneak into the house if it could, nor to enter my bedroom if it went undetected, nor to grab a sleeping dog and make off if nothing stopped it.

With bleeding pride Orion stared at the lion. He had not smelled the lion, not wakened to the soft padding of its paws as it entered the house or the little bedroom. He was humiliated by being snatched up in his sleep, then dropped in the dust. He barked fiercely, demanding a rematch.

We reached the animals, a composite of light and shadow in the beams of our torches. I ordered Orion into silence and was surprised when he obeyed.

The red-maned lion stood calmly. Scarlet dripped from the wounds Orion had managed to inflict.

My father pressed his torch into my hand. Slowly he raised the rifle to his shoulder.

Why did you do this? I asked. No reply.

"It's not going to charge," I whispered. Togom's training told me, not anything I heard.

Before I finished the words, the cat melted into the night.

The next morning I forced a sulking Orion to stay at the farm while I disobeyed my father and went to the village. The dog's neck was torn open in many places from the lion's teeth, but most of the wounds were not deep.

I had seen what a lion could do, what the red-maned lion had done when its purpose was death. It had not dragged off Orion in order to slay him. It had not taken him because he was a fierce dog who killed cats for the challenge. That was Orion's right as a hunter. The lion had another purpose. I was a child and wished I had Togom's wisdom so I could understand.

"The lion would not tell me why," I complained to Togom after telling of the attack. The *ol-oiboni* and I shared a breakfast of fruit and flatbread baked from flour Father had sent some time ago as a present.

Togom sat cross-legged and rocked slightly in thought. "Perhaps the lion is saying, 'I do not like what is happening. I do not like what these human animals do.' "

"Then why didn't it just tell me instead of hurting poor Orion?"

"Perhaps the message was not for you." He rocked and pursed his lips. His hard eyes grew soft at the edges. "I will think of this, Elisbet. I will think like a lion, then the meaning will come to my mind."

I didn't go hunting that day. I followed my own trail back to the farm to nurse Orion.

A battered blue truck sat in the bare space before the house. It was an ancient, wasteful vehicle without a fluid unit to store energy when it idled or went downhill. The official seal on the door was unreadable through the thick coating of reddish dust, but it must belong to a Nairobi magistrate. No other official would come to Njoro.

A Black man, tall and thin as most natives with the sculptured features of the Kamba tribe, stalked from the house, a piece of paper clenched in his hand. He folded himself into the truck, and it took him away with much chugging and complaining.

My father stepped onto the veranda. His boots made solid clomps on the cedar boards. He put his hands on his hips and watched the dust plume grow thin.

I came up beside him. Although he didn't look at me, he knew I was there. I slipped my hand through the triangle his arm made and placed my small fingers on the back of his hand.

"They can't order me off my own land," he said softly. The more angry my father was, the lower he spoke. The quiet of his words made me shiver. "I chose this country and earned my keep. I've no intention of leaving."

Sayid was at his other elbow. "What will we do, *Bwana* Burton?"

My father, Sayid, and myself. Whenever I think of the old Africa, my memories are always of the three of us and the house as it used to be. I can close my eyes now and feel as I did at that moment, with my hand touching my father's and the fragrance of curry that lived in Sayid's flowing clothes. This is the last of those memories.

"Pack my bag," my father told Sayid. "I'm going to Nairobi to straighten this out."

I didn't expect Father to come home that night. When he didn't return the second night, I could do little except sit on the veranda and watch the road until long after sunset.

Sayid tucked me into bed. Orion, much recovered and burning with the desire to kill a cat, took his usual place on the rug. The guards Father posted patroled the immediate grounds of the house and stable. The red-maned lion roared just before I fell asleep.

Sayid woke me by the light of a small torch. I reached for the lamp switch, but he grabbed my hand. "There are headlights on the road," he said. "They do not belong to your father's truck." I couldn't tell if his hand shook or if it was mine wrapped in his that quivered.

My knife and spear lay in the rippled folds of my covers, placed there by Sayid.

"Go to the village," he said. "Not to worry. They are only government officials come to make you leave. I will tell them *Bwana* Burton went to Nairobi two days ago and has not returned, for that is the truth. And if they know that a daughter lives here also, I will say that little Elizabeth went to England with *Bwana* and *Memsahib* Finch. If they search your room, I will say you took little because these things are not what young girls wear in England, and these things are not what young girls play with in England."

His quick cadence told me it was a well-rehearsed speech, something he and Father prepared before Father left.

In a sharp flash I heard the approaching intruders. Their thoughts were simple and loud. They had not come from the government at Nairobi to enforce an evacuation of the White farmers. They came only to destroy.

I gripped Sayid's sleeve with my free hand. "Order the horses released, and the chickens. Send everyone away. You must go too."

Sayid looked deeply at me. In the torch's glow his face was round shadows and curved dark skin. He seemed relieved that I knew what he tried to hide from me, that we parted without a lie between us, even one meant in kindness. I hugged him completely and forever.

I dressed quickly and took up my weapons. Then I opened the door to my chameleon cage and left, warning Orion to be quiet. I went as far from the farm as the dog could lead me in the dark. I heard the confusion of the horses as they were turned out into the night. "There is danger here," I told them and the other animals. "I flee from it myself. Move quietly, now, away from this place."

I stopped to wait for the full moon to rise, so I could find my way to the village by its light. From my hiding place I watched the farm.

Four Jeeps roared like blind elephants into the yard and abruptly halted. The headlights turned movement into a grotesque dance. The shadows of men jumped from the Jeeps. They fired guns into the air, large guns, the kind carried by the man with the magistrate. I buried my face in Orion's scarred coat and held him fiercely to me.

A growing brightness came too soon and harsh to be the gentle moon. The stable glowed, then exploded in heat. Flames waved like wheat stalks. The house burned with the reflection; the reflection became flames. Timbers crackled, cracked, and fell. I heard rifle shots but could not guess what they meant.

From an adjoining hill the roar of the red-maned lion shook the earth. I watched until the slanted roof over the veranda crumbled to meet the cedar boards. "*Kwaheri*," I told Njoro. Farewell.

The moonlight was soft. I blinked until the images of flames dissolved, then crossed over the hill into the valley. I passed through the blurry illusion that surrounded the village, barely aware of the distortion.

In the center of the circle formed by the huts stood Togom. Moonlight spread from him and filled the village.

Beside him stood a man and a woman I did not know. The man seemed older than Togom, wrinkled like a dried creek bed, hair grayed to a cloud of white. The woman was smooth-skinned. At the focal point of what must be a ceremony, she was composed beyond her youth.

The villagers sat in the worn dirt, forming a thick moat of dark water around the island of soft light occupied by Togom and his companions. But there were far more people than this village usually held, and there were many faces I did not recognize.

Togom held out his hands to me across the moonlight and gestured. Waves passed through the water and a path opened. I walked through to the center, Orion at my heels. The dog held his head high, aware that there was honour in this. I took my clues from him and from the young woman beside Togom. I would not let the sorrow of Njoro that cried out for comfort mar my behavior.

"*Koaribu,*" come you are welcome, Togom said. "We have been waiting for you, Elisbet. Maina," he gestured to the old man, "has brought his people. And Jebbta," he moved a hand toward the young woman, "has brought her father's people that we might unite the power of the Nandi against this war that has no honour."

I entered the island of light and stood with the straight posture of a muran.

Togom spoke to the valley. "In the timeless past the Nandi walked Africa, moving as the hunt and grazing land for our cattle took us. But the government of Whites and the government of Blacks who had given up their tribes told us we must live on only one part of the land, that only certain places in Africa were ours and only the game on that land was ours, and that we must live by these laws."

The *ol-oiboni* gave a little smile. "To their eyes, we obeyed; but we are Nandi and will not be ruled by others." The smile dissolved into pain. "Now they invade the little plots of land they said were ours, with their bombs and their guns and their war. We must protect ourselves from their foolishness until Africa is again ours to walk as we will.

"Elisbet, call the animals into the Rongai. Say they must come over the top of the hills and onto the slopes that bend to the valley." Togom's eyes had grown soft, as if he dreamed. "Tell them that this is Africa now. Life and death hold equal honour here."

I listened. Panic echoed from the farm and from other places I could not identify.

Come, I called into the moonlight. It is not a child who calls to you but the noble Nandi. We invite you to this valley, to the land we have shared with you since before time. And we will hunt. And you will hunt. Here, all will be as it was.

Silence. Silence. Silence. My heart stopped beating.

The red-maned lion roared, accepting the bargain.

Leopards snarled, elephants trumpeted, zebras neighed. I covered my ears against the answers but I could not keep them out of my head. Nor did I want to.

Up in the hills the jungle rustled slightly with eland and impala as if no more than a breeze stirred. Under my feet the ground quivered. In my mind I heard animals crest the hill, heard the horses from the farm, heard the ones already in the valley adjust to make room.

They took positions watching the village. And waited.

I nodded to Togom, but he already knew.

Togom spoke to the humans and the animals. "What we do has not been done since before the birth of my father and his father and his father and more fathers before that. One *ol-oiboni* cannot accomplish it alone. This is why *ol-oiboni* Maina and his people have come. This is why Jebbta and her people have come. Jebbta's father is dead, killed by a bomb dropped from the sky. It is a bad way for a Nandi muran to die, and it is bad for an *ol-oiboni* to die so young without another ready. Jebbta takes his place tonight. Although female and not formally trained, she knows her father's work and she will do well."

The three formed a circle, arms outstretched, palms upward, fingertips touching. The moon floated above as if its light fell only on the Rongai.

The drums began a slow rhythm. The assembly seemed gently pulled to its feet. Ruta came forward and took my hand. He led me into the gathering of villagers and those newly arrived. With the others I swayed and danced to the drums.

Orion sat and watched the three immobile *ol-oiboni*, as if it were his duty to witness for his kind. But I knew what the dog did not. The red-maned lion stood in a moon-cast shadow on the nearest slope, *ol-oiboni* for the animals.

The moon slid behind a hill. The drums stopped in the darkness. Togom broke the circle and smiled tiredly, sadly at Maina and Jebbta. "The valley is sealed. The outside cannot see us, can no longer touch us. So it will be until the time arrives for us to take back what was once ours."

Togom carried me into his hut because I was too tired to make my own way. I dreamed of hot flames and cool moonlight and quivering earth.

In the morning the village was busy accommodating its new residents and setting up a system for handling the limited resources.

"Elisbet," Togom said, "you must help the animals establish territories that will keep them from arguing with one another. Their numbers must be balanced so every kind will survive."

I called Valiant Lady and the other horses to the village. They were beautiful and strong and very fast, but they didn't know how to protect themselves against cats and boars. I loved them so and was glad to stroke Valiant's silky coat.

Their lives were now changed as much as mine. They would be useful. There were many places they could not go because of the dense growth, but also many in the valley and up the steep hills where they could carry a rider. I didn't think beyond that. Not then. I didn't consider that their descendants would be useful to my descendants. But I think in such terms now.

I ride a three-year-old stallion, one of Valiant's line, to the crest of the hill nearest where the farm used to be. The same hill I scrambled over in the moonlight with Orion nine years ago when I was eight. The dog slowed with age, and on one of his cat hunts he lost the battle. I have no interest in another dog.

I was such a small child, my father would be surprised to see how tall I have become. I am as long-legged and straight and graceful as any Nandi.

I stretch out a hand and touch the smooth, hard nothingness of the elongated bubble that separates the winding valley from the charred wasteland beyond. I stroke the ancient protection that Togom called up, as I call animals, from the depth of the Nandi heritage. It is not magic. It is something more solidly rooted in the earth and the rightness of things and the place where life began and will not let go.

I close my eyes and concentrate as hard as I can. I listen beyond the barrier, hoping.

Nothing.

I turn and gaze across the valley thick with green, noisy with life. A patch of moisture at the top of the otherwise invisible dome forms a cloud that will become rain.

Very close I feel the presence of the red-maned lion, although he doesn't speak to me. Old enough to be immortal, he often stalks the perimeter, as I do, to assure himself that it still stands and that all is well.

Some day the descendants of the three *ol-oiboni* will open the bubble; and the Nandi will reclaim the wounded world, heal it with their own health. By then I will be dead for centuries.

No matter. Although at times I dream of more, of what used to be and what could have been, this is enough. This valley is my world.

This is my Africa.

About the Authors

A potter by profession, RAY ALDRIDGE first began writing in 1985 and since then has published stories in *Aboriginal SF*, *Amazing Stories*, and *The Magazine of Fantasy & Science Fiction*. He is also the author of "The Emancipator" series of novels, which includes *The Pharaoh Contract*, *The Emperor of Everything*, and *The Orpheus Machine*. Ray, his wife, Nancy, and their two children live in Florida, where Ray continues to make pots and write fiction.

KEVIN J. ANDERSON is the author of fourteen novels, including *Assemblers of Infinity*, *The Trinity Paradox*, and *Lifeline* (co-written with Doug Beason) and *Afterimage* (co-written with Kristine Kathryn Rusch). His short fiction has appeared in many magazines and anthologies, such as *Full Spectrum 1* and *Full Spectrum 3*, *Analog*, *The Magazine of Fantasy & Science Fiction*, *Amazing*, and *The Year's Best Fantasy Stories*. He is currently at work on three *Star Wars* adventures for Bantam Books. He and his wife Rebecca live in California, where he works part-time as a technical editor for the Lawrence Livermore National Laboratory.

As a scientist, DAVID BRIN studied comets and varied projects for NASA, and taught university physics and writing courses. David has won the Hugo, Nebula, Locus, and John W. Campbell Awards for his novels and short stories, which include *Startide Rising, The Uplift War, The Postman*, and his ecological thriller, *Earth*. His wife, Dr. Cheryl Brigham, is also a space scientist. They have a new son, Benjamin Robert, to whom this story is pledged.

STEPHEN R. DONALDSON is fond of saying that he has no useful biography. Born in 1947 in Cleveland, Ohio, he lived in India (where his father was a medical missionary) until 1963. Donaldson made his publishing debut with the first "Thomas Covenant" trilogy in 1977. His chief ambition in life, however, is to learn to play Liszt's *Harmonies du soir* on the piano. He also wants to sing *Rigoletto* at the Santa Fe Opera, but that is never going to happen either. He now lives in New Mexico. Everything else is just a figment of someone's imagination.

L. TIMMEL DUCHAMP's stories have appeared in *Pulphouse: The Hardback Magazine, Memories and Visions*, and *The Women Who Walked Through Fire* (ed. Susanna J. Sturgis, Crossing Press 1989 and 1990 respectively), *Starshore*, and Pulphouse's Short Story Paperback Series. More of her stories are forthcoming in *The Magazine of Fantasy & Science Fiction* and *Pulphouse*. She lives in Seattle.

JEAN-CLAUDE DUNYACH, born in 1957, has a Ph.D. in applied mathematics and works in the aircraft division of Aerospatiale, in Toulouse (south of France). He has been writing science fiction since the beginning of the eighties, and has already had published four novels and two collections of short stories, garnering him the French science fiction award in 1983. He also writes lyrics for several French singers, which served as an inspiration for his upcoming novel about a rock 'n' roll singer touring in Antarctica with a zombie philharmonica orchestra. . . .

GREGORY FEELEY has published science fiction in magazines and anthologies, as well as essays in *The Atlantic, Saturday Review, The New York Times*, and elsewhere. His first novel, *The Oxygen Barons*, was nominated for the Philip K. Dick Award. He has recently completed a contemporary novel, *Exit Without Saving*, and is working on *Neptune's Reach*.

ELIZABETH HAND spent her wonder years in Yonkers and Pound Ridge, New York, where some of the odder people from the Sixties washed up just in time for her to babysit their kids. She studied acting and anthropology at Catholic University in Washington, D. C., and worked for a number of years at the National Air & Space Museum, Smithsonian Institution. She now lives on the Maine coast with novelist Richard Grant and their children. She is the author of the novels *Winterlong, AEstival Tide* and *Icarus Descending*, as well as numerous articles and short stories. She is completing two contemporary supernatural novels, the goddess-inspired *Waking the Moon* and *Black Light*, a dark fantasy about the Warhol Factory.

HOWARD V. HENDRIX previously appeared in *Full Spectrum 1* with a short story, "The Farm System." The novelette "Ah! Bright Wings" is from a cycle of stories linked by their shared concern with sibyls, shamans, altered states of consciousness, and the pursuit of a seamless mind/machine interface—as well as by the fact that most of the works in the series are short stories with long titles. Among the stories in the series that have already appeared are "Singing the Mountain to the Stars" *(Aboriginal SF)*, "The Voice of the Dolphin in Air" *(Starshore)*, and "At the Shadow of a

Dream" (*Aboriginal SF*). Mercifully shorter-titled works in the series include "Almost Like Air" (*Amazing*), "The Art of Memory" (*EOTU*), and "The Unfinished Sky" (*Starshore*). He is currently at work on *Psychopomp*, a novel that further investigates the concerns raised in the stories. In a previous life he held a Ph.D. and was a professor of English literature at a small liberal arts college in the Midwest, and in a life prior to that he held a degree in biology and managed a fish hatchery, but now he just does what he can to make money and month match up.

BONITA KALE has sold stories and verse to *Aboriginal SF, Isaac Asimov's Science Fiction Magazine, The Magazine of Fantasy & Science Fiction*, and *Pulphouse*. She lives near Cleveland with her husband, sons, and daughter, and works in a public library. Currently, she's writing a fantasy novel for young people.

NANCY KRESS is the author of seven books: three fantasy novels, three science fiction novels, and a collection of short stories. Her most recent novel is *Beggars in Spain* (Avon/Nova), based on her novella of the same name, which won the 1991 Nebula and Hugo Awards. Her short fiction appears regularly in all the usual places. She was awarded the 1985 short story Nebula for "Out of All Them Bright Stars." A former advertising copywriter, Kress is currently the monthly "Fiction" columnist for *Writer's Digest* magazine and frequently teaches seminars in writing science fiction. She lives in Brockport, New York, with her husband Marcos Donnelly and two sons Kevin and Brian.

JOHN M. LANDSBERG, a practicing family physician, has published fiction in *The Magazine of Fantasy & Science Fiction*, and in the first two volumes of Silverberg and Haber's *Universe*. He and Jonathan Ostrowsky created, edited, and published *Unearth*, in which they published the first stories of William Gibson, James P. Blaylock, and

Paul DiFilippo. Landsberg recently completed directing his first feature film, "Confessions of a Marriage Junkie."

Born in Berkeley in 1929, URSULA K. LE GUIN has been publishing poetry since 1959 and fiction since 1961. Her awards in the science fiction and fantasy field include five Nebulas, four Hugos, and a Gandalf. Her most recent book is *Searoad: Chronicles of Klatsand*. She is currently working with an Argentinean poet, Diana Bellessi, on a mutual translation project.

DANITH McPHERSON lives on the shores of a Minnesota lake. Her published works include short stories, novels, poetry, and educational materials. Currently she is researching genetics for a science fiction novel in progress.

A. R. MORLAN's work has appeared in *Weird Tales, Night Cry, Iniquities, The Magazine of Fantasy & Science Fiction, The Twilight Zone Magazine, Eldritch Tales, The Horror Show*, and many other magazines; the anthologies *Women of the West, Cold Shocks, Obsessions, The Year's Best Fantasy & Horror 1991, The Ultimate Zombie*. She is the author of the Bantam novels *The Amulet* and *Dark Journey*. This is her first appearance in the *Full Spectrum* series.

"Foreigners" is MARK RICH's first professional fiction sale. His fiction, essays and verse have appeared widely in the small press in the United States, France, and Britain. His first book, *Lifting*, published by Wordcraft of Oregon, won the Leslie Cross Fiction Award from the Council of Wisconsin Writers. He lives in Stevens Point.

BRUCE HOLLAND ROGERS's short story, "A Branch in the Wind," was a prize winning entry in the Writers of the Future Contest. He has sold fiction to magazines and anthologies such as *The Magazine of Fantasy & Science*

Fiction, Amazing Stories, Ellery Queen's Mystery Magazine, Quarterly West, The Quarterly, and *Flash Fiction.* He writes occasional reviews for *The New York Review of Science Fiction.*

DAVE SMEDS is the author of the high-fantasy novels *The Sorcery Within* and *The Schemes of Dragons.* His short fiction has appeared in *Isaac Asimov's Science Fiction Magazine, Dragons of Light, Ghosttide, Hot Talk, Pulphouse—A Fiction Magazine, Sword & Sorceress, Far Frontiers, In the Field of Fire, Mayfair,* and an array of other magazines, anthologies, and comic books.

MARTHA SOUKUP sold her first story to Terry Carr's *Universe 16,* and since then has published fiction in *Asimov's Science Fiction, The Magazine of Fantasy and Science Fiction, Amazing Stories, Analog, Aboriginal Science Fiction, Twilight Zone,* and a number of anthologies. Her stories "Over the Long Haul" and "Dog's Life" were finalists for the Hugo and Nebula awards. She has lived in Chicago and Albuquerque, and currently lives in San Francisco. For her day, evening, and night job, she serves as one of the sysops on Genie's Science Fiction RoundTable.

DEL STONE JR. is thirty-six and single (as of this writing) and works for a newspaper where he designs pages, writes what passes for a humor column, and generally adds to his gray-hair collection. As a service brat, he saw most of the U.S. and some of the world. He finally settled in Florida, however, where he lives today. He began writing in the eighth grade; his motivation was a story he read in a *Twilight Zone* anthology that didn't end the way he wanted it to end. He's been writing off and on since.

About the Editors

LOU ARONICA is Vice President and Deputy Publisher of Bantam Books and Publisher of Bantam Spectra. He lives in Connecticut with his wife, Barbara, their daughter, Molly, and their son, David.

AMY STOUT is a Senior Editor at New American Library. She lives in New York with her husband Alan Rodgers, and their daughters Alexandra and Andrea.

BETSY MITCHELL is Editor-in-chief at Warner Questar Books and has published short stories in *Analog* and *Twilight Zone*. She lives in Brooklyn with her husband, Gene, and their son, Shawn.

"[Silverberg and Haber] have chosen to revive the late Terry Carr's Universe series of experimental anthologies.... This is a good idea."—*The Chicago Sun-Times*

UNIVERSE 3

edited by Robert Silverberg and Karen Haber

Here are fifteen new stories from the brightest and boldest voices of contemporary science fiction. Collected and edited by award-winning author Robert Silverberg and science fiction writer Karen Haber, the tales of **Universe 3** stretch the limits of the real and the possible.

With stories by:

Brian Aldiss * E. Michael Blake * Terry Boren
David Ira Cleary * Nicholas A. DeChario * Paul Di Filippo
Joe Haldeman * Alex Jeffers * Phillip C. Jennings
Barry N. Malzberg * Will McCarthy * Jamil Nasir
Mark Rich * Larry A. Tritten * Mary A. Turzillo

— — — — — — — — — — — — — — — —

Buy Universe 3, on sale now wherever Bantam Spectra paperbacks are sold, or use this page for ordering:

❏ **Universe 3** (56580-X * $5.99/$7.50 Canada)

Send to: Bantam Books, Dept. SF 238
      2451 S. Wolf Road
      Des Plaines, IL 60018

Please send me the items I have checked above. I am enclosing $_____ (please add $2.50 to cover postage and handling). Send check or money order, no cash or C.O.D.'s, please.

Mr./Ms._____

Address_____

City/State_____Zip_____

Please allow four to six weeks for delivery.

Prices and availability subject to change without notice.   SF 238 3/94